People
of the
River

People of the River

W. Michael Gear
and
Kathleen O'Neal Gear

TOR

A TOM DOHERTY ASSOCIATES BOOK
NEW YORK

PEOPLE OF THE RIVER

Copyright © 1992 by W. Michael Gear and Kathleen O'Neal Gear

Maps and interior art by Ellisa Mitchell
Production manager: James Forbin

A Tor Book
Published by Tom Doherty Associates, Inc.
175 Fifth Avenue
New York, N.Y. 10010

TOR® is a registered trademark of Tom Doherty Associates, Inc.

Library of Congress Cataloging-in-Publication Data

Gear, W. Michael.
    People of the river / W. Michael Gear and Kathleen O'Neal Gear.
        p.   cm.
    "A Tom Doherty Associates Book."
    ISBN 0-312-85235-5
      1. Indians of North America—Fiction. 2. Mound-builders—Fiction.
I. Gear, Kathleen O'Neal. II. Title.
PS3557.E19P46 1992
813'.54—dc20   92-2968
                                                CIP

First edition: August 1992

Printed in the United States of America

10 9 8 7 6 5 4 3 2 1

To Harold and Wanda O'Neal

For all of the years you spent sitting in the dust, explaining potsherds, yucca sandals, styles of architecture, and the astronomical alignments at prehistoric sites.

Those wide-eyed children never lost their sense of awe.

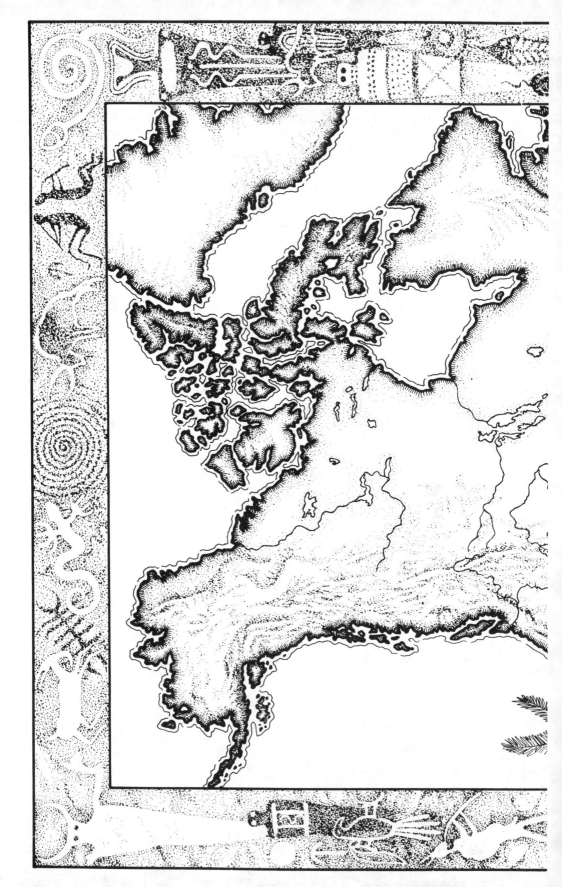

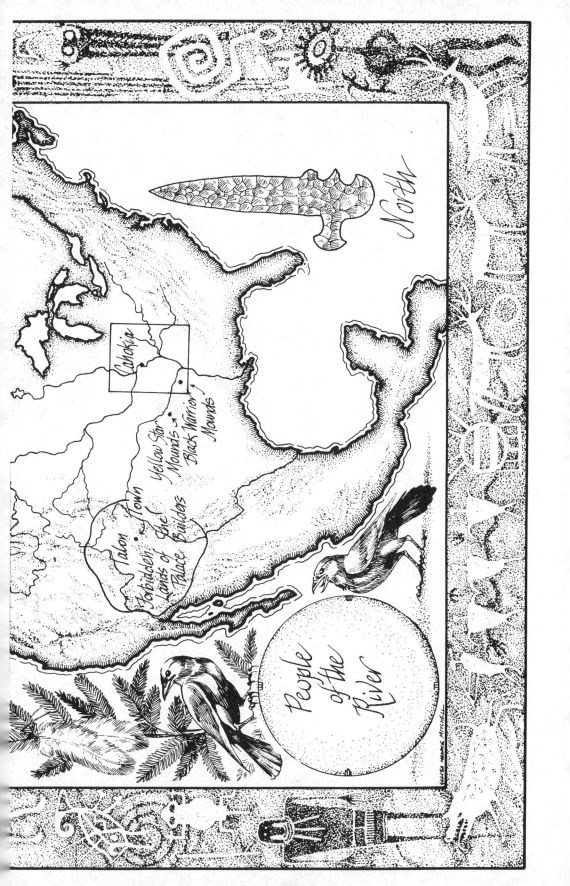

North

Cahokia

Yellow Star Mounds
Black Warrior Mounds

Talon Town
Forbidden Lands of
The Palace Bundles

People of the River

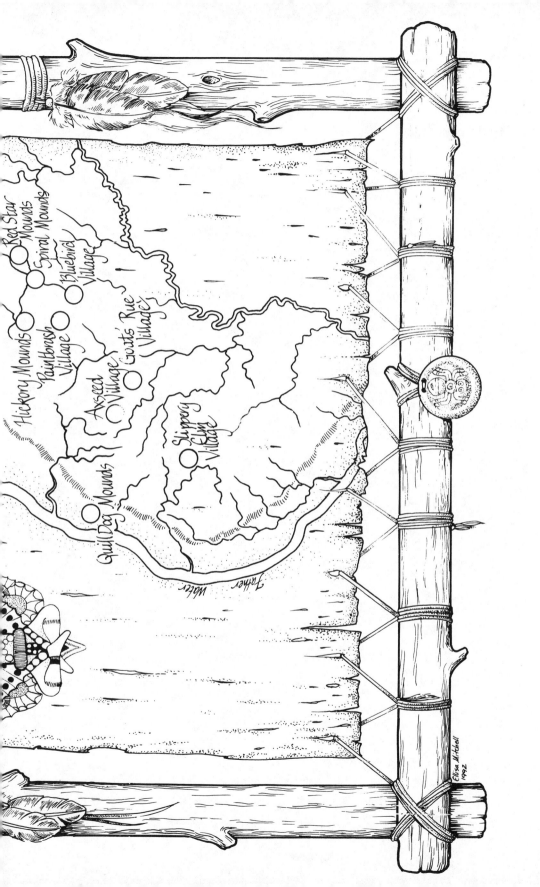

Acknowledgments

Ｎone of the books in the First North Americans series could be completed without the extensive fieldwork of our colleagues in the archaeological community.

We would like to thank Drs. James B. Griffin, Melvin Fowler, Robert Hall, Richard Yerkes, John Kelly, Thomas Emerson, R. Barry Lewis, Neal Lopinot, Christy Wells, William Wood, Timothy Pauketat, George Milner, George Holley, Fred Finney, James Stoltman, Henry Wright, and Bruce Smith for their comprehensive work on Cahokia. And P. Clay Sherrod and Martha Ann Rolingson of the Arkansas Archaeological Survey for their work on the archaeoastronomy of the Mississippi Valley.

Special mention goes to Ray Williamson for his thoughtful comments on prehistoric North American astronomy over dinner in New Orleans at the 1991 Society for American Archaeology meetings. Bill Butler of the National Park Service provided us with source material on Plains/Woodland trade patterns. John Walthall has done superb work on aboriginal trade in North America, and we have drawn from his material.

In addition, National Forest Service archaeologists H. Gene Driggers and Anne Wilson spent hours in researching and procuring books and articles for us. Many thanks.

Dr. Dudley Gardner, Sierra Adare, Jeff Corney, and Bill Blow of the Cahokia staff graciously helped us hone the ideas. Katherine and Joe Cook of Mission, Texas, and Katherine Perry provided encouragement and critique. Special service was done by Harold and Wanda O'Neal, who ransacked their library for archaeoastronomy information.

Michael Seidman made this series possible during his days at Tor Books. We would also like to acknowledge Linda Quinton, Ralph Arnote, and the field force for their hard work. Tom Doherty, Roy

Gainsburg, and the staff at SMP/Tor have believed in the project and given us unflinching support.

Last, we offer our deepest gratitude to Harriet McDougal, the finest editor in New York. We couldn't do it without you, Harriet.

Foreword

During the Archaic, around five thousand years ago, the native peoples of the Eastern Woodlands were hunter-gatherers. They lived in small, scattered villages and subsisted on a diet of white-tailed deer, wild turkey, opossum, raccoon, turtle, and other animals, supplemented with native plants. The introduction of corn, about 1500 B.C., dramatically changed that life-style and led to the rise of an agricultural civilization that embraced not only the most complex religious ceremonialism, social organization, and economic sophistication ever seen in prehistoric North America, but also the most expansive political influence heretofore known. We call these people the "Mississippians."

Mississippian culture flourished from roughly A.D. 700 to A.D. 1500. During that time, the largest earthen structures in North America were built, mounds a hundred feet high and containing over 21,000,000 cubic feet of earth.

The domestication of corn gave the Mississippians a high-energy food resource and heightened the carrying capacity of the land. Probably for the first time in North American prehistory, people could reliably produce an annual surplus of food. This surplus resulted in a population explosion. Village size went from a few hundred people to perhaps ten or twelve thousand. The diet became almost 90 percent corn. This stable economic base provided the conditions necessary for social stratification. Powerful chiefs arose and consolidated the scattered villages into vast chiefdoms whose tribute to the Great Sun Chief—a tax—funded widespread communal activities. Labor became specialized. Certain artisans produced magnificent arrow points, ax heads, shell beads, and perhaps the very special pottery that was traded over thousands of miles.

Mississippians established trade routes that spanned the continent, bringing olivella shells from Florida, obsidian from the Yellowstone region of the Rocky Mountains, alligator and sharks' teeth from the Gulf Coast, copper from Ontario, Canada, and Wisconsin, silver from Michigan, grizzly bear teeth from Montana, conch shells from the Carolinas, mica and quartz crystals from Virginia, chalcedony from the Dakotas, pipestone from Ohio and Pennsylvania. They may have even traded with the high civilizations of Mexico.

From Archaic roots—as is evidenced by the Poverty Point site in Louisiana—Mississippians inherited, and then improved on, a body of mathematical and astronomical knowledge that allowed them to plan their towns with a standard unit of measurement and to align each of their mounds according to solar and stellar positions. At Cahokia, in Illinois, the mounds were arranged so that it was possible for them to chart the exact position of the sun when it rose and set on the equinox and solstice. At Toltec Mounds in Arkansas, they knew the azimuths of Vega, Aldebaran, Rigel, Fomalhaut, Canopus, and Castor, and built their towns and ceremonial centers accordingly.

The Mississippians understood the basic principles of celestial mechanics. For example, they observed that the full moon always rises at precisely the same time the sun sets, which is why the lunar disk is completely illuminated. They charted the 18.6-year lunar cycle and positioned their mounds so that the time the moon reached its most southerly position in that cycle could be ascertained.

It is not an exaggeration to say that the Mississippian peoples knew more about astronomy than does the average modern-day American.

So, we must ask, given the sophistication of their culture, what happened to them?

By 1541, when Hernando de Soto came up the Mississippi River, the mound-builders' civilization had all but disappeared. The massive population centers were abandoned, the thousands of acres of fields left fallow. Why?

The answer revolves around corn and climate.

The rise of Mississippian culture corresponds to what we call the Neo-Atlantic climatic episode. Beginning about A.D. 900, the earth experienced a global warming, which brought moist, tropical air into North America. This extended the length of the growing season and increased the summer rainfall, allowing for substantial crop yields and fostering a massive increase in population.

Then, between A.D. 1100 and 1200, the climate changed again.

The Pacific climatic episode, which lasted until about A.D. 1550, brought strong, dry winds and drought. Rainfall declined by as much as fifty percent. Crop yields plummeted. To sustain their population, Mississippians expanded their trade routes and cleared more land for crops. Deforestation increased erosion, which caused catastrophic flooding when the rains did come. Around A.D. 1150, the people were recycling wood. Red cedar had become so scarce that they were unable to refurbish their sacred structures. Flooding resulted in stunted corn growth, with ensuing malnutrition. Burials from the period are rife with pathologies, including decreased stature, tooth loss, and arthritis. Famine likely ravaged the population centers.

By A.D. 1200, all of the major towns and many of the small, surrounding villages had been palisaded, surrounded with walls twelve to fifteen feet high, and mounted with shooting platforms on all sides. War followed. In one Illinois cemetery, dating to around A.D. 1300, thirty percent of all adult deaths were due to trauma and mutilation resulting from warfare.

Outlying villages began to disperse, and this led to changes in the economic system, as well as in the varieties of plants cultivated. The complex Mississippian way of life, with its emphasis on intensive agriculture, was replaced by a simpler tribal structure. Once again native American peoples mixed hunting with horticulture. Large temple towns vanished and society devolved.

The story you are about to read is set in the vicinity of Cahokia, Illinois, at the peak of the crisis. The rains won't come, the corn won't grow, the people are hungry and desperate. . . .

People
of the
River

Introduction

"Hell, I don't know," old man Mac Jameson grumbled as he steered the John Deere tractor onto the dirt road that led through the center of his barley field. The warm breeze fanned the stalks until they waved like a blanket of gold. Illinois was mighty pretty at this time of year, but hot. Hotter than Hades today. Sweat had matted his faded red shirt and well-worn jeans to his arms and legs. At the age of seventy-five, he still had a whip-thin body, though his muscles had mostly evaporated over the years. He wiped the back of a dusty hand over his sweating forehead to push the wisps of gray hair back from his deep-set brown eyes. "Bunch of goddamn government people called me up to talk about something they call a National Register of Historic Places district. That don't mean nothing to me. Does it mean something to you? You're the one who's always going out hunting arrowheads and pots." He twisted around to peer at his son-in-law.

Jimmy clung to the seat of the tractor as it bounced over the deeply rutted road. About forty, he had a face like a Pekingese, squashed and ugly, with a mop of red hair that hung over his ears. He cocked his head. "No, I ain't never heard of no National Register, but if it's historic sites they're after, they must be coming to see that mound you got at the southeastern corner of the farm."

"What for?" Mac demanded, irritated. He didn't have time for any government bullshit. The harvesters would be coming in tonight to start cutting his barley. God Almighty, he had things to do!

"Who knows?" Jimmy shouted over the growl of the tractor. "Maybe some archaeologist wants to dig it up or something."

"Dig it up? Why?"

"Jesus Christ, Pa! You live damn near on top of Cahokia mounds, that's why."

Mac said gruffly, "What the hell is a Cahokia?"

Jimmy shook his head, which rankled Mac. The damn boy had been in trouble for practically his whole life—stealing, or smacking folks with tire irons—and now he could shake his head like that at his father-in-law? He damn well ought to knock Jimmy off this old John Deere and go on about his business.

"Pa, Cahokia's the biggest mound site in America . . . maybe in the world. They call it a 'World Heritage Site,' I guess it probably is the biggest in the world. A hell of a lot of Indians lived there maybe a thousand years ago."

"Indians!" Mac scoffed. "What have they got to do with this?"

"I don't know, but the tribes have been raising seven kinds of hell in recent years. I heard they even forced a bunch of museums to give back some broken-up bones 'cause they said the bones was from their ancestors." Jimmy chuckled disdainfully. "Can you believe that? They fought for a bunch of bones?"

Mac's eyes darted over the rolling swells of land while he mentally cataloged all of the graves that dotted this quarter section. Up on the rise stood two lonely crosses, tilted sideways now after a hundred years of rain and wind, marking grandparents who had passed on from smallpox. And scattered irregularly along the edges of the fields lay tiny mounds of earth,—the resting places of babies who had died for no good reason at all. Every year Mac and his wife Marjorie went out and set the border stones straight again to prevent some field hand from running over them with his plow.

He peered hostilely at Jimmy. "You think those government people want something out of that mound? I won't have no painted-up buck on my land. Good white folks had enough trouble with them over fishing rights up north. Hell, the Indians think they own the whole world. Well, they don't own my farm! My family's been plowing this hundred and sixty acres for two hundred years!"

"Now, don't get pissed off, Pa. Not yet." Jimmy tried to smooth him down. "Them government people probably just want to ask you some questions. You know, stuff like what kind of arrowheads you been pulling up under your disk, or if you've ever hit any human bones or the like."

Had he ever hit bones? Mac's chest tightened. Why, every time he evened up the border at the base of that mound, he hit bones. He figured they were deer bones, but they might have been human. How would he know?

"You know how it is, Pa," Jimmy continued in that annoying voice meant to comfort. "Some archaeologist probably got a bunch of taxpayer dollars and decided your mound might be important or something. Don't worry about it. This is America. If you want to tell 'em to go shit themselves blue, you can do it, 'cause this is *your* land."

Mac nodded sternly, but as he fought the wheel to guide the tractor up the last hill, his guts started to roil. What right did these government bureaucrats have to come and tell him what to do with *his* land? Well, Jimmy wasn't right about much, but he was right about this being America. By God, there were laws against trespassing, and if Mac didn't like what the bureaucrats had to say, he'd damn well throw 'em off his property.

By the time the tractor crested the hill, Mac had a knot in his stomach the size of that damned mound. They topped the crest, and the tractor launched down the other side toward the mound and the county road that skirted his farm. His eyes narrowed when he saw the State of Illinois Bronco sitting at the bottom next to what looked like . . . hell, a *federal* truck? He scowled at the lettering on the side: Department of the Interior, National Park Service. Shit.

Mac jerked the wheel so hard in front of the mound that he nearly tipped the tractor over. It lunged sideways, and Jimmy yelled before it righted itself next to the state vehicle. Tan dust billowed around the two as they climbed off the tractor.

Mac tramped across the soft earth toward the Broncos, glaring out of the corners of his eyes at the mound that stood like a small mountain beside the road. Trees covered the top of the mound, their red, gold, and green leaves fluttering in the breeze. His family had been climbing that mound for years to have picnics. He'd watched his daughters roam the top in the springtime, gathering handfuls of flowers for their mother. Why, his own grandfather, Samuel Jenkins Jameson, had proposed to his Grandmother Lily up under the spreading limbs of that tallest poplar. And, yes, Mac had even buried a child up there. A girl of twenty. Killed in a damned car accident. Pain constricted around his old heart, and he wondered how that loss could still grieve him after thirty-five years. This mound represented *his* family history, not some damn Indian's who lived a thousand miles away.

Mac rounded the nose of the state Bronco, his hair prickling, and stopped dead in his tracks when a blond woman opened the door and jumped out. She carried a brown box under her left arm. "Mr. Jameson?" she called. "I'm Karen Steiger, archaeologist for the Illinois Historic Preservation Agency. You spoke to my colleague, Rick Williams, on the phone."

She walked forward with a warm smile that set Mac back some. And she was a pretty little thing, which made it worse. Thirty, maybe. She wore a lavender-and-tan plaid shirt with jeans and hiking boots. A mass of blond curls framed her oval face, highlighting her tanned complexion and turquoise-colored eyes. When Jimmy came up behind him, he could hear a low whistle escape his son-in-law's lips.

"Goddamn, Pa," Jimmy whispered eagerly. "Let me talk to this one. You take the Indian."

"What Ind—" Mac saw the tall man coming around the side of the federal Bronco. Indian all right. Tall and thin, but he had the moony red face of most of the tribes that loafed around these parts. He wore one of those off-green uniforms that federal employees loved as symbols of their authority.

Steiger strode up with her hand extended. "Thank you, Mr. Jameson, for agreeing to come out and talk to us." She nodded toward the Indian. "This is Dr. John Thecoel, chief archaeologist for the Office of the National Register of Historic Places. It's part of the Park Service."

Mac shook Steiger's slender fingers and nodded in the most courteous manner he could manage, then silently shook the Indian's hand.

"Mr. Jameson," the Indian said in a deep, cultured voice that sounded like he'd come from Boston or some other hole for liberal asses back east. "Thank you. You have a very important site here that we'd like to help you protect."

"Help me?" Mac squinted at the Indian. "I always get real nervous when people from the government say that to me, so why don't you hurry it up and tell me what you want? I've got harvesters coming in at dusk. I'd appreciate it if you'd be taking up as little of my time as possible."

Steiger nodded apologetically. "Yes, I'm sorry about the timing, Mr. Jameson. We know this is a busy month for farmers. Could you come over here, please?"

She stepped out, the Indian at her side, and headed for the southern edge of Mac's mound. He'd have to be squaring that up again. He hadn't been out here for a while, and a half-ton of dirt had sloughed off into a pile at the base. Odd, though. It must have happened recently, because the rich soil hadn't sprouted any grass yet.

Steiger knelt by the pile and rummaged in it for a moment before she came up with a fragment of shell that gleamed like molten ivory in the afternoon sun. She rose and handed it to Mac. He turned the small object over and over in his hand, studying the beautiful designs that had been carved into it. Looked like some kind of stylized spider, he thought.

"That's part of a gorget, Mr. Jameson. A necklace," Steiger explained. "The Mississippian people who lived here in the twelfth and thirteenth centuries imported that shell all the way from the Gulf Coast so they could engrave it and wear it as jewelry."

Mac shrugged. "Mississippian? Is that Indian?"

"Yes, sir," the Indian responded matter-of-factly. "Classic Mississippian culture flourished in the American Bottom area from approximately A.D. 900 to A.D. 1350. It was an extremely advanced culture, with trade routes that spanned the country. We think—"

"Well, that's mighty fine," Mac interrupted, "but what are you interested in my mound for?"

Jimmy sneaked up behind him to eye the shell, and Mac noticed Steiger's brow lift in what he assumed to be a mixture of speculation and disdain. The Indian just looked on stoically.

"Let me see that, Pa." Jimmy grabbed the bit of shell to eyeball it carefully.

Steiger's blond curls flipped around her shoulders as she turned to point at the pile of dirt. "We came to know about your mound, Mr. Jameson, when we caught a thief stealing artifacts from another site on state land. He had an entire array of looted arrow points, celts, pots, and other artifacts at the time we apprehended him. In the process of the investigation, he admitted to plundering a number of sites on private land in this vicinity. He pinpointed yours on a map."

Mac straightened indignantly. "Are you telling me that some son-ofabitch came out here to dig up my mound without my permission? Why, that's robbery!"

"What was his name?" Jimmy inquired with a practiced nonchalance. But his eyes had taken on a gleam. "The thief's name. What was it?"

Steiger responded, "Franklin Jessaby. Why? Do you know him?"

"Ah . . ." Jimmy backpedaled, acting as guilty as Judas. "No. No, ma'am. I was just wondering, that was all."

The Indian's mouth pursed as he scrutinized the fresh pile of back dirt. "Yes, Mr. Jameson, it was robbery. America is one of the few countries in the world where antiquities can belong to individuals. Usually countries consider archaeological and historical sites to be national treasures, not private property to be destroyed or saved as the landowner sees fit. This mound does belong to you, and that's why we're here. We'd like to enlist your cooperation in protecting it." His voice had a hint of pleading, as though he took the damage done to the mound as a personal matter.

"What tribe are you?" Jimmy asked haughtily. "I bet you're Cherokee or something, ain't you?"

"No." The Indian shook his head. "My heritage is Natchez. That's one of the reasons I'm so interested in protecting sites like this one. The Natchez are probably the descendants of the Cahokians."

"Probably?" Jimmy taunted, and from the corner of his mouth he whispered to Mac, "Archaeologists. They can't decide about nothing."

Mac shoved Jimmy away so he could get some breathing room before he turned back to the archaeologists. "Well, I don't understand all this 'protection' talk. You mean you'd punish people for digging up my land?"

Steiger nodded. "Among other things . . ."

She paused when a sixty-eight Chevy truck rattled by on the county road, honking, its occupants waving. Mac waved back, not knowing who they were, but in these parts, people did that—waved to you just because you were human. In the distance, a curl of smoke rose from one of the plants in St. Louis. Mac studied it briefly, watching the gray spiral across the expanse of blue sky. Damn pollution got worse every year. Pretty soon there wouldn't be any farmland, and not just because farmers hung on the edge of starvation. All of the land would be taken up by industries and condominiums. He wondered what would happen to the mounds then.

Steiger began again. "Yes, if you allowed us to list your archaeological site as part of the National Register district that Dr. Thecoel is proposing for this region, we could prosecute anyone who vandalized this site—and do it under both state and federal laws for the preservation of antiquities."

"Mr. Jameson." The Indian squared his shoulders and straightened up to his full height. He towered over Mac and Jimmy. "We've selected a number of important mound sites that we would like to help protect. Right now we're attempting to gain landowner permission to include the sites in our district nomination—that's the paperwork we have to fill out. We can't list your site without your permission, sir."

Jimmy fidgeted like a toad leg frying in hot oil. "Wait a minute," he said. "What's my pa have to agree to if he goes for this nomination crap?"

Steiger bristled at the last word. She fixed Jimmy with a look that would have liquefied metal. Mac squelched his amusement when his son-in-law unconsciously took a step backward. That little woman might look frail, but Mac suspected that she could take on a grizzly and come out about even.

"I don't think we've been introduced," Steiger said stiffly to Jimmy as she extended her hand.

Jimmy shook it once and quickly withdrew, moving to stand halfway behind Mac. "I'm James Andrew Ortner. I work this farm with Mac."

Work? You mean you lay around on your fat ass while I work this farm! Mac scowled unpleasantly at his son-in-law. "What do I have to agree to, Miss Steiger?"

"Just keep doing what your family has been doing for generations. Don't plow up the mound. Don't build on it. Don't disturb it in any way. Just leave it as it is. That's all you have to agree to, and there might be some tax breaks in it for you if you do. Congress is debating the issue." Half under her breath, she hissed, "Like they do every year."

Steiger and the Indian seemed to be waiting breathlessly for Mac's answer. He fingered the gray stubble on his chin while he watched a gust of wind sweep over the mound and rustle through the trees. The sweet scent of ripe barley pervaded the air. "That's it?"

"Yes," the Indian said, and almost as a goodwill token, he turned to Steiger. "Karen, could I have that box, please?" She took it from beneath her arm and handed it over. The Indian opened it gently and lifted out a beautiful black pot bearing spiral designs around the shoulder. "This is yours, Mr. Jameson. We confiscated it from the thief who robbed your mound." He handed the artifact to Mac. "Please let us help you protect this site."

"Well, I . . . I don't know," Mac hedged, not sure that he really understood all the government jargon. It sounded like they were offering to pay him, through a cut in taxes, for doing what his kin had been doing for centuries. And he knew for a fact that the government only took, it never gave. Some people might have accepted subsidies, but he never had. He knew that somewhere down the line, the conniving bureaucrats would figure out a way of getting it back fourfold. That was just the way the government worked. "Why don't you send me all the information and I'll talk to my wife and kids about it. This land'll be theirs one day, so they ought to have something to say in the decision."

The Indian nodded before extending his hand again. "Thank you for considering it seriously. We know you're busy, and we'll be going now. If you don't mind, could I call you next week?"

Mac nodded as he shook the agent's hand. "I guess that would be all right. Most of the crop should be in by then." For an Indian, Thecoel seemed all right.

"Thank you again, sir." The Indian nodded with extreme politeness to Jimmy before he walked away, back to his Bronco.

Steiger took Mac's hand in a strong grip, but her eyes went to Jimmy, sharp, alert, though she spoke casually. "Mr. Jameson, just so you'll know, Jessaby implicated a number of other people in his crimes. We've no evidence against them yet, but if we get any, we'll certainly inform you. We believe that you have a right to know the names of the people who have stolen your property and plundered part of the heritage of all Americans." Her eyes tightened when Jimmy gave her a broad, macho grin. She said, "We'll be in touch, Mr. Jameson. Good day to you," before she walked back to her Bronco.

"Hey!" Jimmy shouted as he half-ran after her. "Wait a minute. What kind of pot is that? The one you gave my pa."

Steiger propped her hands on her hips as though reluctant to say. "We call it Ramey incised ware."

Jimmy's mouth gaped, but he quickly closed it. He waited until the two government vehicles rolled out onto the county road, plumes of dust following in their wake, before he reached out and ripped the pot from Mac's hands.

"Good God Almighty, Pa," he breathed as he stared unblinking at the black pot. "*A Ramey pot!* They made these special at Cahokia. Traded 'em all over kingdom come. We can get forty thousand dollars apiece for these in Japan! Holy Christ." He rubbed a hand over his sunburned face. Sweat had matted red hair to his temples in greasy strands. "I can't believe it. You ain't never gonna have to face no more hard times on the farm, Pa. Why, next week we'll bring the disk out and start taking that mound down inch by inch until we've found every one of these! We could be millionaires!"

Mac shifted uneasily. "But what about protecting our American heritage and all that?"

Jimmy's mouth puckered as though his father-in-law were stupid. "Come on, Pa! Don't you want to leave anything to your kids? This piece of sod ain't gonna be worth nothing in five or ten years. You know that! Why, what's a 'heritage' compared to a pretty dress for your daughter Janie? And how about a college education for little Matthew? Huh? James Junior could use a red Porsche, for God's sakes! He's almost sixteen. Come on, think!"

Jimmy slapped Mac on the shoulder so familiarly that it made the old man rear up like a mad bear. Mac jerked the pot back. "Boy, when I need your advice, I'll ask for it. And I don't! Get back to the north forty and wait for the harvesters to come in." When Jimmy stood there with his jaw clenched, staring at the pot like he was about to make a dive for it, Mac shoved him so hard that they both stumbled sideways. "Get moving, goddamn it! I'll fire you right now, boy, even if you are my daughter's husband!"

Jimmy backed away, then spun and started stalking up the dirt road, but Mac could tell from the expression on his mad-dog face that the boy's thoughts had gone rough.

Mac sucked in a deep breath to steady himself as he watched Jimmy disappear over the crest of the hill. *Little sonofabitch. I ought to disinherit him just because.*

He quietly ambled over to the pile of dirt where the thieves had been digging. Carefully he made his way down into the hole they had carved out of the mound. "Forty thousand?" he murmured, giving the pot he cradled in one arm a quick glance. *That's almost unbelievable. For an old Indian pot? Why would the Japanese care about old pots?*

Laying the artifact aside, Mac sank down against the slope of the hole. He could see bits of shell and fragments of pots scattered everywhere in the back-dirt pile. He let his hand sink into the rich soil that his family had damned near worked itself to death over during the long years when prices soared and then plummeted. Mostly plummeted. He gripped the dirt in a tight fist and brought it up to his lips, kissing it gently. *My farm. Mine and Marjorie's.* Something poked out of the dirt, jabbing into his thumb.

Mac slowly uncurled his hand and squinted down at the tiny black wolf that gleamed in the sunlight. Made of polished stone, the shape had been smoothed over the centuries. It might have been a raven, but it looked more like a wolf. Then he glanced down at the place where he'd found the wolf, and his eyes narrowed. A rib marred the soil in a rounded arc. He rubbed his fingers over the area, revealing two more ribs, and a skull with a round hole in one side. Perfectly round. As if the hole had been deliberately drilled for some kind of brain surgery. He looked again at the stone wolf, still in his hand. It would have been resting just about over the heart—like the pendant of a necklace.

"Did you wear this, honey?" he asked softly, not knowing why he thought the skeleton belonged to a woman. Maybe it was just the delicacy of the bones, and maybe it was because he knew that this mound held his own daughter's body. A tingle shot out of the wolf and played over his fingertips. Mac tilted his head when the wind started to sound odd, like flutes lilting high and sweet, as if calling to him from a great distance.

He shook his head. Strange, the way sounds echoed down here close to the road. Gently, he put the stone wolf back in place between those narrow bars of ribs, then brushed the dirt over the skeleton, leaving her as she was before somebody tried to rob her grave.

Grave robbing. His jaw tightened.

He got to his feet, picked up the Ramey pot, and trudged up out of the hole, where he stood in the lengthening shadows cast by the trees on top of the mound. He let his eyes drift over the grassy contours of the slope, noting each bush and rock. Beautiful. It always had been. For as long as he could remember, that mound had provided the only shade for miles. *And Jimmy boy wants to disk you down, old gal. Well . . .*

Mac tipped the Ramey pot sideways to get a good look at it. It almost glowed beneath the sun. He wondered how the Indians got it so black. Had it belonged to that dead woman? Might have. The robbers had taken it from pretty close to her grave.

His faded eyes drifted to the top of the mound, where his daughter lay. He tried to imagine how he would have felt if the thief had started digging at the top of the mound instead of at the bottom. Far back in his mind he could hear Marjorie crying—just as she had cried on that terrible day thirty-five years ago when they'd lain their Katherine Jean in that dark hole. Anger mixed with hatred, stinging his veins. Why, he'd have found the bastard that dug up his girl's grave, and he'd have been carrying his old thirty-thirty when he did. He turned and glanced uncomfortably at the Indian woman's grave.

"How'd you get that hole in your head, honey?" he found himself murmuring. "Didn't you have any folks to protect you? Where was your daddy when you needed him?"

Mac patted the John Deere affectionately before he fired her up and started lugging down the road for the house, the black pot snugged under his left arm. Hell, Jimmy could handle the harvesters. Mac wanted to go home. His old body felt suddenly too tired to work. And he knew that Marjorie would be waiting for him, waiting to welcome him home like she had for fifty-two years.

"Forty thousand dollars," he whispered as he shifted into third gear. The memory of those delicate ribs had imprinted itself on his very soul. *Good Lord. That's two years' worth of work on this old farm. Well, hell . . . maybe we could just disk down part of that mound. You know, just enough to find two or three more of these pots . . .*

Prologue

Unseen presences moved through the village of Talon Town, whirling in time to the beat of a pot drum, brushing ghostly shoulders with the human Dancers whose fluid movements brought life to the forces of the stars, clouds, lightning.

Long Horn had come, and the Mudheads. The War Brothers Danced behind them, their invisible arms reaching for the sky. They'd climbed down out of the Shining Mountains to join humans in celebrating the Spring Corn Dance—and to watch the happenings on this critical day in the history of men. They spun to the lilt of the flute, their spectral feet pounding out the same cadence that had created the world.

Unseen, unheard—except by one little girl who Danced with her head thrown back, her voice rising like wings into the deep blue of dusk. . . .

The wind came up suddenly.

Plumes of dust rushed down the sheer flanks of the tawny sandstone cliffs, hurling themselves at the people gathered in the central plaza of the giant pueblo. A few of the elderly yelled and ran for doorways as the battering veil of crimson struck. But everyone else kept Dancing, even the little children in their bright kirtles and doll moccasins. Fires sputtered, throwing the shadows of the Dancers like amorphous monsters on the clay-washed faces of the buildings.

Yarrow and Crane Girl trotted into the lee of a white-plastered wall to avoid the stinging bite of windblown sand. Only here, at the southern edge of the sprawling complex, could a person escape the brunt of the dust storm. Talon Town spread in an enormous crescent moon around the central plaza, its five-story height throwing long shadows across the towering red cliffs at its back. A chunky vista of buttes and ridges stretched to the west and curved around the south like a lover's cradling arm. The vanished sun threw a pink haze over the jagged drainages that wound through the valley bottom.

Yarrow and Crane Girl crouched down as best they could, given their child-heavy bellies. The excitement made them laugh out loud. Yarrow threw her head back, sniffing at the odor of warm desert dust mixed with the pungency of chamisa, greasewood, and sagebrush.

"Look at Nightshade!" Crane Girl said, squinting her slanting brown eyes against the windblown locks of short black hair that slapped her in the face. She drew her turkey-feather cape over her head for protection. "She looks like she's been Dancing for twenty summers! Perfect!"

Yarrow shouted against the tempest, "She's been practicing. She said she didn't want to look stupid this time."

Her four-summers-old daughter Danced near the front of two serpentine lines composed of men, women, and children. Naked to the waist, Nightshade wore white moccasins, a red-and-green kirtle, and a yellow cap decorated with copper bells. A turquoise pendant bounced over her bare chest, while waist-length black hair whipped around her shoulders, tangling in the sprig of pine she carried in her left hand. Her right hand shook a gourd rattle. Yarrow could not hear her daughter, but she could tell that Nightshade Sang with all her heart. Her little head rocked with the effort.

The brunt of the dust storm passed. Yarrow watched as the swirling wall of red raced through the sage in the distance. The wind died down to a warm caress punctuated by occasional gusts.

The two lines of Dancers flared outward, turning, dividing, linking themselves into four slow-moving circles. Nightshade seemed confused by the action and let out a small yip. Then her eyes widened as she raced around, shoving through the closest circle to join the correct one.

Yarrow clamped a hand over her mouth in embarrassment. "Well, almost perfect."

Crane Girl laughed and patted her belly. "I hope my child works as hard at her age. Nightshade is always trying to fit in."

Yarrow's brows pinched together, but she tried to smile. Crane Girl didn't realize what she'd said, though her words affected Yarrow like a fist in the stomach. *Yes, Nightshade tries hard to fit in. Too hard. She's always been different. She never plays with other children. She's forever locked inside her own soul, talking to Spirits no one else can see. It's my fault, for having inherited the Tortoise Bundle.*

Yarrow's mother and grandmother had been great shamans, but not she. She had inherited the Bundle, as was her right as the eldest daughter, but she had never been able to coax life from it. It sat, quiet, dead, in her room, as if waiting for some cataclysmic event to free its Power. Only Nightshade seemed to hear the Bundle's voice. The little girl would stay up all night sometimes, listening to it, telling the Bundle the childish secrets she ought to have been sharing with her mother.

And Sun Father knew, Yarrow could have used the companionship. Since Red Cane's death last autumn, she had been more lonely than she'd ever admitted. Losing her husband had gouged a wound inside her that had never stopped bleeding. Strangely, Nightshade seemed hardly aware that her father had vanished from her life. It worried Yarrow, but she couldn't bear to force her little girl to face that terrible truth, especially when Yarrow herself could scarcely face it.

A layer of purple swelled over the ridges, pushing up the pink of dusk until Sky Boy's darkening belly devoured it. A few stars already peeked through the blanket overhead. As night deepened, the tangy scents of piñon pine and juniper grew stronger. Yarrow inhaled them, letting them soothe her aching body.

She had been working day and night, making clothing, cooking food, seeing that all of the correct ceremonial admonitions were obeyed by her clan members. Yarrow belonged to the Hollow Hoof Clan. As Keepers of the sacred Tortoise Bundle, they had to do everything just right, to set an example for the rest of the community. The slightest dietary violation or an emotional outburst could cause the Bundle to abandon the people. If that happened, the rains would stop and the land would blow away, taking the crops and people with it.

Yarrow forced her thoughts back to the Corn Dance, not wanting to think about the Bundle or its constant needs anymore. She had grown tired to the bones of taking care of it, smoking it every day in sweet grass, sprinkling it morning and evening with corn pollen, Singing over it to keep it happy.

Yarrow had to admit shamefully that had it not been for Nightshade's unflagging attention, she might have cheated on the ritual mandates.

The Dancers stopped and fanned out into a gigantic circle. They hooked their arms together and started kicking their legs out as they bobbed up and down. A hoarse trill began, rising until it echoed through the night like a flock of newborn meadowlarks.

The excitement felt palpable on the warm night air. The lilting of flutes and the chanting of voices soared. Hundreds of feet stamped and shook the earth with the force of Thunderbird's roar, preparing the world for the entry of the gods.

The wail of the flutes changed, intensifying, the notes dropping into a low, ominous range. Old people ducked through the doorways again, laughing, coming out to huddle together along the curve of the wall. In their pale shawls and snowy doehide boots, they looked ghostly.

"It's almost time!" Crane Girl cried happily.

"I'd better get the Bundle. I'll be right back."

Yarrow braced one hand against the wall and the other on her huge belly as she pushed to her feet. Awkwardly she ran around the end of the building and ducked through the T-shaped doorway into near darkness. Only the starlight streaming through the high windows lit the passageway. Her steps pattered lightly on the hard-packed dirt. She took the first left, ducking through another doorway to enter her room. The Bundle sat in the eastern wall niche, its polished hide gleaming in the starlight that penetrated the window.

Yarrow chanted reverently as she approached it. When she picked up the Bundle, a slight tingle prickled her fingers, but nothing more. She turned it over to admire her artistry. Red, yellow, blue, and white spirals alternated around the edge, imitating the designs on tortoise shells. In the middle she had painted a red hand. An eye glared out of the palm, black, glistening as though alive.

"Are you ready?" she asked softly. "It's time to renew the world."

She clutched the Bundle to her breasts and made her way down the dim hall and out into the evening again. In the sky, dust-spawned halos encircled the flaming points of stars. Eerie light penetrated the haze, turning the firelit faces of the Dancers from gold to a smoky crimson. Yarrow wet her lips and trotted back to sit beside Crane Girl. She snuggled down against the white plaster, waiting.

A sharp yell eddied through the crowd.

Then another.

Old man Carrying Wood shuffled backward across the plaza, sprinkling the hard-packed soil with bright yellow cornmeal to sanctify the way. His gray hair hung like a cape down his blue-painted back.

People surged forward to get a look at the spectral figures that glided up from the subterranean ceremonial chambers. Then the crowd rolled back before them in whispering waves, readying a path for the gods.

Silence fell, heavy, expectant. Not even the wind breathed as the six figures floated into the plaza, the bells on their moccasins tinkling, their magnificent capes of blue-and-red parrot feathers swirling about them.

The boom of the pot drum began again, slow, infinitely patient, leading the gods into the flickering light of the fires. Swaying, dipping, taking shape, the gods coalesced into twenty-hands-tall figures with no arms or legs. Their masks caught the light and held it captive in glistening turquoise eyes and twisted mouths of pounded copper. Buffalo horns curved up like supplicating hands, while long wooden beaks made a *clackety-clack* in perfect time to the drum.

The *thlatsinas* had been created in the beginning of the world, when the people were tramping along the sacred Road of Life searching for the Middle Place. On the forty-ninth day of their journey, they had been forced to cross a raging river. Some of the children slipped off their mothers' backs and tumbled into the water, where they changed into strange creatures before swimming down the river to the Lake of Whispering Waters and establishing a town beneath the surface. In answer to the prayers of their mothers, they promised to come back once a cycle to the world of humans and Dance to bring fertility to the fields.

Yarrow could not suppress a smile at the expression on Nightshade's face. Her daughter stood riveted in the middle of the plaza, alone, her young knees trembling as she stared up into those oddly deformed masks: human, bird, and wolf.

Then a strange thing happened. Nightshade turned slightly to peer out at the darkness that cloaked the towering cliffs. Her mouth opened, her jaw hanging soundlessly for a moment before her scream broke loose.

People laughed, pointing as Nightshade threw down her pine sprig and gourd rattle and darted out of the plaza, running headlong for her mother. Many children reacted that way to the Dancers, but it puzzled Yarrow. Nightshade had never before been frightened during a ceremonial. In fact, she usually seemed unnaturally calm.

Yarrow rose to her feet just before Nightshade grabbed her frantically around the legs, shrieking, "Mother, run! Run!"

"Shh, Nightshade. The Dancers won't hurt you." She stroked her daughter's bare back. "They've come to help us, to bring life to the—"

"*No!*" Nightshade gripped her hand, tugging with all her young strength. "Hurry! They've come for *me*! They're almost here! Mother, please!"

Yarrow stumbled beneath Nightshade's tugs and almost dropped the Tortoise Bundle. "Nightshade, stop this! You're embarrassing me. Come on, let's—"

Movement stirred the sage at the edge of Yarrow's vision. She whirled and saw shadows careening through the brush beyond the plaza. The truth didn't register until the enemy warriors loosed their war howls. They burst into the plaza bellowing, shooting arrows, swinging clubs.

The crowd went wild, scrambling to get away. Yarrow fell back against the wall, dragging Nightshade with her. One enemy, a tall youth, swung his war club into the head of the lead Dancer, knocking the sacred mask into the dirt. Then he brought his club down on the old man's head. The sickening thud carried over the shouts and screams. Yarrow watched the *thlatsina* fall to his knees, gaze pleadingly at the sky, and silently topple into a heap of red and green feathers. She stared at the mask lying in the dirt, and her soul cried out in anguish. *Who could do such a thing?*

The warriors were cutting like wild dogs through the scattering crowd. Yarrow did not recognize their clan symbols or their hair styles. Tattoos covered these gaudy demons, and copper spools gleamed from their stretched earlobes. They had shaved their heads except for a bristly ridge that ran down the center, while their forelocks had been braided with shell beads. They wore long warshirts decorated with strange stones and the feathers of birds that didn't inhabit this part of the world.

A warrior ran at Yarrow and Crane Girl, his war club raised. He let out a bloodcurdling yell, his grisly face contorted.

Crane Girl lurched to her feet, struggling against her bulk in an effort to run. The warrior gripped her arm and swung her around. She screamed as his club smashed into her head. When she remained standing, he turned the club and used the jagged chert points embedded in the side to slash her throat. Crane Girl staggered, clutching at the blood that spurted from her neck before she wheeled and fell.

"Crane Girl!"

The warrior jumped over her corpse to fall on an old woman who had managed to crawl halfway into a doorway. He yipped shrilly before he dragged the woman back out and bashed his club three times into her gray head.

"Mother! Come on!" Nightshade sobbed. She clawed a gash into Yarrow's arm, and the stab of pain forced her mother into action.

Yarrow grabbed Nightshade's hand and dashed away, trying to reach their doorway. They rounded the corner, their skirts flying around their legs—and ran headfirst into three of the hideous, tattooed warriors. They'd been waiting there. How could they have . . .

Yarrow backed up, her knees almost too weak to support her. "Don't hurt us!" she begged. "Who are you? What do you want?" She shoved Nightshade against the wall behind her, trying to protect her daughter.

The warriors spread out into a semicircle. The leader stepped forward, fear and desperation in his black eyes. He was a big man, young, with a squat toad face and the burly body of Grandfather Brown Bear. The blue spiders tattooed on his cheeks twitched as if alive. He eyed the Tortoise Bundle fearfully, then scrutinized Nightshade's tiny face as she peered from behind the folds of Yarrow's skirt. Gesturing with a spike-studded club, he said something guttural, rough, which made the short warrior on the left—a man tattooed with frightening, forked eyes—swallow convulsively. The pale shell gorget on the man's breast jerked with the effort. Then the warrior on the right pointed at the designs on the Tortoise Bundle, nodding as though he recognized those colorful decorations and what the Bundle meant to Yarrow's people.

The muscular leader tensed, his glittering eyes slitted as he studied the Bundle. Then he nodded and barked a command.

The short warrior lunged for the Bundle, tearing it out of Yarrow's hands before the muscular leader shoved her away to get to Nightshade. He slung the squirming little girl under a massive arm as Yarrow stumbled to regain her balance. Yarrow barely noticed the third warrior draw his bow, the chert point oddly luminescent.

"*Mother!*" Nightshade cried. She kicked her legs in terror.

"Leave her alone!" Yarrow wailed as she threw herself on the men, beating them with her fists, raging, "Let my baby go! Let her go!"

She did not even feel the arrow that pierced her breast clean through, but the force of the impact sent her pitching sideways, and she struck the wall hard. She had to dig her fingernails into the mortar to keep from falling. Blood flooded into her throat, choking her. She fought to swallow it, but it welled too fast. The baby filling her belly kicked, and kicked again. From somewhere deep inside her, a pathetic little boy's cry rose. Panic held her for a few seconds, then faded into a curious sensation of acceptance. A gray haze swam around the edges of her vision, sapping her strength. She caressed the bright feathers protruding from the shaft buried in her chest as she slumped slowly down the wall. Her feet had become tangled painfully under her, and she couldn't move them. She sat, stunned.

Nightshade shrieked, *"Mother! Mother, Mother! Help me!"* Yarrow looked up to see her daughter's wide black eyes disappearing into the starlit darkness of the desert.

And something else . . . something that made Yarrow shake her head weakly to try to clear her eyes. A huge figure pranced after Nightshade, half transparent in Yarrow's wavering sight. It towered over the enemy warriors. Pivoting on one foot, the creature spun low to the ground, like Weasel chasing his tail, and Yarrow saw its massive, twisted face, colored with the pink clay of the sacred lake. One of the Dancers?

No. No, she could tell now.

A *Mudhead!* He Danced suspended between Earth and Sky, the undulant swaying of his arms sweeping clouds in and out of existence, parting the veil between Life and Death, Light and Dark.

Yarrow's body went completely numb, unfeeling. She sagged forward and sprawled over the cool ground. Since she could no longer blink her eyes, the windblown sand glued itself to the orbs, but through the gritty film she could still see the Mudhead. As the last breath escaped her lungs, he smiled grotesquely at her—sealing a bargain.

One

Lichen, daughter of the Morning Star Clan, ran along the ridge top, dodging the bristly arms of dogwood and beaver root until she found the trail that skirted the edge of the cornfield. The faded leaves of last cycle's crop snatched at her dress as she jumped a deep gully and angled down the incline, heading for the tan humps of limestone in the distance. Her friend Flycatcher's steps pounded behind her. She glanced over her shoulder to make sure that he could jump the gully. Flycatcher was a summer younger than she, barely nine, and he had the shortest legs she had ever seen on a boy. He took a flying leap and made it, but stumbled on the other side and fell to his knees. Dust plumed up around him. Flycatcher made a low sound of disgust.

Lichen laughed. "That was a deep one, wasn't it?"

"Who cares about deep?" he asked as he pulled himself to his feet. "It was as wide as the Father Water." He brushed the dirt from his bare legs and straightened the blue headband that kept his shoulder-length black hair out of his eyes. He had a round face and a small, forever-wiggling nose. Flycatcher liked to smell things—some of them pretty putrid, Lichen thought. Once last spring he had taken her to a recently abandoned bear den to prove to her that he could distinguish the cubs' sleeping places from the sow's just by the smell of the urine. Lichen couldn't see any use to such knowledge. She could tell the difference just by the look of the feces. Who wanted to smell urine?

As Flycatcher trotted toward her, Lichen turned and sprinted on down the trail. She passed the far boundary of the cornfield and descended the slope through a garden of boulders. The irregular surface bit at her moccasined feet. The trail had been worn into the stone here and was polished smooth by thousands of feet. But Wind Mother blew enough sand and gravel into the trough to make the going miserable until the traveler climbed up the next hill, where the rains swept the trail clean. Lichen moved along as fast as she could.

When she crested the slope, the beauty of First Woman's land lay spread around her, vast, and carved into odd shapes by the Ice Giants who had once roamed this swampy river country. In the rich bottom-land below, water rushed down dozens of creeks and flowed into a strewn handful of ponds and lakes. Women sat on the shores washing clothes. Men labored farther north, felling the scraggly trees that grew along the bluffs. The trees would be taken back to the mound construction sites in the great village of Cahokia. Everyone else had stopped building mounds long before Lichen had been born. Only the Sun Chief still worked to lift Mother Earth so she could touch fingertips with Father Sun.

Across the Father Water, to the west, tan-and-gray bluffs thrust their blunt noses into the turquoise sky. Lichen had never been there, but she knew that Pretty Mounds sat on the highest bluff. She had a cousin of the Grasshopper Clan who always came from Pretty Mounds to visit during the Green Corn ceremonial. To the south, the direction in which Lichen and Flycatcher ran, a bank of blue-black clouds trailed filaments of rain over gnarled limestone spires.

"How much farther?" Flycatcher panted.

"Not much." She pointed ahead. The irregular line of the bluff climbed to the tallest spire, which thrust out over the sheer cliff like a long snout. On the ledge beneath it, a thick copse of bare-branched oaks hid Wanderer's rock shelter. "Wanderer's house is in the side of the cliff, just past those oaks."

"Lichen?" There was hesitation in his voice. "Are you sure we should go see him? My mother says he's a crazy old witch."

"I have to talk to him, Flycatcher," she threw over her shoulder as she trotted on. "He's the only one who understands about my Dreams."

"But Mother says the village elders banished him from living with humans because he has the soul of a raven."

"He does," she answered blithely. "At least for the moment. He says his soul had many shapes before it became a raven. You'll like him. He tells great stories."

The pounding of Flycatcher's feet stopped. Lichen paused and looked back at him. He stood awkwardly at the bottom of the slope, the flap of his tan breechclout waving in the breeze that swept the bluff top. A morose expression contorted his face.

"What's wrong?" Lichen called.

Flycatcher gazed up speculatively from beneath his long lashes, but he didn't answer.

"Flycatcher! He's not as crazy as people say. Wanderer is just . . . different, but he's not bad. Come on, you'll see." She waved him forward, but he stood as though rooted to the tan limestone.

He wet his lips. "But what if Wanderer does something to us, like casts a spell on us?"

"A spell? What for?"

"I don't know! Maybe he'd witch us to make us lose our human souls so he can put raven souls in our bodies."

Lichen spread her arms and whirled on her toes, imitating the soaring flight of a bird. A sense of freedom possessed her as she spun, her tan dress fluttering around her skinny legs. "I've always wanted to fly, Flycatcher. Haven't you?"

"No!" he answered firmly, but he seemed to be trying to nerve himself for the last part of the journey.

Lichen put her hands on her hips and shook her head. The curtain of rain had drawn closer, blotting out the sun as it came. She felt the first drops, cool and wonderful, on her face. "Then go home," she taunted. "I'll go by myself. Just like always. But I'm telling you the truth. Wanderer's no witch, and he's not crazy either . . . mostly." She said the last in a voice so low that she knew he couldn't hear it.

Thunderbird chose that instant to bellow, and she saw Flycatcher leap two feet off the ground. His mouth dropped open as the roar rolled over the rocky prominence and down the flanks of the limestone into the bottomland below.

"See?" Lichen grinned. "Even Thunderbird agrees with me. You're a coward, Flycatcher!"

She turned and raced for Wanderer's rock shelter. Rain began falling in earnest, drenching her dress and the long black braid that bounced against her back. She tipped her pretty heart-shaped face so she could offer a soft prayer to Thunderbird, thanking him for the storm, praying he would bring more rain during the summer. The past few cycles had been so dry that the land desperately needed it, as did the animals and her people. Thunderbird's voice drove away the final chill of Frost Man and awakened First Woman so she could begin to tend the land. Soon the shaggy coats of the few deer left near the bluffs would turn glossy. Fawns would be born. And Lichen's people would throw off the bitter faces of winter and smile.

"Wait!" Flycatcher yelled. "Wait for me, Lichen. I'm coming!"

She slowed her pace but kept walking purposefully. She could see the outline of Wanderer's rock shelter, hidden in the tangle of branches ahead. The hair on the nape of her neck had started to prickle. Power did that; it rode the wind like tiny teeth until it could find a human and eat its way inside to coil around the soul.

That had happened to Lichen long ago. She had been just four summers when the first Spirit had walked in her Dreams. It had crept like tendrils of blue light from the tiny Stone Wolf that Lichen's mother guarded and had coalesced into a majestic Bird-Man, with an eagle's head and wings but the skin of a snake. The creature had knelt by the side of her bed and gazed at her through gleaming black eyes. *"Do you know why owls die with their wings outspread, little one?"*

She had shaken her head, too afraid to speak. She remembered trying to crawl deeper into the mound of worn hides covering her.

Bird-Man had gently touched her cheek with a snakeskin hand and murmured, *"Because they try to fly until the very last. They never give up and close their wings. They know that flight is their only hope of survival. In the beginning of the world, when Earthmaker formed the clay into mountains and deserts, humans used to have wings . . . like mine. It was in the time when animals and men lived together. A person could become an animal if he wanted to, and an animal could become a human. Would you like that, Lichen?"*

"Yes," she had responded timidly.

"The world needs you. There is a terrible war coming. First Woman has grown angry with humans. She wants to abandon the world and let all of you die. You will be able to save the world only if you can grow wings and fly to her cave in the Underworld to talk to her. To do that, you must learn to view life through the eyes of a bird, a human, and a snake. It's very difficult. The worst part is that once you open your wings, you will never be able to close them again—just like Owl."

"Would that be bad?"

Bird-Man had smiled sadly and bowed his head, staring at Lichen's bare toes, which had poked out from beneath her hides. Moonlight streaming in the window over her bed glinted off her toenails. *"Sometimes, Lichen, an owl longs with all its heart to be a snake so it can crawl into a hole and hide in the darkness."*

"Do I have to learn to fly now?"

"No." He had shaken his head mildly. *"Soon. You'll know when."*

Then Bird-Man had risen, opened his wings, and soared out her window into the starry night sky, going higher and higher until she lost sight of him.

Lichen still did not understand what he had been trying to tell her, but she had never forgotten his words. Her mother had explained that Spirits often spoke in riddles and that one day, when Lichen was older, she would understand Bird-Man's message.

Flycatcher interrupted her memories when he rushed up and bumped into her. He looked like he'd fallen again. Rain washed the bloody scratches that marred his elbows and the narrow gash that zigzagged down his right arm.

"Did you hurt yourself?" she asked, taking his arm to scrutinize the wound. Seeing that the blood had clotted, she released her hold.

"Your legs are too long," he commented by way of answer. "And I wish you'd act like a girl."

Lichen cocked her head. "What does a girl act like?"

"How should I know?" Flycatcher was always testy when he was scared.

Lichen shrugged and took him by the hand, confidently leading him toward the oaks beneath the spire. The trail split, one path leading up over the bluff top and across the overhang, the other angling down through the trees and onto the ledge where Wanderer's house sat, tucked into the hollow in the cliff face.

The rain had increased from a few pleasant drops to a blinding wall of water. They had to step carefully over the slick limestone as they made their way to the copse of oak.

Lichen ducked beneath the boughs and called, "Wanderer? It's Lichen. I've brought Flycatcher with me. Are you here?"

Wanderer had built his house in the dry, scooped-out area beneath the overhang so that he had needed to cut logs for only two sides. He had covered the upright poles with a thick mat of tan clay, which kept the house invisible unless one knew where to look. A tiny doorway and one window graced the front. Lichen pushed through the branches and trotted for the dry ground, glancing briefly at the brier of chokecherry bushes that fringed the rim of the ledge. Flycatcher scampered at her heels, looking like a frightened rabbit that had just escaped a flooded burrow. Wet straggles of black hair framed his face.

"Where is he?" Flycatcher whispered. "Is he here?"

"I don't think so." Lichen peered through the low doorway. Wanderer's house always smelled odd. The scent of cedar smoke, rich earth, and Spirit potions hung in the air. The room was a small, irregular rectangle, twenty hands by about fifteen. Because Wanderer had plastered the inside with white clay, it seemed to glow even in the dim light of the cloudy day. Covering the walls were power symbols: green squares and red spirals, black crescent moons, and purple starbursts. The old man's woven rabbit-fur blankets lay in a tumbled heap in the northern corner. All along the back wall, brightly colored baskets of coughgrass root, dried cactus blossoms, fish scales, snake heads, and other things that Lichen couldn't remember made bulges in the shadows—but Wanderer was gone.

Lichen sighed in disappointment and slumped down on the cattail mat that lay before the door. "Oh, Great Mouse, what am I going to do now? I *need* to talk to Wanderer."

Flycatcher eased down beside her, his brown eyes wide and wary. He propped his elbows on his drawn-up knees, and Lichen could see that blood still oozed from the scrape on his right arm. She decided not to say anything about it because she didn't want to embarrass him. Flycatcher got teased enough by his friends over his height and his awkwardness.

They sat in silence, watching the waving curtains of rain that moved over the river in the distance. Flashes of lightning darted at the bluffs as Thunderbird took the storm west. The chill in the air bit at Lichen's face and hands.

"What's that strange smell?" Flycatcher asked finally, his nostrils flaring as he scented the air.

"Wanderer probably made another potion for his aching joints. He tries new ones all the time. Nothing seems to help, though. I think he's just getting old."

"How old is he?"

"I don't know. Maybe fifty summers."

Flycatcher nervously picked at a loose thread on his breechclout. "What's he like?"

"He's a good man. He loves everything. And he's smart. I helped him fix a robin's broken leg last spring. We tied twigs around it to keep it straight. Then Wanderer built a cage and caught worms and insects for the robin to eat."

"He *fixed* its leg instead of eating it? He doesn't sound very smart to me," Flycatcher grumped. "Roasted robin tastes great." He sniffed the air again, obviously unimpressed with this place and Lichen's reasons for being here. "So what was this Dream you had that you have to talk to Wanderer about? Why couldn't you just tell your mother? She's the Keeper of the Stone Wolf. She's supposed to understand Spirit things."

"She does," Lichen affirmed, but she laced and unlaced her fingers uncomfortably. Her mother didn't have Wanderer's knowledge of other places and people, or his Power. But Lichen couldn't explain that to Flycatcher, because he would think she meant something bad about her mother, and she didn't, not really. Her mother had actually studied with Wanderer for a while, so she had to know some important things about Dreaming. "But I've missed talking to Wanderer, Flycatcher. He's my friend. I haven't been here in about three moons, and I—"

Scratching sounded on the rock ledge above their heads as a flock of cawing ravens swooped out of the clouds and dove for the cliff face. Flycatcher grabbed Lichen's arm in a death grip. The birds pulled up just before the shelter and floated on the air currents, clucking to each other as they eyed the two children.

"Who are they?" Flycatcher whispered hoarsely. "Part of Wanderer's family?"

"If they are, I've never met them here before."

Sand trickled over the ledge as something heavy moved across the stone above. Lichen and Flycatcher craned their necks to look.

"What is it?" Flycatcher hissed in panic. "A cougar?"

Lichen shifted to get up. "I don't—"

A shaft of sunlight pierced the clouds, lancing the rock shelter, and a loud *"There it is!"* split the day.

Flycatcher let out a hoarse scream as he and Lichen crashed into each other lunging to their feet, shoving and pushing, frantic to get away. But before they had taken three paces, Wanderer's tall, lanky form dropped from the overhang and landed like a thrown rock. Dust encircled him as he staggered sideways, his scant gray hair spiking out in wild disarray.

"Look at it!" Wanderer shouted and began grabbing up rocks and smashing them into the side of his house. "Hurry! Get some rocks. We have to kill it. It pounced on me first thing this morning! Tried to eat my feet!"

Lichen's body jerked with each impact of stone against wall. Flycatcher had clutched her shoulders and hidden himself behind her. She could feel his heavy breathing warm on her upper arm. They stared in utter terror at the house, against which the long, dark shadow wavered in the sunlight.

"Wanderer!" Lichen blurted. "That's your own shadow. Look how it moves when you do."

The old man stopped throwing in midswing. His rock-filled hand hovered over his head. He bent forward cautiously and squinted his faded brown eyes at the suspect darkness, then slammed his rock down and declared, "I wish you'd come earlier, Lichen! I wouldn't have wasted all day following it over the bluffs."

He strode forward in a tattered swirl of heavily painted wolf-hide robe and lifted her off her feet to hug her. "In fact, I wish you'd come moons ago. I've done some very strange things this winter. I think I'm changing form again."

Lichen pried herself loose from his grip when she heard Flycatcher make a strangling noise behind her. "Wanderer, we'll talk about it later, all right? I want you to meet my friend."

She turned and extended her hand to Flycatcher, who had flattened himself against the side of the house and was panting as though he had just finished a tough race.

Wanderer cocked his head and blinked at the boy like a demented owl. "Why, it's Flycatcher, isn't it? From the Serpent Clan. I remember the night you were born. What a nasty windstorm that was. It actually blew boulders off the ridge tops and sent them crashing down on people below." He shook his head and clucked noisily. "Yes, I recall that well. Course, I wasn't much help with the cleanup. I had the soul of a vulture at the time, and—"

"Wanderer!" Lichen cut him short when she saw Flycatcher's mouth gape. "Why don't we have some tea? I need to talk to you. I had a bad Dream."

"Oh, of course. You've come such a long way. You must have risen before dawn to get here so early." He knelt and gestured to his door. "Please, go on inside."

Lichen winked encouragingly at Flycatcher before she dropped to her knees and crawled into the cool, odd-smelling womb of the house. She went to the southern wall and sat cross-legged on a soft pile of fox hides. She heard Wanderer say, "Come on, Flycatcher, you little snake. I've got baskets full of your dead kin in there for you to look at. Hurry it up! Do I have to cast a spell on you to get you into my house?"

Flycatcher dove through the doorway in a flying whirl of arms and legs. He scrambled up beside Lichen and whispered "Not crazy, huh?" before he sank back into the shadows, wishing he could disappear.

Wanderer ducked through the entry and smiled in that lopsided way of his. "My, it's good to have someone come to see me again. It's been such a long winter. How's your mother, Lichen? Did she ever go on the vision quest you mentioned last fall? As I recall, she was still struggling to tap the Power in that Stone Wolf of hers."

"Yes. I guess the vision quest worked a little. She says that sometimes, after she's fasted and prayed for six days, she can feel the feathery touch of harmony coming from the Wolf."

"Well, she's making progress then, though she has a long way to go to reach the Land of the Ancestors in the Underworld. I wish her well. And how about you? You had a bad Dream? A Spirit Dream?"

A single raven, a huge bird with a gnarled beak, fluttered down to sit on the windowsill. It peered suspiciously at Flycatcher and Lichen. Flycatcher sank his fingernails into Lichen's arm, and she wrenched away in self-defense. Red crescents marred her smooth skin.

Wanderer cawed to the creature, moving his head in a birdlike fashion. The raven cawed back. Wanderer cocked his head. "Why, thank you, Crossed Beak. No, I didn't know that," he said.

Lichen peered at the bird from the corner of her eye. "Yes," she replied as she watched Wanderer move about. Because of the low ceiling, he had to stand in a hunched position while he gathered the makings for a fire. "A Spirit Dream."

Wanderer's rumpled shadow swept the room as he arranged the twigs and kindling in the stone-lined hearth in the middle of the floor and used his firebow to get a small blaze going. Flickers of light pranced across his long, beaky face. Then he propped two stumpware supports on the outskirts of the flames and braced his pot on top of them. After that, he wilted onto his tumbled blankets.

"Well," he said, "let's hear about it while we wait for the water to heat up. The Dream must have been frightening to drive you to me again."

Lichen cast a sideways glance at Flycatcher. He sat rigid, his eyes on Wanderer. He had twined a hand in one sleeve of her dress, grasping it tightly lest she try to get too far away from him. He seemed to be examining the Power designs on Wanderer's robe. A stylized tortoise spread its red legs across the old man's chest. From the end of each red leg, a green spiral spun out.

Lichen leaned forward eagerly. "I heard a voice calling me, Wanderer. I followed it through a dark mist where fireflies flashed all around me, until I saw wooden stairs built into the side of a huge mound. When the mist cleared, I walked up the steps into this big, round room. Seashells lined every wall. It was beautiful. Firebowls streamed out around a raised platform like sunbeams."

"Ah . . . the Sun Chamber at the Temple Mound in Cahokia."

Lichen's heart stopped. In hushed awe, she whispered, "You've been there?" Only the greatest holy people were ever allowed to enter that forbidden space.

"Oh, yes, many cycles ago, when I was teaching Nightshade. That was before Tharon cast her out of Cahokia, of course. It's a magnificent place." He shoved a larger piece of oak into the fire and prodded the kindling until the flames leaped beneath the pot. "I wonder what the Cahokians want with you. Tharon, the Sun Chief, is not a good person to be wanted by. Many people call him a sorcerer."

"I've heard my grandmother speak of him. Didn't he burn up Hickory Mounds this winter?"

"Yes. Great wickedness walks with him." He reached into a blue-and-red basket, pulled out a handful of leaves, and dropped them into the boiling pot. Steam rose in a glittering veil around his face.

"What's that strange smell?" Flycatcher sat up straighter to sniff the flowery fragrance that filled the room.

"My own tea mixture," Wanderer answered. "It's made from mint, elderberries, and prickly pear blossoms."

"What does it do to a person?" Flycatcher demanded.

"Do? Why, it clears the head and takes the soul up—"

Wanderer stopped abruptly to scowl at a fly buzzing around the ceiling, and Flycatcher quit breathing. To make matters worse, the raven on the windowsill let out a low shriek and took wing, squawking as it soared away.

Flycatcher rose to his knees, clearly getting ready to bolt. "Up where?"

"Up where?" Wanderer repeated as if he had never heard the words before. He snatched at the fly, missed, and grumbled, "Where what?"

"You said that your tea takes the soul up somewhere. I want to know where." A tremor had invaded Flycatcher's voice.

Wanderer broke into a broad grin. "You're an inquisitive little reptile, aren't you? Did you know that a person's entire future can be read in the wrinkles of dried elderberries? I've spent the past forty cycles making collections for nearly everyone in Redweed Village—barring the youngest babies, of course. I couldn't know about them. Here, let me see if I can find yours. If I recall correctly, it's . . ." He grabbed a basket and proceeded to ransack it, sending black, shriveled berries jumping like popcorn. "Great Mouse! I hope I didn't throw any of those berries into my tea."

"Wanderer," Lichen sighed, "we were talking about my Dream. About the Sun Chamber."

He studied her as though he hadn't the vaguest notion of what she was talking about. "Were we?"

"Yes."

"Well, what was I saying? . . . Oh, wait! I remember." He threw the basket down, heedless of the fact that about twenty berries bounced out onto the hard-packed surface. Flycatcher looked appalled, as if half of his life had just rolled into the crevices in the floor. "That's right, we were talking about Tharon. His madness started with Night-shade . . ." A distance filled his gaze, as if he looked back across time. His voice gentled. "Yes, Nightshade."

"Who?"

Wanderer made a delicate gesture, the way he would push aside a cobweb. "Twenty or so cycles ago, the great priest, Old Marmot, had a Dream that the reason Mother Earth had turned against the Cahoki-ans and the corn couldn't grow anymore was that the people needed to go south and west, into the Forbidden Land of the Palace Builders, to steal a little girl and a Power Bundle. The great warrior Badgertail led that battle-walk. But Old Marmot got more than he bargained for in Nightshade. By the time she'd turned ten, she had more Power than Marmot had ever dreamed of. Gizis, Tharon's father, had hired certain artisans to produce his famous Wellpots—those are the black ones Tharon trades to special leaders—but when Nightshade got hold of the pots, she started breathing terrible Power into them. Gizis forced her to teach all of the other priests and priestesses how to do it too, of course, but Old Marmot hated—"

"She breathed Power into them? Power to do what?" Lichen asked softly.

Wanderer jerked his chin up, startled by the question. "Why, Power to swim to the Underworld. Everyone has his own method of getting there, and the Wellpot is Nighshade's method. Anyway, Tharon went mad when he sneaked into Nightshade's chamber one night and dared to gaze into her Wellpot. He said his heart started jumping around in his chest so badly that he almost died. He claimed that a pink-faced Spirit had tried to devour his soul."

Flycatcher hunched forward slowly, looking like a vulture spying on a dying rabbit. He whispered hoarsely, "Nightshade breathed evil Spirits into those pots?"

Wanderer matched Flycatcher's expression and posture, staring back breathlessly at the boy for a moment. "What would make you think that?"

"Well, you just said—"

"Come here."

When Flycatcher flung himself back against the wall, Wanderer crawled across the floor, grabbed Flycatcher's recalcitrant head, and started rapping on the top of it with his knuckles, as though sounding it out. "No, too bad," he pronounced and promptly duck-walked back to study the boiling pot.

Flycatcher croaked, "What? Too bad what?"

Wanderer waved a careless hand. "Oh, it's just that humans are born with a soft spot in the top of their heads through which they can communicate with Earthmaker. In most people, the spot closes up when they're very young and reopens only at death to let the soul depart to the Land of the Ancestors. But!" He shook his finger emphatically. "A person can learn to keep it open if he tries. I thought maybe you'd been getting messages from the Spirits about Nightshade. Turns out you were just guessing." He paused, frowning thoughtfully. "But you know, I do brain operations. I could fix that for you."

Flycatcher sat rigid with terror as Wanderer took a wooden cup and dipped it into the pot, smelled the aroma appreciatively, then handed it to Flycatcher, who vehemently shook his head, then to Lichen, who took the cup gratefully. She'd had the tea before and knew how sweet it tasted. Nothing had ever happened to her soul because of it.

Wanderer dipped some of the brew for himself and lounged back on his blankets. "Tell me more about this Dream, Lichen. Did you see people?"

"Yes. A little girl. About my age. She was wearing a painted mask with black-and-white squares on it, but I knew she was crying, even though I couldn't see her face."

"Was she the one who called out to you and led you to the Sun Chamber?"

"I think so."

"Why was she crying?" He took a long sip of his tea and smacked his lips as he grinned at Flycatcher.

"I'm not sure, but I felt something horrible. A group of old, gray-haired shamans were hunched on the floor around her. I—"

"Priests," Wanderer corrected. "At Cahokia, they call them priests and priestesses. So . . . what were the priests doing?"

"Singing, and I saw this huge blackness rise over the temple on the tallest mound. It hovered for a little while, then flew north, like the smoke of a forest fire pushed by the wind."

Wanderer set his cup on the floor with a sharp crack. "The blackness flew north?"

She nodded.

Wanderer shot to his feet and turned first one way and then another. "No, no." His stooped position and the curious tilt to his head made him look like a gawky heron. "It doesn't necessarily mean they're coming for us, but if they are, we'd better . . ."

His voice trailed away, and Flycatcher cupped a hand to Lichen's ear. "He's as crazy as a rabid skunk! I'm getting out of here. Are you coming?"

"Just a little longer," she whispered back.

Wanderer moved erratically around the room, touching the colorful Spirit symbols on the walls and blowing at the fly that buzzed around his ears. After a few moments, he stopped and his eyes cleared. His madness disappeared, replaced by a seriousness that frightened Lichen. When he turned to gaze at her, a prickle climbed her spine.

"What is it, Wanderer? What are you thinking?"

"Hmm?" he asked, studying her with unnerving concentration. "Thinking? Oh, I wasn't thinking at all . . . except, well, last week Crossed Beak brought me news about a series of murders at Cahokia. All of the priests and priestesses who could breathe life into the Wellpots were killed—except for Nightshade. I was just wondering about the murders. And why the little girl in your Dream is crying."

"Do you think they're connected? Maybe somebody's killing people who can breathe life into the pots, and the little girl is sad because somebody she loved was murdered?"

His bushy gray brows lowered. For a moment their gazes held, and Lichen's heart pounded against her ribs in anticipation. "I pray not. Nightshade lives at River Mounds now. I don't know what she'd do if someone had the boldness to make an attempt on her life." He fumbled uneasily with his cup. "She might just rip the world asunder in rage."

"So why would the little girl be calling me, Wanderer? How could I help her?"

Wanderer blinked suddenly. "Why, I haven't the slightest notion." Throwing up his skinny arms, he blurted, "Now, where was I? Oh, I was looking for that bowl of berries I collected on Flycatcher's life. Where could I have put it?"

Flycatcher pinched Lichen's arm so hard that she yipped. "I'm getting out of here before he can find it!" he announced.

Wanderer was shuffling through a tangled clump of parfleches, mumbling to himself, when Lichen said, "I guess we should be going, Wanderer. We have to be home before sundown." She finished her tea in three long gulps and handed her cup to him. "Thank you for the tea and for talking to me about my Dream."

Flycatcher scrambled across the floor, crawling madly for the doorway. He was out into the sunlight before Lichen even got to her feet. She heard the cawing of ravens and the mad pounding of his moccasins.

Lichen walked over to Wanderer and patted his arm. He grinned. In the wavering amber glow of the fire, his face seemed older, more wrinkled and gaunt, but the twinkle had returned to his eyes. "You take care of yourself, Wanderer. I missed you this winter."

"Oh, I've been fine, really. I'm just a little disturbed about this weasel that's trying to take over my soul, but I guess if First Woman's set on it, there's nothing I can do to stop it." His face slackened. Vulnerability and an odd tinge of fear entered his voice. "Lichen, about your Dream . . . I want you to talk about it with the Stone Wolf. Maybe it can help. The darkness moving north worries me."

Her hand quaked before she let it fall to her side. "But Mother doesn't like me to get near the Wolf, Wanderer, and it's never called out to me before. What makes you think—"

"Power has taken to the wind again. The Wolf will know that. There's no saying who or what it's trying to corner. Maybe you, my only friend." He rapped the top of her head, listened speculatively to the hollow sound, then smiled approvingly. "You'd better go. Flycatcher's probably to the cornfields by now."

Lichen laughed. "Yes, I'll bet he is. Thank you again. I'll try to come back soon."

"Good. I've missed our talks."

She ducked out the doorway and into the slanting rays of afternoon sunlight, shielding her eyes to see if she could spot Flycatcher. A flock of ravens soared over the trail in the distance, and beneath it, curls of dust sprouted. She thought she heard vague shrieks.

Lichen picked up her feet and began running with all her might, flying over the wet limestone, trying to catch up with Flycatcher before he could hurt himself again.

Two

More than one hundred war canoes sliced through the predawn mist that rose in ghostly streamers from Marsh Elder Lake. Curving prows cut acute chevrons into the glassy water as they slipped silently forward, phantoms in the wavering haze. The red-and-blue animal figures painted on the hulls of the slim dugouts gleamed as darkly as old blood in the dim light. Paddles flashed, powered by muscular arms sending the craft onward. The tattooed faces of the warriors displayed a variety of emotions: unease on some; here and there, anticipation; grim purpose, or fear; and, finally, the thin-lipped tension of distaste.

Night still cloaked the water, but a faint slate-blue glow shone on the eastern horizon. The scent of fish mixed pungently with the odors of frozen mud and dead grass.

The great warrior Badgertail crouched in the bow of the lead war canoe, feeling ill, shivering. His heavy brows lowered as he squinted into the chilly mist, vainly attempting to penetrate its twisting veil.

Defeated, he raised his gaze to the purpling sky. Grandmother Morning Star hung above. Her bright countenance tarnished the land with a silver sheen. A few of the Star Ogres' constellations huddled around her. Faint outlines betrayed their identities: Hanged Woman, Wolf Pup, and Great Deer. But most of the Ogres had retreated to their caves in the Underworld to catch some sleep before Father Sun ordered them to rise again and light the evening skies.

"I hate this," Bobcat murmured behind Badgertail, keeping his voice low lest the other six warriors in the canoe hear him. "I wish we could run away."

Badgertail exhaled, his breath clouding in a wreath around his face. "You're young. Battle is as much a part of life as eating or breathing."

"And you, my brother, are getting old and blind. This is not battle. It's slaughter! The Sun Chief has truly gone mad this time."

"Tharon frightens me, too, Bobcat. But I don't think he's mad. I'm inclined to believe he's a boy in a man's body. Petulant. He's—"

"He's my age! Twenty-eight summers. How can you call him a boy?"

"He may be twenty-eight, but he's been locked inside the palisades at Cahokia for nearly his entire life. How would you feel if you'd never even been able to dip your fingers into the creek a hundred hands behind your house? He knows nothing about the outside world. He's as much a prisoner of the Sun as the Star Ogres are."

"That may be," Bobcat scoffed, "but if he doesn't learn about the outside world, his idiocy is going to destroy our people. And Blessed Moon Maiden knows he'll never be able to marry again. Who would have him? If he can't marry, Cahokia will be cut off from the world."

Badgertail nodded somberly. "I know."

"He's so hated by the other Sunborn that I don't see how his clan elders can ever approach the others about an alliance through one of their daughters. And you, my dear brother, don't help him any. You're always coddling Tharon's weaknesses, bringing him little gifts from every battle-walk."

"We need the chief on our side. Tharon will not last forever, but neither will the chiefdom unless we are allowed to—"

"We can all pray that Tharon will not last forever. The sooner he goes, the better."

The harsh tone made Badgertail swivel his head. Bobcat met his gaze briefly before looking away in shame. Though Bobcat had turned twenty-eight two moons ago, he looked much older than that. Lines had etched the corners of his dark eyes, giving his handsome oval face an air of seriousness—unlike Badgertail, whose toadlike, bemused face tended to make people think he was smirking at them when he wasn't.

Both he and Bobcat had woven shell beads into their braided forelocks. The remainder of their skulls had been shaved, except for a bristly ridge down the center. Copper ear-spools the size of large nuts filled their distended earlobes, the sign of wealth and status. Tattoos adorned their bodies. Badgertail had blue spiders on his cheeks; black-and-blue mazes covered his chest, arms, and legs. He wore a fabric warshirt, dyed in brilliant colors by the master weavers of Cahokia. Heavy, shell-beaded necklaces hung at his throat, the insignia of his hard-earned rank.

Red concentric squares blanketed Bobcat's forehead. His warshirt bore his personal Power symbol: the red image of a snarling wolf. Barely visible under the fine fabric lay his conch-shell gorget with its interlaced woodpecker heads, the badge of the Woodpecker Warrior Clan.

Badgertail's hand drifted to his own chest to lightly caress the green image of a falcon that overlay his shell gorget. His fingertips tingled from the Power there. "I cannot disobey my orders, Bobcat. What would you have me do? Help destroy our way of life . . . and bring the wrath of the Sun Chief down on all of us?"

"No, brother. I would have you grab your pack and run away with me after this battle-walk. Moonseed will agree. She's an obedient wife to me. We could do it, Badgertail! We could run away. Then neither of us would have to obey his foolish orders ever again."

"And where would we go?" Badgertail asked in a melancholy voice.

"Anywhere. It doesn't matter."

Is that how Keran's legacy would end? Badgertail's muscular hands tightened on the carved wood of his oar. Keran, Tharon's legendary grandfather, had welded the small chiefdoms together through a cunning campaign of diplomacy, trade, marriage, and, of course, the Woodpecker Clan—the elite warriors born of Commoner and Sunborn. Men like Badgertail and Bobcat.

Keran had overcome the jealousies and established Cahokia as the major center of power, dominating not only the Father Water, but the Mother Water and the Moon Water rivers. In most cases, Keran had been able to cajole, threaten, bribe, or wheedle the other mound centers into his alliance, but when that failed, his warriors, led by the Woodpecker Clan, had forced the recalcitrant chieftains into compliance, and often into forced marriages to create kinship bonds, with their important obligations.

For two generations, the Sunborn had ruled the chiefdoms, each marrying its young men off to the other mound centers, strengthening the ties of clan and family. And for two generations, the heavy canoes of the traders had plied the waters from one end of the land to the other, bearing a variety of wealth: conch shell and sharks' teeth from the sea to the south; buffalo hides from the plains far to the west—and obsidian from the mountains beyond them. Traders even brought olivella shells from the southeastern seas. Corn traveled back and forth on heavily laden canoes when harvests failed. Red pipestone and steatite soapstone traveled down from the conifer forests, and copper from the western shores of the Great Lakes in the north. Similarly, mica was brought from the southern tributaries of the Moon Water, as were fluorspar, barite and salt. From the far reaches of the Moon Water came granite, gneiss, and schist, to be ground into maul heads, celts, maces, and ax heads. From the west, beyond Pretty Mounds, came ocher, hematite, and galena. From the mountains a moon's journey to the southwest came large quartz crystals.

In return, the artisans of Cahokia worked the raw materials, creating stunning shell beads, nets, fabrics from basswood and cottonwood bark. From weed stems they created silky, soft textiles, dyeing them in colors as brilliant as the rainbow itself. Effigy pipes and delicate ceramics were produced to repay the surrounding chiefdoms with luxury and status goods.

So much had been gained from Keran's vision. *Is it all to come to an end now? Could Badgertail run away? Desert great Keran's grandson in this terrible time of failed harvests?*

Paddles splashed around them, timed to the lilting wail of a flute. The notes gained a ghostly resonance as they traveled over the expanse of water. A few of his warriors Sang, their voices rising and falling in a haunting melody that echoed from the towering banks.

> *We pray for victory, Thunderbird. Give us victory, victory, victory.*
> *Let us die and be reborn at will, as lightning is.*
> *Against the great darkness, we are falling, into its center, falling.*
> *Let us drive our arrows into our enemies' hearts as you drive lightning into the breast of Mother Earth.*
> *Give us victory, Thunderbird, victory, victory . . .*

The words touched Badgertail with the strength of rosin weed, clinging powerfully to his thoughts. Victory? Over what? Over who? He frowned. Ahead, still out of sight, lay the thatched houses in the village of River Mounds. People there would be waking, cooking meals, saying prayers to the rising face of Father Sun.

Bobcat is right. How can you do this when you know it's wrong? These are not enemies! What has happened that we've come to attacking our own people?

Badgertail and Bobcat had relatives in River Mounds—members of their Squash Blossom Clan. Perhaps even a niece or nephew. Their great-grandmother had been born in River Mounds.

He turned to glance at those who rowed behind him and caught Locust's stare on him: hard, unforgiving. Thirty-four summers old, she had a face like a field mouse, narrow and pointed, with black, glistening eyes. She had cut her black hair so that it brushed the shoulders of her warshirt. They had grown up together, witnessed their families killed, their homes ravaged, in the last days before Keran's vision of peace had been fulfilled. Locust knew Badgertail better than he himself did. Long ago, when they'd both been young and rash, he had wanted to marry her. Probably he still did somewhere deep inside, although it had been twenty-two long cycles since that day. They were cousins—each of the Squash Blossom Clan—and such a marriage was taboo. Forbidden.

Since then, Locust had taken a wife, as was customary for a warrior of her status. To have taken a husband would have demeaned her and forced her into the traditional role of a woman, that of cooking, cleaning, and bearing children.

As in all things, the clan ruled. Just as they made decisions about what to plant and who would tend the fields, so did the old women decide when a man should marry. Noticing Badgertail's attraction to his cousin, his grandmother had taken matters into her own hands. He had been forced to marry a woman of the Deer Bone Rattle Clan named Two Tassels. His marriage had been arranged by his grandmother and great aunt, each powerful in clan politics at the time. Since Badgertail had built a reputation as a warrior, and since the Squash Blossom Clan had desired a trading relationship with Flying Woman Mounds, to the east on the Moon Water, they had arranged the union.

The memory prickled in Badgertail's thoughts the way wild rose scratched the skin. Accompanied by some of his kin, he had ridden one of the bulky trade canoes down to the mouth of the Moon Water, then pitched in, rowing the heavy cottonwood canoe for two weeks upriver to Flying Woman Mounds, the bride price stacked behind him.

He could still picture Two Tassels' face: sullen, distrustful, annoyed at having to marry an ugly warrior like him, when her heart yearned for another. Nevertheless, Badgertail had fulfilled his duties; he had labored for a season in her fields, lived in her house, and cared for her young son.

And then I left. He dug deeply with his painted oar, driving the war canoe forward. The dull, traditional life at Flying Woman Mounds was not for him. Not after the excitement of bustling Cahokia. A year after he'd returned, word had come through a young man of the Deer Bone Rattle Clan that Badgertail was divorced—but to maintain the kinship relation so important to the clans, the young man would "adopt" Badgertail as his brother.

Everyone had ended up content, but Badgertail had never quite accepted Locust's marriage. Oh, it comforted him that she was happy, but she'd taken a *berdache* wife: a woman in a man's body. Physically, Primrose was a man, but his soul was female, and therefore he wore his hair long and braided, like a woman, and adopted female dress, going about in a skirt. Primrose cared for Locust's house, tended the fields with the other women, and served as her lover . . . though in the fifteen cycles that Locust and Primrose had been married, Primrose had planted no children in Locust's womb.

Badgertail didn't understand it. Perhaps when a man had a female soul, he had no semen. Who knew?

He had almost overcome his attraction to Locust. The old fire returned to haunt him only on rare occasions now. Sometimes, when they had the leisure to lounge around camp, laughing and talking, he fell in love with her all over again, though he rarely admitted it to himself. She loved Primrose, and Badgertail would not disturb her happiness by intruding his own selfish desires.

Despite his hidden longing, over the years Locust had become his best friend. Being close to her soothed something deep inside him.

Badgertail dipped his paddle to keep the canoe skimming close to the bank. Glistening curls of black water trailed in the wake of his stroke. Warriors whispered behind him, their voices low, twining with the lapping waves until he could decipher only a few of their words. Someone boasted of how good it would be to sink a knife into Jenos' gut and feel the Moon Chief's life drain away. Another man laughed and uttered a brutal threat of what he would do to the women they captured.

Fools. Do they think that Nightshade will stand by and watch us destroy her home? . . . And later, will she follow Tharon's orders and return to Cahokia with us?

And if Nightshade knew of their plans, she would have told Hailcloud, Jenos' cunning and dangerous war leader. Once, in a kinder day, Hailcloud had saved Badgertail from a terrible defeat. They had shared the rigors of the battle-walk, and a friendship based on mutual respect had flowered. That, too, would die on this day.

Badgertail grimaced at the fading Star Ogres. Hanged Woman's face dimmed with each moment—like his sense of self-respect.

How many villages had he attacked in the past cycle? The killing and kidnapping sickened his soul, though he knew the reasons for them. The tribute system served as the sinew that bound their society. But it had been established hundreds of cycles ago, before drought and famine had stricken the land. In the old days, when First Woman guided them, villages could afford to contribute half of their corn and squash crops to sustain the trade and redistribution programs administered by Cahokia's Sun Chief. But not in these hard times. How could Tharon expect the lesser villages to keep tendering the same amount they always had? Especially when "redistribution" had ceased, because Tharon needed the crops to feed his own burgeoning populace of ten thousand at Cahokia.

First Woman has truly turned her face from us.

Badgertail had stood on the shooting platforms of the palisade during the dark days when Winter Boy breathed snow over the land and thousands came to slam their food bowls against the walls, begging for corn to feed their children.

"Tribute!" Bobcat hissed, as though reading the tracks of Badgertail's soul. "How can Tharon keep calling it that?"

"It's what it's always been called."

"Yes, and in the days when the Sun Chief's power protected the people, it had a meaning. But now? It's become a bribe. A ransom paid to stave off *our* attacks, brother. Have you forgotten the days when we *defended* our sister villages from outsiders? Have you? Keran's dream is dead. They are no longer our sisters, and we are snakes!"

Up on the banks, a lone owl hooted, and Badgertail caught sight of dark wings flapping over the water. For a moment, his soul ached at the bird's freedom.

He wanted to escape. But the chiefdom needed him. Thousands of people depended upon his ability to maintain order. And anyway, where could he go? He toyed with his paddle, rowing halfheartedly as he listened to the sweet notes of the flute in the growing light. He had sat around a hundred camp fires telling stories about his experiences far to the southwest in the Forbidden Land, where people grew corn on the bluffs and lived in stone palaces. He had even heard Nightshade herself spin legends about the gods who roamed the cactus-and-sage-covered deserts there. Sometimes, in his dreams, he lived there with them—as free as the eagles who soared over the red buttes.

Nightshade. Her enigmatic image haunted him. Beautiful Nightshade—eerie, frightening. Brave men lowered their voices when they spoke her name. *And once I carried her over my shoulder. Why are our paths always threaded together like a weaver's pattern in a fabric?*

He forced the unsettling thought from his head. "I'm far more worried about Tharon's obsession with Power objects than I am about tribute, Bobcat. What does he think he's doing by stealing every Power Bundle and coveting every ear-spool that's ever been proclaimed to have Power? It doesn't make any sense."

Bobcat gave him a disbelieving look. "It does to me. He's trying to gather all the Power in the world to himself."

"But why? Does he feel threatened if such objects belong to the shamans or the priests? What does he want with such a wealth of Power?"

"Who knows? Maybe he's trying to learn to dive into the Underworld himself."

Badgertail suppressed a shudder. Four times a cycle, the Starborn, priests and priestesses of the highest order, filled their black Wellpots with sacred water and dove into the Well of the Ancestors, swimming through the layers of illusion woven by First Woman to prevent the unworthy from finding the pitch-black Cave of the Tree, where she dwelt. First Woman knew the magical Songs to keep Father Sun and Mother Earth happy in their marriage. Without those Songs, Mother Earth would grow lonely, and in her despair, the crops would wither.

The chiefdom had been suffering under the brunt of Mother Earth's discontent for cycles. The large game had almost completely disappeared. He had been five summers when he had last seen an elk—though the legends told of a time when millions of them had dotted the prairies.

Badgertail had heard Old Marmot say that it was Nightshade's fault, that she'd begun to breathe *death* into the pots, not life. Marmot had claimed that Nightshade had blocked the entry to the Underworld through witchery, and he had admitted that he could no longer pierce the layers of illusion in the Underworld to find First Woman. Perhaps Bobcat's suggestion wasn't so farfetched. Did Tharon want to try it himself? Someone needed to do something—and fast. Oak and hickory had almost vanished from the uplands. In spring, the rivers and creeks flooded and drowned the crops, stunting their growth. The cornfields yielded barely enough to feed the thousands of hungry mouths. Old Marmot had declared that Mother Earth had fallen into despair.

The haunting notes of the flute died away as the flotilla rounded the last bend in the lake. Badgertail cocked his head. He could hear faint sounds from the village: dogs barking, the cry of a child. That pathetic wail knotted in his gut.

"Do you think Jenos suspects that Tharon has sent a thousand warriors to 'encourage' him to turn over the tribute he claims he does not have?" Bobcat's tone was bitter.

"If Nightshade knows, Jenos knows."

Bobcat froze, his oar lifted half out of the water. "You mean you think that she's foreseen our coming? That she knows we've orders to drag her back to Cahokia with us? If you really believe that, turn these canoes around and let's go home!"

"We can't be sure. Since Marmot died, we've no priest strong enough to send his soul swimming to see what she's up to. We'll know soon enough."

"Yes, when Hailcloud sends arrows flying over the palisade walls to land in our bodies. I like Hailcloud, I don't want to fight him. Badgertail, this is madness!" Bobcat banged his oar against the side of the canoe.

Very quietly, Badgertail responded, "I know that, brother."

The warriors had begun to stare. Bobcat noted their gazes and muttered something inaudible before stabbing his paddle back into the quiet water.

Badgertail's eyes barely brushed Locust's, and then he focused on the horizon. A dusty lavender glow washed the heavens and spilled over onto the land, flooding the beach ahead. "There," he ordered, pointing to the place on the shining sands where they would land. "Put in there."

When the bow grated to a stop, he jumped out into the cold water. The others leaped out and helped him drag the narrow hull onto the sand.

Up and down the shore, canoes landed and warriors armed themselves, slinging brightly painted quivers over their shoulders. Without a word, they ghosted away into the dawn to surround the village as Badgertail had planned.

He watched Woodchuck's warriors disperse, noted their positions and numbers, then bent to pick up his own weapons. His quiver felt heavy, pressing down on his shoulders as though already soaked with his relatives' blood. He hooked his bow on his waist thong.

Do not fight me, Jenos. No matter how good Hailcloud is, I'll win, and you know it. Give me a way out of this lunacy!

"Locust?" Badgertail called. She trotted up to him, her body taut as she searched his eyes. Badgertail gestured toward the mounds. "Bobcat and I will go alone. I want you and your men to wait here and watch for my signal. You know the plan."

"I do." Locust gestured to a hillock that jutted up from the bank. "I'll be there, watching." She waved an arm to her war party, and they followed her into the brooding shadows.

Badgertail grimaced at the east before forcing his reluctant feet up the slope toward the village. As he walked, frost from the dry grass dusted his wet hide boots. He had two fingers of time before Father Sun slipped over the horizon. It would have to be enough. The Sun

Chief's orders had been explicit. He wanted Badgertail and his flotilla back at Cahokia by tomorrow, *with the demanded tribute.*

Bobcat trudged by his side, wearing an expression of disgust like a badge of honor. Their fringed boots squished on moist sand as they crested the slope and strode out into the open expanse of winter-tan grass. Badgertail's skin prickled, vulnerable throughout the long walk to the palisade. The main gate made a dark square in the wall, defiant and dangerous. Badgertail extended his hands, palms up, in front of him, letting Jenos know that he had come to talk for one last time.

The palisade consisted of upright poles that rose twenty hands high around the central section of the village. The wall had been thickly plastered with clay and baked as a protection against fire, insects, and rot. Badgertail knew that away from the lake, on the western side of River Mounds, the Commonborn fended for themselves, unprotected by either palisades or professional warriors, though every male would be armed with a club and bow. He hoped they had witnessed his approach and fled into the hills.

"They're up there," Bobcat warned, indicating with a tilt of his head the shooting platforms that had been erected along the length of the palisades.

"I see them."

Faces glowed, the pale blue of flesh just visible over the sharpened ends of the poles. Four warriors occupied each platform; that would make nearly six hundred in all. More would be huddling inside, using the forty-five mounds in the village as cover. Badgertail anticipated around eight hundred armed opponents: desperate men and women who must win this battle if they were to feed their families through the rest of the winter.

He halted and called up to the platform over the main gate: "Leader Badgertail wishes to speak with the great Moon Chief. Will he open his arms to embrace his relatives this day?"

Jenos' rusty voice shouted back, "Will my father's obscure cousin order his warriors to lay down their bows until we have finished speaking?"

Bobcat huffed indignantly, "That old bear-bait!"

Badgertail smiled grimly at the insult. The people of the mounds traced kinship through the females. A man belonged to his mother's clan, disciplined his sister's children. When he married, he went to live in his wife's house and work her clan's fields. He had no say in his wife's household and could not speak to his mother-in-law, but must avoid her at all costs, not even meeting her eyes.

The Warrior Clans consisted of men and women born through the mating of the Sunborn with the Commonborn. Such mating had taken place when Badgertail's mother coupled with his Sunborn father. Jenos had just insinuated that no one believed the claim of Badgertail's mother—and this, if true, would have stripped Badgertail of his warrior's status and privileges.

Badgertail called back, "Your obscure cousin will—for one hand's worth of time, Jenos. No more. *If* you will guarantee my party's safety for the same length of time."

"I will."

Badgertail turned cautiously and signaled Locust to obey. Through the long years of warring, she had never let him down. He knew that she'd be pacing now, anxious, upset by this development. She liked "clean" hit-and-run battles, where no foolish diplomacy twisted the circumstances out of her control. Badgertail touched Bobcat's shoulder reassuringly and faced the gate. He could hear his war leaders calling out in the voices of their Spirit Helpers—Owl, Falcon, Wolf—to signal they'd dropped their bows.

The gate slid back to reveal three lines of warriors, kneeling, bows drawn. Badgertail and Bobcat extended open hands before them and stalked boldly forward.

Four men and one woman fell out of the first line, surrounding them and forcing them down a narrow pathway that wound through the village. Badgertail noted that Jenos took another trail. Why? Was it a trap? Or perhaps Jenos needed to get to the rendezvous point ahead of him to . . . what?

Grass-mantled mounds rose darkly against the pastel glow of dawn. Each mound had been crowned with a plastered wall, and beyond that, thatched roofs rose sharp against the dawn: the proud houses of the elite clans. How many of them would remain standing when night settled on the wounded land?

His people constructed three kinds of mounds: platform mounds, which rose like truncated pyramids and supported prestigious buildings such as temples and the houses of the elite; conical mounds, where the most important leaders were buried; and ridge-top mounds, which served as markers for the village boundaries. Only great warriors were granted burial in these mounds, so that they might forever guard the village. Badgertail gazed appreciatively from the mounds to the silver circles of ponds that dotted the trampled winter grass. Despite the tension of the situation, their ethereal beauty soothed him.

In the Beginning Time, Mother Earth and Father Sun had been married. But some cataclysmic event had torn them apart and cast Father Sun into the sky. Mother Earth had twisted herself out of shape trying to reach up to touch Father Sun so she could ease her need for him. Then, when First Woman and First Man were born, they had commanded all of their children to help Mother Earth. For three hundred cycles, Badgertail's people had been carrying baskets of dirt on their backs, trying to bridge the gap that kept Mother Earth and Father Sun so far apart.

The guards led them past the mud-plastered houses of the craftsmen and across the central plaza with its tall poles, the top of each carved into a clan totem. People garbed in brightly dyed fabrics watched anxiously from the peripheries as they crossed the chunkey court. Last summer—no more than nine moons past—he had played on this very clay, wagering his skill and some of Tharon's finest goods, in competition with Jenos' champion, Mallow.

How had the world gone so wrong?

Before them rose the tallest mound in the village, the Temple Mound. Squared steps of red cedar had been placed in the steep ramp, and Badgertail ascended, his booted feet patting quietly against the wood. By the time he had made it halfway to the top, he could see the temple. It spread two hundred hands long and fifty hands wide. The peaked roof jutted fifty hands high.

He and Bobcat passed through the final gate in the wall that guarded the truncated top of the mound and crossed the flat past the effigy pole that rose the height of ten tall men. Offerings had been left at the base to appease Spider, the Spirit Helper carved into the pole top so high above.

Mallow waited for them, standing before two brawny men who stood on either side of the main door of the huge temple building. Each man was dressed in the flashy robes of temple guards. Thin triangles of pounded copper covered the arms and chests of their red garments. Hardwood clubs hung from their belts.

Recognition glimmered in Mallow's obsidian gaze. Were those warm summer nights no more than fading memory?

Mallow dropped his lance across Badgertail's path. The barest odor of smoke from the sacred fires inside escaped on the morning breeze.

"Stop, War Leader of Cahokia. I've been instructed to tell you to remove your weapons."

Bobcat stuck his chin out. "Why? Leader Badgertail swore no bows would be raised until he'd finished speaking with the Moon Chief. Does Jenos doubt his word?"

Mallow stiffened. "You may ask him yourself—once you've removed all of your weapons."

"You want us to go inside your temple, out of sight of our forces, unarmed? Ha!"

"Do as he says," Badgertail directed. "*I* trust the Moon Chief." A pause. "And I trust Mallow. He is a man of courage and honor."

Something flickered behind Mallow's stone-hard control.

Bobcat's eyes flamed. "But Badgertail! We can't—"

"Do it. Now."

Bobcat grudgingly unslung his quiver and bow and kissed them before placing them gently on the bosom of Mother Earth. Badgertail put his weapons beside Bobcat's and took a step backward, dragging his brother with him. "That's all of our weapons."

Mallow scrutinized them suspiciously. He was taller than Badgertail, and in the subtle light, his beady eyes seemed too small for his round face. "You brought no knife?"

Bobcat took a hostile step forward. "Don't insult my brother! If he says that's all, it is!"

Badgertail gripped Bobcat's shoulder and tugged him back reproachfully. "We brought no knives. But you may search us if you want."

Mallow signaled one of the other guards to come forward and cover them while he knelt and patted down their legs and arms. Rising, Mallow said, "Go ahead, War Leader. The Moon Chief is waiting."

Badgertail inclined his head respectfully and strode to the door. He stopped to bow to the east, north, west, and south, and to cast a glance heavenward and then downward, acknowledging the Six Sacred Persons who held the winds in their hands. Then cautiously he pulled aside the woven-bark hanging to enter the temple.

He heard Bobcat's sharp intake of breath as he stepped within. Badgertail's eyes widened. He had been inside the temple before, ten cycles ago, but he had forgotten the magnificence of the place.

A dim hall stretched fifty hands in front of them, lined by doors that diminished in size, drawing the eye inevitably to the huge room at the end, where dozens of firebowls gleamed. Badgertail's gaze lingered on the bright symbols running the length of the hall: the stylized images of Eagle, Father Sun, and Serpent, the odd, concentric squares painted in black and encircled by rings of white eyes. Intricately carved stands dotted the way, topped by bird-headed effigy bowls and beautiful offerings such as exotic necklaces and bracelets.

Badgertail might have forgotten the majesty, but he had not forgotten the tingle of Power that filled Nightshade's temple. He shook his head. Tharon had been an idiot to cast her out of Cahokia. Of course River Mounds had accepted her with open arms. Nightshade's reputation spanned half of the world. But he wondered how she had ever learned to live without her Tortoise Bundle. Old Marmot claimed that after Nightshade left, he had barely been able to use its Power at all; it was as though the Spirit of the Bundle had retreated . . . or had died from grief. The Bundle still graced the main altar in the Great Sun Chamber, but Badgertail rarely heard anyone mention it these days.

"Come. We haven't much time." As Badgertail walked, his thoughts went to Nightshade. Was she here? He hadn't seen her in ten cycles, and the last time there had been so much hatred in her eyes that he'd been unable to gaze at her directly. She must have passed twenty-four summers now, and her Power had increased with each one. A flutter, like butterfly wings, titillated his stomach.

Bobcat's eyes swept the hall as they walked. "I've never felt Power like this," he whispered. "Not even in our own Great Temple."

"Our temple does not have Nightshade, brother."

"Not yet," Bobcat said bitterly. "Not until we've gutted Jenos completely."

Badgertail could sense her here, everywhere. Her soul lived in the cedar poles and dirt. Seeing, hearing, *watching* through the very fibers of the cattail-mat walls. Her presence throbbed as they neared the inner chamber, and Badgertail heard the soft beating of a drum. Or was it

Nightshade's heartbeat pounding through the veins of halls? He bowed to the Six Sacred Persons again before stepping over the threshold.

"You're a bold man, Leader Badgertail." Jenos' scratchy voice echoed in the golden warmth of the chamber.

Badgertail saw no drummer, yet the faint beats continued. The drummer must live in one of the adjacent chambers. He let his gaze drift. Firebowls radiated outward from the central altar like sunbeams, twelve in all. Their light caressed the plastered walls and lit the intricate designs painted on the white clay.

The altar rose four hands high and spread twenty hands in diameter. Three steps led up to the altar and the sacred pedestal. Carved from the trunk of a long-dead cypress tree, the pedastal's brilliant red, purple, and yellow concentric circles formed a halo around the pink face of Nightshade's Spirit Helper. Just gazing at that twisted face left Badgertail uneasy. The pungent fragrance of columbine seed mixed with sweet-flag plant wandered up from the incense bowls on the altar, where Jenos stood, his arms crossed over the pedestal. A hard glint sparked in his brown eyes.

"Not bold, cousin," Badgertail corrected. "Obedient."

Jenos snorted. "Obedient to Tharon? Then you're a fool. Look at the catastrophe the boy chief has already wrought. I've heard that the babies at Hickory Mounds are starving. Doesn't that bother your soul, Badgertail? How many villages have you attacked in the past two moons? Three? Or is it four now? How long does the Sun Chief think he can keep forcing our people to feed his before we rise up against him? We would give the tribute if we could. We can't!"

Jenos stood barely ten hands tall, but he had the gruff voice and distinctive triangular countenance of all of the Sunborn. His face had been tattooed in a black band that reached from ear to ear. His thin nose rode over even thinner lips above a pointed chin, and his high cheekbones bore black crescent moons. He had pinned his shoulder-length gray hair on top of his head in a bun and adorned it with copper pins and the drooping feathers of a tan-and-white owl, the sort that lived in holes in the ground. A palm-sized shell gorget hung around his neck, blazing against the background of his golden robe.

Badgertail walked forward through the flickering glow cast by the firebowls. He noted that Bobcat remained by the door, guarding the main entry. Badgertail would watch the tiny portal that broke the wall near the point of the northernmost sunbeam.

He knelt before the altar, paying homage, then rose and pinioned Jenos with his gaze. "Where is Nightshade, Moon Chief? We've orders to take her back with us to Cahokia."

Jenos' face slackened. "*What? Why?*"

"Old Marmot is dead. The Sun Chief needs a new priestess. He wants Nightshade."

Jenos clenched one shaking hand into a fist at this unexpected outrage. "He would strip us not only of our food, *but of our Power?*

What kind of monster has he become? We've all heard the stories about Marmot and Tharon's wife. They say *he* killed them, you know—for finding out something forbidden. Hulin, priest at Spiral Mounds, claims that Tharon is to blame for Mother Earth turning against us. He says that Tharon has committed some terrible sacrilege and that Marmot and Singw found out about it."

Badgertail looked away. Had the rumors spread so quickly? Twelve people, including Singw and Marmot, had died only five days ago. There had been no marks on the corpses, but all had been staring wide-eyed when they were found, as though terrified by whatever specter had wrought their death. Badgertail's breathing went shallow when he recalled that terrible night. Moon Maiden had shrieked at the murders and ordered the Six Sacred Persons to unleash the winds. Thatched roofs on hundreds of houses had been ripped off. Their fragments had tumbled through the village, lumbering like beasts, and piled against the bases of the mounds. And each victim, except for Singw, had been Starborn: members of the religious elite who tended the temple and presided over critical ceremonials. Nearly the entire hierarchy had been killed.

"Where is Nightshade, Moon Chief?"

Jenos deflated a little and slouched over the edge of the pedestal. "She's not here. She's gone away for a few days. Her lover, Bulrush, was killed in an accident seven days ago. Thunderbird sent a bolt of lightning to strike the tree beneath which Bulrush slept. It fell on top of him. Nightshade . . . she needs time to mourn."

Badgertail bowed his head. He remembered Bulrush. Fun-loving, always playing practical jokes. No one could believe he had taken up with Nightshade. But they had been together for what? Ten cycles now? "Time is something none of us have. Especially you, Moon Chief. Will you turn over the tribute? Or force me to take it from your storage huts?"

Jenos slammed his fist into the sacred pedestal. His nostrils quivered in rage. "We have another moon of winter left. Without that corn, my people will go hungry! We're in the midst of the Starving Time. You know that. We've hunted out all the animals for days of travel in every direction. There are almost no fish left in the Father Water. I can't turn our corn over to you." He extended his hands in a pleading gesture that made Badgertail's soul go cold. "I beg you, Badgertail. *Please*. Go back and tell Tharon we cannot do as he commands. If he would just give us another season, we would pay him twice the tribute he demands."

"I'm sorry," Badgertail said distastefully, and caught Bobcat's disgusted glare, "but Tharon has grown tired of your insolence. You have about one finger of time left. What is your choice? War or peace?"

"Badgertail, do you realize what will happen to us if you attack? It's not just the tribute. After you're finished tearing River Mounds apart, killing our warriors, we'll be completely vulnerable to attack from anyone who wants what little we have left. The independent chiefdoms south of the confluence of Moon River have become more daring. Rumors of your raids travel on wings faster than Swallow's. If any of those chiefs should become bold, we're no more than a month's travel away. You'll doom every man, woman, and child in this village."

The words came hoarsely. "It's not my decision, Moon Chief. If it were—" Bobcat's boots scuffed the floor, causing Badgertail to whirl. "What is it?"

Bobcat's eyes narrowed as he peered into the dimness of the hall. "People. Six of them. They just ducked under the hanging. They're coming."

Badgertail glared at Jenos. A small, bitter smile curled those thin lips. "What is this, Moon Chief? You would betray your promise of safety?"

The old man's shoulders hunched, making him appear frail and decrepit. His mouth puckered as though he had swallowed something sour. "You've left me no choice, Badgertail. We are a desperate people. In a few moments I will take you to the gate platform and you can signal your warriors to call off the attack. Then I want you to summon one of your warriors and order him to take my plea for more time to Tharon."

"Tharon won't listen. And within two days my warriors will figure out the sham and attack you anyway. You've nothing to gain by taking us hostage."

"Time, Badgertail. Time. Perhaps in two days I can sneak out the mothers and children. Maybe the elderly. Then . . ." He exhaled despondently. "Well, your warriors may do what they will. We will fight you until we are all dead." He lifted a hand and moved it futilely. The fire had gone out of his dark eyes, leaving only hatred. "We will die anyway if you take our food and our source of Power. Better quickly than a lingering death that eats our souls with its pain."

Jenos lifted his gaze expectantly to the doorway. Badgertail prepared himself. The blaze of the firebowls blinded his eyes to the hall, but his keen ears picked up the soft hissing of moccasins against dirt. Bobcat had flattened himself against the wall by the entry. His chest heaved with anxious breaths as he nodded to Badgertail. Then his glance touched on Jenos.

They had warred together too long for Badgertail to miss his brother's meaning; he waited until the first enemy warrior came through the door.

When Bobcat yelled "Go!" and swung a fist brutally into the man's throat, Badgertail dove for the floor, crawling frantically for Jenos.

Jenos vaulted off the altar with the vigor of a boy and sprinted for the tiny door in the northern wall. His golden robe waffled around his legs as he ran. Screams and angry shouts flooded the Sun Chamber. Badgertail caught sight of Bobcat whirling to knee a man in the stomach before two warriors jumped him. An invisible fist constricted Badgertail's heart . . .

"*Moon Chief!* Stop!" Badgertail cried as he leaped forward, tackling Jenos and knocking him to the floor.

Jenos screamed and pounded his withered fists into Badgertail's face and back, shrilling, "No! *No!* Badgertail, have you lost your human soul? Let me go!"

Bobcat uttered a garbled scream.

Desperation drove Badgertail to grab Jenos' throat in a crushing grip. "Tell your warriors to stop! Now, or you're dead! You hear me?"

Two men slammed into Badgertail like a rushing rock slide, propelling him off Jenos. He struggled wildly, grabbing red tatters of clothing, gouging with his fingers, until he got an opening and bashed his knee brutally into the groin of one of his opponents. When the man gasped and slumped to the floor, Badgertail leveled a lethal kick to the warrior's temple. The man toppled sideways, his wide, dead eyes staring, as the second warrior twined his fingers in Badgertail's black hair and wrenched him backward.

Badgertail recognized Mallow's burning eyes. They struggled, kicking, rolling over and over. When they reached the edge of the raised altar, Badgertail gripped Mallow by the shoulders and shoved him over the short drop with all his might, pitching headfirst after him. He landed a knee in Mallow's face, pulverizing his nose. A jagged scream erupted. Badgertail clenched his fists together and hammered Mallow's skull again and again until the warrior stopped flailing. He reared back, preparing to thrust his fist into Mallow's vulnerable throat . . . but his arms went weak.

A wrenching sob diverted his attention.

Across the room, Bobcat writhed weakly in a pool of blood. A blazing golden light glimmered from the copper shaft of the lance that pierced Bobcat's stomach, pinioning him to the dirt floor. Two warriors stood over him, laughing, their lances poised for thrusting.

Oh, Blessed Sun, no. "Bobcat!" Badgertail screamed as he lunged away from Mallow, racing across the floor.

As he jumped over a hideously sprawled corpse, the two warriors spun, reaiming their lances at his chest. Heedless, he threw himself at them, howling his rage like a wounded wolf. "Leave my brother alone! Get away! Get back or I'll kill you!"

The sharp point of a lance sank into his right forearm. A haze of arms and legs flashed around him. Then he vaguely glimpsed one of the men pull his club and felt the first blow strike low on his spine. His legs went numb. Before he knew what was happening, he collapsed, landing hard on the floor. The warrior beat him unmercifully. Badgertail writhed, trying to shield his head with his arms. When he struggled to twist sideways to get away, a stunning blow landed at the base of his skull.

"No!" he heard Jenos scream. "Don't kill him. We need him!"

Just before he blanked out, he heard Jenos scream something else, and he made out the rising clamor of terrified voices in the village below.

Dimly, he heard the war cries of his own warriors coming closer.

Three

Nightshade moved silently, sensually, on her bed of dried maygrass, oblivious to the wails that carried on the morning wind. Her own whimpers barely penetrated her dream.

She smoothed her hands over Bulrush's muscular back, reveling in the corded sinew, gently touching each well-known scar. His hand crept slowly down her bare side, massaging enticingly. She laced her fingers behind his neck and pulled his face down to stare into the warm depths of his dark eyes. He smiled.

Inexplicably, she longed to sob into the curtain of his hair as it tumbled around her face.

"Bulrush, I'm frightened."

Don't be. I'm here. Do you feel me?

He traced a finger down the smooth line of her jaw and pressed his mouth against hers, kissing her with all of the passion she knew so well. His tongue explored, moving over hers, thrusting deeper.

The maygrass beneath Nightshade crackled softly as she wrapped her arms forcefully around his back and crushed his tall body against her. Fear lay behind her hurry, as if some monster lurked, waiting to pounce on them. She whimpered, unknowingly sending a cry through the brush hut she had constructed on the bluff above the Father Water. Bands of golden light shot through the structure, falling over her thick blankets and dancing in the long feathers of black hair that spread in a halo around her beautiful face. Nightshade opened her legs and felt Bulrush there . . .

From somewhere far, far away, the shrill cacophony of screams eddied.

Nightshade jerked involuntarily, shattering the dream. She felt her soul being pulled up through layers of sleep and became aware that a wash of sunlight shone greenish-gold against her closed lids. *No!* She fought, struggling to force herself back into the dream—back into Bulrush's arms.

But the light grew more brilliant, and Bulrush slipped away into the haunted shadows of her soul.

Nightshade's heart pounded sickeningly.

She opened her eyes and peered at the blurry patches of Father Sun's light visible through the rents in the rounded dome of her hut. She had erected a pole frame and then woven handfuls of red hay into the lattice for protection against the elements. But she had been so weary from despair that she'd done a poor job.

"Thank you, Winter Boy," she murmured softly, "for holding back the snow and rain while I've lain here sleeping twenty hours a day."

Her breath misted in front of her. She studied the shimmers of silver as they wafted upward, then let her gaze drift over the rest of the hut. It spread about twelve hands in diameter. At the foot of her bed, her painted Power Bundle and water jar sat silhouetted in the shadows. A few tufts of grass spiked from the wall above them, ready to fall at the first gust of wind.

How long had she been here? Six days? Her thoughts rambled over the sunrises and sunsets she'd witnessed. Yes, six. A sacred number, that. A healing number. Bulrush should have finished his journey down the Dark River of the Underworld and arrived at the Land of the Ancestors by now.

Nightshade imagined him there, laughing, talking to all of the precious relatives who had gone before him.

Six. A healing number.

Grief tightened like Eagle's talons around her chest, crushing the life from her. Why didn't she feel healed? The pain had only grown worse. Like shocked flesh awakening from the keen slash of an obsidian knife, her soul screamed. The pathetic sound wound down and around through the recesses of her memories of Bulrush, seeking comfort there. And sometimes she found it, in his loving voice, his wry laugh, the joy in his smile. The scream would fade to a dull whimper for a time, until her body overrode her soul and tried to wake. Then it would rise again, swelling to a wail as it fled through the recesses, searching, searching for him.

Every morning when she drifted at the edge of sleep, she felt the warmth radiating from his body, heard his heart beating slightly out of rhythm with hers, as she had thousands of mornings in the past ten cycles. She would lie drowsily, enjoying his presence beside her, the softness of their bed, the songs of the birds perched on the peaked roof of the temple, the sweet pungency of the old red cedar poles supporting the walls. Then she would reach out to touch him and awaken, startled, to find him missing. For the briefest moment, she would think that he must have gone out to catch fish for breakfast.

Then the terrible knowledge would return, and she would realize anew that his body lay beneath ten feet of earth in one of the ridge-top mounds at the edge of the village.

Nightshade squeezed her eyes closed. "Don't . . . don't think about it."

Sounds from River Mounds rode the shoulders of the breeze. Occasionally, when the drafts swirled around and swept up the bluff, she thought she heard screams. But it must have been the music of flutes, or the cries of children at play.

She tried to force her soul to swim into the sounds to locate their source, but with Bulrush's death, her Powers had withdrawn into the darkness of despair. She sensed nothing beyond her own anguish. She rolled to her side and fiddled aimlessly with the dry grass of her bedding. Memories fluttered, unbidden, agonizing.

She had seen fourteen summers when she'd met Bulrush; it was just after Tharon had banished her from Cahokia. Bulrush had cared nothing of her reputation, or of her abilities to dive into the Well of the Ancestors and pierce the layers of illusion spun by First Woman to guard the Cave of the Tree. He'd just cared about her.

For a few cycles, happiness had breathed from every rock and tree, as if each persimmon blossom and misty morning had received Father Sun's special blessing.

Nightshade tugged the worn softness of her blanket up around her throat. The tan fabric caught the morning glow and sparkled like Raven's wings as he dove between flashes of lightning. Her heartbeat had slowed to a dull jolting against her ribs.

"Why didn't you foresee his death, Nightshade? Why didn't Brother Mudhead warn you?" She had gone over and over the question, trying to understand why Mudhead had abandoned her. She'd even tried diving into the Well to ask him face-to-face, but she hadn't been able to get through the gate. First Woman had barred the entry to her, and she didn't know why. For the past five cycles it had become ever harder to gain entry. What had she done to deserve such punishment? Mudhead had told her in a Dream: *"Humans have thrown the world out of balance. Nothing will be as it was."* But she hadn't understood at the time.

Bulrush . . .

Perhaps now. It had been six days.

She braced her arms to sit up. Her muscles burned as though set afire by grief. She pulled the warm blanket around her shoulders to fend off dawn's chill breath. She'd been sleeping in her red dress and deerhide boots for so long that they seemed a part of her, like thick folds of aged skin. Though she had slept almost constantly during the past six days, her body cried out for more sleep. But the possibility of seeing Bulrush drove her on. Wearily she crawled across the soft, grass-covered floor to grasp the Mudhead Power Bundle.

Sinking back, she held it protectively to her breast while she traced the blue spiral of Moon Maiden with her fingertip and followed it through the four concentric circles of Father Sun to the fat bodies of the Hero Twins, one white, the other black. One of Light, the other of Darkness. In the Beginning of the World, they had led humans up through a hole in the ground to this lush home and taught them how to live in harmony with the land.

Her hand edged down to the contorted face of Brother Mudhead, and she lifted her voice in an ancient, lilting Power chant:

> *I am calling, First Woman, calling. I wear the mighty colors of Bird-Man, the Serpent of the Sky. Crimson, Emerald, Sand.*
> *Open the gate to me. I am calling, calling. I would descend from the high land,*
>   *into the Underworld to speak with you.*
>   *First Woman, help me. Bird-Man, help me.*
>   *I am calling, calling.*
>   *Open the Gate of the Well.*

Nightshade reverently kissed the Mudhead Bundle and unlaced the leather ties. Father Sun had risen higher. His rays no longer struck her in the face. They penetrated the lodge in a thousand places, streaming down to speckle her tangled hair like copper dust. She cautiously pulled a small basket and a black bowl from the Bundle. She set them gently on the floor before kissing the Bundle again, then setting it aside.

"I'm coming, First Woman. Help me, help me."

She picked up the basket, surveyed its faded red swirls, and removed the woven lid. A gray smudge of powder smeared the bottom. Nightshade offered a small prayer of thanks to Sister Datura. Traders brought the precious seeds up from islands in the Great Salt Water far to the southeast. The seeds cost a fortune, but two of her bowls could purchase enough of them to last her a lifetime. She reached for her water jar and splashed a meager amount of water into the powdered seeds, then half-filled her black Wellpot.

Nightshade took a deep breath. The damp morning air felt sharp in her lungs. She forced her soul into calm patterns before she dipped her finger into the gray paste in her Power basket and began massaging it into her temples.

"I am coming, Bird-Man. Help me. Help me. Help me."

When she let her hand fall to pick up her Wellpot, a gust of wind teased her long hair. Not until the breeze had wandered through her dwelling and scampered away did Nightshade dare turn her eyes to the water in the Wellpot.

Her reflection transfixed her. Midnight snarls of hair framed her face, accentuating the purple circles around her eyes. Her full lips and turned-up nose looked pinched, as though she battled to keep something locked inside that bronze prison of skin. As she stared into the water, she felt Sister Datura seeping into her bones, catching hold of her soul with a granite hand to shake her fears out . . . or to kill her because of them.

Nightshade shuddered when the sickness started. Her soul reeled as she began the Dance of Death with her Sister. They twined souls like lovers, rocking, fighting, delighting and terrifying each other as they Danced over the deadly gate that led to the Well of the Ancestors. Nightshade pirouetted carefully over that bottomless pit, following Datura's lead through the darkness. When the nausea swelled, Night-shade battled it by chanting, chanting with all of her strength, into the Wellpot, praying for help and guidance from Bird-Man and Brother Mudhead.

. . . And at last her soul cut loose from her body. She felt it spiral out through her navel and ooze into the Wellpot like wispy threads of azure light.

I am coming, Mudhead. I am coming. Bulrush, can you hear me?

Sister Datura released her hold, and Nightshade melted into the water. Her reflection wavered around her, cool and caressing. She could look upward at her own face, though it appeared blurred through the water, and downward. Down, down through the gate, into the brilliant darkness of the Well of the Ancestors. She prepared herself and dove, scattering the colors of her reflection like leaves in warm autumn winds.

Lichen woke with a start, staring wide-eyed at the golden veil of light that fell over her room.

"Dawn," she whispered.

She had been dreaming of playing ring-and-pin—a game that consisted of flipping a perforated bone up in the air and skewering it with a sharpened stick—with Flycatcher, when an unknown woman had shouted her name. It had been so loud that Lichen imagined it had come from this world.

But only the far-off mournful howls of a coyote disturbed the morning's quiet.

She snuggled deeper into her precious buffalo robe—her mother had received it as a gift from a trader after having performed a healing ceremony—and blinked at the chestnut poles that formed the ceiling of her room. The pole on the far right, the one over her head, had a large knot in it that thrust out into the next row of poles, slightly skewing the whole roof. Clusters of eagle feathers dangled here and there, each a prayer for someone sick or gone hunting. They twirled in the cool breeze that roamed the room.

Lichen yawned, a wide, lazy yawn. Who could have called her? Her gaze drifted over the interconnected line of painted yellow spiders that crawled around the clay-washed walls. Their red eyes glowed in the light spilling through the window. She hadn't recognized the voice. That had scared her. And she had the vague feeling that the voice had come from far away.

Lichen followed the spiders from one to another until she came to the wall niche that gouged the plaster at the foot of her mother's bed. The Stone Wolf stared at her. Black, tiny, it glimmered like a speck of molten obsidian.

She scooted deeper beneath her robe and peered at the wolf through a kinky horizon of black buffalo fur. Should she try talking to it? Wanderer had told her to.

But the Stone Wolf terrified her. Her mother forbade her to touch it because, she said, the Power in the wolf could kill Lichen, though Lichen thought that maybe it could do that without being touched. She could feel its Power radiating all the way across the room, like the prickly feel of a cricket's legs on her arm.

Bravely she shoved her robe down a little to look the Stone Wolf straight in the face. "Do you know who called me?" she asked. "Do you know anything about that Dream I had two days ago?"

The sensation of Power grew. Lichen thought she could hear something, like the faint rumble of a flash flood before it wiped the face of the land clean. Fear gripped her. She swallowed hard and dove beneath her robe, shivering.

From the blackness, she heard her mother stir. An elbow thudded against the wall. Sleepily, she heard her mother's voice. "Lichen? Did you say something?"

"Yes!" She threw off her robe and flew across the room as fast as she could. The hard-packed dirt floor stung her feet with cold. "I'm scared!"

Meadow Vole sat up in bed, her black hair falling about her shoulders, and opened her robes for Lichen to crawl in. Her daughter scooted back against her as tightly as the narrow platform would permit before heaving a sigh of relief.

"What scared you, Lichen?"

"The Stone Wolf. It was looking at me."

"Well, don't worry. It's quiet this morning."

Lichen frowned as she twisted to gaze up at her mother's round face, full lips, and slightly hooked nose. "Didn't you feel the Power?"

"No. I didn't feel anything. Maybe you were dreaming."

Lichen kept silent. She still felt it, all around, like a noose being pulled tight.

"Lichen?" Her mother's voice changed. "Did you go up to see Wanderer yesterday? Flycatcher's mother said he came home as white as clay and hid in a corner until she coaxed him out for dinner. Do you know anything about that?"

"No," she answered truthfully. She hadn't seen Flycatcher since they'd come back, but she couldn't believe he would have tattled on her. Except for Wanderer, Flycatcher was her best friend.

"Did you go up to see Wanderer?"

"Well . . . Mother, he gets lonely. He needs people to come see him every now and then."

Vole sighed and rested her chin on top of Lichen's head. "How many times have I told you that he's dangerous? You never know what Wanderer will do. His moods change as fast as Grandfather Brown Bear's. I wish you wouldn't—"

"Was he as odd when you studied with him?"

Lichen felt Vole's muscles tighten for an instant before she nodded against Lichen's hair. "He's always been strange. He taught Nightshade for many cycles before he taught me. I think she cast some spell on him that knotted up his soul. That's why I wish you'd stay away from him."

A shaft of light climbed the wall, glaring in the face of one of the spiders. "But I like him, Mother. Didn't you ever like him?"

"Oh, yes, but that was a long time ago, before . . . well, before a lot of things happened."

"Before my father died?"

Her mother hesitated for so long that it made Lichen fidget. She rolled over in bed and gazed up into Vole's troubled eyes. "How come you never tell me very much about my father?"

"There isn't much to tell. We were married for only a cycle, and he was gone most of that time."

"To go on battle-walks." People in Redweed Village told stories on long winter nights about how great a warrior her father had been. She beamed up at her mother in pride, but found Vole's eyes focused somewhere far away and unpleasant.

"Yes, battle-walks. He was always fighting." Vole turned away. "Why don't you try to sleep some more? We'll have to get up soon."

Worried by her mother's sudden coolness, Lichen tried to think of something else to talk about to make her happy again. "Is that when you studied with Wanderer, Mother? When my father was gone raiding?"

"Yes. Wanderer taught me many things. He—"

"Why did you stop studying with him? He has great Power. I'll bet he could have taught you a lot more."

Her mother's eyes sought out the Stone Wolf. "Yes, I'm sure. I just didn't know how to deal with his soul being an eagle one day and a pack rat the next." She laughed softly and playfully tugged Lichen's nose. "Now, let's sleep for another two fingers of time. We've a long day ahead of us. I have to start making preparations for the Beauty Way Ceremony, and you have to help me."

Lichen wiggled closer to her mother and buried her face against Vole's soft breasts, where she felt safe. She tried to force herself to sleep, but her mind kept drifting to the frantic sound of the unknown woman's voice.

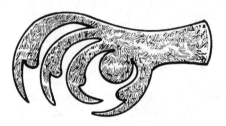

Four

B adgertail?" Locust called.

Where he lay in the glare of the Inner Chamber's firebowls, he could hear the fear in her voice. Shrieks and pleas for mercy reverberated through the temple.

"Badgertail! Can you hear me?"

Then she was bending over him, her frantic fingers lifting an eyelid to see if he lived. Badgertail scratched at the dirt floor with trembling fingers. The pungent tang of blood mixed miserably with his throbbing headache. "Help . . . help me up."

Locust slipped an arm beneath his shoulders and cautiously lifted him to a sitting position. The wound in Badgertail's forearm stung, but worse was the bitter acid of bile clinging to his tongue. It made his stomach want to heave. His vision swam, producing double images. "Quickly, what happened?"

Locust crouched beside him. Spatters of blood flecked her cheeks and warshirt. "When one hand's worth of time passed, we attacked. We overwhelmed Jenos' forces like wolves among fawns. I brought my war party directly here, thinking you might need help."

Badgertail nodded weakly as he touched Locust's arm in gratitude. "And Woodchuck?"

"He's killing as many warriors as he can, to pay them back for perfidy. Elkhorn's raiding the storage huts to collect the Sun Chief's rightful tribute." Her jaw went hard as she cast a malicious glance at the other side of the chamber. "We caught Jenos and his Starborn trying to run for the river."

Badgertail's gaze lingered on Bobcat's dead body. Tears of rage and hurt welled in his eyes before he lifted his head to seek the man responsible. But only Locust seemed to take note of his pain. She rose and took a hesitant step forward before Badgertail shook his head to make her stop.

The blazing firebowls blurred into a connected necklace of amber stones. Beyond them, at the edge of the western wall, twelve priests and priestesses in red robes huddled in a semicircle around Jenos. Through Badgertail's hazy vision, they looked like fuzzy patches of flame. Only a very small priestess, with knee-length black hair, stood out.

He put a hand on Locust's shoulder and struggled to stand. She gripped his elbow to support him until he got to his feet. His knees wobbled as he half-staggered toward Jenos. He made it to the sacred pedestal and leaned heavily against it. "Moon Chief, where is Nightshade?"

Jenos' gray bun had come undone, and the ornate, double-lobed copper pin had vanished. Wisps of hair matted his cheeks. He shook his head wearily. "I don't know."

"She wouldn't have gone anywhere without telling you. *Where is she?*"

"She was *grieving*, Badgertail. I did not demand that she provide me with the details of her plans."

Badgertail's hand tightened on the cool wood of the pedestal. As his senses returned, his body howled for him to lie down. But he couldn't. Not yet. Not until he had accomplished this final task. He inhaled a breath to steady himself and almost gagged. The scent of urine pervaded the air here. Badgertail shifted to look around the pedestal. Mallow sprawled on his side. His intestines had been ripped out and strewn like gray ropes around him. His bladder must have let go at the last.

On that hot summer day not long past, Mallow had played chunkey on the side of Light, his muscles rippling as he hurled the polished stone disk down the court. Friends . . . they'd been friends.

Badgertail wiped a trembling hand over his sweat-drenched forehead as he spread his legs to brace himself. The impact of Bobcat's death began to sink in. He motioned to Locust. "The young priestess. Bring her."

The girl cried and fought as Locust dragged her out of the circle of the Starborn and unceremoniously threw her at Badgertail's feet. Terror tightened her pretty face.

"Who are you?" he asked, forcing his voice into a calmness that he didn't feel. He wanted Nightshade in his hands now, so that he and Locust—and Bobcat—could leave this forsaken village and go home.

"I am Goldenrod. Please, I've done nothing. Don't kill me!" She prostrated herself before him. *"I've done nothing!"*

"Where is Nightshade, Goldenrod?"

She shook her head so violently that a black shroud of hair tumbled over her face, half hiding her eyes. "She didn't tell any of us where she was going, Leader Badgertail. I swear it!"

Locust and four men eased up behind Badgertail. He could smell the acrid odor of their sweat, see the light glinting off the deer-bone stilettos on their belts. Locust had been through this same process with him half a dozen times. She responded automatically to the tone of his voice, the slight tilt of his head.

Badgertail extended a hand and commanded the young priestess, "Stand up, Goldenrod."

She hesitantly complied, glancing from Badgertail to Locust and back again. Her thin robe, woven from the soft inner bark of the sacred red cedar tree and so rare now, clung to the curves of her body, outlining her breasts and hips.

Badgertail did nothing for a time but gaze across the room at Jenos. He could make out Jenos' shaky intake of breath; the Moon Chief's jaw quivered before he clamped it tight. The holy members of the Starborn encircling him had backed away, as if abandoning their chief to Badgertail's wrath. In the weaving firelight, the painted images on the walls seemed to move and shift uneasily.

Jenos lifted his chin and met Badgertail's gaze. "So," he whispered, "you've killed my people, robbed my food reserves, and now you want to steal the only strength that River Mounds has left. We won't tell you, Badgertail. None of us. When Nightshade returns and finds what you've done, you'll wish you'd gutted yourself."

A puff of wind penetrated the chamber, and the firebowls hissed, wavering so badly that they almost went out. Where had the draft come from? A door-hanging being pulled back?

Locust cautiously drew her bow, nocking an arrow before she dropped to one knee. The tawny light danced over her short locks. The other warriors warily nocked arrows and glanced around, muttering uncomfortably to each other. High overhead, something rustled in the thatch.

Badgertail strained his ears, listening for footsteps or voices. An eerie prickle fluttered up his back, as if Nightshade had just stepped into the room and the hem of her robe had swept the winds before her.

Jenos pressed a fist to his thin lips. "We won't tell you." Pure loathing quavered in his voice. "If you kill us, Nightshade will find you. She'll avenge us."

Badgertail returned his gaze to Goldenrod. She clamped her hands over her folded arms so tightly that her knuckles went white, as if she knew the final moment had come.

"I don't want to kill any of you, Goldenrod, but I must find Nightshade. And if it takes killing all of you, one by one, I will do it." Badgertail lifted a hand to Locust. "See that priest on the far left?"

The white chert point on the tip of Locust's arrow sparked as she shifted her aim. "I do."

Badgertail let his hand hover while he pinned Goldenrod with his eyes. "Tell me now, Goldenrod. I've no time for more games."

She wrung her hands and sobbed, "I don't know! I don't—"

Badgertail sliced the air with his fist, and Locust let fly. A wrenching shriek echoed through the temple as the arrow pierced the man's chest. Goldenrod covered her face as the priest stumbled forward, dropping to his knees before he crashed face-first onto the floor, writhing like a skewered bug. Screams and shouts erupted, the Starborn shoving each other to get farther away. The dying priest tried to speak, to call out to Badgertail, but blood clogged his throat. He choked on it, his eyes growing wider until he collapsed into a pile of tousled red robes.

Jenos' elderly face had gone pale.

Badgertail raised his hand again, and Locust nocked another arrow. "Moon Chief? How many more would you have me kill?"

Jenos turned his head against the question.

The posture galled Badgertail like a cactus thorn in his palm. "Moon Chief, you're a fool! We'll find Nightshade anyway! She can't be far, and as soon as we've collected our tribute and disarmed the prisoners here, we'll go hunting for her. Fifty warriors combing the hills—"

"Will find nothing," Jenos said miserably. "She'll turn herself into a cougar and tear your men to pieces."

Nervous murmurs broke out behind Badgertail. He turned sharply to glare at his warriors. They shifted from foot to foot, as terrified as if Father Sun had just swooped out of the sky to scorch them all. "No one has that Power!" he shouted at them. "Not even Nightshade!"

At their expressions of disbelief, Badgertail whirled and commanded, "Locust, aim at Goldenrod."

The young priestess shrilled and fell to her hands and knees, crawling toward Jenos, crying, "Oh, no, no, no! Please, I've done nothing!"

Badgertail lifted his hand.

Goldenrod grabbed Jenos' ankles and buried her face in the hem of his robe, sobbing wildly. Jenos flinched.

"Moon Chief?" Badgertail let the question dangle for a few seconds, then started the downward plunge of his hand.

Jenos yelled, "*Wait!* . . . Wait."

Locust held her fire but kept her aim fixed on Goldenrod's narrow back. The priestess's wails came muted now, muffled by Jenos' robe.

"Where?" Badgertail demanded.

"I . . . I'm not . . . somewhere up in the western bluffs on the other side of the Father Water. I don't know exactly where. It's a secret Power place that she goes to for privacy. No one knows its exact location." Once the words had been uttered, Jenos seemed to deflate like a porcupine bladder pricked with a quill. His shoulders sagged in defeat as tears welled in his eyes. He reached down to rest a soothing hand on Goldenrod's hair. "That's all we know."

"Locust," Badgertail ordered, "give me your ax. Bring . . ." His voice cracked as his self-loathing rose to a crescendo. He could order one of his warriors to complete this final duty. It would make it easier . . . but he couldn't condemn someone else to the memory. *He's a relative! Kin! We . . . we're family . . . family.* "Bring me the Moon Chief."

Jenos' mouth gaped. "What? What's happening?"

Locust dragged him stumbling across the room and released him six hands from Badgertail. She took up her place directly at Jenos' back. "Is this another of Tharon's attempts at coercion?"

Badgertail tested the weight of the unfamiliar ax as he muttered, "No. It's his method of assuring future obedience. Where is your son, Moon Chief?"

Jenos' jaw quaked. "My son? Why?"

"Where *is* he?"

Jenos tilted his head. "Petaga's room is five chambers down. He was . . . was playing the drum earlier, praying to Father Sun for peace."

Badgertail nodded to Locust, and she trotted out. The silence intensified, until Badgertail could distinguish the labored breathing of each person in the chamber. The shocked cry of a young man rang out from the hall; then Locust returned, shoving a youth of perhaps sixteen summers before her. She stopped two body lengths away, holding Petaga firmly by the arm. The youth, a virtual twin of his father, had a slightly more rounded face. His long black hair hung free over the shoulders of his yellow robe.

Jenos exchanged a warm, confident look with his son before turning back to face Badgertail. He opened his mouth to ask some last question, but Badgertail brought the ax around in a powerful swing, slamming it into Jenos' neck, breaking it immediately. Jenos crumpled to the floor. Petaga's screams could barely be heard over the cries of the Starborn.

Badgertail lifted a hand. "Stop. *Stop it!* Listen to me!"

The Starborn, accustomed to obeying commands, hushed, but Petaga continued to sob and tear at Locust's restraining arms.

"Let him go, Locust," Badgertail said softly.

She released the youth, and Petaga ran forward, dropping to his knees to gather his father in his arms and weep into the shroud of gray hair that fell around Jenos' face. "Oh, Father, Father . . ."

"Petaga," Badgertail said respectfully, "you are the new Moon Chief. I bring you a message from the Sun Chief. Tribute is due after harvest during the Moon-of-Flying-Snow. If it is not received at that time next cycle, your fate will be the same as your father's. Don't force the Sun Chief to treat you as badly. Now get up. Leave this sacred chamber before I must carry out my final orders."

Tears rolled down Petaga's pointed chin when he looked up. "What orders?"

"Locust, take Petaga and the Starborn down with the women and children. Then . . ." His voice faltered. "Take . . . take Bobcat back to my canoe and meet me at the west gate. I'll organize a search party. We'll find Nightshade."

When the last of the people had left the Inner Chamber, Badgertail knelt and rested the ax on Jenos' bare throat. A trickle of blood swelled beneath the sharp chert blade. "Forgive me, cousin," he murmured as he began hacking through the muscle and ligaments. It took a full finger of time to sever the head.

Badgertail tore a wide length of golden fabric from Jenos' hem, spread it out on the cold floor, and placed Jenos' head in the center. Awkwardly, he tucked the gray straggles of hair into a bun and fastened it with the owl-feather roach before he brought up the corners of the golden fabric and neatly tied them.

Badgertail carried the head pressed against his chest as he strode out of the chamber, trying to ignore the warm rivulet of blood that soaked his warshirt and leaked down his muscular belly.

Before he exited the temple, he stopped at one of the intricately carved stands to pick up a rare necklace of marine shell and amethyst. He tied it onto his belt, and never looked back.

Leaning over the side of the canoe, Badgertail dipped his hand in the cold river. Ice clung in the shadowed niches along the shore, silver and lumpy. He splashed his toad face and washed the wound in his arm. It burned as though set afire by the coolness. But his headache had eased some. Only the constriction in his chest continued, almost unbearable. Bobcat's body lay in the rear of the canoe, wrapped in a splendid red-and-gold blanket, his head propped next to Jenos'. Badgertail could not bear to look at his brother. In the back of his soul, he kept hearing the words, *"I hate this . . . I hate this . . . I wish we could run away."*

Badgertail fumbled to dry his numb hand on his boot and squinted at the bluff that jutted up before them. Locust and young Flute scrutinized it, too. Flute sat on his knees in the rear, just behind Bobcat, his seventeen-summers-old eyes haunted, not liking this duty at all. His throat bobbed as he swallowed.

"Is this the place?" he called to Badgertail.

"This is it."

Flute jerked a quick nod and paddled too briskly. Locust had to fight the bow to keep it aimed at the foot of the bluff. Dead grass and a few patches of prickly pear rambled down the sandy flanks. Rose and chokecherry bushes poked bare red arms from the crevices, as though reaching out to the life-giving water in the swirling river below. To the north, a haze of blue smoke drifted above the burning houses in River Mounds.

Badgertail turned away, glaring down at the blood that soaked his warshirt. Falcon's green beak hid behind a crimson splotch half a hand wide. *"We could run away . . ."*

"I wish it were so, Bobcat," he whispered softly. "But I'm a warrior.

It's the nature of my soul to kill." *Is it? Is it your nature to kill your own relatives?* He caressed the blood-stiff painted feathers on his shirt. No tingle of Power remained. Even his Spirit Helper had abandoned him.

"How about this cove, Badgertail?" Locust pointed her paddle at a tiny inlet. A dried clump of pussy-toes nestled against the rocky bank, their spoon-shaped leaves curled like fists.

"Yes. Good."

Locust jumped into the river and guided the canoe forward. Badgertail eased over the side, gingerly finding safe footing in the knee-deep water. Together they hauled the boat up onto the sand. Bobcat's head rolled loosely in the process.

"Flute," Badgertail ordered wearily, "stay here. Guard . . . guard the canoe. If we're not back by sunset, go home."

Flute nodded heartily. "I will." A brief smile split his face until he glanced down at the dead body in the boat with him; then he sank back against the hull and apparently found something very interesting on his knee.

Badgertail grabbed up his bow and quiver. He understood Flute's dilemma only too well. The soul split in two at death. The first part separated from the body and roamed the hills, eating from the remnants left in cooking pots, or jangling jewelry to frighten people. The second part clung to the body, awaiting proper burial, when it could embark on the long journey down the Dark River to the Land of the Ancestors. If given a choice of watching over an anxious ghost by himself or trying to capture the most powerful priestess in the world, Badgertail would have chosen the former, too—but not very happily.

Locust scrutinized the steep bank. "I think we can climb up that ramp of dirt that's sloughed off. Are you strong enough to try?"

"Yes, let's go. I want to get this over with."

He led the way, tramping up the irregular slump, his boots making a soft swishing in the dew-soaked dead grass. So much of his stamina had vanished that when he reached the top of the first terrace, he stood panting, studying the lay of the bluff that stretched above them, a series of rounded domes dotted with knotweed stalks.

Locust's black eyes narrowed speculatively as she looked him up and down, appraising his locked knees and the tremble in his hands. Her mouse face was stern with worry. "Why don't you let me go alone? I can search by myself."

"No, you might need me."

"We're not going to find her anyway, Badgertail. This is *Nightshade* we're talking about. What's the point in having you faint halfway up the bluff?"

He lifted his brows. "Your confidence in me has always been such a comfort, Locust."

She folded her arms gruffly as she threw him a sideways glance. "Well, all right, if you insist on torturing yourself. Where do we start? Nightshade could be anywhere."

Badgertail scanned the crevices and slopes, looking for the best way up. "She'll be on top. It's closer to Father Sun and Moon Maiden. Let's try that gentle slope to the west."

"If you say so. Personally, I think we should have brought twenty warriors with lances and bows. Hunting down Nightshade isn't my idea of a pleasure walk."

"I thought you just said you could search for her by yourself."

"I didn't say I'd like it."

Badgertail chuckled. Locust had always done that to him. Made him laugh when he felt the least able to. He said, "There was too much to take care of at River Mounds after the battle. I thought we could find her by ourselves. But if we haven't found her by sunset, we'll come back with fifty warriors tomorrow."

"What made you think we could find her? Her soul rides the waves of the Underworld. If anyone can hide from us, she can."

"She's grieving and off balance. I doubt that she's keeping her eyes open for strangers."

"Well," Locust sighed doubtfully, "we'll see."

They started up the slope, Locust quickly taking the lead, stepping around loose rocks and dead stalks of knotweed. Sunlight had breathed so much life into the stones that Badgertail felt warm for the first time all day.

He halted on a flat spot and gazed around. From this vantage, he could see River Mounds clearly, though the afternoon breeze swept away the sounds. Beyond an endless patchwork of dead cornfields, the forty-five mounds of the village spread in a vast semicircle at the southern end of Marsh Elder Lake. Smoke twisted from the temple, caught the wind, and smeared the denuded bottomland with a broad streak of bluish gray. Badgertail could just make out the location of Cahokia, farther to the east.

He thanked Father Sun that his parents had died cycles ago and he wouldn't have to bring them the news about Bobcat. He couldn't have borne their sorrow. Bobcat had been their favorite son, always boisterous and playful, while Badgertail had been the serious one, forever troubling people to teach him how to weave fishing nets, or how to cord clay for pot-making, driving the elders crazy with his questions about the Beginning of the World. But he would still have to tell Bobcat's wife, Moonseed. Blessed Sun, how would he do it?

"What's that?" Locust asked with such apprehension that Badgertail crouched in self-defense.

"Do you see it?" Locust demanded. "There, on the ridge top near that boulder."

Badgertail squinted against the sun at the squash-shaped boulder. Against a background of cerulean sky, a slender blade of red wavered as it moved down through the rocks. "A man?"

"I don't know," Locust answered, "but he's coming at us. Right at us. Can't be one of ours. Too far from River Mounds. And that color marks him as one of the Starborn."

Badgertail straightened and braced his legs to wait. "Well, whoever it is, he's alone and saving us a walk. Let's catch our breath."

Locust did not respond, but her hand dropped to the bow tied to her belt. Her gaze remained glued to the mysterious figure.

Badgertail took the opportunity to rub his gritty eyes. He felt drained beyond exhaustion, like a punky log. All of his pith had been eaten away during the fight in the temple. He kept seeing Bobcat lying on the floor, dying, and his muscles would go wobbly. He needed sleep badly, though he dreaded closing his eyes. He knew he'd relive this day a thousand times in his dreams.

Locust took a fearful step backward. "It's a woman. Look at how she moves."

"You think it's Nightshade?"

"Who else would be out here alone?"

Badgertail nodded mildly. "Kind of her to save us a trip." Curiously, the scars on his wrists began to itch. Nightshade had clawed those gashes when he had swung her up under his arm that night twenty cycles ago.

"You think so now," Locust said. "Wait until she blows corpse powder on you and kills your soul."

The figure angled around a deep crevice in the stone and floated toward them. The woman moved with uncommon grace, especially for one so tall and willowy. Every so often she would nod, or turn to say something to the air at her side. Badgertail clamped his jaw, trying not to think about it.

"What's she doing?" Locust hissed. "Who's she talking to? There's no one there!"

"No one we can see," Badgertail answered glibly and wished he hadn't. Locust jerked as though he had struck her in the stomach with a war club.

"What should we do?" she whispered frantically. "What if she's brought an army of Spirits with her? We can't fight that!"

"We should stand here very bravely, cousin, and wait to see."

"Wait?" Locust's hands roamed her bow and club before she lifted them to touch the Power totem of Muskrat on her shirt. "Yes, I'll be brave," she said. "Right up until the moment that something invisible touches me. Then you're on your own . . . cousin."

Badgertail smiled agreeably, but the hair on his neck prickled as if stroked by an unseen hand. He could make out Nightshade's face; it was beautiful, with its turned-up nose and full lips, but puffy around the eyes. Waist-length black hair rippled over her shoulders. A small Power Bundle was attached to the belt of her red dress. She carried nothing else, no blanket, no robe, not even a pack for items such as a firebow and food.

How could she have survived out here with no provisions? And in winter. He glanced at Locust and found her glancing at him. They both straightened uneasily.

Badgertail cupped a hand to his mouth and called, "It's Priestess Nightshade, isn't it?"

She continued down the slope, as fluid as a ghost, her red dress whirling around her hide boots. She marched deliberately toward Badgertail, her eyes on him alone. Passing Locust without a glance, she stopped and searched Badgertail's face, as though measuring his soul. The rare turquoise pendant that had never left her neck since her childhood gleamed opalescent in the sunlight.

"Yes," she whispered hoarsely to the air on her left side. "He's just as big and fierce as I recall." Her eyes slitted. "I remember you, Leader Badgertail—murderer, thief, and kidnapper."

Badgertail gazed into those huge, haunted eyes with the paralysis of a rabbit facing a copperhead. Her pupils filled the orbs, as black as coal, and cold, so very cold that his soul frosted. He shivered. She didn't blink, and Badgertail cocked his head in wonder. He knew that the Starborn bartered with the Spirit of Sister Datura to help them break through the gate that led to the Well of the Ancestors, but he had never witnessed anyone possessed by the Spirit. Badgertail was fairly sure that he saw it now.

He searched for his voice, saying reverently, "Forgive us if we disturbed your sacred journey, Priestess. The Sun Chief, Tharon, sent us to—"

She took another step, moving so close to Badgertail that he could feel the warmth of her body. Wisps of her hair touched his face. A strange, pungent scent radiated from her, part sweat, part the tang of dry grass, and part something else, something old and bitter, like mold that has been growing beneath a log for a thousand cycles.

"I know why you came, and I know what you did to River Mounds." A flame of sorrow animated her words. She suddenly turned to her left again, peering thoughtfully at nothing. "Yes," she said softly. "I am aware of that, but it *is* his fault! Badgertail obeyed those commands, didn't he?"

Locust stuttered, "Wh-what's happening?" She drew her club, holding it at the ready, and started circling Nightshade and Badgertail with the wary movements of a cat stalking prey. Nightshade appeared totally unconcerned as her eyes came back to Badgertail, wide and accusing.

Badgertail frowned out over the shining ribbon of river. Fish jumped here and there, sending widening rings across the surface. "You are born to send your soul swimming with Spirits, Priestess. I am born to fight. Not out of hatred or vengeance, but because it's the nature of my soul and my duty. A swan is a swan. A bear is a bear."

He could feel her stare boring into his face, but when he turned back to face her, he discovered that she was examining the blood on his warshirt in minute detail. She touched each spatter that marred

Falcon's image with such aching gentleness in her fingers that it set Badgertail's heart to pounding.

"When you did your duty, Badgertail," she asked, "which of my friends did you mutilate? Which . . ." The fierceness in her voice dwindled as she cocked her head, seemingly listening to her unseen companion again. Her mouth puckered. "Yes, I know, Bobcat. He could have run away. I'm not a monster. If he still wants to, I won't stop him, but I doubt that he has the courage. *A bear is a bear.*"

Badgertail stood rooted to the ground, not breathing. He stared at the empty space she had spoken to, unable to take his eyes away as Nightshade swept around him to glide down the slope toward the river.

Green Ash, a woman of the Blue Blanket Clan, tugged her rabbit-fur cape more closely around her throat while she studied the smoke rising from River Mounds. The chill breath of the Six Sacred Persons flitted gently over the icy water of Cahokia Creek and moaned through the few green plants along the banks.

People around her muttered and shielded their eyes against Father Sun's glare. Green Ash's brother, Primrose, anxiously surveyed the stringers of gray that curled upward, spiking the lavender gloss of dawn. Primrose's husband, Locust, would be in the battle. Worry lined his forehead as he lowered his eyes and stared at the fishing net they had dropped into the water. A medium-sized man with a delicate bone structure, he had well-developed muscles that bulged where the fabric of his green dress touched his calves and arms.

"Badgertail had no choice," Nettle said ominously. "He had to go after our tribute."

Green Ash glanced at her husband-to-be. Though he had the gentle soul of a puppy, Nettle loomed over almost everyone in the village. He stood eleven hands tall and had the face of Sister Cougar, round, with a flat nose and piercing eyes. He had twisted his black hair into a bun at the base of his skull and pinned it with a rabbit-bone skewer. The cloth fringes on his brown sleeves fluttered when he folded his arms to hug himself.

People stared at the smoke with hope in their gaunt faces. Especially old Checkerberry, whose cheeks had gone so hollow that the bones stuck out like a skeleton's. Winter had been unusually hard. The meager amount of corn, sunflower seeds, and dried squash that they had managed to stockpile last autumn had been gone early on. Hunger had been tramping tirelessly through Cahokia for three moons.

Only Badgertail's incursions for tribute had fended off catastrophe. *But for how long?*

Green Ash put a hand tenderly on her child-heavy belly and offered a silent prayer to First Woman. *My baby will need food. Let the rains come, First Woman.*

A soft voice echoed from the nether regions of her soul, and she closed her eyes to listen. The baby spoke to her frequently, sometimes in a deep, ominous voice, other times in a voice so sweet and high that it made the hair on Green Ash's arms stand on end. Occasionally she thought she could grasp words, like now: *Petaga comes . . . south . . . south we must go . . . find an end to the blowing snow . . .*

Tendrils of fear wriggled through her stomach. Petaga? The Moon Chief's son? The Moon Chief. Poor Jenos. How would he feed his own people?

Harvests had been bad everywhere in the last cycle. The ears of corn had been stubby, no longer than a woman's finger. Green Ash did not enjoy taking food from the mouths of her relatives, but what else could they do?

"Well," Primrose said with a long exhalation, "I don't like it, but I'll be standing in line tomorrow morning waiting for our share of corn." He bent to the fishing net, testing the tension, looking to see if any fish had swum into the deadly weave. The water rippled in colliding silver rings.

"So will I," Nettle agreed, twining his fingers in the weave to help Primrose.

Green Ash awkwardly knelt beside Nettle. Her belly protruded so far now that she couldn't see her toes over the bulk. Among her people, a woman could not become pledged to a man until she was pregnant and had proven her worth—unless she were *berdache*, like Primrose.

She gripped the edge of the net to help tug. Primrose had always been odd, touched with Spirit Dreams, and much too gentle for this harsh world. Some of her earliest memories were of Primrose crouching down and covering his head to shield himself against the beatings of the village children, who were terrified by his strange ways. Green Ash had been his protector. More than once she had gotten in trouble for using her fists to drive away Primrose's tormentors.

"I don't feel anything," she admitted apprehensively to Primrose.

"Let's bring it all the way in and see."

They dragged the net, hand over hand, until it lay in a knotted web on the sandy bank. Empty. Again.

"Mother Earth hates us. She's trying to kill us for the way we've treated her," old Checkerberry mumbled. Her wrinkles had pulled as tight as a fresh rabbit hide drying in the sun. "We need to play net-stick and ball . . . to heal the Earth. A big game with a hundred warriors on each side. Play to twenty." The old woman smacked her lips. "We need to call a powerful shaman from one of the small villages. Forget these elite Starborn priests and priestesses . . . bet all the clan fields . . . everything we own. If we don't . . . starvation! War! Disease!"

Nettle glanced at Checkerberry, then quickly looked away. Primrose drew magical signs in the air to ward off the ghastly prophecy.

Green Ash's gaze drifted over the stark hills, seeing the deep gashes cut by ordinary rainstorms. No trees remained to slow the runoff, and the water rushed down the hills in torrents, taking the soil and crops with it. Cycles ago, Cahokians had started trading with the Lakes People far to the north for hickory oil, sugar-maple sap, linden sap, and sacred red cedar—not to mention hides of all kinds, for when the trees went, the animals had not been far behind. The elk had been gone for so long that children under fifteen summers couldn't even describe one.

Green Ash exchanged a consoling look with Primrose before her eyes again sought the smoke spiraling in the distance.

Five

Lichen hunched behind a limestone boulder, peering around it at Wanderer, who was sneaking through the tawny remains of last cycle's cornfield. His shrill whistle carried, a *shree-shree* like the triumph call of Hawk after he'd caught Ground Squirrel. Wanderer moved cautiously, slapping the dead stalks with his stick.

Summer Girl had roused a little from her nine-moon slumber and sent a breath of warmth over the land. That happened occasionally during the Moon-When-Thunder-Walks, but this spell had lasted for three wonderful days. Lichen tipped her face to the sun and basked in the splendor. A bead of sweat had formed under her left arm, and now it trickled coolly down her bare side to soak into the waistband of her yellow skirt. She had gone bare-chested yesterday, too, letting the warmth prick at her bones.

Not a single cloud adorned Father Sky's bosom. An unending blanket of pale blue arced across the world, melting into the spaces between the buttes, outlining the tufts of trees on the crests. Down in the river bottom, the barest hint of green whiskered the banks of the river. First Woman had begun to tend the land again.

Lichen smiled and started to suck in a deep breath of the damp, earth-scented air, but she stopped when she caught a hint of movement near the edge of the cornfield—just a flicker of leaves moving where they shouldn't have. She slowly lifted her bow, nocked her arrow, and sighted it in.

Wanderer kept walking and whistling, his gray hair swimming around his head like handfuls of frosty twigs. He wore only a breechclout. Lichen thought his tall, lanky body looked poorly after the long winter. Knobby ribs stuck out from his chest, and he'd been acting strangely. She couldn't quite figure it out. Worry lined his forehead and ate into his gaunt cheeks. He kept turning to look over his shoulder, as though he expected to see some monster rise up from the crevices in the weathered limestone. He had spoken little since she arrived, asking her only if she would help him hunt for dinner. Absently, he had told her where to sit in the garden of boulders, patting her head and then ambling off to find a stick to beat against the stalks.

Two ravens soared up from below the rim of the bluff, their midnight wings flashing in the sun. Wanderer waved a hand when he saw them and let out a low *cawww-thock-thock*.

One of the ravens swerved to drift over his head. They carried on a whimpering conversation for several seconds before the raven darted away to skim the cornfield. When the gleaming bird reached the edge, a cottontail burst from the field and raced toward Lichen.

She jerked up her bow too quickly. The cottontail spied the motion, lurched sideways, then veered behind a bristly curtain of dead grass to stop, almost hidden, in the tangle of tan and brown. Lichen slipped behind the boulder again and got down on her stomach. She slithered across the warm limestone, pushing herself forward with her toes while she pulled with her elbows. A patch of gray-brown moved slightly in the grass. The rabbit's swift breathing made its sides puff in and out. Lichen began the agonizingly slow process of lifting her bow to aim. The rabbit seemed to know it. It pulled its head back to peer at her through the blades.

Lichen held her breath. As always, this moment of eye contact seemed timeless. She could sense the rabbit's terror and confusion, the silent "Why?" And her young soul cried out that she didn't know. It was just the way Earthmaker had made things.

The rabbit didn't blink. Its stare intensified as it probed her eyes, waiting for her to make the first move. The longer Lichen gazed into those soft brown depths, the more anguish she felt. A passageway seemed to open in the air, allowing their souls to commune. The rabbit's terror became hers. Lichen closed her eyes and softly Sang her love to Rabbit, explaining her need to eat, asking him to give himself to her so that the One great life of all might continue.

As though they had exchanged souls for the briefest of moments, Lichen saw herself through Rabbit's eyes, lying like Snake on the limestone, her bow half lifted, her black braid tumbling over her left shoulder. She felt Rabbit's heart fluttering wildly in the narrow cage of his chest, and she grieved, and promised to aim well, to do it right. She pleaded for forgiveness. A thread of trust built between them, strengthening with each moment, until Rabbit's voice whispered all around her, *"All right, human. I see your need. I give myself to you, but do what you must do quickly. Do not make me suffer."*

"I won't, Brother Rabbit. I promise."

Rabbit hopped out into the open space on the gray stone and turned his side to her. Lichen aimed, sucked in a steadying breath, and let her arrow fly. When it pierced Rabbit's heart, she felt it like a dagger in her soul. She burst into tears. Dragging herself to her feet, she trotted over to where Rabbit lay. His hind legs still kicked, trying to run, but the eyes that gazed up at her told her it was all right, that she had kept her promise.

When finally his body went limp and the glow of life faded from his eyes, Lichen propped her bow on a clump of grass and knelt down to caress Rabbit's silken fur. "I love you, Rabbit," she whispered. "Thank you."

She did not look up at the pat of Wanderer's steps on the limestone. She just kept stroking Rabbit's side.

"Your shot was perfect," Wanderer praised softly. "Come. We'll take him home and Sing his soul to Rabbit Above."

Lichen sniffled. "All right."

Wanderer tugged her arrow from Rabbit's side with as much tenderness as he could, then picked Rabbit up. They walked side by side through the scattered boulders. A flock of ravens squawked and cooed overhead, gliding on the air currents like the blackened, windblown leaves of deepest winter. Lichen ached inside. She had never known why killing did that to her. Most people seemed to be able to do it without feeling anything. Some even seemed to enjoy it. But to Lichen, the act always burned with the strength of Rattler's venom in her veins.

It reminded her of the story of Wolf Slayer and Bird-Man. Sons of First Woman. Just after the people's emergence from the Underworlds, monsters had roamed this fourth world of light. Big Giant, Rock Monster Eagle, Big Horned Monster, and all the others drove people crazy, troubling them, eating their children for breakfast. First Woman told Wolf Slayer and Bird-Man to go ask Father Sun how to get rid of the monsters. So they walked for six days, stepped on blue crosses going up through the sky, and climbed onto the back of a rainbow. The Cat Tail People, Water Bug People, and Rock That Claps Together People tried to shoot the brothers off the ridge of the rainbow, but they hid in the bands of light and scrambled up on their stomachs until they reached the top.

Father Sun said to them, "I will tell you how to kill the monsters. But you must promise to hand the telling down, so that my wisdom will always be on the earth with my people. Humans have many monsters, both inside and out, to kill."

Wolf Slayer and Bird-Man traveled far, far to the south, to the Black Mountain, where Big Giant, the chief of the monsters, lived. They threw arrows of lightning at Big Giant and killed him.

Then they slew all of the other monsters, killing and killing until their people were safe. But the brothers had killed so often that their souls sickened and almost died in the shells of their bodies. The Six Holy People prescribed a ritual for them, *Where the Brothers Climbed the Rainbow.* All humans alive in the fourth world of light joined in the Sing, and Wolf Slayer and Bird-Man got well.

Lichen wondered why her people didn't perform the ritual every time a rabbit or a squirrel died. Maybe the killing wouldn't sear her soul so badly if they did.

They trudged up over the crest of the slope and plodded down the other side, their cattail sandals scuffing softly on the sand-filled parts of the trail. Wanderer ducked through the copse of oak first, then held the branches back so she could come through behind him.

"It's so warm today," Wanderer said. "Why don't we build a cook fire outside? Can you gather some of the dead branches from the chokecherry bushes while I clean Brother Rabbit?"

Lichen went to the edge of the cliff, where the chokecherry grew in scraggly clumps, just barely clinging to the rocky ledge. She twisted and yanked until she had gathered a pile half her height, then lugged it back and thrust it down beside the wall of Wanderer's house.

He glanced at her while he gingerly slit open Rabbit's belly. The intestines squirmed out around his chert knife like living serpents. Rabbit did not look the same now that he'd been skinned and had his head removed. He lay there skinny and pink, like a dead baby Lichen had seen once. Its mother had died, too. She'd bled to death. Lichen's mother had been called in the last moments to Sing for the woman. Lichen remembered the frantic run across the plaza, the screams of the relatives, the crawl through the dark lodge . . . and the huge pool of blood that had glistened around that dead baby.

Just like the pool on the stone at Wanderer's feet. Her heart thumped as she looked for the hide. It lay cradled in the reddish arms of a leafless rosebush. A short distance away, Rabbit's head perched on a rock, staring out at the western horizon, gazing sightlessly at the Road he would have to follow tonight.

"Are you all right?" Wanderer asked.

"Can we pray him to Rabbit Above now?"

"Of course." Wanderer carefully placed Rabbit's corpse on the pile of chokecherry limbs, dried his bloody hands by rubbing them in the sand, and walked over to the severed head.

Lichen stood on the right, in the place of Grandmother Morning Star, and Wanderer took the left side, representing Grandfather Evening Star. Together they mimicked the line of the Road of Light in the sky that Rabbit must run to find his way to the Land of the Ancestors just over the western horizon. Humans had to venture down the Dark River, but animals ran the brilliant Road of Light.

Lichen squinted at a puff of cloud that grew, twirling and swelling, above the river. Then she closed her eyes. The words of the sacred Song rose from the depths of her soul, eddied around the rock shelter, and seemed to hang like a veil just beyond the edge of the cliff. Wanderer's deep voice joined her childish one.

Look yonder, Brother Rabbit, to the life-giving Road of Earthmaker.
We pray Rabbit Above will come and take your soul flying,
    to clasp hands with the stardust,
    and lead you over the western horizon,
    to the House of Father Sun,
    where you'll never be hungry again,
    where it will always be warm and you'll never have
to shiver in the snow.
    We thank you, Brother, for giving your life
    that the One great life of all might continue unbroken.
    Come, Rabbit Above. Come, come, come, come.
    Take the soul of our Brother flying.
We add our breaths now, to give you the strength.
    Come, Rabbit Above, come, come, come . . .

Lichen sniffled again, but she felt better. She could sense Rabbit's soul rise and run toward the Road of Light. Wanderer put a hand against her back to guide her toward his house.

She slumped down by the wall and watched him build a hot, hot chokecherry fire. Flames crackled, shooting out sparks in extravagant wreaths of gold. Wanderer tossed rocks atop the sizzling sticks, then brought a willow tripod from inside his house. He gently pulled Rabbit off the pile of branches, skewered him with a dry stick of chokecherry for flavoring, and set him atop the tripod to roast. When he came to sit down beside Lichen, she rubbed a hand beneath her runny nose to avoid his questioning gaze.

She knew Wanderer well enough to be certain that he wouldn't bother her until she told him she was ready. He sank back against the wall and waited, his leathery hands folded in his lap. Lichen scooped up some sand, letting it trickle through her fingers while she studied the way the grains glimmered. Finally she said, "Wanderer? Why do I cry when I have to kill?"

He peered at her seriously. "Oh, I think it's because for you, hunter and hunted are the same. Just as they are for me."

"I don't understand."

"I mean that every good hunter takes the soul of the animal into himself before he kills. You know how you feel when the animal turns and stares you in the eyes for the first time during the stalking?"

"I can feel its fear and confusion."

"I know." Wanderer squeezed her sandaled foot. "You remember what Bird-Man told you the first time he came, when you were four summers old?"

"What?"

"That in the Beginning Time, humans and animals lived together. Animals could be humans if they wanted, and humans could be animals."

"Yes, but what does that have to do with hunting?"

Wanderer took a twig of chokecherry from the remaining pile. He bit off a thin strip of bark and chewed it thoughtfully. "For most people, the only time that happens now is when they hunt. When the eyes of predator and prey meet, they exchange souls. So when a hunter kills, a part of him dies with the animal. And it should, because he's done something terrible. Necessary, but terrible."

"But why do we have to kill, Wanderer? I could live on plants, the way Deer does."

He brushed the twig lightly over his cheek. Sweat matted his gray hair against his temples and forehead, forcing it to lie flat for a change. His beaked nose looked longer as a result. "Ah, but you're not Deer, Lichen. You have the body of a human. Earthmaker designed it that way for a reason. Deer eats grass and wildflowers. Humans eat wildflowers, grasses, and animals. Everything has a specific duty—for a reason." He paused. The lines between his dark eyes deepened. "Do you know who the ultimate hunter is, Lichen?"

"People?"

"No."

"Who?"

"Mother Earth. She stalks us constantly. All of us. Plants, animals, humans. It is only through our deaths that she lives. Our bodies provide her with sustenance. That makes dying *more* sacred than living. When we live, we live for ourselves. But when we die, we give to everything in the world. It's the most important thing we do, eating and being eaten. Do you understand what I mean?"

She lifted a shoulder noncommittally but responded, "Yes, I think so. But . . . but, Wanderer? I always feel guilty. My soul burns and aches. If it's so important to Mother Earth, why don't I just feel good? Do you know old Bone Whistle? He really likes killing. He boasts about it all the time. Why doesn't Mother Earth make us all feel that way? She'd be a lot happier, wouldn't she?"

His eyes narrowed. "Bone Whistle is a fool. If you love and respect what you hunt, you can't be happy at its death. And boasting of it . . ." He spat on the ground violently. "Hunters aren't murderers! And murderers aren't hunters."

Lichen shrank at the vehemence in his voice. Wanderer slammed down his twig before getting up to turn the rabbit. The sweet scent of roasting meat pirouetted around her head as she watched the reverent way he treated the sizzling rabbit, touching it delicately as he shifted the roasting stick on the tripod.

"What's wrong, Wanderer?"

"Nothing, Lichen. I'm sorry. Don't worry about it."

"Did you have a bad Dream?"

He had his back to her, but she saw his arms sink slowly to rest at his sides. "Don't . . . I . . . I don't want to talk about it. I need more time to think."

Lichen nodded, though she knew he couldn't see her. "All right."

Sometimes, when she had a really bad Dream, she liked to think about it for a long time before she talked to him. She understood. But she hurt for him, knowing the gnawing terror of those Dreams. Lichen sat quietly, playing with her skirt, creasing it between her fingertips.

Wanderer stepped away from the fire and went to the edge of the cliff and stared out across the flat river bottom. His gaze focused on the tan-and-gray bluffs to the west, where Pretty Mounds nestled. She saw him shake his head—thought he exhaled a tense breath—before he looked back over his shoulder at her. In those dark, troubled eyes, Lichen felt Power surging and withdrawing, frightened of itself.

She pulled up her knees and hugged them to her chest, giving him time. With the toe of her sandal, she drew a spiral into the thin veneer of sand that had eroded from the limestone, while she prayed to Moon Maiden to help Wanderer. Only Moon Maiden had the Power to do that—to penetrate the darkness. Oh, the Star Ogres could shed some light, but only Moon Maiden could dispel the dark shadows that imprisoned a person's Spirit.

Rabbit fat dripped into the fire, bubbling on the hot rocks, causing the flames to crackle. The sound seemed to wake Wanderer. He came back and knelt before the tripod. He checked the rabbit, apparently decided it had cooked enough, and removed the stick from the tripod. Blowing on the dark, steaming flesh of Brother Rabbit to cool it, Wanderer carried it back and sat down cross-legged beside Lichen.

He had one of those strange looks in his eyes. Far away. He blew on the rabbit for an unusually long time, until fat had congealed on the meat again. But she didn't say anything, though she preferred it hot and juicy. She let her gaze drift over the irregular line of the cliff and settle on the rock where Rabbit's head drooped sideways. His right ear sank lower and lower, first touching the rock, then bowing against it.

"Forgive me, Lichen." Wanderer tore off a leg and handed it to her. She took it gratefully. It had been a long day, and she needed to eat. Fat smeared her mouth as she bit into the succulent flesh. It tasted rich and earthy, like a mixture of sweet grass and corn.

Lichen wiped her mouth with the back of her hand. "Do you know that we're doing the Beauty Way Dance tomorrow?"

Wanderer stopped in mid-bite. "Yes, it is tomorrow, isn't it?"

"You should come."

He closed his eyes and leaned back against the wall, resting the skewer of rabbit on one raised knee. Lichen hoped he was thinking about the curative properties of the ceremonial. The Dance brought the world back into harmony and healed the wounds inflicted by humans on Mother Earth before the people planted their fields again.

"I can't come, Lichen. You know they wouldn't let me."

"Oh, yes they would. If my mother invited you," she asserted boldly.

Wanderer smiled for the first time that day, and it warmed her soul. "And how could we get your mother to invite me? The last time I saw Meadow Vole, she called me some things I'd just as soon forget."

"I'll tell her I want you there. She'll do it. You just come. You know it starts at nightfall. You can Dance beside me. I'll hold your hand. Then you'll feel better about your Dream."

Wanderer's smile faded. "Lichen, have you talked to the Stone Wolf yet?"

She squirmed uneasily. "I tried. It wouldn't talk to me at all. It didn't even attempt to answer—at least I don't think it did. Why do you ask?"

"Ever since we talked about your Dream," he whispered in a low, savage voice, "I've been having the same nightmare. I don't think it's a Dream—not really. It's more like a . . . a 'shout.'" He shrugged his shoulders in futility. "I don't know how to explain it. But I'll be lying half awake when a smothering shroud of black falls over my face. I have to fight to get it off before it suffocates me. And I keep hearing this voice. I . . ." His mouth pursed. "I think it's Nightshade's voice, calling me."

Lichen licked the sheen of fat from her fingers. Fear nipped at her belly, but she tried not to show it. "It's a woman's voice?"

"Yes."

"Kind of deep and very beautiful?"

Wanderer blinked before he turned to her. "Have you been hearing the same voice, Lichen?"

"I think so. But I'm not sure. I don't know who she is, but she called my name and woke me up."

"She just called your name? She didn't say anything else?"

Lichen shook her head. "Just my name. Maybe our souls are sick, Wanderer. What do you think? I could have my mother give us a Sing. If our souls are sick—"

"No," he interrupted sternly. "I think it's more than that."

Wanderer ran a greasy hand through his gray hair while he stared absently at the fire. The chokecherry had burned away into a pile of gray ashes dotted with crimson coals. Thin wisps of smoke curled upward, adding a new layer to the already thick patina of charcoal blackening the rock overhang. "I'm worried, Lichen. Maybe . . . maybe I will come to the Beauty Way. Even if people drive me out of the village . . . well, at least I'll get to see your mother again. Maybe even talk to her for a while." A wistful nostalgia gleamed in his eyes.

Wanderer put an arm around Lichen's narrow shoulders and hugged her. She fit neatly into the crook of his arm, like an eagle chick sheltered under the wing of its mother. She tilted her head and rested it against his bony chest. She kicked one foot back and forth while she finished her meat. Clouds had started to gather, crowding the sky like lumbering beasts. She laughed at them. When she leaned forward to wipe the fat from her hands onto her skirt, Wanderer's stick of rabbit appeared before her eyes.

"Share this with me?"

"Sure!" Lichen tore out a chunk with her teeth and flopped back into the crook of his arm.

"Maybe I will come tomorrow," he said, as though trying to convince himself. "Maybe it'll be all right."

Petaga's golden robe brushed his legs as he circled the irregular splotch that marked the floor of the Inner Chamber. In the flickering mustard glow, it looked like nothing more than a spill of dye made from sumac berries, dark and brown.

Jenos' body had been prepared, left in the House of the Dead on the charnel mound, with food and drink for his Spirit. Slaves had washed his headless flesh and left it to cleanse in smoke from the red cedar-bark smudge pots. After the six ritual days had passed, Jenos would be buried in a log-lined tomb in the conical mound next to the temple. With him would be placed his wife . . .

According to custom, she, and all the others, should be strangled by a relative—in her case, by Petaga's own hand. *And I can't do it. I'm weak at the thought. My blood becomes water.*

Jenos' slaves and those who were indebted to the Moon Chief would also offer themselves for strangulation. Sunborn would be buried around the edges. The Commonborn among them would be cremated, their ashes scattered over the burial mound. Finally, earth would be piled over the entire mound, adding yet another layer—tribute to a hideously murdered leader.

Burdened by such responsibilities, as well as by his grief, Petaga had only now gathered the courage to reenter this sacred room. A terrible presence pressed down on him, heavy, suffocating. The Starborn murmured softly on the altar, where they talked to the war leader of River Mounds, the great Hailcloud.

Petaga's memory kept replaying that last warm, confident look his father had given him, and his stomach knotted with so much anguish and hatred that his knees began to tremble. He made two more revolutions around the blood stain before he stopped. His brooding gaze locked on the sacred fires flickering in the broad pottery dishes that surrounded the altar.

Polluted! Badgertail had brought blood and violence here. Here, to this sacred place. Too many men had died in this room for it to ever be pure and clean again. At the Green Corn Ceremony, they would ritually extinguish the fires with water and then relight them after Nightshade

Sang the rituals and the appropriate sacrifices had been offered. And to purify the walls and roof would mean another . . .

Purify? How? Wasn't the pollution too great? Hadn't the entire building been violated and mired in filth? The very mound top needed to be cleansed—burned to bare dirt and capped with hard clay before another layer was added.

He glanced around, aware of the subtle touch of evil. The painted figures of animals, monsters, and the Long-Nosed God watched, challenging, from their places on the whitewashed walls. Petaga lifted his hands and studied the patterns of fine lines on his fingers and palms. Closing his eyes, he curled his fingers into fists, clenching them until the muscles in his forearms ached.

With those hands, he would have to strangle his mother at sunrise the following morning. And how many others? His vision blurred and he ground his teeth. *I can't! I'll shame myself and my clan—and all of River Mounds.*

If that happened, Jenos would go to the Afterlife alone, mocked by the other Spirits. On top of the humiliation of going to the Underworld without his head, Jenos would be further shamed when the other Spirits thought that his wife had deserted him and that his eldest son was a coward.

Petaga turned, thinking to summon Nightshade to ask her advice, only to remember the reports he had heard. Commonborn, trembling in fear and hiding in the grass beside the Father Water, had watched her rowed upstream in Badgertail's canoe. What had happened to her? Had Tharon killed her, or just kidnapped her? Petaga's heart ached for the tall priestess. She had faithfully advised his father for cycles. Petaga had grown up depending on her . . . loving her.

"I'm coming for you, Tharon," he said viciously. "And I won't be coming alone. . . . Hailcloud?"

The burly war leader rose and strode to the edge of the altar to peer down at Petaga. A tall man with a slender, aquiline nose, he had the coldest black eyes Petaga had ever seen. The crest of dark hair on his shaved head shone orange in the light, and his copper ear-spools glinted. The lower half of his face had been tattooed in black. "Yes, my Chief?"

"How many warriors survived Badgertail's attack?"

"He left us about a hundred, mostly the old men and young boys." Hailcloud's tone went bitter. "He gutted our ability to make war, my Chief. If you're thinking of returning his attack, don't. We can't."

Petaga tightened his leg muscles to halt the shaking in his knees. "How many warriors survived at Hickory Mounds, Red Star Mounds, and the other villages Badgertail has ravaged this cycle?"

Hailcloud's eyes narrowed as he followed Petaga's line of thought. "It might work, my Chief. If we can draw the other leaders out of their cowardice—if we can convince their people to fight with little food in their bellies."

"The Starving Time will be over soon. By the Planting Moon, butterfly weed and lamb's quarter will be up. There are always rabbits."

Hailcloud nodded uneasily, clearly disturbed by the prospect of waging a long series of battles. "Well, if we're going to do it, my Chief, we'll need to act quickly, before Tharon and Badgertail catch wind of what we're up to. If Badgertail strikes before we're ready, his rage will leave all of our villages scorched husks."

Petaga lifted his gaze to Hailcloud. "Then let's begin. Assemble a war party to escort me. I want to speak to the chiefs myself. We'll leave as soon . . . as soon as . . ." Images of his mother's face splintered his resolve.

Hailcloud's callused hand settled lightly on Petaga's shoulder. "You know how the Warrior Clans were formed, my Chief?"

"Of course. First Woman prescribed them for unions between Sunborn and Commonborn as a way of mixing their strengths."

"My Chief . . ." Hailcloud shifted his gaze uneasily. "My mother . . ."

"Claimed Jenos as your father. Yes, I know."

Hailcloud took a deep breath, and his voice lowered to a whisper. "I saw your expression today. Your mother . . . well, the thought has unnerved you. Tomorrow the entire world will be watching."

"Hailcloud, I—"

"I would ask the honor, my Chief." His voice hardened. "Do you understand?"

Petaga gave him an uncertain glance. "You would achieve a great deal of status. You would become as good as Sunborn." But not quite. Hailcloud's membership in a Commonborn clan would never be erased unless he were officially adopted. Nevertheless, Hailcloud's words after the ritual performance would carry increased weight with the other chiefs and war leaders.

"Very well, my friend. Tomorrow you may perform the ritual duties." A cool breeze of relief blew through Petaga. Hailcloud had freed him from the horror. It was one less torment for his excoriated soul. He clenched his fists and walked down the line of firebowls toward the door.

Behind him, speculative whispers broke out among the Starborn.

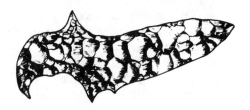

Six

*L*isten to them, Nightshade. Do you hear their words? They killed the only family you've ever known."

The voice of Sister Datura gusted like a dark wind from the depths of Nightshade's soul. She fought to ignore her, to break the stranglehold they had on each other, but her Sister fought harder.

"They destroyed your village. First Bulrush dies, then this. Whose blood is that on their warshirts? Listen to them! They boast of it!"

Raucous laughter, like a foul miasma, surrounded her as warriors called back and forth from the brightly painted war canoes that glided close to the mint-bearded shores of Cahokia Creek. The air had become tainted by a bluish tint of smoke from cook fires and heating smudges. Word had already spread, and hundreds had come running from the outlying cornfields to line the bank and watch the return of Badgertail.

"Ha!" one of the warriors crowed behind her. "I killed seven men and took three women! I'll have sons there next winter!"

Nightshade knelt in the middle of the lead canoe, her bound hands dangling numbly behind her back. The stench of the warriors packed around her made her stomach roil. Odors of blood, urine, and torn guts bombarded her. She tried to hold her breath, but the effort only heightened the presence of Sister Datura in her body. The colors of the river began to swirl together, blue melting into brown in curling stringers, then going green and pale yellow before leaping up again to coalesce into sky, plants, or earth. Against Nightshade's will, Sister Datura plucked the hues of sunset from the clouds and cast them down like liquid jewels on the waves eddying around the boat.

Her stomach heaved suddenly. She shoved her way to the lip of the canoe, shouldering aside two warriors so she could vomit into the churning river. She hung there, weakly suspended between water and sky like a banished god, her body trembling. She vomited until her empty belly could only contort in dry agony.

"Now you pay the price for our sacred Dance. Feel the pain, Nightshade? I'm still here . . . still here . . ."

The warriors around her were silent, watching with strained eyes. Though Nightshade tried to pull herself up, to bring her head back into the boat, her muscles refused to obey her commands. She braced her knees against the hull, feuding with her body; but she only succeeded in tumbling half out of the canoe. Her long hair spilled into the water, swirling just below her face in writhing, serpentine patterns. With her hands tied behind her back, she did not have the leverage necessary to rescue herself.

"Help. Help me. Someone . . ."

Warriors frantically pushed each other to get away, eager to avoid having to touch her Spirit-possessed flesh. So many of them crowded against the opposite side of the canoe that the boat listed sharply. A hushed murmuring broke out. Up and down the river, men stared, waiting to see whether Nightshade could save herself by calling out to the Water Spirits who haunted these muddy banks, or whether the river would swallow her whole.

Sister Datura laughed.

Nightshade's red dress had tangled around her legs, making it difficult for her to move. In sheer exhaustion and futility, she wept. The curtain of her hair shielded her face, but her shoulders shook, revealing her shame.

Whispers pulsed behind her, and she felt the canoe rock with a man's unsteady gait. Someone bravely slipped his arms around her and lifted her back into the boat. She stared up into Badgertail's pensive eyes. He studied her for a moment through the frame of his shell-heavy forelocks. "Are you all right? Is it the Spirit of Sister Datura?"

Nightshade let her head fall forward. She said simply, "She always wrestles me for my life."

"Is there something I can do?"

"No. It's between her and me—an old Dance. We know each other's steps too well."

"Would it help if you lay down?"

Nightshade gazed speculatively into that squat face with its too-large eyes, wondering why he would offer. This was the man who had kidnapped her from her home, dragged her to this foreign land, and offered her up to the malignant arms of the Sun Chief, Tharon's father—Gizis. "Yes," she answered.

Badgertail put a hand behind her shoulders to help ease her down into the bottom of the canoe, where she could nestle against the hull. Blood speckled his leather boots in dark brown splotches. Her soul cried out. Sister Datura murmured: *"It's probably Jenos' blood, or Goldenrod's, or . . ."*

Badgertail rose. The canoe swayed. "We're almost home."

"Cahokia has never been my home, Badgertail. You know that better than anyone."

He stood quietly before turning and going back to the bow.

"Why didn't you go home, Nightshade? When Tharon first threw you out of Cahokia, why didn't you return to Talon Town? You're such a coward."

"I was a child," she mouthed the words. She had desperately wanted to go home, but at the age of fourteen, she had been too afraid to make the long journey by herself—a decision she had never stopped regretting. Talon Town's sun-reddened cliffs still danced in her Dreams, ethereal, beckoning.

Nightshade slitted her eyes. Ahead, the yellow rays of sunset slanted down, striking the Temple Mound, which rose in the distance like an improbable mountain. It had taken three hundred cycles and fifteen million baskets of dirt to erect that stunning monument to Mother Earth—and now she had abandoned them.

"Yes, of course," Datura hissed. *"First Woman refuses to speak to Mother Earth or Father Sun if it will benefit Tharon. It's something he's done. You have to find out what. That's why First Woman has locked the entry to the Land of the Ancestors and barred it with a wall of darkness. You know what Mudhead said. Somebody has to find out and make it right."*

She nodded, whispering, "I know."

When Nightshade had slammed up against that midnight wall, she had screamed for help, sending out a call to every Powerful Dreamer in hearing range, but only silence had met her pleas. Hadn't anyone heard? She'd wallowed there, banging her spiritual fists and crying out for an eternity—until Brother Mudhead had come to tell her that she must return to the world of men to meet Badgertail and go back into Tharon's cage. She had begged him to let her see Bulrush for just a moment before she accepted her fate, but Brother Mudhead had told her that First Woman had slipped into her cave and refused to open the Underworld to any human.

Tharon. Nightshade tried to smother her dread. He had beaten her repeatedly when they were children, for no reason other than that he was bored with his protected life. Once he had blacked both of her eyes and hit her in the head so hard that her soul had separated from her body for two whole days.

Her hatred for Tharon had fermented over the cycles into a roiling brew of scorn and malice.

The canoe veered left to skirt a flotilla of slow-moving rafts heaped with poles that had been cut from the upland ridges two days away from Cahokia. With every cycle, people had to roam farther away to find wood. Saplings still sprouted along the riverbanks, but they rarely grew for more than two moons before being cut down for building or for cooking.

As they rounded the final bend, the river assaulted her with the pungent scents of fish and new plants. Turtles lumbered down the muddy shores to splash into the water. Reeds had resurrected at the edge of the water, shooting green tendrils up through the tawny bones of last cycle's dead plants.

Ghostly fear clutched at Nightshade. She shook herself, not understanding, until a pitiful whimper struggled up from a long-hidden compartment in her soul.

"*No . . .*" she begged through gritted teeth. "No, my Sister, not this."

But the memories gripped her in leaden fists, dragging her back to a time twenty cycles before, when warriors had surrounded her on another trip. The images flashed haltingly at first; then they began to flow—and the scene returned with horrifying power: the mad flight from Talon Town; being handed from one warrior to the next; being carried for half the night, then forced to run until she thought her heart would burst. She lived again the desperate battles waged as they crossed the Land of the Swamp People, skulking through slimy water that came up to her chin, the snakes, the biting bugs, the blazing fires that certainly belonged to enemies, the screams of wounded warriors carrying through the hot, muggy nights—the wrenching loneliness.

Only Badgertail had talked to her, taught her the language, soothed her at night when the Dreams came. He had held her, his the only warm body in a cold and frightening world. Now he had come for her again—still the only kind voice here to comfort her.

Nightshade saw the landing loom up through the eyes of a terrified four-summers-old girl. She huddled in upon herself as the warriors jumped out and tugged the canoe up onto the sand, laughing, calling rude jokes to one another.

Her gaze fixed on Badgertail, barely seeing the gray strands in his braided forelocks or the lines that now etched deeply around his eyes. He picked up a bloody bundle, rose, and stepped out onto land. As he trudged up the muddy slope to the first terrace, he gestured for two of his warriors to bring Nightshade.

The men, one very young and the other about twenty summers, leaned over her, trying to coax her into getting up so they wouldn't have to touch her. She peered at them in terror. When the young one kicked her lightly in the foot, Nightshade screamed, "No! Please don't make me! Leave me alone! I just want to go home. I want my mother! Take me home! Take me home, takemehome!"

Badgertail spun where he stood on the terrace, silhouetted against the dying flames of sunset. He cocked his head as though baffled, and then slowly understanding dawned.

"Get away!" he shouted at the warriors. "Leave her alone!" He ran back toward the canoe, slicing through the crowd of warriors that milled on the banks, unloading supplies and gathering belongings.

The warriors around Nightshade stumbled out of the boat, and she buried her face in the dirty folds of her red skirt. "Mother?" she choked. "Where are you? Why did you let them take me?"

Sister Datura seized images from that forbidden storeroom of Nightshade's soul and flung them against Nightshade's closed eyes, forcing her to remember Badgertail in his youth—tall and commanding as he had been on the night they had spent at Black Warrior Mounds, just below a big river. The village had been abandoned long before—grown over with trees and brush—and it was the first time she had seen sparkflies. They'd come out at sunset, glittering through the grass and climbing into the tops of the trees like a brilliant net of fallen stars. Badgertail had buried a warrior in one of the conical mounds . . .

When he knelt before her now, taking up all of her vision, horror swept her. She struggled to crawl away. "Leave me alone! I want my mother! I want to go home. Please," she cried, "take me home."

Badgertail's eyes softened. "I'm sorry, I don't understand your words. No more now than I did twenty cycles ago."

"Please, *please!*"

He reached out, letting his hand hover uncertainly, as if to brush her hair; then he withdrew it and clenched it into a fist at his side. "Nightshade, I don't know what Sister Datura is doing to you, but—"

"Twenty . . . cycles?"

A cry echoed in her memories. She saw her mother's face, her mouth gaping, eyes dusted with sand where she lay, blood drenching her ceremonial dress . . . and Nightshade sobbed. She would never go home. Everyone she loved was dead, and only Brother Mudhead cared about her.

"Nightshade?" Badgertail's voice sounded so gentle that she almost didn't recognize it.

Sister Datura faded back, Dancing away to twirl just out of reach. Nightshade swallowed her tears.

Badgertail leaned closer. Fear and bewilderment strained his features. "I don't know what to do, Nightshade. Tell me what to do."

She shook her head. "Just . . . just help me stand up."

He tucked his bloody bundle under one arm and gripped her elbow to support her while she got to her feet. On wobbly legs she stepped out of the canoe and onto the soft sand. A brier of arrowleaf snagged at her dress as she climbed the steep incline to the first terrace. Warriors shuffled backward, their silent glares as powerful as shouts.

From the terrace, Nightshade could see the people tilling the northern fields with chert and clamshell hoes. They'd already started to plant, dropping seed kernels into the long, ridged rows that would sprout four different kinds of corn: pop, flint, flour, and sweet. Around the fields, blackberry vines twined over ancient stumps, forming a natural fence. The new green leaves stood out against the rich black soil.

Dozens of mounds were scattered in the west and south, but her gaze skipped over those formidable legacies of the elite, resting on an area where a Commonborn family was constructing a new house. The grandfather had a work line going. Children peeled chestnut logs to make them more resistant to insect attack. Then they fire-treated the ends of the logs to protect the wood from ground moisture before handing them to two men who sank the ends into a trench in the ground. At the rear, three women, apparently grandmother, mother, and granddaughter, sat weaving cattail leaves for the mats that would serve as walls once they had been daubed with clay. Two sides of the house had already been completed.

Nightshade frowned. Between this terrace and the high palisade that surrounded Cahokia, hundreds of new houses dotted the flats between mounds, their shaggy roofs spreading as far as she could see. Even the spaces between houses had been tilled, and fresh furrows waited for the seeding.

No wonder that Mother Earth had abandoned them and that First Woman refused to intercede on their behalf! How could Tharon possibly hope to feed this multitude? They had replanted the fields so many times that the crops never grew very tall anymore, though everything that could be tilled had been tilled: bluff tops and bases, as well as the broad expanse of rich bottomland. Yet Cahokia never had enough to eat, not even with the boatloads of tribute that came up the creeks from villages too frightened to refuse Tharon's demands. Trade provided exotic items such as dried abalone, hides, copper, and pipestone, but the Commonborn immediately exchanged such expendable goods for what food they could get. Only the elite could afford those luxuries now.

The spectators were pointing and nodding as the heavy canoes beached, each piled to the gunwale with tribute from River Mounds.

"Locust?" Badgertail yelled. "Pick twenty warriors. I want them to spread out around Nightshade for the walk into the city. And I'll have no accidents! If any of the Commonborn so much as raise a bow, I expect your warriors to kill immediately!"

Badgertail came to stand at Nightshade's side, glancing at her uneasily as warriors formed around them in an irregular diamond, with Locust in the front.

The group began moving, cutting a swath through loops of warriors to the main pathway that led into the city. Nightshade felt desperately tired. With every ounce of strength remaining, she forced her feet to plod forward. A pack of dogs careened up the trail to greet them, barking, wagging tails, vanguard for the horde of children that followed. The children peered at Nightshade like hunting weasels, asking a thousand questions of the warriors surrounding her.

"Who is she, Locust? Why have you brought her?" a little boy demanded.

"Where are you taking her?" Another bobbed his head up and down, trying to get a good look at Nightshade. "Did you catch her in the battle at River Mounds? Is she a sacrifice?"

A girl of about fourteen summers ducked low to peek around the warriors' legs. Her eyes opened wide before she shrieked, "It's Nightshade! Run! *Run!*" and the children scattered like a school of fish at a thrown rock, racing away to shout the news. It seemed only moments before a crowd had gathered along the route. Even the old and sick were hefted onto shoulders and carried out to watch the spectacle of Nightshade's return to Cahokia.

"Stay close to me," Badgertail ordered.

"I've nowhere else to go." She noticed that he had taken his chert-studded war club from his belt before they even reached the storehouses.

The ring of carved and painted cedar posts forming the Sky Circle appeared on her left. Old Marmot had been adamant about charting the exact courses of Father Sun, Moon Maiden, and the Star Ogres so that he could determine the correct days for planting and harvesting, as well as the great ceremonials—and other things. Marmot had believed that if you could chart the sacred Dance of the sky gods, Bird-Man would help you decipher all of the mysteries of Light and Dark in creation. Legends said that Bird-Man had been evil in life, that he'd fought a devastating war against Wolf Slayer and been condemned after his death to helping humans stay on the path of Light and Harmony. Part of his duty was to carry messages between humans and the sky gods and the Underworld.

Nightshade bitterly recalled the winter nights when Old Marmot had forced her to sit in the freezing cold waiting for Father Sun to climb over the Temple Mound so he could pinpoint the position on the leather sky map that he guarded with his life. He had been keeping that map for forty summers before Nightshade's arrival. With it, a priestess or a priest could chart the precise path of the sky gods on any given night during a period of nineteen cycles.

"Look! It *is* Nightshade. Oh, Blessed Mother Earth! Why is she back?" someone wailed, and Nightshade turned to see an old woman with gray hair fleeing through the crowd, running with all of her strength. People surged in to fill the old woman's place, but Nightshade peered after her. Did she know her? Checkerberry, perhaps? The old woman had taken care of her in the first cycle of her life in Cahokia. But perhaps it hadn't been. Nightshade hadn't known many of the Commonborn. Old Marmot had forbidden it, saying she hadn't time for the lowly tillers of the fields, the makers of crude pots and ugly arrow points. The only Commonborn she had been acquainted with had been the clan leaders, or the privileged artisans paid by Gizis himself: the flintknappers of special points and ax heads; the stone grinders, who polished celts, hand maces, and effigy pipes; certain gifted potters; and the shell-bead workers, who produced almost all of the necklaces, ear-spools, and bracelets worn by the elite in the city.

"Locust," Badgertail called. "We'll enter the outer palisade through the west gate." He motioned with his head to the left, indicating that they should take the narrow path that led around the base of the westernmost charnel mound. Here the houses and storage buildings gave way to open space.

Locust veered away from the houses of the Commonborn to skirt the small plaza before the charnel mound, but a hooting mob followed them. A few rocks flew into their procession, and the warriors shouted threats, but Nightshade paid no attention. Her nose had picked up the sickly sweet odor of the dead. In the big house on the mound, the Starborn kept the bodies of important people while they prepared them for burial by dressing them in fine clothing, painting their faces in scarlet pigments, and rubbing their flesh with a precious mixture of sacred cedar bark and hickory oil. On the hottest days of summer, the stench became overwhelming, forcing people to drape their sleeves over their noses as they passed. Old Marmot used to tell her that Mother Earth found the odor of death pleasing and that Nightshade, as an adopted member of the Starborn, should, too. But she could never manage it. She recalled running more than once out of the charnel house to vomit.

"Badgertail, who died?"

He shrugged, his gaze combing the mob. "Tharon will tell you."

Nightshade sucked in a deep breath when the great palisade appeared before them, tall, white, made of upright logs daubed with clay before fire-hardening. The walls towered twenty-five hands high and guarded the ceremonial centers and the houses of the Sunborn, Starborn, and other elite. Warriors manned the shooting platforms. Behind them, the tops of several mounds thrust up squarely against the purpling sky. Her gaze fixed on the tallest mound and its giant temple that seemed to slice Father Sky's belly. The building even dwarfed the high Spirit Pole, made of the tallest tree that had ever been found, and carved in the likeness of Bird-Man. Tharon would be waiting there, dressed in his finest clothing, wearing a magnificent headdress. Everything would be orchestrated for appearance and effect.

From this angle, the great temple glimmered with a brazen glory. How well she remembered that huge building; it spread in a thousand-hand square and rose a hundred hands high, towering over everything and everyone. She could make out the carved effigies of Eagle, Deer, and Rattlesnake that perched atop the temple's high ridge pole. Even from here, she could see that they needed painting. The slate-blue gleam of dusk played like whips of fire in the copper amulets that adorned the monumental building's grass roof and walls. The Lakes People in the north exchanged nuggets of copper for chert hoe blades. Tharon's metal workers pounded the copper into thin sheets and turned them into jewelry and ornaments.

The huge mound and its stunning temple took a person's breath. All the Power in the world might have been here. For a single breath, she saw the temple through the eyes of the girl she had been twenty cycles ago, and it terrified her all over again. *Oh, Bulrush, what's happened to*

*me? My blood has gone as weak as an old woman's. I can't seem to face
anything without you.*

Nightshade squeezed her eyes closed to bolster her courage. When
she opened them, she found Badgertail giving her a curious sideways
glance. Did he know? Could he guess her anguish at walking this path
as a captive for the second time in her life?

He hung his war club back on his belt and lifted a hand to signal the
guards over the gate. While men scurried to obey, Badgertail took
Nightshade's arm, leading her forward as his warriors regrouped into a
crescent moon around them. The crowd pressed as close as it could,
murmuring, standing on tiptoes to get a glimpse of the sacred space
enclosed within the palisades—perhaps hoping to see the Sun Chief
himself.

With a bang and a thump, the log gate slid back, revealing an
L-shaped entryway. Badgertail clutched Jenos' head beneath his left
arm as he pushed Nightshade through the entry, then waited while the
warriors closed the gate. The beauty here eased something weary in his
soul. Gardens encircled the bases of the mounds in pale-green fringes,
while wreaths of smoke hovered near the summits. The flickering glare
from cook fires reflected on the smoke in ruddy patches.

Nightshade shook off Badgertail's restraining hand, and he met her
eyes. They seemed to swirl and tug at a man, pulling him down into
dark, frightening depths. When he couldn't bear it any longer, he let his
gaze rise over the tangled mass of her still-damp hair and shift to the
gatekeeper.

"South Wind, how is everything here?"

The short, stocky warrior gestured noncommittally. His clean
warshirt hung to his knees and sported the face of a fox on the chest.
"As well as can be expected after the events of last week. People have
been staying inside for the most part, afraid to come out."

Badgertail nodded solemnly. He could feel it. He had been gone for
two days, but the pall hadn't lifted. The city huddled under a
smothering blanket of quiet. No one walked the winding paths through
the eighteen mounds inside the palisades, though he could see the
orange gleams of firebowls lighting the houses on the crests of the
mounds. Occasionally a human voice penetrated the soft noises of
the crickets hidden in the grass, or rose above the distant barking
of dogs—but not often.

"Where's the Sun Chief?"

"*In the temple,*" Nightshade whispered.

South Wind paled, and his hand crept to his knife. "In the . . . the
temple, Badgertail. We thought he would have his guards carry him
down here on his litter, but he's been waiting there for you all day."

Badgertail gave South Wind a confident nod. "Thank you, my
friend. Go back to your platform. We'll talk more in the morning." He
turned back to Nightshade. She stood glaring at the stairs that rose up

the front of the Temple Mound. Made of polished cedar logs, they shone with a reddish tinge in the fading light.

Badgertail shifted uneasily, giving her time to sort through what must have been a haunting mixture of memories. Little had changed in the time she had been gone. A few more mounds had been completed; three more ponds had welled in the holes excavated to fill the necessary baskets of dirt. But not much else was different . . . except that Badgertail now had a house on a small mound on the east side of the temple. Involuntarily he tried to peer through the earthen wall to see it. Oh, how he would love to be coming home with Bobcat to sit before the fire and sip anise tea while they discussed the insanity of the past cycle. Who could he talk to now? Who could he ever confide in again?

He squinted at the sky. The most Powerful of the Star Ogres had awakened. Wolf Pup's long nose dipped down to sniff at the peak of the temple, while his tail brushed the noose around Hanged Woman's neck.

"The cage is locked, Badgertail. Can you untie me now?" Nightshade asked in that startling, beautiful voice of hers.

"Of course." He slipped a flake of pale chert from a pouch on his belt and cut the cord that bound her hands. Nightshade winced as she rubbed her wrists. When she had the blood going again, she rested her palms on the painted Bundle tied to her belt, touching it almost apologetically.

"You remember the way?" He gestured openhandedly, an eyebrow raised.

"I've walked this path a thousand times in my nightmares. I don't think I'll ever be able to forget it."

She strode purposefully along the dirt trail that led to the base of the stairs. There she paused for the briefest of instants to wet her lips before climbing. Her deerhide boots *shished* on the sand that had blown into the crevices in the logs. Badgertail silently followed her.

As they ascended, the magnificence of the city emerged. One hundred and twenty mounds rose from the flat river bottom, speckling the land like gigantic anthills. Wide plazas and small, thatched-roof houses filled the spaces in between, interrupted only by the winding traces of creeks and the glistening dots of ponds. Everywhere, fires glowed.

They passed the first terrace, and Badgertail glanced at the small temple on the southwest corner. The structure rested on a platform, and from the center, a man could look out over the city at morning or at night and tell what day of the cycle it was, for the entire Cahokia complex had been laid out as a three-hundred-and-sixty-five-day calendar.

When they reached the highest terrace of the mound—two hundred hands above the floodplain—and stood before the door in the final palisade, Nightshade was gasping for breath, though Badgertail could not be sure how much of her effort came from exhaustion.

A call rang out. "Who comes?"

"War Leader Badgertail! I come according to the Sun Chief's orders, and I bear him good news. All that I was ordered, I have done!"

The heavy gate swung open on thick leather hinges.

From the corner of Badgertail's eye, he noticed a shiver wrack Nightshade as she stepped inside the final courtyard.

The giant temple rose before them, blotting away the night sky. For the first time, a tendril of anxiety crept into Badgertail's soul. What was it? Where did this sense of rot and corruption come from?

You're uneasy. It comes from the presence of Nightshade so soon after Bobcat's death. That's all.

To one side, the huge effigy pole of Bird-Man rested like an arrow pointed into the sky. Around the base of the giant shaft was placed a ring of offerings. Several lengths of colored cloth had been tied around the girth, each bearing a message to Bird-Man.

Badgertail averted his eyes as he grabbed Nightshade's hand and hurried forward, almost pulling her off her feet. At the doorway to the temple, Nightshade jerked loose and stopped. Badgertail could see her knees trembling beneath the red fabric of her dress.

"The Sun Chief is waiting. Can you make it, or would you like help?"

She inhaled deeply, as though using the rich scents of smoke and river to fortify her will. "I have obligations to the gods, kidnapper. I'll manage." Then she bowed to the Six Sacred Persons, a soft lilting chant issuing from her lips, the sound unearthly in the hush.

Badgertail lifted the door-hanging out of the way so she could enter the main hallway, then ducked through after her into the warm radiance. The temple was an intricate maze of light and shadow. Twelve corridors intersected this main one, six coming in from each side, creating blots of darkness in the halo cast by the firebowls that sat at the bases of the walls; the spiced hickory oil they burned sent a fragrant current through the temple. Six red door-hangings shielded the rooms of the Blessed Starborn, who inhabited this foremost section of the temple.

They walked side by side past the spectacular wall paintings of Bird-Man, Spider, Rattlesnake, Wolf, the Eye In The Hand, Wood Duck, Woodpecker, and all the others. Carved faces of Tharon's ancestors had been placed along the route, their old eyes watchful. Had their expressions always been so distasteful, or had the carvings begun to change?

Every so often Nightshade would lift her hand to smooth her fingers over one of the wall figures, usually that of a serpent or a spiral. Affectionately, she patted the faces of Grandfather Brown Bear and First Woman. The tenderness of the gesture made Badgertail wonder whether she hadn't painted some of those hallowed images herself—a very long time ago in another life.

Nightshade bowed again when she reached the entry to the Great Sun Chamber. Before she straightened, Tharon's shrill, childish laughter wafted into the hall. Laughter, and the soft, muted cries of a little girl:

Tharon's nine-summers-old daughter Orenda, no doubt. An odd child, she seemed to cry constantly. Nightshade flinched. She threw Badgertail a dull glare before she squared her shoulders and stepped into the brilliance beyond. Her steps did not even slow as she strode to stand directly in front of the raised altar where Tharon lounged insolently over the sacred pedestal. The twelve sacred fires cast yellow light on the wealth of Cahokia: a radiance shone on polished sheets of worked copperplate; on exquisite wooden statues and masks painted in glossy colors; on nacre conch shell and endless strings of shell beads. The finest pottery in the world circled the room, the pieces decorated with incised swirls, punctations, or effigies, the finish pearlescent and shining. Beautiful fabrics, each dyed in a brilliant color and bearing a complex design woven in contrast, covered the walls and floor.

"Tharon," Nightshade said to him, "I see you've changed very little. You're still blaspheming the gods."

Tharon looked away, whispering, "So . . . you're here at last."

Over twelve hands tall, Tharon had the triangular face and sharp nose of a bat. Red concentric circles tattooed his cheeks, the lines running all the way to the copper ear-spools dangling from his lobes. He looked irritable and tired tonight. Indigo smudges of exhaustion darkened the puffy flesh beneath his brown eyes, accentuating the prominence of his cheekbones. A headdress of bright yellow tanager feathers caged the black coils of hair piled on top of his head. Mica beads, the stone from their local quarries fashioned by Tharon's artisans, encircled his hem and collar, glittering wildly with his every move. Galena bracelets and anklets covered his arms and legs. Any other man so ostentatiously attired and bejeweled would have been thought contemptibly effeminate—but not the Great Sun Chief.

Tharon fumbled for his handspike, then tapped it irritatingly against the pedestal. The spike, a stylized war club, was sculpted from the finest white chert; it served as his symbol of office. It flared at the top and narrowed to a point. He tapped the spike four more times and apparently gained the courage to speak again, but as he opened his mouth, Nightshade turned away to the Tortoise Bundle, which sat on a tiny table at the edge of the altar. Its red, yellow, blue, and white spirals had faded to near nothingness, as though untended for cycles. The hand that Nightshade extended to stroke it with trembled.

In the heavy silence, Badgertail walked between two of the twelve spokes of firebowls that radiated out from the raised altar. The bowls' artist had sculpted the clay so that a variety of birds' heads rose above the lips of the vessels: eagles, falcons, and occasionally the head of a dove appeared. Father Sun had created birds to serve as assistants to Bird-Man, carrying messages between humans and other types of beings. Legend foretold that if any of the bowls in this sacred chamber ever went out, Father Sun would flare and the world would die.

"Oh!" Tharon had spied Badgertail. He dropped his handspike, trotted down the three steps from the altar, and ran across the floor. He began clapping his hands as he jumped up and down like a five-summers-old boy. His eagle-feather cape fluttered extravagantly. "Oh, Badgertail, I'm so glad to see you! What did you bring me? Where is it? Where is it?" He scrambled around Badgertail, touching his warshirt and boots. Badgertail lifted his arms, the way he always did, to let Tharon search him. "I know you have something. What did you bring me? Give it to me. I can't wait!"

Badgertail drew the amethyst-and-shell necklace from his belt, and Tharon's eyes widened. He grasped the necklace and took a step backward. "Oh, it's magnificent! Thank you. Thank you, faithful Badgertail. Here, put it on me."

Tharon gave it back, and Badgertail kissed the necklace before cautiously draping it over Tharon's head. Great care had to be taken, since the Great Sun Chief's moods could change as rapidly as the clouds. The slightest touch in the wrong place or the merest tone of voice could throw him into a lethal rage.

"There, my Chief."

Tharon ambled back toward the altar, fingering his gift appreciatively as he climbed the steps.

On the far western side of the chamber, Orenda sat cross-legged, watching her father intently. Six members of the Starborn stood behind her, men and women, each young and dressed in a bright scarlet robe. Badgertail knew the six, but not well. They were the eldest sons and daughters of the victims of last week's mad murders. At least they had siblings to comfort their grief—unlike Orenda, who was an only child. In a semicircle around them lay an array of Power objects: eleven Power Bundles, several eagle-feather prayer fans, a necklace of perfectly round white stones, an amethyst bracelet, owl-talon headdresses, and elaborately beaded moccasins.

Nightshade was looking at the objects, too. Her gaze rested on one particular Power Bundle, a curious, fat-bodied creature without legs and a long, flat tail painted in gray on the outside. She cocked her head as if she heard muted voices coming from it.

Badgertail cautiously spread his hands. "My Chief, aren't you forgetting something?"

Tharon gave him a blank gaze. "Forgetting . . ."

Badgertail mouthed the words, "The drink."

"Oh! Yes!" Tharon clapped his hands. "War Leader Badgertail and the great Nightshade have come! Bring us the holy white drink!"

One of the Sunborn, a young man, slipped into the back. Nightshade seemed unaware of the awkward silence, her attention rapt as she stared sightlessly at the Bundle.

The young man returned, walking in slow, measured steps, a huge, beautifully etched conch-shell cup in his hands. He Sang, reciting the story of how First Woman had brought the gift of white drink to humans to clear their thoughts and give them insight. The word "white" referred to the purity of the beverage, not to its color, for that was a deep black. Only as he came close did Badgertail notice the trembling in the youth's hands and the tense set of his jaw.

Tharon took the offered bowl and drank deeply before handing it back, a preoccupied frown tightening his face. The youth approached Badgertail, who accepted the cup with two hands and admired the etchings on it: interlinked figures of Rattlesnake that formed a cross, their tails bending off to the left in right angles. Badgertail drank the bitter, black brew; it was tepid and oily. Nagging unease ate at him. The drink, properly served, could have been poured over a finger without scalding it, but just barely.

He returned the heavy bowl to the youth, who gave it to Nightshade. She absently took the shell, drinking at first with reluctance, then with firmer resolve. A light had kindled in her eye when she finally handed the bowl back and thanked the youth. One by one, the others drank, and the youth retreated with the vessel.

Ceremony observed, Badgertail knelt before the pedestal. "Blessed Tharon, Great Sun Chief, we have returned in triumph. Your tribute is being unloaded as we speak." He cautiously placed Jenos' head on the altar at Tharon's feet. "And I have brought the head of your 'cursed enemy,' as you demanded."

"Did you?" Tharon wet his lips, as if frightened by that fact. He tugged at his necklace. "I'm surprised. I thought . . . well, I'd no idea my cousin would have the courage to face you." He flicked a hand anxiously. "Unwrap it."

Badgertail untied the ends of the stiff golden fabric and peeled the blood-caked cloth back to reveal Jenos' face, hideously distorted by the tight folds that had bound it. The crescent moons tattooing the cheeks had shriveled to black pits, but the eyes were glaring defiantly.

Tharon's thin lips pursed in revulsion. "The fool, he should have known better than to oppose me. Did he die well, Badgertail?"

"He died bravely."

"You forced his son—what's his name?—to watch?"

"Petaga, yes."

"Well, Jenos deserved it. He shouldn't have opposed me. His son will know better." Tharon nodded vehemently. "Yes, the boy will obey now, just like everyone else. Won't he, Badgertail?"

"Yes, my Chief."

Tharon's eagle-feather cape swayed around his legs as he stepped away from the pedestal to look at Nightshade, whose stunned eyes had focused unblinking on Jenos.

"So," he said, his voice brittle, "you are mine again, Nightshade. It seems I can cast you away or drag you back at my whim."

She stood silent for a moment before a deep-throated laugh escaped her lips. When she caught Badgertail's warning glance, she laughed louder, letting her mirth twine rampant through the bright stillness. Even the whimpering Orenda hushed in shock.

"It was hardly you who dragged me back, Tharon, but your whims are certainly the reason I'm here," she said smoothly. "So you killed Old Marmot. What—"

"You liar! How dare you suggest such a thing?" he thundered, his eyes darting to the Starborn, hovering hesitantly over his child. They whispered among themselves.

Nightshade paced lithely before the pedestal, her dirty red dress adhering to the curves of her body like a second skin. "It wasn't a 'suggestion,' and I doubt very much that Marmot's Power Bundle would lie to me. It was there, after all, when he stumbled back into his room after you poisoned him."

Badgertail rose to his feet so fast that he tripped over his own boot and had to grab the altar to keep from falling. Nightshade's demeanor had changed dramatically. Was this the same woman who had lain sobbing like a child only a short time ago? Power now emanated from her, lacing her deep voice and adding a sensual fluidity to her movements. Could this be another of the faces of Sister Datura? When she smiled, a haunted gleam entered her eyes.

"What did Marmot find out, Tharon? What is it you've done to anger the gods so much that they've abandoned us?"

Tharon leaned on the sacred pedestal and picked up his handspike, lifting it as if to rap it, but he didn't. His mouth puckered into a pout. For a long time he stood absolutely still, studying her.

"Do you know that Old Marmot believed you were a witch?" Tharon's teeth flashed. "He said that you were breathing death into the Wellpots. I could have you killed on that suspicion, you know." He made a wide, sweeping arc with his hand. "Everyone would approve."

Nightshade lifted a brow challengingly. "I'm the only one left who can breathe life into the pots, Tharon. Kill me and you'll cut yourself off from the Underworld forever. And without First Woman's guidance, you'll doom your people to oblivion."

Tharon slammed his spike down onto the pedestal and fought to suppress tears. "We're already doomed! Look at what's happened to us!" he screamed. "M-Mother Earth refuses to grow trees. First Woman won't send rain, and when she does, the floods kill our crops!" He flung his spike across the room. It hit a firebowl and tumbled end over end until it struck the wall with a dull thud.

One of the Starborn, a homely young woman named Kettle, gasped as oil trickled out of the bowl. She ran to grab another off the altar and replace the cracked one, chanting frantically the while. Kettle must have become the new Firebowl Tender. If so, she would never set foot outside the temple, forever monitoring the Sun Chamber's bowls to assure that nothing snuffed their light. Tharon watched her with disgust on his triangular face.

"Enough!" he shouted. "Bring me my handspike."

Kettle finished replacing the bowl and carefully shifted the wick before she scampered to return the spike. She bowed as she handed it up to Tharon. He jerked it from her fingers, ordering, "Now go back to your place with my child."

"Yes, my Chief." She ran back to the western side of the chamber, her feet pattering like a frightened squirrel's.

Tharon toyed with his spike, tapping it into his palm before he gained the courage to descend the altar steps and approach Nightshade.

She watched him silently as he circled her, a speculative quirk to his mouth.

"I'd no idea you'd grown up into such a beautiful woman," Tharon said furtively. "I've heard that your Power has grown by equal bounds." He circled her again. "Do you know what I did for you?" he asked with a mixture of childlike joy and apprehension. When Nightshade did not answer, he shouted, "I had your old room prepared!"

Nightshade glared at him from the corner of her eye. "Why did you order me brought back here, Tharon?"

His mouth opened and closed. "I . . . well . . ." He shrugged and smiled, circling her once more. "We grew up together, you and I. Remember when you taught me how to make grass bracelets?"

Nightshade responded softly, "I remember."

His face lit with a pained warmth. "And remember when you taught me the steps to the Spring Corn Dance that your people used to do?"

"Yes."

Badgertail cocked his head. It was curious that he had never considered the probability that Nightshade and Tharon had been friends. He had never thought of anyone as being Tharon's friend, but Tharon had been eight when Badgertail had brought Nightshade to Cahokia; she had been four. Both of them babies. Both lonely. Of course they would have sought out each other.

Tharon chanced a smile. "I wanted you here, Nightshade. I'm sorry I banished you ten cycles ago, but you made me so angry when you beat me in that chunkey game!" He sulked for a moment before glancing up at her from beneath his lashes. "Maybe we could be friends again. You could breathe life into the Wellpots and talk to the Spirits, and I'll rule the land. Would that be all right? What do you think? Hmm?"

Had it not been for the silence that smothered the chamber, Badgertail would not have heard her response: "Tharon, answer me. Why did you kill Marmot? Did he find out what you'd done to turn First Woman against us?"

"Nightshade!" Tharon's hand shot out with the quickness of Snake to snatch a handful of her dark, tangled hair. He yanked her face up to within a handsbreadth of his own. "Don't . . . don't ever ask me that again. Do you understand?"

A smile curled Nightshade's lips. "Let me go, Tharon. Or shall I call out to the hundreds of Spirits who inhabit the Power objects you've stolen? They won't be as gentle with you as I will. They'll gladly eat your soul."

Badgertail's muscles tightened at Tharon's answering laugh. For several moments, no one moved—and then something subtle changed in the room. As if the Ice Giants had strode back into this world, bringing glacial cold with them, Badgertail shivered. The light started to spin in little whirlpools at the edges of his vision. He could almost see Power seeping out of the Bundles to infuse the golden glow that pervaded the room. He took a step forward.

"Don't threaten me, Nightshade!" Tharon glanced around fearfully. "You don't *ever* threaten me! I'm the Sun Chief. You have to obey me. That's all you have to do!"

"I won't obey a fool, Tharon."

Tharon raised a fist over his head, poised to strike. Badgertail broke into a run. Nightshade hunched down as the blow descended, and Badgertail caught Tharon's fist in mid-swing, holding it tightly against his blood-soaked warshirt.

"Don't do this, my Chief," he whispered insistently. "You're tired. Get some rest and think . . . before you do something you'll regret. You know that Nightshade doesn't deserve this kind of treatment."

Firelight sparkled on the beads of sweat that trickled down Tharon's throat. His sudden laughter grated eerily. "Yes. You're . . . you're right, Badgertail. I'm just worn out. And it's been a terrible week."

Badgertail released Tharon's hand and backed away. "No one sees rightly when he's tired. With your permission, I'll escort Nightshade to her room so that you can rest."

Orenda whimpered again, muted, half-choking. Tharon gritted his teeth and gave his daughter a look that would have melted snow. Orenda buried her face in her little hands and sobbed almost soundlessly.

"Go ahead, Badgertail. Take Nightshade to her chamber." Tharon wiped his mouth with the back of his hand as he stared at Nightshade. "Go on. Take her away."

Badgertail quickly ushered Nightshade from the Sun Chamber into the dimness of the hall. In the living quarters around the chamber, firebowls glowed only at the intersections of the corridors, leaving most of the temple ominously dark. They walked in silence until they reached the correct passageway and turned left.

Badgertail inhaled his first easy breath of the night when they stopped before the door to her old room. "Nightshade—"

"You're not planning on defending him to me, are you? Don't make pretenses with me. You hate him just as much as everyone else does."

He nodded mildly. "Perhaps, but you must understand that he's lost his wife and eleven friends in the past seven days. He's—"

"He murdered Old Marmot, Badgertail," she said unemotionally. "I don't know why. But I must find out. If someone doesn't heal the wound that Tharon's ripped in the soul of First Woman, she'll never speak for us again, and Mother Earth will let us all die."

The wild glow of Sister Datura had faded from her powerful gaze, replaced now by something softer and a little frightened. Grief had once more imprinted its tracks on her beautiful face, tightening around her mouth.

He straightened up and bowed slightly. "Have a good rest, Nightshade. We'll see each other again."

Badgertail started down the hall, anxious to leave so that he could go to Bobcat's home and tell Moonseed the things he must. Already his ears rang with her cries.

"Badgertail?" Nightshade called.

He stopped but did not turn. "Yes?"

"Bobcat wanted me to tell you that he forgives you."

Like a knife in his heart . . . Badgertail clamped his jaw before he swiveled halfway around. "For what?"

"For not leaving when you had the chance." She pulled back the door-hanging and vanished into the darkness of her room. The hanging swung erratically, revealing glimpses of her red dress.

Badgertail braced his hand against the cedar wall as memories of his brother swept over him. Softly, he said, "Tell Bobcat I'm sorry."

Green Ash shoved her way through the crowd, calling, "Aunt? Aunt, what is it!" Her child-heavy body made maneuvering difficult. "Move," she shouted at a big man who blocked her path. "Move, please!" Green Ash shouldered by him, aware that her breath had begun to cloud as the air cooled with the coming of night. Around her, a babble of voices rose and fell as people discussed the meaning of what they'd just seen.

Green Ash broke out of a thick knot of people, and rounded one of the houses, stepping carefully to avoid freshly turned rows of soil where someone had started a small garden. A brown-and-white cur barked and nipped at her. Finally, Green Ash caught sight of her aunt.

Checkerberry wailed as she ran through the lavender veil of dusk, a high, breathless sound that traveled eerily on the still air. People made a small path for her, barely glancing as she rushed by. Everyone's eyes were still fixed on Badgertail's warriors, who lounged haughtily outside the palisade, boasting of their exploits at River Mounds.

Green Ash followed and turned the corner at the end of a thatched wall. Ahead, Checkerberry, gray hair tumbling over her withered face, had fallen to her knees to scramble into her house.

"*Aunt?*"

Green Ash put a hand on her protruding belly, and crawled through behind Checkerberry. The house consisted of one room, twenty hands by fifteen. As the powerful and respected leader of the Blue Blanket Clan, Checkerberry's house reflected her status. Sacred masks of the gods covered the walls, glinting with copper and shell inlays. A ladder led up the left wall to a narrow platform that served as a bed; it sat close to the juncture of the roof and wall, where a slit allowed the breezes to repel the smoke from the firepit.

Green Ash blinked in the near darkness. Finally she spied Checkerberry in the rear, hunched in a pile of blankets and jerking spastically at a banded red, blue, and tan blanket, attempting to cover her face. When she had tugged the blanket into place, she sat trembling, only one eye showing.

Green Ash extended a hand. "Aunt? Are you all right?"

Checkerberry spoke in a barely audible whisper. "She's come back."

"If it was her."

"Evil . . . evil walks with her. Couldn't you feel it?"

"Well, even if it was Nightshade, what difference—"

"*Difference?*" Checkerberry shouted, and her blanket slipped down to her shoulder. "She killed my entire family! My poor little Hopleaf. Oh, Hopleaf . . ." Checkerberry fell into choking sobs.

Green Ash closed her hands on air. She hadn't even been born then, but she knew the old stories. About how the Great Gizis had chosen Checkerberry—respected and renowned even then—to teach Nightshade the ways of her new people. Less than two moons after Checkerberry had taken on the task, her husband had perished in an accident while hunting. Within the cycle, all three of her children had died one by one from strange fevers. Checkerberry's soul had come unhinged. She had never been quite right since.

"Oh, my niece, my niece. She was bound and surrounded by guards. She didn't return of her own free will. We are doomed! There'll be no more rains. The crops will wither in the fields!"

Green Ash edged forward until she could touch Checkerberry's knee gently. "No, they won't, Aunt. You know that First Woman will protect us. She—"

"Nightshade is more powerful than First Woman. She'll throw corpse powder on us and kill us all! She's a witch," Checkerberry hissed. "A witch! Wait. You'll see."

Seven

Lichen panted as she scrambled up the gritty rock outcrop that encircled half of Redweed Village. Flycatcher and two other boys climbed above her with the agility and speed of frightened pack rats. The dirt cascading beneath their sandals spattered her like hailstones. A smoky film had already built up on her red-and-tan skirt. Lichen spat gravel from her mouth and climbed faster.

On the banks of Pumpkin Creek, fifty hands below, people laughed and raced around the central plaza, preparing for the Beauty Way Ceremony at nightfall. Fifteen houses with shaggy thatched roofs framed the plaza in a long rectangle. Turtle and bluegill lay naked on drying racks before them, their sweet flesh desiccating in the bright afternoon sun. Farther out, at the edge of the village, storage huts sat on raised poles. Beneath a hut near the bend of the creek, a raccoon struggled, trying to climb one of the greased poles and reach the rich supply of corn inside. It jumped valiantly, attempted to sink its claws into the wood, and scratched wildly at the bear grease before toppling backward to land in a soft bed of knotweed.

Someone shouted, and the raccoon, realizing its chances of winding up in that selfsame storage building—albeit skinned, gutted, and dried for someone's supper—bolted in a ring-tailed streak for the low brush and a longer life.

"Hurry up, Lichen!" Flycatcher called from the top of the outcrop. His shoulder-length black hair glistened with sweat. He waved impatiently. "We're going!"

Screechowl, the biggest boy in the village and meaner than a mating mink, propped his fists on his hips and sneered over the edge at Lichen. He'd broken his nose as a baby, and it still zigzagged as sharply as a lightning bolt. He had small dark eyes and a mouth like a catfish's, but his shoulders spread as wide as a man's—and he was barely eleven summers. He scared Lichen half to death. "Come on, girl!" he yelled, then turned to his companions. "Let's leave her. She can't keep up."

"I'm coming!" Lichen cried as she watched the boys charge away in a cloud of dust. "Flycatcher! I'm coming!"

She slid her knee onto a ledge and dug her fingers into the crevice above, pulling up frantically. The cracked stone gave way, coming off in her hand, and she slipped and fell, landing hard on a lower ledge. She grabbed at the rock to keep from falling all the way and managed to hook her thumbs into a weathered hole. Blood trickled warmly from a scraped knee. She bit her lip to drive back the hurt and tackled the rock face again, climbing until she could slither over the top of the last shelf.

Lichen rolled over to catch her breath. Sand stuck to her bare, sweaty back in itchy patches. She scratched at them while she studied the clouds that brushed the turquoise sky in long streamers, sweeping southward toward the great villages that lined the Father Water.

The hooting laughter of Screechowl made her turn onto her stomach. The boys huddled together, shoulder to shoulder, behind an upright boulder in the distance. They butted each other playfully as they fought for the best position. Lichen got up and trotted toward them, but her steps faltered when she realized where they were. They must be looking down on the dressing area of the Masked Dancers, who would conjure Beauty from the earth and plants in tonight's ceremonial. She bent low and sneaked up on cougar-silent feet to see what occupied them so thoroughly. In the grassy space at the rear of the temple, two women stood naked, painting each other's breasts with bright red ochre. The spirals fanned out from their nipples to blossom in the center of their chests as majestic images of Thunderbird in flight. His wings swept up in a rounded arc until the tips of the feathers connected with the Dancers' earlobes.

Everyone was curious about the sacred painting ceremony that accompanied the Beauty Way. Legend said that Wolf Slayer himself came to help the Dancers with the artistry, but it was considered bad luck to see the painted designs before the Dancers made their appearance on the night of the ceremony. Lichen lifted a brow at the boys. She whispered, "You turkey brains! Do you want to ruin the ceremony? You know nobody's supposed to see the Dancers until they come out of the temple tonight. You're bringing bad luck. Terrible things could happen!"

Flycatcher shrugged in shame and slid backward on his hands and knees, but Screechowl grabbed him by the thongs on his breechclout and hauled him back. Flycatcher let out a yowl while he chopped at the bigger boy's meaty hands. "Quit that, Screechowl! Let me go!"

"Well, what are you doing listening to a *girl*? What does she know?"

Lichen clamped her teeth and narrowed her eyes. "A lot more than you do, ugly boy . . . at least about ritual. My mother's the Keeper of the Stone Wolf."

"So what?" Screechowl jeered. "She doesn't have any Power. My father says she's the Keeper just because some old man named Left Hand got the Wolf a million cycles ago and said only his family could take care of it. That's stupid. I bet my father could take care of it a lot better than your mother does. He's the great-great-great"—he waved his hand to indicate a bunch of "greats"—"grandson of First Woman herself."

"That's stupid!" Lichen pronounced. "Nobody's the relative of First Woman!" She hesitated, not quite sure of how that could be, but it sounded potent, so she continued, "My mother knows all the sacred stories. What does your father know about the Emergence from the Underworlds in the Beginning Time, or about Wolf Slayer's battle with his dark brother, the Bird-Man? Nothing, I'll bet."

Screechowl got to his feet. He threw his huge shoulders back and stalked toward Lichen like Grandfather Brown Bear walking on his hind legs.

She let out a yell and ran.

Her skinned knee told her in no uncertain terms how bad an idea that was. Her leg got weaker with every step, and Screechowl's long gait was rapidly closing the gap between them. Lichen forced her knee to work even harder. When she jumped a squat papaw bush to reach the trail that led the long way back to the village, her knee gave way. She tumbled ankles over snarled hair to land hard at the base of a pile of boulders, a little dizzy.

Screechowl bawled in triumph as he dove for her, but Lichen somehow scooted out of his way, rolled to her feet, and stood with her jaw thrust out and her fists up. "Stop it, Screechowl, or I'll break your nose again!"

Flycatcher and young Wart raced up as Screechowl kicked Lichen in her sore knee. When she screamed, he grabbed her hand.

"Now I've got you! You'll never be talking bad about my father again."

He swung his clenched fist at her cheek. Lichen ducked and rammed her head into his stomach, then sank her teeth into his side for good measure before flinging herself backward to break his rawhide grip.

Screechowl started to bellow in pain but caught himself and straightened up. To his friends, he said, "Come on! Let's get her!"

Flycatcher stood dumbly, casting covert glances at Lichen, while Wart jumped from foot to foot, waiting for somebody, anybody, to tell him what to do. Only seven, he didn't have much sense yet. He didn't have much chin, either. Just doe eyes and a forehead that took up most of his face. His long black braid dangled in a fuzzy mass over his left shoulder.

Lichen braced herself for the battle. "Flycatcher! You're my best friend!"

"I know it!" But he made no move.

"Your best friend's a girl!" Screechowl taunted. "You've got the testicles of a worm! Come on, Wart, help me get her!"

Wart gritted his teeth so hard in indecision that his head shook. Finally, on the verge of bursting from sheer lack of action, he took a hesitant step forward, then yielded and ran to Screechowl's side.

Lichen almost lost control of her bladder. She glared at Flycatcher, trying to look fierce but knowing that her expression quickly changed to pleading. "Flycatcher? Your grandmother was my great aunt's sister!" If nothing else, kinship might work.

His eyes darted calculatingly over the clouds, apparently trying to remember if that was right; then he grudgingly nodded and trotted to stand beside her. Throwing out his chest, he declared, "Don't shove my cousin around!"

Lichen grinned at Screechowl, but he didn't seem to appreciate her accomplishment. He hunkered down, spreading his arms like Falcon ready to soar into the sky, crowing, "All right. We're coming!"

Wart scampered to follow Screechowl's lead as he lunged for Flycatcher. Flycatcher brought up his foot, catching Screechowl in the shoulder, but he only succeeded in throwing himself off balance so that Screechowl could slam a fist into his butt and knock him flat. Flycatcher sprawled across the gray stone like a dead spider, roaring, "Ach!"

Lichen hopped around anxiously, trying to figure out how to protect herself from Wart's attack. He flew at her, yelling, his mouth wide open, so she took her fist and jammed it down that black hole. His teeth made a crunching sound at the same time that her hand erupted in agony. They shrieked simultaneously.

Lichen stared at her bloody knuckles, shook them to fight the pain, and spun to face Screechowl, who had managed to drive Flycatcher at least ten paces up the slope.

Screechowl's lips twitched as he turned to face her.

"Don't do it, Screechowl!" she threatened. In a stroke of genius, she pointed at the sky. "Bird-Man is my Spirit Helper. If you hurt me, I'll call out to him and he'll come and carry you up to the stars before he drops you on Redweed Village!"

Screechowl laughed . . . a low, disbelieving laugh. He sauntered forward menacingly, but Lichen refused to give ground. She grabbed up a rock and stood with her knees trembling, thinking it was probably a good day to die.

As his shadow fell over her in a cool wash, Lichen's throat traitorously contemplated screaming again, but before the sound could clear her lips, a large rock plunged out of the blue and smacked Screechowl in the ear.

He whooped, "What the—" and staggered backward. A tall figure wearing a raven mask rose with ghostly stealth from behind one of the rocks up the slope. Black feathers sleeked down over its face and formed a ruff around its neck. Its huge wooden beak slowly creaked open, showing glimpses of a puckered mouth beneath. Then a shrill caw flooded out, sounding so real that Screechowl stood petrified.

In a flash, the figure swooped down the slope, holding out the woven edges of its rabbit-fur cape like wings, screaming something nobody could understand. Screechowl clutched at his heart with one hand and his wounded ear with the other before flying down the path toward the village, Wart wailing and stumbling behind him.

Lichen and Flycatcher grabbed each other in terror as the figure turned and propped age-spotted hands on bony hips.

"Lichen," the Raven-Man said, "you should stay away from Screechowl. He's got bad blood. Did you know his grandmother used to suck toad eyes for fun? She kept a batch rolling around in her cheeks all day long. I never did like her." One hand reached up and tugged off the mask, revealing a face painted with alternating stripes of red, yellow, and blue. A single black spot covered the middle of the forehead.

"Wanderer!" Lichen shouted in glee as she pushed Flycatcher from her to grab the old man around the right leg. "When did you get here? I thought you would wait until nightfall, when people couldn't see you so well."

Wanderer grinned. "No, no. I came early to talk to the rocks."

Lichen exchanged a prudent look with Flycatcher. "What for?"

"Why, to hear stories about the Beginning of the World. Come on, I'll show you." He spun in a whirl of glistening rabbit fur and tramped back up the slope.

Lichen followed in his moccasin prints, taking two steps for each one of Wanderer's. When she reached the highest cluster of rocks, where Wanderer crouched, she turned to speak to Flycatcher, but the space behind her was empty. She stretched her neck and saw him dashing down the trail in the distance, his short legs pumping as fast as they could.

"I guess he didn't want to talk to the rocks," she said.

"Oh, most people don't," Wanderer observed. "It's a curious prejudice. They'll talk to themselves with no hesitation, but when it comes to communicating with higher Spiritual forms, they go deaf and dumb. Come over here, Lichen . . . let me show you this."

He ducked low and wiggled through a wide crack between the rocks that led into a sort of cave, then extended a hand to her. Lichen tucked her fingers in his and allowed him to pull her into the darkness. Only a tiny dimple of sunlight penetrated the fissure, lancing down between two upright slabs of gray stone and striking the far corner. Wanderer slid into the light and crouched so that it hit him squarely in the chest.

"What now?" Lichen asked as she snuggled up beside him.

"All of these rocks have voices," he answered. "But not everybody can hear them. You have to listen very carefully."

The fissure smelled mustily of pack-rat dung. When her eyes

adjusted to the dimness, she could discern the rat's nest of evergreen twigs and shiny bits of mica stuffed under a narrow shelf in the back. It looked abandoned. Too bad. Her stomach had been growling since noon. She could have used a snack before tonight's big feast.

She wet her chapped lips and gazed around. They looked like ordinary rocks to her, gray and lumpy. "I'm listening, but I don't hear anything."

"Wait." Wanderer reached around the side of one of the slabs and pulled out a gray rope of braided human hair. He wrapped it around the uppermost rock, which protruded just over his head, and hoarsely whispered, "Are you ready?"

"Yes. I want to talk to the rocks."

Wanderer started pulling the hair rope back and forth, back and forth. A soft, protesting moan resulted. He breathed, "Can you understand what they're saying?"

She concentrated on the variations in sound, trying to decipher words. "No. What?"

"They're telling the story of Father Sun's first mating with Mother Earth. You see, these rocks are very old. They were alive untold cycles ago, so they remember."

Lichen canted her head, straining to understand. She could hear something, but not words so much as notes in a Song, rising and falling, twining in an ancient melody. "They're Singing about the Beginning Time, aren't they?"

"Yes." Wanderer smiled broadly. "I thought you'd hear them. Most people can't, but the hole in the top of your head is still partly open."

"What are they saying now?"

"Hmm? Oh, they're telling the story about Bird-Man fighting his brother, Wolf Slayer. It was a great battle of Light and Dark, which sundered Mother Earth and created the hole through which our people emerged from the dark Underworlds to this world that is both Light and Dark. Like all things here, half this, half that, always in harmony unless we do something to upset it."

Lichen scooted closer to the rope. "Wanderer? Could you ask the rocks something for me?"

"Ask them yourself."

"All right." Lichen hesitated, not sure of how to put the words so rocks would understand. "You rock people," she began, "I sort of hear your Song, and I am grateful for your Singing. Since you know about the Beginning Time, maybe you could help me. Bird-Man came to me once when I was a little girl and told me I had to learn to see life through the eyes of a bird, a human, and a snake. Do you know what he meant? I think the time has come when I need to know how to do that."

Wanderer had a look of engrossed concentration as he sawed the hair rope back and forth. Lichen brought up her knees—careful of the stiff one—so she could wrap her arms around her shins. The rope looked like a glimmering icicle, the way it moved in the gloom.

"Ah," Wanderer said thoughtfully. "I understand."

"What?"

"The rocks say that you should take heed of putting on Bird-Man's wings without a resigned will."

Lichen blinked at her knees. The bruise had turned into a black knot that felt hot. "But Bird-Man told me I had to learn to fly . . . so I could go talk to First Woman in her cave."

The rope continued to Sing, sounding more and more like a swarm of grasshoppers sawing their legs in the weeds. "Yes, the rocks say that's true. But to do it, you first have to empty yourself of your humanness, so you can be Snake, who lives in the dark Underworld, and be Hawk, who roams the brilliant light of the sky. When you can unite all three worlds in yourself—Snake, Bird, and Human—then First Woman will let you enter her cave."

"Well . . . but . . . I don't know how to do that. Can Bird-Man come and help me?"

Wanderer frowned. His bushy gray brows drew together as he listened. "The rocks say that he's never left you."

"So, where is he?" Lichen looked around warily, searching the dark cracks in the rocks for any hint of shiny snakeskin or the flutter of feathers.

Wanderer pulled down the hair rope and quietly coiled it in the shaft of light. "They stopped talking."

"Why?"

"I don't know."

"They didn't want to tell me?"

"Perhaps Bird-Man won't let them. And then, rocks don't know everything, though they're always listening and learning when people least suspect it."

Lichen squinted one eye to peer up at the sky, visible through the rent overhead. A puff of cloud sailed across the space, its edges tinged with the palest of pinks. "We should be going, Wanderer. It'll be sunset soon. We can't be late for the Beauty Way. It took my mother half a day to convince the people in the village that it was all right for you to come."

His face darkened as he looked down at his rope. "It was kind of Meadow Vole to ask them. And kind of you, Lichen, to ask her for me."

She patted his arm affectionately and crawled out of the rocky fortress into the waning daylight. The crimson face of Father Sun hung a handsbreadth from the horizon. In the purpling stillness, she could hear voices climbing the slope—soft, reverent voices, as if the approach of the ceremonial turned the world as frail as a plum blossom, so that it had to be treated gently.

"What were you and the boys doing up here?"

"Playing chase. But then, when the boys got to the top, Screechowl wanted to look down on the women painting themselves. I said it was wrong, and we got in a fight."

Wanderer's mouth puckered like a corded bag pulled tight. "Bad blood! Well, I pray Power is lenient with him."

"Lenient?"

"Yes. Power always gets back at people."

Lichen looked at the boulder, and a tickling feeling grew in her stomach.

Wanderer—his mask tucked under one arm—came up beside her, and they took the trail down to Redweed Village, twining around clusters of vine-covered stone. A coolness had climbed onto the shoulders of the air, so heavy that Lichen shivered. When Wanderer noticed, he lifted his rabbit cape and spread it around her to shield her from the coming night.

"Wanderer," she asked, "what am I going to do? About learning to enter the Cave, I mean?"

"Do you want to enter it?"

"Yes. Bird-Man told me I needed to, or First Woman was going to abandon the world and let us all die." She looked up into that long, beaky face with its unruly frame of gray hair to see if he wanted to make fun of her. Grown-ups usually did when she told them about Bird-Man coming to her. Even her own mother laughed at her.

"Well then," he said, "I guess we just have to teach you how to turn into Snake and Hawk, so you can go searching for Bird-Man."

"Will I have to give up my human soul, like you have?"

"Yes, for a while."

Lichen grabbed onto the fringe of his deerhide sleeve while they maneuvered through a thorny bramble of rosebushes. Her heart had started to jam against her ribs. "Wanderer?"

"Yes, Lichen."

"What if I'm scared?"

He smiled. The growing bonfire of sunset cast such a lurid halo over his face that his wrinkles stood out like dark cobwebs. "Oh, don't let it trouble you. Being human isn't all it's made out to be. You might be surprised at what Hawk can teach you about Earthmaker. I just wish . . . well, I wish you could come and live with me for a while, so I could teach you all the little things about changing souls." A pause. "But I doubt your mother would approve of that."

Lichen stepped over a rock and tried to imagine what it would be like to live with Wanderer instead of with her mother. She didn't know if she liked the idea. She had always lived with her mother, beneath the watchful eye of the Stone Wolf, and close enough to Flycatcher to hit him with a rock if she wanted to. But she loved Wanderer just the same. Maybe she could do it. "Am I allowed to pick the kind of bird and snake whose soul I get? Like maybe I could get Water Snake's soul or Falcon's soul?"

"You can try. But sometimes when you're swimming in the Silence looking for a soul, one comes to you that you didn't expect."

"You mean like the weasel that's been trying to take over yours?"

"Yes, just like that."

Lichen ran a hand under her itchy nose. What would it be like to have to fight a weasel for her soul? She had seen weasels attack animals ten times their size, pull them down and chew their throats out. They were so fast, so ferocious and deadly. She wondered if it worked the same way with souls.

They reached the foot of the trail and walked out through the cornfields that led to the village and its central plaza. In the fading beams of sunlight, the straw roofs of the houses glittered as though coated with honey. Lichen sniffed at the tangy fragrances of clover and smartweed. They passed the raised storage hut where Raccoon had been struggling earlier in the day, and Lichen detoured for a moment to examine the claw marks in the bear grease. Bear grease was expensive. They found so few bears now that they had to buy grease from the traders who went north to the Great Lakes.

As they walked on, Lichen asked, "Wanderer? What do you think the rocks meant when they said that Bird-Man had never left me? I saw him fly away through my window."

He glanced up at the people who had begun to gather around the edge of the plaza, surveying the magnificent colors and shapes of their sacred masks. Voices had dropped to murmurs, though a dog barked, breaking the spell of quiet. Wanderer's eyes narrowed in thought. "Oh, I think they were trying to tell you that Bird-Man lives inside you as well as outside. When he flew away, he also flew into you."

"I don't understand. What does that mean? Where is he inside me?"

"Ah," Wanderer breathed and shook his finger right in her face as though the action imparted a great truth. "If we knew that, we wouldn't have to go looking for him by changing ourselves into Snake and Hawk."

"What if we don't find him? No matter how hard we try."

"I wouldn't worry about that," he said mildly. "It's usually when you give up searching for your Spirit Helper that he pounces on you like Grandfather Wolf—with his teeth bared."

Lichen hung her head to watch the slanting sunlight play in the blades of new grass. She decided not to ask him the next question, but it repeated in her soul anyway. *And chews you up? Does he chew you up, Wanderer? Is that how he kills your human soul?*

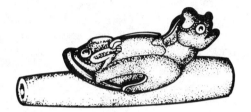

Eight

Hailcloud stood rigidly by the door. The council lodge of Hickory Mounds had suffered in the recent fighting. Poles dangled from the wounded roof, letting thatches of cattail slump precariously into the room. Five-hands-wide gaps gashed the walls. Badgertail's attack had devastated the village. Over seventy percent of the population had been killed, and all of the food reserves had been plundered. Hailcloud anxiously fiddled with his war club, running his fingers over the deadly chert studs. *Will they never come to any decisions? What is there to discuss? If we don't fight, we'll surely die. Why can't these elders see that?*

Moonlight streamed through the fissures, falling in veils of silver over the men and women who sat in a circle on the floor. From one hand to another, they passed a large steatite effigy pipe, carved in the form of a warrior decapitating an enemy. The scent of tobacco rose pungently on the air. In the shed behind the council, four women tended a fire, brewing strong white drink, straining it as they poured it into conch shells, each shell decorated with fancy designs.

A woman, one of the clan leaders, walked into the circle. She cupped the drinking shell in reverent old hands as she Sang the Song of First Woman's gift. First she handed the vessel to Petaga, then to Hailcloud. The hot black liquid nearly burned the war leader's mouth and settled firmly in his stomach. His limbs began to tingle. As this bowl was drained, another of the old women entered, Singing, ensuring that no participant wanted for sacred white drink and the Power it brought to minds, and to words.

"So," Naskap, chief of Hickory Mounds, finally said. A short man, he had a bulbous nose beneath bushy brows that met in a line over his eyes. For this council session, he had braided his silver-shot black hair into two long ropes and had worn a blue-and-red-striped kilt. A thick necklace of marine shells hung down over his bare chest. "My young cousin, Petaga, wants a hundred warriors to add to his ragged group. Tell me, how many do you think it will take to face Badgertail? Hmm? A thousand? Two?"

Hailcloud saw a swallow go down his chief's throat. He wanted to jump to Petaga's aid, but that would humiliate the young leader. The youth had been pushed too far already. Petaga had mustered courage from somewhere, watching with a stoic expression that only Hailcloud had been able to pierce, as the sacrifices were made for Jenos. Petaga had not been ready to assume the mantle of Moon Chief, but he had done it anyway. Knowing what this visit cost the young man, Hailcloud's fingers tightened around his war club. He watched intently as Petaga smoothed clammy hands over his golden robe, summoning his best argument.

"Fifteen hundred, cousin," Petaga answered in a strong voice. "Badgertail's warriors are tired. They've been raiding all winter. If we hit them soon, before they—"

"How soon?" old Rainbow Woman demanded. She had twisted her white hair into a bun at the base of her skull. When she lifted her chin to glare at everyone in the room, Hailcloud respectfully lowered his eyes. She had been a cunning warrior in her day—and the true power in Hickory Mounds. No one would want to argue with her.

Petaga answered, "Within a moon."

"You think Badgertail will stay put that long?"

"I do, Grandmother. Cahokia has all the food it needs. They've already planted corn and squash. I don't believe that Tharon has any intention of going to war again until next winter."

Rainbow Woman rocked back on her heels and puffed the long pipe for what seemed an eternity before cocking her head to glower at Naskap. "I say we do it."

Naskap inhaled haltingly. "You think we can beat Badgertail? With a hastily formed—"

"Yes." She pointed a firm finger. "Somebody has to try. Or would you have us wait until next cycle to defend ourselves? We've barely two hundred warriors left at Hickory Mounds, Naskap. Alone, we're dead. Together, maybe we have a chance of winning."

Naskap raised a hand to the gathering of honored elders. "Who disagrees? Who wants to wait?"

A low rumble coursed through the room. Hailcloud gritted his teeth. *Fools!* Men and women leaned sideways to chat privately. Some nodded, while others raised fists and shook them with soundless ferocity.

Hailcloud gazed longingly through the largest gap in the western wall. Wisps of cloud drifted through the indigo sky, glowing like polished galena. As Moon Maiden slowly sank in the west, the shadows of the trees shot tendrils of black filigree over the land. He didn't want to fight either; no one with half a soul did. But they had to gut Badgertail's forces before the next Moon-of-Flying-Snow. They couldn't count on the corn crop. Already people had begun to comment on the unusual heat and lack of rain. Hailcloud doubted that any of the people would be alive come spring if the corn produced poorly again this cycle. *We have to act now.*

"I would have just one question," Loon said loudly, and the ruckus died down. The oldest man in the village, sixty-two summers, he had an overgrown nose and thick, bloodless lips. Forked-eye tattoos and coiled serpents covered his cheeks. "Once we have assembled this army, who will lead it?"

Petaga met each council member's eyes in turn before extending a hand toward the door. "Hailcloud. He's fought beside Badgertail . . . and against him. He knows Badgertail's weaknesses."

The confidence in Petaga's voice made Hailcloud's stomach churn. Did he? He searched his soul, trying to find any evidence to support that claim. Yes, somewhere, probably he did, though he couldn't think of any weaknesses at this moment. But as a roar of approving voices sprang from the gathering, Hailcloud realized that he had better come up with some.

"And what will you do, Hailcloud," old Rainbow Woman challenged him with a hard gleam in her eyes, "to those villages that won't join us? After talking to them, can we trust them to keep their mouths shut about what we're up to?"

Hailcloud looked around the room, his gaze lingering on the charred patches of roof where flaming arrows had landed. "That is not a decision for warriors, Grandmother. I will do whatever my elders tell me to."

But he could see the decision on the stony faces that gazed at him, and it made his breathing go shallow.

As Moon Maiden slowly sank, the shadows of the mounds stalked across the village, snuffing the glimmers of grass and cattail roofs, until they flooded over Locust's house. She tipped her chin—trying not to wake Primrose—to peer out and watch the sky. Their bed of hides and blankets was spread atop a raised platform at the intersection of the wall and roof. Through the gap in the wall she could watch the world grind in its eternal and ponderous motions. Wisps of cloud sailed through the leaden sky, glowing with a pale wash of moonlight.

She had not been able to sleep, though her tired body cried out for rest. Images of the battle-walk kept repeating themselves in her mind. Again she saw Badgertail's anguished face when he first gazed upon his dead brother. The flame had gone out of his eyes—as though a part of his soul had died with Bobcat—and a matching flame had entered

Locust's soul, burning, aching for Badgertail. Who would he turn to now? Who would the great Badgertail allow to comfort him? Even though she was probably his best friend, he rarely allowed her to see him hurting. Her, or anyone else. Badgertail could not risk such vulnerability. With Bobcat's death, he would truly be on his own.

Locust shifted her head on Primrose's muscular arm so she could look at him. His deep-set eyes and delicate bone structure gave his face a frail, innocent quality. He had washed and brushed out his long hair in preparation for her homecoming. It spread over their blankets like waves of pitch-black silk. She extended a hand tenderly to stroke the glistening strands.

"Still awake?" Primrose whispered.

"Yes."

"Worried about Badgertail?"

"I can't stop thinking about him."

Primrose always seemed to know what troubled her. It was as if so much of his soul lived inside her that he couldn't help but know. When she had first taken him for wife, her relatives had scoffed and snickered behind their hands. "You're taking a *berdache* for your wife? Ridiculous! Find a good woman who will care for your house and can bring you children." Every woman warrior had a female wife, and most of those wives had borne babies through lying with select men—generally Sunborn. But Locust did not want a pack of brats running around her house; she wanted the freedom of a quiet life with Primrose. Now she lifted a finger to trace the smooth line of his jaw. The boyish purity of his face belied the strength of his female soul.

"He's alone, Primrose. And he's never been alone before. I don't know what he's going to do."

"Being lonely is terrible."

Locust squeezed his hand. Primrose knew about loneliness. Most people found him an enigma, others feared him. Many, like her, knew and reverenced the special Power bestowed upon him by Earthmaker. He was a bridge between the worlds of male and female, Light and Dark. But few people felt comfortable in his presence. That meant he forever hovered at the edges of society, respected by some and hated by others, never fully admitted to any group.

Primrose braced himself on his elbows to peer down into her face, and the curtain of his hair tumbled around her in a shimmering wealth. Locust let herself drown in the warmth she saw in those deep-set eyes. "Badgertail will learn to survive, believe me."

"You sound so certain."

"I am. He's a strong man. He'll find someone else to confide in. I hope it will be you, Locust. You're his only real friend now."

She turned away uneasily. The breeze that blew through the gap chilled the sweat that had pooled on her throat. Though she desperately wanted Badgertail to rely on her, she feared it, too. They'd never quite managed to quell the childhood attraction they had felt for each other, and sometimes, when Badgertail looked across the fire at her after a difficult battle-walk, she could see pain in his eyes and desire for her—and then she longed to soothe him in the only way she knew how.

Incest! The people would kill you for it.

Only Primrose would understand. He was *berdache*, half-man, half-woman. He understood human weaknesses better than other people did. Primrose would know that the melding of flesh was nothing more than an attempt to ease two aching souls.

Nevertheless, it would hurt him.

Like a warshirt torn in the heat of battle, the magic would go out of their precious life together. Locust knew it as surely as she knew that she would never stop seeing the effect of her betrayal in Primrose's eyes. Some men took great pride in their invincibility, in their stalwart skill at allowing no injury to penetrate their soul. But Primrose was *berdache* and held nothing of himself from her. Every ounce of his strength and love, his entire soul, he gave willingly—because he trusted her with it.

For that reason, he would forgive her for breaking his heart. He would find some way to blame himself, or to explain it away by saying that things just happened on battle-walks. And they did. Men and women pushed to the limit of endurance often took momentary solace in each other's bodies. It meant nothing to the warriors involved except the chance to escape the horrors of war for the blink of an eye. Locust had seen it often enough to know. Battle-walk romances flared—and then died the instant the palisades of home came into view.

Locust would never tell Primrose, of course. She could never deliberately hurt him. But he would know. Just as he had known tonight that her thoughts lingered on Badgertail.

"How is Green Ash?" Locust asked, changing the subject.

Primrose pursed his lips as he trailed his fingers over her bare breast. "Not well. She's only seven months, and the child is so large that . . . well, the old women have begun to say that something might be wrong."

"You mean they think she might die?" Locust asked in her usual direct manner.

"It's just talk. I . . . I don't believe it. Some babies are larger than others. Nettle is a big man, he must have planted a big child."

"When are they to be married?"

"When the baby is born. Not long. Locust, I sense something odd about the baby."

"Odd?"

"Yes. I don't know how to explain it, but I've been having Dreams." He paused. "Strange. I see huge creatures Dancing around two cradle boards. The creatures are wearing brightly colored animal masks, coyotes, wolves, ravens . . . but the beings have no arms or legs. I don't know what to think about that."

"Have you told Green Ash about the Dreams?"

"I don't want to frighten her any more than she already is."

Locust frowned. Memories tugged: something Badgertail had told her he had seen in the Forbidden Lands when he'd gone to steal Nightshade. What had it been? "What does Checkerberry think about the baby? She's seen dozens born. Is she worried?"

Primrose settled himself into an easier position on their worn hides. "Checkerberry hasn't been 'right' since she saw Nightshade."

"What do you mean, not 'right'? Do you mean she's angry, ill, what?"

"I'm not sure. Checkerberry ran like a hunted mouse at the sight of Nightshade. I think the shock—she hid in her house and refused to come out for an entire day."

Locust had heard the old stories told time and again, when the tales of the clan were being chanted around the winter fires. Stories of how Checkerberry's family had died during that first cycle when she had cared for Nightshade. "Do you mean she's afraid that Nightshade will witch her again? To hurt the Blue Blanket Clan?"

"Yes. That very fear seems to have unhinged her mind. She sits for hands of time just staring at nothing while she mumbles about terrible things happening in the future: famine, floods, and war. I don't know what to think. Green Ash is terrified."

"I don't blame her," Locust said. "Given what's happened this past cycle, Checkerberry's predictions aren't too outlandish."

Primrose toyed with a lock of Locust's hair, but she saw that anxiety had etched crow's feet at the corners of his eyes. "Locust?" he said timidly. "I heard a rumor this morning. It frightened me."

"What was it?"

Primrose sank down beside her and snugged his forehead into the crook of her neck. He hesitated, as though not wanting to tell her, afraid of her response. Locust waited, picking tawny sheddings of deer fur from the soft mass of Primrose's hair. In the moonlight that streamed through the gap in the wall, the fur shone silver. Their hides had grown old and brittle, but new ones were scarce. Three times a cycle, traders shipped canoe loads of pelts in from the western plains, where elk and buffalo still roamed in vast herds. These days, no one but the elite could afford such luxuries.

"Promise you won't get angry?" Primrose asked. "This is only your second night home, and I couldn't bear any harshness from you. Please?"

"Primrose, tell me. I'm too tired to be angry. What is it?"

"I was coming back from the squash fields with Green Ash, and two warriors were lounging around the palisades. They were talking about Badgertail."

He raised his eyes to her face, checking to see if she had adopted the characteristic defensive squint that boded ill for all concerned. Locust diligently kept her expression blank, but a hot tide of alarm warmed her chest. What had these warriors said?

"And?" she prompted.

"They whispered that Badgertail had lost his nerve. One of them said he'd seen Badgertail weeping and scoffed that maybe Cahokia needed a new war leader."

Locust fought to keep her breathing even, but rage seared her veins in a fiery wash. "Did he?"

She saw again the look on Badgertail's face when he had first gazed upon Bobcat's bloody corpse, and the tears that came to his eyes pierced her heart like an obsidian-tipped lance. She threw off her hides and rose to climb down the ladder. When her feet touched the cold dirt floor, she shivered.

Primrose hurriedly followed her down. He stood in the tarnished light streaming through the window, his muscles bulging out in hard swells. Their house spread in a rectangle around them, fifteen hands by ten. Everything occupied its rightful place, arranged with care by Primrose's loving hands. Four rows of colored baskets hung on the long south wall, each ordered according to size and shape: round on top, then square, oval, and the curiously formless on the bottom. Along the northern wall, two shelves held their cooking pots and spice storage jars. Primrose must have replenished their supplies while she was gone. The savory ghosts of dried spiderwort and lavender hyssop mixed fragrantly with fresh mint.

As Primrose folded his arms protectively across his naked breast, his sad eyes glinted with a silver-silk flash of moonlight. "Locust, please, I didn't want to upset you. I just thought you ought to know what's being—"

"Of course I ought to know what's being said behind Badgertail's back! Who were the warriors? What were their names?"

"I don't know. There are so many warriors, I can't know them all."

Locust glared at him with impotent fury. In the quiet depths of his eyes she detected pained understanding and sympathy. Shame reddened her cheeks.

"I'm sorry I hurt you," she said softly. "My anger isn't directed at you."

"No, I . . . I know that."

She held out her arms, and Primrose quickly came to hold her tightly. He nuzzled his cheek against her hair, and his muscular body felt suddenly frail in her arms, too frail to endure her bouts of rage. Locust patted him absentmindedly while her thoughts raced over the implications of what he'd told her. So the warriors had started to accuse Badgertail of sentimentalism. Well, what if it were true? Did that make him less a leader? With a sinking stomach, she realized that the answer to that was "Yes." A war leader had to maintain a hard, practical exterior. Any display of weakness shook the confidence of every warrior around him. Vulnerability made a leader unpredictable, and therefore unreliable in times of stress.

The fact that she understood that truth did not make it any easier for her to condone disloyal remarks from other warriors.

Locust tightened her grip around Primrose's waist. "Thank you for telling me. I need to know such things. It gives me time to prepare in case . . . well, in case something comes of such talk."

He pushed back slightly and gave her the boyish smile that always overturned her heart. "Locust? Could we go back to bed? I want to love you. I missed you when you were gone."

"I missed you too, Primrose."

He bent to kiss her gently. The feel of his arms around her, the steady rhythm of his breathing, comforted her—as it had for fifteen treasured cycles.

Nine

The lilting flute called to Lichen where she sat shivering in her blanket at the northern edge of the plaza. Several other children dozed around her with their backs against the houses, or entwined with their dogs for warmth. The old people and mothers with tiny babies sat hunched against the houses on the south side of the plaza. Moon Maiden had peeked over the eastern horizon, but her light cast no warmth on this cold night. Lichen pulled her blanket up over her icy nose so she could breathe down the front and warm her chest.

The fire where white drink was made had begun to die down, and the last of the sacred drink had been exhausted. Several times Lichen had heard men complaining that in the old days, traders had brought enough of the herb from the southern coastal lands that the drink could last all night. For the last couple of years, it was said, Redweed Village had paid too much corn for the little they had received.

Lichen sighed. White drink was for grown-ups. She and the other children had Danced until very late, then been sent out of the plaza to nap while the grown-ups finished the ceremonial. Lichen could see the

Dancers, silhouetted before the flames of the fire, Singing as they bobbed up and down. Six circles of people wove about like a tangle of snakes.

Old man Wood Duck, with his maimed leg, stood at the edge of the circles and Sang, shaking a gourd rattle as he swayed back and forth. The firelight reflected in his reverent eyes. He had the scratchiest voice in the village, but it didn't matter. The only thing that mattered tonight was that First Woman see the goodness in their hearts. If they kept their souls pure and treated each other well, First Woman had taught, she would go to Mother Earth and Father Sun to speak for humans. Then the rains would come and the crops would grow tall.

Flycatcher mumbled something in his sleep and elbowed Lichen before he rolled to his side, dreaming. She squirmed to get the kink out of her back.

The Dancers blurred together in her tired vision, seeming to sink into the darkness and cold. Only their voices and the tinkling bells on their moccasins assured her they hadn't been sucked up by the Water Spirits that haunted the ceremonials. All of the pigments that humans used for painting their bodies came from the bones of the Water Spirits, and on nights like this one, when so many colors flashed, the Spirits were drawn to the souls of their dead ancestors. They came to watch from the shadows, sometimes to Dance, sometimes to steal a bad child and take him to their home beneath the lakes.

A gust of wind swooped over the rock outcrops and soared down, blasting the plaza. Lichen closed her eyes against the whirling ashes and sand. The fire sputtered, sending a shower of sparks upward into the blackness.

Flycatcher rolled over and scooted forward so he could lay his head in Lichen's lap. "I'm cold," he whispered. "I wish it was over."

She stared down at his round face. Ice had formed on the tan edge of the blanket closest to his nose. "I'm cold, too. But you know we can't go in until the Dance is done. First Woman might get mad."

"I know," he said. Morosely, he snaked a hand out of his blanket and held it up before her face. "Lichen, could you breathe on my fingers? They feel like frozen sticks."

She took his hand and held it to her lips, breathing steadily. Flycatcher shivered with delight.

"Lichen, what did the rocks say to you this afternoon?"

"Oh, nothing much. They just talked about the Beginning Time." She decided not to mention the part about how she needed to give up her human soul.

"You could hear them, really?"

"Sure. Wanderer made a rope for them to talk through . . . though it sounded more like Singing to me than words."

"He's weird, Lichen. I don't think I like him."

She lifted her eyes to study Wanderer. He stood a head taller than anyone else in the village, so it was easy to spot him. Also, his raven mask glinted in the flames. He looked skinny, the way he twisted in the Dance. He had been Dancing next to her mother all night, which Lichen found very odd since her mother didn't like Wanderer either. "I might go live with Wanderer for a while, Flycatcher."

He shot up out of her lap to peer at her nose to nose. His eyes looked like huge moons. "What for? You might never come back!"

I might never come back as a human, you mean. "There are things he needs to teach me. And I don't think I can learn them from anyone else."

"What things? You mean Dreaming things?"

"Mostly." She drew her blanket more tightly around her shoulders. "And stories. He knows lots of stories that nobody else does. I think it's because he's so old."

"And he talks to rocks."

She nodded.

"Do you *want* to go live with him, Lichen?"

"I don't know. I miss Wanderer when I'm not around him, but I think I'd miss my mother more. She's taken care of me my whole life."

"Wouldn't you be scared to live around somebody who wasn't human?"

She shook her head valiantly. "No. I live around birds and raccoons and other animals right now. They don't scare me. Do they scare you?"

"Well, no, not when they're in their own bodies," Flycatcher replied sarcastically. "Why can't he come and teach you down here . . ." He paused and scowled. "No, that would never work. Somebody would whack him in the head before long, and you'd probably feel bad."

"Yes." She sighed glumly. "I would."

Flycatcher rolled the edge of his blanket between his fingers, as though thinking hard. "You know what, Lichen? I'd miss you if you went away. I don't want you to go live with Wanderer. Is your mother going to make you? What if—"

They both started when Wood Duck let out a shrill cry of joy. Awkwardly, he tried to Dance as he shook his gourd rattle in time to the pounding of the drum. The Dancers separated, falling back, splitting into two groups to line the way from the temple at the eastern side of the plaza.

"Here they come!" Flycatcher said excitedly. He jumped to his feet and ran out to stand by old man Wood Duck. Lichen raced behind him, eager for this final moment of the ceremonial. All around the edges of the plaza, old people and children roused to look.

It began slowly. A rumble like an earthquake trembled on the cold air. From inside the temple, a chant echoed, deep and powerful, hailing softly the Spirits of the plants and animals.

Lichen lifted her voice to join that somber call. People all over the village added their voices until the resonant chant rose like thunder over the fire-lit plaza.

The temple door-hanging was swept aside, and twelve Corn Dancers emerged into the pewter flood of Moon Maiden's light.

Lichen's voice faltered as they Danced into the plaza on whirling feet, their masks glowing as though cut from Father Sun's rays. Pounded copper covered their faces, reflecting the flames in spectacular patterns. Ears of last cycle's corn hung from their necks and bounced against their naked, intricately painted bodies. They carried eagle feathers in their right hands.

The lead Dancer spread her arms and spun like a wingseed, circling around and around as if spurred by the wind. She dipped sideways to brush the ground with her fingertips, and Lichen knew the Dancer reached for the Power that lived in the roots, summoning it into her body.

The other Dancers followed, touching the ground and Singing as they twirled.

When they reached the central fire, they formed into a circle and began spinning around the flames, darting and leaping like wayward moths confused by the light.

The people rushed to join in. Dozens of outspread arms spiraled in the flickering light as people Sang their thanks to First Woman and Mother Earth.

Lichen whirled alone, watching the Star Ogres rotate above her. The longer she Danced, the more their bodies ceased to be made up of points of light but melded into gigantic, glowing circles—rings of silver. Music sounded in her ears, rising and falling as the rings slid over each other. It rang like a hundred bells struck all at once. *Thank you, Star Ogres,* she prayed, *for sharing your music with me. Someday, if I learn enough and if I can find Bird-Man, maybe I'll grow falcon wings and I can fly up to Sing for you.*

She smiled as she spun with all of her strength, spun until her feet started to stumble—just like everyone else's. People fell down all around her, clutching Mother Earth to their breasts while they kissed the ground. Finally Lichen toppled sideways and dug her fingers into the cold dirt. Her vision swam.

The Corn Dancers ran through the crowd, sprinkling everyone with cornmeal so that each person could carry the meal prayers showered upon them to First Woman in their Dreams. Perhaps, if they all Dreamed well, First Woman would hear them this time . . .

Lichen rolled onto her back to peer up at the Star Ogres again. A veil of meal-dusted hair tumbled over her eyes. Through it, the Ogres seemed to shimmer more brightly, as though pleased by the ceremonial. Lichen laughed when a huge raven leaned over her. Wind fluttered in its black feathers. Through its open beak, she could see Wanderer's grin.

"Come on," he said. "Your mother invited me to have nutcakes and tea, and I'm starved."

"Mother *invited* you?" she blurted as she struggled to sit up.

"Yes. She hasn't been herself tonight," he answered blithely. "I don't know what's wrong with her, and I'm certainly not going to ask."

He extended a hand to pull Lichen to her feet. They held on to each other as they made their way across the plaza. People swerved wide around Wanderer, still not sure that he ought to be allowed in human company, even though he had Danced with all his raven soul.

The avoidance made Lichen angry. "I watched you. You were the best Dancer here."

"I watched you too, especially when you were talking to the Star Ogres. They heard you, you know."

"How do you know?"

"Oh, I could feel it." He tapped his chest. "In here. What did you say to them?"

She lifted a shoulder. "They sent me their music. It was beautiful, Wanderer, so I thanked them and told them that someday I'd try to sprout falcon wings and fly up to Sing for them."

Wanderer squeezed her shoulder as they started down the path that led to her house. Moonlight blazed so brightly that it shadowed each blade of grass. "I'm sure they'd like that. They get lonely up there. Very few humans talk to them anymore, though Eagle and Hawk still do, of course."

"I'd talk to them more if I could."

Out in the darkness, a wolf yipped, and a whole pack joined in to serenade Moon Maiden. Now that the ceremonial was over, Lichen felt cold to her bones, and very sleepy. She twined her fingers in the soft fur of Wanderer's rabbit cape for warmth.

When they turned the bend in the path, she could see that light already gleamed around the edges of the door-hanging. The scents of Pumpkin Creek—water and wet earth—hung heavy on this side of Redweed Village. But Lichen smelled something else. She sniffed noisily.

"That's Mother's special raspberry tea, Wanderer."

He sniffed too. "Um, smells good."

Lichen gave him a quick look, wondering why her mother would make it for Wanderer when she wouldn't make it for Lichen except on important occasions. She slipped out from under his arm and trotted forward to duck beneath the hanging. Her head brushed against two of the clusters of eagle feathers that dangled from the ceiling.

"You looked beautiful tonight, Mother," she said as she ran across the house and dove beneath her warm buffalo hide. It felt good to be home. The house spread in a thirty-hand square around her. The firelight from the slab-lined hearth in the middle of the floor shimmered over the yellow spiders on the walls and flickered in the eyes of the Stone Wolf that nestled in the wall niche at the foot of Meadow Vole's bed. Along the southern wall, at the foot of Lichen's bed, several cooking pots sat atop each other. Next to them, three large storage jars huddled, filled with the seeds of giant ragweed, corn, and sunflowers.

Vole smiled. She wore a white dress with black and red spirals dyed on the hem and across her chest. She had pulled her long hair away from her face, fastening it over her ears with shell combs. The style made her hooked nose seem smaller. But her eyes looked large and dark, darker than Lichen thought she had ever seen them. "So did you, Lichen. I was proud of you. I—"

Wanderer called softly from outside, "It's me, Meadow Vole. Are you ready for me yet?"

"Come in, Wanderer. We're ready. The tea isn't, but we are."

Wanderer ducked under the hanging. He had taken off his mask and was holding it reverently. His gray hair spiked out around his long face. He winked at Lichen before crouching by the fire, where the pot of tea sat propped on two pieces of red stumpware. Flames licked up around the sooty bottom of the pot. The steam that rose saturated the air with the scent of raspberries.

Wanderer smiled awkwardly at Meadow Vole, and she smiled back before rising to fetch the plate that had the nutcakes on it.

"Are you hungry, Lichen?" her mother asked.

"No, I'm only tired."

"Why don't you try to sleep? Wanderer and I are just going to talk for a short while."

Wanderer's absurd grin faded. He hung his head. "Yes, you sleep, Lichen. We won't be long."

Lichen wiggled deeper into her hides, frightened by the hurt expression on Wanderer's face, but she kept her eyes slitted to watch what happened.

Her mother knelt beside Wanderer and offered him a nutcake, which he accepted gratefully. "Thank you, Vole. It's been a long time since I've had one of your cakes." He took a bite and smiled wanly. "They're as good as I remember. . . . Thank you," he repeated.

They stayed quite for a time, and Lichen felt the tension rise between them. Finally Meadow Vole said, "Wanderer, I wanted to talk to you about something that's happening. I don't understand it."

His eyes widened. "What?"

"Well, it has to do with Cahokia and with Tharon's mad attacks on the surrounding villages. Did you know he attacked River Mounds a few days ago?"

"No, I . . . I thought I felt something, but . . . what happened?"

Her mother ran a hand through her hair. "I'm not sure. I heard that Jenos refused to deliver the tribute that was owed to Cahokia and that Tharon went crazy. He—actually, it was Badgertail. Badgertail killed Jenos and took his head to Tharon."

"Oh," Wanderer said so softly that Lichen almost didn't hear. Grief twisted his face. "Jenos was a good man, and a good chief. I've never forgotten his kindness to Nightshade when I asked him to take her in after Tharon banished her."

"You did that?"

"Oh, yes. She had nowhere else to go, and I knew that Jenos needed her and her Powers."

Lichen's mother lowered her eyes uncertainly at the word "Powers," as if she expected Wanderer to shout at her for not having any Powers herself. "Well, the worst part is that rumors say Petaga has gone crazy, too. He was at Hickory Mounds yesterday, raving about joining forces with all of the surrounding villages and waging battle against Tharon. It's silly. Redweed is so small, yet he sent runners to ask us to join him. Tharon has too many warriors. Even if we all banded together, I don't—"

"Where's Nightshade?"

"I've heard that she was captured and returned to Cahokia, but I'm not certain that's true. I got the story from a trader who was passing through yesterday. He could have been wrong."

Wanderer sat so still that his dark eyes caught the firelight and held it as unwaveringly as mica mirrors. "Tharon must be crazy, all right. Either that or he's looking forward to having his heart cut out in his sleep."

Lichen's mother extended her hands pleadingly. "What are we going to do, Wanderer? Tomorrow we're meeting to discuss whether we should join Petaga or not. Do you think we should?"

He sighed. "If you asked me here because you hoped I'd Dreamed something, I haven't. I'm sorry. I didn't know about any of this. Except . . ." He took another bite of nutcake and chewed it thoughtfully. "Except that I keep hearing Nightshade call me, as though she needs help. But I don't know where she is, and no matter how hard I try to find her, I can't. It's as though she's lost herself, and I can't grasp onto anything to follow." He methodically finished his cake and brushed the crumbs from his hands onto the hard floor.

Her mother rose to pace before the fire. Orange flickers played in her hair. "Well, thank you anyway. If you do Dream anything—"

"I'll tell you immediately."

"I'd appreciate that."

Wanderer's eyes flared disconcertingly for a moment before he said, "There's something else I'd like to talk to you about, Vole."

"What is it?"

"It's about Lichen. Do you know she's been having Dreams? Powerful Dreams."

Her mother frowned in bewilderment. She swung around to stare at her daughter, but Lichen quickly closed her eyes to avoid that wounded look. It made Lichen feel bad inside, but she couldn't have told her mother. Vole always made fun of her Dreams, that or told her to go outside and play. Wanderer was the only grown-up she knew who listened to her seriously.

"No," her mother said quietly. "She didn't mention them to me. What sort of Dreams?"

Wanderer's lips pressed into a tight line. "It doesn't matter. What does matter is that she's old enough now to start learning how to manage them, and . . . and I'd like to teach her." He glanced up hesitantly. "Will you let me?"

"Well, I . . . I don't know. I'll have to think about it."

Wanderer stood up and faced her. "Every time I've ever heard you say that, it meant 'no.' If that's the case, tell me now, Vole."

"If you're going to push," Vole replied with hushed violence, "then the answer *is* no!"

"Please." Wanderer stepped to the door-hanging and pulled it aside. "Come outside with me so we can talk about this more thoroughly."

"I've already told you my decision, Wanderer."

His gaze rested on Lichen again. She lay absolutely still. His wrinkled face softened, and in the depths of his eyes, worry flickered, as if he saw something so terrible in her future that he almost couldn't bear it.

"Vole," he whispered, "don't I even have the right to teach her how to be happy? You know she'll be miserable if she can't control the Dreams. Soon they'll begin *stalking* her." At the hard look on her mother's face, Wanderer said, "Please, Vole. You've denied me every other right. Just let me—"

"She's *my* daughter, Wanderer. You have no rights regarding her." She folded her arms and turned away. "Please go."

Wanderer closed his eyes wearily for a moment before ducking beneath the hanging and disappearing into the night. Lichen listened to his footsteps fade away, and her stomach clutched. She waited until her mother turned to pick up the plate of cakes before she slipped completely under her buffalo robe to cry.

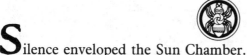

Silence enveloped the Sun Chamber.

As Tharon wove between the firebowls, the whorls of shell on his golden robe glittered with a torrid light. Too quiet! He could hear the individual breathing of each person who slept in the temple. It haunted him, hissing at him like the viperous warning of a hundred menacing serpents.

Yes, they're sleeping while you're up walking the floor. What sort of servants are these Starborn? Negligent. They're no better than the last batch. Well . . . perhaps I'll have to find new priests and priestesses sooner than I'd thought.

Tharon peevishly wandered the sacred room, pounding his hand-spike into anything that happened to come within reach: the sacred pedestal, the altar, the seashells on the walls. Already a line of crushed shell glittered along the floor. This handspike was his favorite. Over four hands long, the head arched like a spreading morning-glory blossom, while the edges scalloped the stone to a fine and lethal point.

Tharon took a long drink of galena tea and smacked his lips in satisfaction. When crushed and mixed with the seeds of morning glory, galena had a potent metallic flavor that the Starborn proclaimed a remedy for almost everything . . . though few could afford it. And Tharon had not been feeling well lately. Bouts of weakness and severe headaches would come upon him out of nowhere and with such ferocity that he would start to tear his black hair out in handfuls.

Even now as he gazed around the room, the glow of the firebowls hurt his eyes. The painted figures on the walls seemed to grin malignantly at him, and the wooden faces of the carved effigies mocked him. Daggers of pain shot through his head whenever he looked directly at the flames.

"Stop it!" he shouted at the firebowls. "I hate you! People are always feeding you oil and watching over you like their lives depended on you—while I'm left to wander the temple in pain!"

He glared at them.

"Such superstition. Firebowls and Father Sun's wrath. Ridiculous." Leaning forward to emphasize his words, he said, "Don't you think I know Father Sun's mind? Why, I'm his own son! Born when a shaft of his light penetrated my mother's womb."

Tharon haughtily traipsed down the seventh line of firebowls, the line that aimed at the door, dribbling spittle into each as he passed. The flames sizzled and popped; the light wavered so violently that it threw his shadow in multiple images across the walls.

He laughed as he whirled to stir the images. The sight pleased him. Why, it gave him a ghostly army at his beck and call! He needed one these days, when everyone had fallen to plotting against him.

Everyone except Badgertail. The burly warrior obeyed Tharon's slightest whim. Down to bringing him Jenos' bloody head. Fool. Did he think such subservience gleaned Tharon's respect? Ha!

"But it does keep Badgertail alive," Tharon mused. "Yes. Perhaps he's more canny than one realizes."

The queasy sensation possessed Tharon for the third time that morning. Angrily, he bent forward to clutch his stomach. "Well, if Badgertail's so canny, perhaps one should keep a better eye on him. No telling when he'll decide he can start making decisions for himself."

Tharon tilted his head speculatively. "You don't think he's doing that, do you? I mean, right now? He could be. Why, of course he could. He's a *warrior*. They're always scheming, the bloodthirsty brutes."

Slyly, Tharon tipped his chin to examine the Power Bundles and sacred headdresses and necklaces that huddled together on the west side of the room. "What do you think? You're supposed to know things like this. Is Badgertail conspiring behind my back?"

He waited for an answer until he couldn't stand it. "What's the matter with you?" he demanded of the Bundles. "I know you can speak. I *order* you to answer me!"

They stared at him malignantly. Yes, he could *feel* their gaze on him, insidious and hateful. Especially Old Marmot's Power Bundle. The blue hawk's head painted in the center glared as though readying itself to spring.

"You can't hurt me! I'm the Sun Chief! While *you*—" he gestured smugly with his handspike "—you are nothing more than strips of hide wrapped around silly bits of bone and stone."

When he sensed their indignation, Tharon fell into suffocating laughter. The mirth shook him with such force that he threw back his head to chortle, "Foolish, foolish things! Did you think you could frighten me? Me? I fear nothing." But as he said the words, the queasiness grew more severe. He straightened up and blinked at the flickering light. "Except . . . Nightshade, of course."

Tipping his cup, he drained it and threw the clay vessel across the room, where it shattered, its pieces falling atop the broken seashells that lay scattered on the floor.

The shuffling of sandals against dirt echoed in the halls outside. Tharon tensed. His blasted knees started to shake. "Oh, Blessed Moon Maiden, not another bout of weakness! What's happening to me?"

All of the fire in his soul drained away of a sudden, leaving him barely able to stand. His hands had begun to tremble. Angrily, Tharon bellowed, "Kettle! Thrushsong! Shagbark!"

In moments, all three priestesses rushed into the chamber and threw themselves at his feet. Their hair lay in tangles over their shoulders. They hadn't even combed it before coming into his presence? Tharon eyed them threateningly. Fat, every one of them. Look at the way their thighs bulged through their red robes. And ugly. Not one had a face he could bear.

"I don't know how your parents could have borne you!" he roared, forcing his shaking knees to hold him up. "Look at you! Your parents were good and loyal members of the Starborn. They tended to my every need. I never wanted for anything while they lived. But you . . ." He kicked Thrushsong in the stomach and sent her toppling sideways. When she let out a small cry, it fired his anger. "None of you care about me! You're all waiting for my death so you can flee Cahokia forever!"

Kettle mustered the courage to look up at him pleadingly. Her homely face had flushed with a mottled red. "No, my Chief. That isn't true. Tell us what you need. We will bring it immediately."

"What do I need?" Tharon raged. "What have you ever given me? Nothing! I need everything! My—my tea cup was empty and so I smashed it into the wall!" He lifted a quavering arm to point at the remains. "My body is wasting away before your eyes from this—this *illness*, and you've not mixed a single Spirit potion to help me!"

"I'll mix one, my Chief." Kettle hurriedly rose and started to trot for the door.

"Not now! I don't want it now! Did I grant you permission to go?"

Kettle fell to her knees on the spot, her hands over her face in humiliation.

Tharon strutted before Thrushsong and Shagbark. As he scrutinized their prostrate position, his head started to pound and he felt so nauseous that he wanted to vomit. He knotted his fingers in the golden fabric over his belly.

A voice whispered from somewhere. He jerked his head to listen. "What? What did you say?"

"What, my Chief?" Shagbark responded timidly.

"Not you, you silly fool. There's a Spirit speaking in my head. But I . . . I can't quite hear it. Shut up, all of you! Don't even breathe!"

The room went thick with silence. A faint repetition of *don't, don't* whispered in his mind. But the firebowls continued to pop and hiss, making it impossible for him to decipher the rest of the Spirit's words. "Be quiet! I command you to stop that noise!"

The firebowls defiantly refused, and Tharon sprang forward like a famished cougar. He swung his handspike back and forth, demolishing every firebowl he could. Bird heads tumbled across the floor, ceramic fragments rolling fiercely as if trying to escape his wrath. Scented hickory oil spattered his face and hair and ran in rivulets down his neck.

"*No!*" Kettle shrieked as she lunged to her feet. "No, stop. Stop, my Chief. Father Sun will kill us all! Stop this madness before you cause the end of the world!"

Tharon checked his handspike in mid-swing and rose with the slow deliberateness of Grandfather Brown Bear rearing up on his hind legs. Kettle's mouth gaped in terror as she took a step backward. Not moving a muscle, Tharon scanned the room through narrowed eyes.

Shagbark's ragged breathing sawed the air behind him while he studied the oil that stained the floor in splotches as dark as spilled blood. Clay shards fanned out in a rough circle around him, and from their midst, disembodied bird heads peered through glistening bead eyes. Sinister. *Wicked.*

Tharon forced a swallow down his dry throat. The army of ghosts that had protected his back earlier had vanished. Now the shadows of Kettle, Thrushsong, and Shagbark loomed over his own shadow like gigantic Underworld beasts.

"All of you. You're—you're trying to kill me!"

The tangles of their hair protruded from their shadows like claws, flexing open and closed as they reached for Tharon. Shagbark took a step, and her shadow lunged for him.

He stumbled in horror, screaming "No!" as he whirled and drove the point of his handspike into Shagbark's chest.

When she staggered face-first into him, her forehead slamming against his shoulder, Tharon wrenched his handspike free and shoved her away. Kettle let out a choking scream. Shagbark crumpled to the floor with the quiet of a feather alighting on a bed of tawny grass. Blood gushed rhythmically from her chest while she writhed weakly under the veil of death that descended like a black curtain.

Tharon could see the curtain coming down, down. He backed up until he collided with the raised altar and sat down.

Odd. His nausea had vanished.

Calmly, he said, "You think I don't know that you Starborn imbeciles are trying to Dream my death? Well, every time you have a Dream about me, you had better remember that I know."

Kettle closed her eyes and stood with her mouth puckered against sobs. Tharon sucked in a deep, soothing breath, rose, and crossed the room.

"Clean up this mess, Kettle," he ordered as he passed. A new spring had entered his step as he headed to his bed chamber. *I should sleep well tonight.*

Ten

Starlight glistened on the yellow wall spiders over Meadow Vole's head. She lay in her robes, watching the light, listening to the broken words Lichen spoke to Wanderer in her sleep. Lichen's voice sounded so breathy and tearful that it made Vole's soul wither. She rolled to her side to study her daughter. Only the top of Lichen's head showed over the edge of the buffalo hide. Her long braid snaked across the sleeping mat like a fuzzy lasso of summer ermine fur.

Lichen whimpered and turned over onto her stomach, her little hands digging frantically into the cattail mat as if she were trying to flee some terror.

Vole threw off her blankets and went to kneel by her. She put a tender hand on her daughter's cheek. "Lichen?" she called softly. "Lichen, wake up. It's all right. Lichen?"

"Mother?" Lichen whispered, her voice muzzy.

"I'm here. You're safe."

Lichen reeled sleepily to her feet and stumbled into Vole's arms. "Oh, Mother, I had a terrible Dream. There's a girl who keeps calling me, and I—I don't know who she is. And I saw this man, a terrible man . . ."

She buried her face in the shroud of Vole's dark hair. Vole stroked Lichen's back gently and made soft shushing sounds in her ear. "What else did you see in your Dream?"

Lichen took a breath as if to speak, then shook her head. "I . . . it . . . never mind. I'm sorry I woke you."

Vole propped her chin tiredly on Lichen's head; her heart sank. Lichen didn't want to tell her, and she knew why. Vole feared real Dreams. She had never learned how to control them. So on the few occasions when they came to her, they controlled her—with such terrifying Power that she often wondered whether the Dreams hadn't ripped her soul from her body. Vole had spent half of her life fighting to obliterate her own Powers and the other half trying desperately to protect Lichen from her inheritance by shepherding her away from anything remotely to do with Dreaming.

Lichen disentangled herself from Vole's arms and quietly sank back into her bed and tugged the robe up over her shoulders. She squeezed her eyes closed, a clear signal that she didn't want to talk any more. "Thank you, Mother, but you can go back to sleep now. I'm all right, really."

Vole let out a tense sigh. She touched the frizzy end of Lichen's long braid. "Lichen? Do you want to go live with Wanderer?"

A pause.

"Do you want me to?"

"Not really," Vole admitted. "But he could teach you a great deal, and maybe . . . well, maybe I've been wrong in thinking that if I tried hard enough, I could kill the Power in you. It seems, my poor daughter, that First Woman has condemned you to be a Dreamer. I pray she has mercy on your soul."

Lichen's eyes shot open. The two stared at each other for a long time before Vole gathered her daughter into her arms and held her close. From the wall niche across the room, Vole thought she heard the Stone Wolf call out for the first time in cycles—as if in approval.

"Sleep now, Lichen. Tomorrow we'll pack your things and I'll take you to him."

Wanderer balanced on his navel on a spire of rock that jutted from the ledge above his house. The rock curved out over the cliff face so that he could see two hundred feet straight down. *What a feeling of freedom!* Wearing only a deerskin breechclout, he spread his arms and legs out over thin air to imitate the movements of the flock of ravens soaring above him. The birds squawked and floated on the warm air currents that swept up the side of the bluff. Wanderer inhaled deep breaths of the grass-scented air and squawked, too. The sound resonated a bit too high until he began to draw it from the very back of his throat. He squawked again, bolstering his concentration by focusing on the silver ribbon of the Father Water that slithered across the treeless bottomland in the distance.

Crossed Beak, the leader of the flock, swooped down and hovered in front of Wanderer's face. He tipped his wings illustratively. Wanderer swiveled his arms in the same way, but couldn't quite get it right.

"My soul wants to, Crossed Beak," he explained in pained embarrassment, "but my human body is stubborn."

Crossed Beak eyed him before letting out a guttural *cawww* and sailing up into the cloud-strewn sky in disappointment.

"Maybe in my next life, Earthmaker will let me have wings so I can fly better," he called to the flock. "I—"

"I doubt it," a familiar-sounding voice wafted up from his house on the ledge below. "You'll probably be a rat's liver in your next life."

His concentration shattered, Wanderer lost his balance. He listed sideways precariously before he slid off the point of rock. Only by sheer luck did he sink his fingers into the right crevice to keep from plunging off the cliff to his doom. He hung there for ten heartbeats, staring down wide-eyed at the limestone boulders that looked like ants below. Finally he managed to swing his legs up and edge down to the overhang that formed the roof of his house. Beneath him, Vole and Lichen stood awkwardly. The packs on their backs made it difficult for them to crane their necks to peer up at him. Their bare chests gleamed with a coppery sheen in the midday sunlight, Lichen's breasts not yet budded, Vole's full and high.

"Hello!" Wanderer yelled in surprise. After that last night in Redweed Village, he had never expected to see Vole again—at least not unless he sought her out. His gaze took in the packs again, and a tiny dagger of hope pierced his heart. "What are you doing here?"

Vole cocked a brow. Her long hair, as blue-black as magpie feathers, fluttered about her shoulders. "Walk down here like a human and we'll discuss it."

"Oh, of course!" Wanderer raced down the narrow trail to the lowest place on the overhang, where he jumped off. He landed hard in front of his house and stumbled several steps sideways before he caught himself. "My, it's good to see you both! Come in. Have some tea."

He hurried forward, but Vole's voice halted him before he could duck through the doorway.

"Wanderer . . ." she began. Then the words flowed out of her in a worried stream, as though she must speak now or she would never be able to. "You've been right all along. I'm sorry I tried to prevent Lichen from becoming a Dreamer. I was just trying to protect her. You know—"

"Yes." He gave her a kind smile and waved down her explanation. "I know. The life of a Dreamer is very hard, and you love Lichen very much. I know that. Thank you for letting Lichen make her own decision."

Vole made a gesture of futility. "I'm giving you ten days. You should be able to teach Lichen the basic skills of Dreaming in that time. Is that fair? Is it enough time?"

"I'll do what I can. It would be easier if I could teach her for three moons straight . . . but it will be enough." He extended a hand toward his house. "Now, please come inside and have a cup of tea. You've walked a great distance today."

Vole wet her lips nervously, as if after all these cycles, she still feared him. "No. Thank you. I must be getting back. The village council is meeting late this afternoon . . . and you know how important our decision will be."

Vole slipped the pack from her back and dropped it in the shade of the rock overhang, then knelt to hug Lichen desperately. "Learn as much as you can," she whispered into her daughter's ear. "Perhaps you'll be able to teach me the things that Wanderer couldn't." She threw Wanderer an apologetic glance that made his heart pound.

"Yes, Mother," Lichen answered in a small voice. She kissed Vole's cheek, and two tears left Vole's eyes, tracing fine lines through the dust on her round face.

Wanderer turned away and gazed out at the fluffy clouds that scalloped the bluff over Pretty Mounds while Vole finished saying good-bye to her daughter. He could hear their hushed words entwining: Vole giving orders and reminders, Lichen responding obediently, a hint of sorrow in her voice.

His thoughts returned to the cycles long before, when Vole had first come to him, begging to be taught, on the verge of madness from the Dreams that tormented her sleep. She had been so young then, fifteen, and so frightened that of course he had agreed—even though he knew that it would take precious time from his own search. But things had not gone at all the way he had planned. Rather than using the things he taught her to deepen her Dreaming skills, Vole had used them to build a wall so high around her soul that she had cut herself off from Power. Then when her husband, Shouts-At-Night, had gone on that last battle-walk, Vole had asked Wanderer for something he had never planned on giving any woman. Sexual intimacy lessened the ways of Dreaming, forcing Power to disperse in order to handle the thousand problems such intimacy brought. But, for a few moons, he had allowed himself to love her. She had left him when news had come of Shouts-At-Night's death, but she would have left him sooner or later anyway. Vole feared Dreamers more than the invisible talons of death itself.

Lichen sniffed and patted Vole's cheek gently. "I'll be all right, Mother," she said bravely. "Wanderer will take care of me."

"I know he will," Vole answered. She rose slowly to her feet. When she turned to him, he could see the pleading in her face. "Should I come and get her in ten days, Wanderer?"

"No, let me bring her home."

Lichen objected. "I can go home by myself. I've done it a hundred times."

"Yes, but things change once you sprout a Dreamer's wings," Wanderer said with a wink. "Your soul will be concentrating on other things. I don't want you to get lost. I'll take you."

Lichen blinked, curious and not understanding, but accepting his decision just the same.

Vole touched Lichen's hair lovingly before she began backing away. "Good-bye. I'll see you before the next new moon." She ran through the oak thicket, leaving the branches flailing against one another. Wanderer watched her until she vanished over the crest of the hill.

Lichen bit her lower lip as she looked up at Wanderer. "Well, I guess I'm here."

"Yes, and I'm so glad. How did you manage it?"

"I had a bad Dream last night—the one about the little girl. I woke Mother. After that, she decided it would be all right."

"Um," Wanderer murmured, studying the anxious twist to her mouth. "And how about you? Do you think it's all right?"

She flapped her arms helplessly. "I have to find Bird-Man, Wanderer. You know I do. I want you to teach me how."

"I'll do my best. Why don't you take off your pack? We'll get started."

Lichen looked startled. "Right now? So soon?"

"Yes. This is as good a time as any. We've a long way to go in the next ten days."

Lichen hesitantly unslung her pack and dropped it atop the one her mother had left. When she came back to stand beside him, she wrung her hands nervously. "What do I have to do?"

"First," he said, "you learn to fly."

"Already?"

"Oh, yes. I was doing it this morning. The ravens were teaching me. But I'm not nearly as good at it as you'll be. Come on, let's go back up to the overhang and I'll show you."

Lichen stopped dead in her tracks. "Is that what you were doing when we got here? When you were balancing on your stomach on that pointed rock that hangs over the edge of the cliff?"

"Yes."

Astonished, she said, "That didn't look like flying, Wanderer."

"No? What did it look like?"

"Well, I don't know exactly. Mother said you were thrashing around like a turtle whose head was being chewed off by a wolf."

"Ah!" he exclaimed in sudden delight. "That's exactly it! Learning to fly is like having your head chewed off. Come on. As soon as your human head gets devoured, you'll grow bird eyes and be able to see the road that ties the sky to the earth."

"Wanderer," she remarked reprovingly, "maybe you shouldn't put it that way. I don't like the idea of getting chewed up."

He grinned as he hiked toward the path that zigzagged up the dusty overhang. "No one does, Lichen."

Eleven

"Tharon *murdered* your own brother, Uncle!" Petaga slammed a fist into the wall poles. "Are you such a coward that you'll do nothing to avenge my father's murder?"

Aloda, Star Chief of Spiral Mounds, slitted his ancient eyes. "Do not call me a coward, young chief, or you'll get more than you expect here. I may be fifty-two summers, but I can still swing a war club."

Petaga gritted his teeth to hold back his anger. He began pacing the council lodge, his sandals scraping on the uneven dirt floor. He had dressed simply, wearing a golden robe with a red band of squares decorating the hem. His headdress of owl feathers accentuated the triangular shape of his face and made him seem a little older, an attribute he needed just now. Hailcloud guarded the door. The tall warrior bore a stoic expression, but his eyes glared.

The room spread around Petaga in a hundred-hand square. Newly built after Badgertail's last attack, it had almost no adornment. Hardwood benches lined the walls. In the four corners, fetishes of hawk feathers hung from the ceiling poles. Four finely woven baskets with red and black designs sat on the floor near Aloda, who reclined on a thick pile of old buffalo hides. The traditional conch shell, traded up from the southern coast, rested beside the chief's elbow, half full, and growing cooler by the moment. Patches of hair had fallen out of the hides, leaving them ratty. Smoke from the pipe curled in fragrant wreaths through the room. Aloda's elderly body had grown as thin as a spruce needle since Petaga had seen him last, three cycles ago. But his black eyes had not lost their keenness. He wore only a finely tanned deerhide kilt and a necklace made of galena and copper nuggets.

"Hickory and Quill Dog Mounds have agreed to join us, as have several of the smaller villages," Petaga explained tightly. "We have over nine hundred warriors committed already. If you would join us, Uncle, we'd—"

"Petaga, please, you must understand." Aloda made a weary gesture. "During the Moon-of-Flying-Snow, we had four hundred and thirty-two warriors. Two moons later, we had seventy, and half of our village had been burned to the ground. I have been praying we can survive for just one more cycle."

Aloda inhaled deeply from his giant effigy pipe. The piece had been carved, ground, and polished from solid granite to represent a man kneeling in prayer, his face lifted to the sky. The stone bowl was so heavy that it rested on an ornately carved wooden disk and was spun about to present the stem, a piece of hickory as long as a man's leg, to visitors.

Now Aloda deferentially blew a cloud of smoke toward the ceiling, carrying his prayers to Father Sun. "My people have already begun preparing to separate into their clan groups and leave Spiral Mounds if we can't grow enough corn this summer to pay Tharon's tribute and still feed ourselves next winter. Of course," he added bitterly, "Badgertail made that easier. He killed half, *half* of our people—and almost all of the men. This is a terrible time for us."

Petaga studied him from under brooding brows. A ring of cane had been placed in a circle around the center post and lit to provide illumination. The newly cut poles gleamed whitely in the light.

"So you refuse to join us? You refuse to help your relatives when they are in need?"

"If we could, we'd—"

"Just commit fifty warriors, Uncle. Just fifty!"

"Petaga," Aloda said, "can't you understand? My warriors are at this very instant out working their clan cornfields. We can't spare a single hand. Without everyone here pulling together from sunrise to sunset, we won't be able to meet our obligations when the Moon-of-Flying-Snow comes."

"But, Uncle," Petaga charged angrily, "can't *you* understand that if we can gather enough warriors to destroy Cahokia, none of us will ever have to worry about 'obligations' to Tharon again?"

Aloda smoked his pipe for a while, pinning Petaga with hard eyes. "Do you know the cost of what you're suggesting? What happens if you win?"

Petaga straightened. A gust of wind penetrated the door, dancing in his headdress and cooling his sweaty face. "Then we're free. Each village can govern itself independently. There'll be enough food. We can live in peace with each other."

Aloda shook his head. "No, my young nephew—though I wish that were true. If it were, I would commit all five hundred men, women, and children who are left at Spiral Mounds. I hate Tharon as much as you do, but if you destroy Cahokia, all of the villages that make up our great chiefdom will collapse."

"What are you talking about? We'll just reorganize."

"Will we?" Aloda shoved himself to a sitting position. "Tell me, why do you think Cahokia became the center of our world?"

Petaga forced himself to respond politely to this irrelevant question. "Why?"

"Look at where it sits." Aloda bent forward to draw a series of wavy lines on the dirt floor.

Petaga recognized the rivers. "You mean because it's at the confluence of the major waterways?"

"Yes. And what do we do on the waterways?"

"We fish, we war, we trade, we—"

"Stop." Aloda raised a withered hand. "*We trade.* Yes. Everyone who goes up or down the Father Water has to pass within reach of Cahokia. Our great chiefdom controls the river—and not just the Father Water, but the Mother Water, and even Moon River, and everything that floats down the tributaries that feed them. Just as an example, what's River Mounds' job in the hierarchy?"

Petaga shook his head, irritated. "You know our job, Uncle. We make certain that every trader who passes stops and trades, or else he pays for the privilege of passing us by. With Tharon and his thieves gone, River Mounds will be free to control the river better, because we won't have to answer to Tharon. We can—"

"Ah." Aloda sat back, nodding. "There it is. The beginning of the end. Do you see? Over hundreds of cycles, we have worked out a way of trading that benefits every village in the chiefdom. Cahokia organizes and funds the chiefdom's traders. River Mounds and Pretty Mounds ensure that the river traders comply with our laws. Cahokia redistributes the exotic foodstuffs and materials. We trade the exotic items for whatever we want. We pay tribute to Cahokia to keep the entire system working. And in the past, when food grew short in the winter, Cahokia's storage huts of tribute were opened to feed the hungry wherever they happened to be in the chiefdom. Because Mother Earth has turned against us, that sharing has ceased, but . . ." Aloda lifted a finger. "But when we chop off the head of our chiefdom, every village will think it can do it better. We'll be at each other's throats in only a few cycles, warring, killing—worse than now. No trader will risk coming up our waterways. We'll be isolated and more desperate than we've ever been. Consider this . . ."

As Petaga listened, he found himself increasingly astonished. The acrid smell of smoke had yet to vanish from Spiral Mounds, and Aloda could speak in this way? As if he wanted the brutal system that had destroyed his own village and killed over half of his people to continue?

"Uncle," he interrupted, "Badgertail killed your own brother to feed Tharon's need for blood. What are we talking about?"

Aloda stared at him unblinking. "*You*, my dear nephew, are talking about revenge. *I* am talking about survival."

Petaga leaned down with fire in his eyes. "I won't stand witness to the murder of any more of my people, Uncle. I'm fighting. Will you join us or not?"

"I can't."

Petaga straightened with a slow deliberateness. "That is your decision?"

"It is."

Petaga tramped toward the doorway, his anger rising to near hatred. Memories of his father's murder replayed in his soul. And until death stole over his exhausted body, he would remember the look in his mother's eyes as she knelt at Jenos' log-lined crypt and Hailcloud walked up from behind, the supple black cord to strangle her in his powerful hands.

Petaga motioned for Hailcloud to leave before him, then grabbed the door frame and turned for one final time. "This day will bring you woe, Uncle."

He went out into the bright noon sunlight, but as he left the mound, he heard Aloda shout: "Maybe I should just disband my village now? Eh, Petaga? It will happen in the end anyway!"

Mother Earth baked in a blinding heat wave. Sunlight lanced through a layer of clouds and fell in stifling sheets of gold across the corn and squash fields belonging to the Blue Blanket Clan. Those first fragile green leaves, ripe with so much promise, were wilting before Green Ash's eyes. The water level in the creek had gone so low that the irrigation ditches had dried up. Already people had begun carrying baskets from the creek with which to water the crops. Two lines of women moved with the efficiency of ants, one going to the creek, empty baskets propped on top of heads, one returning from the creek to pour the contents of brimming baskets into the long, ridged rows.

"Oh, First Woman," Green Ash whispered, hoping that Primrose, who labored on the next row, could not hear. "What are you thinking? We can't survive without rain."

She propped her chert-headed hoe on the ground and stretched her aching back. Her unborn child had grown very large now. Often the back pain kept her awake all night. She had fashioned new skirts, short and loose-fitting, to ease the discomfort during the long workdays. The sunny yellow color made by boiling the fabric with lichen brightened her soul, but nothing helped the pain very much. Her naked breasts hurt, shining full and coppery beneath the glare of the sun. This was her first child, so she knew little of what felt normal and what did not. Women with large families told her not to worry, that every baby nearly broke its mother's back just before birthing.

She wiped her sweating forehead. Insects buzzed in glittering clouds above the cornfield; their spiraling columns curled upward into the sky as far as she could see. Mosquitoes, flies, and gnats had been tormenting her since before dawn.

Wearily, Green Ash bent over her task again, using the hoe to thin the corn plants. Last week they had been able to perform the same labor with mussel-shell hoes—but not anymore. There had been no rain. The rich soil had transformed itself into mudstone before their eyes. They needed stone for stone. Each swipe of her hoe made a crackling sound, sharp, as ominous as clods of dirt being shoveled into a grave.

Checkerberry worked twenty hands away, slamming her hoe into the hard soil with a vengeance. Her elderly back seemed to have hunched more in the past week. Her gray hair slicked down over her head, accentuating her bulbous nose and undershot, toothless jaw. Since Nightshade's arrival, Checkerberry had been unnaturally quiet, as though waiting for the end of the world.

Over the western bluff, a thunderhead built up; clouds piled atop each other in gigantic opalescent tufts. "Look, Aunt," Green Ash called joyfully and lifted her arm. Primrose glanced up. "Perhaps it will rain after all." She laughed gaily, hoping to pull Checkerberry from her gloom.

The old woman bashed her hoe down with all of the force she could muster. The earth groaned beneath the blade. "No," she said tersely, "it won't."

Primrose's boyish face tensed before he cast Green Ash a comforting look and went back to work, his blue-and-tan dress straining over his shoulders.

Disheartened, Green Ash peered at the clouds, praying Thunderbird would prove Checkerberry wrong. Sucking in a breath, she attacked the weeds again.

Twelve

As dawn seeped beneath the window-hanging of Tharon's room, a gray veil fell over the Tortoise Bundle, which sat on the platform beside his bed. He had placed it there the night before, curious whether the bundle would affect his Dreams. It hadn't. The spirals around the edge had faded so much that he could barely see them, but the eye in the center of the red hand had focused on Tharon, as though alive and studying him.

"Don't stare at me, you evil thing," he growled as he dressed. "I'm taking you back to Nightshade. You ought to be happy about that. You've missed her, haven't you? Old Marmot used to say you did. Marmot said that was why you refused to let him use your Power."

He strode across the room, picked up the Bundle, and ducked beneath the door-hanging. His steps echoed in the quiet. From somewhere came sounds of a priestess chanting her morning prayers to the unrisen sun. The scent of spiced hickory oil mixed with dust as he walked by the Sun Chamber and turned left, striding down the hall toward Nightshade's room.

Tharon clutched the Tortoise Bundle to his chest, took a deep breath, and slipped silently beneath her door-hanging. The firebowl in the middle of the floor had gone out, leaving the windowless chamber cloaked in darkness. He could just make out the line of multicolored pots sitting along the right wall, one stacked atop another. Each brimmed with a seed or plant that he knew Dreamers liked: morning glory, toadflax, the dried leaves of foxglove, mistletoe berries, and the shriveled black seeds of Sister Datura from islands in the Great Salt Water. Tharon knew Dreamers liked such things because he had taken these pots from Marmot's room. *The filthy old meddler didn't deserve the benefits of my wealth.*

Marmot's intricate starmap blanketed the entire left wall over Nightshade's sleeping bench. Points of silver revolved in interconnected circles, representing the sky gods during each moon of the cycle. A jug of water and a washing bowl sat at the foot of her bed, half full. She must have bathed before going to sleep. In the transparent halo of light that crept beneath her door-hanging, her skin and hair gleamed. He could hear her breathing, the sound soft, deep with the rhythms of slumber.

He tiptoed across the room and sat down cross-legged on the floor beside her. Very gently he placed the Bundle on the silken veil of black hair that tumbled over her mats. She didn't move. Grinning, he leaned close, so close that he could feel her breath warm on his triangular face. He wanted to clap with excitement! She had no idea that he sat there! He couldn't wait until she woke and discovered him.

Tharon let his gaze wander her body. She lay on her back, her ivory-and-green blanket pulled up so that it just covered her bare breasts. The thinness of the blanket revealed her sensuous curves with brazen clarity. He had to fight his hands to keep from reaching out to touch her naked shoulders. Yes, she had grown into quite a woman. Her large eyes, full lips, and turned-up nose were perfect in her oval face.

And you cast her out of Cahokia? Idiot. You could have married Nightshade instead of that tittering little fool, Singw. You know how much Nightshade loved you when you were young. He smiled to himself, smugly recalling the adoration in her eyes when she had looked at him.

Nightshade stirred, rolled to her left side, and her forehead touched the edge of the Tortoise Bundle. Tharon slapped a hand to his mouth to suppress his mirth. Would she awaken now?

No, she slept on; but her eyes had started to move erratically beneath her lids.

He leaned back and straightened his lace tunic. Thanks to the richest brew of bloodroot and hematite that his textile specialists could concoct, the crimson color stood out regally against the golden background of his robe. The lace had been created with the delicate thread spun of cottonwood seeds; it sported tiny circles in a flowery weave. It came from the south, from Yellow Star Mounds, the village closest to the Forbidden Lands of the Palace Builders. He had given small segments of the precious cloth to his own weavers to see if they could duplicate it, but their crude imitations failed to satisfy him. So Tharon's traders continued to pay a chief's ransom for the lace. But he loved it too much to do without it—even if it meant that he had to force his galena or chert miners to work all day and night to quarry the necessary trade goods to pay for it. He could always threaten to withhold corn from their clans to get them to work harder. Lazy. Everyone these days had grown slothful. That's why the people were starving.

Tharon straightened the coils of black hair on top of his head. He had adorned the elaborate style with the inner spirals of conch shells and with copper clips engraved with the images of Father Sun, Moon Maiden, and First Woman. He wanted to look his best this morning to impress Nightshade.

She stirred again, nuzzling her forehead against the Tortoise Bundle as though it were a lover's cheek.

Tharon leaned forward until his nose was poised only inches from hers. A broad smile split his face when her eyes fluttered briefly open and closed. He thought he would burst from suppressing his laughter!

When finally her lids opened fully, she didn't react at all in the way he had expected. Instead of jumping or crying out in surprise, she stared unblinking into his eyes, the black of her pupils boring so deeply into his soul that he felt he had been skewered by a dull lance. The hair on his arms began to stand on end.

Tharon threw up his hands in exasperation. "Nightshade! You never play right! Not even when we were children. Can't you ever let me have fun?"

She shoved her blanket away and rose from her bench like a dandelion seed borne on a lazy summer breeze. Her grace, mixed with the perfection of her naked body, struck Tharon like a physical blow. His mouth gaped while he watched her slip on a clean red dress, then braid her long hair into a single cord that hung down to the middle of her back.

Tharon clumsily got to his feet and stood with his fists clenched at his sides. "Nightshade, talk to me. Oh, come on!" A pause. "Nightshade, you can't treat me this way. I *command* you to speak to me!"

She strode back across the room, reached around him, picked up the Tortoise Bundle, and stroked it reverently. "I'm going to spend the day in Old Marmot's Star Chamber, Tharon, Singing for the Bundle. I'm surprised it's still alive after what you've done to it. Don't disturb me."

Then she crossed the room, ducked under the hanging, and vanished.

Tharon stamped his feet. "Nightshade, I hate you! I hate you, *I hate you!*"

His voice echoed around him. Humiliated and angry, he fled the room, running wildly down the halls until he reached the front doorway of the temple, where he burst out into the daylight.

Badgertail and Locust stood at the edge of the playing field in the center of the plaza. Leaning on their gaming poles, they were breathing hard from their seventh straight game of chunkey. Badgertail had suffered so many nightmares about Bobcat that he had been unable to sleep. Nervous and irritable, he had awakened Locust hours ago to challenge her to a game, hoping the physical activity would drive away the grief that knotted his stomach. They had dressed in brown breechclouts and begun playing as soon as the first lavender rays of dawn poured over the palisades onto the plaza. The light glistened on the sweat covering Locust's small, bare breasts.

In the past two fingers of time, the rest of the village had roused. From the distance came the rhythmic thumping of pestles being driven into hollow-stump mortars as corn was processed into flour. Smoke from cook fires curled into the silent morning sky. Soft voices and the sweet scent of corn gruel carried on the stillness. Badgertail allowed himself a few moments to appreciate the shadows of the mounds that lay in long black fingers over the plaza. Then he turned to Locust. "Ready?" he asked as he lifted the round chunkey stone to start the eighth match.

Locust wearily braced herself on her beautifully decorated pole. Sixteen hands long, it had a red-and-blue serpent painted up the length of the shaft. "No. Give me a few more moments to catch my breath." She had pinned her short hair behind her ears with wooden combs, but strands had come loose, fluttering around her flushed cheeks. "That's the sixth game you've won," she panted. "I'm beginning to feel like an amateur."

"Don't be modest. You're the best chunkey player in the chiefdom, and everyone knows it—including me."

"I used to think so, too. But I'm not so sure now. Maybe I should try playing on Wolf Slayer's side." She gestured toward the white band tied to his upper arm.

The game had ancient origins, representing the primeval struggle of the Heroes to kill the monsters who had inhabited the world in the Beginning Time. One player took the side of Wolf Slayer, the other took the side of Bird-Man. The chunkey stone symbolized the monsters, while the players' lances represented the bolts of lightning that the sacred Brothers had thrown.

With a flourish, Badgertail took the white band from his arm and presented it to Locust. "There. All yours."

She gave him a wry look as she tied it to her arm. "Leaving me no excuses, eh?"

He smiled and gazed down the length of the field. It stretched two hundred hands long and forty hands wide. A white clay line cut across each end, twenty hands from the edge. The game began when one player hurled the chunkey stone to roll down the field; then both players raced to the throwing line and cast their poles, trying to hit the speeding stone. The player who managed the feat scored two points, but if neither hit it, the player whose pole landed closest to the stone when it quit rolling scored one point. If the poles lay at an equal distance, neither scored. Whoever achieved ten points first won.

Locust sucked in a few more deep breaths. "All right. I'm ready."

Badgertail brought his arm around in a complete circle to fling the stone underhandedly. When it hit the ground rolling, he and Locust charged for the throwing line, already calculating the speed and motion of the stone. They cast simultaneously as their toes touched the line, then raced over it, eyes on their poles, trying to influence the flight by chanting their own special Power Songs. Badgertail slowed to a half-trot when he saw his pole making a perfect arc toward the chunkey stone. Locust let out a frustrated cry as his pole struck the stone and sent it careening sideways.

"I don't believe it!" she shouted. "I quit! I'm not playing with you anymore."

Badgertail laughed. He slapped her on her bare shoulder as he stooped to pick up his pole. "I'm just lucky today." More softly, he added, "Maybe Bobcat's helping me."

Locust searched Badgertail's face worriedly before lowering her gaze to the hard-packed ground. "There's nothing you could have done, Badgertail. Stop blaming yourself." She picked up the chunkey stone, then marched the short distance to retrieve her pole.

Badgertail rolled his pole in his fingers. The hollowness in his chest had begun to throb, like the punky sound of the mortars in the distance. He studied the pink clouds that drifted westward over the village.

Nothing I could have done. "I—I know," he lied.

Locust came up behind him and put a comforting hand on his forearm. "I could use some breakfast."

"So could I. Too bad we don't have Primrose to cook for us. His corn cakes are wonderful."

Locust nodded. Primrose had taken Green Ash to see the birthing women this morning. Green Ash had been having severe pains for two days. Badgertail understood Locust's anxiety about the safety of her sister-in-law. The child had swelled Green Ash's belly so much that rumors had been flashing through the village that she might die.

Locust gave him a weak smile. "Well, perhaps tomorrow . . . if Primrose is home."

"You may be an aunt tomorrow," Badgertail replied encouragingly and patted her on the back. Her face went wan, filled with fear.

As they started off across the plaza, Badgertail noticed Tharon standing on the top step of the temple mound. "Locust," he called. "Wait."

"What is it?" She followed his gaze and fell silent.

Tharon stood rigid at the crest of the mound, his face set like granite, his red-and-gold garments shining. Behind him, the temple rose in a glittering wealth of copper-studded walls and roof.

"He looks angry," Locust observed.

"Yes, he does."

"They say he murdered young Shagbark yesterday. For no reason."

"I heard that, too. I think he's finally slipped into complete madness. Kettle told me—"

Badgertail stopped in mid-sentence. Tharon had plunged down the steps, taking them three at a time. Badgertail's gut writhed when Tharon sprinted across the plaza toward them.

"Locust, give me your lance!" Tharon ordered, and jerked it roughly from Locust's extended hand. "Badgertail, I want you to play chunkey with me."

"Of course, my Chief," Badgertail responded with a slight bow. He gave Locust an apprehensive glance as he reached for the chunkey stone. She gave him the stone and the arm band, but let their fingers touch for a moment—a warning, a gesture of silent support.

Tharon fidgeted beside him, stabbing Locust's pole into the ground and roughly jerking it out. Locust cringed at the mistreatment of the pole she had taken such care to breathe Spirit into.

"Do you want to play on the side of Wolf Slayer, my Chief?"

Tharon cocked his head slowly. His right eye twitched. "No. I hate Wolf Slayer. He condemned people to this world where everything is so hard. I'll fight on Bird-Man's side. He never wanted humans to enter this world."

Badgertail inclined his head obligingly and walked back to the field, Tharon tramping along behind him. "Should I roll the stone, my Chief, or do you want to?"

"You do it." Tharon set himself, lifting his lance as he bent forward. "Go on. Throw it!"

Badgertail flung the stone, and Tharon charged forward. Badgertail quickly caught up. When they reached the throwing line, they both cast, but Badgertail deliberately threw his pole short. He loped leisurely down the playing field, letting Tharon take the lead. When Tharon's pole landed twenty hands closer than Badgertail's, Badgertail clapped approvingly. "An excellent throw!"

As they walked toward their poles, Badgertail watched Tharon closely. The Sun Chief's eyes roiled with such dark thoughts that Badgertail's skin started to creep.

"I hate Cahokia. Did you know that, Badgertail? I hate my home."

"No, I didn't know that," he answered lamely.

As Badgertail picked up both poles and the chunkey stone, Tharon blurted, "You're always letting me win this game, Badgertail. Why is that? Don't you think I can beat you fairly?"

"I didn't let you win, my Chief."

"You did so. I've never seen you miss by so far!"

"I've been playing all morning. I'm tired. Maybe we should compete again later in the day. My aim will be back by then."

Tharon scuffed the toe of his cattail sandal on the ground, looking much like a petulant child. "No, I—I don't want to. I'm not feeling well."

"I'm sorry to hear that. Perhaps if you would go rest, soothe yourself with—"

"Oh, Badgertail," Tharon whispered miserably, "I need to talk to someone. Would you come up to the Star Chamber?"

"Yes, of course, my Chief," he answered too quickly, then flinched when Tharon's eyes slitted. No one sane wanted to be caught alone with

Tharon. Anything, the slightest tone of voice or tilt of the head, could throw him into a calamitous fury. "I mean, I'd be happy to. What . . . what will we be discussing?"

"I'm confused about Nightshade. I tried to surprise her this morning, and she . . . well, she wasn't surprised. She was very mean to me."

"She's undoubtedly unused to being back in Cahokia. And then, too, she lost her lover recently. I'm sure she's still hurting. She probably didn't intend to be unkind." He wondered idly how Nightshade had the bravery to commit such a slight.

He shifted both poles and the stone to his right hand and followed Tharon across the plaza, where he handed the chunkey equipment to Locust. She glanced at Tharon's back and mouthed the words, *"Be careful!"* Badgertail nodded and started up the steps of the Temple Mound behind Tharon, trying to figure a way out of this madness—knowing that he couldn't.

Their feet tapped out a dissonant rhythm against the cedar logs. Over the top of the palisades, Badgertail could see the Commonborn going about their early duties. Women already worked the fields, plucking every weed, thinning the sprouting corn with chert hoes. Men lined the riverbanks, their fishing poles bobbing here and there, while others used nets to reap the catfish and carp that liked the mud on the stream bottom. No one was catching much. In the dirt paths, children played under the watchful eyes of the elderly. Their laughter rose with bell-like beauty. A perfect day.

But Tharon didn't seem to notice, and his expression had hardened again. They reached the top step, and Badgertail saw Jenos' head sitting on a tall pole that rose from the palisade. The ravens had been at it. They had eaten the eyes first, leaving hollow, black pits that stared through a dry web of gray hair. Strips of flesh hung in tatters down Jenos' cheeks. Badgertail could feel the ghostly condemnation coming from that head.

Tharon laughed. "I put it there myself. I had that ugly Kettle bring me the pole."

Badgertail nodded, unable to find words. They stepped into the compound.

"Don't you like it?" Tharon demanded.

"Yes, my Chief. Well done."

They curved around the temple and headed down the worn path in the grass that led to the Star Chamber. Badgertail could see the chamber ahead at the northern edge of the mound; it was nothing more than a clay-plastered ring of upright posts laid out in a perfect circle, the roof open to the broad expanse of sky. Old Marmot used to sit up all night diagraming the positions of the Star Ogres—and other things that Badgertail didn't grasp.

Abruptly, Tharon stopped ten paces from the chamber. "I . . . I've changed my mind. I don't want to go in there. Let's just sit down out here and talk."

"That's a good idea. From this vantage, we can see halfway across the chiefdom."

Tharon slumped down against the wall of the temple. Glumly, he brought up his knees and propped his pointed chin on them. Badgertail sank beside him. The shaded wall felt cool against his sweaty back. Plucking a blade of grass, he chewed it as he gazed westward. Heat waves blurred the horizon, changing the bluffs above the Father Water into pale, floating ghosts.

"What's it like out there, Badgertail?" Desperate longing invaded Tharon's voice. His eyes drifted over the rolling green hills.

"Oh, it's not as pleasant as it appears from here. You're not missing much."

"Don't tell me that. I know I am. I wish I could go outside. But I—I'm afraid to. Do you remember twenty cycles ago, just after Nightshade arrived, when I ran away and those warriors from Dark Water Mounds wounded me before you came and killed them?" He jerked up his sleeve to reveal a long scar.

Badgertail surveyed it. Little more than a scratch, it was the most traumatic thing that had ever happened to Tharon—including the death of his wife, Badgertail suspected. When Badgertail had attacked the hidden camp of the Dark Water warriors, he had found Tharon tied to a tree, weeping. All the way back to Cahokia, Tharon had clung frantically to Badgertail's warshirt, refusing to let go. "Yes. I remember. You had everyone terrified for three days."

"It was Nightshade's fault. She was always tormenting me!" Tharon's chin quivered. "Why do I have so many enemies? Why does everyone want to kill me?"

Badgertail cautiously responded, "Enemies come with power. It's just the way things are."

"But if I wanted to leave, I could turn rule over to one of my cousins and go."

"You could. Yes."

"No, that would never work. You know it wouldn't, Badgertail. My cousins are too young. They couldn't keep order."

"Probably not."

"Only I can do it. That's why I must stay inside the walls, where it's safe. You all need me. Every one of you."

Tharon's eyes misted as he stared at a red-tailed hawk that hovered over Cahokia Creek. The bird's tail feathers shone like polished coral when it angled down through a broad band of sunlight. "Everything in the world is free except me," Tharon whispered.

Badgertail wiped at the dust that covered his muscular arm. The chiefdom balanced on a knife's edge—wavering between existence and nonexistence—and Tharon whined about his own freedom? In the villages beyond Cahokia, rage, hatred, and desperation seethed, fit to explode in revolt. Tharon ought to know full well why his own freedom had been denied. Especially after the insane battle-walks he had ordered last winter.

Tharon lifted the hem of his red-lace tunic to peer at the clouds through the delicate weave. "Nightshade doesn't love me, Badgertail. I've always loved her. Even when we were children. I don't know what I did to make her hate me."

"I don't think she hates you. She's confused right now, and lonely. Give her more time to get over the loss of Bulrush, then maybe . . ." Badgertail fought to keep his true feelings hidden. Nightshade hated Tharon more than anyone else he knew.

"But what if she doesn't come to love me?" Tharon lowered the lace so that it hooked on his copper hair clips and fell in a veil over his face. In the gusty breeze, the edges fluttered. "That's a bad question to ask someone like you, isn't it, Badgertail? You've never been in love. You can't possibly understand what I'm feeling."

Badgertail let out a slow breath. "I was married once. It didn't work." Tharon was too young to remember the rumors about Badgertail and Locust—thank Father Sun. "War has been my passion."

"War? She's not a very warm lover. Aren't you lonely too, Badgertail?"

"Sometimes. I think all humans are."

"But it's worse for warriors, isn't it? I mean, it must be hard to trust people when you know you might have to . . . to kill them someday. And then you lose so many friends. Like Bobcat."

"Yes," Badgertail responded hollowly.

Tharon seemed to sense that he had struck a sore spot. He unhooked the lace and brought it down, staring intently at Badgertail. "Did I tell you that I've decided to adopt Bobcat as a full member of the Sunborn? I've already told the Starborn to prepare a special burial for him inside the palisades. Did I tell you?" He turned sideways eagerly. "Oh, it will be grand, Badgertail. Just you wait."

"Thank you, my Chief. I—"

A deep, beautiful voice rose in Song from within the Star Chamber. Badgertail stopped speaking, startled that anyone was in the structure. Tharon whirled, staring in terror for an instant before he leaped to his feet and ran. His lace tunic billowed behind him as he swerved past the pole bearing Jenos' head and vanished around the front of the temple.

Badgertail's muscles tightened when understanding dawned. That rich voice belonged to Nightshade. Had she overheard their conversation? Is that what had frightened Tharon so, that she might have heard him say he loved her? Or had something else prompted Tharon's abrupt departure? Not that it mattered. Badgertail sank back in relief that he was gone.

Smoke spiraled up from the Star Chamber, redolent with the tang of burning cedar.

Badgertail eased down on his back in the cool grass and granted himself one hand's worth of time to drift with the beautiful lilt of Nightshade's Song. In the distance, he could see laborers digging a hole in the farthest ridge-top mound. Dust swelled around them while they worked to prepare Bobcat's resting place.

"Hurry, Aloda!" Black Birch, the war leader of Spiral Mounds, yelled as he pushed aside the door-hanging to Aloda's bed chamber. "They are already upon us! They sneaked up the drainages like cowering dogs!" He ran away.

Aloda threw his long shirt over his gray head, reached for his bow and quiver, then ducked outside into the night.

The cold ground bit at his bare feet as he followed the swaying shadow of Black Birch across the top of the mound. Starlight drenched the world, turning the thatched temple into a hunching beast. Before he had even rounded the corner of the lodge, he heard screams. They swelled in the darkness—jagged with terror, coming from nowhere, from everywhere at once.

"Traitors! Filthy, treasonous dogs! They are worse than Badgertail!" Black Birch proclaimed. He joined a huddle of warriors who peered over the edge of the mound, surveying the happenings below. "At least with Badgertail, you can understand his reasons, but this . . . !"

"I understand Petaga's reasons," Aloda panted as he stopped behind them. "If we survive, one of us *must* go to Tharon. That's what he fears."

Streaks of fire sailed through the sky, landing on top of the thatched houses. The bone-dry structures burst into flame. People fled wildly through the village, half-dressed, dragging shrieking children. Behind them, pursuing warriors let out piercing war cries.

"Follow me. Hurry! Let's at least try to protect the children!" Black Birch shouted as he led his warriors forward.

Aloda braced his elderly legs. The full impact of the attack sank in. His seventy warriors could not even fight a delaying action against Petaga's nine hundred. This was pure butchery, merciless and brutal.

Petaga, you fool. You come spouting words of cooperation and unity, and then you attack us in the middle of the night. If our survivors go to Tharon begging protection, it will split our people down the middle. What a trap you've laid for us. You little fool.

A woman carrying an infant was cut down in her tracks by a flaming arrow. Aloda's old jaw quivered. She shrieked when her dress caught fire. The flames leaped into her long hair and turned her into a living torch. She threw her child from her and rolled frantically in the dew-soaked grass before her body went limp. The child toddled to its feet, crying in the glare of the blazing houses, reaching out blindly to every warrior who fled past. Aloda watched in anguish as a man bounded by, stopped, and slammed his war club into the baby's head. The child fell, kicked, and went still.

Blessed Earthmaker. Does Petaga plan on killing us to the last child? What harm could a baby do him? When the other villages find out . . .

Aloda stumbled forward as Hailcloud sprinted over the crest of the mound, his bow raised.

Thirteen

Sunset lay like a golden mantle over the land. Mourning doves cooed from rock perches, their calls mixing oddly with the undulant buzzing of cicadas in the marshes below. Lichen trotted across the bluff behind Wanderer, trying to match his long strides. She could see clear to the edge of the world. Redweed Village lay in the distance. Smoke from its evening cook fires smudged the sky with a ripple of gray. She let herself drift for the briefest of instants, thinking about her mother, missing Flycatcher.

A hollowness had grown inside Lichen's chest. She loved Wanderer, but she missed her family. And learning to Dream came so hard. Only a few days ago, she had felt that she knew herself and her place in the world. But now everything had changed. Her old Dreams had come effortlessly. This new Dreaming often terrified—or amused—her. She never knew for certain what madness Wanderer would suggest next.

Lichen smiled to herself as she glanced at the back of his long head with its spiky gray hair. He carried a thick coil of rope looped over his shoulders and a box trap in his hands. Unfamiliar emotions scurried through her chest, tingling like sticky ant feet. Things had changed between them. He no longer treated her like a child. He treated her like a Dreamer. She didn't know how to feel about that.

In past cycles, she had visited him for a few hours, but she had never spent the night before. Only since she'd left Redweed Village two days ago had she really come to know him in all of his amiable craziness. They talked constantly about Dreamers he had known and the trials they had faced, about the nature of Spirits and Spirit Power. He was always challenging her to go farther, to "step into the mouth of the Spirit that wants to chew you up," as he put it. She hadn't accepted that teaching yet. Who would want to?

Narrowing her eyes, Lichen grimaced at the slope they climbed. The limestone had been carved by the Ice Giants and smoothed into mounds like those on a buffalo's back. The *need* to Dream tormented her, calling out in unfamiliar voices, showing her flashes of places and things she had never seen before. She longed to give herself up to the ways of Power.

But it took so much courage.

"All right, here we are. This is it!" Wanderer cried in elation. "Sit down, Lichen."

She sat. The gray prominence of rock formed the highest point on the western bluff. Her blue dress and her braid had acquired a fuzzy patina of dust in the past hour of climbing. Wanderer knelt beside her. His buckskin shirt and pants looked just as dirty as her clothes did, but his gray hair appeared surprisingly clean.

"Are you ready, Lichen?"

"What can we catch up here, Wanderer?" Lichen scrutinized the place. Not a sprig of grass sprouted anywhere. "A lizard? A snake? This is barren rock."

His wide eyes flared, rearranging the wrinkles of his long face. "Oh, just wait. You'll see soon enough."

She watched him carefully as he took the box trap they had spent all morning making and prepared to set it up. Laying the lid flat on the ground, he tilted the box up so he could prop a flimsy stick beneath its lip. He laughed slyly as he got to his feet; then, his eyes still on the box, he pulled on the length of rope that hung over his bony shoulders. The action sent a mass of coils spiraling down around his tall body. "Oh, my," he said in distress.

"Aren't you going to put any food in the trap, Wanderer?" Lichen asked, attempting to ignore his embarrassment.

"No, no. We won't need any." He began stepping this way and that, trying to extricate himself from the tangles of hemp.

Lichen glanced back at the trap. It didn't make any sense. Why would an animal go into the box if there was no bait inside to lure it? But after the "flying" episode two days ago and the "slithering" yesterday, she was not so sure that she wanted to press Wanderer about the trap. Her belly still stung from the cactus she had accidentally slithered over when Wanderer had been showing her how to "snake" through the brush in the moonlight.

Lichen sighed.

"There!" Wanderer had finally unraveled the mess. He quickly tied one end of the rope to the stick and seized the other in his left hand. "Hurry! We haven't much time."

He took two long bounds, grabbed Lichen by the arm, and raced down the rocky slope, trailing the long rope behind. She ran to keep up. When they reached the bottom, they were both breathing hard.

"Hide behind that blackberry bramble," Wanderer panted, pointing to a bristly hedge. "Quickly!"

Lichen leaped over a bush and ducked down. Her heart had started to patter at her ribs. Thousands of tiny thorns poked out of the brier, warning her not to get too close to the handfuls of white blossoms that covered the vines. Wanderer scooted in beside her and swiftly began taking up the slack of the rope.

Lichen stretched her neck to peer through the tapestry of leaves. The rope was trailing down the slope, the curls unwinding with each of Wanderer's tugs. The damp scents of night pervaded the air. What could they possibly trap this late in the evening? What prowled the rocks at dusk? Sister Cougar? No, their trap was too small.

"Lichen, get down! We don't want him to see us!"

"Who?" she cried as she dodged behind the highest arc of the bramble.

Wanderer's mouth dropped open expectantly. "Shh. Here he comes."

She searched the rocky parapet, trying to see something moving out there, but all she spied was Father Sun's glowing face as it disappeared into a thick layer of clouds that lay like a lumpy blanket over the horizon. The clouds blazed, changing from pale pink to a lurid violet.

"Wanderer? What did you see? It'll be dark soon. Don't you think we ought—"

"*Hush!*"

She lowered her voice and leaned over to cup a hand to his ear. "Well . . . are we trying to catch a bat?"

"No." His gaze fixed on the trap as his fingers tightened around the rope—like he was almost ready to jerk the stick out. A wild gleam had entered his eyes. "We're trying to catch Father Sun."

"Father . . . Sun?" She gave him a sidelong look.

"Yes."

"Won't he get mad?"

"Oh, don't worry. By the time we've let him loose in the morning, he'll have forgotten all about it."

Lichen nodded shortly. Her gaze slid back to the gray hump where their trap sat silhouetted against a luminous wash of lavender. A thin strip of clear sky spread between the clouds and the rock. When the first sliver of molten gold edged beneath the clouds, Wanderer tensed, and Lichen found herself holding her breath.

"Just a little more," Wanderer whispered hoarsely. "A little more . . ."

Father Sun descended until his face shone full and round in the gaping mouth of the trap. In a flash, Wanderer tugged the rope and the box slammed closed. He let out a shrill cry of triumph as he flopped on his back, kicking his long legs in joy. "We got him! We got him!"

Lichen lunged to her feet to run and see, but Wanderer caught her arm. "No, wait! He has to thrash around for a while trying to get out. See? Look at the sky. When he quiets down, then we'll go."

Lichen frowned at the horizon. Clouds roiled, twisting madly as they changed from gold and pink to an angry crimson. A low roar started in her ears, but she didn't know whether it was just the hush of twilight settling over the land or Father Sun's rage. When a family of frogs in the meadows burst into song, she grabbed Wanderer's shoulder hard. He jumped at her touch, but his mouth quirked knowingly when the croaking chorus continued, its throaty tones floating skyward on the cool draft that eddied up the bluff.

Lichen's face flushed. "Sorry."

"Oh, it's all right. It happens to everyone their first time. Here, hold this," he said and thrust the end of the rope at her. Startled, Lichen grasped it. "Good girl. I'll be right back." He vaulted to his feet and ran headlong up the slope.

When Lichen realized she held a rope that no longer had a purpose, she threw it down and ran after him. "Wanderer, wait! I want to see, too!"

The sky had gone a dark indigo by the time she crouched next to him beside the box. She could not remember Father Sun vanishing so quickly . . . *maybe we really did trap him!* Excited, she shouted, "Can I see? Please, Wanderer, let me look?"

"Oh, not yet." Wanderer crooned softly as he picked up the box and held it tightly against his chest. "Later tonight. First we have to prepare ourselves. Come on, let's take him home."

In the corner of Wanderer's house, Lichen sat on the pile of fox hides that had become her bed. She stared at the Power symbols on the walls, just as Wanderer had commanded her. In the dim glow of the fire, they gleamed as though alive. The black crescent moons seemed to be leaning sideways, whispering secrets to the purple starbursts. But the red spirals . . . oh, the spirals! She bit her lip as she gazed at them. *They moved tonight.* Spinning, rising and falling over the wall, pulling at her with invisible hands.

Wanderer's chanting only intensified the sensation. He sat on his blankets on the opposite side of the room, hunched over the trap like a vulture. He had been painting it for hours, until the spirals, serpents, and faces of Father Sun, Moon Maiden, and First Woman looked perfect. When not absorbed in his artwork, he spent his time glancing at Lichen . . . measuring, appraising.

When he at last picked up the trap and stood, Lichen turned—
"No, don't look at me," he said quietly.

Lichen returned her gaze to the spiral in the center of the back wall.

But from the corner of her vision, she saw Wanderer reach into the green-and-red basket where he kept shavings of butterfly-weed root. A Power plant. In Redweed Village, only her mother had the right to keep and guard it. The ceremonials surrounding the digging, drying, and distributing of the root took six full days in the spring. Wanderer dipped a bristly handful into his water jar, shook off the excess water, then sprinkled the shreds of root on the flames. Steam and smoke exploded, filling the room. The fragrance encircled Lichen as sweetly as a rain-soaked forest.

Wanderer closed his eyes and began chanting again while he waved the trap through the sacred smoke. His feet moved in a Dance step that Lichen didn't know—*but the spiral on the wall did*. It bounced from place to place in perfect rhythm. Her breathing went shallow as she watched it. She became so entranced that she barely noticed when Wanderer stepped away from the fire and came to kneel before her.

"What do you see, Lichen?" he asked in a soothing voice.

"The spiral . . . Dancing." Her mouth didn't want to work. And her body felt numb, floaty. With every breath she took, the sensation deepened. How long had she been staring at the spiral? Half the night? Or for only a few moments? She didn't know—but she could no longer take her eyes from it. It had begun to expand and contract in time to her heartbeat.

"Good. Keep watching it." Wanderer lowered himself and sat cross-legged in front of her, the trap held protectively in his lap. "All right, Lichen. I want you to look at me now."

It took great effort to force her head to turn. Wanderer's eyes shone as black as the darkness, deep-set and piercing under tufts of gray brows. Sweat covered his beak nose. In the glimmers of firelight, his gray hair blazed like polished threads of silver.

"Now look at the trap, Lichen."

She did and found another spiral there, spinning, as red as blood, just like the one on the wall.

"What do you hear, Lichen?"

"You."

"Listen harder. Listen to the motion of the spiral. Listen . . . listen . . ."

Wanderer's voice faded, going so low that she could barely hear it. At the same time, blackness closed in around her, swallowing everything except the spiral on the trap.

She *did* hear something—or rather, she felt it, warm and soft, like the water in the hot pools that lined the Father Water. The "sound" swirled up out of the spiral, enveloping her. Lichen's body at first seemed to rise off the floor and hover; then it evaporated into nothingness. Her soul floated alone in the silence of the spiral. *Silence?* A tingle of longing went through her. Could she find Falcon's soul here? Or maybe Water Snake's?

Bird-Man? Are you here? I need to talk to you. Can you come and talk to me? I—

"Lichen? Lichen, look at the trap." Wanderer's kind voice came from a great distance.

She hadn't even realized that she had closed her eyes, but now her lids felt as heavy as granite. She fought to open them. When she managed a slit, she saw Wanderer smiling gently.

"Not at me," he whispered. "At the trap."

She lowered her gaze and noticed that he had placed his hand on the edge of the lid. His fingernails had gone white. Then she heard the leather hinges creak when he slowly lifted the cover.

An amber shimmer glided from the crack. Lichen watched in awe as the shimmer slithered down over Wanderer's legs and formed a pool on the floor.

"Lichen?"

She saw Wanderer opening the trap wider. In a sudden flood, light gushed out, fountaining up in blinding golden waves. Lichen gasped when it touched her. It felt cool. The light Danced, forming into strange, birdlike patterns that flapped across the room, circled her head, then hovered to stare at her through glittering eyes. Bird-Man's Helpers. They carried messages. Lichen waited for them to speak.

"Don't be afraid," someone said.

Lichen did not understand what she should be afraid of. This was beautiful. The Light Birds fluttered closer, coming so near that she could feel the puffs of their wings on her face. Suddenly she felt the wings flapping inside her chest, soft, erratic, and her body lifted off the ground, rising higher and higher. Then the deep rumble of Thunderbird echoed through her soul, and the light changed, forming into the face of a man. He had eyes so kind that they tore at her heart. His smile turned forlorn. *Remember the owl, little one. Remember . . .*

The light burst into flame around her. It engulfed the Power symbols on the walls and spread down to explode in Wanderer's blankets. Thunderbird roared again, the sound deafening amidst the crackling of the flames. Fierce yellow tongues licked toward her, devouring her hair, burning her flesh until it peeled from her bones!

"No!" Lichen screamed. "Stay away!"

She lunged for Wanderer's door. The light pursued in a vast golden torrent. "Help! Help me!"

She dove out into the darkness and weakly got to her feet. Like a pouncing beast, the light swallowed her up again—glittering in a blazing whirlpool. Lichen ran, heedless of direction. She screamed, "Wanderer? Wanderer!"

Something heavy tackled her and knocked her to the ground. "Lichen, it's all right. You're all right! It's Wanderer. Shh . . . shh!"

She saw his face hanging in the blaze, but the light faded like paint diluted by water, thinning until nothing remained but the darkness.

"Wanderer?" she called weakly.

His eyes had gone owlish. Behind him, in the house, Lichen could see the trap lying on its lid by the side of the fire. No light streamed from it now. She looked up at Wanderer and started to sob in great choking gulps.

"Oh, don't do that. It's all right." He gathered her into his arms, where she buried her face in the folds of his buckskin shirt. He smelled pleasantly of smoke and sweat. "You don't know what you did, do you, Lichen?"

"What?" She gazed up at him through blurry eyes.

Wanderer smiled. "You *flew.* I've never seen anyone learn to fly so quickly. You'll have Falcon's soul before you know it."

"Maybe I don't want it anymore, Wanderer. The light hurt me!"

"I know," he said as he stroked her hair. "That was my fault. I shouldn't have pushed you so fast. But you did it, Lichen. For just a moment, *you flew!*"

Long before dawn, they put on heavy coats and hiked to the gray hump to let Father Sun go.

Badgertail stood stiffly atop the mound, watching the burial procession move past the line of torches that marked the route across the starlit plaza. Chanting undulated on the still air. Six warriors, three men and three women, conveyed the litter bearing the body. They moved like ghosts in the windblown glare of the torches, visible one instant, gone the next. Behind them came Moonseed and her clan members, with all of the servants who had ever attended to Bobcat's needs. Their wailing rose on the quiet night, as pathetic as a newborn's mewl. There must have been ten in all—most of them young women.

Badgertail gritted his teeth, trying not to think about it . . .

Eighteen members of the Sunborn followed next in line, beating drums or shaking gourd rattles, waving prayer feathers over their heads. Nightshade led the group. She looked ethereally beautiful. Her red dress had been painted with pigment made of crushed galena mixed with oil. The resulting silver color gave the stylized serpents, crosses, and hand symbols a gaudy splendor.

Lastly, Tharon rode in a curtained litter, borne on the shoulders of eight muscular attendants, their hickory-oiled skin gleaming as they approached.

Badgertail waited at the northern end of the log-lined tomb excavated into the mound. He refused to look down into that terrible glittering darkness. Tharon had ordered that Bobcat be placed on a blanket of twenty thousand shell beads, dozens of chunkey stones, and arrow points. It represented the finest work of special artisans—ten lifetimes' worth of wages for a single corn farmer.

Bobcat would have hated it.

The bare breeze whispered forlornly to Badgertail, and he thought he heard Bobcat's voice calling out in a final good-bye.

"Burials are savage," Badgertail whispered bitterly to Locust. "Don't let them do this for me when my time comes."

"You mean that Tharon's burials are savage," Locust clarified.

She exchanged a pained look with Badgertail. They had worn their finest warshirts, Locust's a pale gold deerhide with intricate quill work that accentuated her breasts and hips, Badgertail's made of white moose hide and covered from knee to shoulder with green falcons, wolves, and badgers: predators held sacred by warriors. Copper beads sparkled in their braided forelocks.

"I won't. Not if I can prevent it," Locust replied softly, but her eyes narrowed.

When the procession began climbing the mound, Badgertail clasped his hands in front of him. It seemed an eternity before everyone took their proper place around the trench, but at last Tharon's litter sat on the east side. Nightshade stood on the west side. Everyone else grouped along the southern edge.

Badgertail mustered the courage to look at Bobcat's oiled and painted body. The face had been painted in bright red, with lines of yellow crossing his breast and black zigzags streaking down his legs. The corpse had bloated and deflated from the heat and the tending in the charnel house. It didn't even look like Bobcat.

Attendants threw back the curtains of Tharon's litter, revealing him sitting there regally, dressed in gold and with a pounded-copper headdress that flashed in the night. He wore a beautifully crafted mask of Long-Nosed God—not really appropriate for this ceremony. He looked around haughtily before he inclined his head to the Six Sacred Persons, raised his handspike to the Star Ogres, then lowered it to point at the Underworld. A giddy excitement filled his voice when he addressed the mourners: "We come to pray for a great warrior of our people! Worthy Bobcat, of the Squash Blossom Clan, brother to Leader Badgertail, is about to start his long journey down the Dark River to the Land of the Ancestors. Who will accompany him on his journey?"

The drums began, low at first, then rising to boom like thunder when the first cries erupted. Moonseed's cries.

Two of Moonseed's kinsmen brought her forward. Her face had gone pale, and her legs wobbled as she walked. She wilted in their arms, weeping incoherently. Her black dress blended so well with the night that she almost vanished when they yanked her away from the glare of the torches and forced her to stand at the edge of the burial trench. To her credit, she did not plead for life. The blow came quickly, the hammer smashing the back of her skull as it would a ripe melon.

Badgertail flinched at the sound of the blow. *Moonseed, why didn't you let them buy your life, or provide a substitute? Would it have been so hard to live without Bobcat?*

Moonseed's clansmen carefully lowered her over the edge of the trench, where one of the Sunborn gathered her in his arms and laid her out on the sparkling bed of shell beads.

When they brought up the attendant who would serve Bobcat in the Underworld, Badgertail looked away. The servant could not have been more than twelve. Her cries shredded his soul before the cord strangled her.

It's only the death of the body, not of the soul. His eyes darted over the stars, moved to the mounds huddled within the protective walls of the palisades, touched on the torches in the plaza, and finally came to rest on Nightshade. *And considering what lies ahead for us, perhaps they are the lucky ones.*

Another young girl screamed.

But the world had gone quiet around Badgertail. Though he could sense people moving, he saw only Nightshade's black, luminous eyes sucking him in, devouring his soul.

When she started toward him, he frowned.

"What's she doing?" Locust demanded. "She can't do that! The priestess has to stay in the west until the ritual is finished!"

The mourners pointed, whispering behind their hands. Badgertail glimpsed Tharon lunging to his feet in indignation.

Nightshade stopped no more than a handsbreadth away and placed slender fingers over Badgertail's heart. A tingle went through him.

"What is it, Nightshade?"

"Wanderer," she said softly. Her beautiful face tensed as she searched Badgertail's eyes. "You must not kill him. Bring him to me. He has found the way to First Woman."

"Wanderer? I thought he was dead. Where is he?"

She shook her head as she started to back away. "I don't know. We'll know in a few days." She returned to her place in the west.

Badgertail braced his feet as if to steady the world. Another woman's body was lowered into the tomb. A chill played along his spine like dancing mice feet. *Wanderer? The old lunatic?* Bobcat was lifted and carried forward, lowered gingerly, and placed beside his wife. Badgertail battled to keep tears at bay, trying to still the turmoil inside. *Yes indeed, the lucky ones.*

Perhaps it was just the glare of the torches, but he swore that a huge, transparent figure stood at Nightshade's side, swaying in time to the beat of the drums.

Fourteen

Dusty afternoon sunlight streamed across the cornfields in the basin
below, reflecting from the mist that twined through the short stalks.
Shimmering, interconnected rainbows arced over the crops.

Lichen smiled. She stood half-hidden in a fortress of rocks, her bow
up and ready. Though they had been hunting all morning, they hadn't
found anything that Wanderer would let her shoot. He seemed to be
waiting for some specific game, but he wouldn't tell her what it was.
She had been pretty angry when he refused to let her aim at a grouse
that strutted over the top of her feet. She sighed and studied him as he
tiptoed across the bluff, his eyes on the ground.

Lichen frowned when he froze with one foot in the air. Slowly, he
knelt, brushed at the ground, and whispered, "Come look at these
tracks, Lichen."

She lowered her bow and trotted through the dense shadows cast by
the towering rocks. She slid to a halt and braced a hand on Wanderer's
arm to look where he pointed. Bare rock, covered with a scattering of
old needles, met her gaze.

"I don't see any tracks, Wanderer."

"Ah, you're not looking very hard. Look again."

Lichen crouched to bring her eyes within a handsbreadth of the stone.
The fragrant scent of cedar met her nose, but there weren't any tracks.

"What tracks?"

He jerked around and peered at her like a startled stork. His
rabbit-fur shirt and breechclout shone whitely in a lance of light that
penetrated the rocks. "Lichen, you're smarter than this. What do you
see down there?"

"Rock."

"And what else?"

She glanced at the stone again. "A few cedar needles that were probably blown off in the gale this morning."

"Yes!" He bounded to his feet and slapped her affectionately on the back. "Now keep your bow up. She's around here somewhere." He started off, taking one careful step at a time while his eyes diligently scanned the terrain.

Lichen threw him a glance. *Blessed Thunderbird, we're not tracking a tree, are we?*

She shrugged and fell into line behind him, tipping her face to the cool wind. It had tousled her hair all day as they climbed.

The afternoon smelled damply of water, as though it might rain. Clouds meandered across the tarnished amber sky. Two full moons had dragged past begrudgingly since they'd had a soaking downpour. The few sprinkles that cooled the evenings did little for the crops. It worried Lichen. This moon had started out even drier than the last one.

"Ha!" Wanderer blurted. "More!"

Lichen trotted up to peer over the top of his gray head. He tapped a finger next to another cluster of cedar needles.

"We're close, Lichen, so be quiet. You'd better stay back and let me lead the way."

"Go ahead."

He gave her a confident wink before tiptoeing forward like a long-billed sandpiper in a shallow pool of water.

She crept along behind, trying to peer around his lanky body to see where he was going. Every so often he would stop and point out more cedar needles.

Lichen shook her head. They sneaked through a cluster of boulders where Wind Mother had laid down a thin layer of soil. Roots laddered the path. Wanderer thrust out a hand to stop Lichen from coming any closer. Then he knelt to stroke the roots reverently. When he turned, he stared at her so hard that she was afraid to breathe.

"I have to tell you something," he murmured just loud enough for her to hear. "You know that red cedars are sacred, but this tree is special. You have to hunt her correctly, with the proper ritual intent—or she'll kill you. You understand."

"Why is she special?"

He leaned close and breathed, "She's First Woman's tree. She grows in three worlds. Her roots are buried deep in the Underworld next to First Woman's cave, but her trunk and branches stretch up through the earth and into the sky. Thunderbird lays his eggs in her branches."

Lichen listened in fascination. "And I'm supposed to kill her? I don't think that's such a good idea."

"Oh, we just have to be careful and do it correctly."

Lichen wet her lips. "Are you sure? What if one of Thunderbird's eggs falls and breaks?"

"That would be very bad. It might never rain again. And we're having enough trouble these days as it is."

She nodded in fervent agreement. "I know it. So, you know what, Wanderer? I don't think I'm the one to do this. Here—" she thrust her bow into his hands—"you do it." Lichen took a step backward, swiftly clasping her hands behind her back lest he think of returning the bow.

Gently, Wanderer said, "I can't. You're the one who wants to find Bird-Man."

"Is he in that tree, too?"

"Oh, yes," Wanderer responded positively. "He's there."

"Well, why can't he just come out and talk without me killing First Woman's tree?"

Wanderer lowered his head and gazed contemplatively at her small bow. He plucked the tightly braided hair bowstring and canted his head to listen to its responding thrum. Lichen watched his bushy gray brows raise and lower expressively. "Well, at least your bow knows why."

Lichen scowled at it. "It does? What is it saying?"

"It said that you have to prove your courage to Bird-Man before he'll talk to you face-to-face. You do want to talk to him, don't you?"

"Yes, but . . . well . . ."

"Lichen?" he asked reprovingly.

"I do," she announced against her better judgment. "All right, Wanderer. How do I hunt First Woman's tree?"

His dark eyes narrowed. "She's just behind that rock. When you go in, you have to shoot straight into her branches. Don't aim at her trunk, or Thunderbird will feel the tree shudder and send lightning shooting out the ends of the branches to get you."

"Because he'll think I'm trying to disturb his nest?" Lichen asked reasonably. She had been pecked in the back of her head once when she'd reached into a finch's nest to steal eggs. The mother finch had chased her all the way home, twittering and diving.

"Yes, that's right." Wanderer lifted her bow and handed it back. "Can you do it?"

She felt as though maggots were crawling around in her stomach. "I guess so," she admitted morosely. She took the bow and nocked an arrow. "Just one arrow will be enough?"

"It should be. But if she comes after you, shoot her again."

Comes after me? "Sure."

Wanderer sat on his haunches and lifted his voice in a strange Song that had no words, just beautiful, lilting sounds.

Lichen bravely stalked toward the rock. She eased around the gritty side, and a shadow fell over her face as a dark cloud wandered over the bluff.

Lichen edged farther, then jumped back. The cliff fell away in a sheer drop of a hundred hands. *Wanderer, there's no tree here.* But when she craned her neck to explore over the edge, she saw a tiny cedar tree clinging to a patch of soil no bigger than her foot. The tree couldn't have been taller than her knees.

This was First Woman's tree?

Lichen didn't see any of Thunderbird's eggs in the top. She frowned over her shoulder at Wanderer, then sighed, lifted her bow, and shot into the branches. The tree flailed mildly, as though trying to dislodge her arrow.

She turned. "Wanderer, I did it. What should . . ."

A flash of lightning crackled through the air, striking the bluff a thousand hands away. Chunks of stone exploded like huge hailstones. The roar of Thunderbird that followed shook the ground so violently, it knocked her off her feet.

"Lichen!" Wanderer shouted.

"I didn't hit the trunk!" she yelled.

Thunderbird's growl subsided, rolling away into the setting sun. Lichen lay panting, staring up wide-eyed at the cloud. A drip of sweat tickled her neck. "I didn't," she vowed. "I *didn't* hit the trunk."

Wanderer ran up and clutched her tightly against him. "Are you all right?"

"Yes, but I don't know what I did wrong."

"Oh, Thunderbird is contrary. Sometimes he just does that to scare people. Did you kill the tree?"

"I think so."

He released her and slithered forward on his stomach to see. "Oh, yes. You did very well. Why don't you sit in the shade while I cut off her top."

Lichen slumped down against the rock and wiped her drenched forehead. Hunting Spirits took a lot of strength. "Just the top? Why don't we take the whole tree?"

She could hear a soft *zizzing* as Wanderer sawed with his knife.

"It takes only a very small portion to open a tunnel through which you can speak to Bird-Man."

"A tunnel?"

"Yes. These branches are like hollow reeds. They connect the Underworld with humans and the sky."

"Do I have to crawl into the tunnel?" That possibility frightened her more than Thunderbird's wrath.

"Oh, yes, just like Snake. Tonight we're going to prepare you to die and—"

"*What?*"

Wanderer looked up with sudden surprise, his knife halted in mid-motion. "Didn't I tell you?"

"No!" she protested. "You didn't tell me anything at all about having to die!"

"I'm getting so forgetful." He shook his head and turned back to finish sawing. When the very top of the tree came off in his hand, he placed prayer feathers near the trunk and Sang a soft Song of thanks to First Woman.

Gingerly, he used his toes to pull himself backward. He grinned as he extended the fragrant branches to Lichen. "Well, anyway, we have a lot of work to do. Let's go home. We have to build a death litter and prepare food for you to take on your journey to the Underworld."

"Wanderer, I don't want to die tonight."

"Just wait, you will."

Lichen sat cross-legged on the floor near the fire. The flames crackled and spit, throwing Wanderer's gangly shadow over the walls. He bustled around the house, Singing softly while he arranged Lichen's hides and blankets on the death litter. Consisting of two side poles, the litter had hair ropes laid out across the floor in front and a net bottom made from the woven undercoats of wolves.

Just what I need, to go into the Underworld on scraps from Wolf Slayer's Spirit Helper.

Wanderer's eyes had gone bright and alert, like Raven's when feeding on a week-old carcass. He grabbed a yellow basket covered with red and black designs and filled it to the brim with rabbit jerky, sunflower seeds, and a healthy sprinkling of corn pollen. He set the basket on the foot of her death litter.

"Now, Lichen, you have to remember that *if* Bird-Man decides you're worthy, the journey will have stages. At first the road is easy, but the problems increase as you get closer to the Land of the Ancestors. There's a wide, rushing river that blocks the entry—or sometimes it's a high wall. Only a very good Dreamer can pass—"

"Well, that lets me out, Wanderer. What happens if I can't?"

His lips pursed speculatively. "Why, I don't know. I suppose you just come back. But something might eat you."

"Like what?"

"Oh, there are strange creatures down there. Snakes with wings. Buffalo that live under the water. I once had a toad with antlers try to gore me." He gazed absently at the ceiling, as though remembering. "Hmm. Well, so, when you get to the river, or whatever, let your team pull the weight of the litter. Don't—"

"What team?"

Firelight reflected in his dark eyes. "Your wolf team. It will pull the litter through the Underworld. That is, if Bird-Man agrees. You'll have to ask him to harness the wolves for you before you set off. Wolves almost never let Dreamers touch them."

Lichen squirmed, not liking this even a little. The closest she had come to learning how to be Snake was the slithering incident, from which she still had cactus spines festering around her belly button.

She twisted her hands in her lap. "Wanderer, are you sure I'm ready for this?"

"No," he said curtly. "But if we don't try, we'll never know, will we?"

"No, but—"

"So, let's get you started on your journey." A twinkle lit his eyes when he leaped over to her. "First you must go and lie facedown on the litter."

Lichen nodded sullenly. "All right. I guess I'll have to do it sometime anyway. First Woman's cave is in the Underworld."

She stepped forward and stretched out on the litter. The fox fur glistened in the firelight as though drenched with morning dew. She nuzzled its softness. "How's this?"

"Oh, that's good. Your chin is right over the cedar we cut from First Woman's tree. It's hidden under that top hide. Now turn your face so that your mouth rests against the fox hide."

Lichen did. "The fur tickles my nose, Wanderer."

He came and crouched by her side. "That's all right, you'll get used to it. Now, you just have to stay on your stomach with your mouth against the hide and call to Bird-Man all night long. If he wants to, he'll answer you."

"And then I have to ask him to harness the Spirit Wolves to my litter."

"That's right. Now," he said, patting her foot, "you'd better get started."

Lichen pressed her mouth to the hides and called, "Bird-Man? Bird-Man, it's me. I need you to come and talk. Bird-Man . . ."

She tilted her head and saw Wanderer crouched barefoot in the middle of his blankets, laying Power objects in a circle around his bed. Briskly, he arranged painted rocks so that they alternated with eagle-feather fans, skulls from predators like Marten, Badger, Coyote, Weasel—no, he hastily thrust Weasel's skull back into its basket. Instead, he picked up a huge bear paw and placed it next to where his head would rest. The long claws glimmered in the crimson glow of the fire.

"Wanderer? What are you doing?"

"Hmm?" He swiftly rearranged a rock and a skull. "Don't concern yourself with it. It's for protection, that's all."

A small thread of panic stitched her chest. "Protection? From what?"

He grinned like Coyote baring his teeth. "Bird-Man is your Spirit Helper, not mine. I don't know him as well as you do." He flicked a hand emphatically. "Keep calling him, Lichen."

"Bird-Man, Bird-Man, Bird-Man . . ."

Wanderer sprawled fully clothed on top of his blankets and closed his eyes. In almost no time, snores erupted from his mouth.

"Bird-Man, can you hear me? Bird-Man? Bird-Man?"

Lichen had to breathe through her mouth or the fine red fox hairs that had glued themselves inside her nose made her sneeze. It gave her voice a nasal quality. "Bird-Man? I don't like this any more than you do, but it looks like we've got to do it, so why don't you come and bring the Spirit Wolves? Bird-Man, Bird-Man . . ."

Her chant became a singsong. She called for what seemed an eternity, until her soul felt numb and her body had gone past aching. Her neck burned so badly that she feared it might snap in two if she moved.

Shadows clung in black welts along the ceiling. The flames had died down long ago, leaving freckled red eyes to glare at Lichen.

She shifted to bring up her knees, feeling sneaky since Wanderer had told her to lie on her stomach. But she conscientiously kept her mouth pressed over the cedar. "Bird-Man? Remember when you said that I needed to learn to see through the eyes of a bird, a human, and a snake? Well, Wanderer's been trying to teach me how."

The Power symbols on the walls peered dismally at her, looking through the eyes of Spirits long accustomed to failed Dreamers.

I'm trying, Spiral. Can you help me? The Symbols stayed mute, hostile, wishing she would go away, trying to lull her to sleep. Antlered monsters who lived under water lurked just beyond the horizon of her drooping eyelids, secreting themselves in the brooding shadows of her thoughts. She dared not sleep.

"Bird-Man? Why won't you come?"

She slid out flat again, in the manner of Ground Squirrel sunning himself on a log. The tuft of branches beneath her chin made a lump under the sleekness of the worn hides. Lichen blinked lazily at the coral threads of light reflecting on the wall.

"Bird-Man . . ." Gritting her teeth, she growled, "Bird-Man, Bird-Man, *Bird-Man!*"

A lonely wolf barked sharply, trying to locate its pack in the gloom of midnight. From across the bluff, answering yips echoed. The first wolf let out a delighted howl, and a chorus rose in eerie cadence. Lichen yawned deeply. Her tired body floated on the sound, rocking like a leaf in a peaceful stream. The padding of paws approached with the gentle rhythm of sacred drumbeats, soothing, echoing . . .

A whisper of sound came from the branches beneath the hide. Lichen stiffened, too afraid to move. Timidly, she called, "Bird-Man?"

"I hear you, Little One. I brought the wolves."

Lichen heard an animal snuffle. She twisted around and saw two huge black faces silhouetted in the door. They had pushed the hanging aside with their noses. A fiery sheen glowed in their yellow eyes. One of the wolves took a step into the room, a paw lifted, waiting.

Lichen got to her knees. Her throat had gone as dry as cottonwood leaves in the dusty radiance of autumn. Frightened, she croaked, "Can you harness them for me, Bird-Man?"

"Yes, if you think you're ready."

"Don't you?"

"You've sprouted the wings of a Dreamer, but they're wet and frail. The journey will be hard on you."

Lichen swallowed the lump in the back of her throat. "I have to learn sometime, Bird-Man."

"Yes, but you're so young. And brave. All right. Come down through the tunnel. Come. I'll be waiting for you, Lichen."

The wolves padded across the floor, their nails clicking on the stone, and dipped their muzzles through the nooses that Wanderer had braided from his own hair.

She took a last look at Wanderer's slack old face. His mouth hung open. Softly, she called, "I found Bird-Man, Wanderer. I'll try to come back to you."

The wolves lifted their snouts and gazed at her. One wagged its tail as though waiting for instructions. Lichen gripped the side poles of her death litter in tight fists. "Let's go."

The blackness rippled around her as they dove.

Fifteen

Checkerberry's ancient voice droned on to the accompaniment of precocious giggles. Surrounded by twelve children under the age of ten, the old woman seemed truly happy. For the first time in weeks, her withered cheeks glowed pink, drawing attention away from her bulbous nose and hunched back. She had pulled her gray hair into a neat bun and fastened it with tortoiseshell combs. Her orange dress added brightness to the overall effect.

Green Ash shifted miserably on the thick cushion of blankets near the front door of Primrose's house. Because *berdache* were technically female, the Blue Blanket Clan had given this plot of land and the adjacent fields to Primrose. Locust, his "husband," had moved here and now worked the fields for the clan—on rare occasions, given her obligations to the Woodpecker Warrior Clan.

Ordinarily the children's laughter would have brought Green Ash joy, but not today. Over the past week, her pain had grown to incapacitating levels, and the birthing women had been unable to ease it. She distracted herself by watching Primrose huddle over the central firepit, stirring a soup of ground corn mixed with the green leaves of lamb's quarter and flavored with mint. He wore a simple tan dress with fringed sleeves, but his long hair glimmered with seashells.

Locust napped on the high sleeping platform behind Primrose, the tips of her moccasins visible. Green Ash noticed that Primrose kept glancing up affectionately, as though to reassure himself that Locust still lay there.

Green Ash let her gaze drift to the long rows of colored baskets on the walls. Where had Primrose gotten that talent for coordinating color and shape? A round red basket sat perfectly over a square green one. No two similar colors were allowed in close proximity. It pleased the eye and calmed the soul.

Green Ash could use a good dose of calm. Her unborn baby had started kicking so violently that she had grown ill with panic. Was the baby all right? The birthing women didn't seem to know. She had been questioning the other pregnant women in the village about how they felt. Four of them were seven moons along, just as Green Ash was, but none of them reported such pain as she was suffering.

Blessed First Woman, don't let my baby die.

The words, seeping up from a cold pit where she had buried them, goaded her to face the fear. Had Primrose not pleaded with her to come today, she would have stayed home, sleeping to avoid her desperation. But his anxiety about Checkerberry had prompted Green Ash to walk halfway across the village to attend this round of Taletime.

Once a moon, each of the clan leaders collected the youngsters and told them the Old Stories. When the children became adults, at thirteen or fourteen, they would be expected to recite the sacred stories flawlessly.

As it turned out, Primrose's worry about Checkerberry had been unfounded. The instant the children had crowded around her knees, the old woman had roused and thrown off her dread like Badger shaking a blanket of spring snow from his glistening coat. Checkerberry seemed more her old jovial self than Green Ash had witnessed in moons. Her wrinkled lips had curled into a full smile.

Checkerberry leaned forward and pointed at Little Burrowing Owl. ". . . And what happened then?"

The five-cycles-old boy clapped his rapture at being given the chance to answer. "Tortoise brought up mud!"

"That's right," Checkerberry praised. "Tortoise brought up mud from the depths of the oceans, and Earthmaker fashioned the mud into the land and kneaded it into shape for the trees, animals, and humans. Then what happened?"

Hyssop scrambled to her knees. "Earthmaker breathed Spirit into the world, just like we do with arrow points! And all living things chose their own colors. The trees turned green, and the animals—"

"Good. You've got it." Checkerberry rocked back on her hips and smiled broadly. "And after Earthmaker had finished his creation, he realized with a shock that he'd forgotten to leave room for the rivers and creeks—but by then, he didn't know where to put them. He'd made everything so perfect that he hated to start ripping ditches so that the water could flow. He vacillated so long that the trees started drooping and the animals were dying of thirst. Muskrat came to him with his tongue hanging out and told Earthmaker he'd better do something fast."

"So Earthmaker made rivers!" two-cycles-old Buzzard slurred around the finger in his mouth, only to be shouted down by the other children yelling, "No, he didn't! Stupid! Not yet."

"You, Big-Nosed Rattler," Checkerberry singled out the older girl. "What did Earthmaker say to Muskrat?"

"He said he didn't know where to put the rivers."

"That's it. Earthmaker said, 'Yes, yes, you're right, Muskrat, but where shall I put the rivers and creeks? Do you have any ideas?'

"So, together, Earthmaker and Muskrat went to the rim of the sky to peer down upon the world. From their height, the only things they could see clearly were the huge serpents that Earthmaker had created. They slithered all over the land, creating squiggles everywhere. But when a dark shadow skimmed over the face of the world—it was Red-Tailed Hawk looking for dinner—the serpents instantly froze. Only their forked tongues darted to scent the air for danger."

"Ha!" Big-Nosed Rattler blurted in delight. "They were beautiful squiggles!"

"Yes," Checkerberry agreed. "Muskrat pointed at the snakes and said, 'There! Look at those magnificent patterns! Put the rivers where the snakes are. Isn't that beautiful? Not even you could have found better places than Red-Tailed Hawk.' So Earthmaker turned all the giant serpents into rivers—and the trees, animals, and humans have been able to live well ever since."

Hyssop let out a happy shriek and threw her arms around Checkerberry's neck. "Tell us another one, Grandmother," she begged, and all the children joined in.

Checkerberry laughed and patted Hyssop. "All right, sit down. I'm going to tell you about how Giant Beaver witched Bear and forced Bear to build dams for him. This was in the days when beavers grew as big as bears . . ."

A staggering pain ripped Green Ash's belly. Bending over, she clutched at the yellow fabric of her dress.

"Green Ash?" Primrose called. He knocked over a water bowl in his hurry to reach her. "Are you all right? Is the baby coming?"

The room had gone silent, and dozens of wide eyes had fixed on Green Ash. Locust leaned over the edge of the sleeping platform, her lean, tattooed face creased with alarm. Short black hair spread in a halo around her head. She shot a glance at Checkerberry.

Checkerberry sat like a statue carved of weather-beaten wood. Only her nostrils flared to show that she breathed. "Witched . . ." she whispered. The old woman's thoughts had gone dark.

Primrose raced to the fire to fill a cup with herbs and hot water. Green Ash rocked back and forth, moaning. Her whole body burned as though the invisible creatures of the Underworld had crept into her womb to bite her with teeth of fire.

From the silence, Checkerberry's hoarse voice rose. "Come and listen to me, children. I'm going to tell you a story of long ago. A true story of Nightshade and the evil creatures that come at her bidding . . ."

Reluctantly the youngsters tugged their gaze away from Green Ash and stared at Checkerberry, who had leaned forward into the midst of their circle, her eyes blazing.

"I heard her calling," Checkerberry began. "It was in the middle of the night, and I thought she was calling to me. She'd only just come from the Forbidden Lands—four cycles old, she was, and helpless. I'd decided to sleep in the temple for a few nights in case she needed me.

"The wind battered at the temple as I walked through the dim corridors, following her voice. Nightshade was crying. My heart ached for her. I had a little girl of my own at the time. Pretty, with big brown eyes, and I kept imagining how my own Hopleaf would feel if she'd been dragged away to a strange land, with no family or friends.

"In the corridor that led to Nightshade's room, all the firebowls were out. I couldn't see my hand in front of my face—but I kept marching, pushing on through the blackness to get to her.

"Her door-hanging was swinging when I arrived, as though someone had just entered. A thin line of light seeped around the edges, lighting the floor at my feet."

Little Hyssop's face had slackened in terror. She had begun to wring her hands in her lap.

"I heard Nightshade laugh. A gay sound, as if all her fears had been swept away. When I pulled back the door-hanging and stepped into that firelit room, my heart rose into my throat. I don't know what they were. Huge things, with no arms or legs. They Danced around her bed, their beaks clacking like thunder while they spun and leaped in time to music I couldn't hear."

Primrose dropped the cup, and it smashed on the floor. Green Ash's gaze darted back and forth between her aunt and her brother. Primrose stood rigid, as though the words had torn the threads of his soul.

Checkerberry's mouth hung open for so long a time that a bead of spittle formed at one corner and dribbled down her chin. Big-Nosed

Rattler cast a pleading look at Primrose and mouthed, "What's wrong with her?"

Primrose shook his head; Checkerberry blinked herself awake as though returning from a long Soul Voyage.

"I . . . I cried out—in fear, you see. And the dark shadows . . . That pink demon with the twisted face flew at me. He drove me down the hall, clutching at my hair and dress while I screamed my throat raw. The next day, my baby—Hopleaf—she died. *Witched.* Witched by Nightshade, because I'd seen the evil Spirits she'd called to keep her company."

Checkerberry lifted her head and stared straight at Green Ash. In the pause, Primrose touched his mouth with quaking fingers. Locust's eyes had narrowed to slits where she peered over the sleeping platform.

"Witched," Checkerberry repeated. *"My baby died!"*

Green Ash jerked as a warm flood poured from her vagina, soaking her yellow dress. "Oh, Primrose! Help me! I have to get to the birthing women. I think . . ."

But when she had stumbled to her feet, she saw that it wasn't water that trickled down her legs, but blood.

A low groan worked its way up Green Ash's throat. "Hurry. The pain. Ah!"

The room whirled around her, but she didn't realize that she had fallen until she heard the children's shrieks and saw Primrose lean over her, his face wild with fear as he called hoarsely for Locust. Primrose slipped his arms beneath Green Ash. In a voice that shook, he said to Locust, "Get old woman Nit. Quickly. She lives near the southern end of the palisades."

Locust sailed out the door, her black hair flying in the sunlight. Green Ash barely realized that she had gone until she heard the scritching of sandals on gravel.

Primrose stroked Green Ash's hair. "It's all right. Everything's going to be fine. Stay calm."

Beneath the soothing words, Green Ash could hear Checkerberry murmuring, "Nightshade . . . she's a baby killer."

But Green Ash's baby didn't come, and the pain eased by dusk. She spent the night tossing and turning in horrifying dreams wherein armless creatures Danced in the moonlight and children fell dead in the streets.

Tharon tiptoed through the dim halls, blowing out the flickers of light in the beautiful ceramic firebowls as he went. Kettle would assume that a gust of wind had snuffed them. She would grouse tomorrow as she went about relighting the wicks. Oily blue smoke rose in Tharon's wake.

When he stopped before her door, a bout of nerves mixed with his eagerness. Sweat drenched his back and beaded his face. He scanned the halls, making certain that no one wandered about at this hour. Then he seized the hanging, jerked it aside, and ducked under.

She lay asleep on her bed, her black hair haloing her swollen face. She must have cried herself to sleep. He smiled with disdainful amusement.

Around him, corn-shuck dolls watched through unblinking, obsidian-bead eyes. She had arranged them with precision so that they sat side by side along the walls, going from tallest to shortest. One doll, a huge thing twelve hands high, slumped beside her bed, within reaching distance. Did she coddle it, tell it secrets? *Probably. Well, you know what I do to people you tell secrets to.* Evil came from that doll. Yes, Tharon could sense it glowering at him. One of these days he would have it burned just to show her what he thought of her "companions."

With the stealth of Wolf, he stalked across the room and clamped a hand over her mouth, lest she scream and alert the guards outside the temple.

She woke in terror, her brown eyes jerking wide as she flailed wildly at him. But her pathetic strength was no match for Tharon. A muted cry breathed against his hard hand. Then her tears started to flow, warming his fingers.

"Don't make a sound," he warned.

Sixteen

Nightshade knelt on a mat in the stifling darkness of the sweat lodge. A small, conical structure, it spread ten hands in diameter. She had been here since before dawn, Singing, talking to Brother Mudhead, who came and went like a breeze over a meadow. The Tortoise Bundle nestled on a tripod to her left. It shot out frail fingers of Power to touch her skin, as though desperate to be close to her. She reached back with her soul, soothing, assuring it that she would never leave again.

"I'm here, Bundle."

The bitter ache in her soul had eased. Her vigil had almost silenced Bulrush's laughter and the joy of his smile. Though occasionally, for the briefest of moments, it would be spring again, and she would find herself lying in Bulrush's arms, gazing up at billowing clouds that floated through deep azure skies. The pungent scent of the river would fill her nostrils, the gaiety of his voice would sound in her ears . . .

Then a terrible shroud of weariness would descend. Nightshade wielded it as she would a knife, concentrating on it, using it to separate her from herself so that her memories drifted with a detached quality, as if someone else's.

He who loves is lost and gone, an old woman's voice echoed in her mind. *Render of the fair heart's Song. Woman weep, for not you know . . .*

Nightshade dipped her cup into the red pot of cedar-scented water beside her and slowly poured the cool liquid over the hot rocks in the center of the floor. An explosion of steam erupted. Sweat drenched her, cleansing, purifying. She tipped her chin to let the rivulets of water stream from her face and trickle down over her breasts to the flat of her stomach.

Brother Mudhead's twisted face wavered in the glistening veil of steam—huge, and pink with the clay of the Sacred Lake. His dark eyes shone with concern. *"The time has come. You must renew the Bundle by tying your Spirit to it once and for all. The Bundle needs you."*

"Yes," she whispered, her voice sounding far away and unreal to herself.

Laughter penetrated from outside. Players called scores in a chunkey game.

Mudhead vanished, leaving only swirling mist.

Nightshade lifted her deep voice, Singing the Beginning Song. The notes lilted in the cramped lodge, seeming to hang on the mist like shimmering gems.

When she had finished the Song, she reverently reached for the Tortoise Bundle and placed it on her knees. The freshly painted red, yellow, blue, and white spirals that encircled the edge shone dimly in the shreds of light penetrating around the hide hanging over the door. The black eye in the center of the red hand stared at her, unblinking.

"Let's go back to the Beginning Time together."

She Sang her own personal Spirit Song as she cautiously untied the damp lacings on the Bundle. Power drifted up, muted, almost dead. The "Thousand Voices" had waned to a few whispers, the words indecipherable.

Tears stung Nightshade's eyes. "What did he do to you?"

All of the other Bundles and Power objects that Tharon had collected had been in the same condition, their souls withered to near nothingness, even Old Marmot's. How could one man kill so much Power so quickly? Or had the Power been dwindling for cycles? If she could only strengthen the voices of the Bundle, they might be able to answer that question—and tell her what Tharon had done to anger First Woman so much that she would abandon them.

"Help me, Tortoise Bundle."

With the tenderness of a lover, Nightshade pulled back the hide covering, revealing the sacred contents. Her fingers smoothed the edge of the long dart point with the fluted base. In the Beginning Time, humans had hunted gigantic, two-tailed monsters with such points, though it seemed impossible now. Tiny bits of bone lay scattered on the bottom of the Bundle. Old, brittle beyond belief. Her mother had told her they had come from a Spirit Wolf that had helped Wolf Slayer. A smooth, black rock—no, a shark's tooth, but this was definitely stone—rested on the left side. It had been drilled perfectly before being strung on a leather thong, so ancient that it crumbled before her eyes. Only the stone shark's tooth retained enough Power to touch her deeply. She rested her hand on it, feeling its coolness, exchanging Spirit for Spirit while she gazed at the other relics. A beautiful tortoiseshell gorget inscribed with the face of Thunderbird lay next to the shriveled head of Rattlesnake.

No matter how often she had gazed on these ancient Power objects, she had always felt that something was missing—some bit of stone or shell that would rouse the sleeping Spirits to full life again. What had happened to the absent object? Had it been lost somewhere? Or had the gods hidden it from her people to punish them for a crime committed so long ago it had been forgotten?

Cycles ago, Nightshade had Dreamed of a homely man with a silly smile. He would come to open the Bundle and gently touch the stone tooth. Then he would turn, looking at the rising sun, wondering. A reddish-yellow halo would form around him, as if spun by the very sun, and with his strong left arm, he would point . . . eastward. Then the yellow-red halo would engulf him, like flames devouring a tree.

After that, she had always sensed that the missing object and the tooth remained tied somehow, joined by a thin strand of Power that spanned centuries.

Carefully, Nightshade removed each object and passed it six times through the purifying steam of the lodge, rejuvenating its Power in the fragrance of cedar. After each pass, she brought the object to her mouth and softly breathed Spirit into it, promising her life to protect it. The "Thousand Voices" cried out weakly in relief.

When finally she had breathed Spirit into each object, she rearranged them on the sacred hide and hesitantly slipped her turquoise pendant over her head. She had worn it for that last Corn Dance at Talon Town. Nothing in the world contained more of her soul than this tiny slip of stone engraved with the image of the wolf *thlatsina*. Clutching it tightly to her breast, she Sang a soft Song of praise to the *thlatsina*, then placed the pendant on the hide with the other objects, tying her soul once and for all to the Tortoise Bundle's soul.

She blinked, heat smothering her. Her vision began to blur as sweat poured down her body. Light-headed, she pulled up one knee and propped her forehead against it. The hiss of the steam pulsed . . . pulsed . . . voices whispered . . . *"First Woman killed our Power deliberately. To keep it from Tharon. He has polluted the temple . . . killed Marmot and Singw . . . and all the others . . ."*

Her stomach twisted, and her head throbbed with each beat of her frantic heart. The voices faded as a misty grayness settled like a suffocating blanket on her soul.

B adgertail charged headlong down the steps of the Temple Mound and hit the grass running. Breath tore at his lungs as he swerved around the eastern corner of the mound and raced past his house toward the low, rounded dome of the sweat lodge ensconced against the rear palisade wall.

Nightshade's red dress hung from a peg on the outer wall, the hem swaying in the warm breeze. Badgertail slowed his steps to a trot. Fist-sized stones lay in a bed of glowing coals just outside the entry.

"Nightshade?" A long silence answered. "Nightshade . . . I'm sorry to disturb you. The Sun Chief demands your presence in the temple. We've just received a messenger—"

"Yes, yes," she replied wearily. "And Tharon wants to know what I've Dreamed about Petaga."

Nightshade emerged from the lodge, her naked body drenched in sweat. She had pinned her long hair on top of her head, but wet ringlets curled over her ears and down her back. Her movements betrayed deep exhaustion, but a strange glitter possessed her eyes, as if something more than Nightshade inspected him.

She tilted her head back, her eyes closed, mouth open, and breathed deeply, as if revitalizing herself. Sunlight glistened on her flesh, sparkling, and Badgertail's heart raced at the sight of her.

He averted his eyes to kill the sudden attraction he felt and bounced nervously on his toes, attempting to appear nonchalant.

"Throw me my dress." Nightshade's voice sounded normal, but some underlying Power caused Badgertail to jump, as if an order had been barked.

He groped for the garment, removed it from the peg, and forgot what he was doing as he ended up staring again. He shook himself irritably and tossed the garment to her without a word. *Blessed Sun, I'd no idea such magnificence existed in the world. Beautiful and terrifying. . . . How did she know what I wanted to tell her?*

Nightshade slipped the dress over her head and reached back into the lodge to grab the Tortoise Bundle. Cradling it in her arms, she started off, as straight and deliberate as an arrow, the fatigue that had weighted her somehow vanished.

Badgertail kept pace at her side, throwing her alarmed glances. "Do you also know what news the messenger brought?"

Nightshade's eyes tightened. "Tharon is such a simpleton. Does he really think I would tell him anything that would betray Petaga?"

Badgertail marshaled all of his strength to keep from shouting at her. Dread had fermented into a sickening brew in his stomach. Blue wildflowers splashed the slopes of the mounds. Above the blossoms, clouds of insects swarmed, their iridescent coils unfurling into the sunlit heavens.

"Nightshade," he said quietly, "if Petaga attacked Spiral Mounds, he's surely planning on attacking us—maybe not now, not until he's raided the other villages and gathered enough supplies and warriors, but soon."

She just kept walking.

When she rounded the eastern corner of the Temple Mound, he stepped in front of her, blocking her path. Out in the plaza, people whooped and clapped; wagers were being shouted back and forth on the chunkey game in progress. Clans had been known to win or lose entire tracts of land, buildings, food stocks, even the clothes on their backs—or, on rare occasions, their lives.

Badgertail spread his hands wide. "Don't you see that you're in danger, too? And what of every other innocent person here? Do you hate these people so much that you'd—"

"I do not hate, Badgertail. I just see more than you do." She slipped lithely past him and hitched her skirt up to start climbing the mound.

He trotted beside her, his woven cattail sandals clacking on the wooden steps. Anger stirred in his breast. "What does that mean? That you see the patterns of the future?"

When she did not respond, he grabbed her shoulder and spun her around to face him. They stood there, gazes locked, breathing hard. He knew that he ought to be terrified by the look she was giving him—as dangerous as a wounded bear's—but he could only think about the effects of another war, the probability of total destruction, the death, and the horror. It ripped him inside out.

"Nightshade," he implored, "is Petaga truly mounting an army against us?"

She chuckled softly at first, then louder, and the sound drove him to near madness.

"Please!" He extended his hands to her. "Talk to me. Just . . . talk to me."

Nightshade's gaze drifted from his fingers, up his tattooed chest, to his eyes. "We've nothing to discuss, Badgertail."

"I *beg* you," he implored. "Give me just one hand of time. Let me talk to you."

"All right, War Leader. But not now. Later. Tharon—"

"Tonight? At my home. I'll send a warrior to escort you."

"Tomorrow. There are rituals I must perform tonight. Now we must go. I have to discover what orders Tharon is about to give you."

"Orders?"

"Of course," she responded coolly. "Did you think he could hear about Spiral Mounds and not consider sending you out on another battle-walk? It will make him a hero."

The very thought of initiating another attack so soon after River Mound sent Badgertail's soul reeling. "What?"

Nightshade examined his squat face and began climbing again. She had entered the temple before he could force his feet to follow. He took the steps in leaps, bowed to the Six Sacred Persons, and sprinted inside to catch up with her.

Orenda peered from one of the doorways, her young face swollen from tears, her nose red. She clutched her huge doll against her breast. Her mouth opened. Feebly, she called, "Nightshade . . ." then glanced at Badgertail and vanished. The door-hanging swayed behind her.

Badgertail shook his head. In Orenda's entire nine cycles of life, he had heard her speak no more than three or four sentences. She never left the temple. She never played with other children. The little girl's only solace had been her mother, Singw. With Singw gone, how would the child survive?

They proceeded down the long hall in silence, toward the angry voices coming from the Sun Chamber. Nightshade bowed again and stepped over the threshold.

Tharon was glaring at the messenger, the war leader of Spiral Mounds, Black Birch. Young, he stood a hand taller than Badgertail. His high brow accentuated the flatness of his pug nose. His now-pale flesh made the tattoos of parallel lines across his forehead and cheeks stand out starkly. He wore a blood-soaked warshirt cut from pale leather.

"I did not say that, Sun Chief!" Black Birch responded, his voice tight. When he saw Badgertail, he swung around. "War Leader, surely *you* see that Cahokia cannot simply sit by and let her sister villages be ground to dust beneath Petaga's heel! Where will your tribute come from next cycle? You know you can't survive without us!"

Nightshade walked quietly to the ring of Power objects that lay on the edge of the altar. She reverently placed the Tortoise Bundle near Old Marmot's and seated herself beside it. The light from the firebowls reflected like honey in the ringlets of her hair. But the flames did not shine with their usual luster today. The dull, rusty glow barely crept halfway up the walls, leaving the high ceiling in utter blackness. Not even the new seashells glittered.

"Is that what's going on, my Chief?" Badgertail asked. "Are our sister villages being ground to dust, or is it just Spiral Mounds?"

Tharon strolled across the altar to the sacred pedestal and propped his elbows on it. His golden robe and tanager-feather headdress made him seem a figurine carved of pure amber. He had rubbed oil into the red circles on his cheeks to give them a sheen. "Just Spiral Mounds, for the moment. But Black Birch says that everyone is turning against us. Even some of the smaller villages have sided with Petaga. He says that Petaga is planning on attacking us once he gets enough warriors. Do you believe that?"

Badgertail glanced at Black Birch. He had fought against the man only moons ago and knew that he was arrogant and reckless. Could he be trusted? What if he was in league with Petaga and trying to lure Badgertail into some sort of trap? A deadly keenness, like freshly struck chert, animated Black Birch's eyes, and Badgertail knew that look. "Yes, my Chief. If Black Birch says it is so, I believe it."

Tharon's gaze slid to Nightshade. His lips quirked in amusement. "And you, Priestess? What have you seen regarding this?"

Nightshade softly stroked Old Marmot's Power Bundle. "Nothing, Tharon. That's what I see."

"Nothing?"

"Nothing."

Tharon ground his teeth. "What kind of priestess are you? My people are plotting behind my back, and you . . ." Nightshade canted her head, and he swallowed his words. Even Badgertail flinched at that deadly glare. "Well," Tharon retreated, "Black Birch says that places like Redweed Village have gone over to Petaga's side."

"Redweed Village?" Badgertail gestured dismissal. "We don't need to worry about them, my Chief. If they have more than fifty warriors, I'd be surprised."

Black Birch interjected, "Petaga is massing forces, War Leader. He has already gleaned over nine hundred from the southern villages. If he keeps receiving pledges of fifty here and fifty there, soon no one will be able to stop him."

Black Birch turned to glare at Badgertail, and the unspoken words, *even you,* hung like a war club over Badgertail's head. He folded his arms and stared at the floor. Even with nine hundred warriors, Petaga could not have molded men and women from different villages into an "army" so soon. The warriors would still be studying each other, scrambling to gain position for themselves and their clans in the coming war. And Petaga was so young. The older village leaders would want to test him, to make certain he had the courage and stamina of his father. Badgertail could almost pity the boy—if this weren't such a deadly serious game. And if Black Birch were telling the truth, the game grew more deadly with each passing moment. Badgertail could not give Petaga the time he would need to turn his warriors into an army.

He forced his mouth to say, "I think Black Birch is correct, my Chief. We must stop Petaga now."

"You're recommending attack?"

"I am." When he glanced at Nightshade, he found her watching him unemotionally, as though she had known all along that he would say those very words. He wanted to slam his fists into something, or to shake her until she told him every vision she had ever had.

"I see," Tharon said. "Well, all right, but first, before you attack Petaga, I want you to strike Redweed Village."

Badgertail's thick brows drew down over his nose. "But . . . why?"

"They've turned against me! I want every traitor there wiped from the face of the earth."

"But, my Chief . . ." Badgertail shook his head in disbelief. "They are inconsequential. Let me concentrate my forces—"

"No!" Tharon shouted imperiously. "You will attack Redweed Village and . . . and bring me the Stone Wolf that resides there."

"The *what?*"

"The Stone Wolf. A trader told me about it. It's supposed to have great Power."

Unable to contain his incredulity, Badgertail blurted, "You have dozens of such objects, my Chief! What good would another do you? And a Stone Wolf? How would I even recognize it? It could be a necklace, a bracelet, a pipe, anything! Why are you so interested in these Power objects?"

Tharon's face reddened, and Badgertail braced himself.

Nightshade laughed. "He's trying to protect himself. That's it, isn't it, Tharon? You think that if you can mass all the Power objects in the world around you, you'll be shielded from First Woman's wrath." Understanding dawned in her eyes. "And that's why she's draining their—"

Tharon's eyes darted wildly over the room, as though he feared everyone was laughing at him. "I *want* that Stone Wolf! Badgertail, you *will* attack Redweed Village and get it!"

His heart thundering, Badgertail bowed very properly. "Yes, my Chief."

Black Birch turned eagerly to the sacred pedestal. "And then Badgertail will join forces with the rest of us to destroy Petaga?"

Badgertail's stomach cramped. Already his mind had begun running battle plans, and he could see *cycles* of war, one after another, not ending until thousands had died. Bile rose in his throat.

"Yes," Tharon agreed. "Then he can help you. Is that understood, Badgertail?"

"Yes . . . yes, of course."

Tharon stepped from the altar and left the room, his head high. When he had vanished down the hallway, Badgertail rubbed a hand over his face, as if to wake himself from a wrenching nightmare. "Black Birch," he said softly, "let's meet tomorrow. It will take time to organize. We'll talk about details."

"It can't take too much time, Badgertail. Petaga's next stop is Red Star Mounds. They've three hundred warriors left there. If he manages to convince—"

"I understand," Badgertail said shortly. "We'll discuss it at dawn."

Black Birch cast a wary look at Nightshade before he bowed and left.

Badgertail's eyes focused blindly on a single firebowl that flickered on the verge of going out. He couldn't muster the will to call Kettle to come and fill it.

Nightshade rose.

She came to stand in front of him. "Tomorrow, after Wolf Pup rises. Send the escort. I'll be ready."

*S*ister Datura's knowing laughter echoed.

Nightshade exhaled slowly. Her fingers traced the designs on her sacred basket before she put it down by her knee. The soft sounds of the sleeping temple crept into her room: someone snoring, poles creaking and moaning, the rustling of the wind through the roof thatch. Nightshade leaned forward. Her Wellpot sat on the floor in front of her, its black shape almost invisible in the darkness.

"I'm coming, First Woman. I'm coming. Open the Gate to the Well of the Ancestors."

The water had a faint yellow sheen from the light that seeped beneath her door-hanging. Images flashed across the surface: Singw violently shaking Orenda . . . Orenda fleeing through the temple, searching one room after another until she found a stack of blankets to crawl behind . . . Old Marmot staring into his Wellpot like a wounded vulture . . . and Tharon . . . Tharon stalking the halls . . .

"What is this, my Sister? I must talk to First Woman. These glimpses tell me nothing. Let me go deeper."

"First Woman has closed the gate. No one may enter. It's just you and me tonight, Nightshade. Here, in this world."

"What? Why? What have I done to deserve—"

Nausea overwhelmed her. She rose to her feet and reeled across the room, trying to reach her bed. Halfway there, she vomited onto the floor. She sank down, pressing her hot cheek to the cool dirt. "Oh, my Sister, be gentle with me."

Seventeen

The long, deeply blue twilight of the Planting Moon had settled over the countryside, bringing with it Wind Mother's fury. A gale had come up last night, roaring, blasting everything in its path. Now a potent gust slapped at Wanderer's fringed sleeves as he paced the ledge in front of his house; then it tormented the chokecherry bushes before soaring over the precipice into the meadows below. As Wanderer surveyed the land, his thoughts hardened like raindrops in the grip of Winter Boy. Smoke drifted in the south, rising from Spiral Mounds. A great purple smear trailed across the horizon. *War!*

. . . And Lichen hadn't awakened in two days. He ran a hand through his matted gray hair. She lay lifelessly on the litter inside his house.

Wanderer had checked for a heartbeat. He had placed a mica mirror beneath her nose. Nothing.

"Oh, Lichen, what have I done to you? I . . . I just wanted you to see the tunnel. I never thought you'd be able to—"

His words were torn away by the wind and blown into the green distances.

Wanderer hugged himself as he ambled to the very edge of the cliff. Cornfields dotted the bottomland in emerald patches. Weaving between them, the Father Water cut a blue swath of hope in a land already wilting from the heat of early summer.

He had sent Lichen on this journey. But he had never imagined that she had the ability to enter the Tunnel to the Underworld. He'd prayed she would just be able to peer over the edge into the darkness. It took even the greatest Dreamers cycles to gain the skill and courage to actually plunge down that spiraling black throat.

"You underestimated her, you old fool."

The truth seared his soul. He knew better than anyone that gaining entrance to the Land of the Ancestors required strength beyond measure. The Underworld creatures devised terrifying traps with which to capture the Dreamer's soul.

"And you . . . you didn't even warn her about the traps."

Wanderer looked up when three ravens swooped down from the hazy sky, eying him curiously. Crossed Beak fought to balance himself in the gusting wind. He cawed, and Wanderer cawed back. The bird fluttered into the oak thicket, his black feathers shining with the frosty iridescence of seashells.

"I'm so glad to see you, Crossed Beak. I've never been this frightened in my life."

Crossed Beak *thocked* softly, tilting his head first to the right, then to the left.

"Yes, I know. But waiting is so difficult. I've been half crazy since I found her."

A deep-throated caw rumbled as Crossed Beak fluffed his feathers, then used his beak to pluck at some irritation beneath his right wing.

Wanderer expelled a breath and nodded. "You're right. Many Dreamers stay in the Underworld for days, talking to Spirits, visiting with old friends. But Lichen is so young, and I—I'm worried, that's all." Guilt constricted around his heart, making it pound nauseatingly.

"How could I have done that to her, Crossed Beak? She's the most important thing in my life."

Crossed Beak whimpered and sprang from the tree, challenging the wind before flapping over the crest of the bluff. The other two ravens tipped their wings and followed. Wanderer shielded his eyes to watch their sinuous flight. The way they circled into the sky, they could have been chips of obsidian borne on the breath of a dusty whirlwind.

What am I going to do? If she hadn't awakened by tomorrow morning, he would have to do something. What? Danger lurked in even the slightest interference. If Lichen were struggling against some Underworld creature and he so much as called her name, the distraction could cause her doom. But if she'd had an accident, if her litter had overturned and she was fleeing . . . well, she would be running through a country that had no landmarks . . . a country haunted by horror. His voice might help lead her back to the tunnel, from which she could come home.

"But you can't know which it is unless you go yourself."

He hadn't been to the Underworld in cycles. But if Lichen had not awakened by tomorrow, he would go. It might do no good. The Underworld spread infinitely in all directions. Finding her would take a miracle.

He folded his arms, his thoughts twisting like Snake caught in the jaws of Badger, while he studied the smoke from Spiral Mounds.

What was happening out there?

Could it be Badgertail again? Why would Tharon order his warriors . . .

Petaga?

Wanderer's hands dropped limply to his sides. The smoke had thinned to streaks of pale gray that stroked the gentian fabric of evening like wispy fingers. Why would Petaga have attacked Spiral Mounds? To steal supplies? Wanderer had heard that after Badgertail's attack, Aloda had barely enough to fend off starvation. What political motive—

A sound penetrated his thoughts. Wanderer cocked an ear. It barely carried over the wind, soft, mewing.

Then he clearly heard a cough and a wheezed, "Wanderer?"

"*Lichen?*"

Ducking beneath his door-hanging, he saw her lying on her side, her body dripping wet. Strange bits of moss clung to her tan sleeves. She coughed again, desperately, and tried to raise herself on her elbows but weakly fell back against the fox hides.

"Oh, Lichen." Wanderer scooped her up in his arms and frantically kissed her soaked face. "Thank First Woman, I was so afraid."

Lichen tried to speak and fell into a violent coughing fit. A trickle of water ran from her mouth. She fought to catch her breath and started choking. In terror, Wanderer laid her facedown on the floor. Straddling her, he firmly pressed against her back. More water gushed from her lungs, forming a small, crystalline pool on the dirt. He pressed again and again, until she seemed to be breathing easily; then he stretched out on the floor beside her to study her face. She smiled weakly. Wanderer lifted a hand and stroked her sopping hair. "Are you feeling better?"

"Yes," she whispered.

Her pretty face, with its full lips and button nose, had gone as pale as clay. But her eyes gazed at him steadily. A luminous serenity lit their mahogany depths. "I fell into the river, Wanderer."

"You did? How did you get out?"

"I was . . . was drowning. I saw something in the waves. It came and slithered inside me."

"Snake?"

She nodded. "Water Snake. I . . . I got Water Snake's soul, Wanderer. Then . . . I could swim to shore."

"Oh, that's good, Lichen. You wanted Water Snake's soul. How—"

"I saw Wolf Slayer. He came . . . to . . ."

"Wait, Lichen," he said gently, seeing how hard her words came. "You need to rest and eat. We'll talk about it when you're stronger."

Lichen's hand crept spiderlike across the floor until she could twine her fingers in his buckskin shirt. "I tried very hard . . . to come back to you. I love you, Wanderer."

Tears welled in his faded eyes. "I love you, too, Lichen. You sleep now. When you wake up, we'll eat and talk."

The sweetness of roasting grouse pervaded the air. Wanderer crouched before the birds, turning their stick carefully on the tripod so they would cook on the other side. Lichen knelt on her knees before the firepit. He had bathed her and combed her long hair until it crackled. The green shirt with red spirals that draped her skinny body came from his ritual attire—specially blessed by Raven Above. It hung down to her ankles.

She'd been quiet, deep in thought. Her dark eyes fixed on the sparkflies that glimmered beyond the doorway like Dancing suns. He had tied up the hanging so that the cool, rain-scented breeze could blow through the house. Raindrops patted softly in the dust outside. Not much, but enough to wet the world. The wind had died down to a rippling breeze. The richness of damp earth smelled so good, so soothing, that he longed to run out and Sing his thanks to Thunderbird. Any other night, he would have.

But he dipped a horn spoon into the pot of tea, stirring it for the twentieth time, waiting for Lichen to speak.

After every Power journey he'd ever undertaken, he had needed time to just sit and look at the world. Talking to Spirits did that. Left a Dreamer drained of physical vitality, but filled with a silence so profound it felt downy against the soul.

Wanderer rose and went to sift through the basket of phlox blossoms near the back wall. The delicate, flowery scent swirled up when he grasped a handful.

Lichen blinked. Slowly, she turned her head to gaze at him. Her eyes gleamed like sunlight on snow. He smiled as he stirred the blossoms into the boiling blend of roots.

"I saw Wolf Slayer, Wanderer," she repeated softly.

"Did you? When?"

"After I swam to shore. He was sitting on the bank, waiting for me. He's beautiful, Wanderer. He glows like Father Sun."

Wanderer listened intently. He had never seen Wolf Slayer—but each Dreamer met different Spirit Helpers in the Underworld. Lichen had clasped her hands in her lap. She fumbled with them vulnerably. "And?"

"We sat by the river and talked. He told me things . . ."

When her eyes went vacant, unblinking, Wanderer filled two wooden cups with tea, then slid the grouse from their roasting stick and put them in clay bowls. He carried Lichen's over and set them by her knees. She didn't even seem aware of his closeness. He returned to pick up his own dinner and stretch out on his bed.

Gently, he said, "Tell me about the journey. Bird-Man came up through the tunnel in the cedar branches?"

"Yes. He brought the wolves for me. They put their muzzles into the nooses you made. Then . . . then we started down . . . into darkness."

Steam rose around Wanderer's face as he sipped his tea. "Eat, Lichen. We have lots of time."

She plucked a leg from her grouse and chewed it thoughtfully while her gaze touched each Power symbol on the walls. The spirals and purple starbursts listened especially intently tonight.

"The wolves had a hard time pulling the litter in the river, Wanderer."

"They always do. It's so deep and wide."

"And fast. It rushed so fast."

"So you fell in and had to turn back?"

She finished chewing and swallowed. "No. On the other bank, we started seeing signs of people. Footprints—"

He sat forward, shocked. "On the other side? I thought you fell into the river on the way across."

"No, on the way back."

Wanderer straightened slowly. She had made it across into the Land of the Ancestors and returned! At her age? Almost unbelievable. It had taken him eleven cycles to accomplish the feat.

"Anyway, we started seeing things like old firepits, aspen stumps with ax marks. And the trees, the trees, Wanderer! They were so tall, their tops disappeared into the clouds. That's when Bird-Man appeared. He soared down from the sky. He was so beautiful. His wings shone like a rainbow."

"Did he take you into the Village of the Ancestors?"

Lichen gobbled a chunk of meat, barely chewing it. "A little way. Bird-Man told me he wanted me to talk to some people and to see a vision."

"What vision?"

Lichen's lids fluttered before she lowered her eyes. Tears glistened in those dark depths. "People dying. The land dying. Just like here. But this was a place far to the south. I think it's where the Palace Builders live. There were huge buildings made of stone. Bird-Man said that they had wounded Mother Earth just as badly as we have and that they need a Dreamer too, to set things right again."

Wanderer methodically gnawed at his grouse, but his attention stayed on Lichen. She had changed. She sounded so different, older. But that happened when a Dreamer got a new soul. They became disoriented for a time, seeing an old world through strange new eyes. He had known Dreamers who'd gone mad from fear. Others would leave their homes, searching to fulfill the visions that suddenly filled them with longing. Dreamers like Wanderer just delighted in the bizarre thoughts that came to them. After he had gotten Pack Rat's soul, he'd had the unquenchable urge to poke his nose into dark crevices, looking for shiny objects. He had spent an entire moon sleeping in the day and poking around at night—collecting bits of mica, and crystals. Then one night he'd poked his head into a hole in the ground where Weasel lived. He'd pulled his head out quickly, but not before Weasel had sunk his needle teeth into the top of Wanderer's skull. He'd had problems with weasels ever since.

"Lichen, did you tell Wolf Slayer that you wanted to go see First Woman and talk to her about the land dying?"

"Yes, but he said I couldn't. Not yet."

Lichen sipped her tea, watching Wanderer with the bright, unblinking eyes of Water Snake. When she set her cup down, she brought up her knees and wrapped her arms around them. "Wanderer? Why didn't you ever tell me you were my father?"

His hand stopped midway in bringing his cup to his mouth. "I . . . Lichen . . ." He fought to swallow past the knot in his throat. "Your mother never claimed me. She wanted people to believe that Shouts-At-Night was your father. It made things easier for her."

"How did you know you were my father?"

He smiled. "Oh, I knew. I felt the instant you were conceived. I could see your glow in Vole's womb. I even knew you'd be a Powerful Dreamer because of the colors of your soul, blue and red so brilliant they shimmered purple."

"Why didn't you tell anyone?"

"I couldn't. You belong to your mother's clan." Tea sloshed onto the floor when he tried to set the cup down, because his hand was shaking. "It would have been embarrassing for Vole. I wasn't well liked. People feared me. And . . . I loved your mother. I didn't want to hurt her."

As the flames died down in the firepit, smoke curled upward in billowing clouds. It hovered, roiling along the ceiling before being sucked out the doorway.

Lichen's mouth quirked. "You know what, Wanderer?"

"What's that, Lichen?"

"I wish I'd known a long time ago. Maybe I could have come up to see you more often."

Wanderer bowed his head. "I would have liked that. I got lonely for you."

Lichen bit her lower lip uneasily. Her fingers had knotted in the green fabric over her shins. "What am I going to do, Wanderer? Mother won't like me having Water Snake's soul. I don't . . ." She fidgeted. "I don't want to go home now. I want to live with you. You understand about things like this."

"Yes, I do. And then, too, you still have to try to find Falcon's soul. Maybe we should talk to Vole about it when we take you home."

"She won't let me, Wanderer. She thinks you're bad for me."

He let out a sigh. "Maybe I can convince her anyway. She has listened to me once or twice before."

A sparkfly had flown in through the window. It blinked over Lichen's head. For the first time that day, Wanderer heard Lichen laugh that childish laugh that warmed his soul.

She tipped her face to watch the sparkfly's erratic path. Slowly, she lifted a finger. The insect flitted down and sat on the tip. Her mouth gaped. A joyous expression came over her face as she examined the yellow designs on the fly's back while it crawled over her hand and up her arm.

When it finally winged away toward the ceiling, Lichen propped her chin on her drawn-up knees and gave Wanderer an affectionate gaze. "I'm glad you're my father, Wanderer. There's nobody else I'd want for a father."

Emotion swelled at the back of his throat. He tilted his head awkwardly, and Lichen jumped up and ran across the room. Her green hem swung around her legs as she crawled into the circle of his arms and snuggled against him. Wanderer kissed the top of her head and hugged her close.

What if Vole wouldn't let Lichen stay with him? How could he take her home in three days and just walk away? The thought twisted like a serrated chert blade in his gut.

"Lichen?" He couldn't help but ask. "Who told you I was your father?"

"Wolf Slayer. He said that's where I got my ability to Dream—from you."

"What else did he tell you?"

Lichen pulled Wanderer's arm over her so she could hold his hand against her chest and pat his fingers gently. The sparkfly caught her attention for a moment while it blinked near the door-hanging, trying to find a way out.

"Wanderer, you have to promise not to tell anyone. Wolf Slayer told me it was a secret."

"I promise. What did he say?"

Her brow puckered. "Well, he said that you and I, we have to go to Cahokia. Bulrush told me that Nightshade needs us. I don't—"

Wanderer's sudden jerk silenced Lichen. He squeezed her hand tenderly, trying to conceal his alarm. *To help Nightshade? Is that why she's been calling me?* "Did he say why?"

"No, he just said that one of these days soon, Foxfire would call us."

"Who is Foxfire?"

She shook her head. "I don't know. A Dreamer. Haven't you ever heard of him?"

"No. But if Wolf Slayer warned you he would call, we'd better be prepared."

"Why?"

"No Dreamer wants to be called by a Spirit Helper he has never heard of, Lichen. It's a little like meeting Grandfather Grizzly unexpectedly in the forest. You never know whether he'll just turn and walk away—or force you to run for your life."

Nightshade walked the long halls of the temple, her red dress fluttering around her legs in the muted light. The fragrance of spiced hickory oil rose especially strong tonight; even the delicate scent of the cedar poles was overpowered. Frightened murmurs drifted out of the rooms. From somewhere far off, she could hear Tharon's high, shrill laughter.

In the afternoon—and for the first time—the Starborn had come to her, begging her to breathe life into their Wellpots so they might see into the future and discern the patterns of the battles to come. They were desperately trying to please Tharon. Nightshade had laughed. What a fool Tharon had been to think that she would ever agree to help him, or his priests and priestesses.

She had earned herself twelve more enemies today. *But you knew it was coming. Unavoidable.*

Nightshade turned down the hall to her room . . . and stopped dead in her tracks. Orenda lay curled on her side in front of Nightshade's door. Asleep? The child clutched a huge doll to her chest. The toy stared at Nightshade from its black-and-white mask. A masterpiece of carved cedar, it represented the triumph of Light over Dark in the Beginning Time.

How odd that Orenda would have gathered the courage to approach Nightshade's door. No one else possessed such boldness—not after the past week—including Tharon.

She knelt by Orenda. The girl's pretty face looked haunted, her cheeks unnaturally pale against the tumbled frame of her hair. Her closed eyes and mouth twitched. Dirt and soot spotted her golden robe. Nightshade frowned. Didn't Orenda have attendants? Was there no one to make certain that she ate and dressed properly? Strange. When Nightshade had been nine summers, she'd had two attendants who slept in the room with her, there to take care of her.

Nightshade stroked Orenda's hair delicately.

"No! D-Don't!" Orenda scrambled back against the wall in terror, dragging her precious doll with her.

"Orenda, it's Nightshade. It's all right. I'm not going to hurt you."

Orenda's mouth trembled, moving with silent words while she stared wide-eyed at Nightshade. "You . . . can I . . ."

"What is it, Orenda?" When tears filled the child's eyes, Nightshade smiled gently.

Shivering all over, Orenda managed to say, "I—I wanted to know . . ."

"Yes?"

"Could I . . . I want to sleep in your room!" She burst into choking sobs.

A tickle of premonition played at the edges of Nightshade's soul. *Something's not right here. Why would she choose me, of all people?*

"Of course you can. And I'd actually enjoy the company," she said as she rose to her feet. "I've been lonely since I returned to Cahokia. I'll rearrange the hides so you'll have a place to sleep."

Orenda darted forward and twined a hand in Nightshade's skirt. She looked up with her whole tormented heart in her eyes. "Can . . . can we go in now?"

Nightshade pulled aside the door-hanging. "Yes. I even have some fish soup left that we can share."

Eighteen

I'm really frightened this time, Badgertail. What in the name of Moon Maiden are we fighting for?" Locust shook her head and flopped back against the wall. To escort Nightshade, she had dressed plainly, wearing a simple blue-and-tan kilt. No adornments hung in her stubby braids, which made her stern expression seem all the more stony.

"The chiefdom," Badgertail said fervently. "We're fighting to keep the chiefdom intact. To protect our way of life."

"Then why doesn't it feel like it, cousin? Do you know that Tharon called me to the temple five times today? You know what for?" Locust shook a fist angrily. "To rant and shout, vowing to obliterate his betrayers."

"He did the same to me."

Badgertail paced the shabby hides that lay on the floor. His house was a long rectangle, forty hands by thirty. A variety of war coups decorated the walls. The entire western side was covered with shields painted in bright yellows, reds, and blacks. Stumpware sat in every corner, supporting exotic pots and baskets acquired during battle-walks. His sleeping platform stood along the northern wall at the junction of the wall and roof. A ladder led up to it. The doorway opened to the east, facing the palisade wall and Father Sun's first morning rays.

On this warm night, Badgertail had pinned the door-hanging up so the light of the moon could drench the interior. A liquid silver film poured through the opening, so radiant that it sparkled in every hair on the elk hides that lay strewn across the floor. By comparison, the firebowl sitting in the southern corner seemed a pale caricature.

"Badgertail, tell me what we're going to do."

"We're going to obey the orders of our chief, Locust."

"How *can* we? He just commanded us to destroy a little village of a hundred people and then kill anyone who won't join forces with us! It's insane! It will destroy the chiefdom."

"No." Badgertail massaged his forehead. "No, I don't think so. We'll have to initiate the attacks properly, but if everything goes as I'm planning, the only thing we'll destroy will be the troublemakers."

"Who *isn't* a troublemaker these days?" Locust shouted as she shook her fists in frustration. "*Who?*" She clenched her teeth so tightly that her jaw stuck out.

"Locust . . ."

For a long time Badgertail evaded her gaze. He had been fighting a losing battle against a tide of despair ever since the attack on River Mounds. His dawn discussion with Black Birch had only augmented the sense of futility. The man had lost his sense. He just wanted revenge—and revenge was the business of the clans, not of the chiefdom. Badgertail had left the meeting with an overwhelming urge to slam his fists into something, preferably Black Birch.

To calm the sick dread tormenting him, Badgertail had gone to walk the shooting platforms that lined the palisades. And all day he had listened to his warriors laugh about the war in the offing, cursing Petaga and the traitorous villages that had joined his cause, boasting of their prowess and of how quickly they would destroy these upstart enemies. Every warrior had hung on Badgertail's words, most of them staring at him through eyes reverent with faith. They believed he could lead them to victory and honor. Others, however, had studied him with a measured . . . what? Skepticism? He batted away the thought. *Too much is happening for you to heed absurd notions.*

"Badgertail, *listen to me.*" Locust leaned forward. "Our warriors do not understand yet what sort of orders Tharon is giving. When they do . . ."

Badgertail lifted his hands and shook them helplessly. "What would you have me do, Locust? Shall I join forces with Petaga? Do you want me to assassinate the Sun Chief? *What?*"

"I don't know, cousin. I just want you to think about it. You know I'm on your side, no matter what you decide."

By the Long-Nosed God, she meant it! Badgertail's soul shriveled, twisting like a slice of meat tossed carelessly into the middle of a blaze. Did everyone have faith in him except himself? He had never felt so alone in his life. Desperation began tugging at his guts with the keen talons of Eagle.

"I'll think about it, Locust. But you know what my decision will be in the end."

Locust glanced uncomfortably at him. Badgertail had seen that same look once before, the night they had carried Bobcat's body from the Inner Chamber at River Mounds. Forced loyalty—the loyalty of a warrior who knows that what she is doing is wrong but feels she owes too much to her war leader to back out of the battle, no matter that it might cost her her soul.

Locust lowered her eyes and sighed. "Wolf Pup has risen. I'd better go to escort Nightshade."

"Thank you. Maybe she can help untangle this mess."

Locust stood. "Do you really believe that?"

"I want to believe it."

"She hates us, Badgertail. If she could influence your actions to our doom, she would."

"I know that, cousin. Leave it to me. I think I'll be able to tell if it's the latter."

"I certainly hope so," Locust growled as she left.

Badgertail paced aimlessly for a few moments, shaking his head, fighting with himself. Then he went to pull the jug of tea from the shadowed niche in the south wall, where he'd left it to cool. Fumbling, he knocked it sideways so that a splash darkened the floor.

Calm down, he told himself. *Do you want Nightshade to think you're a fool?*

Carefully, he poured the tea into a small falcon-headed pot. Made from birch twigs steeped in hot birch sap, the tea tasted of wintergreen and honey. He placed the pot and two cups on the shell-inlaid wooden platter that sat atop a thick pile of hides.

Badgertail resumed his restless pacing. When he caught his image in the mica mirror suspended near the doorway, the reflection stunned him. Bulging brown eyes gazed back at him from a weave of deep wrinkles. The tattoos on his cheeks, once bright blue, had dulled to a melancholy indigo. Gray shone in his hair like strands of Spider's web shimmering in the sunlight.

When did you get so old, Badgertail? And when did you start fighting wars that had no honor in them?

Roughly, he massaged the back of his neck to lessen the tension.

Tharon had ordered him to hurl their entire army of a thousand at Redweed Village. Badgertail had protested, convincing Tharon that prudence dictated he leave at least two hundred warriors to guard Cahokia. But eight hundred battle-hardened warriors against a hundred corn farmers? How could Badgertail convince his warriors to go through with it? Locust was right. Once they understood the brutality of the order, only a few of them would like it. He would have to figure something out, maybe split his forces into small groups and take only the most "hearty" warriors to Redweed with him.

Soft voices rose outside. Locust called, "I've brought Priestess Nightshade, Leader Badgertail."

Badgertail nervously straightened his tan-and-black kilt. His shell-heavy forelocks swung with his movements. "Enter."

Nightshade ducked through the door-hanging. Beautiful long black hair spilled around her shoulders; her red dress was belted with a delicate cord woven of milkweed threads. It highlighted the narrowness of her waist and the fullness of her breasts. A shell gorget engraved with a human hand draped her neck.

"Please, sit down."

Nightshade kept standing, rigid, vigilant.

Locust leaned through the doorway. "Will you need me for anything else?"

"No, thank you, Locust. I'll escort the priestess back to the temple. Go home and get some rest. You'll be needing it."

"Yes, cousin. I'll see you tomorrow. Good night." She vanished like smoke in the wind.

When Badgertail turned, he found Nightshade staring at him intently. What was it about those eyes? So black and unforgiving, they made a man feel as though he had been castrated with a dull chert flake. And yet so magnetic; it was like looking into the eyes of a coiled rattlesnake.

"Could I get you something to drink?"

"You could. Thank you."

"I have a wonderful tea . . . and, of course, white drink."

"Tea would be fine."

He knelt on the hides and poured two conch-shell cups while he surreptitiously watched Nightshade wander his house. She scrutinized the shields, touching the painted designs with the intimacy of a mother tending a hurt child. Did they speak to her? Could she discover their bloody history just by laying a hand on them?

"Why don't you sit down, Nightshade?"

"I don't plan on being here long."

"Please stay long enough to finish a cup of tea."

She came across the room like Weasel stalking Mouse, unnaturally quiet, fluid. Her red dress spread in a circle around her when she sat down opposite him. Through the doorway behind her, sparkflies danced against the pearlescent background of night.

He handed her a cup, noticing how quickly she took it. Their fingers brushed for less than a blink of time. *Trying not to touch me. Am I so tainted?*

Badgertail sank back, bringing his cup carefully to his mouth to sip. The wintergreen tasted rich and sweet. "Nightshade, I wanted to talk to you to—"

"Tell me about Orenda."

"Orenda?" He gestured aimlessly. "There's not much to tell. As you've noticed, she's a bizarre child. I don't think she's left the temple in four or five cycles. She never plays with . . . with anyone, children or adults. She just skulks around the temple."

"Is she Spirit-touched?"

"No, no. I don't think so. Although—"

"Have you ever heard her speak to anyone but Tharon?"

"To Singw, when she was alive. I even saw her whisper to Old Marmot once."

"How long ago?"

Badgertail drank leisurely while he thought about the implications of Nightshade's questions. Why was she so curious about Orenda? The child had never been more than a trace of mist at Cahokia, less visible than that, if the truth be known. Badgertail remembered being startled several times by coming upon Orenda hiding in the temple, usually crying—startled, because he had forgotten she existed. "I saw her speak to Old Marmot for the first time just a few days before his death. Why do you care?"

"She's been hurt, Badgertail. By Tharon, I'm almost certain." Nightshade lifted her eyes to gaze at the wall behind him.

Uneasily, he turned to examine the space himself. The square of moonlight that penetrated the doorway had transformed her shadow, changing it into an amorphous creature, dark, huge. Badgertail suppressed a shudder, worried that it might not be a shadow after all, but her Spirit Helper, Mudhead. He had listened many times to Old Marmot whisper about the enormous demon with the twisted face who followed Nightshade everywhere. Old Marmot, the great and powerful priest, had feared that Helper as though his own soul were in jeopardy any time it appeared.

Nightshade said, "So, Badgertail, you called me here to ask me about Petaga's war plans."

"I'm not asking you to betray him, Nightshade."

"No? What are you asking?"

Badgertail met her stern gaze and noticed for the first time the puffiness of fatigue that encircled her eyes. Had she been walking the floor at night worrying, as he had? "Tell me how to stop the killing. Can you? Do you know how I can save the chiefdom without . . . without doing what Tharon has ordered me to?"

"No."

He paused. "You don't know—or you won't tell me?"

"I don't know."

Badgertail frowned into his tea. "How can you not know? I mean, I don't understand very much about Dreaming, but I thought—"

"You thought right. I should have been able to dive through the Well of the Ancestors and walk the path in the Underworld to ask First Woman."

"And you haven't?"

"No."

"Can I ask why not?"

She ran a hand through the wealth of her black hair. "Apparently First Woman has closed the Underworld . . . out of anger."

"At us?"

"Yes. For destroying the land. And in punishment for something that Tharon has done. I wish I knew more, but I don't."

Nightshade shifted sideways to bring up her knees so she could prop her cup on them. Moonlight fell over her face, silvering each curve, highlighting the shadows of her cheeks and nostrils. She seemed frail and half-afraid. Her face touched something deep inside him, some illogical need to hold and pet her.

"Nightshade," he said, "if *you* can't get in, who can?"

"A woman whom Wanderer is teaching. I don't know her name, but she's Powerful. More Powerful than I am."

"I didn't know there was anyone more Powerful than you."

She fumbled insecurely with her cup, as though his words had wounded her. He couldn't imagine how. Bulrush? Had he said something that reminded her of Bulrush? Or perhaps it was just being alone with a man for the first time since her lover's death.

"And that's why you want me to bring Wanderer here? So we can find out who this woman is?"

Nightshade nodded. "Yes. She's the vital link."

"To what?"

"To stopping this war."

Badgertail exhaled in relief. "That's all I needed to know from you, Nightshade. Thank you for telling me. I'll bring Wanderer here as soon as I find him . . . and I'll guard him with my very life."

Nightshade took a long drink of her tea, and Badgertail expected her to set her cup down and leave. But she didn't. Instead, she pointed to the falcon pot. "May I have more tea?"

"Of course," he said in surprise and refilled her cup, then poured his full again, too.

She smiled, and the softness of it built a warmth under Badgertail's heart. He noticed that her breathing had gone shallow. The red fabric over her breasts rose and fell swiftly.

"I also didn't know that you feared anyone," he said softly. "Least of all, me."

"*If* I feared anyone, it ought to be you, my kidnapper."

Badgertail looked down at the scars on his wrists. "I didn't do it out of malice, Nightshade. Old Marmot had Dreamed that you and the Tortoise Bundle could bring Mother Earth back to life."

"He didn't understand the problem here."

"You mean that his Dream was wrong?"

She set her cup on the floor, where it cast a long shadow. "Not wrong, just . . . incomplete. He didn't see far enough, or he would have known that I wasn't the one he needed. And he would have seen that your people—"

"You still don't consider us your people, after all these cycles?"

Her brow furrowed, as if the question upset her. She picked up her cup again and took four long sips to drain it, then set it back on the platter. "You will never be my people, Badgertail. You've forgotten First Woman's Dream. 'Find a new way,' she said, or we'd all be dead. 'Learn the grass, the root, and the berry.' Your people abused her Dream. You decided it was all right to take and take."

Wearily, she braced a hand against the hides and stood up. "Thank you for the tea, War Leader." She turned to the doorway.

Badgertail stumbled over the platter as he rose and lunged for her hand. "Nightshade, please . . ." They stood toe to toe, staring at each other. She glanced down at his hand, holding hers in a hard grip, then scanned his face, waiting. "If you Dream anything . . . could you . . . I'm not asking that you help me, but there are people out there, many of them children, who don't deserve what's coming."

Desperation taunted him. He needed her help—but she would never help him. His gaze traced the smooth line of her jaw, remembering how she had looked as a child: terrified, clinging to his warshirt for entire days and nights while they skulked through the swamps to find the Black Warrior River. He had never meant to hurt her. He had only been trying to save his people. Impulsively, Badgertail gently caressed a lock of Nightshade's hair. She had grown into such a beautiful woman . . .

Nightshade shivered, as though cold. Instinctively, he lifted an arm, then hesitated to slip it around her shoulders, letting it hover awkwardly. For several agonizing moments, she held his gaze. Then her eyes changed, going soft and more vulnerable than he had ever seen them. She took a step forward and eased into his arms.

"Just hold me," she said.

He pulled her close. The scent of her hair and the feel of her breasts against his chest left him off balance. How long had it been since he had held a woman? Twenty cycles? Yes—Two Tassels. But it hadn't been like this. Holding Nightshade comforted him deep down, like a warm blanket on a cold winter night. He brushed his chin over her hair, and for a timeless moment let himself drown in the feel of her body against his. Why had she asked him for this? Was she as lonely as he was? As worried about tomorrow?

Slowly, fearful of her response, he leaned down and kissed her. The touch of her lips against his sent a fiery wash through his veins.

Nightshade pulled back. Her eyes searched his face. "Bulrush still lives in my soul, Badgertail. But . . . I thank you."

He straightened. "Let me walk you back to the temple."

"It's not necessary."

"But I think it wise. The village is confused. Tempers are running wild—if you'll recall the reaction upon your arrival. You might need me."

She inclined her head. "Thank you."

Badgertail walked at her side, parting the net of sparkflies that glittered above the grass. Tomorrow he would have to sit down with Tharon and Black Birch and lay out his final plan for annihilating Petaga's army. If he could just get to the chiefs of the northern villages, especially the larger ones such as Bladdernut and Henfoot, he might be able to end this before it boiled into full-scale warfare. Perhaps he could even talk sense into White Clover Mounds; they had at least four hundred warriors. Petaga would never bargain as long as he had superior numbers, but if Badgertail could equal the odds, he might.

Badgertail found himself watching Nightshade's hair flutter in the wind. And something soothed in his troubled soul.

In a hidden valley to the north, nine hundred warriors camped, their robes thrown on the soft grass. The pungent scents of sweating bodies and human wastes pricked the breeze, wafting up to the guards who stood on the bluff, silhouetted against the moonlight.

Petaga clapped his hands as he peered over the crackling camp fire at Hailcloud. Moon Maiden's glow illuminated the war leader's face, shadowing his eyes and mouth. "That's three hundred more, Hailcloud! With Red Star on our side, that makes twelve hundred. We can do it. *We can beat Badgertail!"*

Hailcloud's brows drew down over his slender nose. "I pray that you are right, my Chief."

Petaga's joy died at the apprehension in that voice. "You don't think so?"

"Maybe. If we can keep our warriors together. They come from so many different clans." He gestured weakly. "I don't know. It will be a trial. We still must recruit more warriors and gather supplies quickly, praying that we haven't lost the element of surprise. And I think we have."

"Why?"

"Too many people escaped our attack on Spiral Mounds. Any one of them could have fled to Cahokia. I fear, my Chief, that Badgertail has already started assembling his warriors."

Petaga lowered his eyes and squinted at the wavering flames. The orange light drenched the brush around them like thick amber resin. "What will Badgertail's strategy be? Can you guess?"

Hailcloud lifted a burly shoulder. "Were I him? I would make a play for all the unaligned chiefs. Every small village we haven't approached yet, and those that have refused to join us—they'd be my target. I would tell them that the chiefdom was at stake and that they had to choose sides."

"And if they refuse? As most did our offer."

Hailcloud propped a fist on his knee. "He's *Badgertail*. The small villages will go rigid with terror the moment they see him coming." He fixed Petaga with stony black eyes. "They'll either flee instantly or want to please him."

"But if he surrounds them with a full force of a thousand, how can they flee?"

Hailcloud's fist tightened. "I don't . . . I'm not sure, but I don't think Badgertail will approach it that way. If he really does want them on his side—and he does—he'll send less-threatening emissaries. It would be more like him to split his forces into smaller groups. That way, he can discern very quickly which villages are friends and which are foes."

Petaga exhaled wearily. "Then we must stop him."

"Yes . . . if we can. He'll make it easier for us if he does split his forces."

"How do you mean?"

"Small war parties are easier to confuse than large ones. If we use quick hit-and-run tactics . . . well, I'll have to think about it more. But the first thing we must do is to cut off his lines of communication."

"So we'll need to station lookouts on every possible trail, you mean?"

Hailcloud nodded. "And in groups of three or four . . . just in case Badgertail decides to send guards with his runners."

Petaga stared out into the cool darkness where the sparkflies twinkled. The distant muttering of wind in the valley below sounded ominous, like demons whispering secrets to each other. His father's smile, knowing, reassuring, lurked bittersweet in the back of his memory. He heard Jenos' words: "No one can lead without risk, boy. The difference between a great leader and a fool is knowing when to act and when not to."

But how do I know, Father?

Jenos' gentle eyes had gone sad, shrinking blackly into hollow orbits from a sun-bleached skull that stared out over an empty land. Tattered strips of desiccated flesh clung to the bone here and there. They quivered and trembled in a hot breeze that gurgled like his mother's throat had on the day Hailcloud strangled her.

Petaga rubbed his brow, dropping his hand to his temples to mask his troubled eyes. "Let's get the lookout parties organized first thing tomorrow, Hailcloud. If what you say is true, Badgertail will be on the move soon."

"As you wish, my Chief."

"Is there a way out, Hailcloud? Or was Aloda right? Are we all trapped in the end?"

Hailcloud filled his lungs and exhaled, a vacant smile on his lips. "I am only a warrior, my Chief."

Petaga nodded. A warrior always had a way out . . . in the end. The acrid smoke of Spiral Mounds—so many days behind them—still burned in Petaga's nose. Would he ever be free of that stench?

Nineteen

Lichen blinked herself awake in the warmth of her blankets. A cool breeze meandered through the window and sniffed at the colorful baskets along the back wall. The Power symbols, particularly the black crescent moons, observed it with a detached bemusement, as though intrigued by the curious habits of Wind Mother.

Outside, Hanged Woman shone dimly above the cloud-puffed horizon. Lichen stretched while she stared at the eight twinkling points of light sewn on the lilac canvas of predawn.

Wanderer's bed lay empty. Where could he be? Lichen studied the shadows that flowed into the folds of his tumbled blankets, then rose and slipped on her dress and sandals.

She took the trail that wound over the top of the rock shelter, considering all the places Wanderer might have gone. The waking sun sent shafts of light to pierce the drifting clouds. Far down on the western horizon where Hanged Woman's feet had disappeared, the irregular skyline of the bluffs glimmered purplish. Shadows lengthened in the floodplain below, blurring the bristly outlines of goosefoot and starwort.

Lichen yawned as she walked. The fragrance of blossoming gayfeather clung to the air. Delicate stems heavy with purple flowers survived undaunted along the sun-blasted knoll tops. Lichen wished she had brought along a digging stick. She could have pried out two of the long roots and roasted them over a fire for breakfast. This early in the spring, gayfeather had a sweet, earthy flavor, but in another moon, it would have gone pithy and unpalatable.

She squinted at the trail. Moccasin prints dimpled the sand. Lichen called, "Wanderer?"

Caws punctured the morning stillness, and Lichen tipped her face to watch the ravens. They flirted with the ragged edge of the bluff, diving close, hovering on the updrafts, then canting their wings to soar away.

She cupped a hand to her mouth and yelled, "Crossed Beak, is that you?"

One of the ravens swooped over her head, and she could tell that it was indeed Crossed Beak. He *thocked* at her.

"Where's Wanderer? Have you seen him?"

The voice that eased up over the edge of the precipice made her jump. "I'm over here."

Lichen trotted forward and peered out into near nothingness. The limestone dropped away in a cliff that plunged to the ground two hundred hands below. Six hands down, Wanderer sat cross-legged on a narrow ledge that perched over thin air. He had wrapped a red-and-brown blanket around his shoulders to fend off dawn's chill.

"That looks pretty scary, Wanderer."

"Does it? I hadn't noticed," he responded cheerfully.

"What are you doing out there?"

He extended a hand to her as he slid over a few feet. "Come down and I'll tell you."

Lichen put her fingers in his and let him support her weight while she scrambled over the gritty edge of the bluff to sit beside him. She scooted as far back as she could, making certain she had solid rock behind her before she relaxed. The three ravens glided down to float on the ocean of air before them.

"This is a Power place," Wanderer explained. "I come here a lot to think about Earthmaker, the Spiral, and the One." He grinned and untucked his blanket to wrap it around her shoulders. She snuggled against him, glad for his warmth. He'd worn his tattered wolf-hide robe, painted with the red tortoise and the green spirals. It smelled of wood smoke and odd spices.

"What are those things? I mean, I know who Earthmaker is. I've heard stories about him all my life. About how he made the world covered with water and told Tortoise to dive down and pull up dirt"—she illustrated Tortoise's journey with a plunging hand—"so that he could mold land and people. But what are the Spiral and the One?"

Wanderer's wrinkles rearranged into sober lines. "What are they? Why, they're everything."

"The Spiral is everything?"

"Yes." He waved a hand at the blue-shadowed valley below. "The Spiral is all that is."

"And what's the One?"

"All that is . . . and is not."

Lichen tucked the edge of the blanket around her chilly toes. "That doesn't make any sense, Wanderer. All that *is not* isn't anything at all."

"Good thinking! Tell me, what else comes to your mind?" He shifted to peer at her.

"Well, if the One isn't anything, what is it?"

"Nothing."

Lichen grimaced, and Wanderer's face lit as though he anticipated great thoughts from her. "Nothing can't exist, Wanderer. I mean . . . it's nothing."

"Exactly! That's why the One is the heartbeat of the Spiral. If it was *something*, it couldn't be the basis for everything. It can be the basis for everything only if it isn't anything at all."

Lichen opened her mouth, then closed it and shook her head. "Wanderer, that's silly."

A lopsided grin split his face. For several moments he squinted out at the strengthening glow of Father Sun. He chuckled softly, then smiled, then chuckled again while he watched the veil of translucent amber creep higher and higher into the lavender belly of the sky. Rays from the unborn sun tinted the basin, painting the silhouettes of rocks and bushes with an opalescent fringe of fire.

"You know, Lichen," Wanderer said at last, "there are Dreamers who believe that all of the Spiral is illusion."

"You mean they think the world is illusion?" She snorted her disgust. "Do you believe that?"

Wanderer leaned close and whispered, "Lichen, do you really want to get to the Cave of First Woman?"

"Yes," she answered fervently. "I have to."

Wanderer's eyes twinkled. "What if I told you that no matter what I teach you, no matter how hard you try, all the knowledge and skill in the world won't be enough to take you there?"

Lichen frowned. "I don't understand, Wanderer. Isn't that why you're teaching me? So I'll learn how to Dream better? Isn't that what trapping Father Sun and hunting First Woman's tree was all about?"

"No, Lichen. I was trying to teach you that you have to let go of the idea of *you*."

"If I let go of *me*, how can *I* become a Dreamer?"

Leaning back against the limestone, Wanderer laced his fingers around one knee and watched the splinter of sun peek over the horizon. A glorious flood of yellow drenched the land. Plants cast off their shadows and stood naked in the splendor, their arms lifted high to receive Father Sun's morning blessing. The ravens soared and dove in delight.

"Poor Lichen," he said as though speaking to someone who wasn't there. "She thinks she can Dream her way to the Cave." He grinned wryly at her. "Don't you?"

"Sure. I thought that's why I was here."

"No. *You* will never find it. There are no tricks or methods for getting there. When you learn that everything you want, everything you crave and believe, is just sparkflies flitting through the darkness— then you'll find First Woman's Cave."

"Sparkflies?"

"Yes," he chuckled. "Knowledge and skill are nothing more than sparkflies darting through the evening sky with Bat in hot pursuit. They lead Bat a merry chase, don't they?"

Lichen nodded. "So what?"

"When Bat catches them, what happens?"

"He gets to eat, which keeps him from dying."

"Yes," Wanderer said sadly. "Bat spends a great deal of time chasing sparkflies so he won't die. And if he would just let himself die, why, he'd find out that he didn't need those glittering flies at all."

"Of course not!" Lichen blurted in irritation. "He wouldn't need sparkflies, because he'd be dead."

Wanderer grinned. "You don't follow this at all, do you, Lichen? Oh, well . . ."

He hopped to his feet and began scrambling back up over the edge of the bluff. His moccasins sent a shower of sand over Lichen's head. "And you did so well in the Underworld! But never mind, you'll understand the One eventually. That is, either you will or you won't. And if I'm any good at all to you, you'll . . ."

His voice faded as he strode across the bluff in that ungainly, long-limbed walk, his tattered sleeves swirling about him.

The flock of ravens flapped to glide around his head, cawing as though giving advice. Wanderer yelled back at them, waving his arms for emphasis while he strode headlong back toward his house.

"Wait! Wanderer?"

Lichen tied the blanket around her waist and warily eased up from the limestone lip, sliding her back against reliable rock until she could dig her fingers into a crevice and brace her feet. By the time she managed to clamber up onto the crest, Wanderer was no longer in sight.

Green Ash ducked and waddled through her doorway before she inhaled a breath of the heavy night air. The pain in her womb throbbed with each step she took, leaving her weak and trembling. The odor of smudge pots wafted on the breeze coming up from the river. Dogs barked and yipped somewhere. A baby crying, voices of a man and woman having a loud argument, and frogs croaking could be heard. Other than that, the houses of the Commonborn had gone ominously quiet. She let her eyes adjust to the night. Fires gleamed like strewn drops of honey, reflecting from the thatched houses and somber faces of people cooking dinner. But no laughter carried on the cool evening wind. This night, no one dared breathe. Today Badgertail had left with over eight hundred warriors, and then the traders had rushed in, brimming with terrible news of Petaga.

More war. How can we bear it?

Green Ash carried her plate of corn cakes across the hard-packed ground toward the elders sitting outside of Checkerberry's house. A pile of corncobs lay stacked near the central fire. The cobs burned hot and fast, but wood was too precious to use for a simple warming. The people in the outlying villages could still scavenge oak, hickory, and dogwood, but it was a full day's walk for people here.

Green Ash eyed the powerful women around the fire warily. They'd come to talk of the future, to decide what the clans should do. Tharon might be the Sun Chief, but these women held the ultimate fate of Cahokia in their hands. The decisions they made on this night would determine the course of the future.

The four clans controlled all of the fields within walking distance of Cahokia. They farmed them, gave half of their crops to the Sun Chief to keep the chiefdom going, and stockpiled the rest to feed their lineage, or to trade for needed goods. In the past five cycles, the stockpiles had been pathetically small. By the Deep-Snow-Moon, no one had been above begging the Sun Chief for a bowl of corn. Discontent had been growing.

Sandbar, from the Squash Blossom Clan, sat next to Redhaw, from the Deer Bone Rattle Clan; and Tickseed, leader of the Horn Spoon Clan, hunched beside Checkerberry, maternal elder of the Blue Blanket Clan. Each had a prunish face and almost no teeth left in her head. Old, so old. Their heads glimmered with a frosty sheen in the firelight. Behind them, a ring of men and women sat quietly, waiting in the hope of being able to express their views.

Green Ash stepped over a dog sprawled at the outer edge of the circle and hurried to set the plate of corn cakes in front of Checkerberry. Then she backed away to sit down between Nettle and Primrose, each of whom wore a dark expression. Nettle opened the tan-and-red blanket over his shoulders to enfold Green Ash in the warmth. Snuggling against him, she whispered, "Have they started yet?"

"No. They're just vying for position—boasting of how many children have been born to their clans this cycle, of how many marriages are in the offing."

"What has Checkerberry said?"

He glanced at her. "Nothing."

"What? Doesn't she realize that if we don't present a strong face, we'll be dragged into this like a rabbit to slaughter? I can't understand—"

Primrose bent sideways. Softly, he said, "Checkerberry has been staring at nothing ever since Redhaw arrived."

"But I—"

Green Ash hushed when Redhaw pulled herself up straight. Redhaw wore a beautiful deerhide dress covered with shiny beads of galena—a sign of wealth and status. Green Ash thought of how much food Redhaw could have purchased for her clan last year if she had sold that dress. She could have fed fifty for another moon. Only one tooth remained in Redhaw's mouth, hanging in the front like a rotting fang.

She waved an arm authoritatively. "Deer Bone Rattle Clan has six new husbands coming from Yellow Star Mounds. They're bringing lace and thousands of seashells with them as dowry. We'll be able to trade far to the south and east next cycle."

"So?" Tickseed snorted disdainfully as she lifted her flabby chin. Her gray hair had grown so sparse that it looked as wispy as a spiderweb spun about her round skull. The firelight reflected with snowy radiance in her blind eyes. "What good are such things when the trade routes are cut off? Eh? You heard what the traders said today—that Petaga has cut off our trade routes!" Over the murmurs of outrage, Tickseed shouted, "There will be no more hickory oil from the east. No more sacred red cedar will be rafted down the river from the north. Where will we get maple sap? Not to mention all the baubles like pink stone for our pipes, or seashell for our bead workers!" She rocked forward, pinioning Redhaw with her white-filmed eyes. "*You* won't be able to trade at all, unless we take some action here!"

A hollow pit of cold grew in Green Ash's belly. She shuddered. Nettle hugged her more tightly, whispering, "Wait. She may not mean what it sounds like."

Green Ash nodded, but she knew Tickseed better than he did. Green Ash had served as Checkerberry's messenger to the other clans for five cycles. Tickseed rarely attempted misdirection. It might take her a little time to lead up to what she wanted to say, but her words were always straight.

Sandbar's eyes narrowed over the broad lump of her nose. "What are you suggesting, Tickseed?"

"All of us know what the Sun Chief did to our sister villages this winter. We—"

"He retrieved the tribute that was owed Cahokia!" Redhaw shrilled in a voice like sand against stone. "That corn was ours!"

The dog that had been sleeping at the edge of the circle yipped and sprang to its feet in alarm. Primrose waved a hand to it, calling it over. The dog sniffed the air with a dusty nose, checking for danger, before wagging its tail and trotting over to flop down on the spreading hem of Primrose's tan skirt.

Sandbar shook her head. On the eastern horizon, Moon Maiden timidly peeked over the bluffs. A milky flood tarnished the land, shadowing every house and mound in the village. "It doesn't matter whose corn it was. Our sister villages needed it to survive. We took it from the mouths of their children to feed ours. We—"

"Mother Earth is dying," Checkerberry muttered. She fumbled with a stick, trying to draw spirals around her extended foot. In the warm, amber glow, her unblinking eyes shone with madness.

Gazes darted around the gathering before falling to stare at nothing. The words echoed everyone's darkest fears. What had happened to the priests and priestesses who rode the waves of the Underworld? Rumors had rushed like wildfire through the village that none of the Starborn could get into the Underworld now—that First Woman had closed the Gate to the Well of the Ancestors.

Blessed Star Ogres, what will we do if it's true? If the gods have abandoned us, how can we possibly survive?

Redhaw wet her withered lips nervously. "I don't think Petaga can keep the trade routes closed," she began, trying to change the subject. "Badgertail will slice his army—"

Checkerberry cut her short. "It's Nightshade! She's a witch. She's cursed us! She's always hated us—ever since Badgertail stole her from her home when she was a child. She's killing us!"

Frightened cries and shouts broke out. People wanted someone to blame for their misfortune, and Nightshade's reputation blew like a black wind through their souls.

Redhaw thrust up her hands. "Stop. Stop it! We don't know this. If it were true, why has the Sun Chief not already killed her? It makes no sense!"

Checkerberry hunched forward. The fire that had briefly lit her eyes dwindled to nothingness. "Still," she whispered, "it's Nightshade. She's killing us. Wait. You'll see."

A difficult swallow slid down Sandbar's throat. Fumbling with the hem of her green dress, she said quietly, "Tickseed, earlier you sounded as though you wanted us to choose sides in the upcoming battle. Do you?"

Tickseed lifted a narrow shoulder. "Want has nothing to do with it. Sooner or later, we'll be forced to. You've seen how the corn grows. Everyone knows it will be stunted again this cycle."

Redhaw said, "Maybe, yes, but what—"

"Just this! If Badgertail wins, next season will be worse than last. No one will want to give tribute. We'll have to kill to the last child to take the stockpiles we need to survive." Tickseed pointed a crooked finger at Redhaw's heart. "If Petaga wins, the system will be changed. You heard the traders talk! Petaga is saying that each village should handle its own affairs, that we should reorganize so that every village looks after itself. If we don't want to trade south, we can save our goods and use them for other things—things we want—not things the Sun Chief thinks are good for the chiefdom!"

Redhaw shook her head violently, while Sandbar's wrinkled mouth pursed. Checkerberry didn't even seem to have heard the argument; she gazed fixedly at the toe of her sandal.

Green Ash's heart went out to her aunt. It wasn't Checkerberry's fault. Her soul seemed to hover half in her body and half out, as though it thirsted to leave, to travel down the Dark River and find her family again. It made Green Ash frantic. She loved her aunt, but she didn't know what to do to ease Checkerberry's distress. *And I'm not sure she's wrong. Perhaps Nightshade is to blame for some of our problems. Not all, but . . .*

"So you want to join Petaga?" Redhaw asked, glaring at Tickseed.

"It will have to be a unanimous decision by the clans," Tickseed replied cautiously. "Tharon will have to accept anything we decide here tonight—as long as we all agree to the same decision. What warrior—even Badgertail—will leave on a battle-walk if his clan tells him not to? Where will Tharon find men and women willing to empty our storage buildings if we tell our people not to? Nowhere! That's where. Our people owe their kin before they owe the Sunborn."

"That's true," Sandbar muttered, waving a withered hand. "We know our power here. Go on with what you were going to say."

Tickseed steepled her fingers, choosing her words carefully. "I think we should consider all of the alternatives. The Sun Chief did not consult us last cycle before he decided to attack our sister villages—where we have *kin*! Remember, elders? For generations, we've been marrying our men off to those very villages! Now we're killing them! Yes, think back to the old days . . . to the great and wise Keran. Keran would have asked us before he even thought about ordering an attack. Gizis would have talked it over with us after he'd thought about it. Today our men—our sons—are dead from arrows made at Cahokia." Tickseed paused. "I think we've seen the beginning of something unbearable."

Sandbar fingered her lumpy nose in thought. "Yes. I think Tickseed is right. We should watch and consider. Let us wait to see what happens between Badgertail and Petaga. Then, if—"

"*Traitors!*" Redhaw snarled. She stood up on tottering legs. The galena beads on her dress shimmered in the firelight as she lifted a fist high over her head. "The Deer Bone Rattle Clan will be no part of plotting against the Sun Chief! I have spoken!"

She tramped away into the night, the six delegates of her clan following behind.

"Wait!" Primrose shouted as he leaped to his feet to run after them. "Wait, please! No one here is suggesting treason. Come back! Redhaw!"

Green Ash stole a glance at Nettle. He had closed his eyes in agony.

Twenty

Wanderer stretched out on his side and gazed across the room at Lichen. He had been deliberately waking himself every few fingers of time to make certain that she was all right. When she had first crawled under her blankets, she'd been afraid that the monsters of the Underworld might rise up from the darkness and capture her soul.

Hot wind seeped through the window, rocking and spinning the eagle-feather prayer fans Wanderer had hung with such care over her bed. Lichen lay curled securely beneath them, her body illuminated in a shaft of starlight.

The Power symbols on the walls observed in silence, pensive, uncertain about Lichen now. She had gone far beyond their expectations. Wanderer could sense the awe of the Spirals, and he knew how they felt.

The starlight had tipped Lichen's long lashes in silver and flowed into the twists of braid that fell over her bare shoulder.

Oh, how he loved that child. He had always wondered what it would be like to be her father, not just her friend. But he'd never conceived of this joy. Every time she gave him one of those wry, reproachful looks that said, *Wanderer, you're not serious, are you?* his soul soared. When her brows drew together and she listened to him as breathlessly as if he knew more than Earthmaker—well, Wanderer didn't know what to do. It left an uncomfortable tickle at the base of his throat. How did parents handle that? Such unwavering trust made him feel as though he carried a frail pot in his trembling hands, a vessel that he dare not break. Lichen demanded more of Wanderer's soul than he'd ever had to give to anyone or anything . . . except to Power.

It frightened him.

The call of Power eddied at the edges of his soul, reminding him that he had been neglecting his own Dreaming.

I haven't forgotten you. It's just that she needs me more right now.

Great Deer's hooves twinkled through the window. The Ogre perched upside down on his nose, his feet in thin air. Wanderer smiled. How did the Ogres do that—tilt themselves into such awkward positions? He would have to see if he could manage it sometime. His thoughts drifted, contemplating all of the rocky places where he might be able to string the necessary ropes.

Wolves howled faintly in the distance. Twelve of them had roamed around the rock shelter all day, spying on Lichen and himself from behind rocks or brush. Every time he had told a story, they'd pricked their ears. Odd. He had never seen so many so unafraid.

Wanderer slipped his arm under his head, floating on the memory of those burning yellow eyes. They had been trying to tell him something. What was it? He let himself drift, thinking about it. Tension trickled from his body, leaving him feeling as light as a hovering milkweed seed. Into that peace a Dream swelled with the rumbling Power of Thunderbird's roar . . .

Snow blasted Wanderer, shoving him sideways into an outcrop of boulders sheathed in ice. He fought to gain a handhold, but as he clawed at the transparent surface, his feet slipped. He tumbled down the slope, over and over, head over heels. When he saw the towering snowdrift loom up before him, he raised his arms to protect his head. Flakes gushed around him as he struck it.

Wanderer lowered his arms slowly. Glittering apparitions of ice spread for as far as he could see. To the west, plains collided with indigo peaks so jagged and lofty that they lanced the bellies of the Star Ogres. But . . . the Ogres looked different. Their shapes had changed. Wolf Pup's leg stuck out more. Hanged Woman's neck bent almost double.

"Where am I?" he cried in fear.

Blood oozed from a gash in his arm, soaking his worn cottonwood-bark shirt. Under the brilliant bands of light that wavered in the heavens, the drops of his blood shone like black tears.

The wind seized his plea and blew it out across a wasteland of glacial hills.

Wanderer's toes had gone numb. He had to find shelter or he would freeze to death. His steps squealing on snow, he dodged out of the protection of the drift to get a better look at the terrain.

Southward, stringers of foam rode the fins of waves on a vast, churning sea. The lights battling in the sky cast an opalescent sheen across the dark surface.

"Hello! . . . Anybody? Where am I?"

"In the land of the Long Dark, Dreamer."

The sky flared, exploding in silent bursts of purple, green, and azure. Wind Mother held her breath in awe. Stillness. The colors hung like splashes of paint. Then, as though warmed by Wolf Pup's breath, they trickled through the glistening net of stars and fused into a rainbow that arched across the bosom of the night.

"Come, Dreamer, we must talk, you and I."

The gentle voice reverberated from the snowdrifts. On the crest of the rainbow, a tall youth stood. Wanderer stared up in awe. "Who are you? What do you want?"

"Power has need of your strength. Come. Climb to me. Talk to me. Lichen may be a great Dreamer, but she will need your help."

"How?" The word lodged suffocatingly in Wanderer's throat. He gazed up at that glowing figure. "How can I help her?"

"Teach her that to step onto the Path, she must leave it. Only the lost come to stand alone before the entrance to the Cave, and only the defenseless step over its threshold. She is young. Surrender does not come naturally to one so full of life. Teach her that in Union she will find the light, though it appears as darkness, nakedness, nothingness."

"Who *are* you?"

"Your people know me as Wolf Slayer. My people called me Wolf Dreamer. I Dance with Power."

"Wolf Slayer?" his voice quaked. "Are you the Spirit who spoke to Lichen in the Underworld?"

"Yes. Hurry . . . hurry . . ."

Wanderer forced his wobbly legs to carry him to the edge of the rainbow, where he sank his fingers into the bands of light and hoisted himself onto the arch. A thrill filled him as he ran up the center. By the time he reached the crest where the youth waited, he was panting. Glorious colors curled up around him with translucent splendor.

Wolf Slayer's body radiated a golden light, as if Father Sun lived inside him. Black eyes stared out from either side of his straight nose. The grief and concern in those eyes rent Wanderer's soul. Wolf Slayer's smile turned wistful.

"Do you hear them, Dreamer? Listen."

Faint screams crept up from every sparkle in the rainbow. Agony clutched at Wanderer, a pain so overwhelming that he crumpled to his knees and dug his fingers into the red-and-purple bands.

The colors swirled and twined, solidifying into war. Sparkflies glittered in the air, seemingly unaware of the tattooed warriors who raced through a plaza with their chert-studded war clubs raised. And the fires! Flames vaulted from house to house before catching in the bone-dry grass. The fire swelled to a brilliant orange wall as it consumed the underbrush and swept into the parched cornfields like a raging beast.

Wanderer felt himself descending, being pulled into the midst of the battle. Women and children lunged out of their blazing homes and into the haze of smoke that billowed into the starry sky. The pungent odor of fear-sweat sickened Wanderer. Shrieks and shouts tore the air as people rushed around him, their terrified faces bleached by the flames engulfing the night.

"Where is this, Wolf Slayer?"

"You don't recognize it?"

"No, I—" Another thatched house ignited, and Wanderer glimpsed the looming shape of a mound. "Cahokia?"

"Yes. The time is short. Prepare yourself, Dreamer. When Gizis' father, old Keran, decided that his people could pillage the land, he tipped the Spiral out of balance. But when Tharon broke one of the people's most sacred taboos, the Spiral flipped. And now war has sprung from the drought and famine. First Woman has turned her head. She believes humans deserve to tread the path of Mammoth and Saber-Tooth Cat. She has spun such a veil of illusion around the entrance to the Cave that no Dreamer has been able to pass to talk to her.

"Badgertail left today. Petaga will be waiting for him. Beware. Mother Earth's hold on life in this land is frail, and growing more so the longer First Woman bars the entry to the Cave. If Lichen cannot enter the Cave, First Woman's wrath will sweep humans from this land like bits of goosedown in the wind."

Wanderer gasped when red Spirals burst from Wolf Slayer's chest to unwind into arms and legs. The tall youth vanished, and a huge red spider rose on those spindly limbs. It loomed over Wanderer, leaning close to peer into his eyes. Wanderer fell to his knees. "I'll help you! I promise. Just tell me what to do! Don't hurt me!"

"Watch . . . see the future that will come if Lichen cannot enter the Cave."

The spider turned and raced up the rainbow, then leaped into the frosty, twinkling heart of Wolf Pup.

"Wait. Wait!" Wanderer shouted, startled. "Don't leave me! Wolf Slayer? Come back! How much time do I have left to teach Lichen? How much time remains?"

Wanderer glanced in fear at the battle raging around him. The wild flames silhouetted a crowd of people rushing up from the bottom of Cahokia Creek . . . and he recognized Nightshade. Her expression could have been molded from white clay. Hard, unforgiving. But if the shrieking warriors frightened her, Wanderer could not see it. When she reached the palisades, she ran around to the gate, her long hair streaming out behind her.

A horde of enemy warriors flooded over the top of the palisade. When they saw Nightshade, they whooped and pursued her. One shouted, "It's her! The traitor. Kill her quickly!" The lead warrior dove and tackled Nightshade, knocking her to the ground. A second warrior lifted his war club over her head. Nightshade screamed.

Wanderer cowered as an earthquake shook the rainbow. Glistening threads shot through the stars, crackling like lightning as they lanced across the sky. One bolt soared straight toward Wanderer's chest. Beady spider eyes grew larger and larger as the thread approached, until Wanderer could see the web spinning around him in rainbow shades, drawing so tight that he couldn't move . . .

He bolted upright in bed, screaming, "Wolf Slayer! No!" Cold sweat drenched his body. Outside, an owl hooted as it glided through the darkness that capped the bluff.

"Wanderer?" Lichen called.

He turned and saw her kneeling in bed, an eagle-feather fan clutched to her bare chest. Her braid draped over her shoulder, the tip touching her green-and-tan kilt. She gazed at him through wide eyes.

"Wanderer, are you all right?"

"Lichen, a . . . a *spider* is trying to take over my soul!"

"What? Just now?"

"Yes, it sent out a web to catch me."

Lichen bounded to her feet like Deer does when an arrow *thwoks* the tree at her back. Her feet thudded on the hard floor until she leaped into bed with him. With fumbling fingers, Wanderer pulled his blankets up around her chin, then snuggled close to her. *Oh, Nightshade . . . so much rests on my daughter. Am I good enough to teach her in time?* The Power symbols watched in stunned silence.

"It didn't have antlers, did it?" Lichen inquired in a small, anxious voice. "The spider, I mean. Did it have antlers?"

"No, just beady eyes."

She relaxed a little. "But it was a Dream? A Spirit Dream?"

"Yes."

"What was it about?" She flopped onto her back to listen better.

"War . . . mostly."

"You shouted 'Wolf Slayer!' when you woke up. Did he come to you?"

Wanderer smoothed his sweaty gray hair. "Yes. Yes, he did. But Lichen, let's sleep. I'll tell you about it tomorrow, when I take you home. Dreams have so many hidden meanings. Spiders and rainbows and warriors. I need time to think."

Lichen nodded and nuzzled more deeply into the shelter of his arms. "I guess it was pretty bad, huh?"

"Pretty bad."

Wanderer fiercely kissed her temple while his eyes drifted over the room, taking in the firepit, the prayer fans, and finally the rip in his sleeve. Blood. Through the hole, he could see the gash that tore his arm.

Tharon grabbed one of Orenda's dolls and brutally tore it in half before throwing the pieces across the room. Breathing hard, he began kicking the rest of her toys with all of his strength. Fragments of corn shuck and silk fluttered in the thin glow. Where was that big doll? He searched every shadowed nook. Gone. The little wretch had taken her favorite "companion" with her.

"You've asked for it," he rasped. "When I find you, Orenda, you'll wish you were dead with your despicable mother!"

In rage, Tharon overturned Orenda's bed, then methodically broke every pot and piece of jewelry he could find. His rage escalating, he snatched back the door-hanging and stamped into the hall.

Light the color of fresh maple sap coated the walls near the dimly burning firebowls. Kettle had thinned the width of the wicks since they had been unable to get more hickory oil from the last traders. Apparently Petaga had cut off their trade access. Well, Badgertail would fix that. Badgertail always fixed things. Tharon smiled. What a superb trained bear the burly warrior made.

"Just you wait, Petaga. I'll take great pleasure in watching Badgertail cut out your living heart. Oh, yes, I ordered him to take you alive, Petaga. I want to see you die myself!"

Tharon strode through the burnished auras from one mat-lined hall to the next. He'd worn his red-lace tunic tonight. The tiny holes in the weave let the gold of his robe come through in flashes like darts of lightning. Where could that demented child have gone? She hadn't escaped to the outside world, had she? Perhaps hidden in the flood of Badgertail's warriors?

His rage towering, Tharon turned a corner and jerked open the first door-hanging he came to. Boldly, he strode into the room. Before his eyes fully adjusted to the darkness, he heard a woman gasp.

"My Chief!" Thrushsong pulled herself upright in bed, hastily attempting to blink the sleep from her eyes. Ugly and skinny, Thrushsong would never have ascended to the position of priestess had it not been for her mother's and aunt's deaths a few days earlier. Black hair fell over her face, and she sputtered, "What—"

"Where is my daughter?"

"I . . . I don't know. I haven't—"

"*Find her!*" Tharon gritted his teeth, watching maliciously as Thrushsong lurched out of bed and frantically began throwing on her clothes. "I want her in my room in less than one hand of time. Search the south half of the temple, Priestess. I'll search the north half. Wake all the other Starborn if necessary."

"Yes, my Chief!"

Tharon ducked back into the hall and raced to the next curtain. Beyond it lay a storage room, filled with vessels containing rare seashells, pounded sheets of copper, galena nuggets, and finely woven blankets. Roughly, he searched the room, shoving aside the largest jars so that they crashed to the floor and spilled their contents in a glittering wealth across the dirt. Tharon slammed his fists into the walls while he screamed, "I want Orenda! Bring me my daughter! *Bring me my daughter!*"

He heard Thrushsong's feet thudding down the hall and heard her awaken another of the Starborn. Voices rose urgently.

Tharon charged out of the storage room, blood pounding. He raced down the hall and turned the corner, but here his steps faltered. The only room still occupied in this corridor belonged to Nightshade. All of the other Starborn had moved out when Nightshade moved in.

Tharon pursed his lips, trying to overcome his panic at the thought of challenging her. Nightshade had been acting very strangely in the past two days. She ghosted through the halls long after everyone else had retired, no more than a shadow in the darkness, as though looking for some malignant Spirit that stalked the night.

Tharon had watched her surreptitiously from behind his door-hanging. She seemed to spend more and more time outside his room, and the thought terrified him. Why? What purpose could she have other than to intimidate him? For all he knew, she might be out tonight. Furtively, he examined the hall behind him and heaved a sigh of relief when he saw that no one stood there.

He had awakened yesterday morning to find a raccoon-skin pouch tacked over his door. When Kettle had taken it down and slit it open, she'd screamed from the Power that inhabited the evil device. A shriveled tumor lay on a bed of cedar bark. Hair and teeth had grown inside the monstrous bit of flesh. And someone had painted his likeness on one of the teeth.

Tharon had been enraged. Throwing things and shouting for over two hands of time, he had forced all of the Starborn to huddle, terrified, in the Sun Chamber, but his heart had begun to jump around in his chest like a flea on a hot rock. Even now, his queasiness would not leave him alone. He felt so weak that he could barely walk up the temple steps without reeling.

He had no evidence that Nightshade had witched him through that pouch, or even that she had put it there. But he *believed* she had. He had been gulping cups of galena tea to cure himself, but it only seemed to make the weakness worse.

"*Witch!*" he hissed. "Old Marmot was right. I should have killed you when you first arrived."

Tharon squared his shoulders. She had no right to make him afraid of her! He was the great Sun Chief! He ruled thousands. She was a—a *woman*—that was all!

He strode to her door and gripped the hanging. But it took several moments before he gained the courage to ease it aside a crack and peer into the darkness. While his eyes adjusted, he scanned the black shapes of pots on the right wall, then drifted to Marmot's starmap. It etched faint silver rings over the tripod that supported the Tortoise Bundle. Finally, Tharon squinted at Nightshade's bed. Black hair hung over the bedside, brushing the floor with nearly invisible strands.

Tharon pulled the hanging back far enough that he could stick his head into the room. Darkness lay like thick cobwebs in the corners, but the light from the corridor illuminated the bed.

Violent rage overwhelmed him.

Orenda? In Nightshade's bed? He saw her ugly doll slumped sideways to the left of the door. A blanket had been tucked around the bestial toy very carefully. The eyes peered malevolently at Tharon. Did Orenda think she could escape him so simply?

"Orenda!"

His daughter leaped up, terrified, and threw herself back against the wall. He laughed raucously.

"No, no, nonono!" Orenda sobbed.

Tharon lunged forward, a knotted fist raised to beat her for this outrage. Then the faint whisper of clothing rustled in the northern corner. Tharon whirled so fast that he staggered sideways.

From the dark corner, Nightshade's eyes gleamed. Plated with a silverish cast, they shone like frozen lakes.

"Nightshade!" he snarled. "How dare you kidnap my child!"

Her low laughter echoed, and her eyes disappeared.

Tharon backed up until his legs struck the foot of her bed. Why couldn't he see her? Where was she in that smear of shadows? "Nightshade, answer me! I command you—"

A sound, a sandal scraping against dirt, sent Tharon lunging for the only thing he knew Nightshade valued: the Tortoise Bundle.

Clutching it to his breast, Tharon panted, "There! Now I've got it. Come any closer and I'll . . . I'll burn it, Nightshade! Do you hear me? I'll kill it!" His eyes darted wildly in the darkness, seeking a hint of her location.

"Put it down." Her voice was unnaturally quiet.

"No! I—I want my daughter, and I want to leave. That's all. Stay back!"

Tharon reached out and snatched Orenda by the hair. The child shrieked and fought as he dragged her out of the bed and onto the floor. Like a terrified mouse, Orenda buried her face in her hands to bawl. "Shut up!" Tharon ordered.

Nightshade's low laugh bludgeoned him. "Go ahead, Tharon. Keep holding the Bundle just like that."

"W-Why?"

"Because you have it centered over your heart . . . and it will kill you."

"You can't frighten me, Nightshade. I won't put it down! I know that if I do, you'll . . ."

A chill crept into the room, like the damp cold in the bottom of a burial pit. Tharon shivered. Icy fingers penetrated his robe to clutch at his belly and loins. When the cold knotted in his chest and his heart lurched, he abruptly released Orenda's hair and, stumbling, knocked over the Bundle's tripod. It clattered to the floor.

"Do you see, Tharon?" Nightshade sounded mockingly tender. "They've come for you."

"Who . . ."

Voices whispered around Tharon, eerie, *familiar*. He opened his mouth to shout. But the voices rose to a roar. They rode the darkness like falcons, soaring, then diving at him. A thousand of them, they came from everywhere.

"What's happening?" he screamed.

Faces blossomed in the darkness, white and transparent, before becoming part of panoramic scenes: an old woman dragged a young man across a snowdrift in a dark land where lights Danced in the sky; a beautiful woman soared over the top of the world on the wings of Thunderbird; a little boy sobbed that his mother had killed herself . . .

The scenes faded, leaving the faces hanging alone in the darkness of the room. They swayed toward Tharon, angry, demanding that he put down the Bundle. He let out a shriek and slammed the Bundle on the floor. Nightshade gasped. He saw her stagger and vomit as he ran for the door.

Tharon seized Orenda's big doll by the throat and plunged out into the hallway with it, yelling, "Kettle! Thrushsong! Help! Help me!"

Orenda's wails echoed up and down the temple corridors.

Twenty-one

Lichen tugged up the hem of her green dress—actually, Wanderer's shirt with the red spirals—to avoid the tangle of dewberry vines that crept across the path. Fragrant white blossoms scented the air. She had pinned her braid on top of her head with a wooden comb, but now straggles crept down to tickle her ears. In the pack on her back, she carried all of the sacred things that Wanderer had used to teach her:

Father Sun's trap, the cedar from First Woman's tree, a hollow tube to blow away bad Spirits; and the clothes she had brought with her.

Wanderer walked beside her in his gangly, springing stride, his head tilted so far to the left that it looked like it hurt. He had been thoughtful all morning while they followed the irregular edge of the bluff down into the bottomlands. As the heat of the day increased, sweat dripped from his long nose and splatted in the center of his red shirt. He had hung Power pouches and shell bells on the ties of his breechclout—to frighten away rambunctious souls, he'd said.

"So the rainbow wasn't a regular rainbow?"

"No." Wanderer shook his head. "It stretched across the entire sky. And the bands of light felt warm when I touched them." His wrinkled face had a preoccupied expression, as if he were plumbing the depths of an intricate problem.

"So what did Wolf Slayer say about the war, Wanderer?"

"Oh, he just showed me Cahokia during the battle. It was terrible, Lichen. It frightened me. I . . ."

Lichen swerved around a thistle patch, and Wanderer's words faded away. She turned and saw him stepping off in another direction, still talking while he waved his arms.

"Wanderer? No, not that way! *This* way."

Lichen trotted over to grip his hand and guide him back to the trail. He'd ambled off in the wrong direction five times since dawn. Once he had almost stepped off the edge of the bluff. "Just try to follow me, Wanderer. All right?"

"Oh, did I do it again?" he asked in bewilderment as his eyes went wide to study the land. "I'm sorry, Lichen."

"You were thinking. It's all right."

"I'm not very good company today, am I? I'm still trying to figure out that Dream."

"I know. Tell me more about Wolf Slayer. He was a glowing man, you said. I wonder if Foxfire will be?"

"I don't know. First Woman doesn't glow at all."

Lichen stared, open-mouthed. *"You've seen her?"*

Wanderer peered back with aplomb. "Why, yes, a very long time ago. When I was first learning to Dream."

"Wanderer, why didn't you ever tell me? I need to know things like this—you know, for when I see her. What's she like?"

"Cantankerous. I never even saw her Cave. She ran at me, swinging her walking stick to drive me away."

"She did?"

"Yes. I don't think she liked me." Wanderer's bony shoulders slumped when he sighed.

The wilted remnants of lamb's quarter, strawberries, and windflower drooped across the black soil. Morning glories huddled at the base of rocks, cautiously twining their purple blossoms in the sheltered crevices. A few hearty sunflowers stretched their leaves to the sky, pleading for a drop of moisture. But not a cloud blemished the expanse of pale blue.

Father Sun beat down on Mother Earth with clublike intensity, blinding the people who worked the fields that outlined the meandering traces of creeks. The soil had shattered where it lay exposed to the burning rays.

Lichen led the way across a stretch of trail where the ground had shrunken and cracked like pieces of fat frying over a chokecherry fire. *I'm coming, First Woman. I'll be there to talk to you as soon as I can. But won't you let even one good rain fall before I get there?*

Lichen winced at the thought of going into the Underworld again. Memories of her litter overturning in the river had been haunting her. In her nightmares she still gulped mouthfuls of chilling water and felt her lungs go cold before she jerked awake. With Water Snake's soul, she knew that she could cross, but what if she had received a new soul by then?

"Wanderer?" she asked with trepidation. "What happens if I get Rock's soul before I have to go back into the Underworld?"

"Hmm?" Wanderer grunted absently. "What?"

"I said, what happens if I have to cross the river in the Underworld with Rock's soul in my body?"

Wanderer squinted. In the sky behind him, a bald eagle circled lazily, flapping only when it needed to change altitude. Its flight inscribed a lilting Song across the blue. "Rock's soul?"

"Yes. You know, or something else that would sink. I'm worried that—"

"Oh. . . . Oh, I get it. Well"—he gestured airily—"I suppose you'll have to roll along the river bottom until you find a firm enough place to climb ashore. You'll want to avoid all the mucky places, of course, because if you get stuck, you won't have any hands or feet to push out with. Not having eyes will be the real problem, since you won't be able to see where you're going. But I suspect that if you *feel* your way, paying attention to the flow of the current, you'll make it." His bushy brows lifted abruptly. "Well, I mean unless one of the grouse with fish fins dives down to gobble you up for its gizzard."

His eyes were unnervingly intent. Lichen frowned sullenly and walked off. Her sandals crunched on the baked soil as she descended into a hollowed niche where cool shadows fell over her. *Blessed Thunderbird, I hope no worm souls try to get me before I have to talk to Bird-Man again.*

Wanderer trotted up behind her. "What really worries me about the Dream, Lichen, was that the whole countryside had been set afire. If the crops and land burn, there will be no more us. Life is so precarious now that such a loss would be fatal."

"Did Wolf Slayer tell you how to stop it?"

Wanderer gazed down at her with so much worry in his eyes that her stomach muscles went tight. "Yes, my daughter. He told me to teach you that to step onto the path, you must leave it. Only the lost come to stand alone before the entrance to the Cave, and only the defenseless step over its threshold. Wolf Slayer said to tell you that in Union you will find the light, though it appears as darkness, nakedness, nothingness. He said that if you can't enter the Cave, First Woman's wrath will sweep humans from the face of the land."

A prickle of panic climbed Lichen's spine. She shifted the weight of her pack, and the trap clunked against the hollow tube. "Wanderer, why me? Why does it have to be me? Why can't you do it? Or Nightshade? You've both been to the Underworld lots more than I have."

"Power makes its own choices. No one can fully understand its ways. I just wish I knew how much time I have left to teach you. I don't want to push you, but, Lichen—"

"We'd better do it, Wanderer." She bit her lip, recalling how the light had roasted her soul the last time he had pushed her. Could she stand that again? "It might take me longer to learn than we expect, so—"

"Oh!" Wanderer shouted. "There he is! Wait, Lichen! I've been trying all morning . . ."

Wanderer thrashed his way through a brier of withered nettles. He jumped first to the right, tried to grab something off the ground, then jumped to the left and grumbled, "No, no, come here! I'm not going to hurt you!"

Lichen resignedly sank to the ground in the thin shadow of a buffalo-bean bush. Stems decked with long, hairy leaves and a few shriveled beans sprawled around her. She plucked one of the beans and popped it into her mouth. Sweet wateriness coated her tongue.

Wanderer dodged out of the thistle, hunched over and snatched at something in the weeds. "Ha!" he blurted in glee and tramped back to Lichen with a horned toad in his hand. The creature's throat puffed in and out angrily while Wanderer stroked its prickly head with a dirty thumb.

"There, there," Wanderer cooed. "It's all right. We just need your help for a little while." He dropped in the shadow beside Lichen and sat cross-legged. "Horned toads are very secretive. But they have remarkable eyesight."

"Better than Antelope?"

"Oh, yes. Much better."

"Is it going to tell you about something it saw?"

"I doubt it. They hate it when people do this to them."

Wanderer handed the toad to Lichen so he could tug a red thread from the sleeve of his shirt. Horned Toad gave her an evil look and started to slime her hand. She shifted him to her other hand and wiped her fingers on the grass but had to switch him back almost immediately.

"Wanderer . . ."

"Hold on just a little longer, Lichen."

She lifted Horned Toad and squinted threateningly at him. He glared back, looking so mean that Lichen resignedly lowered him to her lap.

"All right, Lichen. Let me have him."

Horned Toad shot out of her hand like a slippery fish and into Wanderer's. Lichen rubbed her fingers in the dirt to clean them.

"Quiet, quiet," Wanderer cooed softly to Toad. "That's it. We're not going to hurt you. Wolf Slayer said that Badgertail had left Cahokia yesterday and that Petaga would be waiting for him. We need to know where those warriors are now."

He stroked Toad's head until the creature calmed down and stopped sliming. Very gently, Wanderer set Horned Toad on the ground and tied one end of the red thread around Toad's throat, the other end to the tip of his own first finger. Then he picked up Toad and started walking.

Lichen trotted behind. "Where are we going?"

"Up to that high point."

"What for?"

Wanderer trudged up a small rise that overlooked the bottomland. Redweed Village sat at the base of the rocky outcrop to the southwest. Lichen joined him among the sunflowers. She thought she could see people moving in the fields along Pumpkin Creek, but the heat waves that rippled the distances could have transformed boulders into looking like humans. Still, her eyes lingered on those black dots.

Her chest tingled with sudden longing for her mother and Flycatcher. She had even missed Screechowl and Wart. Lichen had the urge to run all the way home—until she imagined her mother's face when she told her that she had Water Snake's soul. But maybe she didn't have to tell her mother right away. Maybe they could just sit around for a night . . .

"All right," Wanderer whispered. He held Horned Toad high over his head and closed his eyes. "Let's see what's happening out there."

As Wanderer turned in a slow circle, sunlight transformed his gray hair into a snowy halo. Lichen gazed up at Horned Toad. His throat puffed as he scanned the rolling hills. Whenever Horned Toad blinked, Wanderer stopped suddenly, as though he could no longer see, then rotated another hand's worth.

After he had finished three full circles, Wanderer's brows drew down over his long nose. He lowered Horned Toad, untied the thread, and let him go. Toad scampered back into the grass, blades bending this way and that as he ran.

"Could you see anything?"

Wanderer wet his lips. "Petaga. He's still in the south, but it looks like he's moving north. From the smoke patterns, I would say that he's attacked several villages along the way." The red thread dropped from Wanderer's finger and fluttered into the weeds. "But I couldn't see anything to the north or west. I don't understand."

Lichen edged closer to him. "What don't you understand?"

"If Badgertail left Cahokia yesterday, I should have seen . . .

something. Warriors, or scavenger birds following the warriors. Where could Badgertail be? He must be traveling with nearly a thousand." He frowned. "Do you think Wolf Slayer was wrong?"

Lichen shielded her eyes to examine the west. The bluffs along the Father Water were nothing more than an ethereal smudge of gray. But the longer Lichen gazed at them, the more uneasy she felt. When the wind stirred the sunflowers, she thought she heard a voice calling to her, desperately. "Wanderer? Something's wrong out there. Can you feel it?"

"Yes." He nodded. "I've been feeling it all morning."

"Let's hurry!" Lichen trotted down the hill to the trail, Wanderer close on her heels. Over her shoulder she called, "When can you teach me more, Wanderer? Tonight?"

"If your mother will let me, yes. In fact, doing this lesson in your own house might be best. You'll feel safer there than anywhere else."

Lichen broke into a hard run, her legs pumping while the pack slapped her back. Bristly nettles snatched at her sleeves as she flew past. In the distance, the trail wound downward. "What will you teach me, Wanderer?"

His sweat-damp gray hair flopped with each long, ungainly stride. "I was thinking that maybe you're ready to learn about surrender—about stepping into the mouth of the Spirit that wants to chew you up."

Locust's boots squished in the moist sand as she walked along Pumpkin Creek behind Badgertail. Patches of mint filled the air with a savory tang. Every so often Locust plucked a leaf and chewed it gratefully. They had marched half of last night and all of today, gnawing dried fish from their packs and making do with what plants presented themselves along the way. But their speed could not keep Locust from worrying about her sister-in-law. The birthing women had said that Green Ash's time was close, and Locust desperately wanted to be there when the child pushed from the world of darkness into this world of light. Primrose might need her if something went wrong.

She glanced at Badgertail's broad back. But Badgertail needed her, too . . . especially now.

Fifty warriors followed in single file behind Locust, quiet, cautious. To either side, the creek's banks rose steeply, shielding them from all but the highest points on the bluffs to the east. But nothing was certain. Curls of smoke sprouted for as far as the eye could see.

What is Petaga doing? Burning every village in the highlands?

"We'll be there by moonrise," Badgertail called softly over his shoulder. He lifted a hand to point. "The village sits at the base of that crescent-shaped outcrop."

The fires of sunset reflected from the flat faces of the rocks in a play of colors so dazzling that it hurt her eyes, an iridescent mosaic of lavender, indigo, and fallow gold.

"Will we attack tonight, Badgertail? Or wait for sunrise? The warriors are tired. It's been a long, hot march."

"It depends on what we see when we arrive. I won't know until then. Remind the warriors again that we're looking for two things: a tall old man with gray hair, named Wanderer, and—"

"You're going to save Wanderer, as Nightshade asked?"

"Yes. She wouldn't have asked unless that old man played some important role in the future."

Locust gestured apprehensively. "But what if the role he plays is *against* us, Badgertail? How can we know—"

"We can't, cousin. But we can always kill him later if it turns out that he's supposed to help Petaga. Anyway, tell the warriors not to hurt Wanderer and to find that Stone Wolf. Since we don't know what the Wolf is, tell them to protect anything that might be it."

"I will. . . . Badgertail?"

Locust sprinted up beside him so she could look him in the eyes. Dirt had sloughed off the bank and formed a pointed mound that they had to step around. Locust took the time to inhale a deep breath. "Badgertail, what should I . . . If Redweed Village did join Petaga, the only people who will be left there are the very old, the sick, and a few women and children."

Badgertail stopped so suddenly that he forced Locust to sidestep. "I already told you, Locust. The Sun Chief wants the village wiped clean—as a sign to others who might have treasonous notions. Make it clear."

"I know you picked these warriors carefully, Badgertail, but most of them have human hearts. They won't like it. You know how they feel about—"

"*I* don't like it either!" Badgertail's face contorted.

Locust's stomach tried to tie itself in knots. He had not been thinking well during the past several hours; he'd been making mistakes, misjudging the difficulty of the terrain, had even gotten lost once—a thing unheard of for the great Badgertail on a battle-walk.

Now he laid a hand on Locust's shoulder and for the first time in years, gently caressed her skin. "Sorry if I sounded harsh. I—I'm worried about Petaga. Tell the warriors to . . ." Breath went out of his lungs. "Just tell them to do their duty."

"I'll tell them."

But she stood watching Badgertail plod forward, walking as though he wanted to be out of earshot when Locust relayed the order to the men. Badgertail came to a curve in the bank, where a thick slab of rock protruded over the creek. Locust watched him lean against the stone, bracing himself with a hand.

Under her breath, she whispered, "Seeing the faces of the dead, Badgertail?"

All night and through today, when she least expected it, voices from past battles would eddy up through her soul: a woman begging her not to kill her husband, the sudden silencing of a child's laughter, a dying warrior cursing her with his last breath. Images flared and died, and Locust recoiled from the charred skeletons of houses wrapped in pale, smoky haze, the corpses staring up in hatred.

Oh, Badgertail, what are we doing? Why aren't we trying to talk to Petaga? Why . . . Don't. Don't even think it!

Locust expelled a breath. Useless.

At dawn Badgertail had split their forces, dispatching several scouts, then separating the remainder into war parties of about seventy-five each and sending them as emissaries to the major villages in the north. He had ordered them to stay under cover, to creep along the drainages.

But Locust knew that it would not be enough. Even if they managed to escape Petaga's lookouts, day after tomorrow the foundations of everything Locust *and Badgertail* held precious would be rent asunder.

Badgertail's strategy seemed solid. If the northern villages joined them, they would incorporate new warriors into their ranks, and the war parties would link up south of Bladdernut Village and form an unbreakable chain a half-day's walk in length—then sweep southward to confront Petaga.

Locust's eyes narrowed. Badgertail's hand slipped from the rock and fell limply to his side. It looked as if he had to force his reluctant feet to walk forward.

Twenty-two

Meadow Vole knelt on a mat outside her house, rubbing a handful of milkweed against her bare thigh, separating out the inner fibrous material for thread. Children shrilled happily in the plaza, while their parents labored over fires where evening stews of turkey, spring-beauty corms, and tubers of pepperroot bubbled on pots over the flames. Dogs barked in joyous accompaniment. A feathery draft eased up the creek bottom, tugging at Vole's hair.

She smiled. Across the endless blue above, clouds swirled into massive thunderheads that gleamed violet in the last rays of sunset.

Her eyes kept straying to the trail. *They're coming. One thing you can say about Wanderer, he keeps his promises. He's bringing Lichen home right now . . . providing he's not lost.* She tossed the milkweed fibers into the basket at her side.

All day she had been fighting her desire to run up the trail and meet them halfway. She had missed Lichen more than she'd ever thought possible. In the ten days since her daughter had been gone, Vole had felt empty and purposeless, as though without Lichen, nothing meant very much.

Now she rose, stretched her tired back muscles, and walked out into the plaza. Flycatcher and Screechowl were involved in a wrestling match near the central firepit. Screechowl's bulk kept Flycatcher pinned to the ground, although his arms flailed wildly. A huddle of old people clustered around the fire, watching the match in delight while they placed bets.

"Screechowl, get off me!" Flycatcher yelped breathlessly. "This isn't fun anymore."

"Not fun for you." Screechowl chuckled. "But lots of fun for me." He gripped one of Flycatcher's arms and wrenched it hard.

Desperate, Flycatcher squirmed to throw Screechowl off balance and then slammed his knee into Screechowl's groin. The bigger boy let out a yowl and fell back. Flycatcher scrambled up and darted into the brush like a jackrabbit, Screechowl hot on his trail.

People laughed and shouted encouragement to one boy or the other, while Vole took in the quiet beauty of the evening. The fifteen houses that formed a rectangle around the plaza stood like shaggy beasts, their door-hangings tucked up to admit the breeze. Along the glistening ribbon of the creek, women crouched to wash clothes, soft *clap-claps* sounding as they pounded the garments with rocks before dipping them back into the water to rinse away the dislodged soil and yucca soap.

The day had been so hot that the old people who had been out carrying water to the corn and squash fields sat with sweat runneling the dust on their naked chests. No young male voices stirred the air. All of the able bodied men and four of the young women had gone to fight with Petaga. Only sixty-two people remained in Redweed Village.

Vole strolled over to Flycatcher's mother, Star Bulb. The flat-nosed, pudgy woman had coiled her long braids on top of her head to keep them out of the way while she pierced her youngest daughter's ears. Little Teal crouched tensely, her hands twisting in her lap.

"Do you need help?" Vole asked as she knelt by Star Bulb.

"No, this will just take a moment. Teal is two summers, old enough to have her own ear-spools. I traded for some small greenstone spools last month. Just the right size to start with."

Star Bulb carefully surveyed her awl, made from the wing bone of a golden eagle, then slipped a small piece of wood behind Teal's ear to use as a stop. With a quick thrust, she punctured the lobe. Teal jerked, but didn't cry out. Her dark eyes stared unblinking while Star Bulb pierced the other lobe and laced short lengths of porcupine quill through the holes to keep them open.

"All right," Star Bulb said as she patted Teal on the arm. "Go play."

The little girl raced away to join the children playing ring-and-pin near the central fire. The "pin" was a sharp stick with a string tied to one end. The other end of the string had the "ring," a hollowed-out bone. The game involved tossing the bone upward and attempting to catch it on the point of the stick. One of the children managed the feat. The others clapped and jumped up and down. In the distance, Screechowl continued to chase Flycatcher through the brush. Their boyish shouts echoed in the plaza.

"So, Lichen should be coming home today?" Star Bulb asked.

"Yes. I'm sure they're coming." Vole's eyes traced the winding curves of the trail that led up over the half-moon-shaped outcrop that encircled the village. "They're probably almost here."

Star Bulb gave her a suspicious glance. "You don't sound certain about that. I wouldn't be either if my child had gone to learn Dreaming from old Wanderer. He's as crazy as they come. I don't know why you let Lichen go."

"Two reasons. Lichen loves Wanderer, and he's the best Dreamer in the land. He taught me. He taught Nightshade. And his Powers have grown in the past ten cycles. There's no one better for Lichen to learn from."

Star Bulb rocked back on her haunches. "If he's such a good Dreamer, why didn't he know about Petaga attacking all the surrounding villages?"

"Dreamers don't know everything, Star Bulb. Sometimes Power prevents them from seeing certain things—for its own reasons."

"Probably because Power knows Wanderer isn't human. I don't like looking into those raven eyes, either." She picked up her bone awl and tucked it in the small red pot resting by her knee. "I always thought that old man was strange, even when he was teaching you. I never trusted him."

Vole brushed away the sweaty strands of hair from her forehead. "I did. And he never let me down."

"Then why did you stop studying with him? I thought he'd done something terrible to you."

"No." She hesitated. But then, perhaps the time for honesty had come. Meadow Vole lowered her eyes, her hands fidgeting. "His Powers were so great that they . . . they frightened me. I wasn't ready to learn the lessons he wanted to teach."

Vole sighed and closed her eyes. *I wasn't old enough to understand his love for me, either—gentle, unbinding, holding me as delicately as a spiderweb that ties two spring leaves. And my love for him was so childish, half worship, half infatuation for an older man who could and did ride the waves of the Underworld. And I'd felt so much guilt over Shouts-At-Night.*

Star Bulb studied her, eyes neutral.

Vole shrugged. "Now I wish I had forced myself to learn those lessons. Lichen's been having strong Dreams for years. If I'd learned more from Wanderer, I could be teaching her."

"You still could," Star Bulb said. Her wide nostrils flared as she lifted her head to sniff the turkey stew. Steam whirled in silver wreaths over the pots.

"Me, teach Lichen? No. My daughter is already a better Dreamer than I am, Bulb. *She* should be teaching me."

"She's barely ten summers!"

"Yes, ten. Power cares little for a person's age. It's the quality of the soul that matters. She'll be a great Dreamer, if she can stand the pain."

Dusk was deepening into night, rousing the animals of darkness. On the other side of Pumpkin Creek, a skunk wandered the grass, turning over damp pieces of wood in search of grubs. Its black-and-white body waddled behind a bush, only to reappear on the other side. A great horned owl hooted from the dogwood trees on the next bend in the creek, and Vole caught sight of a ghostly form flapping low over the land.

She slapped at the mosquito that probed her wrist. "Come on," she said. "It's time to go sit next to the fire, where the smoke will keep the bugs away."

When she stood, she saw two black dots descending the trail on the top of the outcrop. Against the slate-blue horizon, they moved steadily. Flycatcher's voice affirmed Vole's hope.

"Lichen!" he screamed. "It's Lichen! She's come home!" Flycatcher flew up the trail, leaving a gasping Screechowl far behind as he dodged brush and leaped rocks to welcome Lichen.

Vole knotted a hand in her tan skirt and started up the trail herself, forcing her feet to plod slowly . . . lest Lichen see her desperate happiness.

Lichen let go of Wanderer's hand when she saw Flycatcher racing up the hill, her mother following behind. She flashed down the trail to meet them, her green hem fluttering around her legs. The vista of the village rose before her. People stood up in the plaza to look. Wind lifted their soft voices upward and bathed her face in the pungent scents of home and night. She could smell the cooking stews, and her empty stomach growled in delight.

"Lichen! Lichen!"

"Flycatcher!"

"I'm glad you're home, Lichen!" He threw his arms around her and hugged her tightly. They tussled for a while, trying to throw each other off balance, laughing. Even though she stood a hand taller than he and usually won this contest, Lichen's pack made her so awkward that she staggered sideways and lost.

"What happened to you up there?" Flycatcher's blue headband had slipped up on his forehead, pushing his hair higher on one side. Grass and twigs protruded from the tangles. "What kind of things did you learn? Are you still human?"

"I . . ."

Her mother, panting, came up behind Flycatcher and opened her arms wide. "Lichen, come let me look at you."

Lichen dove to wrap her arms around her mother's neck. It felt so good to be close again. Her mother kissed Lichen's hair and face, and Lichen's soul ached with happiness. "Oh, Mother, I missed you."

"I missed you, too," her mother said, and Lichen heard the tremor of tears in her voice.

Lichen patted her mother gently before she pushed back to stare into those dark eyes. "Mother, guess what? I went into the Underworld! Wanderer made a death litter for me, and Bird-Man brought Spirit Wolves to pull it. And on the way back, I fell into the river—"

"You . . ." Her mother blinked thoughtfully, then lifted her gaze to Wanderer, who had come to stand behind Lichen like a tall, willowy tree. Lichen saw Wanderer nod. Her mother stroked Lichen's hair in amazement. "I'm so proud of you, Lichen. I've known only one Dreamer in my life who could visit the Underworld." She smiled at Wanderer.

"Yes, well," Lichen blurted happily, "Wolf Slayer told me that not many Dreamers can, but I got my Dreaming Power from Wanderer."

Her mother's smile faded, then hardened into anger as she looked at Wanderer. A dreadful silence fell. Flycatcher stood as rigid as a startled goose, his eyes going back and forth from one to the other.

"I kept my promise, Vole," Wanderer said softly. "I didn't tell her. Wolf Slayer did."

Her mother lowered her eyes disbelievingly before she straightened. "We'll discuss it later, Wanderer. I'm sure Lichen is hungry. I have a fresh pot of rabbit stew waiting for her."

Wanderer patted Lichen's head as he passed her to stride down the hall at Vole's side. He murmured so low that Lichen couldn't make out his words, but she could see that her mother's shoulder muscles had bunched. They marched straight through the plaza without saying a word to anyone.

"I guess I shouldn't have said that," Lichen told Flycatcher.

"What did you say? I didn't understand why your mother got mad."

"Oh . . ." Lichen adjusted her pack and started down the outcrop. "When I was in the Underworld, Wolf Slayer talked to me about my family, that's all. He told me some things I didn't know before."

"Like what?"

She lifted her hands aimlessly. "Like he told me my mother could have been a great Dreamer. Wolf Slayer said that he had picked my mother to save our people—but in the end, Mother couldn't do it. She was too afraid of Power. So Wolf Slayer said that he and the Wolf Bundle had to make sure I got born."

"Why?"

"So I can find First Woman's Cave and talk to her."

Flycatcher pulled one of the blades of grass from his tangled hair and put it in his mouth to chew. "I've never heard of those things. What's the Wolf Bundle?"

"I don't know. I guess I'll find out."

"What else did Wolf Slayer say?" Flycatcher skipped by her side, a broad smile on his dirty face.

"I don't think I'd better tell you yet, Flycatcher. Even if you are my best friend."

"Why not? I wouldn't tell."

"I know, but I think people in the village might be mad at my mother if they found out."

Flycatcher kept giving her sideways glances as they descended. She felt guilty in not telling him about Wanderer being her real father, both because the fact made her proud and because she usually told Flycatcher all of her secrets. But she didn't think it would be a good idea just now. She avoided the questions in his eyes by gazing out across the land. At the biggest bend in the creek, a pelican was stepping slowly through the water, its beak clamped on a fish. Beyond, swallows darted like black daggers over the spreading expanse of floodplain.

"I'm sorry, Flycatcher," she said when they reached the plaza.

Flycatcher flapped his arms awkwardly. "Well, I should probably go and eat dinner or something."

Lichen gave him a quick hug and said, "And I should go see what my mother and . . . and Wanderer are saying." As Flycatcher raced away, she shouted, "We'll play ring-and-pin tomorrow, all right?"

"Yes!"

Flycatcher trotted up to the central fire and squatted next to his mother and Teal. The old people watched Lichen as she headed for her house. Firelight flowed into the brown seams of their weathered faces, highlighting their curiosity.

Lichen felt ill. She had been so afraid of telling her mother about having Water Snake's soul that she had forgotten that she wasn't supposed to know about Wanderer being her father. What would happen because of her slip? She picked up her feet and sprinted home.

By the time she reached the doorway, the barest sliver of Moon Maiden's face had crested the eastern horizon.

Hailcloud clutched his bow to his chest as he made his way down over the edge of the bluff toward a rock shelter where his warriors waited. Dusk had settled over the land like a dark blue cape. For a while, as the blue deepened to a smoky indigo, he forced himself to forget about the terrible days to come and drifted on the beauty around him. Scents of toadflax and kicked dust twined up with the darkness.

He angled down, jumping to a lower ledge that jutted out from the slope. Massive chunks of limestone had broken from the cliff and tumbled into a jagged pile in the meadow below. The dying light shimmered off the torn faces of the rocks. As Hailcloud watched, a flock of bats erupted from one of the darkest crevices and flooded the sky in a serpentine sheet of black.

Hailcloud worked across the narrow lip of rock, softly calling, "Basswood, it's me," before he jumped down into the rock shelter.

The twelve men who slumped wearily along the back of the shelter turned to examine him. Their dirt-streaked faces wore the strain of deep fatigue. None of them had slept in two days. Sweat gleamed on their heavily tattooed bodies, staining their breechclouts. Basswood, a medium-sized man built like a block of granite, shoved himself to his feet and crossed the shelter to embrace Hailcloud so hard it drove the air from his lungs.

"We were growing worried. What took you so long?"

Basswood backed away to look Hailcloud up and down, making certain he was all right. Basswood's body bulged with muscles. His eyes were red-rimmed and submerged in a face as dark and wrinkled as aged leather. He might have been thirty, but he still possessed a fire for battle, as well as the sense to know when to fight and when to run for cover. He had fought at Hailcloud's side for fifteen cycles.

"Bluebird Village took longer than expected," Hailcloud said. "After the young went to join Petaga, the few old people who remained had to scramble to help us find wood. Some even tore down their own houses to contribute to the bonfire."

Basswood slapped his shoulder approvingly. "Good. Surely Badgertail will think the bulk of our forces is still hanging around Red Star Mounds."

Basswood led Hailcloud across the dusty floor to a soft bed of grass piled against the rear wall. They both dropped tiredly atop it and leaned back against the stone—cool and comforting against Hailcloud's bare shoulders. Young Bull Tine swiveled around to gaze at them. Seventeen summers old, he had bushy, drooping eyebrows that contrasted with his girlishly long lashes. When he spoke, his voice grated from too much running and too little rest. "With the Bluebird fire, that makes fourteen in all. Will it be enough? Will Badgertail be fooled?"

"Into thinking we're still in the south?" Hailcloud asked.

Basswood added, "In the south and burning our way north."

Hailcloud balled his fists. For two days he had been asking himself the same agonizing questions. How many fires are enough? Will too many look suspicious? How are the small harassment parties doing? Have our lookout parties managed to capture and kill each of Badgertail's runners to keep him from gaining any information? If Badgertail falls for our ruse, where and how will he position his warriors?

"I don't know," Hailcloud said. "We're counting on him going north. I pray he does that. If he goes south instead . . ." He shook his head.

Bull Tine ran a hand over his dirty ridge of hair. Dislodged dust swam in the fading light. "When do we join forces with Gourd's warriors?"

"Tomorrow—if everything goes as planned." *Father Sun, let it be so.* "We need to hear what's happening in the north."

"I'm sure Petaga has everything organized."

"Yes," Hailcloud assured him. "Of course he does."

But doubt gnawed at his ribs. When Petaga had ordered him to lead the diversionary war parties, Hailcloud had objected, arguing that Petaga needed him close at hand in case something went wrong with their plans. *The instant we engage Badgertail, something will go wrong.* There were too many variables in warfare to be certain of anything. But Petaga had maintained that he could handle the initial attacks if Hailcloud would just create enough confusion to keep Badgertail wondering what they were up to.

Basswood leaned forward to unlace his water sack from his pack, which lay against the back wall. He opened it and took a drink, then handed the sack to Hailcloud. "Everything is a gamble. Let's all pray that Father Sun agrees with our cause. Did anyone catch sight of movement in the bottomlands today?"

Heads shook all around, and worry sank knives into Hailcloud's gut. Where could Badgertail be? *What trap was he laying?*

Twenty-three

Lichen sat on her bed, her chin propped atop her knees. The yellow spiders on the walls whispered to the Stone Wolf, barely audible, brooding. She strained to understand their words. Strange that she had never heard them talking before, though she had slept in this room thousands of times. But Power was loose on the night. She could feel it nipping at her flesh with tiny fangs.

She fiddled with the red spirals on the hem of Wanderer's green ritual shirt, creasing them between her fingertips while she studied Wanderer and her mother. They sat cross-legged near the dead fire in the middle of the house. They'd lit no firebowls and had lowered the door-hanging for privacy. Opaline shadows, soft and translucent, fell over them.

If Lichen had to listen to their silence much longer, she wouldn't be able to breathe. What had they said to each other before she'd entered? Something bad, she guessed. Her mother's face looked stormy. Wanderer smiled sadly while he drew magical signs in the hard-packed dirt of the floor.

Is that what the Stone Wolf and the spiders were discussing? Their voices had dropped even lower.

Lichen turned away to gaze out the window. As she watched, Moon Maiden's face slipped above the craggy skyline near where she and Wanderer had talked to the rocks. The tumbled boulders stood like dark sentinels against the silver undercoat of moonlight.

Can Bird-Man come and help me? The rocks say that he has never left you . . . but I saw him fly away through my window.

This window.

Lichen tilted her head inquisitively. Maybe Bird-Man did live inside her—like the shadow of her soul, always there, but not really. She'd known in the Underworld that he was coming, even before she'd seen him flying through the sky. As if their souls touched somehow.

"Vole," Wanderer said very softly. Lichen's heart started to pound. "You don't have to believe my Dream, but—"

"I *don't* believe it," her mother responded in a low, shaky voice. Anger and hurt flashed in her eyes. "I think you've taught Lichen enough. Maybe I won't let her go back to see you ever again!"

Wanderer's fingers continued to draw magical designs in the dirt, but the deep wrinkles around his eyes tightened. "Dreamers are not made in ten days, Vole. Thunderstorms do not come from wisps of cloud. Lightning is more than a tongue of fire. If Lichen has to learn on her own, the pain will probably drive her away from Dreaming. Power has *chosen* her. This is not something you or I have a say in. She will *be* a Dreamer. The only choice we have is whether we help her . . . or leave her to stumble around trying to find her own way."

"Some people do better stumbling around than being guided by a crazy old . . ."

Her mother suddenly stood up, and Lichen jerked involuntarily. Tears stung her eyes. She pulled her lips in between her teeth and clamped them tightly to keep them from trembling. She just wanted to live with Wanderer for a little while longer—she didn't want to hurt her mother.

Crossing the room, her mother tugged the Stone Wolf from its niche, then strode back past Wanderer to kneel before her daughter. Lichen fought to suppress her tears while she gazed into her mother's stern face. Vole's eyes looked blacker than black, and the nostrils of her hooked nose had started to flare.

"See this, Lichen," her mother said as she held up the Wolf, but she seemed to be holding it up for Wanderer's benefit. "I braided a thong to put the Wolf on, just so you could wear it when you got home." She draped the thong over Lichen's head.

Lichen shuddered when the Wolf fell over her heart. Threads of Power seeped out of the object, penetrating her chest. She barely heard her mother say, "The Wolf will help Lichen, Wanderer. You don't need . . ." because the Wolf had started talking to her, soft and gentle, in the voice of a woman.

"Your mother doesn't realize that her little girl died crossing the Dark River in the Underworld. That Lichen's soul is living down with the waving weeds that grow on the bottom of the river. I, too, crossed a river once—and lost my soul."

Lichen swallowed. "Did Water Snake come to save you, too?"

"No." A soft laugh. *"A Dreamer did—though he didn't know he was a*

Dreamer at the time. He saved me in just the way Wanderer is trying to save you—by taking care of your new soul so it doesn't hurt itself before it can grow strong."

"But what if my mother won't let me go live with Wanderer?"

"Know this, Lichen: Power works toward its own ends . . . even if it has to destroy entire ways of life to keep the Spiral in balance. No single life is sacred to Power. All life is sacred. Humans are no more important than Eagle. Eagle is no more important than a tiny rice-grass seed tumbling over the prairies in autumn. All things have their place on the Spiral. The path that lies before you will be very hard. Are you brave enough?"

"What do I have to do? I know I have to go talk to First Woman in her Cave, but—"

"Before that, you must go to a cave in this world. It will be dark, cold. But fire burns there. As it did on a mountain long ago when another Dreamer had to lose his soul, his family, that he might save the Spiral. Or perhaps . . . perhaps you might find blood there . . ."

"Why me, Spirit? Why not somebody better? Wanderer—"

A laugh again, as gentle as a summer breeze through a field of sunflowers. *"I once asked that question. Perhaps every Dreamer does. Power takes great risks to find the best, the strongest. You are that Dreamer."*

"But I'm scared, Spirit. What if I can't do it? What if I'm never good enough to get to First Woman's Cave?"

Wanderer glanced at Vole, who had eased down to the floor on shaky legs, her eyes glazed, mouth ajar, as she watched her daughter. Lichen's gaze had gone unfocused: Dreaming, though wide awake. Moonlight spilled through the window, cradling her heart-shaped face and flowing into the folds of green fabric she wore.

When Lichen spoke again, her voice sounded miserable: "But what will happen to my mother? What will happen to Wanderer? I can't leave them! I don't want to be alone, Spirit! I'm scared."

Lichen let out a cry and fell forward, burying her face in the kinky fur of her buffalo robe. Wanderer and Vole lurched forward simultaneously, each reaching for the girl.

"What is it, Lichen?" Vole asked as she kissed her daughter's forehead. "Who were you talking to?"

"Mother, oh, Mother!"

Wanderer crept forward and touched Lichen's shoulder. His soul ached for her. "The Stone Wolf told you that you had to leave both of us? Your mother and me?"

Lichen sobbed, "Yes!"

"But why? What's—" Wanderer would never finish his second question.

War cries rose out of nowhere. The high-pitched shrills slipped up and down like someone playing a bone comb with a chokecherry stick. Through the window, he saw the first barrage of flaming arrows pierce the darkness. They sailed in glowing arcs into Redweed Village.

Screams erupted around the plaza. Wanderer's breath caught in his throat.

He whirled and dove for the door, where he jerked the hanging aside to peer out. Moonglow cast the long shadows of warriors over the houses. As Wanderer watched, a shrieking warrior shot an arrow into the temple. The cattail roof crackled to life, sending wands of light to illuminate the outcrop. Houses burst into flame all around him; people scrambled out the doors to run.

The warriors yipped and fell on the old men, women, and children alike, bashing with their clubs, shooting arrows into frail old chests. Bodies tumbled to the bloody grass. One old man, his head bashed in, crawled spiderlike, trying to get away. Contorted faces flickered orange in the blazing glare.

An arrow arced down into the roof of Vole's house. Garlands of red sparks shot upward, spattering the black belly of the sky.

Wanderer dodged back into the house. Already smoke twirled down in a gray haze. "Vole, grab Lichen! We'll have to try to get out through the window."

"But they'll be watching!" Vole cried in terror. "You know they will. They're probably waiting to—"

"Get out! It's our only chance!"

Lichen screamed, "Look!" and pointed at the ceiling.

Wanderer lunged for his daughter and knocked her back against the wall as a burning section of roof toppled into the room. Flames engulfed Vole's bed and licked up the wall, peeling off the clay to get to the hardwood poles beneath. Smoke boiled out in choking black layers. When Wanderer turned, he caught sight of Vole's arm, twisted at an impossible angle in the midst of the flames. Vole was under the blazing thatch.

"Vole?"

"*Mother?*" Lichen shrieked. "Where's my mother? Wanderer, help my mother!"

The fire roared, searing Wanderer's face until he had to close his eyes. Roughly, he grabbed his daughter's hand and dragged her to the window. Lifting her up, he shoved her outside, then turned back.

"Vole? *Vole!*"

Gasping for breath, Wanderer hit the floor on his stomach, sliding beneath the smoke toward the last place he had seen Vole. His scorching lungs screamed for him to get out, but he swept the floor with his hands until he bumped soft flesh. Grabbing Vole's forearm, he jerked with all of his strength to pull her from beneath the sizzling thatch. Her dress burst into flame as soon as the air struck it. Wanderer rolled her in the dirt, then scrambled to get her up in his arms so he could run to the window. Together, they toppled out into the darkness.

Wanderer carried Vole through the brush, away from the burning village, where he could lay her down on a soft bed of grass. The vile odor of singed hair clung to her. Blisters bubbled over her right leg.

Lichen trotted in from the shadows, crying, her face covered with soot. In a choking voice, she asked, "What happened?"

"She got caught under the roof. It must have smashed her against the wall when it fell. I think she hit her head."

"Is she all right?" Lichen looked at Wanderer desperately.

"Yes, I think so, but—"

A hoarse shout surged over the roar of the fire. A dozen people flooded around the husk of Vole's house, stumbling and shoving their way toward the black ribbon of the creek. Wanderer recognized Wart and his mother in the forefront.

Five enemy warriors leaped up from the drainage channel where they had been hiding. The chert studs in their war clubs glittered as they raised their weapons over their heads and charged forward into the fleeing people. The group broke and scattered. A warrior grabbed the racing Wart by the back of his shirt, slammed his club into the side of Wart's head, then tossed the boy's limp body to the ground. The warrior vaulted Wart's corpse and fell on another child.

Screams rode the night wind like circling vultures, growing louder until the very fabric of the darkness pulsed with agony.

"Lichen!" Wanderer ordered in panic. "Run. I said *run*!"

She stood rigid, staring unblinking at Wart, fifty hands away. The boy stared back, his sightless eyes wide and dead.

Wanderer pushed her with all of the strength he could muster. "Run! We'll find you if we can!"

Lichen stumbled and fell to the ground. "But I can't—"

"I said, *go*!"

Lichen put her hands over her mouth to stifle her sobs but dutifully rose to her feet and dashed out into the dark clusters of brush and rock. The anguish on her face had torn Wanderer's soul to dandelion fluff. He watched her disappear, his heart in his throat, before turning back to Vole. Slipping his arms under her knees and shoulders, he staggered to his feet, preparing to follow Lichen.

"Wanderer!"

The familiar voice caused him to hesitate for an instant—long enough for three warriors to loom out of the firelit darkness and encircle him, their bows up, arrow points aimed at his back and stomach. Wanderer's tongue clove to the roof of his parched mouth like a choking root.

A tall, burly warrior swaggered from the shadows. Blood coated his heavily tattooed chest in lurid splotches. The fire flared suddenly as the last of Vole's roof and walls crashed in upon themselves. Wanderer instinctively ducked and clutched Vole's limp body closer to his chest. The light wrapped the warrior in a patina of pure gold. The squat face had grown more wrinkles in the past ten cycles, but the bulging eyes had lost none of their keenness.

Wanderer swallowed hard. "Badgertail!" he whispered.

Lichen thrashed through the underbrush, gibbering to herself in terror, ignoring the stinging nettles that raked at her legs and arms. Firelight reflected across the rock outcrop, swirling like monstrous creatures with fiery wings. From the heart of the flames, a voice called to her, whispering her name over and over again: *"Lichen, Lichen, come this way . . . this way . . ."*

"Who are you? What do you want?"

Lichen stumbled over a black mustard bush. Sobbing, she regained her balance and ran again. Prismatic reflections sparkled through her blurry eyes as she dodged into a thick bramble of berry vines and fell to her knees. Through the dense tangle, she watched in horror as the warriors shoved Wanderer toward the creek, stabbing his back with the blunt ends of their war clubs. Her mother's body, legs dangling, hung limply in Wanderer's arms as the group disappeared down the black throat of the creek bottom. Was her mother dead?

A fist tightened around Lichen's heart. *Mother? Mother, don't leave me!*

The screams were fading now, dying to a few breathless squeals.

Lichen gasped desperate breaths of the cold, smoky air while she tried to spot anyone she knew. Warriors trotted around the skeletons of houses, haughty, one laughing while he checked bodies, kicking them to make sure they were dead.

Flycatcher, where are you? Bird-Man, let him be all right. Oh, Wart . . .

Lichen crawled to the far end of the bramble so she could view the village from a different angle. Corpses lay hideously sprawled across the scorched grass in the plaza. Ashes fluttered down from the sky like horrible snowflakes, covering the dead with sheets of white. Lichen sniffed the pungent odors that oozed from the breeze. Her soul writhed with the coppery scent of blood.

"Stone Wolf? What's happening to me?" she cried.

Eight warriors trotted from the village and began striking the brush with their war clubs. They flushed a rabbit that darted away into the firelit crevices of the rocks. The warriors laughed. But when old man Wood Duck rose from behind a clump of rosebushes and tried to run on his maimed leg, one of the warriors pounced on him. The club smacked wetly against his skull. Lichen's heart thundered.

"They're searching for anyone still alive, little one," the voice said softly in her head. *"You have to run. Run, Lichen. Hurry!"*

"But if I stand up, they'll see me. What . . ." Suddenly, she knew.

She flopped on her stomach and slithered through the brush, as silent as Water Snake, her movements hidden by the wavering dance of shadows.

Twenty-four

Petaga sat beside Gopher in the chief's open-sided shelter north of Red Star Mounds and peered intently out at the darkness. Half of his warriors had come up through Slippery Elm and Goat's Rue Villages, while another third had been with Hailcloud at Axseed and Bluebird before they'd broken off to come join him. The remainder, perhaps three hundred warriors, had coalesced along the river south of One Mound Village—waiting for Badgertail.

No fires burned on this night. Everyone knew that at least three of Badgertail's war parties lurked a day's walk to the north, just over that hump that thrust up on top of the bluff.

Another two days, then Petaga would attack. They couldn't risk being spotted, not now, not when they stood on the brink of battle.

In silver-edged darkness, warriors groped awkwardly for their packs and blankets. Everywhere Petaga looked, black forms swayed as they completed final nightly duties. They moved in grave silence—as silent as the dead.

Father? From your pole high in Cahokia, do you watch us through your empty eye sockets? Coming . . . yes, coming for you, Father. Coming to take your head home and bury it with your body so you can walk in the Underworld with pride and honor.

Old Gopher leaned sideways to look out from beneath the hastily constructed grass roof at Moon Maiden. She hung in the middle of the sky, surrounded by concentric halos of green, orange, and yellow. Far out on the western horizon, lightning bounced around inside the belly of a bank of dark clouds. Petaga strained his ears to see if he could pick up the roar of Thunderbird, but he heard only the pounding of his pulse.

"Gopher?"

The old man cocked his head expectantly. At the age of forty-two summers, his long black hair and bushy brows had grown streaks of gray. He had a broad nose that spread out onto his cheeks like a flattened ground cherry. He had worn an ancient deerhide warshirt painted with the faded-blue image of Falcon—it had brought him luck, he'd boasted, in his early days when he had been one of Red Star Mounds' greatest warriors. But it looked tattered and shabby to Petaga's eyes.

Gopher frowned. "What is it, young Petaga?"

"I've been . . . concerned . . . about something."

"What?"

Petaga ground his teeth. *If you don't discuss it with someone soon, you'll burst from the anxiety. Gopher should be the perfect man to talk to. He was your mother's favorite cousin, and he gave three hundred warriors to this venture. That should be proof enough that he believes in your cause. Still . . .*

Petaga grooved the dirt with the toe of his sandal. In the dusty moon glow, the groove resembled the dark, slithering track of a snake. "I—I was wondering what you think will happen if we destroy Tharon."

"I think we'll be a lot happier."

"Yes, but . . . I mean . . . well, do you think that the remaining villages will work together? After all, Cahokia has been the center of our chiefdom for hundreds of cycles. Trade was handled for the benefit of every village. Cahokia has organized and funded the traders, then redistributed the exotic 'things' we've gleaned so that each village could trade them for what they wanted. And—" he hesitated, struggling to recall exactly how Aloda had put it "—the villages have always paid tribute to keep trade going. What will happen when there's no longer a need to pay tribute?"

Gopher's eyes sharpened. "Ah, you mean to ask, do I think the trade will fall apart?"

"Yes, that's what I mean. Do you?"

Gopher turned so he could study the stars. They twinkled with an uncommon brilliance tonight. His long hair draped over the green diamonds woven into his tan blanket. "Probably."

Gopher had spoken so blithely that Petaga's mouth dangled open. "But if that happens, what will we do?"

"Fight each other, I suspect." Gopher grinned. "Which is nothing new. We've been fighting each other for tens of cycles. That's the way it was before Keran's Dream. That's how it began, with Wolf Slayer and Bird-Man, both brothers, fighting. We've always fought. Never with as many warriors as now, but haven't you noticed? Cahokia's palisades aren't exactly new, and other villages have even older earthen embankments or flimsy stockades—out of fear of their 'relatives.'"

"So you think we'll be at each other's throats? Worse than now?"

"Umm . . . no." Gopher's smile went as hard as a quartzite hammerstone. Even in the darkness, Petaga could see the glint in his eye. "There won't be as many of us when this is over. Those who aren't killed outright will be stupid not to run for their lives. I suspect that two thirds of us will be gone when this war is done." Gopher paused to inhale deeply of the earth-scented night. "You've seen the endless lines of people fleeing with their possessions strapped to their backs. You didn't imagine that they'd come back, did you?"

"But why wouldn't they?" Petaga blurted. "We're building a better life for them!"

Gopher vented a close-mouthed chuckle. "We're building a better life for *us*, cousin. Anyone who can afford to keep trading when this is through will be wealthy beyond his imagining. Prices will soar because unusual goods will be scarce. The Sunborn, with their treasure troves of lace, galena, copper, and seashells, will make out like thieves."

Petaga's stomach knotted. Aimlessly, he formed tiny peaks in the golden fabric over his knee, then smoothed them away again. Anger mixed with disgust within him to form a bitter brew. "Is *that* why you agreed to give three hundred warriors to this fight?"

"Of course," Gopher said. He smirked as though Petaga were a child. "Do you believe that your reasons—revenge and hatred—are more noble?"

Didn't Gopher understand that River Mounds was fighting for the salvation of their way of life? That they hoped to make things easier for everyone, especially for the Commonborn, who suffered the most in times of hunger and deprivation?

Gopher casually turned sideways on his blanket, apparently sensing the emotional waves Petaga was riding. "You're such a boy, Moon Chief. You must learn to see the world through the eyes of a man. We—"

Petaga rose with as much dignity as he could find and bowed at the waist. "Excuse me, cousin. I promised to talk to Hailcloud's son, Spoonbill, before I retired tonight."

Petaga started away, but Gopher's insidious voice stopped him.

"Spoonbill? He's your age, isn't he? Yes, good idea. He'll understand you. All children your age have grand notions of right and wrong."

"At least *we* make a distinction, cousin."

Gopher's mouth quirked. "When you're rich and fat—then we'll talk about it. We'll see if you draw the line in the same place."

Petaga strode out into the darkness, his heart bursting. He had tried so hard to be like his father: honorable, open to new thoughts, sensitive to the needs of anyone in trouble, calculating in war.

But as he sped through a dense brier of buffalo currant, those traits seemed suddenly unimportant. *Oh, Father, I wish you were here.* Like flesh shocked by an arrow point's keen edge, his grief, grief he had been suppressing for days, awakened to choke him. Tears burned his eyes.

"Father," he whispered, "what would you have done? Would you have sat back like Aloda did and hoped for the best? Wouldn't you have fought? Father . . . ?"

A finger of wind ruffled his hair—gently, affectionately—and a sob welled in Petaga's throat.

He broke into a run. His first three paces went unhindered, but then his golden robe caught on a currant branch and ripped. Furiously, he jerked at his hem to tug it loose.

The tearing sound rang like a shriek in the evening quiet. On the hump, he saw one of the lookouts crouch in alarm.

Unable to restrain his grief and doubt any longer, Petaga slowly sank into the shelter of the currant bushes and buried his face in his hands.

W e've gone over this five times, Wrenwing! How many more times do I have to explain?" Black Birch demanded from where he squatted before the fire in the thatched house of the young chief of Bladdernut Village.

Pale moonlight spilled through the window and outlined the simple furnishings at the far end of the house with a soft, dove-colored glow. The ivory blanket draping Wrenwing's sleeping bench faded to a mottled gray, and the five baskets lining the wall above the bench were nothing more than dark shadows. A small shell contained a finger's-full of very weak white drink; it was all that Wrenwing had to offer.

"Until we understand each other," Wrenwing replied calmly. "Or would you have me deny you warriors just because I don't grasp your need? That's what will happen if you keep pushing me." He lay stretched out atop a colorful mound of blankets on the opposite side of the fire, his yellow-and-brown robe flowing around his long legs.

To Wrenwing's right, a beautiful shield made of tanned buffalo hide stood on a tripod. Beaded fringes draped down the sides and swayed delicately in the draft through the window. The drooping white blossoms of a bladdernut plant were painted on the center of the shield—the sole item of any value in the chief's lodge. But then, Bladdernut was one of the poorest villages in the chiefdom.

From the moment his war party had marched into the village, Black Birch's skin had been crawling. Not one person had seemed surprised to see them when they trotted up from the drainages. Had lookouts spotted them and prepared the village for possible attack? Probably. The main path that led through Bladdernut had lain empty to the streaming moonlight—and ominously silent. Too silent. No childish giggles or women's voices had wafted from the houses, though he had occasionally caught sight of frightened female eyes peering through slits in door-hangings.

Black Birch had felt as though he were running through a ghost village as he approached the chief's house, on the hilltop at the northern end of the maze of houses. Then Wrenwing had agreed to meet with Black Birch only if he came in alone and unarmed.

Black Birch felt naked without his weapons. Uneasily, he glanced around. Five guards stood at strategic points throughout the house, their arms crossed, each holding a war club and with a knife sheathed on the sash that belted his tan shirt above his breechclout.

"I'm not trying to push, Wrenwing. It's just that time is so short. We have to move south to join Badgertail day after tomorrow."

"Perhaps you should just move on now, Black Birch, and save us both this trouble. This is your fight, not ours."

In irritation, Black Birch growled, "Let me try again. You've seen the fires in the south. You're far more vulnerable than Bluebird or Paintbrush were. Look around you." Black Birch waved a hand toward the south and west. "Bladdernut has no palisades. You've barely enough warriors to man the high points of the rocks. A strong gale would blow down your defenses. If Petaga comes here with nine hundred warriors, you'll be wiped out to the last child."

Firelight danced over the soot-stained walls behind Wrenwing, silhouetting his twenty-summers-old face and his long braids, fierce eyes, and pug nose. The man had become chief after his father's death last winter, and he'd had little experience in governing.

He's never even been on a battle-walk. How can he understand the importance of this war?

Wrenwing rose to sit cross-legged. Lines furrowed his brow as he tucked his robe around his ankles. "I've no doubt of the truth of that, Black Birch. But what reason would Petaga have for coming here? We've nothing he wants."

"Oh, yes you do. You have forty warriors he might be able to recruit to fight against the Sun Chief."

"So?" Wrenwing spread his hands, palms up. "Forty is a pittance. Would he kill a hundred women and children to—"

"He killed nearly four hundred at Spiral Mounds! And at least fifty at Bluebird, and seventy-five at Paintbrush!" Black Birch replied so violently that the guards shifted and eyed each other as though signaling an alert. Black Birch clenched a fist to still himself. "Look, Wrenwing, we came here in good faith, asking you to help us grind Petaga into the ground so that we might all go back to living in peace. I—"

"Peace?" Wrenwing scoffed. "Keran's Dream died when he did— and it's buried in his mound with him and his servants and his grave goods. Gizis found the Dream convenient to adopt, since it filled his storehouses with wealth and his name with Power. And we've seen Tharon's commitment to peace. No, Black Birch, we've never lived in peace. Why do you think half of the countryside has palisades? *The enemy is us!* It's not Petaga. It's our way of life."

"What are you talking about?"

"Trade . . . mostly. Greed for exotic goods drives the Sunborn.

You've seen it. You know what I mean. To get a shred of lace from Yellow Star Mounds, Tharon will kill babies for a five days' walk around Cahokia so that he can steal enough corn to pay for it. Surely this is not new information to you?"

Black Birch lifted a shoulder impatiently. "What if it's true? Badgertail and I are fighting for the Commonborn, not for the Sunborn."

"Are you? Who will benefit most?"

"Blessed Father Sun!" Black Birch shot to his feet in anger. "The Commonborn will. They'll be alive, won't they?"

"Some things are more terrible than death."

Black Birch snorted derisively. "For instance?"

Wrenwing lowered his eyes and studied the crackling dance of the flames. "Dishonor. Sacrificing dozens of strong people so that two or three may have copper ear-spools to wear—or to keep the war leader inside his plush mound-top house inside Cahokia's palisade. My people are villagers, Black Birch. We're all Commonborn. Perhaps we can see more clearly as a result. Our eyes aren't clouded by living near the Sunborn, who find the lowest class expendable. I want to see my sister's children grow up and make lives of their own. Our clans here have to rely on each other to survive."

"What does that have to do with—"

"Don't you see? If I send my forty warriors to fight with you and they're all killed, then I will have murdered my village as well. Those forty warriors are fathers, farmers, and fishermen—not professional warriors. They are the heart of Bladdernut Village. We can survive without trade, without membership in Tharon's chiefdom, but we can't survive without our forty warriors."

"I suspect that Bluebird and Paintbrush felt the same way, young chief. That's why they're dead."

Wrenwing pinned Black Birch with worried eyes. "And if we don't join you, Black Birch, what are your orders?"

He fidgeted nervously, refusing to answer. The guards had unfolded their arms and were holding their war clubs at the ready. Their eyes glistened in the mauve shadows, making Black Birch wish he were anywhere but here. Outside, in the open, he might have a chance. *The idiots. If they know that dissent means death, why don't they at least pretend to go along?*

"My orders are to move south, with or without your help," Black Birch said ambiguously.

Wrenwing steepled his fingers over his lips. "I see. I take it that means that Bladdernut is dead, no matter whose side we choose." Black Birch held his tongue. Then Wrenwing inquired, "Will you kill my people, Black Birch? In the same way that Petaga murdered yours? What if I promise not to take up arms against Badgertail? Hmm? If I give you my word that my people will scatter to the winds until this madness is over and then return to their homes only with the Sun Chief's approval . . . what then?"

In a low voice, Black Birch responded, "You would let your sister villages be destroyed without lifting a finger to help them? What kind of chief are you, Wrenwing? Are your people cowards? Can't you understand that unless we all pull together—"

From outside came a frantic shout. "Black Birch! Black Birch, quickly! They're coming!"

Whirling breathlessly, he faced the door as an elderly bald-headed warrior, named Bucktooth, dipped beneath the hanging. Panting, Bucktooth explained, "The enemy came up from the south, following our trail. It's surely Petaga."

Black Birch ducked out into the moonlight. Flaming arrows laced the sky like a perverted meteor shower, landing in the roofs of houses and in the parched brush. Blazes crackled to life everywhere. When Wrenwing came out, Black Birch pointed and yelled, "See! What did I tell you? Petaga has no cares for your people! If you don't join us, you're condemning all of them to—"

But Wrenwing darted away into the darkness, his guards following in a semicircle. Black Birch saw their shapes flit down toward the southern end of the village to the mouth of a small drainage. There, dozens of other shadows joined them. All vanished into the blackness beyond.

Had Wrenwing had his village ready to flee all along? Was that the only way out that the young chief had been able to see? Black Birch shook his head.

"Bucktooth, run and find Wasp. Tell her to take twenty and lead a drive along our attackers' right flank. Then find Beehive. I want him to take his men and flank them on the left side. I'll lead what's left of our forces down the middle."

When the old man hesitated, Black Birch shoved him so hard that Bucktooth fell to the ground with a soft grunt. "But, Black Birch, maybe this is just a diversion to draw us—"

"I'll do the thinking! Get up, old man! Hurry! You can see where the arrows are coming from. Petaga's forces are still bunched. If we can surround them before they disperse, we'll have them!"

"Yes, yes, all right. I'm going. I'll tell them." Bucktooth scrambled to his feet and ran away, limping.

Black Birch scowled at the night. Given the narrow swath of land from which the arrows came, it had to be a small party, but he couldn't tell how small. Twenty warriors? Or five, firing in rapid succession? *Petaga, you poor boy. You must be desperate to send such a tiny contingent so far north just to harass us. Well, you can count these warriors as dead. We'll pursue them to their doom.*

Black Birch leaped over a bush and sprinted downhill to gather his forces.

Twenty-five

Lichen's lungs ached, but she dug her toes into the crumbling clay of the trail and forced her body quickly up the steep slope. The bluff loomed above her, a tan wall two hundred hands high. Mist shrouded the cap rock. The thick veil had been rising progressively since before dawn, edging up to become clouds. Scraggly stalks of hyacinth and buckbrush clustered along the ledges, where moisture gathered on damp mornings like this. The pale-blue petals of the blossoms glistened with dewdrops. Lichen fought stinging tears as she panted up the slope. Maybe from the top she could see someone else who had escaped the attack.

Father Sun poised precariously on the crest of the bluff, peering over the edge at the world below. Filaments of mist twined up from the rocks as the day warmed, caressing that glowing amber face with tenuous fingers.

"Mother?" she croaked softly. "Where are you? I need you. Wanderer, can you hear me? I'm calling you! Come and find me."

He had promised that he would if he could. But she had seen no sign of any of her people since last night. Maybe Wanderer couldn't come and find her. What had the warriors done to him? To her mother? A suffocating bubble swelled in her throat, making it hard for her to swallow. Those bad men had killed everyone else in the village. Even old man Wood Duck with his crippled leg—and children like Wart.

During the terror of the night, running, hiding, and running some more, a chasm had opened in Lichen's soul. Every time she thought about her mother, Wanderer, or Flycatcher, her soul gaped like Bear's huge maw, threatening to swallow her.

Lichen shoved her frizzy braid over one shoulder and scurried around a bend in the steep trail that overlooked the bottomlands. The smoke from Redweed Village still spiraled into the crystal sky. When it reached a certain height, it flattened out and pointed westward, like an extended arm, silently accusing the Sun Chief of the crime. Cahokia was the only place those warriors could have come from. The Sun Chief must have been punishing Redweed for siding with the River Mounds warriors. Lichen remembered her mother whispering with Flycatcher's mother. They had been frightened that Cahokia might attack Redweed just as it had attacked Hickory Mounds.

Her legs trembling, Lichen tried to run, but it was hard. As she climbed, mist enfolded her in a shimmering rainbow haze. The coolness felt good on her dirty face and scratched body. When she had raced through the bushes last night, her hem had been ripped to shreds, baring her legs to the thorns. The dried blood that clung to her skin had started to burn every time she took a step.

It pained her to look at Wanderer's sacred shirt. The red spirals hung in sad tatters around her ankles. She remembered the love in his eyes when he had given it to her on the day after she'd come back from the Underworld. He'd been proud of her . . .

Lichen started crying again. The sobs came in terrible waves. "Wanderer! *Come find me!* I need you!"

Terror clutched at her soul. What would she do if no one ever came to find her? Where could she go? Who would take care of her? She was only ten summers! Could she take care of herself?

Lichen pursed her quaking mouth and studied the bluff face, noting the niches where toadflax sprouted. The edible urn-shaped fruits that clustered in the top leaves would not be ripe for another moon. Here and there, clover stretched its willowy arms toward the sunlight. She could dig the roots and eat them raw; the leaves she could brew for tea. She might be able to find some violet wood sorrel down on the moist prairies and dig the bulbs. When she had the time, she would braid strands of her hair into a bowstring and cut a stem of willow for a bow. Then she could hunt. She didn't know how to make arrow points, but a sharpened hardwood stick would work on small game.

Maybe she would be all right.

Maybe . . . *Wanderer, I don't want to live without you . . . or without my village.*

But Redweed was already gone—wiped from the earth forever. She understood that truth, even if her heart shouted that it wasn't so.

The higher she climbed, the farther she could see. From up here it looked like the whole world had burst into flame. Northward, coils of smoke sprouted everywhere. Was that Petaga? Or had the Cahokia warriors split up and gone to murder other villages the way they had Redweed?

Lichen drove her legs up over the crest of the bluff and slumped down on the warm stone. Stretching out on her stomach, she lay quietly for a time, breathing raggedly, stifling her tears. "Oh, Mother . . ."

Her mother's voice echoed in her memories: *"Stop crying, Lichen! How many times do I have to tell you that tears are useless? They don't do anybody any good—least of all, you. If Screechowl kicks you again, pick up a stick and smack him."*

Lichen had never seen her mother cry—not even once. Oh, she had seen tears in her mother's eyes. They'd been there yesterday, when she'd first gotten home, but nothing more. Her mother always faced life with a glare, daring the world to fight with her.

"I can't help it, Mother," she had said.

The more Lichen thought about being alone, the worse she felt. Tears leaked from the corners of her eyes. She braced her chin on her arm and wept softly.

She wished she had had more time with her parents, that she had grown up with Wanderer living in their home. Never before had Lichen missed having two parents—but now, when she might never see them again, she wished with all her heart that she had a whole family.

Wanderer? Are you all right? You don't have to come for me. She rolled to her side and stared out across the sun-washed basin. *Just take . . . take care of my mother. She needs you now. Bird-Man? Take care of my mother and father. I need them to be all right.*

Elkhorn plodded on weary legs to the lone cottonwood tree on top of the grass-covered knoll and leaned a shoulder against the tree trunk. From here he could look down on his fleeing enemies. The fierce afternoon sun had sucked the moisture from his body and spread it over his arms and legs in a thick sheen of sweat. His brown breechclout clung to his loins in clammy folds. On his left, the eastern bluff rose to scallop the sky with humps of gray. Was someone up there, watching? A lookout? Reporting back to Petaga that his ten warriors had escaped Elkhorn's best efforts to kill them?

In the gully below, the warriors dashed about, skipping across rocks when they could, looking as happy as could be. Faint laughter wafted up with the heat.

Five of his own war party trotted into the shade cast by the cottonwood.

"We've lost them." Elkhorn wiped the sweat and dirt from his chevron-tattooed forehead. At the age of twenty-four, he stood only ten hands tall, but his cunning more than made up for his height. New sweat trickled from his matted black hair and ran into his eyes before it pooled on the tip of his stubby nose. He lifted his bow and shook it at his retreating foes. "I can't believe it! I thought we had them."

Soapweed eased up beside Elkhorn. "So did I. If I didn't know better, I'd think they had the attack and their escape route all carefully planned. How else could ten men and women evade our seventy warriors?"

Elkhorn glanced at Soapweed's round face that rarely showed emotion. He had tied a length of green fabric around his head to keep his loose black forelocks from obscuring his vision. The longer Elkhorn peered into Soapweed's deadpan eyes, the more his nervousness grew.

"It did seem that they had it all planned, didn't it?"

Other warriors came forward to cast curses after the escaping enemy warriors, who had now skirted a raspberry brier and jumped lower into the drainage channel. Only the tops of their bobbing heads remained visible.

"You sound like you have an idea," Soapweed countered. "Like maybe you know why they struck our camp at night and lured us way out here."

Elkhorn grimaced. *Lured?* That thought had occurred to him as early as noon, but it annoyed him to have someone else echo his deepest fears.

Heat rolled off of the bare stone beneath his sandals, searing the bottoms of his feet. They had been at Henfoot Village when the attack came. *What are you up to, Petaga?*

"Should we chase them? They look like they're heading toward One Mound Village. We might be able to catch them before sunset," Soapweed pointed out.

Elkhorn squinted after the warriors. "We won't catch them by sunset. They're moving too fast."

He pushed away from the tree and walked a little way down the slope. Cracks and crevices drew jagged lines of shadow over the face of the bluff, creating perfect hiding places. Had Petaga stationed warriors up there with their bows, ready for the first fool who would follow his fleeing forces into the gully?

Elkhorn hiked back up the slope. "Let's stick to Badgertail's original plan. We'll join Black Birch south of Bladdernut Village. After that, we'll meet Amaranth outside of Balsam Village, then head south to join Badgertail near One Mound Village."

Soapweed canted his head inquiringly. "You think that's what this was all about? Petaga is trying to provoke us so that we'll mess up Badgertail's war plans by flying off and getting ourselves killed in an ambush?"

"Might be."

"Then we'd better warn the other leaders of the war parties. We might not be the only ones he's tried this on."

Elkhorn ran a hand through his wet hair. "Where's High Prairie? He's the fastest runner we have. We'll dispatch him to Black Birch to see."

"I'll fetch him." Soapweed turned back into the savage light of Father Sun, pushing through the warriors who were climbing the hill. Soapweed yelled, "High Prairie! Where's High Prairie?"

Twenty-six

Locust paced before the boulders where Wanderer and the woman, Vole, sat with their bound hands in their laps. Badgertail had ordered the prisoners moved downstream into the tiny grove of flowering dogwood nestled within a group of huge, tilted stones slabs, but the ruins of the village could still be seen across Pumpkin Creek. Wolves skulked around the scorched plaza, snarling as they fought over the bloating bodies of the dead. They always went for the gut first, and the intestines and organs were scattered in bloody heaps around the corpses. Golden eagles wheeled on the warm air currents or perched on the outcrop to await their turn. When a gust of wind blew down from the north, the stench was almost overwhelming.

Locust turned her attention to Badgertail, who stood in a huddle of warriors questioning the runner who had come in from White Clover Mounds. She could barely make out their angry voices.

Badgertail asked, "What do you mean, the chief wouldn't even see Woodchuck?"

The runner, Little Paw, lifted his arms helplessly. "There was *nothing* Woodchuck could do! He tried everything, but Chief Pevon refused to even open the gate. Pevon told Woodchuck that White Clover Mounds would not fight on either side!"

Locust sighed and gazed upward at the drooping white blossoms overhead, softening the sharp lines of the rocks that formed a jagged fortress around them. The trees and boulders blocked the view from the eastern bluff, theoretically providing cover from Petaga's lookouts.

To the west, the land fanned out in undulations of wilting green. Heat waves obscured the serpentine line of the Father Water, but the closest ponds shone clear and blue.

Locust threaded tired fingers through her gore-encrusted hair. She had combed the black mass, but the blood clung like a fine spray of filth. It had been so long since she'd slept that she felt weak in the knees.

Then she inspected Wanderer. The old man sat like a gangly stork, his gray head cocked to peer at the ground, strangely engrossed by the lattice of shadows that crisscrossed the grass. Locust scrutinized the lattice but saw nothing particularly interesting in the pattern. Wanderer had aged dramatically in the past ten cycles. Had his eyes and beaked nose grown bigger? They seemed enormously large in the thin frame of his facial bones. His red shirt and breechclout bore streaks of soot.

"Wanderer?" Locust said, and jumped when the old man shouted "What?" as though startled from the depths of his thoughts by a bolt of lightning. He lurched to his feet, his knees knocking together. "What did you want, Locust?"

She surveyed his terrified posture and sighed. "I just wanted to know if you'd ever heard anything about a Stone Wolf that resided in Redweed Village."

"Oh, yes, many cycles ago." Wanderer slumped back to the rock and mopped his forehead with his torn sleeve. "But it's been a long time since the Wolf vanished."

"How long? You mean that it hasn't been here in cycles?"

"Here? No. Someone stole it. Quite a long time ago. Isn't that what happened, Vole?"

The woman moved her bound hands to shield her burned leg while she glowered at the warriors who swarmed the camp. People had been coming and going all morning, whispering news, laughing crudely. Not one had washed the blood from his flesh. When Vole turned to look at Locust, hatred seethed in her eyes. "Yes, that's what happened. The Wolf was stolen."

Locust folded her arms. "I don't believe you. The Sun Chief had word from a trader only days ago that there was a Stone Wolf here that possessed great Power."

"Well, if it was here," Wanderer remarked reasonably, "it certainly didn't possess very much Power. Look at what happened to Redweed."

Locust ignored the logical comment. "We've been searching the ashes of the village all day and have found nothing."

"That's not too surprising, is it?" Awkwardly, Wanderer maneuvered his bound hands to open the pouch tied to his breechclout so he could draw out a handful of dried elderberries. He began sorting the berries, dividing them into piles in his right palm.

"Why isn't that surprising?"

"What?" Wanderer said, his eyes riveted on one pile of four berries. He clucked morosely at it.

"Why isn't it surprising that we haven't found it?"

Wanderer shook his head at the berries. "Locust, are you aware that your sister-in-law is about to have twins? You'd better be getting home very soon or you'll miss the excitement. I . . ." His voice faded as his eyes went huge and frightened.

Locust's breathing stilled. Wanderer looked as though monsters had risen up from the Underworld to claim his soul. "What? What's wrong? Is it Green Ash?"

"No, I'm . . . just seeing glimpses."

"Glimpses? Of what?"

"A thousand tomorrows—and more," Wanderer answered. He peered intently at Locust.

Taken aback, Locust gripped Wanderer's shoulder and shoved him back, sending his handful of berries pattering across the grass. "Listen, Wanderer, we have to find that Wolf. Where is it? What have you done with it?"

Wanderer blinked inquiringly. "What do you think I did with it?"

As the old man bent over attempting to retrieve his elderberries, Locust threw up her arms in frustration. "This is ridiculous. Why am I even trying?"

"Well, most likely because Badgertail told you to. Poor Badgertail. He dimly realizes that this battle-walk will be his last. It must be very hard on him." Wanderer patiently ordered his berries into piles again. "Did you know that the patterns of elderberry wrinkles take five major forms? Sharp zigzags, sinuous slithers . . ."

Locust peered at Wanderer. He was calmly flipping over a single berry so he could examine the wrinkles on the other side. "How do you know that?"

Wanderer looked up, affronted. "Because I've studied them for cycles, Locust. I'm an expert on elderberries. You'd be amazed at how many berries I've analyzed in the past five hundred moons."

Angrily, Locust demanded, "About Badgertail! How do you know this will be his last battle-walk?"

"Well, it doesn't take any special Powers to see that he's lost the heart for war. Even you can see it, can't you? Everyone knows what happens to warriors who lose that."

Locust swallowed hard. This old man had just pronounced Badgertail's doom, and done it with no more alarm than if he had been forecasting a windstorm. Shaken, Locust asked, "What sort of a man are you, that you could talk of Badgertail's death so—"

"Well, for one thing," Wanderer responded, "I'm not a man. You see, years ago when I was swimming in the Silence, a *raven* came and—"

"Oh, Blessed Thunderbird," Vole moaned.

"You know it's true, Vole. As I recall, you were very upset by it—ordered me out of the house when I started picking at dinner before you'd had a chance to cook it."

"I hardly think this is the time to discuss your peculiarities, Wanderer," Vole responded sharply.

"Peculiarities?"

She gave him a sour look.

"It wasn't my fault that the pack rat who'd taken over my soul was afraid of ravens. You should have seen that bird when it first dove at me. It had a wingspan as wide as the Father Water. I couldn't blame Pack Rat for running. Of course, it disturbed me that he picked that precise moment to go, but you said yourself that nothing was happening anyway, so—"

"What does this have to do with anything?" Vole snapped.

"Locust wanted to know. Didn't you, Locust?"

Locust massaged the back of her neck. "You're crazy."

"Yes. Well, anyway . . ." Wanderer very carefully opened the pouch on his breechclout and dumped the berries back inside.

With relief, Locust saw Badgertail break from the huddle of warriors and walk toward the dogwoods. Dried blood still spattered his tattooed chest. He had tied his warshirt into a sash around his waist. He seemed nervous, fidgety.

Badgertail inhaled a deep breath before he said, "Locust, what have you discovered?"

"About the Stone Wolf? Nothing. These two say that the Wolf was stolen cycles ago."

Badgertail turned to peer at Wanderer. The old man's expression didn't change, but as he tucked his bound hands into the folds of his red shirt, Locust saw them shake.

"Badgertail. It's been a long time. How are you?" Wanderer asked in a gentle voice, as though inquiring about the health of a long-lost friend—rather than that of the man who had captured him last night and who would probably be his executioner.

"Well enough, Wanderer. And you?"

Wanderer tilted his head apologetically and lifted his wrists. They had already developed sores from the scratchy rope. "Things haven't been going my way lately."

Badgertail stared into Wanderer's wrinkled face, contemplating each line as if it represented an event in Badgertail's own life. Locust noticed the hard set of Badgertail's jaw sag before he sighed, "Forgive me, Wanderer. I'm not doing this to humiliate you."

"No. You're following Tharon's orders. I know that, Badgertail. What does he want of me?"

"Actually, it's not Tharon who wants you. It's Nightshade. She told me that you'd found the way to First Woman and that I had to protect you and bring you back to Cahokia. Do you know the way?"

Wanderer peered at Badgertail in silence. Locust looked pensively from one man to the other. Knowledge glowed in their eyes—dark, Powerful. The sounds of the day intensified. The call of a meadowlark boomed in Locust's ears, and the whisper of the wind through the dogwoods turned ominous.

"Yes," Wanderer responded.

"You *do* know the way to First Woman?"

"I do."

"Then we must get you to Cahokia quickly. Perhaps, if the rains come and Mother Earth grows fertile again, we can end this madness."

Wanderer stared down at his long fingers. "I don't think so, Badgertail. We need guidance from First Woman, all right, but this 'madness' will not end until Tharon is dead. So long as he's alive, he'll keep knocking the Spiral out of balance. It's his way."

"What are you talking about?"

Wanderer straightened and faced Badgertail. "What does Tharon want with the Stone Wolf?"

"He's on some . . . Power quest. A trader told him about it. I don't know why he wants it—he just does." Badgertail's brows drew together. "Why? Do you know where it is?"

"If I told you yes, what would you do?"

"Demand that you turn it over."

"And then?"

"Then I'd assign a small war party to escort you and the Wolf back to Cahokia."

A gulp bobbed in the flabby folds of Wanderer's throat. "And my friend?" He tilted his head toward the woman, who fought to keep her face impassive, but a flush had crept into her cheeks.

Badgertail turned and glared at the latticed shadows cast by the dogwood limbs. Splashes of sunlight flowed into the spaces of the dark weave, forming a pattern like scattered bits of amber. He said, "She won't be going."

Vole slowly wilted against the rock. Wanderer moved his moccasined foot over so that it touched hers in encouragement, but he spoke to Badgertail. "And if I refuse to reveal the location of the Wolf?"

Badgertail swung around harshly. Locust could see the indecision on his face. Nightshade wanted Wanderer. Badgertail couldn't kill him for refusing. Badgertail's eyes went over Vole quickly.

"You would bargain for this woman's life? Is that what you're telling me? All right, Wanderer. I will grant you that. Tell me where the Wolf is."

Wanderer shook his head. "No. Not you, Badgertail. I can't. The Wolf is a very great Power object. It's not a thing of warriors. But I will tell Nightshade. She's the Great Priestess at Cahokia now. Isn't that true?"

"Yes, but—"

A childish scream tore the day. Badgertail spun on his toes as Locust sprinted to the edge of the rocks. Near the overgrown bank of the creek, Southwind, kneeling, struggled for a moment, then hauled a young boy out of the weeds by the scruff of his neck. The boy twisted wildly, kicking, biting, trying to wrench free of Southwind's iron grip.

When Southwind lifted his war club to kill the boy, Locust shouted, "No! Wait! Bring him here."

"Why?" Badgertail asked.

"Children are less skilled at lying. Perhaps he knows where the Stone Wolf went."

Southwind tramped into the grove and threw the boy on the ground with a grunt. Maybe eleven or twelve summers old, the child was big for his age. He had small, dark eyes and a crooked nose. He scrambled to his knees, breathing hard.

"What's your name?" Locust demanded gruffly.

"Screechowl," the boy responded. He wet his lips in fear. When his gaze landed on Wanderer and Vole, hope blazed in his eyes.

Locust exchanged a knowing glance with Badgertail. "Screechowl, what happened to the Stone Wolf?"

"Why don't you ask her?" the boy responded, jerking his head toward Vole. "She's the Keeper."

Badgertail didn't deign to glance at Wanderer or the woman. He motioned Locust back and knelt before Screechowl, staring hard into those young, terrified eyes. "Which house belonged to Vole?"

"The one at the southern edge of the village—close to the creek."

Badgertail looked up at Locust. She shook her head. "We checked. We found nothing in the ashes of that house."

Badgertail turned back to Screechowl. "Where could it be if it wasn't in the house?"

"I don't know. Maybe Lichen has it."

Wanderer lurched to his feet. Badgertail's jaw hardened. The old man's wrinkled face had gone as white as snow. Through the gaps in the rocks behind Wanderer, in the patches of blue sky, wisps of clouds painted graceful swirls.

"Who is Lichen?" Badgertail asked.

Wanderer said nothing.

Screechowl piped up, "She's *her* daughter." He pointed at Vole, who squeezed her eyes closed in response.

"Where is Lichen, Screechowl?"

"I don't know," the boy said. "I saw her running away last night, but I don't know where she went."

Badgertail rose to his feet and stood stiffly. His mouth twitching, he ordered Locust, "Take care of the boy. Then organize a search party. Tell them they're looking for a little girl."

Twenty-seven

Dawn light threw a pink halo across the bluff. Lichen's breath fogged before her as she leaned forward to prod the coals of her fire with a stick. Orange sparks rose and winked in the morning sky. Amidst the ashes, six egg-sized gayfeather roots roasted. She tossed on a few more chokecherry twigs, keeping the fire small, just big enough to cook the roots and fend off the chill while she beheld the rising sun. She had never seen a sunrise without her mother or father close by.

Lichen bit her lip and puttered with the stick, using the charred end to draw serpentine designs across the limestone while she remembered other mornings. Often she would wake when the fragrance of frying corn cakes wafted to her. She'd half-open her eyes and poke her nose above her buffalo hide to watch Meadow Vole moving silently around the fire. The glow of the flames would be reflecting from her mother's round face, calm and serene as she cooked. Lichen used to lie for a long time just smelling breakfast and watching her mother from the warmth of her bed.

Now she dug her stick beneath the ashes to turn her roots over, trying not to think about those times. But the ache grew worse. Wanderer's beaky face appeared in her thoughts, gazing up at her from the limestone ledge that hung over sheer nothingness. *"You know, Lichen, there are Dreamers who believe that all of the Spiral is illusion."*

Lichen pondered the hunger that gnawed at her stomach and wondered how anyone could think that. Didn't every hurt disprove it?

Are my parents all right, Father Sun? Let them be all right.

She had not given up hope that Wanderer might trudge up the trail at any moment and find her. All night long in her Dreams, she had called out to him. *Wanderer, Wanderer, I'm here, up on the bluff. South and west, near the old burned-out stump.*

The stump stood, huge and black—like a toothy mouth—in a hollow in the tan rock twenty hands away. When Brother Lightning had struck it, the bolt had winnowed out the center, leaving a charred husk behind. Worms had been feasting on it for cycles. Their distinctive trails spiraled through the ancient bark with a woodworker's artistry.

Her parents lived. Last night, curled in the hollow of the stump, she had sent out wisps of her soul, seeking theirs. Wanderer's had been easy to find; it radiated with a gentle blue light. But her mother's had been more difficult. Lichen had searched long into the night before she had recognized that faint yellow glow. But Lichen couldn't tell whether they were safe or hurting.

How bad were Mother's injuries? Smoky odors of melted hair and singed flesh still hung cloyingly in the back of Lichen's nose. When her throat started to tighten, to ache, she swallowed to make the feeling go away. But it didn't help much. Tears blurred her eyes.

Stop it. They don't do any good.

She used her digging stick, a sharpened length of oak, to scoop the gayfeather roots from the ashes of the fire onto the rock. Yellow threads of flame licked up angrily at the disturbance, then died down again to a mellow coral glow. The roots sizzled and bubbled. While they cooled, Lichen watched a doe and fawn graze in the meadow below.

Curious, to see them so close to Redweed Village. Elk, buffalo, and most of the deer had been hunted out long before Lichen was born. Everyone traded for hides now because they couldn't harvest them themselves. But these deer appeared unafraid. The animals had discovered a shady nook where the wildflowers and grass flourished despite the drought. Deer were faithful lookouts. Her ears might miss the approach of warriors, but the deer would scent their coming long before they posed a threat to Lichen. Nothing had spooked them so far. They sauntered lazily amidst the wildflowers, chewing and glancing up, only to bow their heads again while their tails flicked to keep off the biting flies.

The roots had cooled. Lichen peeled off the charred exterior to get to the meat, which she gobbled down greedily. Her stomach had been too knotted up to eat last night, but this morning it whined with gratitude and begged for more.

By the time she had finished all six of the roots, a warm satisfaction pervaded her body, trickling strength into her limbs. She sat quietly, staring out across the vista. On Pumpkin Creek, the white flowers of dogwood gleamed with an unearthly light amidst a jumble of tilted stone slabs.

Somewhere down there, her parents watched this same sunrise.

Wanderer? Can you hear me? I want you to come for me. I'm up here . . . up here.

Lichen took her stick and pushed the fibrous peelings of her roots into the fire. They withered and clenched into tiny, writhing fists.

"When you learn that everything you want, everything you crave and

believe in, is just sparkflies flitting through the darkness—then you'll find First Woman's Cave. Yes, Bat spends a great deal of time chasing sparkflies . . . and if he would just let himself die, why, he'd find out that he didn't need those glittering flies at all."

Lichen's nose ran. She lifted her sleeve to wipe it. "Well, I'm dying now, Wanderer," she whispered as her mouth started to quiver.

Whiffs of smoke fluttered in the northern sky like windswept feathers. How many people had died? Was the war still going on? She didn't know how long such things lasted. Didn't the warriors just attack, kill people, and leave?

Lichen tugged the thong around her neck to pull the Stone Wolf out from beneath the green ritual shirt. The Wolf flashed in the sun.

"Are you in there, Spirit?" she called. "I . . . I need help. Can you talk to me?"

She received no answer.

The deer in the meadow bolted suddenly, bounding among the rocks that skirted the bluff. Frantically, Lichen's gaze raced over the winding path—and there, far below, she saw five warriors trotting along her backtrail. Occasionally they would stop to make sure of the tracks, then take off again.

Panic burned through Lichen's veins like wildfire.

She grabbed the fire sticks she'd made from chokeberry branches, tucked them in her belt, and ran. Her feet pounded the gritty stone as she ran down along the crumbling edge of the cliff, out of sight of the trail. *Are they looking for me? No, no, why would they be looking for a little girl? But maybe they want to kill everyone who lived in Redweed. Maybe they're hunting down the people who escaped.*

"You won't leave any tracks across this stone," she panted to herself. "They won't be able to follow you."

But they would find her smoldering fire.

Then they would fan out to search for her. Warriors knew how to hunt for people. She had heard her mother talk about old battles where warriors crawled into every cranny to catch people they didn't like.

She forced her feet to move faster. Rounding a boulder, she pounded along a shadowed ledge where alumroot sprouted in the tracery of cracks. The shaggy stalks tugged at her tattered hem.

Movement ahead! Lichen grabbed onto a rock to stop herself so she could see. Melting against the rock, she hid in its shadows. With each puff of breath that escaped her lips, a glittering wreath of sand flitted before her face.

They speckled the bluff above her like black ants. Fifty, a hundred? More warriors? Coming up from the south?

Lichen whirled to look back toward her breakfast fire. The five men who had been working out her trail were trotting toward it. She could just make out the top of their bobbing heads.

A cry strangled in her throat. "Oh, what should I . . . where . . ."

She looked over the ledge. There, eight hands below, was a lip of rock no wider than two hands across. Urgently, she scrambled over the edge and landed safely on the lip. Sunlit nothingness spread below. When she moved, gravel scritched under her sandals before rolling over the brink and tumbling a hundred hands to the jagged, uptilted slabs at the base of the cliff.

A war whoop split the air. Lichen clutched the rock face in desperate fright.

Screams and shouts rang out like the baying of coyotes. Were the two groups of warriors enemies? Had they gotten into a fight? Lichen forced herself to inch along the lip, seeking a better hiding place.

A garbled shriek echoed as a man's body rolled off the bluff top and wheeled through the air before her.

Lichen let out a stunned cry and clawed to maintain her hold on the crumbling limestone. For what seemed an eternity, she fought blind, sickening terror as she teetered on the narrow lip. The world swayed with each jolt of her heart. Her sense of balance had fled with the horror. The rock itself seemed to shudder beneath her feet.

"Bird-Man, Bird-Man . . . Bird-Man," she began, a choking litany filled with tears. "Bird-Man, help me. Help me . . . Bird-Man . . ."

While the sounds of battle continued above, Lichen mustered the courage to take another step, and another. She scratched viciously at the limestone to hook her thumbs in the crevices. Her nails split and bled.

"*Help me, Bird-Man!* Where are you? You're supposed to be my Spirit Helper!"

Her questing hand hunted wildly for the next hold . . . and sank into a womb of cool air. Lichen gasped. Her eyes went wide with hope. Patting the emptiness, she carefully lowered herself to peer into the cave.

"*. . . You must go to a cave in this world. It will be dark, cold. But fire burns there.*"

Fear surged in her veins. What was in there?

The screams of the dying still pierced the air above her.

Falling to her knees, she crawled into the cave.

Hailcloud roughly jerked the shell-inlaid war club from the hand of his enemy and tied it to his own belt. The man's body flopped lifelessly, though blood still pulsed around the arrow embedded in his chest. Hailcloud took a deep breath. With a dizzy feeling of triumph, he gazed out at the broken bodies sprawled across the heights. Two enemies still made weak swimming motions while they died. But Hailcloud had lost only one man—young Crayfish. At the age of thirteen, this had been his first battle-walk. Who would tell the boy's mother? Would any of his party be left alive when all this was over?

Hailcloud stepped around the dying and the dead to join Basswood. The elderly warrior's dark, leathery face wore a film of tan dust spattered with flecks of blood. The lead Cahokia warrior had taken five arrows and still fought his way into cruel combat with Basswood before he died.

Breathing raggedly, Basswood wiped the back of his hand over his mouth. "These are no green boys. Badgertail brought his best. He must have left the inexperienced to guard the palisades."

"That's his way. Always prudent, calculating." Hailcloud lifted his chin to the west. "These men came up the trail that leads down to Pumpkin Creek."

"Yes. Are you thinking there may be more warriors there?"

"Perhaps," Hailcloud answered. A pang of dread went through him.

He narrowed his eyes and examined the copse of flowering dogwood almost hidden amidst slabs of stone. Last night, after witnessing the devastation of the village, they had seen a tiny glimmer of fire there—a warrior's fire, built low, smokeless, shielded on all sides by rocks. A bare glint of light had betrayed the man. Hailcloud had been waiting this morning to see if anyone moved in that rocky fortress. When the five enemy warriors had emerged, Hailcloud's war party had crept like weasels to meet them.

"How many? Can you guess?" Basswood asked.

"I don't know." Hailcloud frowned.

"What's wrong?"

"Well, we counted . . . what? Six war parties circling around the northern end of the bluff?"

"Yes, six. One for each of the major villages."

"Why would Badgertail waste warriors on Redweed? There's nothing of consequence here. A few old men and some women and children. What threat could they pose?"

Behind Hailcloud, laughter rose as men and women combed the dead enemies, boasting, stealing anything of value they could find.

"You think it's some sort of distraction? A ploy to draw us away from . . . what?"

"I'm not sure."

Hailcloud's gut squirmed. Northward, black dots were moving across the land, blurred by the heat waves that rose from the warming rock. Walking in single file, they resembled a shaggy string of buffalo plodding over the grass, swinging their heads in unison. But it couldn't be; the buffalo had been gone from this countryside for hundreds of cycles. More likely they were refugees fleeing the war-torn land. But there were so many!

"Do you see them?" Basswood whispered softly.

"Yes."

"Blessed Ancestors. Will there be anyone left in the chiefdom when this is over?"

Fragments whirled through Hailcloud's memory. He heard Aloda saying, "*My people have already begun preparing to break up into their clan groups and leave Spiral Mounds if we can't grow enough corn this summer . . .*" Jumbled images flashed through his mind, coming close and fading away. He lived again the attack on River Mounds, watched his warriors cut down one by one and left bleeding on the dry grass, knelt before Jenos' decapitated body—and wept.

He answered Basswood, "Anything is better than what we've been living through."

"I won't argue with that," Basswood said. "And if the numbers decrease, there'll be more land for our people to farm."

Hailcloud's eyes drifted back to the flowering dogwood where they had seen the light last night. A feathery tickle like a thousand butterfly feelers moving in his chest made him stand straighter. "Do you think he's down there, Basswood?"

"Badgertail? Could be. There's only one way to find out."

Twenty-eight

Primrose knelt by Green Ash's head and fanned her with a woven bulrush fan. His sister lay naked in the middle of the floor on a red-and-yellow blanket splotched with her blood. Green Ash's lips pinched against the agonizing moans that crept up her throat. In the last two hands of time, she had started thrashing weakly, rolling to her left side, then to her right, frantically muttering, "What are they? Huge. Look at them! They're everywhere. They've come to take my baby . . . in exchange . . . exchange . . ."

During the night, Green Ash had simply knotted her fists in Primrose's brown hem and bitten back her groans, but now her nails tore at the fabric.

Primrose writhed inside. How could Green Ash bear it? He would have rather died than witness such suffering. Slivers of late afternoon light penetrated the edges of the lowered window-hanging and streaked his sister's tormented face with bars of gold.

"It's all right," he soothed. "Just keep pushing. The baby will come . . . he's coming . . ."

Primrose had kept up an inane monologue for half the night, because when he stopped, Green Ash would cry, "Please! Talk to me!"

A birthing woman sat on each side of Green Ash, and a third crouched at her feet. In the dim light, their traceries of wrinkles appeared etched into their dark, leathery folds of skin.

Primrose licked sweat from his upper lip. The salty flavor taunted his empty stomach. How long had they been here? Twenty hands time? More? At least the night had been cool. Not like this stifling afternoon heat that made it hard to breathe. Flies buzzed in glittering dances around them, landing on their clammy faces, biting until Primrose thought he would go mad.

"I'm worried," old Nit whispered. Her eyes flitted over the raised sleeping platform behind Primrose, then dropped absently to the rows of grain-filled pots along the walls.

Green Ash's house was simple. Only a few baskets decorated the walls. A weaving loom stood beneath the sleeping platform, a half-finished blanket on it. Folded piles of dresses lay neatly mounded beneath the window. In the slices of window light, their red, green, and yellow colors blazed, providing the only real spots of color.

Nit let out a tired sigh. "She's not opening up like she should."

Fescue bent down to peer between Green Ash's spread legs. The oldest woman there, over sixty summers, she had large black eyes and a moony face. Not a single tooth remained in her head. Her words were always slurred. "I can see the top of the baby's head . . . but there's not enough space for him to come out."

"Wait," Little Rye Grass urged. "Give her a few more hands of time before we start to panic. At least he's not coming out backwards." She shook her head to toss her sweaty black hair away from her face, then nodded encouragingly at Primrose.

His throat tightened. Gently, he stroked Green Ash's wet forehead. Her whole body was sheathed in sweat. "I love you, Green Ash. Don't worry. The baby's just being stubborn. He's taking his time. But he's coming."

When a new wave of contractions struck, Green Ash reared up, pushing with all her might while she gritted her teeth. For the first time, she let out a scream, and Primrose put his arms around her and smothered her head with kisses. "Keep trying, Green Ash. Don't give up! Push! *Push!*"

But she fell back in his arms, panting, and he eased her down onto the drenched blanket. "Primrose! Don't let them take my baby. Stop them! Stop them . . ."

Old Nit growled, "Talk to her, Primrose. Say something!"

He stuttered, "I—I've been thinking about Locust, off and on, wondering where she is and how she's doing." Green Ash let out a shuddering breath and closed her eyes. Primrose smoothed his fingers down her cheek to her throat. "By now, Locust and Badgertail should be ready to join forces with the separate war parties that they sent out to talk to the northern villages. I've been praying that White Clover Mounds and Henfoot Village joined them. Locust figured they could glean about four hundred and fifty warriors from those two places, and that would give them enough to beat Petaga. I don't know. I have misgivings about the war. Who knows what will come of it? I can't see any way that we can have our old lives back. Too many people will have suffered. No one will be happy."

Primrose picked up his fan again and swept air up and down the length of Green Ash's body. The flies rose in an angry torrent. Had there ever been a day so hot or filled with so many biting flies? The insects buzzed incessantly, and though Primrose kept his fan moving to shoo them from Green Ash's naked body, there were so many that he couldn't keep them off. They simply moved to Green Ash's legs, arms, or face, depending upon where Primrose waved his fan.

"*Talk!*" Nit ordered.

"I—I heard a funny story." Primrose laughed nervously. "Did you hear it, Nit? The story about the Sun Chief and the field mice? Apparently the mice have infested the temple with a vengeance this cycle. I guess it's because the plants wilted so early and they're hungry, so they're coming inside, sniffing for bits of corn or seeds. Well, the way the story goes, the Sun Chief woke one night screaming when two mice crawled into the coils of his hair and couldn't get out. Those poor mice got flattened by fists before it was through, and the Sun Chief . . ."

He continued his story, his voice droning in unconscious rhythm with the swarming of flies, but Locust's pretty, pointed face filled his mind. *Be safe, Locust. I need you to come back to me.*

Surely she would be all right. She was cunning, and a perfect shot. No one could come close to Locust when it came to drawing a bow. But . . . what would happen if none of the northern villages had agreed to join them? They would be outnumbered, what . . . two to one?

You don't know that. Stop imagining the worst.

The possibility gnawed at him. Why did people fight wars at all? Couldn't everyone just share what little they had and live in peace? Then he shamefully recalled how desperate he had been last winter—desperate enough to stamp around in front of Locust weeping and pleading for her to do something to get them food. They hadn't eaten in two days. At the time, he hadn't cared in the slightest what lengths she had to go to in order to find food. Threats, theft, even murder, would have been acceptable. But Locust had only shushed him and held him tightly before she'd gone out hunting. When she came back the next morning with two measly pack rats, he had spent all day in bed, crying.

It wasn't long after that that Badgertail had gone raiding to collect tribute. Primrose had always secretly wondered if his own selfish pleas hadn't sparked it. He had felt too guilty to ask Locust whether she'd mentioned his desperation to Badgertail.

"Nothing's happening," Nit murmured as she sank back, so exhausted after the long hours of waiting that she couldn't do anything but stare blindly at the cattail mats covering the floor. Green Ash's cries started up again, pathetic whimpers like a fox trying to chew its way out of a trap. "Little Wild Rye, run to my house and get my bag of poisonous milk vetch."

Rye's face tensed. "Are you sure?"

"We've no choice. Go."

Rye scurried to her feet and ran out the door. For a brief moment, the tarnished rays of afternoon sunlight penetrated the gloom and lit the dust that curled up from the floor in her wake.

"Why?" Primrose dared to ask. "What will it do?"

Nit rubbed a hand over her ancient face. "Sometimes, when the poison enters the veins, it brings the child. We'll see."

"But what does it do to the mother?" Primrose questioned. "If it's Powerful enough to bring the baby, what . . . what happens to the mother?"

"It's a chance." Nit spoke very softly. "Don't question too deeply. We don't want to lose both of them."

"*Both!*" Primrose cried.

Nit glared at him. "Shut your mouth. If Green Ash knows what's coming . . . she's so weak . . . maybe too weak."

Nightshade floated in the glory of the Dream, her thoughts lilting as though borne on the wings of Hawk. Below her, Talon Town stood proudly like a jewel in the desert heat. Near the central plaza, a young woman sat surrounded by the tools of a potter. An eagle-bone whistle draped her neck, hanging down over the blue-and-yellow squares of her dress. The woman used a polishing stone to smooth a piece of coiled greenware before she picked up her bone-incising tool. Around the shoulder of her pot, she etched the delicate, abstract forms of thunderheads and falling rain. When a gaggle of laughing children raced by, the woman looked up and smiled.

Nightshade ached. Dimly, she realized that only her soul witnessed this scene, while her body lay elsewhere.

"But I want to go home," she pleaded of the Powers that she knew inhabited the towering red cliffs surrounding Talon Town. "Let me come home."

"Your life has been as a seed in water—sterile, waiting to strike earth so that it may bring forth fruit. Do not fear. The thlatsinas *will lead you home. The moment of fruition is coming."*

"When? My soul is dying. It's been dying for twenty cycles."

Nightshade shuddered with a bone-deep cold. Talon Town dissolved into a shimmering red haze, no more than a mirage spawned by the longings of her soul.

Brother Mudhead's twisted face, coated with sacred clay, solidified in the haze. *"Mother Earth never rests."* His familiar voice soothed her. *"It is her destiny to give birth unceasingly, to bring life to whatever comes back to her lifeless and sterile."*

"When can I go home?"

"When the waters wash you up onto shore. You were stolen to be delivered by the Father Water. He has done his job well. The seed of your soul has been nourished, strengthened, changed, by drowning in his chilling current. You are a child of the River—and a child of the Desert. Opposites crossed. Like Light and Dark. Good and Evil. Perfect and Imperfect. All things born of reconciliation atone."

"But what am I atoning for? I've done nothing."

Mudhead smiled sadly. The red haze deepened to a mortal shade of crimson, and voices whispered around them. They came from nowhere, from everywhere at once—soft, muted, ringing with desperate hope—and Nightshade knew that the Tortoise Bundle had penetrated the Dream to cry out to them. *"Yes, the Bundle knows. It has seen it all before. Power has crafted you, Nightshade. Like a lance of sunlight through fog, your soul will clear the way and allow the arrow to pierce the layers of illusion spun by First Woman to prevent entry to the Well."*

"The arrow? Is that a person? The woman whom Wanderer has been training?"

Mudhead laughed, raising his massive hands to sunder the image of his pink face from the backdrop of crimson. The *thump-thump-thump* of a pot drum echoed as he began to Dance—or perhaps it was his heart beating in Nightshade's veins. The crimson haze shattered, fragments whirling while Mudhead's sweeping arms reconfigured them into a land deluged by rain, where lightning leaped through moonlit clouds.

"What is this place?" Nightshade asked. She could discern people running, no more than dark shadows flitting through the body of the Dream.

"What might be—if you are willing."

"Willing?" she asked in confusion. Despite the cleansing downpour, the night reeked of smoke, as though fires had been raging for days before the rains came.

"Empty out your heart. Drain your own soul onto the path to prepare the way."

The scent of smoke grew. Through slitted eyes Nightshade saw ghostly white fingers grasping at the dark ceiling of her room.

"Fire! Fire!"

Orenda's cries brought Nightshade up and out of her warm blankets, clad only in her tan sleeping kilt. Her feet struck the cold dirt floor as Orenda crawled from beneath her bed. Smoke billowed around them. Nightshade grabbed the Tortoise Bundle from its tripod and reached down for Orenda's hand before racing with her for the door.

When she threw back the hanging, Nightshade halted so abruptly that Orenda ran into her leg, blurting, "What . . . ?"

Tharon crouched in the hall, his favorite handspike clamped to his chest. Black hair had escaped his copper hair combs and trailed over the sharp angles of his cheeks. He looked weak, ill. His trembling body shook his turkey-feather cape. In the light of the fire he had lit in the belly of Orenda's doll, his face gleamed as white and cold as wind-sculpted ice.

Orenda whimpered and tugged at Nightshade's hand. "Oh, no. Nonono."

Those seemed the only words the child freely spoke. Since she had been with Nightshade, Orenda had said barely ten sentences—and then only in response to a direct question about food or drink.

The doll burned quickly, its corn-shuck body greedily chewed up by the fire. For a moment, flames shot through the empty eye sockets of the doll's black-and-white mask and illuminated Tharon's mouth. A slow smile twisted his lips.

"Didn't I tell you, Orenda?" he hissed. "I told you I'd kill your companion if you crossed me. Now she's dead, just like your mother. And all because you abandoned me when I needed you most. Remember this. The next time you choose a companion to tell secrets to, I'll—"

"Get away from my door, Tharon!"

He looked up at Nightshade, his eyes glittering weirdly. "You can't frighten me anymore, Nightshade. You see, I've been talking to that foul device you tacked above my door. That evil tumor told me that your Power doesn't extend beyond your room. So I'm safe out here in the hall. I can do anything I want and you can't hurt me."

Nightshade released Orenda's hand and told her, "Get dressed. Bring me my red robe."

The little girl darted back into the room. While she waited, Nightshade examined Tharon. He seemed to be looking through her rather than at her. It was as though his soul floated in some disembodied world beyond the gray film of smoke. Nightshade frowned. This detached air bore the mark of a powerful Spirit Plant. What had he been mixing with his tea? Chokecherry leaves? No, he would be a lot sicker if that were the case. *You haven't had the courage to try some of Old Marmot's datura, have you, Tharon?*

"What are you doing, Tharon? Trying to become a Dreamer? I'm surprised that First Woman hasn't already struck you dead."

"You can't scare me. Not anymore. I'm not afraid of you! Your Power can't—"

"*My Power* comes from the Tortoise Bundle. Where it goes, my Power *is.*"

And with those careless words, she realized that she had trapped herself. From now on, day and night, she would have to carry the Bundle with her or Tharon would find a way of capturing and destroying it. No one but Nightshade knew the frailty of the Bundle. Its Power had grown, its voices resonated more strongly, but it still could not defend itself—not alone. *Nor can you. When you tied your Spirit to the Bundle's, you gave it a direct link to your Power—and it hasn't stopped siphoning it off since. Each day you grow weaker and the Bundle grows stronger. That's why you can't get beyond the gate now. You've no Power to spare for Underworld journeys. If the Bundle lives, you live. If the Bundle dies . . .*

Nightshade felt Orenda tuck the sleeve of a robe into her hand. Her eyes left Tharon for an instant while she slipped the robe over her head and unlaced her sleeping kilt to let it fall to the floor. Clutching the Tortoise Bundle in one hand, she gripped Orenda's shoulder in the other and stepped out into the corridor.

Tharon clenched his sweaty hands around his handspike and shifted as if to lash out. Nightshade fixed him with a look that made him freeze like Rabbit when he feels the cool touch of Eagle's shadow on his back.

"Don't force me to kill you, Tharon. I've no intention of doing so unless First Woman demands it. But if you push me, you'll leave me no choice."

Tharon watched through glassy eyes as Nightshade and Orenda walked past him and quietly rounded the corner.

"Hurry," Nightshade whispered to Orenda, and the child charged for the front entry.

Perhaps Orenda had felt it too, that glacial breath of wind against the back of her neck, as though a warning hand had been suddenly raised.

Several members of the Starborn peered through slitted hangings as the two passed. Those who watched had fear in their eyes, and hatred in their hearts for Nightshade, that she had roused Tharon's anger by taking Orenda into her care. Tharon had vented his rage on them.

When they stepped out beyond the highest palisade and into the misty morning, Nightshade filled her lungs, sucking in all the damp air she could hold. Blood rushed in her ears as she looked down at the bustling plaza, where at least a hundred people walked, laughing and conversing.

She had forgotten that today was Barter Day.

Every seventh day of the moon, Tharon's finest artisans spread their wares on blankets at the bases of the mounds. Magnificent pots, tools, and fabrics encircled the feet of the creators, who worked to craft new pieces until onlookers stopped to haggle prices.

The song of a flute wafted on the morning air as Nightshade and Orenda went down the steps, across the lower terrace, and through the gate. Soft and joyous, the notes spun by the flute touched Nightshade's soul, soothing it like a tender hand.

She followed the flute's song across the grass, passing a flintknapper who was heating chunks of brown chert in a small fire so that the stone would be easier to work. An antler flaking tool with a copper tip lay beside his knee, next to a battered hammerstone. Handspikes, arrow points, and long stone knives were displayed on his outspread blankets.

A weaver had set up her loom close by. She worked her colored strands back and forth while blankets and shirts waved gently around her, displayed on a series of wooden racks. One blanket, a magnificent blue creation that sported red, green, and yellow geometric designs, had been woven from the soft undercoats of dogs. Nightshade touched it admiringly before studying the bubbling pots of dye that sat on four fires. Cottonwood leaf buds made the yellow, maple twigs the black, dodder the orange, and bloodroot the red.

As they walked on, Orenda seemed to relax. Her dark eyes brightened and lost some of their usual hunted-mouse look. Nightshade led her to the base of the next mound, where a shell-bead worker was squatting on a cattail mat, with sandstone smoothers, abraders, sawin' tools, and drills scattered around her. Nightshade's memory tugge' *Could it be? Had Pursh grown so old in ten cycles?* The woman h yellowish hair and no teeth. She sucked her gums while she rolle bead in the sizing slot on her sandstone pallet. When she lifted the b to examine its size, the shell gleamed like polished elk ivory.

Nightshade knelt before the array of necklaces displayed on tan-and-green blanket. A magnificent gorget, the size of her h; caught her eye. Spider spread his legs across the shell in breathta' splendor.

"How much for this one?"

The old woman glanced up and squinted her half-blind eye though struggling with recognition herself. The shell bead drc from her fingers as she stiffened her spine. "For you—Priestess deerhide."

"That's half what it's worth, Pursh. I'll send you two."

"Thank you, Priestess," the old woman quavered and hastily] up her shell bead, refusing to raise her eyes again.

Nightshade took the necklace and put it on. The gorget reflec' morning sunlight like a pearlescent mirror.

Orenda fidgeted and yanked Nightshade's red skirt.

"What's the matter, Orenda?"

Orenda cocked her head.

"Are you all right?"

Orenda whispered, "She's coming . . . soon."

"Who? Who is?"

"That . . . little girl. The one who t-talks to me sometim in my Dreams."

Don't you dare cry, Primrose," Nit ordered. "If you cry, I'll strike you with my fist. At least . . . at least they're both alive."

Primrose shook as the old woman handed him one of the deformed babies: a little boy, his face twisted, wrapped in a green swaddling blanket. The baby had a misshapen bald skull—not like other newborns'—ballooned at the top and narrowing sharply to a pointed chin. His eyes were closely spaced, and he had no nose, just nostrils in the center of his face. Primrose's soft moan changed to sobs, but no tears came. His eyes had gone as dry as his throat over the past thirty hands of time.

Green Ash had lived—though she lay as still as a corpse on the soiled blanket. She had collapsed into a sound sleep nearly the instant the infants had been born.

"Will she be all right?" Primrose asked Nit. Rye was throwing back the window and door-hangings to let in the slate-blue gleam of dusk.

"Looks like it. The milk vetch will make her sleep for a whole day probably, but she should be up and around by the end of the moon."

"I'll bet it's sooner," Fescue called from where she stood against the northern wall talking to Checkerberry.

"Perhaps it was the starvation," Checkerberry said. "Hunger does strange things to a woman's body. Maybe, if Green Ash had been healthier—"

"There's no sense in speculating on it now," Nit admonished. "They're here, and they're alive. Be grateful."

Primrose started across the floor with the child. "Here, Checkerberry. You take him. You know babies better than I do. I'm afraid I might do something wrong."

But that wasn't the real reason. The sight of those pathetic stubs of arms tore Primrose apart. And that face. He girded himself and peered at the other boy, nestled on the blanket at Green Ash's side. The child stared back—as though it could see him through those enormous pink eyes. White hair clung to the tiny head in a thick mat, framing a face so strikingly like a wolf's that it terrified Primrose. The mouth jutted so far forward that it resembled a snout. Primrose looked away hurriedly and continued across the floor.

"Here, Checkerberry," he repeated. "You take him."

The old woman gingerly accepted the bundle and held it tightly to withered breasts. "Where's Nettle?"

"I sent Big-Nosed Rattler to fetch him. He should be here soon."

With the coming of night, the broiling heat had dwindled, replaced by a cool breeze that sawed in and out of the window like the breath of a slumbering giant. But instead of soothing him, the breeze chilled Primrose's drenched clothing. Sweat trickled coldly from his armpits, rolling down his sides until it soaked into the waistband of his skirt.

Outside, feet pounded closer, and Nettle ducked through the doorway, his eyes searching for Green Ash. He rushed to her, knelt and clasped her limp fingers safely in his—diligently avoiding looking at the misshapen boy on the blanket beside her. Nettle looked up at Nit.

"Green Ash . . . she's all right?" he asked.

"Don't fiddle with her," Nit ordered. "She's dead tired and needs her rest. And I don't want you troubling her about the babies. I . . . I don't know why First Woman did this, but I sense great Power in these children."

Nettle tenderly kissed Green Ash's fingers, then laid them back at her side before rising. He faced Checkerberry very nobly. "Now that the babies have been born, when may I marry Green Ash? I was hoping—"

"You don't have to do that, Nettle," Checkerberry said wearily. "I know it frightens you. And there's no guarantee that future children won't—"

"I *want* to marry Green Ash," he insisted vehemently. "When? When will you allow it?"

Checkerberry's expression conveyed her deep respect for his brave decision. "Once she's up and around. Don't be overanxious. She'll have preparations to make . . . and she has other things to think about."

Checkerberry touched Nettle on the shoulder and edged around him to stand before Primrose. She looked almost as tired as Primrose felt. Dark circles ringed her old eyes. "With Green Ash down, I'll need a spokeswoman for the clan. I was thinking that maybe you'd like to be it."

Primrose's mouth worked soundlessly. "I . . . it's never been done before." He was awed that she would even suggest it.

"The world is full of strange things, Primrose. And we've important business to take care of. Redhaw has begun openly charging us with treason. I'm worried about what she might do next. You have a female soul—that's all that counts. No one will be crude enough to point out that you have a man's body."

Primrose bowed his head in assent. "I would be honored, Aunt."

"Good. Come see me later in my house. We'll discuss your duties."

Checkerberry cast a final loving glance at Green Ash's sleeping form, then went out into the mauve veil of dusk, leaving Primrose and the others alone with the mews of the newborns.

Twenty-nine

The clouds that sailed westward over Badgertail's camp gleamed with a rusty hue. From where he stood leaning against the rock, he could see all the way to the Father Water. The wind had picked up, stirring the blossom-laden branches that formed the green canopy over his head.

Badgertail forced himself to work on his stiletto, made from the foreleg of a white-tailed deer. The needle-sharp point had a tendency to dull quickly, when it didn't outright break in the process of being withdrawn from a victim. He began to sharpen it, anxious, his heart pounding. He was eager to be away from this "sanctuary." At first it had been a shield against the enemy, but now the tall rocks hemmed him in like a cage. Worse, not even the dogwood blossoms could keep away the odor of death that blew down from Redweed Village when the wind changed. Wolves had growled and fought there all night, tearing the bloating corpses to pieces. Nor had the hot sun brought any relief, for with the day had come the shrill cries of vultures. Badgertail clamped his eyes shut and shook his head. The whole world rang with the sounds of death.

Badgertail's dreams had been haunted, filled with images of Nightshade. The feel of his arms around her had stirred feelings he'd thought his body had long forgotten.

His gaze lifted to where Locust knelt, playing a game of dice with Flute. She had been the only woman in his dreams for over twenty cycles. Guilt filled him. Dressed in a thin warshirt made of woven bulrush threads, the curves of her perfectly toned body riveted Badgertail's attention. Like all vigilant warriors, she had tied her war club to her belt—just in case—though her bow and quiver leaned beside her rolled blanket next to the closest rock. She had washed her hair and left it loose to dry. Sable curls caressed her ears.

Stop it. Badgertail exhaled impatiently. *You can't control your dreams.*

And they had been so vivid. He'd awakened himself several times in the night, always after a bout of desperate lovemaking with Night-shade. They'd been happy, laughing while they chased each other through juniper and piñon-pine forests in the Forbidden Lands. No war tore the countryside in his dreams.

He drew his stiletto tip across the piece of sandstone, honing it back to a lethal point. Around the camp, groups of warriors talked quietly, while others slept in preparation for the long night march ahead. At dusk, not long now, they would angle northward to join forces with Black Birch, Woodchuck, Elkhorn, and the other war-party leaders just south of Bladdernut Village. Then, day after tomorrow, they would start the sweep southward to challenge Petaga.

Badgertail's skin crawled at the thought. The fires in the south had begun to die down, but what did that mean? Had Petaga taken out his rage on everyone who wouldn't join him? Was he even now positioning his forces to repel Badgertail's coming attack?

Of course he is. No matter how carefully Badgertail's war parties had clung to the drainages, someone would have made a mistake by now. Petaga would know that Badgertail was on the move in the north and would be making preparations for their eventual clash.

But where were the scouts Badgertail had sent out? Almost none of them had returned. That fact nagged at him like a festering wound. Had they been killed? If so, Petaga had dispatched scouting parties long before Badgertail had left Cahokia. Why would he do that? Fear of the villagers whose homes he'd destroyed? Or knowledge that Tharon had taken dramatic action?

Too many things didn't fit.

He looked over at Wanderer and Vole, who still sat with their backs propped against an eroded rock. Vole had braced her forehead on her drawn-up knees to sleep. Wanderer gazed around the camp with remarkable mildness, given his circumstances. As Badgertail studied that thin, expressive face with its mop of gray hair, the old shaman turned to look directly at him. Badgertail gazed for a long time into those faded brown eyes, then strode through the weave of shadows to stand over his captive.

"Is there something you need, Badgertail?" Wanderer asked politely, as though addressing a dinner guest rather than his captor.

"Yes, if you don't mind. I was wondering if you knew whether or not Hailcloud is in charge of Petaga's forces."

"Oh, I would think so." Wanderer nonchalantly picked dried mud from his red shirt and dropped the bits at his side. With his hands bound, the effort was awkward at best. "I doubt there's anyone in the world Petaga trusts as much. And Hailcloud's loyalty is certainly beyond question. Crossed Beak told me that Hailcloud himself stran-gled Petaga's mother."

"Crossed Beak? Is this some relation of Petaga's?"

Wanderer's brow lined, then he shook his head. "No. Petaga isn't related to any ravens that I know of, so I suppose he's not related to Crossed Beak either."

"Crossed Beak is a raven?"

"Last time I talked to him, yes. But you know, these things change. Did I tell you I was having trouble with a weasel? It all started when I was Pack Rat and stuck my nose into—"

"Wanderer, you don't doubt that Hailcloud is leading Petaga's warriors?"

"Not at all."

Badgertail folded his arms and hugged himself. His feelings of friendship for Hailcloud had grown over the cycles, as well as his respect and admiration. Hailcloud had an unnatural ability to second-guess his enemy's war plans. Ten cycles ago they had been on a battle-walk in the south, working together to reopen a closed trade route, when Hailcloud had suddenly refused to take his warriors any farther. Badgertail had demanded reasons and was told only that Hailcloud *sensed* something amiss. Badgertail, angry, had finally agreed to send out scouts, and the scouts had surprised the enemy in a narrow defile where they had set up an ambush. Three had lived to make it back to camp and shout a warning. Hailcloud's battle sense had saved Badgertail hundreds of warriors that day. How many would it cost him over the next week?

And surely Hailcloud's battle sense had been responsible for what had happened at River Mounds, too. Nightshade had not been there to foresee their attack, so it must have been Hailcloud who had roused the village and gotten it ready.

Locust laughed, and Badgertail shifted to watch the dice game. Flute shook the decorated bits of clay in a hollow cane container, then threw them out across the dirt. Locust clapped a hand to her forehead, moaning, while the warriors around her chuckled and collected bets.

Vole woke at the noise. Badgertail could tell only because her shoulder muscles tightened. She kept her head down, pretending sleep.

"Wanderer," Badgertail asked, "where are Petaga's forces? Do you know?"

Wanderer regarded him inquiringly. "Don't you know?"

"No."

"You're the war leader, Badgertail. What makes you think I would know when you don't?"

"I was hoping you'd Dreamed something. You are, after all, a greatly renowned shaman—I'm a warrior."

Wanderer's bushy gray brows lowered. "Dreams aren't the province of shamans alone, Badgertail. Why, Spider and Weasel are far greater Dreamers than most humans. Did you know that?"

"Wanderer, do you always answer a question with a question?"

"Don't be silly. What would make you think that?"

Badgertail irritably focused on the sky over the weathered rocks. The molten ball of the sun perched low on the western horizon. Streaks of scarlet light shot out from the fiery fringe, puncturing the deepening blue. All seemed quiet, peaceful. Shadows lengthened across the floodplain in the distance, sending charcoal fingers over the edges of every hollow.

Badgertail returned his gaze to Wanderer and found the old man staring back at him. Their eyes met like the clash of war clubs. Then, just as suddenly, Wanderer's eyes regained their amiable lunacy.

Badgertail lifted a brow. "You know, Wanderer, cycles ago, I used to wonder how much of your curious behavior was feigned and how much was real. You know what conclusion I came to?"

"No. What?"

"I decided that you are the consummate trickster, better than Coyote or Deer at circling and trotting back over your tracks to confuse your hunter."

"Badgertail, do you think I'm being dishonest with you?"

"Are you? I suspect that you'd do anything to mislead me about the Stone Wolf and Hailcloud."

"Well . . ." Wanderer straightened indignantly. "Then why would you ask me about them?"

"I was hoping that I could send you back to the Sun Chief with a message saying you had helped us. The Sun Chief might show you greater leniency."

"Really?" Wanderer scratched his cheek thoughtfully despite the awkwardness of his bonds. "Well, that would be surprising, given that leniency isn't one of Tharon's more noticeable attributes. Besides, you're forgetting that Tharon has always loathed me. Even as a boy, he used to sneak up to poke me in embarrassing places with sharp objects. I doubt that he'd show much reluctance to do the same thing now. Since he's grown into an adult, I'm sure that his toys—as well as his aim—have gotten more lethal."

Badgertail said nothing, remembering what Tharon had done to poor Shagbark with his handspike. And there had been other times when he'd been called to the temple to help remove the bodies of luckless servants.

"Wanderer, do you—" Badgertail's head snapped around. "What was that?"

Through the warriors' voices, he had heard something soft, the crunch of a sandal in the dry plants beyond the rocks, a sandal far too carefully placed to be one of his own warriors.

"*Badgertail!*" Locust shouted in warning as she lunged to her feet.

War cries burst the stillness, and an arrow smacked the rock behind Badgertail. He dove for the ground, rolling and coming up with his war club clutched in his fist.

The rocks came alive with racing men and women scrambling for their bows. Badgertail could see enemy warriors sprinting in from every direction, shooting as they ran. How many were they? Fifty? Sixty? No . . . more. And Badgertail had barely forty-five left.

"Southwind! Take ten people. Climb the rocks. Guard the south side of camp. Flute, you take the north. I'll—"

Out of the corner of his eye, he saw Locust whirl and drop into a crouch as she brought up her bow, aiming over Badgertail's head before she let fly. A shriek, and a man toppled from the jagged rocks, landing on top of Badgertail in a bloody heap.

Badgertail shoved the corpse aside and crawled for his own bow and quiver, resting where he had been sharpening his stiletto earlier. Arrows fell around him. Warriors collapsed, thrashing and screaming where they'd sprawled in the dust. Clusters of dogwood blossoms erupted in a fine spray of white petals that pirouetted around people as they ran.

Blood surged in Badgertail's ears. He slung his quiver over his shoulder and grabbed up his bow. Rolling onto his back, he nocked an arrow while he scanned every possible entry. To his left, Parsnip and Groundsel scaled the rocks to shoot down on their attackers.

A thin cry wavered into oblivion. On its heels, one enemy warrior materialized, vaulting a maze of wounded and dying to leap into the camp.

When the man threw back his head to shrill a war cry, Badgertail aimed and let loose. His victim wheeled, yelling as he stumbled backward and wilted atop the rocks, clawing at the shaft that had buried itself in his belly.

"They're coming!" Southwind howled. He and his people had wedged themselves between stone slabs to guard the south side. "There must be a hundred!"

Badgertail hit the ground on his stomach, slithering until he reached the tumbled stone on the western side of camp. Slinging his bow over his shoulder, he scrambled up the rocks until he could look down over the creek.

Coming up the drainage bottom, in the same way that his own people had ambushed Redweed Village, twenty warriors were splashing through the thin film of water. How had they gotten through? They must have killed the guards he'd posted as lookouts.

The enemy war party charged Badgertail's camp in a screaming horde, shooting into the midst of fleeing warriors and swinging their war clubs for close combat. They came in wave after wave, ten at a time, throwing themselves against the stone fortress.

A glint of black caught Badgertail's eye, and he whirled in time to see a man moving through the rocks behind Locust. "Locust, get down!" he shouted. She dove for cover as Badgertail fired. The arrow took the man squarely through the ribs. He jerked backward and lost his balance on the uneven rocks. Spinning sideways, he fell.

"There are too many!" Badgertail shouted. "Run! Break into groups of five and get out of here! Let's make them split their forces if they're going to hunt us! Flute, go first. We'll try to cover you."

Flute tapped four people as he sprinted by, and they followed him through a break in the rocks, then raced down into the creek bottom. Other parties of five began escaping. Badgertail fired three arrows to hold off pursuers, but only one hit its mark, slashing across a woman's face, blinding her.

Jagged shrieks mixed with the wails of the wounded, and Badgertail's warriors fell back beneath the onslaught.

"Everybody! Go! Go on, get out of here!"

Badgertail climbed higher into the rocks to peer out across the floodplain. The sight that met his eyes made the muscles knot in the pit of his stomach. His warriors retreated in a choking cloud of dust, stumbling through the charred remains of Redweed Village while they fired at the irregular lines of people who followed. But the wounded near the camp kept fighting, drenched in sweat and covered with blood.

"Badgertail?" Locust yelled. She crouched alone in the eastern rocks. Blood soaked her shoulder and sleeve. Hit? Had she been hit? Or was the blood someone else's? "Hailcloud has split his people to chase ours. There's an opening to the southwest. *Take it!*"

"Not without you! Come on!" Badgertail jumped down to the ground and ran for her.

Locust fired a final arrow and sprinted to meet him halfway. They dashed past the place where Wanderer and Vole had sat earlier, leaped over the scattered contents of two packs, and burst out onto the open plain. If they could just get across the creek and into the tall stands of sunflowers and giant ragweed, they might be able to crawl their way to freedom.

"Badgertail? Help . . . help me."

He spun to see Southwind half-staggering, half-running, behind them. Blood drenched the warrior's side around the hand he pressed tightly to his side. Dark, crimson blood, gut blood.

Badgertail slapped Locust on the shoulder. "Get across the creek. I'll join you as soon as I can."

He started back, but Locust caught him by the arm and swung him around. "Don't be a fool. Southwind is dead on his feet! His body just doesn't know it yet. Look at the color of that blood. I won't let you sacrifice yourself to—"

"Maybe it's not as bad as it looks."

"Stop lying to yourself! You've seen too many wounds not to realize—"

"I can't leave him! They'll mutilate any of us they catch alive."

"Mutilation is nothing! Do you know what they'll do if they catch *you?* The great Badgertail! The man who murdered their families and destroyed their homes. They'll make the torture last for days. They won't let you die until you've told them every detail of our battle plan. You'll betray the entire—"

"Go!" Badgertail jerked free of her grip. "I'll meet you!"

Then he was running back, winding around clumps of wild roses, to reach Southwind. The stocky warrior tottered into Badgertail's arms; putting his right arm around Southwind's waist, Badgertail hauled him over the edge of the creek.

Father Sun dipped lower in the sky. Only a sliver of crimson peeked above the gray wall of the western bluffs. Night would drape the land soon. Perhaps if they could find a place to hide until darkness . . .

A flock of grouse squawked and exploded into flight on the creek bank ahead, causing Badgertail to stumble. "Southwind, wrap your arm around my shoulders."

Southwind tried to, but Badgertail had to take the warrior's hand and slide it across his back before quickly beginning the climb up the steeply eroded bank. Dirt sloughed off beneath their thrashing feet, forcing them to work twice as hard.

They had almost reached the top when Southwind sagged against Badgertail, muttering, "Sorry, can't . . . sorry . . ." Southwind's fingers clutched at Badgertail's shoulder as weakly as a newborn's while he sank to his knees in the glittering sand.

"Southwind? Southwind, hold on to me!"

"Can't . . . shouldn't have called. Sorry . . ."

"Come on! You can do it! Live!"

Badgertail lifted Southwind in his arms and climbed over the lip of the creek, where he laid him down in a tall, aromatic bed of golden ragwort. The yellow flowers stood six hands tall, high enough to cloak them temporarily. Badgertail moved Southwind's hand away from his side so he could get a look at the injury. He felt his stomach rise into his throat. The enemy warrior must have used the chert studs on his war club like a saw to carve such a deep wound. The gash extended from just under Southwind's ribs down to his groin. Gray intestines wormed through the opening, green-brown, and oozing where they had been ruptured. The stench forced Badgertail to turn his head.

"I didn't know how bad . . ." Southwind blinked lazily at the purple-rimmed clouds that hovered overhead, as if his vision had started to fade. "Sorry . . . Badgertail. Leave. No use . . ."

Voices came from across the creek, and Badgertail flattened himself in the weeds. Through the fragrant curtain of flowers, he spied warriors flitting past the shadow-dappled stone slabs.

The tallest of the warriors stepped into a patch of wan sunlight, and Badgertail involuntarily dug his fingers into the sand. *Hailcloud!* Was that burly warrior beside him Basswood? Probably, though Badgertail could not be certain from this angle. He concentrated on stilling his frantic breathing so he could hear their quiet words.

". . . says no, but he's still checking the dead."

"How many did we lose?"

"Nineteen. But they easily lost thirty. Bull Tine is still pursuing those who fled. If he can catch them before it gets dark, no one will be alive to report our location."

Badgertail braced his forehead on his fist. *Thirty?* A sick dread gripped him. Which friends? What was Hailcloud doing so far north? Had this been simply a scouting party that had accidentally stumbled onto Badgertail's camp? Or were they part of a larger force? Had Hailcloud *known* that Badgertail would make a play for the northern villages, and convinced Petaga to move his warriors up?

A woman's shout tore the evening, and he jerked.

Hailcloud trotted out of the rocks and shielded his eyes, gazing southward. Two warriors were dragging Locust up from the creek bed. Horror numbed Badgertail. She fought wildly, kicking, wrenching against their iron-fisted grip while she cursed them.

"Locust . . ." His fingers knotted in the golden ragwort. "Why didn't you run?"

What had she been doing there? It wasn't like her to . . . *She was waiting for you.*

Desperately, Locust yanked away from her captors and dashed across the grass-rich terrace, her hair flying. She took barely ten paces before the warriors tackled her and knocked her to the ground. Her enraged scream rang out in the twilit stillness.

Badgertail's gut twisted as he watched the warriors haul Locust through the mauve shadows of dusk toward the rocks where Hailcloud waited.

V̇ole started squirming for cover when the battle exploded and men and women went wild, careening for weapons, scrambling up the rocks to spy on their attackers, shooting back in desperation.

Wanderer landed beside her with sweat beading on his nose. "This way, Vole. Follow me."

"Do you know where you're going?"

"I certainly do," he answered curtly. "Away from here."

Wanderer half-slithered, half-crawled through a narrow opening between the slabs to get out onto the grassy plain. Vole followed him, her blistered leg hurting unbearably. Tattooed warriors raced everywhere, their beaded forelocks glinting as they ran. Lavender light fell in a woolly blur across the fields of sunflowers, thistle, and grass.

Her hands tied, Vole crawled clumsily. Wanderer's frantic feet kicked dirt into her face, forcing her to turn her head. A few hands away, she saw a dead warrior—coagulated blood jelled in his mouth and nostrils—sprawled on his stomach, an arrow protruding from his back. He watched her with wide, sightless eyes.

"Wait! Wanderer . . . ?" She lunged for the knife on the man's belt, pulling it out with her teeth before whirling to drop it in front of Wanderer's nose. "Hurry! Cut me loose."

She extended her hands. When Wanderer had sawed the rope enough that she could pull it apart, Vole jerked her hands free, snatched the knife from his hand and cut his bonds, then tucked the knife in her belt.

Her eyes darted from warriors who sprinted in from the south to those who scrambled up out of the creek bed. The moans of the dying mixed hauntingly with cries of triumph.

"Which way? Where can we go that they won't—"

"This way!" Wanderer got down on his stomach and slid through the wilted grass a hand at a time, going so slowly that it seemed to take forever to get beyond the fighting. Ahead lay the shade of taller plants.

When Vole could stand it no longer, she whispered, "Will you hurry up!"

"I don't think that's wise, Vole. The only way Snail stays hidden from Bluebird is by moving slowly. I learned that when I had Bluebird's soul. He was always annoyed by the stealth of Snail. We—"

"Tell me *later*, Wanderer! *Move!*"

"They'll see us if I go too fast, Vole. That's what I was trying to tell you. We ate a lot of flies and mosquitoes when Bluebird and I were together, because their glittering wings attracted our attention. But snails? Only rarely."

A rush of warriors swerved around the rocks in pursuit of several of Badgertail's retreating men. They shot arrows as they vaulted brush. "Blessed Father Sun," Vole hissed in panic. "They're coming right at us!"

Wanderer changed course, angling sharply to the left into a dense growth of thistles. The thorns slashed at Vole's arms and face as she followed. She lay panting, praying that the evening had grown murky enough to hide them. Though the sun had sunk below the horizon, its brightness lingered on the hilltops in luminous smudges of gray.

War cries rent the air as the warriors approached. Vole held her breath. They sprinted by, one pounding past within six hands of her prone body.

"Let's get out of here!"

"No!" Wanderer flung his arm across her back and flattened her on the ground. Vole stared at him in shock. His wide eyes were fixed on the rocks, where a stocky warrior was dragging out a youth of no more than fourteen summers. Four men and one woman followed, swinging deadly war clubs. The stocky warrior threw the youth to the dirt about thirty hands from where Vole and Wanderer lay hidden.

"Where's Badgertail?" the stocky warrior demanded. "Tell me, boy! Is he here?"

"I don't know," the youth answered in terror. "I swear, I—I haven't seen him!"

"You're lying!"

"No! No, truly, I—"

"We haven't time for this." The stocky one turned to his warriors.

"Kill him. Then search every inch of the brush. I want Badgertail!" He strode away, heading back toward the rocks.

The five warriors fell on the youth with their clubs, first bashing his spine, then beating his head until his face was a spongy mass of red. Soon after they trotted away, another warrior sprinted by and slammed his club into the dead boy's skull. Sickness churned in Vole's stomach.

Hailcloud organized a group of his warriors to search for wounded enemies. They fanned out in a long line and began beating the brush beyond the body, killing anyone who still breathed. As the darkness deepened, the heat of the battle died down and warriors trotted back to the stone slabs to regroup.

Wanderer nudged Vole with his elbow. "Now. Let's go. But we have to crawl. If we stand up, they'll be all over us."

They crawled out of the thistles, heading in an easterly direction.

Thirty

As the evening coolness settled on the land, mist rose from the ponds, twining phantom arms into the twilit sky. The somber shadows of rocks and brush melted under the deepening blanket of darkness, smoothing until they pooled with the night, the croaking of the frogs, and the hum of insect wings.

Lichen lay curled on her side in the entrance of the cave, her head pillowed on her arm, her back to the small fire she had built in the rear. The wood she had gathered at dawn had been damp with dew, and it smoked badly, forcing her to stay near the opening of the cave so she could breathe.

Oh, Wanderer. Where are you?

Would no one ever come looking for her? She had been watching the trails from sunup to sunset, but no one had walked them.

Almost all of the people who fled along Pumpkin Creek had been caught and killed. She had witnessed the entire battle, and had cried when the screams of the dying rang with ghostly resonance from the hills.

What's happening out there, Wolf Slayer? Is the whole world going to die in this war?

To the north, vultures soared above Redweed Village, their black shapes flapping against a gray, sickly sky. The brief battle had forced them to retreat to their hidden perches. But they had returned—dozens of them. Lichen whimpered. She had barely slept in the past two days for watching the birds and listening to their squawks while they feasted on her friends.

Mother? Are you alive?

She tucked her green hem around her toes. Every time she thought about her parents, a chill swelled in her chest and tingled in her hands and feet. The cave did not help. Its oblong womb of darkness was no wider than two of her body lengths, and little taller. Cold seeped in from the rocks. Her teeth had chattered all of last night.

She was tired . . . so very tired. It took great effort to stay awake, to keep watch on the trails.

"Bird-Man, Bird-Man, Bird-Man, Bird-Man," she called desperately to her Spirit Helper, trying to suppress the ache in her heart. "Help me stay awake. I have to wait for Wanderer or my mother. They might not see me here. I have to stay awake."

Her voice faded as though the wind had sucked it away and blown it up to the newborn stars. Lichen fought the heaviness of her eyes, but weariness overcame her. Images danced on the back of her lids, flickering orange and blue as sleep numbed her body and coiled through her thoughts . . .

. . . The hiss of a moccasin against stone startled her.

Lichen scrambled up, panting in terror, to stare at a little boy who squatted in the mouth of the cave. Two black braids framed his oval face and glistening black eyes. He was younger than she, maybe eight summers, and dressed in strange hides. The red face of Wolf adorned his chest.

"Who . . . who are you?" she croaked.

"My name is Foxfire. Your Spirit Helper sent me. Come with me, Lichen. We haven't much time."

"Where are we going?"

"On a Dream-walk. Just like warriors on battle-walks, Dreamers have to confront their enemies, too. I'll take you. Hurry."

But Lichen couldn't move. She scrutinized the curious hides he wore. For all of their beauty, they were thick and mottled in a way she had never seen, as if they came from animals that didn't live in her world.

Lichen cocked her head. "What kind of hides are those?"

"*Mammoth*," he said, lifting his arms. Then he pointed to his braided belt. "*And this is horsehair.*"

"What are those animals? I've never heard of them before."

"*Come with me and you can see them if you'd like.*"

Foxfire ducked out of the cave and stood on the narrow lip of rock that overlooked the floodplain. Gingerly, Lichen followed and stood beside him beneath a vast, glittering bowl of stars. The Road of Light tied the heavens together with a broad band of white. Lichen frowned. Wolf Pup had already galloped two thirds of the way across the sky. How had it grown so late without her knowing it?

"Where do these mammoth and horse live?"

"*Far away . . . and a long time ago. When the threads of the Starweb pulled apart, the world changed and they died.*"

"You mean they're all gone?"

He nodded wistfully. "*Yes. Every time a Dreamer fails, a part of the Spiral dies.*"

Sadness filled Lichen. Her soul seemed to remember Mammoth and Horse, but dimly, like the recollection of birth buried deep inside every living creature. "If they're gone, how can we see them?"

"*Spider will help us. The Circles are coming full again, and you're going to need to see for yourself what happens when a Dreamer gives up.*"

Foxfire extended his hand and blew across his palm. Strands of light shot from his fingertips, spreading across the darkness like a spiderweb iced in blue fire. Lichen's mouth gaped when he trotted out onto the swaying web. "*Please, Lichen, we must hurry.*"

"I . . . I'm coming."

Lichen tested the blue thread with the toe of her sandal before biting her lip and racing out after Foxfire.

Vole woke. Rain drifted out of the night sky in a wind-borne mist. A hushed whisper filled the air as drops pattered on the sunflowers that curtained the undercut hollow where she lay hidden. Soft. Soothing. For a moment she almost forgot her pain. But as she moved, seeking to draw up one knee, the agony returned with a ferocity that left her gasping for breath.

Don't . . . force yourself. Just rest for a while.

They had crawled in the underbrush for half the night, desperately dodging the warriors who ghosted through the darkness. Every patch of cat's claw and stinging nettle had scoured the blisters of her injured leg; now she had to stifle whimpers whenever a blade of grass brushed her. Somewhere in the terror, her fever had begun. It burned bright inside her, leaving her weak and trembling while it seared her soul with its fire.

Vole lifted her head so she could peer at her leg. Despite the poor light, she could see it, clotted with blood, dripping pus, and coated with dry leaves. Shreds of skin hung loose where the blisters had been torn. The sight sickened her. She would have to clean it soon, or evil Spirits would smell the blood and come to feast. Then she would be in real trouble.

As she eased her head back to her rock pillow, she noticed that Wanderer's tattered red shirt draped her shoulders, protecting her against the chill of the mist. Where was he? Her gaze roamed the hollow. Small and gray, the rock shelter spread about twenty hands by ten. The rounded overhang arched thirty hands over her head, protruding just enough to fend off the moisture. No more than an arm's length away, a ragged border of dampness darkened the soil.

Vole looked out toward the field of sunflowers beyond the cliff face and saw Wanderer. He stood in only his breechclout, its attached array of Power pouches dangling like cocoons around his waist. In the sky above him, a single cloud blotted the stars. The rest of the heavens shone crystal-clear and beautiful. Why would he be standing out in the rain? *Don't be silly. That's just the sort of thing he'd do.* But surely fatigue weighed as heavily on him as it did on her—probably more, since he was twice her age.

As she watched, Wanderer tipped his chin to the mist. Water slicked his gray hair against his skull and reflected with an ethereal sheen from his starlit face. He spread his arms, hesitating like a hovering kestrel, then began the fluid motions of the Thunderbird Dance. His ribs stuck out as he swayed and spun, dipping his hands to stroke the earth before lifting them reverently to the sky. All the while, his outstretched fingers imitated the rhythmic sprinkling of rain.

From far off, the distant roar of thunder answered . . .

Wanderer Danced harder, gyrating as he stamped his feet. Mud caked his sandals, leaving dry tracks in the moistened dirt. Power built. Each fluid lacing of his arms quickened it, until the hair at the nape of Vole's neck crawled. When Wanderer began a prolonged spin, his head thrown back, his arms reaching straight up to Thunderbird, lightning flickered through the cloud, gently at first, as though Thunderbird had just awakened and blinked his eternal eyes. Thunder rumbled lazily. Then, abruptly, a lance of lightning split the darkness and zigzagged across the black fleece of night. The flash illuminated Wanderer's skeletal form in a deluge of blue.

From deep inside Vole, awe rose. She felt the same half-worship of him that she had when she'd loved him those many years ago. He had always been able to call lightning from the clouds—at least as long as he'd had a bird soul, whether Eagle, Magpie, Raven, or any of the others who had inhabited his body. She had asked him about it once. Wanderer had told her that all animals of flight, even flying squirrels, had a kinship to Thunderbird. Their calls, he said, resonated more clearly in Thunderbird's soul than the calls of other animals did, rousing him as though they were the muted echoes of his own sacred voice seeping up from the crevices of his thoughts.

Vole sucked in a deep breath of the rain-sharp wind and studied Wanderer as he plodded along the base of the towering cliff. Bushes crowded every shadowed nook. He bent to fumble with the leaves of a scrawny plant, then moved on. He felt his way around the concave curve of the wall, prodding first one bush, then another.

There are warriors crawling all over the floodplain and bluff. Where can we go? We're trapped here.

Who were the warriors who had launched the attack against Badgertail? Petaga's forces? She had not recognized any of them. But the Moon Chief would have gathered hundreds by now, perhaps thousands. She couldn't know all of them.

So much is happening, and, Blessed Thunderbird, I'm tired. She rubbed her eyes.

Badgertail and Petaga had locked themselves in mortal combat, while the small villages lashed out with hit-and-run raids to steal supplies from the camps of the warriors. She had overheard Locust talking about it. A runner had come in from the north to announce that Oxbow Village had joined them. But he had complained bitterly of the traitorous stragglers who had abandoned their homes and taken up bows against both sides, creeping into camp at night, looting, and then fleeing in all directions before the lookouts could decide which thief to shoot at.

Wanderer shoved a thorny rosebush sideways. His chert knife glinted, and the plant quaked. What could he be cutting from the stems? After about a finger of time, he straightened up and awkwardly fumbled with a handful of something.

The rain cloud sailed eastward over the bluff, and the stars returned in a glittering canopy to illuminate the world. Vole saw Wanderer shiver, and guilt darted her. Without his shirt, even the slightest breeze must prick his bones. He hurried, trotting around bushes and jumping fallen rocks, back to the hollow.

"I thought maybe you'd left me for the wolves," she commented.

Startled, he whirled and frowned into the darkness. "Have you seen any?"

"No," she sighed.

Wanderer turned, smiled happily, and knelt to pile his handful of small, round objects on the dirt near an old firepit. The jagged edges of the rock ring scarcely thrust above the surface. "You were whimpering in your sleep, Vole. That's why I left. I thought maybe I could help."

"Help?"

"Yes. You see, these bulbous growths come from the lower stems of rosebushes. When charred and crushed to powder, they take the pain from burns. It's lucky for us that so many rosebushes grow here."

He smiled faintly at her and rose to pull wood and dried leaves from the pack-rat nest clogging a hole in the corner. Using the pointed end of a piece of pack-rat litter, he dug out the firepit before arranging the leaves and wood just so; then he reached for the fire sticks that he had made while she'd been asleep.

For the dowel, Wanderer had stripped the bark from a straight hickory branch as long as his shin. Next, he had whittled one end to a point. The second piece of wood consisted of a section of oak into which he had gouged a round hole. This he now steadied on the ground with his feet and sprinkled punky material in the hole. Taking the pointed hickory dowel, he speared it into the punky stick on the floor and began spinning it as fast as he could between his palms. In no time, the friction had heated the punky wood to the point that it smoked. He quickly bent down and blew on it to bring the embers to glowing life. With great care, he then scraped them against the dry leaves and blew some more, gently coaxing until the tinder caught and he could start adding knots of grass, and finally twigs, and then wood.

"Aren't you afraid that some warrior will see the glow?" Vole asked.

"No," he said reassuringly. "I walked a long way out onto the floodplain to see how well-concealed this hollow is. The sunflowers completely shroud us. If it were day, I'd worry because of the smoke. But not tonight. We'll be all right."

Wanderer carefully arranged the rose burls at the edges of the blaze and sank back on his haunches to watch their thin outer husks sizzle and wither. Exhaustion deepened the web of lines that covered his face. Sitting there like that, the flames dancing in his eyes, he looked very old and a little sad—like an ancient woman peering down curiously at her reflection in water and trying desperately to recall the image that had gazed back at her twenty cycles before.

Tenderly, Vole said, "You're the only man—er, raven—I know who could Dance with such energy after crawling on his belly half the night to escape people who wanted to kill him."

"Really? I'd think anyone would want to Dance after that. In sheer relief, if nothing else." He used the knife to turn the burls. As he did so, his bushy brows plunged down to meet over his nose.

"What is it, Wanderer?"

"Hmm? . . . Oh, I'm just thinking."

"I could see that. About what?"

"Wondering if Badgertail survived. Wondering when you'll be well enough to travel."

"Tomorrow!" She sat up suddenly, but her body mocked her by trembling under the strain. She hastily sank back down.

Wanderer lowered his eyes to his rose burls. "How's your leg?"

"Bad."

"And your fever?"

"Getting worse."

"I thought so. I doubt that you'll be able to travel for days. But I don't know how long we can stay here. If Badgertail is alive, he'll eventually have search parties combing the hills for us. He wants the Wolf." More softly, he added, "And me."

Wanderer gazed in the direction of Pumpkin Creek, his eyes going vacant as if he had sent his raven soul flying to see what creatures skulked along the dark banks. That expression had always set Vole's gut to writhing.

"Forget about us, Wanderer. I'm worried about Lichen."

"Don't be. She's fine. Frightened, hungry, but fine."

A terrible hope tightened Vole's chest. Shakily, she asked, "How do you know? Did you Dream something?"

"No, not a Dream. She's been calling to me."

"Calling . . . ?"

Wanderer scooped the rose burls out of the fire onto the ground, where they rolled in tiny circles before settling down to smoke. Thin gray columns rose. He went to the edge of the hollow and picked up a flat piece of limestone. Bringing it back, he set it next to the fire and began to methodically crush each charred burl into paste. "I mean that her soul has grown Powerful enough to make itself heard over long distances."

"But how is she? What's she saying?" Vole found herself sitting bolt upright, the limestone hollow swimming nauseatingly around her. Her heart jammed against her ribs as the flames of the fire blended into the images of firelit sunflowers, damp earth, and blurs of stars.

"Vole?" Wanderer called faintly through the dark fog that descended on her. "Oh, no."

His face suddenly loomed large, and she felt strong hands grip her arms to halt her fall. Her head bounced limply. Slipping a cool hand behind her neck, Wanderer let her down easily and rearranged his red shirt over her shoulders. She hated it when anyone tried to take care of her. It made her feel weak and helpless. Feebly, she flailed at him.

"Don't . . . touch me."

Wanderer drew back and studied her anxiously. "I'll be glad to oblige, so long as you're not about to bash your brains out on a rock." He pointed at her "pillow."

"Lichen . . . tell me about Lichen. Where is she?"

"I don't know that," he said. "But she's been calling to me steadily. When she stops calling, then I'll panic." He got to his feet. "Vole, I have to wash your leg before I can apply the salve. It'll hurt. Can you stand it?"

"It has to be done soon. . . . What's Lichen been saying to you?"

Wanderer went out to the lip of the overhang and cupped his hands beneath a trickle of water. He carried the cool liquid back conscientiously and dribbled it down her leg. Vole suppressed a cry when the water touched her flesh like a river of fire. The more that Wanderer dribbled on her leg, the worse the pain grew, until she had to bury her face in the crook of her elbow to keep from weeping.

As though he hadn't noticed, he said, "It's not words I hear, it's more like the feathery touch of Lichen's soul against mine." Vole felt him lift the sleeve of his red shirt and heard the squeal of ripping fabric. He kept talking, softly, confidently. "Lichen is a very Powerful Dreamer, so as long as she stays under cover, she'll be safe. I think that by now she can probably sense when enemy warriors are near. All great Dreamers can. It's like . . ."

Vole stopped hearing his words. Only a soft drone penetrated the violence of her pain. It took what seemed an eternity for him to wash her burns. She trembled while he gently dabbed the wet cloth to remove the grime that had melded with old blood. Every grain of sand he touched bit into her flesh like a poisoned talon.

Only at the last, when he started applying the rose salve in cool globs, did she break down and weep . . . in relief that it was almost over. Her shoulders shook traitorously. He stopped for a moment, his hand faltering in its work, and then he finished and stood.

Vole refused to look up and let him see her tears. *Just go away, Wanderer. Don't shame me by asking anything ridiculous, like how do I feel.*

His sandals scraped the stone with his awkward movements. After a time, she heard him kneel beside her and felt a large hand, bony and uncertain, clumsily stroke her hair.

"Try to sleep, Vole. I'll keep watch."

Thirty-one

Around Lichen, brilliant stars twinkled like hoarfrost while darkness flooded outward, rippling in the farthest reaches of the sky. Her skin gleamed blue-white in the eerie light.

Foxfire stopped suddenly and pointed. *"Do you see that, Lichen?"*

At the end of the blue strands they traveled, a forbidding wall of ice spread for as far as she could see. From its belly, water gushed out in a thunderous torrent, carrying gravel and sand down a broad channel that sliced through towering snow-choked mountains. Where the tortured river collided with rocks, water splashed in crystal sprays and froze into odd shapes.

Foxfire trotted forward. Lichen called, "Wait! Where are we going? We can't get past that. Look at how high that wall is!"

"Let me show you. Hurry. Come this way."

Lichen followed him to a jagged crack suddenly visible in the wall. High over her head, sandwiched between two massive bastions of ice, there gleamed a clear patch of azure sky.

"Through here." Foxfire dropped to his knees and scrambled forward into utter darkness. *"This is the way, Lichen."*

Lichen grabbed his hide sleeve and crawled through behind him. Blackness weighed down on her, heavy, taking her breath away while it pounded on her eardrums and pressed on her eyelids. Around her, crusted ice creaked and groaned, the sound echoing like gibbering voices.

Ahead, a tiny spot of light shone, growing larger as they neared it. Lichen stepped out onto a water-smoothed boulder. She inhaled a deep breath of the chill, bright air. Strange scents caressed her nostrils, smells of moss and chokecherry steeped together for a thousand cycles.

"Come, Lichen. It's just a little farther."

Foxfire clambered through the maze of boulders ahead until he reached a ridge where the sun blazed on his black braids. He tipped his face to the light and smiled in joy at the warmth that beat down on him. *"Up here, Lichen. Let me show you what happens when a Dreamer fails."*

She jumped to the next boulder, her sandals crunching on the ice in the shadowed hollows of the stone. When she reached the top, she stared at the majestic land that spread before her. Herds of strange, long-horned animals dotted the rich plain, their ears and tails switching away flies while they inquisitively studied Lichen and Foxfire. Ice-capped mountains thrust up like teeth behind her, their ragged peaks raking the bottom of the clouds.

To the south, hundreds of drainage channels zigzagged through a white maze of ridges. And there, their prey trapped against one of the snow-clad ridges, humans hunted.

An enormous hairy animal with two tails thrashed wildly, flinging its front tail in mad arcs, trying to kill its attackers. Humans dodged and ran, using throwing sticks to launch long arrows into its sides. The animal let out a roar that sounded like a conch-shell trumpet blast. Then it made a feeble run to scatter the humans. But they just circled and kept throwing their arrows, until the creature bristled with them, as if a huge porcupine had been at it.

"Where are we?" Lichen whispered.

Foxfire crouched down, a faraway look in his eyes. *"This is the land of Mammoth and Horse. That two-tailed animal down there is an orphaned mammoth calf. It's the last mammoth alive. Humans killed its mother less than a moon ago. Now they're killing it."*

"It's the last of its kind? Why don't you stop them?"

"We tried to. When the Spiral has been turned upside down, not all the Dreamers in the One can set it right again. Only a living Dreamer can do that. Power makes its choice and tries to hone the Dreamer like a fine arrow point—but sometimes Power loses the gamble."

Lichen squatted beside him, watching as the mammoth calf wailed and dropped to its knees. Even from this distance, she could see the blood that frothed and bubbled at the animal's mouth. The calf shoved itself up on trembling legs, but stumbled and fell, then flopped on its side in the snowfield. Humans shouted gleefully and hugged each other. As they cavorted, Dancing, Singing their praises to the sky, the mammoth calf's huge head sank into the drift, and the snow ran red with its blood.

"How could they do that?" Lichen gasped. "Didn't they know it was the last mammoth alive?"

"No. But even if they had known, it wouldn't have made any difference. They wanted its meat. That's all they cared about." Foxfire let out a taut breath. *"It happens when the Spiral is knocked out of balance. Earthmaker created the universe to have equal portions—Pain and Happiness, Birth and Death, Heat and Cold. That's why the Spiral is so important. Its circles reach from the thinnest roots that dig into the ground to the perfect motions of the stars. Sometimes humans knock the Spiral out of kilter, sometimes animals do it. Every time a coyote runs through a flock of new lambs, killing for the sheer sport of it, without ever eating its prey . . . the Spiral tilts."*

Tears blurred Lichen's eyes as she watched the hunters begin the laborious task of butchering Mammoth Calf. With sharp stone tools, they pulled back the hide, revealing muscles that quaked and jerked even as the blades carved.

"You see that man on the far right? The one with Owl's face painted on his shirt?"

Lichen wiped at her eyes and nodded. The man stood with his shoulders slumped forward, a hand braced on the head of a little girl who bounced joyfully up and down as she watched the piles of meat growing.

"His name is Tusk Boy. Power placed all of its strength and hope in him. He had Owl as a Spirit Helper from the day of his birth. But in the end, when Power called him to enter the Sea of Father Sun's Light so that he might learn the way to set the Spiral straight again, he couldn't do it. He was afraid."

Lichen's eyes widened. "Afraid that the Light would burn him?"

"Yes. Afraid that it would burn away his soul and there would be nothing left of 'him' to return to his family. His wife and children meant more to Tusk Boy than Mammoth Calf did. Humans are like that. It's not their fault that they care more about themselves than everything else in the world. Earthmaker gave them that trait to help them survive. Only a few are willing to

sacrifice themselves so that yellow butterflies may continue to flutter over the wildflowers in springtime. It is those few that Power seeks out. But not even Power can know for certain who will succeed and who will fail." Foxfire gave her a sad smile. *"No one really wants to be a Dreamer, Lichen."*

The grassy plains before her changed, glittering like a million gnat wings before fading into a new scene . . .

White water boiled up from the ground through fissures in the rocks, then spilled down, filling a deep aquamarine pool where people sat around the edges, eating and talking. The chill breeze captured billows of fog and dragged them through the surrounding valley in long streamers. Sitting alone on a rock, away from the rest, a young man cried, *"I'm not the one . . . I'm no Dreamer."*

"Who is he?"

"Wolf Dreamer. He succeeded. He Dreamed humans into the Spiral of this land . . . even though all he wanted out of life was to be a hunter and to raise a family with the woman he loved."

"Power wouldn't let him?"

"He wouldn't let himself. The survival of his people was more important to him than his own wants. Without his Dream, humans would never have found the way here."

Lichen knotted her fingers in her tattered hem. "So Wolf Dreamer understood that everything he wanted was nothing more than sparkflies flitting in the darkness?"

"Yes, but not until the very end." Foxfire methodically traced the face of Wolf that adorned his chest. His finger halted here and there, on eyes and snout. *"When he realized that all of the Spiral was illusion, he knew in truth how much he loved my mother—enough that he could let her go to find her happiness with another man."*

He made a swirling motion with his hand, and the vision transformed into one of drifting clouds that sailed through midnight skies.

Thunder roared, and from its heart a woman whispered, *"I feel lost. It's like being born into a new world."*

The rainy night brightened into day. From the gold-spun rays of sunlight, the image of a man formed. He lay on a spire of rock that jutted up from a high mountain. Below him, to the west, there stretched a broad basin, and purple mountains rimming the incredible vista. Blood oozed from the man's cracked lips when he opened his mouth to speak. *"I can't be your Dreamer. I can't leave Elk Charm . . . or my girls. I love them too much."*

The scent of smoke penetrated the vision. Lichen turned to gaze at Foxfire. His young face had taken on a bittersweet expression that melted her heart.

"No one wants to be a Dreamer, Lichen—but can you be one?" Foxfire's large eyes encompassed her soul. *"Are you willing to give up your soul? It means that you'll have to leave the safety of your cave and go to Nightshade at Cahokia. Alone. Unarmed."*

"But there are enemy warriors everywhere out there. I—I'm only ten summers! I can't go by myself—"

"*So was I,*" he said softly. "*I was ten when Power called.*"

"You were a Dreamer?"

"*Yes. A very long time ago.*" Foxfire rose to his feet and stared down at her. The air wavered around him as heat wafted up from the rocks, blurring his body into bizarre, ominous shapes. "*It was as hard for me as it is for you, Lichen. But I learned that I had to give up all that I was to gain all that I was not. A Dreamer needs to understand both before he can enter the Light and learn what he needs to keep the Spiral in balance. When I came back, I made two sacred Power Bundles—one of Light, the Wolf Bundle that your people call the Tortoise Bundle, and one of Dark, the Raven Bundle. It lives far to the east, along the great shore. I took the last vestiges left by Raven Hunter and Wolf Dreamer and put them into the heart of the bundles. Opposites crossed, you see. Still . . . I was afraid.*"

"How did you get over it?"

"*I united the worlds in myself and became Feathered Serpent. He was my Spirit Helper.*"

"Became?"

"*Some Dreamers are strengthened when they're consumed by fire, Lichen. Fire-Dancer was. Other Dreamers need water. White Ash did. Some, like us, have to drown in blood before they can unite the worlds in themselves. Don't fear it, Lichen. Those crushing jaws will give you Falcon's wings . . .*"

"What do you mean? I don't understand."

Lichen stumbled backward when Foxfire's legs began to writhe in a hideous dance. As she watched, they lengthened and twined into a snake's body, with scales that shimmered a deep blue. Black feathers sprouted from the roots of his arms, stretching and spreading until monstrous wings blotted the sunlight. With wistful, human eyes, he peered down at her. "*Go to Cahokia. Bird-Man waits for you there . . .*"

Lichen bolted upright in the cave. Panting, she looked out at the starry night. Wolf Pup hung in the middle of the sky, his snout pointed straight up as if scenting for danger. Lichen blinked. Something tiny fell from Wolf Pup's paw. It spun gently through the darkness and settled on the lip of her cave.

She crept forward over the cold stone floor to stare at it. The black feather glistened with a leaden brilliance in the starlight.

Thirty-two

Night hugged the land as Badgertail crawled through the tall cane fields that lined the southern meanders of Pumpkin Creek. The thick leaf blades rustled with his guarded movements, but the water should cover the sound. He prayed.

Hailcloud's lookouts roved the darkness. He had crept past three of them in the last two hands of time.

"Locust . . ." he whispered.

On the other side of the creek drainage, camp fires gleamed boldly. He lifted his head to study them, and the moist wind drenched his face with the fragrances of damp mint and newly flowered spice bush. The yellow clusters of blossoms that spotted the creek bank swarmed with blinking sparkflies. Badgertail squinted through the glittering mesh, counting the fires.

Fifteen in all. That meant maybe seventy people.

He sank back to the cover of the cane. *Are you mad, Hailcloud? What are you doing lighting fires? Inviting my northern war parties to swoop down upon you? Or inviting me to rush into your arms in an attempt to save Locust?*

Hailcloud was too shrewd a warrior to light fires with no thought of the possible outcome—unless he knew the precise location of Badgertail's war parties, and they were nowhere close, or unless he knew that the war parties had been neutralized. Petaga would have certainly sent runners to notify his war leader of such crucial information.

Or had the fires been lit as some sort of lure? To pull Badgertail's parties out of the north? A decoy? That would mean Petaga had calculated the most advantageous point from which to ambush Badgertail's forces—and figured a way of getting all of them there.

Fear congealed in the pit of his stomach. Such maneuvering could be done through subtle ways, given a master strategist's hand; but would Black Birch, Elkhorn, and the other experienced war leaders fall for it? Badgertail tightened his fingers around a cool stalk of cane. Yes, they might. Even he himself would have trouble in distinguishing between genuine hit-and-run raids and raids timed and arranged to lead several groups into a clever trap. Only good swift runners relaying information to a central point could prevent such a disaster.

And he'd had but few runners come in . . .

The pieces began to fall into place. Badgertail's gut knotted. *How could you have let this happen?*

His gaze searched the black length of the eastern bluff before returning to the tangle of underbrush that surrounded him. If Petaga had set up an ambush, the best place for it would be somewhere around One Mound Village. There the ravines and rocks provided ideal cover. But Badgertail would never make it in time to warn his warriors.

You walked right into Petaga's arms when you split your forces. Blessed First Woman . . .

He pulled out his deerbone stiletto and clutched it tightly before he crept forward another ten hands through the cane. One of the leaves caught in his warshirt with a soft, tearing sound. Badgertail stopped instantly, but not before he saw movement to his right.

From the shadows, a low voice called, "Very carefully, throw out your weapon and show me your empty hands—or I'll shoot an arrow through you this instant."

Badgertail swallowed down his dry throat and tossed out his stiletto. He heard it land softly in the grass as he raised his hands.

"Good. Now stand up. I want to get a good look at you."

Slowly, Badgertail got to his feet. The camp fires lit his face with an orange glow. He saw his foe rise from behind a bush and stand silhouetted against the sable cloak of night.

Teeth glinted as the man edged closer. Maybe twenty-one or twenty-two, he had shaved his head in the manner of a seasoned warrior. Shells hung from his braided forelocks, swaying with each cautious step he took. Fear was evident in the man's shallow breathing and in the way his arms shook while holding up his bow. He was tall, but gangly. Badgertail's shoulders packed twice the muscle. If he could just get his hands on the man . . .

"You're—Badgertail. Aren't you?"

"Badgertail? Are you joking? I came here to join Hailcloud! Who are you?"

"Come closer. I want to see your face better."

As Badgertail walked forward, his opponent sucked in a breath and stared at him through terrified eyes. "You *are* Badgertail. I saw you once. When I was a boy. You attacked my village."

A familiar ache swelled in Badgertail's chest. There had been so many villages over the past twenty cycles. He could barely keep the battle-walks straight anymore. Oh, here and there a child's weeping face had stuck in his mind, or a man's final screams. But for the most part, all had blurred into a vast din of garbled voices and acrid pools of blood drying in the sun. "Which village was that?"

"Bear Cub Village."

Badgertail shook his head. He didn't remember that one at all. Not even the name cued his memory. Had all of those deaths meant so little to him that he couldn't even recall their location? He lifted his chin to peer at the twinkling Star Ogres. "What's your name?"

"Flaxseed. But you wouldn't remember that. You just killed, pillaged, and ran—though your warriors lingered to rape my mother." Hatred hardened his face.

"Supposing I really am Badgertail? What are you going to do with me?"

Flaxseed pulled back on his bowstring, and Badgertail inhaled in preparation for the impact of the arrow. The muscles beneath his right nipple began to twitch with anticipation. Sixty heartbeats passed, and Badgertail shifted his weight to his other foot. Flaxseed stood like that, poised to shoot, for what seemed an eternity, until sweat rolled down Badgertail's neck. Finally Badgertail demanded, "Well?"

"I . . . I'd probably get in trouble for killing you," Flaxseed said as he lowered his bow. "Most likely Hailcloud wants to torture you for information . . . just like he's doing with Locust."

Oh, Locust, forgive me.

"No," Flaxseed said with certainty, "I'd better not kill you. Not yet." He pointed southward with a tilt of his head. "Turn around and walk. There's a good place to cross the creek a couple thousand hands down."

Badgertail chuckled. "Well, good. Since I'm not your infamous Badgertail, I'll happily accept your escort into camp. Saves me from taking an arrow by mistake." He turned and made his way through the dark cane while he examined Hailcloud's camp. The war leader had selected a small knoll that jutted up along the eastern side of the creek. Knots of warriors eddied around a central fire. Their laughter carried . . . along with something else. The triumphant jeer of warriors was underlaid by a frail sound that made Badgertail's soul recoil, even though his ears couldn't quite hear it.

He hurried toward the creek so he could see the camp better. Warriors whooped and cavorted in the firelight. Every eye had fastened on the ground. Badgertail maneuvered around . . . and saw Locust staked out on her back before Hailcloud. Her naked flesh glowed orange, revealing the puncture wounds on her legs and arms. Blood webbed her thighs.

A small "No!" worked up Badgertail's throat when he saw Hailcloud pull a flaming stick from the fire and bend over Locust.

"Don't force me to do this to you, Locust!" Hailcloud shouted. "Tell me Badgertail's plans and I'll make your death quick. How did he intend to fight me?"

"I don't know!"

Hailcloud thrust the stick against Locust's hip. She writhed, trying to get away, but her bonds allowed her only a few hands of movement. Hailcloud jabbed his brand again, this time at her side. Locust's cries pierced the night—high, breathless, driving Badgertail to near madness.

The crowd went wild, clapping and laughing. Small groups of warriors formed into a Dance line to circle the fire. Their silhouettes had an inhuman quality in the darkness, resembling wolves moving anxiously around a freshly killed buffalo calf.

Frantically Badgertail studied the formation of the camp. Around the base of the knoll Hailcloud had thrown up a six-hands-tall pile of brush. Entering that ring unheard would be almost impossible. But he might be able to create a diversion.

"There. Stop," Flaxseed ordered. "See that dip in the bank?"

"I see it."

"Good. Walk down. The creek is shallow enough there to cross. And remember, I'll be right behind you, with my arrow aimed at your back."

Badgertail scrambled down the crumbling bank and stepped out into the knee-deep flow. The frigid water grabbed at his bare legs so powerfully that it almost toppled him. He glanced over his shoulder. Flaxseed was sliding down the bank, clods of dirt tumbling each time he braced a foot. When he entered the fast-moving stream, the young warrior's sandal slipped on a rock and he dropped his eyes for an instant to catch his balance.

Badgertail dove with lightning quickness. His head rammed Flaxseed's stomach and knocked the youth into the chilling current. The bow swept by Badgertail before he could grab it.

I can't let him scream. Lunging, he splashed on top of Flaxseed and dug his toes into the rocks. At the same time, he gripped Flaxseed's bristly ridge of hair and shoved his face under the water. Badgertail managed to straddle Flaxseed with his broad chest over the man's throat—holding him down.

Flaxseed twisted like Snake beneath him, flopping, kicking, clawing at Badgertail's sides.

Just another finger of time . . .

In a mad gamble, Flaxseed wrenched sideways and thrust a knee into Badgertail's groin. Pain flashed, causing Badgertail to lose his toehold on the rocks. The current jerked them downstream, dragging them over the stones.

Flaxseed's contorted face crested the water, and he let out a desperate cry of *"Help!"* before Badgertail could throw himself forward. His thick fingers groped for Flaxseed's throat to cut off the cry. He crushed with all his might, and felt the bands of Flaxseed's windpipe collapsing under his fingers. Flaxseed choked hoarsely, writhing; then his limbs went still, and he fell back in the water.

Badgertail kept holding Flaxseed's head under the rushing current. Through that gaping mouth, water flooded to fill the lungs. Bubbles broke the surface. Badgertail waited, making certain. Flaxseed's wide eyes stared up at him, chilling in the moonlight that reflected from the stream.

When the throbbing of blood in his ears began to fade, Badgertail could again hear Locust's cries penetrating the raucous shouts of warriors. It drove him like a knife in his back. Exhausted and cold, he tugged Flaxseed's body onto a rock and proceeded to search it. But he found nothing he could use as a weapon; the quiver on Flaxseed's back hung empty.

Badgertail slogged back into the water. Carefully, he searched the downstream bank until he found the bow and, a good distance later, three arrows.

Not much, but it was a start.

Crossing to the opposite bank, he pulled himself up so he could again study the camp. Through a thick wall of brush and grass, he could see the central fire. The shadows of warriors moved wherever he looked.

He lowered himself and laid his cheek against the cool dirt. *What can I do?*

Locust's cries had died down, but Hailcloud's voice rose angrily: "We searched for his body. We couldn't find it. He's alive, Locust. Where would he have gone? Back to Cahokia? To meet with the war parties he sent north? Where was he supposed to meet up with them?"

Exultant whoops and hollers split the air. Badgertail forced himself to concentrate. *Think. Think, blast you! Where has Hailcloud left himself weak?* The enclosure of brush might defeat an opponent trying to slip in soundlessly, but if Badgertail could get a fire going and shoot flaming arrows at strategic locations . . .

Dry grass crackled on the other side of the creek.

Badgertail's gut crawled with fear. Holding his breath, he swiveled his head. Cane and goldenrod rose in dense patches, their stalks weaving a thick curtain above Flaxseed's corpse. Badgertail's muscles trembled as if dozens of bows had just been aimed at his vulnerable back.

More crackling. Then a twig snapped.

"Badgertail?"

Relief vied with terror. It could be a friend, but how many warriors would love to be the hero to capture Badgertail? In the cane field, at least four ghostly figures loomed, bending the stalks with their movements.

A man emerged from the vegetation, but his identity lay hidden in shadow. "Badgertail? It's Flute. Hurry! I've got three other warriors with me. We've found a way in."

We must strike now!" Gopher insisted from his place at the council fire. His silver-shot black hair had gone greasy in the past few days. Dirt puttied the lines of his weathered face as though a thick gray spiderweb had been plastered to his skin. His bushy brows pulled together as he readjusted the filthy blanket over his shoulders. "There they are! We've got three of Badgertail's war parties sitting just outside of One Mound Village and our own forces positioned perfectly around them. What more could we ask for?"

"*Six* war parties," Petaga pointed out softly. "From what our runners say, the other parties have vanished. Which means that they didn't fall for our strategy. Elkhorn worries me the most. Where is he?"

"What *difference* does it make?" Gopher shouted. "Three war parties total only two hundred and fifty warriors. We'll be able to crush them easily!"

The twenty-two members of the council whispered to each other, either shaking their heads in disagreement or nodding fervently. Most of them were old men and women who had joined the fight just to be able to say that they had been on this great battle-walk, a battle-walk that would forever change the face of their world.

Petaga gazed up at the sky while the elders considered. Thick fingers of cloud stroked the face of the crescent moon. They had dispatched war parties to surround One Mound Village, then moved their main camp a half-day's walk northward before resettling in a deep hollow that gouged the highlands. The hollow provided protection from enemy eyes and had a spring in the bottom that not only gave them water, but an occasional duck for dinner.

Moonlight fell over hundreds of warriors where they lay sleeping with weapons in limp hands. Their oblong shadows stretched across the bare gray stone. Somewhere in the maze of bodies, a man snored raggedly.

Petaga cast a glance at Spoonbill, who sat beside him, his calm, clear gaze roving the council. Though he was only fifteen, Spoonbill acted much older. His sallow face and washed-out brown eyes always remained patient and attentive, even in the worst of situations. Tall for his age, Spoonbill had not filled out yet, leaving him as scrawny as a water-starved reed. He had received his first warrior's haircut just before this battle-walk and had proudly woven two small shell beads into his forelocks. The long warshirt, with the image of Eagle on the chest, was still almost clean. Petaga suspected that Spoonbill took great pains to keep it that way.

Warmth grew inside the Moon Chief. He had spent most of last night talking to Spoonbill, working out his worries so that he had them straight in his own mind. He had learned that he could rely on

Spoonbill for solid advice with almost as much confidence as he had in Hailcloud.

"Why not? Tell me!" Gopher pressed. He thrust out his jaw pugnaciously. "We planned on attacking tomorrow. Who objects?"

"I do," Petaga said.

Gopher grunted. "What do you think? That Elkhorn is going to miraculously appear out of nowhere with a thousand warriors behind him? Be realistic. He probably glimpsed our forces and ran off into the hills with his tail between his legs."

Spoonbill straightened his back and quietly noted, "I know Elkhorn. He fought with my father cycles ago. He's not a coward. If he did spot our forces, we could be in more trouble than we know."

"How's that, young whelp?"

Unaffected by the slight, Spoonbill continued in a mild voice. "I suspect that Badgertail left a few hundred warriors to guard Cahokia. It wouldn't be farfetched to assume that if Elkhorn has counted our numbers, he may have gone back to call the others into battle."

"And leave Cahokia unguarded?" Gopher challenged him. "Ridiculous!"

"Don't be an idiot," Mother Sassafras said as she rocked forward on her cracking knees to warm her hands over the flames. Firelight flickered on the human fingerbone beads that formed chevrons across the blue fabric of her dress. Down her sleeves, the drilled canine teeth of wolves were interspersed with tiny seashells. "Spoonbill is right. If Elkhorn knows for certain that we are *here*, there's no reason to leave those forces idle at Cahokia. Of course he would recruit them. What do you think, Spoonbill? Perhaps he could get another two or three hundred warriors if he did that?"

"Yes, Grandmother," Spoonbill replied. "And if he has joined up with the other missing parties, he could have six hundred warriors at his disposal."

Gopher blurted, "Then why haven't we seen them? We've had lookouts perched on the highest points on the bluff, and they've reported nothing!"

"True," Petaga acknowledged. "But our lookouts wouldn't have seen anything if Elkhorn moved his warriors in spurts through all of last night and kept them under cover today."

"Which means"—Mother Sassafras pointed a gnarled finger at Gopher—"that Elkhorn could have already joined up with Badgertail and be flanking us at this moment."

Petaga stiffened. Runners had come in earlier that evening with news that Hailcloud had engaged Badgertail's war party near Redweed Village, won, and captured Locust. Even now, Hailcloud was trying to glean information from her, but Locust was being stubborn. No one had reported seeing Badgertail.

"For that matter," Petaga said softly, "Badgertail could have gone back to Cahokia and gathered those warriors himself."

People muttered uncertainly. No one liked the idea that Badgertail still lived.

"Stop this silly talk!" Gopher called out. "Who cares if Badgertail or Elkhorn returns to bring the last warriors from Cahokia? Even with those forces, we outnumber them by at least two hundred! I think the time has come for us to attack and wipe these thieves and murderers from our land. I'll lead the attack. Tomorrow at dawn. Who will follow me?"

The anxious hush gave way to the hoots of a great horned owl that sailed over their heads before swooping sharply across the face of the moon. People watched uneasily, then lowered their gazes to Mother Sassafras and Gopher.

Sassafras cocked a gray eyebrow. "I'd rather follow a child in diapers than you, Gopher. What do you know of war? You've barely exposed your butt to the wind in the past twenty cycles, let alone organized and led a battle-walk."

A few irreverent snickers fluttered through the gathering.

"And what of Nightshade?" someone murmured from the shadows.

"What?" Gopher demanded. "What did you ask? Who's there?"

Shellgourd, a little old woman with a formal, brittle air and the nervous eyes of one afraid of her own shadow, leaned into the light. It wrapped her white hair in gold, accentuating the length of her overgrown nose, and flashed from the red-and-yellow porcupine quills that ringed her hide collar. She lived in a backward village on the river far to the south, more isolated than any other village in the chiefdom.

Shellgourd lifted her chin. "I said, what of Nightshade? Is she on our side?"

"Who knows if she's even alive?" Gopher responded. "All we hear are rumors."

Petaga had been wondering the same thing. What had happened to her? As a child, he had fallen in love with the tall, willowy priestess who came to sit at his father's feet every night and report on the spiritual life of River Mounds. He had gotten over it—mostly. But his heart continued to need her. For advice. Just as his father had needed her.

Petaga lifted a hand to gain attention. "I believe that she is alive and being held captive by Tharon—but she's fighting on our side."

Shellgourd twisted her hands. "If she's as Powerful as legends say, why doesn't she just turn herself into Raven and fly out of Tharon's hands?"

Petaga bowed his head as murmurs eddied around the fire. "I've seen Nightshade perform some miraculous acts, Shellgourd, but I've never seen her change herself into an animal, though I know that legends say she can. My father used to use the Power of those stories to his own benefit. I assure you, if Nightshade could come to us, she would."

"How do you know she's on our side? She may have turned traitor. If she's fighting for us, and locked in Tharon's temple, why hasn't she just killed him?"

"Perhaps she hasn't had a chance to yet. I don't know. Remember, she fights with Power . . . and Power has its own ways. But I *feel* her on our side." He put a hand over his heart. "In here. She's with us. I know it."

The words seemed to calm Shellgourd. She sank back into the shadows.

Old man Plantroot pulled himself up to his full height of ten and a half hands. "Let's get the question of when we attack resolved. I, for one, agree with Mother Sassafras. We don't know Elkhorn's numbers. What if White Clover Mounds joined him? That would add at least three hundred more to his forces. The warriors of Bluebird Village came on this battle-walk because Petaga and Hailcloud led it. I will follow wherever Petaga leads." He bowed to Petaga before tottering away on ancient legs to find his blankets.

Petaga kept his face blank to hide his emotion. Plantroot had been a boyhood friend of Petaga's father. His loyalty to the Sunborn of River Mounds had clearly not perished with Jenos. That fact eased Petaga's soul.

Gopher snorted. "Plantroot has gotten so old he's feebleminded. Don't listen to him!" The other elders in the circle eyed Gopher scornfully, but he didn't seem to notice. "Red Star Mounds has many great warriors who can lead us to victory tomorrow. You all know their names: Valley Boy, Frogleg, False Face . . ."

One by one, the council members rose, bowed to Petaga, and disappeared into the darkness beyond the tawny halo cast by the fire. When the last one had gone, Petaga tiredly stood up, too. Spoonbill rose beside him.

"The matter has been decided, Gopher," Petaga announced. "We will wait another day before we attack. In the meantime, we'll send out runners to see what's happening at Cahokia and White Clover Mounds. Perhaps by tomorrow night we'll even have reports on Elkhorn's party, or maybe about Badgertail."

Gopher didn't answer, but his eyes narrowed. Petaga turned and walked away, Spoonbill's tall form on his heels. Hostility lingered in the darkness, waiting to pounce with Eagle's talons. Petaga placed his feet carefully, crossing the barren stone as quietly as Lynx, as though his very caution could give him some measure of protection.

When they had descended into the cloaking shadows of the rocks clustered around the spring, Spoonbill murmured, "He's going to be trouble. We'd better watch him."

"I know. I wish your father were here."

"Tomorrow. He'll be here by nightfall."

Petaga cast a glance over his shoulder. Gopher still sat hunched forward over the dwindling flames of the council fire.

Now you will please Man Eagle, eh, great woman warrior?"

The four youths anxiously waiting their turns around the fire laughed as Man Eagle untied his breechclout and let it fall to the dirt. He had a broken nose and arms as big around as her waist.

Locust locked her trembling jaw when Man Eagle dropped on top of her and opened her limp legs so he could shove himself inside. Her vagina burned.

Grunting, Man Eagle brutally groped her wounded breasts as he thrust. "Oh, yes, that's good." The blisters that covered her legs and arms shrieked in pain. "There, see? Man Eagle will make it good for you. Women throughout the chiefdom fight for the attention of Man Eagle. I'll make the last night of your life the best. Yes . . ." he breathed in her ear. "I'll let these others have their chance, then I'll be back. You and me, we'll be happy all night."

Locust turned her face away. Most of the camp slept. People, rolled in blankets, dotted the scrub thickets, while lookouts roamed the high places. Their dark forms wavered in the moonglow. Hailcloud had gone to bed two hands of time ago, leaving her to his warriors, hoping that if torture wouldn't break her iron will, rape might. She had lost count of the number of men who had taken her.

At first she had fought, but the effort had only provided more entertainment, and the rawhide straps encircling her wrists and ankles to spread-eagle her body had cut deep gashes into her flesh. Her whole body flamed in agony. Even her throat had gone raw from screaming.

She had been trying not to think of Primrose, of what he would do without her—because it broke her heart. She could endure losing people she loved. She had lost so many in her cycles as a warrior that her soul had woven an impervious inner sanctuary to which she could retreat until the worst pain had passed. But Primrose would never get over her death. His gentle and tender-hearted spirit would dwindle. The thought of his anguish wounded her more terribly than all of the torture she'd lived through on this night.

Man Eagle began moving faster while he panted warmly against her throat. "Yes, almost there. These other fools . . . might not have been able to do it, but Man Eagle will plant a child in your belly."

The gleaming eyes of the waiting warriors sharpened in the firelight, eager, impatient. She felt Man Eagle's release before he sagged atop her. The next man in line, Wildcat, smiled. Seventeen summers at the most, he had a strong, heavily tattooed body. Red serpents wound up through a blue maze from his navel to his breasts, where their flat heads rested beneath his nipples.

"I will be back, Locust," Man Eagle whispered against her cheek. "Soon. Before Hanged Woman crosses the midpoint in the sky."

Laughing, he stood and retied his breechclout. "Go on—but she's so full of my seed, there's no room for yours," he said as he gestured to Wildcat. The youth stumbled in his hurry to undress and brought forth peals of laughter from his friends.

Wildcat climbed on top of her, and the lances of pain began again. With all of her strength she fought to abandon her body by forcing her soul to concentrate on the beauty of the night.

Tatters of cloud, black and opaque, coasted through the indigo sky along the southern horizon. The irregular rents in the clouds picked up the starlight and gleamed with a gossamer fire like pale, silver eyes in the blackness, looking down on the camp's enclosure . . .

Locust frowned. Weeds rattled like dry bones at the edge of her hearing range. She thought she saw people running, nothing more than dark wraiths in the night.

Wildcat had started to pant and groan, his fingers clawing into the blisters on her breasts. Locust bit back her cries.

"It's an attack!" a disembodied voice shouted from the darkness.

Then came the war whoops of the lookouts. Warriors scrambled from their blankets, yelling. Man Eagle and the waiting warriors stiffened when flames burst to life at different points along the southern and eastern borders of the brush enclosure. Wreaths of sparks whirled into the sky.

"Come on!" Man Eagle shouted. "Quickly, grab your weapons and follow me."

The three warriors instantly lunged for their bows and quivers, but Wildcat kept up his frantic movements.

Man Eagle loomed over Wildcat. "Didn't you hear me, you young fool?"

"Go!" Wildcat barked. "I'll . . . I'll be there . . . in a few instants. Just give me another . . ."

Man Eagle glared but turned to the other warriors and led them running down the knoll toward the closest fire, where figures ran and leaped like white-tailed deer frisking in the spring. Flames shot higher. The crackles swelled into a deep-throated roar as the blaze swept greedily through the enclosure and into the camp itself, consuming blankets and packs before rushing on. Screams laced the air as warriors fled to the fires, leaving Locust alone with her tormentor.

Wildcat did not appear to notice the tumult. He grinned down at Locust through glazed eyes. "Just a little longer. I only need . . . a few more—"

Thick fingers grabbed Wildcat by the hair from behind. A garbled cry escaped his throat. Then gouts of hot blood spattered Locust from the gaping slit that opened below his chin.

Badgertail jerked Wildcat off of Locust and threw the young body aside before he bent to cut Locust's bonds. His toad face, with its bulging eyes, went hard with rage as he surveyed her wounds and the white fluid that trickled down between her legs. "We haven't much time," he said. "I told Flute to light the fires and run for all he was worth."

"Good," she said, but tears rose to choke her. Badgertail did a double take when he noticed. He had never seen her cry. In all of the cycles that they'd warred together, she had never broken down before him. But now she couldn't stop the sobs that lodged in her throat.

Badgertail's eyes softened. Then he swiftly grabbed her by the shoulders and pulled her to her feet. The act of sliding her arm over his broad shoulders flayed her with pain.

"You can run, can't you?" he asked.

"Of course I can."

Shouts rang out as they charged headlong into the darkness, jumping brush and rocks, while a half-dozen men—including Man Eagle—raced across the knoll, yelling as they followed.

Thirty-three

Tharon yawned. He readjusted himself on his carved cedar stool and carefully spread the hem of his golden robe around his feet. Old Redhaw tottered on wobbly legs in front of him, waving her arms as she built up to her real reasons for demanding a meeting with him.

This withered old woman is boring me to distraction.

For over a cycle, Tharon had been refusing all formal requests for meetings with the clan leaders. Oh, he knew his father had routinely met with them once a moon, but what did these hags know? Shriveled gourds with delusions of godhood, that's all they were. But he had been so weary and ill lately that he'd approved this request because it might, after all, be entertaining.

How wrong he had been. The woman's single incisor shone a filthy yellow in the midday sunlight, although her dress glittered immaculately with galena nuggets and shell beads. Behind her, around the edges of the courtyard, twenty representatives from the four clans sat nervously watching Tharon and the ten guards he had recently assigned to accompany him whenever he went outside. From the instant that Badgertail had left, the tension in the village had been rising; it hovered now like the stench of carrion.

Few people walked the plaza below. Most had barricaded themselves in their houses to furtively watch the spirals of smoke rising like wayward dust devils across the eastern bluff. The placement of the fires disturbed Tharon. The blazes in the south had just vanished when the ones in the north began. Had none of the northern villages joined Badgertail? Had he been forced to torch them all? That seemed the only thing that could explain the number of fires.

Absurd. Who would have the gall to stand up and refuse to join Badgertail when they certainly knew it meant death?

"Sun Chief? *Sun Chief?* Are you listening to me?"

Tharon folded his arms and nodded. "I am, Redhaw. Would you get to the point? I have other things to do, you know. We are at war."

The old crone's jaw clenched indignantly. "I am well aware of that, Sun Chief. That's why I urged you to meet with us." She swung around and waved a clawlike hand at the other clan leaders. "Tickseed said that if Petaga won this war, the system would be changed, that each village would be able to handle its own affairs, and that we would reorganize so that every village designed and paid for its own projects."

"That's what the Moon Chief is preaching. So?"

Tharon's attention fixed on the *berdache,* who was whispering into Checkerberry's ear. Strange creatures, the *berdache.* Magical. Filled with Power. Especially Primrose. Tharon had admired him before. Primrose wore a beautiful pale-blue dress decorated across the breast with red porcupine quills. His long black hair draped over his shoulders in thick waves, as though he had braided it while wet, then shaken it loose to dry.

Tharon lifted his chin and studied Primrose intently. Perhaps, if Locust didn't return from this battle-walk, Tharon might consider taking Primrose as a lover. He'd had *berdache* lovers before and found them . . . interesting. His thoughts danced around the images of muscular male arms enfolding him, male lips pressing against his. Primrose had a reputation for feminine gentleness. But perhaps beneath that facade, true male passion lurked. It would be fascinating to find out.

Yes. Tharon decided on the spot. He would take Primrose as his lover, regardless of whether or not Locust survived. He flashed the *berdache* a seductive smile and laughed when Primrose caught his look and straightened in surprise.

"This old woman!" Redhaw walked between Tharon and Primrose to gesture at Tickseed. "She suggested that all of the clans turn against you, my Chief, and join Petaga!"

Caught by surprise, Tharon went rigid. "What?"

"Yes," Redhaw insisted. "Treason! That's what—"

"Liar!" Tickseed rose and waddled forward uncertainly. Her blind eyes shone like frosted lakes in the sunshine. The skeletal prominence of her old cheekbones made her look like a shrunken corpse. "We were discussing the war, that's all. We . . ."

Tharon's mind closed in upon itself. The edges of his vision went dark, and he started to tremble. That had been happening a lot lately, so often that he had begun to believe the common superstition that Father Sun actually could communicate with human beings. A breathy voice spoke in his head: *"Like a corpse . . . a corpse . . ."*

Tharon barely heard Tickseed's voice over the dull thudding of his heart. Her words slipped to the outermost edges of his awareness, where they rose and fell like the dirty foam that rims the surface of a turbulent lake. This world of hot sun and pungent fear-sweat draped around him with the unreality of a vague nightmare.

. . . while his soul looked across a field of mangled yellow stalks, sucked dry by the relentless winter wind.

He held Badgertail's sleeve as they peered over the steep bank into the ice-varnished lake below. Badgertail's face had tightened as the corpse rose, dredged up through the thin film of ice that had formed since the weighted net had been lowered. Thousands of ice shards flickered in the early morning light.

A stifled cry caught in Tharon's throat.

The attack had been brief, brutal. The warriors from Quill Dog Mounds had ambushed the trading party, killing, looting, and then burning the litters and packs. Tharon's father, Gizis, had been the last to die. The enemy had saved him to make sport of him.

The men began reeling in the net. Gizis twisted as if hurt and fighting the diamonds of webbing. His mouth gaped in a soundless scream. Waterlogged wounds crisscrossed his flesh like the swollen bites of monsters.

Voices buzzed around Tharon. Someone sobbed.

The body rode toward him, bobbing on the current as it plowed the ice—a naked blue lump against black water.

"Why did they do this, Badgertail?"

"Because they could, my Chief."

"They could?"

"Yes. Gizis should have taken more guards. He trusted his own people too much. The vulnerable are always the first to die. Quill Dog must have been watching and waiting to find your father exposed. It's part of the price of being Sunborn . . ."

"Redhaw has always been jealous of the Horn Spoon Clan's status," Tickseed raged. "That's why she makes these accusations against us!"

Tharon gasped air explosively when the vision burst—and saw Redhaw eying him speculatively. The sound of shattering ice receded as the hot sun banished his sensation of bitter cold. But the image remained. Gizis' blue corpse overlaid Redhaw's form like a ghostly presence, writhing, twisting to show its ghastly knife wounds, while its mouth screamed for help that would never come.

. . . *reminding Tharon of what every Commonborn person longed to do to the Sunborn.*

Tharon lunged breathlessly to his feet. "Is . . . is Tickseed the only one who was plotting behind my back?"

Redhaw lifted her hands noncommittally. "She's the only one who spoke out against you, my Chief. The others, well, they just sat by mutely. Only *I* refused to take part in Tickseed's plan."

"But, my Chief!" Tickseed hobbled forward, her ancient arms lifted in supplication, while she tried to focus on where she thought he must be standing. "This is sheer fantasy! None of my clan would—"

"You are guilty of treason!" Tharon judged. "Kill her!" He waved to his guards. "I will have no traitors in our midst!"

The Commonborn jumped to their feet, yelling and begging for Tharon to retract his order, shouting defenses. But he turned his back on them and stamped toward the temple doorway. The dry grass crunched under his sandals, increasing his rage. *Would it never rain?*

Only Primrose's masculine voice could have halted Tharon's steps. The *berdache* ran up with his hands outstretched, pleading, "*Please,* please, my Chief. Do not do this thing. Tickseed is innocent! I swear, she never suggested we turn against you. She only—"

"That's enough." Tharon put a hand on Primrose's flushed cheek and caressed it softly. "It's too noisy out here. Come inside and talk to me."

Primrose's face slackened in fear, but he swallowed and nodded. "Yes, my Chief."

Tharon held the door-hanging back for Primrose to enter the amber glow of the temple, then lowered it and turned. The guards held Tickseed's withered arms, waiting. The old clan leader had started to weep from her sightless eyes. "My Chief, please!"

"I'll have no traitors in my village!" Tharon nodded to the guards, then ducked beneath the door-hanging to take Primrose's muscular arm.

Tharon heard Tickseed let out a gasp when the guard's arrow struck her heart.

Elkhorn's sandals raked the gray limestone as he squirmed his way toward a dense clump of rice grass that grew in the cracks of the rocks. The tawny stalks had barely seeded out before they'd withered. Such a dry cycle. Had there ever been one drier? Not in his memory. The grass crackled as he slid through it to reach the crest. Gingerly, he pulled himself up and peered over the edge. A huge camp filled the depression below.

Dread needled his chest. He fought the urge to leave this rock and run with all his might. But to do so would betray the warriors waiting in the distance, depending upon him. He had rejoined forces with Woodchuck and Bittedax.

Black Birch, you fool. Why didn't you stick to the plan and meet me south of Bladdernut Village?

Elkhorn and Soapweed had led their warriors to the specified copse of cottonwoods and found it empty. Not even Badgertail had been there. That, more than anything, terrified Elkhorn. If Badgertail could have come, he would have.

Elkhorn wiped at the sweat rolling off his stubby nose. He had tracked Black Birch's war party, noted their southerly heading, then swung around in a wide arc to see what Black Birch had gotten himself into. In the process, they had cut tracks from several other war parties, and the story had become clear.

A trap . . .

Sounds rose from Petaga's camp: muted voices, dogs barking. But few warriors walked through the intense heat of the day. Those who did moved quietly around the rocky spring in the bottom of the hollow. Elkhorn did not see anyone wearing gold, but perhaps Petaga had dropped the symbol of the Sunborn for this battle-walk.

Elkhorn crumpled onto his stomach. A gust of wind rasped through the rice grass and frosted his arms with a tan coat of chaff while he tried to think his way out of this mess. Flies buzzed and wheeled around his sweaty body.

The floodplain spread to the west, the flat expanse stippled by ponds and isolated trees; a few seedlings had managed to take root far enough away from villages to survive. The western bluff stood as an implacable backdrop to the blue ribbon of the Father Water. Along the shore, ragged squares of cornfields fringed the boundaries of villages.

The highlands to the north and south supported small villages on nearly every rolling swell of land. Elkhorn wondered idly if any of those villages remained intact. He had seen so many refugees fleeing eastward, to get as far away as they could before the slaughter broke loose, that he doubted it.

Slaughter of my *people,* he thought sourly. *I have to get word to Black Birch and the other war-party leaders who've camped outside of One Mound Village. Must warn them before it's too late. . . . And where's Badgertail?*

With the grace of Snake, Elkhorn backed down the incline, hoping the rice grass would cloak his movements.

Thirty-four

A furious gust of wind moaned through the firelit halls of the temple, penetrating the cracks in the roof and walls and chilling Nightshade's skin where she sat cross-legged on the floor of her room beside Orenda. The little girl was watching her own fingers twisting restlessly in her lap. She had been talking, to Nightshade's relief, though her words came with difficulty. Orenda wore one of Nightshade's robes, long and red. Nightshade had rolled up the sleeves and knotted the hem to shorten it to the right length. Orenda's black hair fell over her shoulders, cloaking the misery on her face.

"So Old Marmot was bold enough to accuse your father of sacrilege in public? I'm amazed." Nightshade contemplated the starmap on the wall. The arrangements of the Ogres glittered in the flickering light cast by the firebowl next to the Tortoise Bundle's tripod. "And he said he'd seen the evidence for it in the stars. What happened after that? After Old Marmot called you into his room to question you about your father?"

Orenda inhaled, a short, sharp breath. "I—I cried. Tharon heard. H-He made me go back . . . to my room. Mother came—to s-sit with me."

"What did she say?"

Orenda's little hands began to shake. She hid them in the red folds covering her lap. "She said she would k-kill Tharon."

Nightshade said nothing, fearing that if she questioned too deeply now, Orenda would retreat into silence again. The list of taboos that constituted sacrilege was enormously long, but for Singw to have made such a statement, Tharon's crime must have been dreadful.

She adopted a different approach. "Your mother was a good woman,

Orenda. When I first went to River Mounds, I was fourteen. Singw used to come and talk to me late at night. She was one of the few people my age who had the courage to speak to me."

Orenda's lower lip quivered, and grief shone so brightly in her tear-filled eyes that Nightshade's hatred for Tharon intensified. "What did she s-say to you?"

"Oh, many things. Most of it was about your father. She asked me endless questions of what he was like. Tharon and Singw had been pledged to each other the year before, and your mother was anxiously awaiting your birth so she could marry Tharon and move permanently to Cahokia."

Orenda's eyes widened. "Was M-Mother afraid of him?"

"Oh, yes, very much. I'd told Singw of how Tharon used to hurt me. I'd even shown her the bruises from where he had beaten me with a war club on the same day he'd banished me from Cahokia."

"He beat you?"

"All the time." Nightshade pulled up the hem of her robe and turned her leg so Orenda could see the long scar on her calf. The ridged line of white shone snowy against her brown skin. "I got this when your father received a new knife as a gift. He wanted to try it out on someone. He was so much bigger than I was, there wasn't much I could do to stop him."

Orenda gingerly touched the thick mass of scar tissue. "B-But, Nightshade, you're a priestess. Why couldn't you just k-kill him?"

Nightshade drew up her knees and laced her fingers atop them. Orenda's eyes remained riveted to Nightshade's face, but her hand fell back to her lap and nervously twined in her robe. The tawny light danced fitfully through her long hair.

"Power doesn't work like that. Oh, I could have killed him, but I feared what Power would do to me to exact justice. You see, when Earthmaker created the world, he made sure that Balance stood as the most fundamental law. If I had killed Tharon for giving me that scar, Power might have blinded me, or broken both of my legs—or worse."

Orenda looked away. In a whisper, she said, "He beats me, too."

"I know."

"Nightshade? Did Tharon . . . did he . . ." A glint of terror entered Orenda's dark eyes as she looked up. "What else d-did he do to you?"

"Oh, he hurt me in lots of ways. How did he hurt you?"

"He . . . he . . ." Orenda opened her mouth as though she wanted to answer, but cycles of fear had trained the words to bury themselves.

"You can tell me, Orenda. I promise not to tell anyone else."

"But if he ever f-found out . . . That's why my mother died. She died because I told Old M-Marmot." Orenda bent forward to hide her face in the hem of her red dress and cry.

Astonished, Nightshade's graceful brows drew together. "When he called you into his chamber? That's when you told him?"

Orenda nodded.

"And it was the next night—wasn't it?—that Tharon ordered all of the Starborn to take dinner with him in the temple?"

Orenda didn't respond. She didn't have to.

"Well, your father didn't waste any time, did he?" She reached out and gently stroked Orenda's back. More to herself than to Orenda, she mused, "Your father has always been fond of poisonous plants. When he turned nine, he began collecting things like saltbush, death camas, the pits of chokecherries, and the leaves of hoary peavine. I remember that he used to grind the pits of chokecherries and mix them with death camas to feed to squirrels, just so he could watch them writhe before they—"

Nightshade's ears pricked. The wind whistled shrilly through the halls outside, but beneath the whistling she heard a muffled scream, than a grunt—as though someone had smothered his victim's face with a blanket, then struck him hard.

Orenda lifted her chin to listen.

Racing feet pounded in one of the adjacent hallways, accompanied by panicked voices.

Nightshade rose and went to the tripod to pick up the Tortoise Bundle. It felt light and smooth in her fingers as she tied it to her belt.

"Come with me, Orenda." The girl jumped up and tucked her fingers in Nightshade's.

Together they ducked beneath the door-hanging and into the hall. Two firebowls gleamed, one outside of Nightshade's door and the other at the end of the dim corridor. They walked cautiously, their steps as soundless and calculated as Cougar's.

At the intersection of hallways, Nightshade held Orenda back and peered around the corner. Kettle's pudgy form dashed through the semidarkness toward Tharon's chamber. Two dark shapes stood near Tharon's doorway.

Nightshade led Orenda into the hall. Every firebowl along the way had been snuffed. *Tharon's way of hiding his trail.* The thin, tarnished glow that clung to the walls came from the firebowls in other corridors.

When they were within thirty paces of Tharon's door, Orenda let out a garbled animal sound, tore her hand from Nightshade's grip, and fell back against the wall. "I-I c-can't go down there! That's where h-he—"

"I won't let him hurt you." Nightshade knelt and put a hand on Orenda's flushed cheek. "Would you rather wait here for me? I'll be able to see you the whole time."

Orenda sank to the floor in relief and nodded.

Nightshade rose and proceeded down the hall. The guards posted on either side of Tharon's doorway straightened when they saw her coming and gave each other terrified glances.

Nightshade strode up beside Kettle and pinned the nervous men with her gaze. They kept their eyes averted, as though fearing she might capture their souls if they looked at her directly.

Nightshade turned to Kettle, whose hands were pressed over her mouth. "What's happening? Is that Tharon making those sounds?"

Kettle shook her head. "I don't know. I heard the screams, just as you did."

"Well, don't you think we ought to find out whether the Sun Chief is all right?"

Kettle's mouth worked without producing any sound.

Nightshade stepped around her, calling "Tharon?" as she reached for the door-hanging, but the guard on the right thrust out a muscular arm to block her.

Sweat had broken out across his nose. He swallowed hard. "The Sun Chief is well, Priestess. He gave us orders that he didn't want to be disturbed—by anyone."

Nightshade's gaze hardened, and the guard's arm wavered. He murmured, "Please, Priestess, I beg you. You know what the Sun Chief will do to me if I allow anyone to disturb—"

At that instant, Tharon's door-hanging flew back and the ruler stepped unsteadily into the hall. His golden robe looked disheveled, as if he had picked it up off the floor and hastily thrown it on. Slovenly coils of hair cascaded over his face, but Nightshade could pick out the speckles of blood on his cheeks and chin. His eyes had a crazed gleam.

Like he has done something that surprised even himself.

Tharon glared at them, then waved his arms wildly. "What's everyone doing here? Get away from my door! You Starborn are all alike. When I need you, you're nowhere to be found, and when I don't need you, you're staring over my shoulder like fatted geese. Go on, get away from here!"

Tharon grabbed a war club from one of the guards and charged forward. When Nightshade refused to give ground, Tharon swerved around her and slammed the club into Kettle's upraised arm. Kettle yelled "No, my Chief!" and rushed down the hall.

Tharon followed, howling like a wild beast, but when he caught sight of Orenda, the howl turned into hysterical laughter. He let Kettle go . . .

Orenda gave a high-pitched shriek and stumbled to her feet, trying to flee, but Tharon caught her arm.

Nightshade charged after him. "Tharon! Let her go!"

He whirled and peered at Nightshade. As though in indecision, his lips pressed into a pout. Then he yanked Orenda's arm and threw her against the wall before dashing headlong back toward his chamber, flying past Nightshade with ghostly speed. As he ducked beneath his door-hanging, the guards adopted their former position.

Orenda crawled frantically to Nightshade. She hugged her around the legs so hard that Nightshade almost toppled. "You're safe, Orenda. Get up. We're going back to our chamber."

She grasped Orenda's hand and turned for a final time to peer at Tharon's door.

No sounds came from that chamber now. Not even the patter of footsteps.

Thirty-five

Sunrise shone with a subdued yellow glow on the western bluff. Vole pulled Wanderer's red shirt up to cover her shoulders. It had slipped off in the night. During her bouts of fevered dreams, Wanderer had curled his lanky body around her to protect her from the chill night. He lay next to her now, his back pressed warmly against hers, his even breathing deep and rhythmic.

His closeness comforted Vole, though she spent a good deal of time fighting with herself about it, trying to convince her soul that she felt that way only because she had been weak and ill and he had been fluttering over her like a worried hen. He had cooked, brought her water, cleaned her wounds, and until last night, when her fever had broken, spent hands of time mopping her brow with a cool cloth—which he'd torn from his shirt for that very purpose.

Vole inhaled deeply of the dawn-scented air. Sparkflies continued to dance in the shadowed trough of the floodplain. Vole watched their luminescent arcs while she thought about the war and Lichen.

Yesterday afternoon Wanderer had climbed up onto the bluff to survey the battle situation. He'd seen a number of isolated warriors dashing up and down the drainages, but no war parties. The fact had worried him because it implied that the parties had settled down and gone undercover in preparation for a long and arduous fight.

And somewhere in the midst of the madness, their daughter hid, no doubt frightened half out of her wits.

Night before last, when the fever had come upon Vole like a raging fire, she had mustered the courage to attempt something she had shied away from for cycles: she'd sent her soul out hunting for Lichen. But she'd barely had the strength to get as far as Redweed Village, and the devastation there had wrenched her heart so terribly that her soul had immediately retreated to the sanctuary of her body.

She had awakened from that brief voyage to find Wanderer sitting over her, his bushy brows knitted inquiringly. He had commented, "I didn't know that you could do that, Vole. Have you ever tried visiting the Star Ogres?"

She had evaded a long discourse on the various Ogres—"Hanged Woman is so irritable. But then, I'd be irritable, too—" by blessedly falling asleep.

Vole eased around to study the side of his face. His mouth was half open. His unruly gray hair stuck out every which way. Above the hook of his nose, his closed eyelids twitched with Dreams.

The old lunatic. An uneasy contentment filled her. With a war brewing around them, she had picked this moment to start liking him again. Power played with people's lives in the strangest ways. She wondered what Power's purpose was in throwing her and Wanderer together like this. Could it have something to do with Lichen?

Vole frowned thoughtfully, then gave up. No human could fathom the ways of Power. And it didn't really matter. First she had to concentrate on finding Lichen. Then she had to figure out where they could go to find a new home. Then, if she had the time, she would think about Wanderer. It made no difference which side won the war. Her village and family had been destroyed. They had to move on.

Light crept through the sunflowers and mottled Vole's face with splinters of gold.

A faint squawk carried on the morning air as three ravens glided down past the lip of the rock shelter and flapped to perch on the nearest sunflowers. The stalks bobbed and swayed under their weight. One of the ravens, the one with the ugly, gnarled beak, scrutinized Vole curiously before it lifted its beak and began cawing while it shook its wings. Its midnight feathers glinted in the sunshine.

"What?" Wanderer asked sleepily. "Are you sure?"

The raven cawed louder.

Wanderer sat up and used a fist to rub sleep from his eyes. Cocking his head, he stared into nothingness before he nodded. "I guess you are right, Crossed Beak. Well then, that's that."

Wanderer jumped to his feet and trotted to the sheltered nook where he had stored his Power pouches and began tying them to his breechclout.

Vole propped herself up on her elbows. "What?"

"What?"

"What are you doing?"

"Oh, I'm sorry. Did you want me to leave these?" He graciously extended the pouch with the elderberries.

She scowled at it. "Leave? Are you going somewhere?"

"Yes, I'm afraid it's time, Vole."

"Time for what?"

The ravens let out a series of guttural squawks, and Wanderer nodded agreeably. "I'm hurrying, Crossed Beak. But if she's that close, she'll probably reach Cahokia before we do."

"She . . . Lichen?" Vole sat up and pulled Wanderer's red shirt from her shoulders into a crumpled pile in her lap. "What's Crossed Beak saying about Lichen?"

Wanderer strode out into the brilliant sunshine, where he knelt before the cerulean flowers of a blue flag plant. Dewdrops glimmered on the petals. He picked up a flat piece of limestone and dug around the plant to get to the roots. When he'd succeeded and the roots lay in a wilted pile, he called over his shoulder, "Crossed Beak says that Lichen has started for Cahokia. Which means that I—"

"*What? Why?*"

Wanderer spun around, startled. "Why, because she must! Really, Vole, it's the only way she'll get to the point that she understands darkness, nakedness, and nothing."

Ignoring the gibberish, Vole demanded, "There are thousands of warriors out there. What if she gets captured . . . or what if she gets lost?"

"Oh, let's hope she gets lost, Vole." Wanderer scooped up the blue flag roots and brought them back to Vole's side. He gazed at her with utter gravity. "Getting lost is the only way she'll find the Cave. First Woman has spun an impenetrable fog of illusion around it." He dropped the roots on the ground.

Vole reached out, put her hands on Wanderer's bony shoulders, and shook him until his head bounced. When she stopped, he peered at her as though hanging on her next words.

"What, Vole?"

"I want you to slow down. Pretend I don't know anything about Dreaming. What in the name of Father Sun are you talking about?"

He blinked. "Lichen. I have to go find her."

Vole let her hands fall. "*We* have to go find her."

"But you're still ill, Vole! That's why I picked these roots for you. If you crush them to pulp and smear them on your sores—"

"I'm going with you. That's all there is to it." Bracing her hands, she shoved to her feet. "Let me get my things together. Then we'll—"

Wanderer let out a high-pitched shriek and leaped up into the rocks, clinging like a quaking vine. Vole whirled breathlessly, seeking the source of his fear, searching the field of sunflowers, the rocks, the floodplain visible in the distance. She saw nothing. "What's the matter?"

Wanderer cautiously detached a hand and pointed to Vole's rock "pillow." "Look! There he is. He's come for me!"

Vole bent over to look and saw one red leg tentatively probe from beneath the stone. Then a spider crept out. It was a beautiful creature, with enormous eyes.

"It's a spider, Wanderer."

In a choked whisper, he said, "It—it wants my soul."

"Oh, Blessed Moon Maiden. Another one?"

Vole turned, raised her foot, and smashed the spider to mush. When she lifted her sandal, only a greasy spot remained. "There. Feel better?"

Wanderer gingerly let himself down off the rocks and crept forward to stare at the spot. Inquisitively, he lifted her rock pillow. "I guess that wasn't him. I do hope that Spider Above understands your rash nature, Vole."

"I don't care whether he does or not."

The ravens squawked and shot up into the sky, disappearing above the rocks. Then a gust of wind suddenly battered the sunflowers and sent a spray of petals pirouetting into their shelter, where they settled on Wanderer's gray hair.

Wanderer looked for a long moment into Vole's dark eyes before a grin twisted his lips. "You know, Vole, I've always been intrigued by your impiety. I expect that you're the one who's going to be a rat's liver in her next life." He snatched up the roots and tucked them into one of the pouches dangling at his side. "We'd better be off. Are you sure you're strong enough for this journey?"

"Of course I'm strong enough. My daughter is out there somewhere, and she needs me."

H e's done it. He's done it, my Chief!"

The frantic voice made Petaga bolt up in bed, grabbing for his bow while he blinked into the blackness. He saw Spoonbill sitting up beside him, his war club raised threateningly. A small, dark form stood silhouetted against the vast bowl of stars.

"Please, my Chief, please hurry!"

"Plantroot?" Petaga asked muzzily. "Who? What are you talking about?"

The little old man knelt before Petaga. The wisps of white hair on his head gleamed silver in the starglow. He held out his hands pleadingly. "Gopher. He's gone. He took all of his warriors and left."

Spoonbill's upraised club slowly sank to rest on the stone. "Oh, no." He turned to Petaga. "You don't think he decided he could handle Elkhorn's war parties by himself, do you?"

Plantroot's elderly voice shook. "If he ruins our surprise attack, it will doom us all."

The words sent a tingle up Petaga's spine. He ripped his blanket away and got to his feet. The frosty night wind bit at his cheeks and whipped the hem of his robe around his legs. "Spoonbill, gather the council members. We may have to attack today."

Night grayed into early morning, softly illuminating the rocks and bushes, the village, and the major features of the land. Crickets chirred and clicked in the grass around the rocks where Gopher and his guards lay hidden.

"Tell Gloveseed to start moving," Gopher ordered. "We'll attack the instant we have enough light."

Tobacco Boy grinned and rose. "This is a great day, my Chief. The names of the Red Star warriors will live in legend."

"Yes, yes," Gopher whispered absently. "Go on. Hurry it up. It'll be light soon."

Tobacco Boy took off at a steady lope, his sandals pounding the stone until he veered to the right and descended out of sight.

Gopher ran his fingers over the beautiful fletching on his arrows. Men shifted around him, getting ready. Gopher had yet to go to sleep this night, but he felt no fatigue. Too much excitement pumped in his veins. He had been so angry after the council meeting that he'd sent runners to his already-positioned forces, then gathered those Red Star warriors who waited in the hollow and led them down to join the others in surrounding the enemy encampments south of One Mound Village. It would be Gopher's three hundred against approximately two hundred and fifty from Cahokia.

Gopher smiled to himself. It wouldn't be the rout he had hoped for. He would lose a few more people. But it would be worth it to see the pitiful look on Petaga's face when he told him that he, the great Gopher of Red Star Mounds, had thoroughly thrashed the enemy—and without help from anyone.

People assume that Petaga will rule when this is over. Well, I'll show them. When I win the war, no one will deny me the place of Sun Chief in Cahokia.

In the camps below, black shapes moved in the predawn light. Faint traces of conversation made their way to his ears. Gopher waited, knowing the ways of warriors. As more of them rose and rolled up their blankets, confusion would set in. He and False Face had positioned their forces perfectly, stationing most of them along the rocky highlands from where they could shoot down on fleeing foes. Three broad gulches carved the earth south of One Mound Village. The major thrust of Gopher's forces would rush down from the north, and panic would drive the enemy south, into the ravines. Those who survived the gauntlets would run straight into a wall of warriors.

Gopher grunted as he picked up his bow and nocked an arrow.

Darkness was paling rapidly.

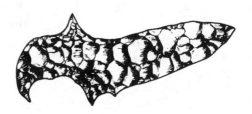

Thirty-six

Someone's fingers ran through Primrose's long hair, combing it over his right shoulder. He fought to return to his dream of Locust's sweet laughter as they lay in the sunrise-painted meadows north of Pretty Mounds. Wildflowers spread in a blue-and-yellow blanket around them, the blossoms wavering in the cool breezes of spring. But the touch intruded again, fingers sensually feathering his hair.

"Wake up, *berdache*," a voice cooed. "I'm not tired of you yet."

Primrose struggled to get his legs under him. His head throbbed violently. He knew that his arms were tied over his head, but he couldn't feel them. Not even a sting of numbness told him they were there—but the rest of his body burned as though he stood in a raging fire.

Primrose groaned softly and opened his eyes. He could not quite focus on the broad, luxurious room. The cattail mats around the bed that he remembered as covered with alternating blue and red diamonds looked like splotches of purple.

Primrose's gaze slid sideways. Tharon's face appeared, a fuzzy triangle, with dark pits for eyes. Hoarsely, Primrose said, "Locust will kill you."

Then his head fell forward, and he saw that he had been stripped naked. Red paint circled his genitals and wound down his legs in sinuous patterns like streaks of blood. Or . . . *was* it blood?

Eerie tendrils of memory tugged . . . knives glinting in moon-light . . . shrill laughter . . .

Tharon swayed closer, baring his teeth in a smile. "What makes you think Locust is alive?"

The fetid odor of that breath made Primrose turn his head. *Like the fermented leaves of a Spirit Plant.* "She's too good a warrior . . . to be dead."

The Sun Chief clapped his hands and did a little dance. "Oh, you're priceless, *berdache.* Do you think that Locust will come rushing in to save you? I have guards posted all around the temple. No one can enter or leave without my permission."

Queasiness sank claws into Primrose's gut. He braced himself by imagining Locust's rage when she found out that he was being held captive in the temple. She would burn the place to the ground, if necessary, to get him out. Yes. *Yes, she would.* His love for her swelled, firing a hope that had perished sometime in the terror of last night. "Why are you doing this to me, Sun Chief?"

Tharon smoothed clammy fingers down Primrose's chest, and an animal gleam filled his eyes. "I *like* you, Primrose. You're so different. You have that wonderful male body, but everything else about you, your smile, your movements when I touch you—they're all feminine. It's been a long time since I've had a *berdache* lover."

Tharon stepped closer to press his tall body against Primrose, and only then did Primrose realize that Tharon was naked. Primrose could not stop the quiver that ran through his wounded flesh.

"And just so you won't get brave, *berdache,*" Tharon whispered sensually into Primrose's ear, "let me tell you that Locust is dead. I got word yesterday. She was shot through the head."

Dawn spilled through a labyrinth of twisted roots, mottling Badgertail's face where he sat at the edge of a pond studying the calm green surface. The reflections of clouds sailed across the water. He picked up a pebble and tossed it through the roots into the center of a cloud. Rings distorted the peaceful image.

Badgertail let his gaze wander. Frogs croaked and splashed along the shore, startling the turtles that floated placidly with their noses poking up. The pond's wave action had scooped out the bank, providing a perfect hiding place for his small party on the run. But it proved a haunted spot.

Huge roots thrust gnarled fingers out over the water. Especially in the half-light, they looked like skeletal hands groping for him. Badgertail hunched down and propped his elbows on his knees to think.

Locust's nightmares had kept him awake. Twice in the night he had been forced to clamp a hand over her mouth to cut off her screams. Flute and the other warriors had awakened in terror, but Badgertail had just motioned them back down and spoken softly to Locust, telling her that he was close and she need not worry.

What am I going to do? Should I try to sneak through the battlefield and join up with Black Birch and Elkhorn? What will I do with Locust? Her wounds have started to fester. If she doesn't get to a healer soon, she may lose that right leg.

Despite Locust's bravery last night, she had barely been able to run to the ambush site where Longtail, Cloudshadow, and Budworm had been waiting to pounce on their pursuers. Badgertail had carried her most of the way here.

As dawn softened into morning, the turtles began paddling around the pond, snapping at the insects that unwisely landed on the shining surface.

"Flute, loan me your warshirt." When the warrior had stripped, Badgertail ducked under the roots and quietly wandered down the narrow shore. The breeze nipped at his bare chest and flapped his beaded forelocks against his shoulders. He angled toward a beaver run, a tiny dug-out inlet that nicked the bank. Five turtles floated there; through the transparent green, he could see their round shells bobbing just beneath the surface. When his shadow passed over them, the turtles splashed and dove.

Carrying Flute's shirt, Badgertail eased into the cold water, wading out until the ripples came up to the middle of his chest. Then he took a deep breath and dove.

The chill ate into his flesh and curled around his bones. *Blessed Father Sun, this is bitter!* He grabbed onto the plants that grew on the bottom and pulled himself along, stirring the water as little as possible. Dark minnows darted around him through delicate filaments of algae. He curved out into the belly of the pond, then doubled back toward the beaver run.

Ahead, gossamer hairs of mud trailed up through the still water. His eyes followed the hairs to their lumpy source, where the turtles had half-buried themselves in the mud of the bottom.

He eased forward, checked their shells to make certain none were snapping turtles, then began grabbing them and tucking their squirming bodies into Flute's warshirt.

When he broke the surface and slogged up onto shore, the chill dawn air felt wonderfully warm against his wet skin. He headed straight for camp.

Stooping beneath the protruding talons of a long-dead tree, he rounded the bend and saw that the whole camp had roused—except for Locust. Flute and the other three warriors crouched around the fire, feeding it just enough dry sticks to keep the coals hot without smoking. Soft conversation carried to him.

Badgertail knelt beside Flute and began handing out turtles. "Breakfast. It may be your last. You'd better enjoy it." He wrung out the fabric and returned the garment to the warrior. "And thanks for the loan of your shirt."

Locust lay a few hands distant. Her eyes fluttered open. "Always the . . . optimist." She had curled on her side, and her hair fell around her cheeks in a dark, silken veil. His warshirt swallowed her slender body, keeping her warm.

Badgertail smiled, watching as one of the painted turtles peed on Flute when the warrior turned it upside down.

"After the past two days, I think we're all cynical," Flute noted as he gave the turtle a sour glare and shoved it deeply into the coals. To avoid blistering his hands, he held it down with a stick. After several seconds, the animal stopped fighting and Flute laid his stick by the fireside. His seventeen-summers-old face had aged of late. Lines etched his high forehead, giving his round face with its blunt nose a craggy look, like weather-beaten granite. "What are we going to do, Badgertail?"

"I'm not sure yet. Let's eat, then we'll talk about it."

Badgertail poked his and Locust's turtles into the pit of glowing coals, keeping them down with a stick for a sufficient time before he rose and went to kneel at her side. "How are you feeling?"

"Like one of those turtles," she answered feebly.

Badgertail nodded. After a night of chafing in his shirt, her wounds must have been rubbed raw. "Pretty fiery, huh?"

"'Fraid so."

Badgertail looked down at her hands. Blood had clotted in thick circles around her wrists. Softly, he said, "I'm thinking about taking you home—myself."

Locust gazed at him steadily. "You would leave your warriors without guidance?"

"Whatever's happening out there, we're too far away to do anything about it. If we go home, we can gather the two hundred warriors guarding the palisades and return. We'll be of more use that way than . . ."

Locust turned her face away from him, and he saw her jaw muscles jump. "You don't want me to say it, do you?"

He spread his hands wide. "What else can I do? Tell me."

"Take Flute's party and find Elkhorn. He probably needs you desperately."

"And what about you?"

She lifted a shoulder. "I'll be fine here. In a few days, I'll have enough strength to walk home myself. Then you won't—"

"That's not true, and you know it. You're sick and getting worse."

They glared at each other, waging a silent battle of wills, until Locust looked away. Her expression said she knew that he was right—and she hated having to admit it.

Badgertail aimlessly scooped up sand and let it trickle through his fingers. An uncomfortable stinging had started in his guts. Locust watched him worriedly.

He shook his head slowly. "I can't leave you, Locust."

"If I were another warrior, you'd go."

"You're not another warrior."

"Then assign Cloudshadow to take me home." In a whisper, she continued, "He's the least of these warriors. You can do without him. That way, you'll feel better about me and you can go on and do what you know you should."

"But, Locust, I—"

"Badgertail," Locust said with as much harshness as she could muster, "think of how you'll feel if you leave your forces and hundreds die because Elkhorn or Black Birch makes some stupid mistake. I'm one person. There are over seven hundred warriors out there who need you more than I do."

The stinging in his gut grew, as if his intestines had decided to twist into knots. He gazed at her imploringly. In a bare whisper, he said, "But Locust—I'm afraid for you. Please. I want to make sure that you get home safely. Then I'll—"

"And if Elkhorn is trapped somewhere? You may cost him—"

"All right!" Badgertail threw up his hands. But as he did, a tight band constricted around his heart. "I'll . . . I'll assign Cloud-shadow."

Weakly, Locust lifted her hand and patted his bare calf. "I'll be all right. It's only one day's walk from here."

He stared at her miserably. "Those turtles should be done. I'll get them."

Black Birch smiled his satisfaction as he rolled up his blanket. Things had gone well yesterday. They had captured one of Petaga's war parties and killed all of the warriors—even the last, who had groveled before Black Birch, pleading for mercy. Today they would head back north and see if they couldn't join up with Badgertail. What could have happened to him?

Every war party that had regrouped here had been attacked. Perhaps Badgertail hadn't fared as well as these other war leaders. Had something unexpected happened at Redweed Village? *Could* a bunch of corn farmers have thrashed the great Badgertail? Maybe even killed him? Well, Black Birch could lead the Cahokia forces just as expertly as Badgertail could. It made little difference.

Black Birch tied his rolled blanket to the back of his belt, then attached his war club and slung his quiver over his shoulder.

Warriors moved through the dawn around him. Their soft sounds rang through the morning stillness: clubs clattering against knives as they were tied to belts; strains of dialogue; arrows rattling as quivers were picked up.

Black Birch lifted his arms over his head to stretch his back muscles. The hard ground had been full of stones. He'd tossed and turned most of the night, trying to find a comfortable position.

Strands of light crept over the eastern horizon and twined through the transparent gleam of lavender that stretched halfway up the sky. Idly, he noted the positions of his lookouts. They hunched on the high spots overlooking the three major drainages that led into One Mound Village.

Odd, when they had entered One Mound yesterday, they had found it abandoned, forgotten possessions visible like ghostly sentries in the empty sockets of doorways and windows. The inhabitants had left so quickly that they hadn't even bothered to pack their stores of corn. Black Birch's forces had raided every storage hut, filling their warriors' packs and stuffing themselves at dinner last night.

Had the villagers seen them coming? Or had they gotten word from traitors like Wrenwing that Black Birch was recruiting warriors and they knew what would happen to them if they refused to join him?

Black Birch grunted to himself as he strode through a maze of warriors, many of whom he didn't know, toward Wasp and Beehive. They waited at the edge of camp like score sticks at a chunkey game, arms folded, eyes roving the lightening heavens.

Wasp turned when Black Birch strode up. He smiled at her, but she did not smile back. Her beautiful face showed her Sunborn heritage in its triangular shape, high cheekbones, and pointed chin—all framed within a thick tumble of silky, raven hair. The seriousness in her mahogany eyes punctured his confidence. He stopped smiling.

"Have you noticed that none of our lookouts have moved since we've had light this morning?" she asked.

Black Birch looked again. The dark forms still stood vigilantly against the pastel backdrop of morning. "So?"

Beehive shifted uneasily. Medium-sized, he possessed a moony face with soft eyes and a sensuous, heart-shaped mouth. "Maybe nothing," he said. "But it doesn't *feel* right."

Black Birch laughed. "You've got the jitters. Relax. We're going north today to connect up with Elkhorn and the other party leaders. If we meet more of Petaga's forces, we'll kill them, just like we did those yesterday."

Wasp said, "Doesn't it strike you as odd that three of our parties wound up here, in the same place, each chasing different—"

"*They're coming!* Get your weapons!" old Bucktooth shouted, racing down from the north as fast as his ancient legs would carry him.

"Who?"

Bucktooth's response was drowned out as Black Birch's shouting warriors raced from the camp like a terrified herd of deer, careening between people, stumbling over packs, as they fled from the onslaught.

Black Birch grabbed the arm of the lead warrior and swung him around. "What's happening? How many are chasing you?"

The man panted, "Hundreds—I don't know." He shook off Black Birch's hand and dashed for the drainage that led south.

War whoops shredded the peaceful morning as enemy warriors burst over the hill, their bows aimed. Arrows hissed through the air around

Black Birch. He heard Beehive grunt and turned to see the man sink slowly to the ground, a brightly feathered shaft sticking out of his chest. Blood frothed at his quivering lips.

Wasp yelled "Get down!" as Black Birch dove for the ground and scrambled on his stomach to an uptilted slab of limestone, where he could pull his bow and nock an arrow. He fired into the oncoming enemy. A man whirled and fell, writhing on the ground. There were so many of them! Black Birch nocked another arrow.

On his left side, Pipestone's war party rushed into the screaming horde, working their bows, striking with their war clubs.

A choking curtain of dust rose, curling into the scarlet wash of sunrise. Men and women fell like flies at the first heavy frost, sprawling across the ground or creeping spiderlike while they held their wounds. Cries of pain rang out above the tumult of groans and grunts.

Wasp led a group of seven warriors northward, then came racing back. "Black Birch! We're surrounded! There are more warriors streaming down out of the hills. Petaga must have organized the battle in two stages. We've got to find a place and make a stand. How about those rocks at the head of the southern drainage?"

"Yes, go!"

Black Birch lunged to his feet and led the retreat.

Thirty-seven

Lichen stopped in a field on the bank of Cahokia Creek to watch the crimson ball of the sun rise over the eastern bluff. Streamers of orange light fanned out across the clear blue sky before spilling into the floodplain in a deluge of amber. In the field, ancient tree stumps stood amidst the thistles and maygrass.

Lichen wearily sank down on the bones of an old cypress. For as far as she could see, stumps dotted the expanse of land. She wondered idly how many of those trees had been maples. She had heard about maple sap. A trader had let her cousin Claycoil, who lived in Pretty Mounds, taste it once. Claycoil said it was like the dew of melted sunshine, sweet and warm, and golden brown.

Why did you let people cut down all the trees, Mother Earth? Couldn't you stop them?

As she gazed at the jagged gullies that cut the parched land, Wanderer's words echoed through her mind: "*It is only through our death that she lives. Our bodies provide sustenance.*"

Was that what this war meant to Mother Earth? *Hunting?*

Lichen turned. Southward, shadows clung to the lee side of the mounds in the great village of the Sun Chief. So many mounds. Over a hundred. The vague shapes of people moved around the bases. Stunted cornfields covered nearly every hand of tillable ground within one day's walking distance. The leaves on the stalks drooped like long, thin fingers reaching down to Mother Earth in desperation.

What's going to happen, Foxfire? What if I can't get into the Underworld to see First Woman? Will Mother Earth let everyone die in this war? So she can eat?

Lichen rubbed her forehead. In the creek bed below, fog rose from the gurgling water and roiled like earthbound clouds. While she watched, the mist shifted, forming strange, haunting shapes—one of them almost a face that peered up at her through wide, black eyes. Lichen had not slept in two days, not since her Dream of Foxfire, and she had eaten only a few roots found along the way. She felt woozy. She squinted hard to focus on the wavering face in the mist, but her vision blurred with tears of exhaustion. The sun rose higher, piercing the fog with a dagger of light, and the amorphous face glowed pink and seemed to solidify.

Lichen blinked, not certain that she saw it. *Who are you? A Water Spirit? Have you come to take my soul?*

The pink creature lifted its arms and began the steps of a Dance that Lichen had never seen. It pranced on the surface of the water, its feet lifting in high steps before it began to spin.

The mist swirled after the creature as it Danced down the creek.

Lichen crawled over the lip of the bank and jumped to the sandy shore. Silver veils of fog swept around her, clutching with cold, transparent fingers. On her left, the creek ran over a series of rocks. White froth bobbed down the channel until it disappeared in the thick fog.

Lichen filled her lungs with the scents of water and damp grass. She saw nothing now, except fog. But the Stone Wolf resting over her heart had grown warm and heavy. Its weight seemed to be pulling her forward.

Do you know the best way to get there, Wolf?

The weight of the stone tugged at her neck.

Go ahead, Wolf. You lead me there.
She walked forward, parting the mist like an arrow.

They've made it down into the flats!"

At Soapstone's shout of warning, Elkhorn spun around and yelled, "Pick a spot! We're going to have to try to stand them off, or they'll shoot us in the back." Then he ripped his antler stiletto from his belt. The contents of his quiver had been exhausted long ago—like his strength. He locked his knees to keep himself standing.

All day they had been fighting and running, fighting and running. The three war parties under his command had entered the battle late, because it had taken time for them to grasp the layout of the terrain and get into position to shore up Black Birch's failing lines.

But they had failed anyway. Petaga's warriors had just kept coming, roaring through the hills in wave after wave. They fought as fearlessly as enraged wolves protecting their pups.

During the first part of the retreat, Elkhorn had been able to pluck arrows from the battlefield. But the enemy had pushed them far to the south, herding them along the bluff until they had been forced down over the edge north of Hickory Mounds.

Blessed Father Sun, at this rate, they'll have pushed us back to the palisades of Cahokia by midday tomorrow. Then what will we do?

They now fought in a field of pink toadflax interspersed with tangles of buffalo-gourd vines. Elkhorn could barely take a step without his feet becoming knotted in the creeping tendrils.

Soapstone stood a few hands to his right, panting, sweat running down his round face. His warshirt clung to his body in blood-drenched wrinkles. About forty members of their original war party had survived; they dotted the field, their eyes on the slight rise a thousand hands away—back in the direction from which they had come.

War cries erupted, and the enemy warriors flooded down the trail.

Elkhorn made a futile attempt to count them, braced his feet, and fell into a wary crouch, his knees shaking. *Too many . . .*

A tall, burly man targeted Elkhorn and rushed with his war club lifted high over his head. He let out a ululating cry as he dove, tackling Elkhorn and dragging him to the ground.

The world spun crazily around Elkhorn while he and the warrior rolled over and over, each trying to get on top. Vines grabbed their legs and broke with loud pops, crushed in the fury of the battle.

Elkhorn maneuvered his opponent into a patch of prickly pear cactus. As the poisonous spines sank into the man's back, he flinched, and Elkhorn jerked his hand loose and plunged his stiletto deep into the man's side, trying to pierce a kidney.

His enemy shrieked and reared up in panic. Elkhorn drove his weapon into the man's chest, struck a rib, tugged it free, and plunged it down again. Blood spattered Elkhorn's face as he shoved the other over and threw all of his weight behind the stiletto. The man flopped like a fish out of water while his ineffectual war club feebly pounded Elkhorn's broad back.

The instant his enemy stopped moving, Elkhorn was on his feet, bracing for another attack. Woodchuck sprawled a few hands away, his skull split open. Already greedy flies had landed in the thick clots of blood.

All around Elkhorn, war clubs cracked wetly into skulls, or splintered bones apart. Moans and screams rang out.

His warriors were being slaughtered before his eyes. Only one exit remained open: a small creek bed that led back to the north. "Soapstone! Hurry, this way!"

An arrow slashed by Elkhorn's shoulder, and he turned to run, jumping the thick tangles of vines, fighting to close his ears against the wretched screams that rose into the afternoon heat behind him.

Badgertail cautiously worked out the trail that led along the creek. Sweat had laid a fine sheen on his muscular body. Flute, Budworm, and Longtail spread out behind him. They had been heading north when they'd glimpsed the two people but hadn't had a good look at them before they'd lost them. The leader had a talent for obscuring a trail. He had ordered his comrade to circle around on their own tracks, taken them through the creek, then jumped from rock to rock along the bank. But Badgertail had backtracked and spotted the places where their sandals had slipped off the rocks and scuffed the dry ground.

He needed to determine the outcome of this weasel-and-mouse game. If these were Petaga's people and they had recognized Badgertail, they might try to swing around and ambush his party. If they were his own people . . . well, he would find out at last what was happening.

Flute stopped suddenly and knelt down. He waved to Badgertail.

When he knelt by Flute, he frowned. Spots of blood dimpled the earth beside this set of tracks. *Wounded. And limping. Look at how he's dragging that left foot.*

Badgertail scanned the landscape. Though it might appear basically flat, cycles of erosion had cut knee-deep troughs around the creek and created a maze of possible hiding places. Moreover, clumps of flowering saltbush thrust up thickly through the dry crust of earth. In the distance, the gray bluff stood as a silent witness. Overhead, ravens soared and cawed while they flapped across the infinite expanse of blue.

Badgertail motioned to Flute and the others to fan out in a wide semicircle, then went ahead, his sandals crunching on the desiccated gray soil as his eyes flitted from one drop of blood to the next. The trail led down into a jagged erosion channel, where the warrior had slid a good hundred hands on his stomach, leaving splashes of blood as he went. Every nerve in Badgertail's body hummed as he followed the trail up out of the channel and into a dense growth of cattails so wilted that they crackled against his bare legs.

He took his time, letting Flute, Budworm, and Longtail position themselves around the boundary of the cattails. Gingerly, Badgertail pushed stalks out of his way and inched forward. He had lost the blood trail—*but the warrior has to be in here somewhere. What happened to your friend? Did he sacrifice you so he could escape?*

Wind rippled through the dried stalks, rattling them before it swept out into the saltbush and formed into a dust devil that whirled into the sky. Badgertail ignored the twisting column spinning across the edges of his vision.

He knelt. More spots of blood. They stuck to his fingertips. Wet. *On a day this hot, they'd have dried within moments . . .*

Badgertail straightened warily and let his gaze wander the slitted patterns of leaves, searching for any irregularity. The cattails had already started to burst out, weeks early—a desperate attempt by the plants to cast their seeds before they died.

A single stalk shuddered suddenly. Badgertail didn't move a muscle. The same stalk bent sideways.

Slowly, Badgertail lifted a hand and gestured to the location. Flute and the others began tightening their circle, moving into the cattails with the stealth of Cougar stalking Marmot.

Badgertail took another step and caught movement from his left, down at the creek. *So there's your friend.*

He ground his teeth. Through the weave of grass at the edge of the creek, he could *feel* eyes peering out. Powerful. Malignant. The man couldn't have a bow or he would have used it by now.

Badgertail kept glancing at the grass while he moved through the cattails. Leaf blades caught on his breechclout before zipping away to flail back and forth. A percussion symphony resulted as the stalks battered each other.

He took another step—and spied a brown patch of skin through the dried green. Slowly, he lifted his hand to signal Flute that he had located their quarry. Flute nodded and moved in.

As Badgertail quietly slipped his stolen war club from his belt, a clod of dirt whirred through the air and smacked him in the shoulder. Badgertail whirled. A flock of geese exploded from the creek in a squawking flurry, and Badgertail almost swallowed his tongue.

The lanky old man trudged up from the creek bed, his tattered red sleeves flapping.

"*Wanderer!*"

Gray hair matted his temples, highlighting the hook of his long nose. "First Woman is so cantankerous," Wanderer remarked. "I can't figure out why she's convinced that you and I have to enter Cahokia together."

Badgertail's eyes narrowed. "I can't either—since I'm not going to Cahokia."

He scrutinized the aged shaman to make sure he didn't have any weapons, then turned to the cattails again. Flute crept closer to the place where Badgertail had seen the brown flesh.

A woman jumped to her feet and made a mad dash through the stalks. Budworm ran her down with little effort, though she almost beat him to tatters with her fists before he could drag her back.

"Meadow Vole." Badgertail looked at her bloody leg. "What are you two doing here?"

Wanderer gestured aimlessly. "For the most part, we've spent the day watching your warriors flee like rats back toward Cahokia."

Badgertail paled. "What are you talking about?"

"Petaga has devastated your forces, Badgertail. I'm surprised you didn't know. We saw Elkhorn fly past only—"

"Elkhorn?" Badgertail's hand tightened around his war club. If a seasoned warrior like Elkhorn had headed home, Cahokia must be in grave danger. But could it be true? "Where's Petaga?"

Wanderer pointed to the bluff. "About there, I should think. At least that's what Crossed Beak said earlier. You'd better be getting back to Cahokia, Badgertail, or Petaga will arrive before you do."

Badgertail lifted his chin. Could things have gone so terribly wrong that his forces had been unable to hold Petaga for even a few days?

"Well, it's good to see that you're still alive, Badgertail." Wanderer smiled genially as he strode by Badgertail to grab Vole's arm. "Vole and I have to be going now."

Wanderer briskly led Vole off in a westerly direction, engaging her in an animated conversation. Flute turned to gape at Badgertail.

He waved a hand irritably. "Yes, go stop them."

As Flute charged off, swinging his war club, Badgertail's eyes returned to the bluff. *Could Petaga really be up there? So close to Cahokia?*

He kept staring, and caught sight of thin wisps of dust rising from the bluff, shading the blue sky with a hint of gray.

His stomach cramped—as though his body knew something that his soul refused to believe.

Thirty-eight

Lichen trudged up from the mint-scented shore of Cahokia Creek and stopped at the edge of the sprawling settlement to look around. Dusk outlined the mounds with luminous borders of gray. A few children raced up and down the paths that led through the maze of houses.

Awe and fear struck Lichen at once. She had never seen this many houses before. Shaggy thatched roofs filled her vision. How could so many live in so small a space?

She walked on. People barely glanced at her as she passed—but with so many living here, how could they know all the children? The thought made her feel hollow. What would it be like to live in a place where you didn't know everyone? If a little girl were hurt and calling for help, would someone she didn't know come to save her? The thought that they might not sent shivers through Lichen.

She passed an old woman who sat outside her house combing a basketful of dog hair to be woven into the beautiful blanket sitting half-finished on the loom beside her. The colors amazed Lichen. Reds and purples so brilliant they must have been stunning in the full light of day. Did the Sun Chief trade for such dyes? Or did his artisans create special blends that Lichen's people didn't know how to make? Lichen would have given almost anything to have a dress with that rich shade of purple in it.

The mouth-watering smell of corn-and-fish soup filled the air, taunting Lichen's empty stomach. Dogs barked, the sounds soft and indistinct, as though coming from across the village.

Lichen gawked at the mounds as she walked. They rose up like small mountains, hemming her in, making it hard to breathe. Big houses stood on the tops of most of them, orange glows lighting the windows. Wanderer had told her once that the Sunborn insisted the mounds be built to reflect the shapes of the sky gods. The mounds reached up to the sky, and the sky gods reached down. As she gazed around, she thought she could distinguish the major stars that formed Hanged Woman's body, and a series of mounds curved southward to represent the noose around Hanged Woman's throat. Lichen followed the mounds and spied a large group of people gathered in front of a house.

When she was close enough, she could hear the sobs of a woman, and someone screaming, "Keep them away from me! They're not human. Oh, Checkerberry, what are they? Where's Primrose? Nettle? Nettle, where are you? Go find Primrose for me! I want my brother!"

The people outside had their arms crossed tightly across their breasts. They muttered nervously, and Lichen caught half-sentences:

". . . don't know. She won't nurse them."

"I swear that wolf-faced one can see. I was talking to Nettle about taking them out and bashing their heads on the rocks, and I turned around and found those pink eyes boring into me."

On the far side of the group, a big, handsome man leaned wearily against the shaggy roof. Tears traced lines through the dust on his face. An old white-haired woman stood beside him, staring at him intently.

The old woman said, "I don't care what you think, Nettle. This is no simple matter. Who will we find to nurse those babies? Do you think just anybody will be willing to—"

"Stop, please, Nit," the man pleaded. He dropped his head into his hands. "I'll find a way. I don't know how, but I will. Right now I'm more worried about Primrose. Green Ash cried for him all of last night, and none of us can gain admittance to even discuss it with the Sun Chief."

"Tharon has lost his mind. Everyone says so. Get used to the idea that you may never again see Primrose . . ."

Lichen turned cold inside. Tharon had gone crazy? And she was supposed to go into the temple, where he lived?

She reached an intersection of pathways, and to her left, at the end of long lines of houses, she saw the clay-plastered walls of the palisades. Men lounged along the shooting platforms, their bows and quivers slung over their shoulders.

Lichen's soul shriveled. Fear grew with each beat of her heart.

Tightly, she whispered, "What if those warriors won't let me in? If those grown-ups couldn't get in, how can I?"

"Bird-Man waits for you there . . ."

I don't understand anything anymore. I wish . . . I wish my mother were here. Oh, Foxfire, I'm only ten.

"So was I. I was ten when Power called . . ."

In the back of her soul, she could hear Mammoth Calf trumpeting as he tried to run, the long arrows in his body shaking like perverse quills. The village vanished for a moment, and Lichen again watched Mammoth Calf fall to his knees and roll over in the field of snow.

The Stone Wolf radiated warmth against Lichen's chest. "I—I'm going, Wolf," she murmured.

Lichen plodded forward until she reached the gate. Six guards strolled near it. She stopped before a tall man with copper beads woven into his braided forelocks. He peered down at her as though annoyed.

In a quaking voice, Lichen said, "I need to see Nightshade, please."

The warrior's mouth pursed unpleasantly. "The priestess is busy, girl."

"Yes, I know, but could you tell her that Wolf Slayer gave me a message for her?"

The warrior stiffened. The other men, who had been talking together, fell silent. Lichen tried not to think about the looks they were giving her—as sharp as flakes of obsidian.

The tall warrior propped callused hands on his hips, hands that looked suspiciously like a farmer's instead of a warrior's. "What do you know of Wolf Slayer?"

"I talked to him in the Underworld. He—" she twisted her hands nervously "—he seemed nice."

The men burst into laughter. One bent over, holding his stomach. But the tall warrior did not laugh. His eyes narrowed reflectively.

"Why would the creatures of the Underworld let a little girl like you into the Land of the Ancestors?"

Lichen shrugged. The Stone Wolf tugged powerfully at the thong around her throat. She gazed down at the bump it made beneath her green dress. "I—I guess because I'm the Keeper of the Stone Wolf."

That wasn't quite true. Her mother was really the Keeper. Unless . . . *No, don't think about your mother. That hurts too much.*

The warrior's eyes widened. "The Stone Wolf of Redweed Village? The one Badgertail was sent to steal? Where is it? Let me see it!"

Lichen pulled on the thong and brought the little black Wolf out to hold it in her palm. It glinted in the diminishing light.

The warrior took a step backward, as though he could feel the Power that poured from the Wolf. "Stay here. I'll be right back."

Lichen watched him disappear behind the palisades. The log gate slid into place with a loud bang.

She glanced at the other warriors, who were studying her with fear in their eyes, then walked a short distance and slumped down on a patch of grass. The dry blades crackled beneath her weight.

Lichen drew up her knees and propped her chin on them. The red spirals on her tattered hem looked pathetic. They made her heart ache for Wanderer. She remembered his pride when she had returned from the Underworld covered with the strange grasses that grew at the bottom of the river there.

"I'm here, Wanderer," she whispered. "I came, just like you—and Foxfire—said I had to. But I'm scared."

Suddenly a different thought possessed her, leading her to think of that long-ago day when Wanderer had jumped from the rock overhang to throw rocks at his own shadow. *"I wish you'd come earlier, Lichen. I wouldn't have wasted all morning . . ."*

Lichen smiled, but tears filled her eyes. *Lonely. So lonely.*

The gate grated open, and Lichen jumped to her feet.

But it wasn't Nightshade who stepped through. It wasn't a woman at all. Instead, a man stood there—a man wearing a golden robe and a headdress of beautiful yellow feathers. Intricate tattoos covered his face. He wore splendid copper ear-spools, almost as large as his very ears. He lifted her chin and stared at the Stone Wolf with a predatory gleam in his eyes. "Who are you?"

"I—I'm Lichen. I need to see Nightshade."

A groan sounded from behind the gate, and the man turned and said gruffly, "Get him out of here. He no longer entertains me."

Lichen stumbled sideways when two warriors dragged out a woman—no, it was a man, a *berdache*, in a dress. Black lumps covered his face. Bruises—some yellowed from time—covered the rest of the *berdache*'s exposed skin. He struggled weakly, moaned, and gazed at Lichen through fever-brilliant eyes. She thought, but wasn't certain, that he muttered, *"Run!"*

The guards dragged him off down the path that led to the south.

The man with the golden robe looked at Lichen. Waving a hand to his guards, he ordered, "I want her in my chamber. Bring her."

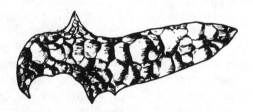

Thirty-nine

A little girl's cries . . .

Orenda jerked her eyes open. She had been half-asleep on the cattail mat beneath Nightshade's bed. She held her breath to listen more closely. Wind worried the shaggy roof, shishing and thumping in the darkness, carrying the yips of a fox down from the north. Maybe the girl's cries had been only a dream?

"Nightshade?" she called. "D-Did you hear that?"

A firebowl made an orange blot in the far corner of the room. At the edge of the glowing halo, Nightshade sat with the Tortoise Bundle cradled to her breast, peering unblinkingly into a Wellpot. The light reflected eerily in her wide, black eyes.

"N-Nightshade?" Orenda slid out from under the bed.

Indigo shadows draped the walls and ceiling like the fluttering hem of a garment. Orenda sniffed to let the pungent fragrance of damp cedar and earth fill her senses. Fog must be hovering around the temple, seeping into the bones of the logs, to coax such sweetness from the old wood.

Orenda trotted across the room, her tan sleeping kilt patting at her knees, and crouched before Nightshade. Curtains of long hair fell over Nightshade's shoulders, framing her slack face. Orenda bent down and stared into her eyes.

"Nightshade? I heard s-something."

Nightshade looked dead.

Orenda wet her lips anxiously. She had been with her mother a few times when they had accidentally disturbed Old Marmot's journeys to the Underworld. Her mother's voice repeated in her thoughts: *"Dreamers look dead when their souls are swimming in the Underworld, Orenda. It's because their bodies are just barely alive."*

Orenda cautiously peeked into the small basket with red spirals on it that sat beside Nightshade's knee. A gray paste smeared the bottom.

"Nightshade. There were s-screams. Did you hear them? I need you. I'm afraid."

When no answer came, Orenda pulled back Nightshade's long hair to scrutinize her temples. Yes, just like Old Marmot's. Gray paste smudged them.

She let go of the curtain of hair and sat back, watching it sway before it settled again over Nightshade's cheeks. Orenda hugged her knees to her chest and tried to force her frightened mind to think. Nightshade had been attempting to enter the Underworld for weeks, but hadn't been able to. Orenda wondered why First Woman had decided to open the gate to the Well of the Ancestors on this cold, damp night.

Another cry echoed through the halls and was abruptly cut off.

Orenda's heart pounded. The sound came again, this time more muted, like a stifled sob. A chill thread of terror coiled in her stomach.

"It is a little g-girl's voice," she whispered to herself in horror.

She put a hand on Nightshade's cheek and patted it hard. "Nightshade? I . . . I'm afraid. There's another little g-girl in the temple. I don't know who . . ."

She tensed. Could it be the girl who had been talking to her in her Dreams? The one who kept telling her not to worry, that she was going to go talk to First Woman and make everything all right again?

But if *he* had caught the little girl . . .

She jumped to her feet, breathing hard. Her mind began spinning panicked images of what Tharon did to little girls, and in the recesses of her soul, a muted voice screamed, *No, no, it can't happen to someone else!*

Orenda threw off her sleeping kilt as she ran to Nightshade's bed. She slipped on her red dress with the rolled-up sleeves, then combed out the tangles in her long hair with her fingers. Before she left, she called again, "Nightshade? Nightshade, please w-wake up."

But Nightshade didn't move.

Orenda peeked around the door-hanging. The firebowl beside their doorway cast a radiant aura over the soundless, deserted hall, but the bowl at the end of the corridor had been snuffed.

Sometimes that just happens. Especially on windy nights. A stray whiff of wind might penetrate the cracks . . .

Orenda tiptoed down the corridor to the first intersection. The darkness wrapped her like a smothering blanket. She listened for any sound. Hearing none, she hesitantly turned into the corridor that led to *his* chamber. No one walked about tonight.

Bracing her back against the cold wall, she slid slowly along while her lungs gasped for air. Passing the entry to the temple, she listened again, then proceeded onward.

Two guards stood on either side of the doorway to Tharon's chamber. The tall, ugly one, named Hoofprint, glared uneasily as she approached. The other, skinny, with a belly that bulged through his warshirt, frowned. Orenda could not recall his name.

From within, a girl's voice begged, "Stop it! Why are you hurting me? I don't understand . . ." Orenda halted six hands away.

"I don't require that you understand, child. Only that you obey," Tharon responded in that mockingly nice voice. "I am the great Sun Chief. Everyone obeys me or they die. You can understand that, can't you?"

A choking sob. Then a small voice said, "Yes."

"Do as I say and get over there on that mat and lie down."

"But why?"

"Because you're a pretty little thing and I want to . . . to look at you." Laughter echoed. "Yes, that's it. I want to *look* at you."

Orenda's knees shook so badly that she could barely remain standing. She looked pleadingly at the guards, but they had turned to stare down the hall, pretending they heard nothing. She fought with herself, twisting her hands, trying to figure out what she could do.

When the little girl inside screamed *"No!"* as though she'd been grabbed, Orenda acted instinctively. She dove and crawled beneath the door-hanging on hands and knees.

The guards bellowed behind her, and one of them clutched at her foot, but she jerked loose and kept crawling. She knew they wouldn't dare follow her inside unless summoned.

In an instant, Orenda had reached the middle of the luxurious room. *His* big bed, mounded high with hides and blankets, sat to her left. Odd pieces of furniture lined the wall beneath the window in front of her, things stolen from faraway places. The window-hanging had been lowered so that only a slit of dusk crept into the room, joining the dozen blazing firebowls that stood in their holders along the walls. Everywhere she looked, Power objects watched her through blank eyes. He had moved them out of the temple. Why? To protect him here in his own chamber? Old Marmot's Bundle, with its blue designs, lay in shreds beside his bed, the contents strewn over the floor in a strange, glittering wealth. On her right, all of her mother's things—jewelry, robes, sandals—had been thrown into a careless pile.

A horrified sob caught in Orenda's throat.

Tharon turned, his golden robe whirling around his legs like sunlit clouds. He carried a war club in one hand and a cup of tea in the other. Orenda recognized the strange, detached expression that creased his face. *He's been drinking that galena tea with crushed morning-glory seeds in it.* On occasion, he had forced Orenda's jaws open and poured some of it down her throat, all the time telling her that she would like it.

And she had. Because the tea had given her the Power to take her soul out of her body and hide it in the dirt floor, a place so hard and dark that his hands couldn't find her there.

He strutted forward with that arrogant tilt to his chin. A deerbone stiletto hung from his belt. "Why, Orenda, I've been wondering when you'd come to your senses and return to me." Then he glanced at the other little girl, who crouched in the corner, half-hidden behind an old, heavily carved maple bench. The front of her green dress had been torn, and Orenda could see the claw marks on the girl's chest.

"I h-hate you!" Orenda blurted.

"You've gotten bold since you've been with Nightshade, Orenda. Well, all the better. Get over there with Lichen. Hurry it up! I haven't got all night."

"No!"

"I *order* you—"

"N-No."

His bat face tensed before he let out an incoherent cry and ran at her with his club raised.

Orenda jumped to her feet and fled across the room. When she dove behind the bench, Lichen stared at her in astonishment. They held each other's eyes as they had a hundred times in their Dreams.

Lichen grabbed Orenda's arm. "Hurry! Maybe we can get to the window."

They scurried like mice, shoving over furniture when they couldn't crawl beneath the legs. His shrill laughter echoed, as though their desperate flight amused him, but Orenda could hear the *crack-crack* of the club smacking his open palm. The firebowls threw his shadow like a flickering giant over the walls. It moved with the stealth of Wolf on a blood trail as it tracked them through the maze of furniture.

"Orenda? Orenda, stop this game and get up. Do you hear me? I'm tired of this. *I said get up!*"

The club came crashing down on a loom over Orenda's head, showering her with splinters of wood. She let out a shriek and covered her face.

"This way. Come on!" Lichen said and dragged Orenda behind a conical fish trap before darting out to make a dash for the window.

When Lichen lunged for the sill, he threw a conch-shell cup so that it shattered against her back and shocked her long enough for him to catch a handful of her flying black hair and jerk her to the floor. Lichen fought, trying to rip her hair from his stony grip.

Rage and terror mixed so blindingly inside Orenda that she didn't know what to do. At last the strain drove her to throw herself at him in a biting, kicking whirlwind.

"*Run, L-Lichen!*" Orenda yelled as she clamped her teeth on the web of skin between his thumb and forefinger. He howled and struggled to shake her loose.

"You little animal!" Tharon raged. "Shall I club you to death like they do snapping turtles?"

Orenda refused to let go. She saw Lichen flit by in a swirl of green. He gasped and lifted Orenda off the ground so he could spin around and smash his war club into Lichen's head. Lichen stumbled in a circle before crumpling like a flower wilting on a hot summer day.

"Lichen!" Orenda cried. Her bite loosened, and Tharon shoved her to the floor. Orenda sat staring in horror at Lichen, who lay on her back at the foot of the bed. Blood matted the hair over her right ear and streaked her pretty face in horrifying patterns. Orenda could not take her eyes from Lichen's hands. They had curled into twitching fists.

From Orenda's tormented soul a wretched cry erupted: "*No, nonono!*" Unthinkingly, she sprang to her feet and attacked, trying to claw him to pieces, but he twined his fingers into the back of her red dress and held her out at arm's length, laughing hysterically.

"Oh, Orenda! You're going to be a great deal more entertaining now. I'm glad that Nightshade stole you away."

Orenda kicked and screamed her hatred.

"Stop it, Orenda. That's enough!"

She twisted, struggling against his hand. Tharon's shadow darkened her face as he bent to stare at her.

"I said, stop it!"

The polished club shone orange in the firelight as it sliced the air.

Orenda didn't even feel the blow. Lost in a floating sensation, she watched him remove his robe, throw it onto the floor, and reach for her. As if in a dream, Orenda tried to crawl away, but his hand knotted in her collar and brutally ripped her dress. Then he forced her down, and his heavy body pinned her atop the soft fabric of his robe.

"So you thought you could get away from this by going to Nightshade. Well, you'll never get away again."

He smashed her head against the floor and used his knee to force her legs apart. Orenda screamed "Nightshade!" and clawed at his face. Tharon struck her so hard that it made her head spin nauseatingly.

"She can't save you." He laughed. "No one can."

Orenda felt his manhood stiffening against her, and madness overcame her. She shrieked, *"Nightshade, Nightshade, N-Nightshade!"* while her hand frantically swept the floor, searching for anything to strike him with. She touched something cool and smooth in the tangle of his discarded robe.

Her fingers tightened around the deerbone stiletto.

Badgertail took the path that angled toward the western gate. Budworm strode beside him, his wary eyes scanning the lifeless houses that lined their route—as if he expected some malignant force to spring out and pounce on him. They had all been edgy, jumping at the slightest movement in the grass.

"Why is it so quiet?" Budworm asked. "We didn't see anyone out working the corn or squash fields."

"Maybe they've taken cover."

And if they have . . . Blessed Father Sun, that means that Tharon already knows of my defeat from warriors who've come dragging in. He's probably been planning my death for days.

Badgertail clutched his club tightly.

This section of the village belonged to the Horn Spoon Clan. Where had the people gone? Window and door hangings flapped in the breeze, revealing empty interiors with baskets and pots still in place. Had they rushed away so fast that they hadn't even had the time to pack?

Wanderer and Vole followed behind them, speaking in low tones, while Flute and Longtail brought up the rear. Though night had settled on the village, only a few stars poked through the charcoal blanket above. The moon hung like a crescent of silver behind the temple mound. Over the field of thatched roofs, he could just make out the sharpened tips of the palisade poles. Warriors walked the shooting platforms.

"Do you think that Tharon could have ordered the Commonborn to flee?" Budworm's round face looked haunted when he turned to Badgertail.

"I hope he did. It would have been prudent." *So he probably didn't.*

Badgertail had to get to Tharon quickly to explain the situation. His gut roiled. He dreaded Tharon's rage more than Petaga's military strength. What would Tharon do? Order him killed on the spot? . . . He might.

Wanderer mumbled something, and Vole responded, "I pray you're right. But what if she's not? I've been *feeling* something, Wanderer. Some terrible—"

"I know, so have I." His voice returned to a low drone.

As they stepped onto the paths that led through the Blue Blanket Clan's section, dogs ran out of houses to yap at their heels. A haze of indigo smoke draped lazily around the tops of the mounds; it smelled brittle and musty.

Firebowls lit luminous lines around window and door hangings—but few voices echoed, and those that did were hushed. Occasionally, a hanging would be pulled back and eyes would peek out at them as they passed.

Normally at this time of year, people would have been sitting outside, laughing and talking, throwing sticks for the dogs, until the nightly chill drove them inside.

Badgertail picked up his pace, hurrying to reach the western gate. When he got close enough, he broke into a trot, and the warriors on the platforms saw him.

"Badgertail! It's Badgertail! *Look!*"

His name swept through the ranks like a tornado. He rounded the corner of the last house and ran head-on into a pack of warriors racing out to meet him. Elkhorn broke through the crowd to hug Badgertail so hard that it drove the air from his lungs.

"Thank Father Sun," Elkhorn said. "We feared you were dead. Locust told us about Redweed, but after the thrashing we took—"

"How is Locust?" he couldn't help but ask. "She and Cloudshadow made it back all right?"

A roar of talk built around Badgertail as a hundred hands thrust through the tangle of bodies to clasp him. He made every attempt to clasp each one in turn while he watched Elkhorn's face darken.

"What is it, Elkhorn? Is it Locust? Tell me."

"She's all right . . . I mean, physically." Elkhorn ran a hand through his bristly ridge of hair and began leading the way toward the open gate. The swarm of hooting warriors followed. "I had to post four guards on her house, Badgertail. She's . . . I've never seen her so enraged. She tried to storm the temple, alone . . . to kill the Sun Chief. It took three warriors to stop her, even with her wounds. At first, well, I thought it was her fever. You understand, I thought it had driven her mad."

Badgertail stopped before the gate. "Say what you mean. What drove her to this?"

Elkhorn looked like he had swallowed something sour. "The Sun Chief captured Primrose while we were out on the battle-walk. Apparently, he . . . he tortured him."

Tortured? Badgertail's heart skipped, his blood pounding in sudden anger. He wondered how three warriors could have stopped her. "Take Wanderer and Vole inside. Hold them by the gate until I return."

"Certainly, but where are you—"

"I'll be at Locust's. Give me two fingers of time." Badgertail ran with all his might, winding down the empty path that fronted the palisades.

Memories flitted at the edge of his soul, memories of Locust's rage. Once a stupid trader from Yellow Star Mounds had dared to laugh and belittle Primrose about the dress he wore. Locust had moved so fast that Badgertail had been unable to stop her. She had leveled a kick to the trader's groin that crumpled him to the ground, then landed a knee in the middle of his chest and dimpled his throat with her stiletto before he had even finished laughing. It had taken Badgertail a full hand of time to convince her not to kill the man. Locust had been angry with Badgertail for a week; she couldn't sleep for wishing that she *had* killed him.

Badgertail slowed to a trot when Locust's white-plastered house came into view. Cornsore and Puffball guarded the front entrance, both of them warriors of repute and special friends of Locust's. Good thinking on Elkhorn's part. Even if she did try to fight her way out, she probably wouldn't kill them.

Relief crossed Puffball's craggy face when Badgertail came to a halt. Pathetic cries carried from inside.

Puffball stepped forward and clasped Badgertail's hand in a powerful grip. Worry lined his high forehead like the deep wrinkles worn into the bluffs by cycles of wind and rain.

"Is she all right?" Badgertail asked quietly.

Puffball shook his head. "Her fever's worse. She refuses to see any healers . . . though Checkerberry has been taking care of her."

Badgertail clapped Puffball on the shoulder before greeting Cornsore and stepping up to the door-hanging. "Locust? May I enter?"

"*Badgertail!* Yes, thank First Woman, come in."

He ducked beneath the hanging and entered the pale amber glow of a single firebowl. Locust sat in the rear of the room on a pile of blankets with Primrose—sobbing—sprawled on the floor with his head in her lap. The curtain of his long black hair spread over Locust's bandaged right leg, but through the glistening strands, Badgertail could see the dark yellow stains that splotched the white cloth. Locust had dressed in a thin white shirt spun from milkweed threads. It clung to every curve of her perspiring body.

Badgertail bowed respectfully to Checkerberry, who was lying on her back near the door, dozing, with two bundles clutched in her arms. Babies? Green Ash's? Why weren't they at home with their mother? Checkerberry nodded a tired welcome to Badgertail and closed her eyes again.

He went over and knelt before Locust. She had pulled her short locks back and fastened them over her ears with copper combs. The style accentuated the lean, pointed qualities of her face. Her eyes had gone vacant, glazed.

Badgertail lifted a hand and put it against her forehead. "You're burning up."

"You heard what happened?"

"I heard."

Locust's jaw trembled despite her efforts to set her teeth. "I'm going to kill him, Badgertail."

He nodded obligingly. "I don't blame you. But let me talk to him first, find out why he—"

"There's no reason for what he did!"

Locust reached down and threw back the black-and-white blanket that covered Primrose's naked body. Primrose buried his face deeper in the white fabric covering Locust's lap and squirmed to hide the most hideous of his wounds. But Badgertail's heart went cold and still. Primrose's testicles had been cut off. Pink wounds marked the places where they had been. Badgertail closed his eyes and turned away.

Locust reached out and grabbed him by the chin, twisting his head so that he met her hot gaze. "I'm going to *kill* him, Badgertail . . . and not you or anyone else can stop me."

Primrose sobbed, "No, no, don't." When Locust put a hand tenderly on his hair, his arms went suddenly around her waist and he bawled openly, "I just want you to stay here with me! Don't leave me."

Locust lifted her eyes to Badgertail's, and in them he saw rage the likes of which he had never seen. Rage that seared his very soul.

Badgertail put a hand on Locust's bare foot. "I don't think you'll have to."

"Why?"

"Petaga will be here by tomorrow night at the latest," he said and sucked in a steadying breath. "There's no way we can hold him off."

"Are you saying you've given up?"

"No. You know me. I'm too bullheaded to give up. We'll fight to our last warrior, but . . ." He shrugged, and all of the weariness he'd been staving off settled on his shoulders like a leaden cape. "Hailcloud has managed Petaga's forces expertly. I don't know how many they lost in the fighting up north, but I wager it wasn't more than two, maybe three hundred. He still has about a thousand warriors. You've been home longer than I have, Locust. How many warriors would you say we have?"

Her gaze dropped away from his. Absently, she stroked Primrose's hair. "We've had very few come in. I don't know, perhaps fifty. I've been locked in here, but Puffball keeps me informed."

"That gives us two hundred and fifty against one thousand. Even with the palisades . . . I don't think it'll be enough."

"What are we going to do?"

"I want you and your family to move inside the palisades—into my house. I won't be there most of the time anyway, what with planning and fighting, and that way I can ask Nightshade to come and care for both you and Primrose. She's a great healer. You know that."

"Badgertail, if you allow me to enter the palisades—"

"Just give me three days. I suspect that Petaga will have overrun the palisades by then and killed Tharon himself. But if not . . . well, we'll discuss it then. Agreed?"

Locust's expression softened, wiped clean of all except fevered exhaustion. "Agreed."

He squeezed her bare foot and rose. "When can you move to my house?"

"I'll need to get word to Green Ash. She and Nettle are supposed to be married tomorrow. I don't know how she—"

"They can be married on the temple mound . . . as long as no arrows are sailing around them. Tharon will agree to that."

Locust's eyes smoldered again, and Badgertail quickly turned away. Checkerberry was staring at him through a wispy veil of gray hair. The old woman said, "I won't be coming to your house, Badgertail, though I thank you for the offer."

"Why not?"

"Because Green Ash will go mad if she has to be close to her babies. And I—I'll go mad if I have to be close to Nightshade."

"I know your fear of Nightshade, Checkerberry, but what do you mean about the babies? I don't—"

"It's a long story, too long for tonight. Is there perhaps another house where I could stay and keep the children safe?"

"I'll find one."

Checkerberry nodded her gratitude. "I thank you. And I'd like to warn you about something."

"What?"

"Tharon murdered Tickseed. If you came up from the west—"

"I did." A cold well grew in his belly. "Is that why the Horn Spoon section of the village is empty? How could two thousand people move so swiftly? Where did they go?"

Checkerberry readjusted the bundles on her arms, and a baby began to mew like a hungry wolf pup. She shushed it and rocked it gently. "I fear, Badgertail, that they went to join Petaga."

Forty

By the time Badgertail returned to the west gate, evening had given way to night. Sparkflies blinked in the grass. The tip of Moon Maiden's face thrust above the temple like a glowing claw of bleached white. Bands of light shot through the spikes on the palisades, scattering the ground with a fringe of silver triangles. Badgertail strode swiftly toward the gate, exchanged a few pleasantries with the guards, and entered.

The mounds loomed quiet and still. Pale amber gleams fell from windows, pooling in the dead grass, but little movement caught his eye. Except for the constant motions of the guards on the shooting platforms, the sacred ground protected by the palisades had the feel of an already empty village. Had the elite fled? The great merchants and wealthy traders who lived here? The Starborn, of course, would have been forbidden that luxury, but the others might have gone, seeking safety until the war had exhausted itself.

As the logs grated back into place behind him, Badgertail searched the darkness for Elkhorn and saw him standing with some others in the long shadows at the base of the stairs that led up the temple mound. Five people? Their clothing melted into the night, giving their movements an unreal quality, like lost souls materializing out of thin air; an arm waved here, a foot stepped there, occasionally a gleam of light would flash from a face.

When he walked into that gauzy blanket of darkness, he recognized Flute standing next to Elkhorn and Budworm. Wanderer stared at Badgertail through wide, inquiring eyes that verged not on madness, but on panic. Despite the chill breeze, Wanderer's wrinkled face glistened with sweat. Dark splotches showed around the collar and beneath the arms of his red shirt. Yet the old man shivered.

"What's the matter with you?" Badgertail asked.

"Power is loose on the night," Wanderer whispered. "Can't you feel it?" His eyes tipped to the moonlit heavens.

Badgertail followed that gaze, but all he saw were a few bats darting through a maze of sparkflies.

Vole edged closer to Wanderer and slipped her arm through his, not so much in affection, it appeared, as to support Wanderer's wobbling legs.

"Badgertail," Vole said, "Elkhorn claims that a little girl came through the gates earlier today. I think that was my daughter. Could we hurry, please?"

"Your daughter . . . Lichen? The one with the Stone Wolf?"

Grudgingly, she answered, "Yes."

Surely, Tharon would have snatched the girl up to take the Wolf from her, but after that . . . Badgertail wondered. Tharon would have had little use for another child in the temple.

Badgertail evaded Vole's request by turning to Elkhorn. "Locust and her family will be moving into my house. Assign two warriors to help them."

"Here?" Elkhorn asked dubiously. "You *invited* Locust into the palisades?"

"Yes, and I want you *personally* to go to the other clan leaders and ask them to bring their clan councils here, too. I'll have to receive permission from Tharon first, but I think he'll agree that they deserve our best protection. We may need them to reorganize people after Petaga . . . when this is all over."

Elkhorn caught the dread in his voice and gave Badgertail a thorough inspection. "I'll take care of it. What will you be doing?"

"I have to deliver these two—" he gestured to Wanderer and Vole "—to Nightshade and then speak to Tharon. After that, I'll be on the shooting platforms. Preparing our warriors."

Badgertail motioned to Wanderer and Vole. "Follow me. It's going to be a long night. Flute? Please accompany us."

The young man fell into line behind Wanderer and Vole while they walked up the log steps.

As they climbed, Badgertail glanced out over the jagged teeth of the palisade wall to where moonlight gleamed on the strips of creeks and tiny awl-points of ponds. Tormented longing rose within him. Thirty cycles ago, those ponds had been lakes. *Why am I still here? Nothing that I loved in my youth is left. I should have run away.* For an instant, the brilliant colors of the Forbidden Lands called to him in silent promise.

They stopped in front of the temple entrance, and Badgertail bowed to the Six Sacred Persons, then stepped aside to allow Wanderer, Vole, and Flute to do the same. While they made their obeisances, he looked up at the sky. Skeletal fingers of clouds drifted through the bodies of the Star Ogres. They pointed southward, as though beckoning him away from this madness.

"Flute, check the Sun Chamber first. If Nightshade isn't there, please escort Wanderer and Vole to her room."

As he started to duck under the hanging, he caught the utter terror on Flute's round face. Badgertail scowled. "She won't kill you for disturbing her, Flute. She asked me to bring Wanderer to her as soon as I found him."

"Oh." The youth's taut shoulder muscles relaxed some. "All right."

Badgertail stepped into the temple, leading the way past the magnificent wall paintings. Most of the firebowls along the floor remained unlit. Because of the shortage of hickory oil? In the dimness, the images of First Woman and Grandfather Brown Bear looked down at them through disdainful, brooding eyes.

They neared the corridor that ran in front of the Sun Chamber, and Badgertail made out the dusky figures of Hoofprint and Black Dog leaning against the wall, their arms folded. When they recognized Badgertail, they both turned sharply and ran toward him.

"Badgertail?"

"Black Dog. Hoofprint." Badgertail clasped their hands warmly. "How are things here?"

Hoofprint's ugly face pinched when he looked over Badgertail's shoulder at the two strangers. Badgertail turned and motioned to Flute. "Go on, Flute. Check the Sun Chamber, then take Wanderer and Vole to Nightshade's room."

"Yes, War Leader."

Hoofprint's tension abated only slightly when Wanderer and Vole passed beyond hearing range. He watched them while they peeked into the Sun Chamber, then turned down the left corridor.

Badgertail frowned. "What is it?"

Hoofprint glanced uneasily at Black Dog, then propped his fist atop the war club tied to his belt. "We don't know. The Sun Chief called us in to guard his chamber. He ordered us not to enter under threat of death. But strange things have been happening."

"What?"

Hoofprint shook his head. "Sounds. Choking sounds. Coming from the Sun Chief's room. For a while there were screams. He ordered us to bring a little girl to his room. Then his daughter, Orenda, came and sneaked in past us."

Badgertail studied Hoofprint's face, then Black Dog's. *Scared to death. Both of them.* "And Nightshade? Where has she been during all of this?"

"We haven't seen her."

Badgertail's thick brows drew together over his nose. Nightshade invisible at a time when Orenda might have needed her? It didn't make sense. Nightshade had begun treating Orenda like her own daughter. "Stay here where you can see the front entrance. Let me know if anyone else comes in. I have to speak to the Sun Chief."

As he walked away down the right corridor, Hoofprint called, "Badgertail? Is it true? Is Petaga going to attack Cahokia?"

Without slowing his stride, he answered, "Yes."

Anxious whispers broke out behind him, but he closed his ears to them, not wanting to think about the actual attack when he had so many preliminary details to work out. Which warriors should he condemn to the first line on the platforms? How would he defend against the flaming arrows that Petaga would certainly shoot into every house he could see? Fire would spread quickly in the dry grass. The sparks might even carry to the high roof of the temple, far out of arrow range. What sort of surrender terms should he beg for? Would Petaga even let him surrender? *Would Tharon?*

Though brilliant light blazed around Tharon's door-hanging, the hall had a deep chill. It nipped at Badgertail, pricking his tattoos like an icy quill.

He stopped before the hanging to listen. "Sun Chief? It's Badgertail. May I enter? I have many things to tell you."

A garbled sob came from inside that sent a prickle up Badgertail's spine. He stepped forward, calling, "My Chief?" and pulled back the hanging . . .

Gasping, he stumbled into the chamber. From the pit of his stomach an involuntary cry broke loose that echoed through the sacred bones of the temple. He shouted, *"Orenda, no!"*

*S*ister Datura's laughter penetrated the Dream.

Nightshade stirred. The firebowl on the floor flickered as though the flame had been brushed by the feet of racing children. She saw it dimly on the back of her closed eyelids—orange and black, orange and black—while her soul rose up through the layers of the Well of the Ancestors.

"Yes," Sister Datura mocked, *"you've done your work. Now go and see what evil the Sun Chief has wrought in your absence."*

Nightshade blinked her eyes open. The darkness of the room rippled around her like waves of black water. Her hearing seemed to have stopped working, and she could see nothing clearly. The starmap wavered into reality as a tarnished smear of sparkling galena paint, and her bed was only the barest gray smudge. An odd hush had descended upon the world.

"Oh, my Sister . . ." she whispered miserably as the nausea began with a vengeance. "Please, let me go."

Datura sank her taloned fingers deeper into Nightshade's stomach. *"Not yet. Our Dance is not done. Get up, Nightshade. You've been doing Power's bidding for cycles. Get up and let me see the cougars fall upon you."*

The taunt was followed by a sound, shrill but barely audible, that caught at Nightshade's heart like a strangling hand.

Then . . .

"Nightshade?"

The familiar voice echoed and shot shimmers of light through the black room. Her vision began to clear. She could make out the starmap now, with its glowing rings of Ogres.

"Who—"

"Nightshade! It's Wanderer."

She turned slightly and saw him duck through the doorway. He stood tall and lanky against the backdrop of Orenda's toys strewn at the foot of Nightshade's bed. Joy and relief filled her.

As her hearing cleared, she jumped at the chaos of shouts and cries that filled the halls. Running feet pounded the hard floors of the temple.

"What's happening, Wanderer?" she asked as she lowered the Tortoise Bundle and tied its straps to her belt with shaking hands. "Is Petaga attacking?"

"No, not yet." He came forward in that gangly walk she remembered so well and crouched before her, examining her eyes. "But there was a scream. Are you strong enough to stand? Or is Sister Datura—"

"If you'll help me up, I think I can walk."

Wanderer gripped her arm while she struggled to find her balance. "Where did the scream come from?"

"Tharon's chamber."

Nightshade's nausea grew worse. She started across the room, calling, "Orenda . . ." but the space beneath her bed lay empty. Her voice faded.

As though a great wind had howled out of the night, Nightshade's ears went deaf again. She could see Wanderer's mouth moving with desperate pleas, but she heard only Orenda's voice: *"Could I . . . I want to sleep in your room!"* The unspoken words "where it's safe . . . *safe* . . ." pierced Nightshade's heart.

She rushed past Wanderer and out into the corridor, almost knocking over an unknown woman standing beside a male warrior. Sidestepping them, Nightshade raced away, her red robes flying about her ankles.

When she turned to the right, a square of bright light suddenly lit the far end, and her steps faltered. Badgertail, silhouetted against a blaze of firebowls, stood in Tharon's doorway. He swiftly let the hanging drop, but not before she saw the bloody stiletto in his right hand, dripping crimson onto the floor. Hoofprint and Black Dog rushed up to him, shouting a hundred questions.

Sternly, Badgertail ordered, "Get out of the temple. If anyone asks, the Sun Chief ordered you away at dusk."

"But Badgertail, what—"

"*Go!* You heard me!"

Like whipped puppies, Hoofprint and Black Dog turned and slunk away, but frightened whispers passed between them.

Sister Datura played tricks on Nightshade. Badgertail's face seemed to balloon and surge toward her before it shrank to almost nothing.

From her left, she heard Wanderer's horrified murmur, "Blessed Father Sun, what's happened?"

Badgertail numbly watched her approach. She walked to stand very close to him so she could see his eyes in the murky light. His face was ashen and strained. He gazed over her shoulder at Flute.

"Go and guard the front entrance. Let no one pass. *No one.* Do you understand?"

Flute jerked a nod and stammered, "Y-Yes. But what if Elkhorn—"

"*No one!*"

"I—I understand, War Leader." Flute ran as though the creatures of the Underworld were snapping at his heels.

Nightshade edged by Badgertail and pulled the door-hanging aside to slip into Tharon's chamber. Her knees went weak. She barely noticed the overturned furniture, the broken seashells, or Tharon's naked body. Her eyes were riveted on Orenda. The little girl sat on the floor with her chin braced on her drawn-up knees, staring blankly at the far wall, where her mother's belongings lay piled. Blood spattered Orenda's face and arms, and soaked into the tatters of her robe.

"Wait here," Badgertail ordered Wanderer and the woman, and the hanging shished when he let it fall behind him. He extended the gory stiletto to Nightshade. "She used this. I found her . . . still stabbing him. I tried to talk to her, but her soul seems to have slipped away."

Nightshade crouched beside Orenda and put an arm around the child's shoulders. "Are you all right?"

Orenda didn't move.

Tharon's wide, dead eyes stared up at her from a face twisted with disbelief, as though even in the last moments, he could not accept the notion that anyone could kill him. One puncture wound had pierced his heart—but the majority of the stabbings centered on the lower half of his body. Intestines had wormed out through the torn flesh where his genitals had been. Now only bloody pulp remained.

"Incest," Badgertail hissed. "No wonder First Woman abandoned us."

Very gently, Nightshade reached out and brushed Orenda's hair away from her face. The girl's pupils had dilated to different sizes. Nightshade remembered very well when Tharon had struck her in the head as a child—the time her soul had separated from her body for two days. She let her hand drop to the Tortoise Bundle. "Orenda needs rest. I'll take her to my room, where I can—"

"Badgertail?" Wanderer's old voice called. "Let us in. What's happened?"

Badgertail glanced at Nightshade, and she nodded. He moved to the door and pulled the hanging aside so Wanderer and the unknown woman could enter. The woman let out a small cry and charged headlong across the room to where another girl lay on her back in a tangle of torn green dress. The woman gathered the child into her arms and wept suffocatingly.

Wanderer ran after her and put fingers on the girl's temple, then very gently opened her lids and peered at her eyes. "She's alive, Vole. But evil has entered her body. Hurry. We may not have much time. I'll—"

"What are you going to do?"

Wanderer's faded eyes narrowed. "We have to release the evil in Lichen's head. I'll need a chert drill and several very sharp obsidian flakes. Someone will have to find an awl and some thread. Vole, I want you to—"

"Wanderer?" Nightshade rose. Memories of her voyage to the Underworld flashed. "Take great care. By now Lichen will have already passed through the Land of the Ancestors and be on her way to the Cave of First Woman. You don't want to shock her body so much that it will distract her. We don't know what kind of terrors she'll be facing."

Wanderer's face slackened. "How do you know she's on her way to the Cave?"

"I've spent the past hand of time leading her through the Well. She couldn't find the way by herself—though she swam the Dark River expertly."

"I'm glad she had you there, Nightshade," Wanderer said as he carefully took Lichen from Vole's arms. "But I have to release the evil soon. The Spirits that get locked in the brain after this type of injury can kill the victim if they're not given a way out quickly."

"I understand. Just—"

With sudden violence, Sister Datura swept through Nightshade's veins in a sickening wash. "Oh, no . . . stop it!" Nightshade staggered, vainly clutching for the wall. Too dazed to stop herself, she fell into the scattered pile of jewelry and clothing. The room spun around her.

"Nightshade!" Wanderer shouted. When he stood up with Lichen in his arms, the motion caused a pendant to fall from Lichen's dress and swing freely—a black wolf. Tiny. Made of stone.

As though Nightshade's gaze triggered it, a halo of gold pulsed around the Tortoise Bundle, growing larger and larger until it encompassed Nightshade in a blazing ocean of light. She gasped when the Stone Wolf responded by shooting a beam across the room to connect with the Bundle. In the middle of that wispy thread of gold, a ball of light, like an egg, grew. From it, a head lifted and peered around until its glowing eyes locked with Nightshade's eyes. She pushed back against the wall in fear as fiery wings unfurled in the slow, delicate motions of a moth emerging from a wet cocoon. A creature stood there on frail, spindly legs, while its talons clutched at the golden strand.

In a voice that sounded like the chiming of seashell bells, the Spirit creature said, *"The seed of your soul has struck earth and brought forth fruit, Nightshade. Go home now. Go home. Take the Monster Twins and follow where the* thlatsinas *lead. They will show you the way."*

Nightshade's eyes widened when the creature dissolved into a glittering spray that fell over the floor like sacred cornmeal being sprinkled by the sky gods.

Then she saw them.

They came Dancing from every shred of shadow in the room—swaying, dipping, twirling—until they coalesced into twenty-hands-tall figures with no arms or legs. The *clackety-clack* of their enormous beaks thumped in perfect time to Nightshade's heartbeat. Tears trailed icy paths down Nightshade's cheeks as she gazed up into those pitifully deformed faces—Wolf, Bird, Badger.

She rose as though in a Dream and waded into their midst to Dance with them, as she had on that long-ago day when her world had been rent asunder.

Badgertail—his gaze riveted on Nightshade—sidestepped uneasily, feeling his way along the wall until he stood beside Wanderer. Nightshade's pounding feet shook the room as she threw her head back and lifted her deep voice in a strange Song. "What's she doing, Wanderer?"

The old man clutched Lichen more closely to his chest and said, "I don't know. Dancing. She's happy, and I've never seen her happy before."

"Will she come out of it soon? How long will Sister Datura control her soul?"

"Five or six more hands of time. I doubt it will be longer than that." Wanderer's voice had dropped to a reverent whisper, and his eyes squinted curiously—as if he saw something faint and frightening moving in the wavering firelight around Nightshade.

"Wanderer, listen," Badgertail implored him. "I'm going to need her. I may have to surrender to Petaga. Nightshade is the only person in Cahokia that Petaga might believe if she brought him such news. Can you wake her sooner?"

"No," Wanderer said mildly and lowered his head to gaze at Lichen's blood-streaked face. "Sister Datura will release Nightshade in her own good time. . . . Badgertail, I must hurry. I'll be in the Sun Chamber, where the firebowls will give me enough light. Will you help me? I must cut a hole in Lichen's skull to release the evil—or she'll die. I'll need tools and herbs. Can you assign two of the Starborn who know where the supplies are in the temple . . . and see that no one disturbs us?"

Badgertail frowned at the little girl in Wanderer's arms. Such a beautiful child. Her heart-shaped face, full lips, and button nose had the perfection of an expertly carved cedar doll. Could someone so young really be traveling through the Underworld to speak to First Woman?

"I'll ask Kettle and Thrushsong—and I'll post a guard outside the temple door." He glanced at Orenda. "Wanderer, you know spiritual matters. What should I do with Orenda? The people . . . if they find out . . . they'll consider her polluted. They'll demand her death. How can I—"

"Wait. Let Nightshade handle it. She'll know what to do." Wanderer started across the floor, careful not to jar Lichen. Vole walked close behind him, her fear-bright gaze shifting from Tharon's brutalized body to Nightshade to Lichen.

Forty-one

Nauseated, trembling, Vole sat on the raised altar beside Lichen and held her daughter's hand. As her eyes drifted over the magnificence of the temple, with its spokes of radiating firebowls and abundance of seashells, she felt oddly detached, as though she were watching this spectacle from somewhere far above—too far away to help.

"Are you all right, Vole?" Wanderer asked. He knelt on the other side of Lichen. His old face had grown a thousand more wrinkles in the past hand of time.

"Worried. That's all."

Wind roared as it battered at the thatched roof.

Wanderer squinted at the bits of cattail duff that floated down like sunlit dust, then turned back to their daughter. Lichen lay on her back, her hair spread in a wealth around her head. Her eyes were sunken in twin black circles, and though her heartbeat was strong, her chest barely moved. The claw marks showing through the tatters of her green dress enraged and terrified Vole.

I wish you were alive, Sun Chief, so I could kill you myself.

Kettle and Thrushsong bustled about, gathering the things that Wanderer had asked for. Clangs and thuds rang out as they pulled tools from hidden niches around the altar. All the while, Wind Mother blasted the temple with her fury, making the structure creak and moan.

Wanderer leaned forward and gently moved his hands through the long strands of Lichen's blood-encrusted hair while he muttered half-sentences to himself. "Well, it's not as bad . . . but the bone is cracked. Yes, yes, that's what that is. A crack. I wish . . . but there's no sense wishing."

"What?"

"Oh, her skull is fractured. We'll have to be very careful. We can't drill too near the crack for fear of worsening it, but we have to drill close enough to let the evil Spirits trapped there escape. They always cluster around the wound. Like wolves around a butchering fire."

Beaver root boiled in a pot propped over a firebowl in the middle of the altar. The Spirit of the beaver root was renowned for driving away the evil that caused convulsions. Its rich, earthy fragrance filled the temple.

"Vole," Wanderer asked softly, "could you get a bowl and dip out one of those rags I put in the beaver root? Don't wring out the liquid. We'll need all of the plant's Spirit before this is through."

Tenderly, Vole squeezed Lichen's hand and went to do as Wanderer asked. As she used a stick to pull the cloth out of the boiling mixture and drop it into a bowl, she watched Kettle deliver a hafted chert drill and an array of obsidian knives and flakes. Kettle laid them out on the blanket at Lichen's side.

"Thank you." Wanderer smiled tiredly at the frightened priestess. "You've helped a good deal, Kettle. Why don't you sit down and rest?"

"No, we—we want to Sing for her, Wanderer . . . if that's all right."

"We would greatly appreciate it, Kettle. Thank you."

The two priestesses picked up rattles and lifted their voices in a Healing Song while they Danced around the central altar. They seemed an odd pair to Vole, Kettle with her pudgy body and homely face next to Thrushsong, who was as skinny as a weasel's tail.

Vole set the bowl at Wanderer's side and went back to holding Lichen's hand.

Wanderer lifted his old voice in Song while he submerged his tools in the sacred beaver-root broth.

When he had finished Singing, he gazed across at Vole, and she could see the fear in his faded eyes. He suddenly looked very ancient. His gray hair hung in tiny, sweat-drenched curls over his forehead.

Vole gave him a brave smile and reached out to take his hand in hers. His fingers felt long and gnarled, but singularly comforting. He tightened his grip, and she said, "I trust you, Wanderer. Tell me what you need me to do."

"Nothing for the moment. I'll have to cut her hair and pull back the scalp before I can drill."

Vole sat quietly, studying him as he used an obsidian blade to shave away a palm-sized patch of Lichen's hair. Each lock that came off in his hand he tenderly placed on a red piece of fabric. When he had finished, he took the steaming cloth from the bowl and without wringing it out, sopped it over Lichen's bald spot. The brownish-green liquid ran down and drenched her hair before it soaked into the blanket beneath her.

Wanderer exhaled a halting breath and seemed to be collecting himself. His bushy brows rose when he focused on Lichen's face.

The pause lasted for so long that Vole asked, "What's wrong? Is something wrong?"

"No," Wanderer replied faintly. "I've done this many times, but I . . . I never imagined it would be so hard when the patient was someone I loved so dearly."

He picked up a stone knife and lowered it to the pale skin of Lichen's head. Vole turned away, unable to watch.

"Vole," Wanderer said after a few moments, "please hand me a dry cloth."

She bent sideways to pull one from the pile to her left and handed it to him.

Wanderer used the cloth to soak up the blood that flowed in a rich, red flood from the skin he had peeled back. "Scalp wounds always bleed like this."

The flap lay like a folded square of deerhide, revealing the blood-streaked skull beneath.

Oh, Lichen . . . Vole swallowed hard. She felt queasy and light-headed.

Wanderer seemed to sense her panic. He looked up in a kindly way. "Vole, I know this is hard. Do you want to leave? Kettle can—"

"No." The thought of entrusting Lichen to a stranger affected her like a cold slap. "No, I—I'm fine. What do we do next?"

"I need to outline the hole with the drill, so we'll know exactly how big it will be before we start."

Wanderer removed the hafted chert drill from the beaver-root broth and sucked in a breath before he lowered the tool to Lichen's skull.

Silent tears rose in Vole's eyes as she watched him spin the drill between his palms to create a small circle of six dots. *Six. A holy number.*

"Now comes the hard part, Vole," he said gently. "There's a thick membrane that lines the interior of the skull. I have to remove this circle of bone without breaking it. And it adheres much more tightly in a child's skull than in an adult's."

"So what will you do?"

"I have to drill each of these holes to just the right depth, then saw through the remaining connecting bone until I can easily lift this piece out."

"And you have to detach the tissue before you can lift it out. Is that right?"

"Yes," he whispered. "But we'll worry about trimming the tissue away from the bone once we've sawed the circle."

"Then what will we do?"

"If everything goes well, the tissue will puff out through the hole, giving the evil Spirits a chance to escape. Then we'll sew the scalp back over the hole."

She blinked. "Without putting the piece of skull back in place?"

"Oh, Lichen won't need it." He gave her a feeble imitation of that old demented smile. "It will just give her another opening through which to speak to Earthmaker. . . . Are you ready, Vole?"

Vole studied his frightened eyes, noting the way they glinted in the burnished gold of the firelight. "Yes. I'm ready."

The cold wind batted at Hailcloud's forelocks, rattling the beads. He leaned back against the sandy bank of Marsh Elder Lake and cupped a knee in his hands while he gazed across the rough water. The gale had ravaged the flowering dogwood trees and strewn their petals over the choppy surface. A few petals still bobbed in the middle of the lake, but most of them had worked their way to shore. In the moonglow, they glistened like a pale blue ribbon stretched along the curving rim of the lake.

"Beautiful," he murmured to himself.

The sharp thumps of a woodpecker began, and Hailcloud turned to see the red-crested bird excavating a hole in an old maple stump. When it had dug it deep enough, the woodpecker thrust its enormously long, sticky tongue through the opening and probed the ant burrows within. A swarm of ants rushed out and scrambled over the stump in a mad horde. The woodpecker seemed undisturbed by the multitude that climbed through its bright feathers. It used its beak to widen the hole and continued to feed.

Hailcloud heard Petaga's footsteps before he saw the young Moon Chief stepping down from the terrace above. The hem of Petaga's brown-and-yellow robe caught on the mint that covered the shoreline. "They're gone."

"And what did the woman want?"

Hailcloud leaned back and looked at Petaga. The black braid hanging over Petaga's shoulder had been freshly combed, but because he'd had no time for bathing, it appeared stringy. His triangular face showed the strain of too many sleepless nights. Purple circles darkened the flesh around his eyes, making them seem wizened, and more deeply set than usual.

"She's the new leader of the Horn Spoon Clan." Petaga dropped down on the sand beside Hailcloud and folded his hands in his lap. "Her name is Currant. Tharon murdered her mother for treason."

"Treason?"

Petaga nodded. "Yes. She dared to suggest in a clan council that perhaps the Cahokia clans should join us. Tickseed was a smart old woman. She knew that the system must be changed or our people will cease to exist." He hung his head and stared at the sand that glimmered with an indigo hue. "Tharon killed her for it."

"And all of the people who came up around Marsh Elder Lake yesterday?"

"Currant talked it over with the Horn Spoon Clan. They decided they would seek us out. She offered over one hundred warriors."

Hailcloud lifted a shoulder. "We don't need them, Petaga."

"No, I—I know. But we must let them do something. They've risked everything to join us, and we can't just turn them away."

"If we put them in the first wave to burst through the palisades, we might take fewer casualties. We can assume that roughly one out of four of Tharon's warriors will have kinship ties."

Petaga gave Hailcloud a sidelong look and snorted his disgust. "You think that kinship ties would keep Badgertail's warriors from killing them?"

Quietly, Hailcloud responded, "They're human, Moon Chief. Just like us."

"Barely human," Petaga corrected. "Don't worry about the Horn Spoon people. I'll think of something for them. I'd rather not have them fight unless it's necessary."

Hailcloud inclined his head agreeably while his eyes turned south-ward to the palisades of Cahokia. They gleamed white and lustrous against the sable background of night. Warriors strode around anx-iously on the shooting platforms. Hailcloud had been counting them off and on from the moment he could make out their shadows. Three hundred—at most. He had over one thousand, and that was without the additional warriors promised by the Horn Spoon Clan. Most of the men and women he had lost had been spent in the poorly planned attack launched by Gopher. Over one hundred of those who had fallen were Red Star warriors. With Gopher's death, the remaining forces had lost their arrogance and started obeying the orders of more prudent leaders.

"Have you figured out our battle strategy?" Petaga asked.

"Yes." Hailcloud used his finger to draw in the moist sand. "Cahokia Creek runs like this past the palisades. We have no quarrel with the people living in the surrounding village. I don't think we even want to enter the village, except as necessary for cover when we're surrounding the palisades."

Petaga's dark brows drew together. "Yes, I agree. I'm surprised that my cousin Tharon hasn't already burned the closest houses just to prevent us from having cover."

"Don't say that too loudly. He still might do it."

Hailcloud drew an arc around the northern edge of the palisades, which fronted Cahokia Creek. "This is where we want to position the majority of our forces, my Chief. Our first goal will be to take the creek drainage. With the drought, there's so little water that it should be only a minor annoyance. Once we've established our warriors in the drainage, we'll have shelter for our best archers. While our front lines fire at the guards on the platforms to keep them down, ax crews will be working at the base of the palisade. We'll have a hole chopped through in no time. Once we're inside, it will be over quickly."

Hailcloud sat back and looked at Petaga. The young chief's eyes gleamed as he gazed southward. Moonlight drenched the Temple Mound like an opaque sheet of silver and blazed from the pounded copper ornaments on the walls. "And Badgertail will be mine. I *want* my father's murderer, Hailcloud. Tell our warriors not to kill him, but to bring him to me."

"Yes, my Chief."

Petaga rose, laid an affectionate hand on Hailcloud's shoulder, and climbed back up over the terrace.

Hailcloud steepled his fingers over his mouth while he listened to Petaga's retreating steps. Bitter bile rose in his throat. For days he had been reliving battle-walks he'd taken with Badgertail, and he could barely stand the thought of the next few hands of time. In the depths of his soul, pain welled. *I know you've just been obeying orders, Badgertail. As we all have. None of this is your fault.*

Petaga would want to make an example of his father's murderer, and the people would love it. In the past cycle, thousands had witnessed their families brutally killed and their villages burned to ashes around them. They would probably start gathering the night before to get good viewing places for the torture ritual.

Two tall poles would be sunk into the ground the width of Badgertail's reach. Next, crosspieces would be lashed on to the poles to make a hollow square. Bound hand and foot, Badgertail would be stripped, fed a final meal, and his scalp would be cut from his head. After that humiliation, he would be tied, one hand to each upper corner of the square, one foot to each of the lower, so that he hung in the shape of an X. For as long as he lived thereafter—days for a man as strong as Badgertail—they would sear his flesh with cane bundles, peel bits of hide from his limbs and belly, burn out his eyes, ears, and nostrils, roast his penis and testicles . . .

Hailcloud closed his eyes, remembering the times that he and Badgertail had laughed together.

Forty-two

Badgertail stepped out of the temple into the morning breeze and watched the rising sun blush pink into the shimmering mist that coated the floodplain, creeping across the ground like a wind-rumpled blanket. Its uppermost tendrils curled in intimate wisps around the sharpened tips of the palisade poles, eighty feet below where Badgertail stood on the crest of the mound. Long before dawn, the warriors on the platforms had started grumbling. Everyone knew that Petaga would use this mist as cover to move his warriors closer.

Uneasy emotions scurried through Badgertail's chest, lunging at his soul as viciously as weasels in a death fight. Fatigue lay upon him like a sodden blanket. All night the Commonborn had been packing up and moving out of the sprawling settlements beyond the palisades. Redhaw, and even Checkerberry, had accepted Badgertail's offer of protection and moved their clan councils within the walls. But Sandbar had refused. She had promised him that none of her people would join Petaga, but she could not support the Sun Chief.

What will happen when I have to tell them that Tharon is dead? Will Redhaw's clan revolt, try to tear us apart from within? Or just try to tear me apart?

The news of Tharon's death would have caused too much commotion and mistrust. He couldn't risk it. Had his warriors known of the sacrilege committed by Tharon on the eve of battle, they would have run like scared mice, believing the Power broken and defeat a certainty.

And poor Orenda. Tainted by incest and murder. The clans would have wanted to kill her immediately. There was no telling what Nightshade would have done to prevent that.

Mindlessly he walked across the courtyard to the upper palisade—the final stronghold. The gaping hole just inside the baked clay marked the location where the pole bearing Jenos' head had been raised. On Badgertail's orders, warriors had removed the pole and placed the Moon Chief's head in an ornate red cedar chest found inside the temple; it was a fitting container in which to take a good man's skull back to his body.

Badgertail rubbed his fingers together, remembering the sticky warmth of Jenos' blood. *Blood . . . everywhere. My soul drips of it.*

He passed the gate and trotted nervously down the steps. On the first terrace of the Temple Mound, Nettle and Green Ash stood with Checkerberry and Redhaw, Singing the Beginning Time stories of Father Sun's marriage to Mother Earth. Within the circle of spectators, Dancers moved in serpentine lines, shaking gourd rattles, beating drums.

Badgertail strode to the edge of the crowd and asked the first person he came to, "Have you seen Nightshade?"

The old man lifted an arm and pointed. "She went to the burial mound. She took those . . . those babies. I don't know why."

Badgertail nodded and backed away, wondering at the awe in the elder's voice. He finished trotting down the steps and broke into a run across the plaza, down the length of the chunkey field toward the conical mound where his brother Bobcat rested. He hadn't been to the mound since the burial. The very sight of it dredged up Bobcat's voice from the depths of his memories. *"We could do it, Badgertail. We could run away. . . . Badgertail, this is madness!"*

"I know that, brother," he whispered, and the agony of that day at River Mounds struck him all over again.

In a pink-tinged patch of mist, Nightshade lay on her side on a blanket, scratching the ears of a dog that huddled in a furry ball in front of her. Two bundles pressed against the dog's belly. As Badgertail drew closer, he could tell that they were babies, like the old man had said. Tiny mouths stuck out of the shroud of blankets, clamped onto the teats of the dog, suckling like pups.

The hair at the nape of his neck crawled, the same way it did when he was in the presence of Power objects. Instinctively he checked the area around Nightshade to see if she had brought the Tortoise Bundle with her, but he didn't see it. Memories flared. Something Checkerberry had said . . . something about Green Ash going mad if she had to be near her babies. His steps faltered. Wouldn't Green Ash nurse the children? Sometimes a mother refused to, but always another woman with a new baby stepped forward and offered to feed the unfortunate infant. He could not fathom why the clan had been forced to resort to suckling the children on this half-wolf dog.

Nightshade tilted her head to look up at him, and Badgertail stood motionless for a moment, holding that charismatic gaze. Something had changed. She looked almost too beautiful. Long hair fell over the shoulders of her red dress in blue-black waves. The sharp wariness that generally filled her eyes had vanished, replaced by a serenity as warm and soothing as the distant deserts of her home in the Forbidden Lands.

Badgertail knelt on the opposite side of the dog and stroked the bitch's back while he spoke. "How is Orenda?"

"She woke this morning. But she went right back to sleep."

"Is she going to be all right?"

"Yes, I've spoken to her soul. She has a raging headache, but she'll be fine." Nightshade cocked her head. "What did you need, Badgertail?"

"Your help."

"What for?"

Even her voice sounded different: calm and deep, like the controlled rumble of the Father Water during spring runoff. He said, "I—I can't win this battle."

Her gaze never wavered. "And?"

"When the time comes—whenever that is, maybe tonight, maybe tomorrow morning—will you take my message to Petaga? I fear that if anyone else delivers it, he will think it's a trick to gain time or to deceive him in some way."

"Petaga would. Hailcloud wouldn't."

"It's Petaga I'm worried about."

"And what will you ask, Badgertail?"

He spread his hands to gesture his frustration. "I know his anger, his hatred. I won't deny him vengeance. He can do with me as he will, but I want my warriors to go free. I want them to be able to go home to their families and take up their lives again. I don't know that Petaga will trust them to serve him in the future, but I think they'll be loyal to the new Sun Chief, whoever he is."

Nightshade smoothed her fingers over the bulrush blanket spread beneath her, tracing the black and green chevrons with her fingertips. "He will want them all killed—for their part in the River Mounds massacre."

Badgertail ground his teeth, loath to hear his deepest fears affirmed. Hot, agonizing flashes of Bobcat's death taunted him. Petaga undoubtedly relived the same sort of nightmare about his father's death. "I know that, Nightshade. But it would be unwise for him to slaughter these men and women. They have too many ties here—spouses, children, and grandchildren. If he kills them, he will never be able to rule this village. He'll have to abandon Cahokia and go back to River Mounds, and if he does that, he'll lose his grip on the trading, mining, and farming. It's the Cahokia clan leaders who have the knowledge to run things. There will be more fighting. The chiefdom will fall apart around his ears."

"I'm sure he knows that."

"Then he'd better start caring about it."

They stared at each other for a time, each silently trying to see the other's soul.

Finally, Nightshade drew a deep breath and nodded. "I'll deliver your message, Badgertail."

"And would you take Jenos' head with you? Tell Petaga I don't expect anything in return."

"I will take the Moon Chief's head." Her eyes seemed to expand, drawing him into their unfathomable depths. "And you'll simply surrender yourself? He will do everything in his power to prolong your death."

Locked in that endless gaze, Badgertail nodded. "I know."

The dog, who had had enough of the infants, tried to rise, and the spell broke like a sheet of pond ice dropped on sandstone. Nightshade ordered, "No, not yet!"

Badgertail grabbed the dog, holding its neck down and whispering in its pointed ear, "It's all right, girl. Shh, lie down. There, that's it. Good girl." He patted its shoulder gently.

The babies had broken into annoyed shrieks when the teats were rudely jerked from their hungry mouths. Nightshade positioned the infants' heads so they could suckle again. But the dog grunted and tried to rise. Badgertail had to lean all of his weight on its shoulders to keep it down.

Nightshade laughed—and it made him laugh. They gazed at each other from no more than three hands away. Warmth grew, like a strengthening fire on a cold winter's night. *How can you look at me like that, Nightshade, when our world is on the brink of destruction?*

"Badgertail?"

Something about the softness in Nightshade's face buffeted him. It was a rare occasion when he couldn't hold an opponent's gaze, but this was one of those times. He dropped his eyes to the dog. "What is it, Nightshade?"

Vaguely at first, then stronger, the din of battle came to him: shouts of surprise, roars of victory and pain. The warriors on the platforms began a ululating battle cry as they pulled arrows from quivers and hunched down to nock them in their bows.

Badgertail lunged to his feet and ran.

Fear propelled Lichen along the narrow dirt trail. Around her stretched a wide expanse of rolling, tree-covered hills. Towering cottonwoods lifted their crooked gray limbs into the sky, creating a woven canopy that filtered the gleam of twilight; it fell across her path in patches of muddy blue.

From the depths of the forest, a chant drifted, deep, rhythmic. An old woman's voice, it lilted on the wind in time to a sacred drumbeat.

"Hello!" Lichen shouted.

Flutes added their wails to the woman's chant, giving it a haunted quality that struck fear into Lichen's heart. The Song reminded her of the Ghost Chants her own people Sang to drive away evil Spirits.

"Hello! Who's there?"

The forest seemed to close in around her, the trees bending down to peer at her more carefully. Lichen shivered. This place was not beautiful, though she had the feeling that it was old, very old, and that living humans had never dared to tiptoe beyond the well-worn trails. Tumbled piles of deadfall choked the forest floor, and wherever light struck, thorny underbrush flourished. Voices murmured in the tangles, low and muted, like the whimpers of coyotes closing in on wounded prey.

Lichen turned around in a full circle. "Oh, First Woman, where are you? I'm scared. I don't know how to find you. First Woman?"

Sobs clutched at her chest as she started to run again, dashing down a dip in the trail and up the other side.

As Father Sun sank in the west, his purple glory was shattered into a thousand pieces by the infinity of branches. It would be getting colder, and she had neither a coat nor a blanket. How cold did it get in the Underworld? Could she just sleep in the grass and . . . *No, you can't sleep! You have to keep going. You know what Nightshade told you. Petaga is going to attack Cahokia soon. Maybe even now! If you don't find First Woman, everyone is going to die!* Hunting. Mother Earth was hunting.

When Lichen's confused soul had first escaped her body, it had been lost and terrified. Then a brilliant white light swam out of the utter blackness and spoke to her in gentle tones. Nightshade's soul had lit the path for Lichen, leading her on like a winter bonfire.

"First Woman? I have to find you. You know I do. Why won't you help me?"

With the deepening of night, the chant grew louder, and life stirred the depths of the forest. But Lichen did not think she knew this kind of life. Gourd rattles sounded in time to the chant. Feet pounded, heavy, thrashing angrily in a Dance that shook the trail where she stood. Trees creaked and cracked as though being torn up by the roots.

Lichen backed away. Then she ran like the wind, trying to get out of this low spot. Shadows moved at the edges of the trail, some of them loping along beside her, keeping pace while they hissed their resentment at her presence. Lichen's fear burst into terror.

"First Woman? First Woman, please!"

She rounded a bend, and one of the Dancers' masks—enormous black eyes, and a protruding mouth shaped from pink pipestone—caught the sunset and held it prisoner. Colorful feathers adorned the Dancer's costume, as if Eagle, Hawk, and Owl had been spattered from different pots of dye. The Dancer dodged behind a tree when Lichen looked at him. But she could see others moving nearby. Their masks glinted as they darted through the thicket.

Lichen ran on, racing down a winding trail through the trees and brush, but she slowed when the undergrowth became denser, the leaves and branches weaving a mat around her.

Could this be the way? If the path became any narrower, she would be crawling on hands and knees on a rabbit run. An owl hooted somewhere, and Lichen scurried on. Suddenly she broke out of the interlaced forest and stood on a slender backbone of ridge. A multitude of trails crisscrossed the slate-gray vista, winding in and out and across each other like worm patterns in aspen bark.

Which one? Which one do I take? They all lead in different directions.

Lichen spun around, checking the weave that dropped into the eastern valley, then examining the trails that climbed the highlands and those that plummeted back into the darkest part of the woods.

From out of her memories, Wanderer's voice instructed: "*. . . To step onto the path, you must leave it. Only the lost come to stand before the entrance to the Cave . . .*"

Lichen's mouth puckered as tears blurred her eyes. She looked back down the trail she had climbed. Even from this distance, she could discern dark shapes moving. "But Wanderer, the only place without paths is that horrible forest."

"*. . . Only the defenseless step over the threshold. Wolf Slayer said to tell you that in Union you will find the Light, though it appears as Darkness . . .*"

"Union?" The word slipped off of her tongue. She didn't know what that meant, not really. Now she wished she had asked more questions when she'd had the chance. "What is that, Wanderer? Did you mean that if I go down there into that darkness, I'll find the light of First Woman's Cave? Will the Dancers show me?"

Foxfire had told her: "*. . . Just like warriors go on battle-walks, Dreamers have to confront their enemies. Are you willing to give up your soul to be our Dreamer? Bird-Man waits for you there . . . waits for you . . .*"

Lichen sucked on her lower lip, fighting the fear, and let her feet take her down, down, into the midst of the woods, where no trails marked the land, where dark trees watched in silence.

The woman's chanting rose to a thunderous roar. It boomed against her ears.

Lichen shouted, "Bird-Man?"

Stars shone through the leaves. Lichen raised her arms in front of her face to keep the vines from raking her eyes. Cool leaves whipped past with a cottony touch. For a while, she thought she might be all right. Then the masked Dancers returned, circling her like a ring of wolves, their feet pounding to the beat of a pot drum and rattles. She couldn't see them clearly. Just flashes of hideous red mouths, or of long noses carved from some kind of pale wood. When she looked the hardest, the

Dancers vanished into twists of brush. Her heart had synchronized to the hollow beat of the drum.

"Bird-Man?"

Her voice echoed.

"Bird-Man! I'm trying to find you! Come and bring the wolves so I can get to First Woman!"

The shadows froze. Lichen jerked around, trying to figure out what they were doing. The chanting had stopped, the forest gone silent.

From the densest weave of trees, something glimmered. It seemed a trick of starlight when the figure loomed up from the heart of the darkness and stepped toward her.

"I hear you, little one."

Relief made Lichen laugh. She ran to him, shoving clinging dogwood and raspberry brambles out of the way. "Bird-Man, thank you. I—"

Bird-Man lowered his head, and his beak opened, revealing sharp teeth. He shrieked like Hawk.

Then he spread his wings and dove at her.

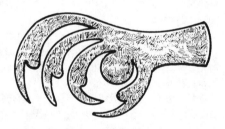

Forty-three

"How long?" Petaga asked, standing on the knoll overlooking Cahokia Creek. While the plants closest to the water thrived, the brush lining the terrace had shriveled in the merciless heat; it was dust-coated and a sickly green. The goosefoot, grass, and knotweed looked as forlorn as the cornfields.

With the slow brightening of day, the mist evaporated, leaving the swarm of warriors clearly visible. Men and women slogged across the shallow water to challenge Badgertail's forces, who had dug in on the opposite bank in front of the northern palisade wall. Arrows glinted in pale streaks, arcing from the shooting platforms, rising from the ground. Above them, the temple gleamed with a gaudy brilliance. *Are you in there, Tharon? Well, you won't be for long.*

"We'll have them by nightfall—I think," Hailcloud answered.

"When will we send in our ax teams?"

"Once we have the creek drainage." Hailcloud folded his arms uncomfortably. His gaze lingered on the temple. "The bank will provide a safe place for our warriors to shoot from. Then we'll start aiming at anyone who dares show his face above the palisade wall. When they're too frightened to stand up and shoot, we'll move."

Petaga paced the knoll, his sandals crackling on the parched, black dirt. To distract himself from the gnawing anxiety in his gut, he dreamed of what he would do when they'd won. It *wouldn't* be the way Aloda and Gopher had thought. Petaga would make sure that things didn't fall apart. He would reorganize the villages; Cahokia's elite would no longer run things. He would pick better people—but who they would be, he didn't know.

Nightshade would know. Nightshade knew everything. Oh, how he longed to see her, to talk with her again and share his hopes. Once things had settled down, he would ask her to journey into the Underworld and tell First Woman that they had won the war and killed the wicked Sun Chief—ask her to beg First Woman's forgiveness for whatever offenses Tharon had committed. Surely First Woman would agree to talk to Mother Earth again, so that the crops would flourish next cycle.

But Petaga dreaded the time until then.

All around him, wilted cornfields lay untended, the stalks barely tall enough to reach his knees. The harvest would be dismal. How would he feed the people this winter? They would have to conserve, to ration food very carefully. So many people had fled. He could send teams to collect from their now untended fields, but he would have to move fast to keep the crops from the raccoons, mice, and crows. Yes, it could be done.

As if to mock him, a new sound rose, shrill, tumultuous. Petaga spun around and stared at the palisades. Flaming arrows lit fiery paths through the sky before they landed in the dry vegetation above the creek and burst into flame.

"No," Hailcloud murmured. "I hadn't thought he'd resort to this so early in the battle. Why—"

Petaga cursed. "Tharon ordered it! He's trying to drive us mad so we'll make a mistake. Well, he can't!"

The fire crackled into an orange monster that drove his warriors back from the creek in a screaming horde. Men and women flooded wildly into the cornfields, watching in horror as the flames rose higher.

"The fool!" Petaga spat. "Tharon is destroying himself. Surely he knows I'll flay him for this!"

Hailcloud shook his head. "It's not Tharon. It's Badgertail. And he knows exactly what he's doing. The more he hurts us, the more time he can buy, and the longer he holds out, the more we'll want the battle over. He's driving a harder bargain for his survivors."

"Well, he won't get it!"

Hailcloud pressed a fist to his lips for a moment, then said, "My Chief, I think we've found a use for the Horn Spoon Clan. If we don't put out those fires before they reach the fields—"

Petaga gasped. "Yes, Blessed Father Sun. Order them to dig a fire line with their hoes and start water baskets moving from the creek to the fields. Hurry. *Hurry!*"

Hailcloud dashed down the knoll to speak to one of his warriors, and Petaga shook his fists in rage.

Black smoke billowed into the blue sky. Moments later, Father Sun's yellow face had changed to a dark, glaring crimson.

The blood thudding in Wanderer's ears all but drowned out the wretched pandemonium of battle outside: the yells, the dull rumbling of feet as they pounded around the shooting platforms, the screams of women, the wailing of terrified children.

He blinked the stinging sweat out of his eyes and forced himself to concentrate as he began to lift the circlet of bone out of Lichen's skull. He had barely moved it before the underlying tissue tugged back. "Quickly, Vole, hand me that knife."

Vole fumbled before her trembling hand could place the blade in Wanderer's bloody fingers. Her round face was pale and drawn.

Wanderer exchanged a confident look with her and paused, mustering strength. Kettle and Thrushsong had grown so weary that their voices moaned the sacred words more than they Sang them. The two priestesses sat on either side of the entry, where they could look down two different spokes of firebowls to the altar where Wanderer and Vole worked. Kettle shook her gourd rattle with a weak-wristed action.

Chips of marrow-pink bone scattered the area around Wanderer, along with gore-encrusted knives, strips of coughgrass root, cactus blossoms, and the crimson-filled bowl in which he had been rinsing out his cloths.

The murky smells of herbs and blood mixed cloyingly with the smoke that rode the wings of the hot wind. Wanderer's nostrils flared as he lowered the knife and slipped the tip beneath the circlet of skull. Exhaustion made his hands shake so badly that he had to brace the base of his palms on Lichen's head to steady them. With the delicacy of a shell-gorget artist, he carved the bone away a bit at a time.

When at last it came loose, the bloody tissue bulged through the hole like a swelling bubble. Vole put a hand to her trembling lips in an effort to still them, but tears rose in her eyes. Wanderer sagged forward and heaved a relieved breath.

"They're leaving," he whispered. "Can you feel it? The evil Spirits are going."

"Yes," Vole said hoarsely. "I can feel it."

Wanderer leaned back and stretched his aching muscles. His shoulders had been on fire for three hands of time. Sweat trickled in cold drops down the middle of his back, gluing his red shirt to his flesh.

"What should we do now?" Vole inquired. "Sew the flap of skin back over the hole?"

"Not yet. Let's give the Spirits a little longer to escape."

Wanderer's gaze drifted over Lichen's pale face, and his ribs seemed to shrink like wet rawhide strips, constricting painfully around his heart. She looked so frail and helpless. *How are you doing in the Underworld, my daughter? I pray that Bird-Man is helping you.*

Lichen's lips parted slightly. As though she had heard him, she groaned. Wanderer laid a hand on her arm and closed his eyes. He gathered every shred of strength that remained in his body and concentrated on pouring it into Lichen.

"Vole . . . help me."

He knew the instant that Vole began infusing her strength. It felt like a warm tide.

Forty-four

Bird-Man's feet thumped the ground behind Lichen as he Danced his pursuit, spinning and leaping, his wings outspread so that the feathers brushed the ground. Starlight coated his body until each feather shimmered like liquid silver.

"No! Bird-Man, *why are you doing this?*" Lichen screamed as she ran headlong through the dense underbrush.

Breath tore in and out of her lungs, while the night grew thicker, the cold heavier. Like sharp quills, the chill penetrated her green dress, pricking at her skin.

A thick root grabbed at Lichen's foot, and she almost fell. She stumbled into a red cedar tree and caught her balance, panting against the worm-chewed bark while her knees trembled. The girth of the tree was enormous; its branches stretched so high into the sky that they vanished amidst the stars. In awe, Lichen stared upward, wondering. First Woman's tree?

Shadows flicked through the forest around her. Every so often she would catch sight of a mask, just a glimpse of jasper or shell beads.

Bird-Man's steps echoed: *thump-thump-thumpety-thump*. "*Do you know why owls die with their wings outspread, little one?*"

Lichen spun and cried out in horror when she saw him perched on the branches of the towering cedar over her head. He had tucked in his wings and bent forward to peer down at her, like a vulture waiting for a wounded deer to die. His snakeskin belly glittered with the majesty of crushed mica.

Lichen choked out, "B-Because they never give up and close their wings!"

Bird-Man's black eyes gleamed as though from an inner fire. He shifted on the branch, stepping back and forth as he began to Dance again. Old needles cascaded out of the tree with each stamp of his feet. Lichen watched the needles twirl through the air in black flashes before they settled on the ground.

"*Why, Lichen? Why won't they give up?*"

"They know that flight is their only hope of survival."

Movement stirred the forest all around her, and six ghostly forms shuffled out from among the shadowed trunks of oak, hickory, and cedar. Some wore bushy-headed masks of beautifully woven cornhusks; others had animal masks, with upcurving horns of buffalo, deer, and elk. The seashells on their leggings glittered extravagantly in the starlight streaming down between the overarching branches. Through the enormous sockets of their eyes, only blackness showed: empty, ominous, with no glint of life.

Lichen shrank back against the cedar trunk as they closed in around her. The Dancers extended their hands and began throwing cornmeal at her. It netted her hair and stuck to her bare arms and legs.

"What are you doing?" she cried, knowing that cornmeal purified and sanctified the way for Power. But she did not understand why they were throwing it on her.

Then, just as suddenly, the Dancers shuffled backward and opened their hands to Bird-Man. They started to chant while they Danced around Lichen. They moved slowly, lifting each moccasined foot and holding it suspended before bringing it down with a powerful thump. Starlight gilded their red-and-black robes. They leaped into the air, looking at Lichen through those hollow eye sockets, and her soul shriveled.

"Will you give up, Lichen? Or will you fly for your people?"

"I want to fly, Bird-Man! I've always wanted to!"

Bird-Man let out a cry of triumph and dove out of the tree, his sharp talons reaching for her. Lichen shrieked when he knocked her to the ground and clamped his talons around her chest, in the manner of Eagle catching Chipmunk.

"Bird-Man, no! You're supposed to be my Spirit . . . Helper." She coughed as the air went out of her lungs in a gush. Her arms and legs flailed weakly while his talons tightened, and she could hear her ribs cracking. Sharp darts of pain shot through her.

The unseen old woman started chanting again, and pounding her drum.

Bird-Man lowered his head, staring into Lichen's terrified eyes. *"Didn't I tell you that sometimes Owl longs with all his heart to be Snake so he can crawl into a hole and hide in the darkness? This is what he's hiding from."*

A gray haze fluttered at the edge of Lichen's vision. She struggled, trying to escape Bird-Man's grip. But with a wrench, he sank his claws deeper into her flesh, and his huge beak dropped out of the gray to tear at her chest and arms. She felt her flesh being torn from her bones as he devoured her.

Lichen's mouth filled with blood from her ruptured lungs. She gave a final gasp as Bird-Man's beak opened and plunged for her eyes. The last of her body began sliding down his throat, into his stomach . . .

"Oh, First Woman, I tried so hard. Wanderer? Wanderer, I'm sorry."

Eternal night enveloped her.

Lichen's soul separated from her body and sank into the pool of her own blood.

From out of the darkness, the old woman pounded her drum, and her cackle penetrated the black. *"The One Life. It's all a Dance, and you have to feel its motions before you can understand it."*

The pool of blood began to sway, rocking Lichen back and forth in time to the drumbeat. It washed over her and filled her with warmth. The fluid motions of the Dance seeped into her soul. She began to float with them.

"Free yourself," the old woman instructed. *"Move with the sounds. Dream this world away. It doesn't exist. Nothing exists but the Dance."*

Lichen Danced, dipping and swaying to the old woman's monotonous chant.

Like mist dispersing beneath a hot sun, her soul faded, growing thinner and thinner, blending with the Dance itself, until it melted into the blackness . . .

And from that nothingness came light.

As though Bird-Man had opened his beak, a stream of gold flooded down through an opening above. It filled her with a bright glow, and Lichen reached for the warmth, but her fingers were . . .

different . . . like, yes, like wings. They prickled as though circulation had just been restored, frail Dreamer's wings strengthening, growing. She shook herself, and white bits of down fell away, revealing brown-speckled feathers.

From deep in her throat, Prairie Falcon's shriek rose: *kree, kree, kree!*

Lichen spread her wings and soared upward. The opening above acted as a lure; it was round, and so brilliant that it hurt her eyes. She flew out into a vast sea of amber sky. Clouds twisted and tumbled in the high winds. Lichen tested her wings, diving and sailing on the warm air currents, feeling the way that each feather affected her flight when she flapped, or flexed her tail. Joy brought tears to her eyes. *Such freedom!*

A heron, formed from the gold filaments of sky, stepped lithely across the puffs of clouds ahead, as though walking on the rocks in a stream. *"So you found me,"* the old woman's voice called.

"Are you First Woman?"

"That's what your people call me. And, yes. I was there at the Beginning of this Spiral."

"I need to talk to you."

The heron cocked its head, and a curious glint sparked in its eyes. *"Well, come on, child. You've earned the right to talk. Come and sit with me and we'll discuss it. But don't think you're going to convince me. For thousands of cycles, I've watched humans. Part of my soul died with the last mammoth calf. Another part went with Giant Beaver. When Sloth and Horse were hunted down and slaughtered, the last bit of my sympathy for humans died, too. Mother Earth will be better off without people."*

"No, First Woman, no!" Lichen cried as she flew closer, thinking about Wanderer and her mother . . . and about Orenda, who had bravely tried to save her. They would die if First Woman wouldn't listen to her. And Flycatcher might already be dead—starved because of the drought, or killed because people were hungry enough to slaughter each other for a basket of corn. Her sobs sounded eerie to her ears, as though coming from a great distance. They rolled around the sky like muted thunder, echoing from every shred of cloud. Reluctant sadness entered First Woman's eyes.

Lichen tipped her wings back and softly lighted on the golden-hued puff of cloud where First Woman stood.

Get down, Elkhorn!" Badgertail shouted, flattening himself on the shooting platform as another volley of arrows lanced up from the creek drainage. Sheltered by the palisade poles, he heard the arrows *thwok* against the wood.

The horrified shrieks of the crowd huddling in the plaza below penetrated the din of battle. People didn't dare stay in their houses. They didn't know when Petaga would resort to firing the thatched roofs, but they knew that he would do it. Badgertail could not stop thinking about Locust. He didn't know where she was, though certainly she and Primrose would have left his house by now. Only Wanderer and Vole remained in the temple, because they were afraid to move Lichen. The last time Badgertail had run through the dark halls in search of Nightshade, he had checked on Lichen and found the little girl near death—her heartbeat erratic, her breathing so shallow it was almost imperceptible.

Elkhorn pulled himself forward on his elbows, panting, his brown eyes wild with fear. Blood streaked his face and spattered the shells in his forelocks. "What are we going to do? You can hear them down there. If we can't stand up to shoot at them, they'll be through in no time!"

Badgertail licked his dry lips. The pounding cadence of axes and adzes biting into the wooden guts of the palisade resounded through the high wall. His thoughts darted, trying to find a last-ditch strategy to buy time. "Take a third of the warriors we have left. Order half of them to dig shooting pits into the side of the Temple Mound. Tell the other half to build a barricade around the area where Petaga's forces will break through. If we can cage them and shoot down from safe positions—"

"It'll be like shooting netted geese!" Elkhorn smiled in desperate relief, grateful to be taking action. "I'll do it." He quickly backed away and began to crawl toward the nearest warriors.

Badgertail lay alone, dread throbbing in his veins. As night came on, the fires outside the palisade shone clearly. Although Petaga's warriors were tirelessly carrying water, it was not enough. The northern cornfields gleamed red-orange, while moonlight silvered the spirals of smoke rising from the devastated squash fields to the west. A thick smudge of black straggled languidly across the cloud-strewn sky. Lightning had been flickering here and there—nothing more than a vague threat of rain.

He inhaled, and his nose stung with the smoke that pervaded the air.

Below him, warriors flitted through webs of sparkflies like nighthawks in search of mice. Petaga's attack had been relentless, brutal, throwing wave after wave at the palisades; yet all of Petaga's warriors seemed fresh and alert.

He can afford to spell the tired and replace the wounded. You can't. Badgertail had warriors with arm and leg wounds still at their positions, functioning as best they could.

He balled a fist and slammed it repeatedly into the platform. Only when the pain drove him to stop did he look up and see Nightshade climbing the ladder toward him.

Forty-five

Petaga leaned his shoulder against the creek bank where they had established camp. He watched ash twirl and tumble out of the sky, alighting on the tepid brown water. The roar of the fires and the screams of battle had risen to such a clamor that he could hear nothing else.

He tried to contain his nervousness. Clouds had moved in suddenly and blanketed the sky with a silver-tinged wall of black that reflected the flames with a torrid glory. Lightning flashed.

Petaga turned to examine Hailcloud and Spoonbill, both of whom sat beside him in the shadowed niche. Spoonbill looked on with his usual infinite patience, but Hailcloud's jaw had set as he studied the final assault on the palisades, his fingers steepled over his mouth. The team of four had been hacking away at the palisade poles for over a hand of time while dozens of warriors provided covering fire. Badgertail's people dared not expose themselves to that constant barrage. Those who had been so bold had fallen quickly.

Farther down the bank, dark forms dipped baskets into the water, then awkwardly ran back to the fields to dump them. The Horn Spoon Clan had been working tirelessly, but they had been able to save only a few paltry patches of corn. *The land is so dry. The flames move with the speed of Eagle.* Anxiety gnawed at Petaga. Aloda's angry words echoed in his memory: *"Maybe I should just disband my village now. Eh, Petaga? It will happen in the end anyway!"*

How many people had this war left homeless? Thousands. Would they come back? Petaga would make them come back. He'd find a way.

"They're almost through, my Chief." Hailcloud pointed at the small crack of light that showed through the ax hole in the palisade wall. "I think we should fire the buildings now."

"Do you really think that Badgertail has enough warriors left to mount a defensive action when we rush through? I hate to burn the temple unless we have to." Even though Tharon's presence tainted it, Petaga could not help but believe that such an act would further anger the gods.

The lines around Hailcloud's eyes pulled tight. In the orange gleam, his face seemed molded of hard clay. "It's never wise to underestimate Badgertail."

"Then so be it. Give the order."

Hailcloud put a hand on his son's shoulder. "Spoonbill, go and tell Basswood to begin firing the houses within the palisades. Hopefully, the fires will carry sparks to the roof of the temple. If Badgertail has positioned people on the Temple Mound, the fire should divert their attention from us."

"Yes, Father." Spoonbill dashed away through the darkness.

A few more moments, that's all.

Excitement and fear thrilled Petaga's soul. If Tharon and Badgertail had not been killed in the fighting, then Petaga would soon have them.

Flaming arrows arced across the blackness. Screams rose on the tortured air as the missiles dropped on the defenders. Other arrows landed in houses. Tongues of fire leaped into the sky beyond the palisade, as though possessing a malignant life of their own.

Over the crackling din of the flames, Petaga heard a new sound, shrill, as though a hundred people had suddenly gasped in unison.

He looked westward, down the creek. The warriors who had taken refuge along the bank suddenly rose and scattered.

Petaga started to stand. "What . . ."

Hailcloud gripped his shoulder and pulled him down again into a safe position. But Petaga's gaze kept searching. As the warriors fled, leaving an empty swath near the water, he thought he saw a long robe dancing in the wind.

A figure loomed out of the darkness and glided toward them soundlessly. "Who is that?" Hailcloud asked suspiciously.

Petaga frowned. He could see in the firelight that it was a woman, tall and willowy. Long black hair hung in a midnight wealth over her shoulders and framed her full lips and turned-up nose. She bore a beautiful cedar box under one arm.

Petaga's heart almost burst. He leaped up, threw off Hailcloud's hand, and ran. "Nightshade!"

"Petaga?"

He fell at her feet and hugged her around the legs, as he had when he was a child and frightened of the dark. "Oh, Nightshade, I knew you were alive. I knew you were helping us." Petaga desperately kissed the hand that had lowered to touch his hair. "I knew you wouldn't turn against me."

"Your family gave me a home when I had none. I couldn't turn against you, my Chief."

Petaga had never heard her call him by his new title, and the word sounded so magnificent on her lips that he smiled up at her radiantly. "How did you get away? Did Tharon—"

"Tharon is dead, Petaga. Badgertail sent me to you to try to end this killing."

Hailcloud, who had rushed up to stand behind Petaga, sucked in a breath. "Tharon dead? Why?"

"He committed sacrilege. Incest."

Petaga rose to his feet, searching Nightshade's black eyes. "Incest? With who?"

"His daughter."

"Orenda? But she's a little girl! Blessed Father Sun . . . my poor cousin." He had never met Orenda, but he knew the requirement that ritual law would place upon him. To right the sacrilege, he would have to obliterate all memory of Orenda and her father. Petaga lowered his eyes and shook his head.

Nightshade said, "Petaga, Badgertail wants to surrender. He—"

"*What! Surrender!* I won't let him! These are the men and women who murdered our village, Nightshade. I want them dead!"

She stepped closer as she put a graceful hand on Petaga's cheek. "You have won the war, my Chief. Now save what's left of this village. You need a foundation on which to build your new chiefdom. The farmers, artisans, and merchants here have the knowledge needed to help you. And Badgertail believes that his warriors will be loyal to whoever the next Sun Chief is."

"Do you believe it?" Petaga asked, taken aback by the thought.

"Yes. My Chief, the time has come to cleanse and heal."

Riddled with conflicting emotions, Petaga walked a few paces away from her and stood at the edge of the water. A dark oval lay on the opposite shore. He squinted, and in the sudden, livid flaring of the temple roof as sparks ignited it, he saw that the oval was a corpse sprawled among charred weeds. The face had been burned beyond recognition. Anger roiled in Petaga's belly. His need for revenge battled like a rabid wildcat with his understanding that Nightshade was right. He needed the Cahokia clans. All of them. *It's the boy in you fighting with the man.* Despite all of the death and despair he had seen in recent weeks, and all of the difficult decisions he had had to make, only now, when faced with the challenge of being either merciful or spiteful, did he feel like a man.

Petaga bowed his head, studying the obscene film of ash that bobbed on the dark surface of the water. In his dreams, he had been returning again and again to his father during the last moments at River Mounds. He saw his father standing calm and erect, serene with the dignity of his office, no matter that his life was threatened. Nightshade had faithfully advised his father, and his father had trusted her judgment implicitly.

The rear part of the temple roof erupted in a ball of crackling flame. People stood transfixed, watching in awe as the rolling gouts of fire billowed into the sky, scorching the very clouds. And then part of the high roof collapsed in a thunderous blaze. The gaudy light bleached the faces of the warriors struggling at the base of the palisades. They stopped in shock, and then screams of triumph ululated as sweat-gleaming bodies broke into a spontaneous Dance of triumph.

"Petaga?" Nightshade called urgently. "There is something else." She offered the box. "Badgertail asked me to bring you your father's head. He asked that it be returned to the body so that Jenos' Spirit can walk with pride in the Underworld."

Petaga started to reach for the box, and stopped himself. His muscles trembled as he remembered that last encouraging look his father had given him before Badgertail struck. "If Badgertail thinks—"

Nightshade shook her head. "It is his belief that you will torture him to death. He accepts that."

Petaga reverently took the box. As he did so, rain pattered out of the sky, splatting in the bone-dry dust. It so surprised Petaga that he jumped as though he had been struck by a fist. In only a moment, the drops turned into a heavy downpour that drenched the world in an impenetrable wall of water. The sizzling and sputtering of flames grew so deafening that they drowned out all other noises.

Petaga stood in numb confusion, letting the rain soak him to the core. It soothed like cool salve on an aching burn. He lifted his eyes and saw Nightshade climbing the creek bank to the charred terrace. Her red dress clung to her body like a second skin, hanging in drenched folds. When she spread her arms to the storm, lightning danced like a thousand sparkflies through the clouds and bathed her in amber splendor. Thunder bellowed.

Nightshade tipped her face up and laughed. "*She's* done it! First Woman listened!"

The sizzling of the fires rose to a roar. Everywhere, warriors stopped in the middle of nocking arrows to stare in disbelief at the torrent that spilled from the clouds. The ground had begun to shine with a thick, downy sheen where water pooled.

Nightshade lowered her arms and called, "Petaga? What shall I tell Badgertail?"

"Tell him," he shouted back, "tell him yes. I'll accept his surrender. But that applies only to his warriors and the villagers. *He* is another question."

Tears welling to mix with rain, Petaga lowered himself to his knees on the slick mud. With trembling fingers, he stroked the carved surface of the rain-shiny box that lay before him.

A flash of lightning spun an eerie, luminescent web around Wanderer and Vole where they sat beneath a worn buffalo hide at the base of the Temple Mound. Lichen lay wrapped in a blanket between them—still, quiet. Even when he and Vole had lifted the edges of Lichen's blanket and dashed out of the burning temple, she hadn't made a sound. Her hair spread in a wet veil over the blanket. Wanderer reached down to touch her head. The swelling had gone down quickly, and he had sewn the flap of skin back into place just before the temple caught fire. She seemed to be breathing easier.

Wanderer leaned forward and put his mouth close to the flap. "Lichen? Can you hear me? It's Wanderer. It's raining here. The war has stopped. Tell First Woman we send our thanks."

Vole frowned. "Her soul's gone, Wanderer. She can't hear you."

"Oh, you'd be amazed at what the soul can hear when you've got an extra hole in your head."

The temple blaze still cast a lurid halo over the plaza. As the interior walls caught and burned, the flames illuminated the rivulets of water that slithered across the chunkey field like quicksilver serpents. Against the temple's pale yellow glow, warriors stood silhouetted along the shooting platforms. Their hands spread, they warily scrutinized Petaga's jubilant warriors, who raced around confiscating weapons.

"Wanderer?" Vole's voice was fragile. "When will Lichen's soul come back to us?"

He saw the fear in Vole's eyes and patted her hand tenderly, then tugged on the thong around Lichen's neck to pull the Stone Wolf out on top of the blanket. It gleamed a reddish-orange in the light of the fire. As Wanderer stared at it, he felt its Power radiating out, forming an invisible net around Lichen.

Wanderer leaned back and closed his eyes, gazing at the net with his soul. It shone blue, pale blue, and glistened like a spider's web covered with dew on a cool spring morning. Joy crept through the strands, reaching for him like a weak hand.

He smiled. "Soon, Vole. She's on her way back."

Forty-six

I don't know, Nightshade. I'm not sure she'll want to," Wanderer said as he picked his way through the smoldering remains of the temple. Morning sunlight streamed between the charred poles, painting Nightshade's beautiful face with slashes of gold as she stepped over the rubble of a collapsed wall.

Nightshade sighed. "Well, it's up to her. But I think that Petaga will need her help very badly. All of the people will. Could you talk to her about it?"

"Yes, of course."

Nightshade put her basket on the blackened ground and crouched to examine the ashes, as if looking for something.

A few hands away, Orenda sat cross-legged beside a blanket-enshrouded Lichen. Still weak, Lichen could stay awake for only a few hands of time, but her cheeks had grown rosy again, and the sparkle had reentered her eyes. Girlish laughter filled the air.

Orenda's gaze was fastened on Lichen. "So First Woman t-told you that humans could live here for a little while longer?"

"Yes," Lichen said. "But she didn't say for how long. She told me she would watch and wait. If humans keep hurting Mother Earth, First Woman said she would force us to leave."

"Where will she make us go?"

"South. To the Swamp People's lands. First Woman said—"

Orenda blurted, "But there are huge s-snakes there! I heard a trader talking once. He told me the snakes were so b-big that they could swallow a child whole!"

Lichen nodded. "That's just the kind of place First Woman would send humans. She's not very happy with us."

Orenda frowned. Then suddenly a smile lit her face. "You know what, Lichen?"

"What?"

"I'm going south. Nightshade's taking me." Eagerly, Orenda got on her knees and leaned closer to Lichen. She whispered as though it were a secret. "But not to the Swamp People's lands . . ."

Wanderer knelt beside Nightshade, studying the care with which she searched the ashes. Her fingertips brushed the blackened remains of the cattail mats that had once graced Tharon's floor. "What are you looking for?"

"They've been calling me," Nightshade replied softly. "When the fire reached this room, I could hear them screaming my name."

"Who?"

"The Bundles, necklaces, and other Power objects that Tharon stole."

Wanderer cocked his head. A smoke-scented breeze rustled through the gutted remains of the temple, tousling his gray hair around his face. "I don't hear them."

"That's because they're not calling you."

Nightshade's hand stopped moving. Her fingers tightened around something, and she drew an iron-covered human jaw from the ashes. The iron had been pounded into a thin sheet, then wrapped around the bone. Wanderer leaned forward to peer at the place where she had found it. The mummified body of a dog, a puppy, lay beside a stone palette stained with red paint. Nightshade gathered the remains and put them in her basket, murmuring, "Don't worry. We're going away."

She stood up and closed her eyes, letting her soul lead her to the next place. Wanderer followed. Nightshade stepped around a toppled bench, knelt, and gently blew away the ash blanketing a large soapstone pipe. The face of Otter stared up at her, carved expertly from the soft green stone. Inside the bowl of the pipe were two fishhooks and a stone net sinker.

Wanderer heard a soft male voice come from the pipe, followed by the echo of female laughter and the sound of waves striking a shore. "The things Bundles remember," he said. "I wonder who they were."

Nightshade stroked Otter's side fondly. "People of the sea. I can smell the salt in the air—just like the traders describe. And I hear—"

Orenda's giggle made them both turn. She had placed her ear atop Lichen's head, over the bald spot where Wanderer had taken out the circle of skull.

"Do you hear it?" Lichen asked.

Orenda smiled broadly. "Yes. Th-That's First Woman's drum?"

Lichen nodded. "She told me that I would always be able to hear her playing my Death Song, to remind me of how I got Falcon's wings."

"You had to die?" Orenda pulled back. "She killed you?"

"No. My Spirit Helper, Bird-Man, tore me apart with his beak and swallowed me."

Orenda stood rigid, her eyes wide. "I don't think I'd want him for my S-Spirit Helper."

"Oh, it was all right," Lichen said. "I needed him to kill me. When he pecked away my head, I grew bird eyes, and then I could see the Road of Light that ties the sky to the earth."

Lichen turned to smile at Wanderer, and his heart warmed. She had changed. Power radiated from her. He could see it in every move she made.

A commotion broke out in the plaza below. For days people had been straggling in from all over the chiefdom, seeking food and shelter in the aftermath of the war.

Nightshade rose and took a step forward to watch the line of people climbing the steps of the Temple Mound. Meadow Vole led the way, a little boy hot on her heels, taking the steps two at a time. When they reached the top of the mound, the boy broke into a headlong run. Lichen gasped, "Flycatcher!"

"Lichen! Lichen!" Flycatcher yelled as he raced across the charred grass to throw his arms around her.

"Oh, Flycatcher, what happened to you?" Lichen cried, feebly hugging him back.

"We went up and hid in that hole where you and Wanderer talked to the rocks. We stayed there for two days, with no food or water. Then we sneaked away in the middle of the night. We—"

Wanderer walked through the burned debris and stood beside Vole. She smiled up at him.

"Vole," he said, "we must talk. Nightshade is leaving. She wants Lichen to stay on as Petaga's priestess."

Locust set another log into the ground trench she had dug for their new house, then caved dirt in around the base to keep the log in place. Primrose walked toward her, dragging another log down the path that led through the gutted village outside the palisades. His long hair glinted blue-black in the sunshine. He had been wearing the same yellow dress for three days, but it still looked clean and fresh. He seemed almost well again. Nightshade had sent a healing poultice that drew the infection from the flesh. Locust had forced Primrose to use it first; then, when his wounds started to heal, she had placed it on her own leg. Today, for the first time, she could walk without pain.

Locust took a breath and gazed around at her new world. Fire-blackened wall poles thrust up everywhere, like jagged, rotting teeth. People swarmed across the rubble, crying, cursing, searching for the few belongings that might have survived the blazes, calling out the names of missing family members.

A very old man stood beside a mound of charred debris. He shouted,

"Petaga says he didn't mean to burn the village beyond the palisades, but look at this! This was my home! What will I do now? Where can an old man go?"

Primrose's face saddened as he threw the end of the log into the fire a dozen hands from Locust. Sparks spiraled upward into the late afternoon sky. In another finger of time, he would remove the log and give it to her to sink into the trench. Who would have thought things could get so bad that they would be reusing wood? But the log would finish one wall of their new house. Their old house, like so many others, had been demolished in the fighting. Early that morning they had sifted through the wreckage and collected what little they could find of their precious life together.

Locust turned back to her work. Picking up a stalk of cane, she wove it between the logs to add strength to the wall. Freshly cut saplings would have worked better, but there weren't any. Dressed only in a blue-and-tan kilt, she had been working tirelessly to suppress the futility that weighted her soul. She could have stood losing the battle for Cahokia, agonizing though it might be. But just over there, beyond the walls of the palisade, Badgertail was tied up, surrounded by guards—and she had been unable to do anything to help him.

Primrose gave Locust a soft glance as he knelt and turned the log, making certain that it charred evenly. Flames licked up in a crackling serenade.

"I saw him . . . in the plaza," Primrose said. "I think he's all right."

"When is the torture ceremony scheduled to begin?"

"No one has heard. I asked all of the guards around the palisades. I don't think Petaga has decided."

For a moment, Locust couldn't move. Memories of Badgertail rose within her like morning mist off Marsh Elder Lake, weaving images from the past in her head. Her soul overlaid the bittersweet memories with those of the present: Badgertail striding confidently through a village at her side . . . Badgertail smiling at her across a camp fire . . . Badgertail strung up like a dead animal waiting to be gutted. Alone, all alone. Locust squeezed her eyes closed.

"Locust?"

"I . . . I can't talk about it. Not yet, Primrose." *He saved you from Hailcloud's warriors, and here you are, doing nothing to help him.* Guilt smothered her, its power so great that she felt that if she didn't do something, her soul would die.

She lurched to her feet, pulled her war club from her belt, and slammed it into the new wall. Mustering all of her strength, she hit the wall again and again, swinging her club from side to side as though cutting a swath through a wave of enemy warriors. Each of them had hurt Badgertail at some time; she knew their faces, their scars, the look in their eyes. Her sobs began as muffled grunts but quickly rose to suffocating cries. She swung harder, pounding the wall like a madwoman. The hot tears flooding her cheeks made her hate herself—for being so weak, for not being able to save Badgertail.

"Locust," Primrose pleaded. He ran up and stood behind her. "Please. Please don't do this to yourself! There's nothing you could have done."

Finally the despair drained her strength. She let the club fall to the ground, then sank against the wall and leaned her forehead against the cool logs. "I—I'm going to organize the warriors. There are some who'll follow me. We'll get him out. I just have to figure a way of distracting—"

"Locust . . ." Primrose put a hand on her hair. "Petaga has a thousand warriors. Four hundred are walking the shooting platforms, watching everyone who comes or goes through the palisades. You could gather maybe a handful of warriors. None of you would live long enough to get near Badgertail." He stroked her hair gently. "Badgertail made peace. He knew what he was doing."

"No!" she cried. "Offering himself in exchange for us was crazy! I would have rather died at his side than live through this." Locust turned, and Primrose hugged her desperately. For a blessed, timeless moment, Locust let herself drown in the comfort of his arms, the smooth, steady rhythm of his breathing, the feel of his hand stroking her hair. "I can't let him die, Primrose."

"He'd be terrified, you know, if he suspected that you might try to rescue him. He offered himself so that those men and women who've been loyal to him could live. And he loves you, Locust. He always has. He would want to know that his life bought your safety."

Locust's heart pounded, knowing that Primrose was right, hating to admit it. She leaned her cheek on his shoulder and stared hollowly at the scorched fields across Cahokia Creek.

Nothing would ever be the same. Half of the population had fled or been killed. Sandbar had led the Squash Blossom Clan away on the night the fighting began, and now refused to return. Checkerberry . . . poor Checkerberry. She had been injured when a burning roof collapsed on top of her. She lay in Green Ash's home, coughing up blood, moaning in despair about Green Ash's twins. Locust, too, wondered what would happen to the babies if Checkerberry died. Nit was taking care of them now, but if Green Ash became clan leader, no one would be able to protect the children. Would Green Ash give them away? Or order one of her relatives to bash their brains out? Perhaps offer them as ritual companions, to be strangled the next time a powerful Sunborn died?

"I love you, Locust," Primrose murmured. "I need you. Maybe we should leave for a few days. Stay away until the torture is over."

"No. No, I—I have to see Badgertail again. Even if Petaga won't let me speak to him. Tomorrow . . . I'll go tomorrow, when I can stand it."

Forty-seven

A bright, hot day. So hot.

Badgertail hung limply on the rack in the center of the plaza, staring up at his hands tied over his head. For four days Father Sun had been tormenting him, sucking every drop of moisture from his naked body, roasting Badgertail's skin with brilliant yellow rays. Sweat poured down his face, stinging his eyes and occasionally blinding him to the happenings around him. People crowded the plaza, scavenging through the husks of houses for anything that might be usable. Some came just to stare at Badgertail. A few, very few, came to spit on him and curse him for having lost the war.

In the past hand of time, Badgertail had begun to shake. Not from fear, but from the deprivation of food and water for the third day in a row. His tongue stuck to the roof of his mouth like a withered root, and his belly roiled with sickness.

Just get it over with, Petaga. At this rate, I won't have the strength to die bravely, and you'll have very little entertainment from me.

He struggled to get his feet under him so he could ease the unbearable pain that lanced his back. An involuntary groan escaped his lips.

Petaga glanced over from where he sat on a fabric-covered bench twenty hands away, listening to the complaints of the villagers. Badgertail had watched the people come and go, begging remuneration for crop losses, pleading for corn to feed their children, or, if they were Starborn, just complaining that Tharon had waged a war without consulting them first.

Tharon. May your soul be lost forever on the Dark River in the Underworld.

"Hurts, does it, Badgertail?" Petaga asked. Laughter eddied through the people standing nearby. Badgertail saw Hailcloud bow his head and stare at the ground as though he felt ill. "Think of how my father felt."

"Your father felt nothing, Sun Chief," Badgertail replied. His voice sounded so hoarse that it didn't seem his at all. "I had a great deal of respect for your father. I made certain that he never suffered."

"You won't feel anything either," Petaga replied in precise words, ". . . when the time comes. But I don't think that will be for a few days."

Days! Blessed Moon Maiden . . . Badgertail sucked in a breath and fought to lock his knees.

Petaga waved a hand, calling, "Who's next? Hurry up! There are others waiting."

Locust and Primrose stepped out of the crowd. Locust carried a basket. Badgertail's heart ached, knowing how much it would hurt her to see him like this. He gave her a weak smile as she limped forward. Anguish lined her pointed face, puckering her warrior's tattoos. She tried to stop to talk to him, but Petaga ordered, "No one speaks to the prisoner! Step forward, Locust."

Badgertail's gaze held Locust's for a few moments longer, long enough that a lump built in his throat at the love and grief he saw in her eyes.

Then she limped forward to stand beside Primrose and set the basket down at Petaga's sandaled feet. The jarring motion caused a duet of mews to erupt from the bundles lying side by side in the basket.

"What's this?" Petaga demanded.

"Sun Chief, these babies have no family or clan. Checkerberry, their great-aunt and former leader of the Blue Blanket Clan, was killed in the war. The new clan leader, Green Ash, and the mother of these children, has disowned them. What will you have us do with them?"

Petaga looked horrified. He leaned forward to peer into the basket, his golden robe stirring around his feet. "No one wants these babies? But that's . . . that's unthinkable. Surely you can find someone—"

"No, Sun Chief. After these boys were banished from our clan, my wife, Primrose, and I searched throughout the village, seeking to give them to the other clans. No one wanted them."

"But why not?"

Locust gingerly knelt down and unwrapped each of the bundles to expose the babies.

A roar of shock and fear rose from the crowd. Badgertail blinked, thinking his blurry vision responsible for the terrors he saw before him, but when his eyes cleared, his horror worsened.

One of the children had no arms; only fingers protruded from the stumps at his shoulders. And the other . . . he seemed to be looking directly at Badgertail through wide, pink eyes. And something about those eyes was so *Powerful.* They assailed anyone who had the courage to look into them—as though this boy had the soul of a creature foreign to his people and their world. Thick white hair clung to the child's skull, framing a face with a mouth that protruded so far that it appeared to be a snout.

Petaga stammered, "If—if none of the clans will have them, Locust, there's nothing I can do."

Locust rose to her feet resignedly. "Very well, Sun Chief. I will find someone to take them out and leave them for the wolves. I was hoping we could—"

"*I* want them." Nightshade's deep, melodic voice penetrated the silence. People whirled to stare; then whispers hissed like shifting sand as they pointed.

Nightshade approached with a liquid grace, her head high, her eyes on Petaga. Badgertail craned his neck to watch. Orenda walked at Nightshade's side. The little girl grinned happily, as if oblivious to the stares of loathing. People shuffled backward so quickly that they stumbled over one another, many of them making warding signs with their fingers.

Nightshade had rejected the red color of the Starborn for a blue dress, woven from the finest dogbane thread. Badgertail stared unabashedly. He had never seen her wear anything but red since the day he'd delivered her to Old Marmot twenty cycles ago. Her long hair hung down the middle of her back in a glistening braid; a beautifully carved shell gorget lay suspended over her heart.

Nightshade knelt by Petaga's feet to refold the blankets over the babies and pick up the basket. The mews stopped immediately. Orenda continued to smile, her eyes focused on someplace far away, as if she lived a dream.

Badgertail swallowed hard. Poor Orenda. On her head lay the guilt of incest. People muttered behind their hands, pointing at the child, scowling. Cahokia would never rest until her screaming body was thrown on a burning pyre alongside Tharon's.

"But Nightshade," Petaga said, his eyes averted from the tainted Orenda, "what will you do with two babies?"

"They're going home with me . . . where they belong."

"Home?" As the word sank in, Petaga lunged to his feet and stared imploringly into her dark eyes. "Nightshade, you don't mean—"

"Yes, I do, Petaga. My work here is done. Power has its own needs. Orenda and I are leaving tomorrow."

Badgertail felt as though his aching body had received the first death thrust from a lance. *Fool. She has always wanted to go back. You knew she wouldn't stay.* And it didn't matter anyway. He would be dead soon, beyond missing her.

"Burn the child!" an old woman screamed from the crowd. "She's polluted! Her father's semen runs in her womb!"

Petaga stood speechless, his mouth open, suddenly looking like a frightened little boy. "Leave? With Orenda? You can't! I mean, Orenda must die . . . must be purified."

"Burn her!" "Cleanse the pollution!" "She's an abomination!" Cries rose from all sides.

Petaga backed up a step, his uneasy eyes darting from Orenda to the crowd. The smile died on Orenda's lips. Her chin quivered as she looked up at Nightshade.

Nightshade's eyes seemed to grow, dark pools that sucked at the soul. Silence settled like ancient dust. People went still, as though afraid to move. "Orenda goes with *me*."

Petaga shook his head, rubbing his hands on his golden robe as if they had gone sweaty. "You know the laws against incest, Nightshade. The people are right, the girl must be burned. From the Beginning Time, First Woman instructed—"

Nightshade stepped closer and stared into Petaga's eyes. "You will have to kill me first, Sun Chief. Your club lies behind you. Raise it. Strike."

Into the crackling tension, Badgertail shouted, "Let Orenda go! I've been there. Being condemned to the Forbidden Lands of the Palace Builders is the same as death—maybe worse!"

Petaga wet his lips. "Worse than death? Yes! Take her! But she must *never* return!" He faced the crowd, lifting his arms. "I banish my cousin Orenda to the Forbidden Lands of the Palace Builders! Her feet will not pollute the lands of our ancestors ever again!"

Nods of assent went around as cries rose. "Get rid of her *now!*" "Leave! Go!"

Badgertail sighed numbly. *One less victim for Tharon.*

When Petaga turned back to Nightshade, he gestured weakly. "Take her, Nightshade. But I—I don't know what I'll do without you."

Nightshade set her basket down so she could embrace Petaga. Orenda protectively clutched the basket's handle, eyes lowered to avoid the glares from the people.

"Oh, Nightshade!" Petaga whispered against her hair. "I'll miss you. I need you more now than I ever have."

"No, you don't. You just don't realize it yet. I've *seen* your future." She pressed her lips to his temple. "You'll have a priestess who is much greater than I am—if you'll ask her to stay."

Petaga let his arms fall and stared at Nightshade through blurry eyes. "Who?"

"Lichen."

"*Who?*"

"We'll discuss it tonight. I've arranged for you and me to take dinner with Meadow Vole, Wanderer, and Lichen."

Then, as though Badgertail's intense gaze drew her, Nightshade walked across the dirt and stood before him. She studied his eyes, probing so deeply that it felt like a fishhook ripping at his soul.

"So, my kidnapper," she said quietly, for his ears alone. "Do you still believe a bear is a bear?"

He took a breath to steady himself. "Are you asking if . . . if I believe that it's the nature of my soul and my duty to be a warrior?" She only stared. He said, "It is no longer my duty, Priestess. But whether or not it is still my nature, I can't say."

"What is your duty now?"

"My duty is to die as well as I can—for the sake of my warriors. And if Petaga doesn't hurry, I may fail even at that."

Nightshade stepped closer to him, so close that he could smell the sweet scent of mint that rose from her hair. When his heart started pounding, he made a futile effort to straighten his body.

"Badgertail, *I would have you grab your pack and run away with me.*"

The words echoed around a familiar chasm in his soul, circling, returning in Bobcat's voice. Desperate longing surged through him. Softly, he answered, "I would run away with you, Nightshade."

She turned without a word, striding through the buzzing onlookers to pull the hafted chert knife from Hailcloud's belt. Hailcloud cast an inquiring look at Petaga, who shook his head in confusion. Hailcloud made no move to stop her.

Nightshade raised the knife over Badgertail's head and cut his bonds. He fell to his knees, gasping in agony when his arms struck his sides like slabs of dead meat.

Nightshade knelt beside him and slipped an arm around his shoulders, supporting him until he could shift into a sitting position. "Are you all right?"

"I will be."

Nightshade lifted her commanding gaze to Petaga. "Badgertail is also going home with me tomorrow, my Chief."

Forty-eight

I've never heard that story," Wanderer said. "How do you know it?"

The sweet fragrance of bull thistle filled the air as Lichen walked along the terrace of Cahokia Creek behind him. He had been toying with the fringe on his green shirt, studying the thistles' magenta blossoms, or just gazing longingly up at the transparent bands of cloud that streaked the deep blue sky. Not even a breath of wind stirred the weeds this evening.

"First Woman told it to me. She said that Wolf Slayer almost died. He had to jump across the spiny backs of the Ice Giants while he fought Grandfather White Bear. That's how he tricked Bear. Wolf Slayer sneaked down onto a ledge in a deep crevasse in the ice. Bear sniffed him out and tried to follow, but he slipped and fell to his death. Then Wolf Slayer cut off Bear's hide for a robe and his claws for his Spirit necklace."

Wanderer blinked thoughtfully. "Like the claw that First Woman gave you? I was surprised when you woke with it in your hand."

"First Woman said she hoped it would always remind me."

"Remind you?"

"Yes. Of what Wolf Slayer had to go through to find the hole that led to this world of Light."

Wanderer propped his sandaled foot on a rock. "Lichen . . ." He paused. "Have you decided whether you'll stay here or not? Petaga needs you badly. I think your mother wants you to stay, too."

"Do you want me to?"

"If . . . if it's what *you* want." He bowed his head. "I'll miss you. I was hoping that maybe you'd come back to my rock shelter and live with me. You're young, and Power is so unpredictable. Living here in this big village will be far different from living in Redweed. I'm afraid it will be hard for you."

Unconsciously, her hand moved from the Stone Wolf on its thong around her neck, then down to her new Power Bundle, which was tied to the belt of her purple dress. It contained the huge bear claw, as well as the bits of hair and skull that Wanderer had cut from her head. First Woman's soft voice echoed from the Bundle: *"It's like crossing a mountain. The climb is hard. You can't understand anything about the whole world until you see the other side. This is another step on the way to ultimate Dreaming Power."*

Lichen leaned over and sniffed at the wet scents of water and mud. Down in the creek, two turtles paddled along the shore, sneaking up on insects. "Wanderer, do you know what? When I was in the Underworld, I thought I could hear your voice. It sounded like the wind."

He smiled. "Oh, that's because I'd cut that hole in your head and I could talk directly to your soul. It's going to be interesting to see what kind of voices you hear now that you have two holes in the top of your head. I've never known anybody with two."

"Maybe that's why I keep hearing the corn and squash talking to me."

Wanderer glanced at her, then lifted his gaze to the new sprouts of green that dotted the burned fields. "What are they saying?"

"They want to know when there will be more rain. I said it would come tonight."

"How do you know?"

"Thunderbird told me."

He nodded mildly. Since she had gotten Falcon's soul, Thunderbird talked to her all the time, his deep voice rumbling through her head.

Wanderer's eyes suddenly narrowed. Lichen turned to see what he was looking at. Coils of black smoke rose into the still air above Cahokia.

Wanderer said, "Kettle told me that people had been arriving for two days to watch the cremation. They've already started spinning legends about him. Wicked ones, I hope."

Lichen leaned her head back and stared up at the sky. As Father Sun sank lower on the horizon, crimson streaks shot into the hearts of the wisps of cloud, turning them into blazing spirals. They couldn't bury Tharon in the ground, because that would have offended Mother Earth, and they couldn't give him a platform burial, because Father Sun would have been outraged. Burning him was the only way to be rid of his polluted body.

"How long did First Woman say that humans could stay here, Lichen? Did she give you an idea?"

Lichen tilted her head reluctantly. "She didn't say . . . not for certain. Only that she would be watching us closely."

"Well," he sighed, "I hope Petaga runs what's left of the chiefdom better than Tharon did." Suddenly Wanderer skipped sideways, pointing. "What's that?"

Lichen turned her head, staring at the brush. "It's just a weasel hole, Wanderer."

Cold tendrils tightened in his chest. "I thought I saw him . . . sneaking up on me."

"Weasel would be silly if he bothered you, Wanderer. I have Prairie Falcon's soul."

A great weight seemed to lift from Wanderer's shoulders.

Lichen smiled and drew a perfect spiral into the ground with the toe of her sandal. "Wanderer? I think I have to stay here. To help Petaga. Can't you stay with me? Maybe for just a while. Until I get used to things."

He gave her a soft look that broke her heart and patted her shoulder. "I'll stay. For as long as Power will let me." Cautiously, he glanced back at the weasel hole and sighed.

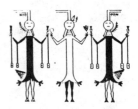

Epilogue

Nightshade moved silently, sensually, on her bed of pine duff, oblivious to the laughter of the children who played in the piñon grove near the drainage. The perfumes of juniper and pine rode the hot wind that swept through the trees.

She smoothed her hands over Badgertail's muscular back, reveling in the bulging muscles, gently touching each well-known tattoo. His hand crept slowly down her bare side, stroking tenderly. Streaks of golden light wove through the branches, dappling their faces.

Nightshade smiled and whispered, "We really ought to be down there helping the children gather pine nuts."

"Orenda is watching the boys. They'll do fine by themselves." He braced himself on his elbows and stared at her through warm brown eyes. He had let his hair grow out, and it draped around her face in a silver-shot black curtain. "Besides, the pine nuts aren't going anywhere. They'll be there tomorrow."

"Tomorrow?" She laughed. "You've grown lazy, my kidnapper."

He absently toyed with a lock of her hair while his eyes caressed the magnificent wind-sculpted red buttes that lined the vista. Jaybirds cawed in the trees as they hopped from branch to branch.

"Yes," Badgertail gently traced a finger along the smooth line of her jaw. "Thank you for that."

From down in the piñon grove, Orenda's joyful laughter mixed with that of the boys, the sound echoing through the forest. In her soul, Nightshade saw them, playing, chasing each other through the trees. Born-Of-Water couldn't see very well through his pink eyes, but he could run like the wolf he resembled so much. Home-Going Boy had to be more careful. With his stubby arms, he had trouble in keeping his balance on the uneven footing. He lagged behind Orenda and Born-

Of-Water, but a broad smile split his three-summers-old face. He called, "Brother? Sister? Wait for me. Wait!" before he charged off after them again.

Badgertail brushed his lips over Nightshade's ear. "I love you, my Priestess."

She wrapped her arms around him and kissed him with all of the passion he had kindled in her soul, leisurely, as though they had hands of time to play. She felt him smile.

Up in the trees, the jaybirds squawked and burst into flight, circling the pines, their blue wings flashing in the glory of the sun.

Selected Bibliography

Baerreis, D.A., and R.A. Bryson.
"Climatic Episodes and the Dating of the Mississippian Cultures."
The Wisconsin Archaeologist, Vol. 46. 1965.

Bennett, Gwen Patrice.
A Bibliography of Illinois Archaeology. Illinois State Museum
Scientific Papers, Vol. XXI, in cooperation with the Illinois
Archaeological Survey. Springfield, Ill. 1984.

Bierhorst, John.
*The Sacred Path. Spells, Prayers and Power Songs of the American
Indians*. Quill, N.Y. 1984.
The Mythology of North America. Quill, N.Y. 1985.

Chapman, Carl H., and Eleanor F.
Indians and Archeology of Missouri. University of Missouri Press,
Columbia. 1983.
The Archeology of Missouri. Vols. 1 and 2. University of Missouri
Press, Columbia. 1975.

Chomko, Stephen A., and G.W. Crawford.
"Plant Husbandry in Prehistoric North America: New Evidence
for its Development." *American Antiquity*, Vol. 43. 1978.

Cohen, Mark N., and George J. Armeloagos, eds.
Paleopathology at the Origins of Agriculture. Academic Press, Orlando, Fla. 1984.

Culin, Stewart.
"Games of the North American Indians." *Twenty-Fourth Annual
Report of the Bureau of American Ethnology to the Smithsonian
Institution, 1902–1903*. Government Printing Office, Washington,
D.C. 1907.

Eliade, Mircea.
    Shamanism. Archaic Techniques of Ecstasy. Bollingen Series
    LXXVI. Princeton University Press, N.J. 1974.
Emerson, Thomas, and R. Barry Lewis.
    *Cahokia and the Hinterlands. Middle Mississippian Cultures of the
    Midwest.* University of Illinois Press in cooperation with the
    Illinois Historic Preservation Agency, Urbana. 1991.
Erdoes, Richard, and Alfonso Ortiz, eds.
    American Indian Myths and Legends. Pantheon Books, N.Y. 1984.
Fagan, Brian M.
    Ancient North America. Thames and Hudson, N.Y. 1991.
Ford, Richard I., ed.
    Prehistoric Food Production in North America. Anthropological
    Papers, No. 75. Museum of Anthropology, Ann Arbor, Mich.
    1985.
Fundaburk, Emma Lila, and Mary Douglass Foreman.
    *Sun Circles and Human Hands. The Southeastern Indians—Art and
    Industry.* Southern Publications, Fairhope, Ala. 1985.
Gardner, A. Dudley.
    "Test Excavations at the Minor Site (40BY28)." Unpublished
    Report for the Department of Behavioral and Social Sciences, Lee
    College, Cleveland, Tenn. 1991.
Gero, Joan M., and Margaret W. Conkey.
    Engendering Archeology. Women and Prehistory. Basil Blackwell,
    Cambridge, Mass. 1991.
Gill, Sam D.
    Native American Religions. An Introduction. Wadsworth Publishing
    Company, Belmont, Calif. 1982.
Gilmore, Melvin R.
    Uses of Plants by the Indians of the Missouri River Region. Univer-
    sity of Nebraska Press, Lincoln. 1977.
Grim, John A.
    *The Shaman. Patterns of Religious Healing Among the Ojibway
    Indians.* University of Oklahoma, Norman. 1983.
Halifax, Joan.
    Shamanic Voices. A Survey of Visionary Narratives. E.P. Dutton,
    N.Y. 1979.
Hayden, Brian, and June M. Ryder.
    "A Graph-Theoretic Approach to the Evolution of Cahokia."
    American Antiquity, Vol. 56, No. 1. Jan., 1991.
Hudson, Charles.
    The Southeastern Indians. University of Tennessee Press, Knox-
    ville. 1989.
Kindscher, Kelly.
    Edible Wild Plants of the Prairie. An Ethnobotanical Guide. Uni-
    versity Press of Kansas, Lawrence. 1987.

Milner, George R., Eve Anderson, and Virginia G. Smith.
"Warfare in Late Prehistoric West-Central Illinois."
American Antiquity, Vol. 56, No. 4. Oct., 1991.

Morse, Dan F., and Phyllis A.
Archeology of the Central Mississippi Valley. Academic Press, San Diego, Calif. 1983.

Muller, Jon.
Archeology of the Lower Ohio River Valley. Academic Press, Orlando, Fla. 1984.

Nabhan, Gary Paul.
Enduring Seeds. Native American Agriculture and Wild Plant Conservation. North Point Press, San Francisco. 1989.

O'Shea, John M.
Mortuary Variability. An Archeological Investigation. Academic Press, Orlando, Fla. 1984.

Roper, Donna C.
Archeological Survey and Settlement Pattern Models in Central Illinois. Illinois State Museum Scientific Papers, Vol. XVI. Kent State University, Kent, Ohio. 1979.

Sherrod, Clay P., and Martha Ann Rolingson.
Surveyors of the Ancient Mississippi Valley. Modules and Alignments in Prehistoric Mound Sites. Arkansas Archeological Survey Research Series, No. 28. Fayetteville, Ark. 1987.

Spindler, George and Louise.
Dreamers with Power. The Menominee. Waveland Press, Prospect Heights, Ill. 1984.

Squier, E.G., and E.H. Davis.
Ancient Monuments of the Mississippi Valley Comprising the Results of Extensive Original Surveys and Explorations. AMS Press, NY, for the Peabody Museum of Archaeology and Ethnology, Harvard University, Cambridge, Mass. 1973.

Stoltman, James B.
"Ceramic Petrography as a Technique for Documenting Cultural Interaction: An Example from the Upper Mississippi Valley."
American Antiquity, Vol. 56, No. 1. Jan., 1991.

Swanton, John R.
The Indians of the Southeastern United States. Smithsonian Institution, Washington, D.C. 1987.
Indian Tribes of the Lower Mississippi Valley and Adjacent Coast of the Gulf of Mexico. Bureau of American Ethnology, Report No. 43. Smithsonian Institution, Washington, D.C.
Social Organization and Social Usages of the Indians of the Creek Confederacy. Johnson Reprint Corp., N.Y. 1970.

Tedlock, Dennis and Barbara.
Teachings from the American Earth. Indian Religion and Philosophy. Liveright Press, N.Y. 1975.

Tooker, Elizabeth, ed.
  Native North American Spirituality of the Eastern Woodlands. Sacred Myths, Dreams, Visions, Speeches, Healing Formulas, Rituals and Ceremonials. Paulist Press, Mahwah, N.J. 1979.
Trigger, Bruce G., ed.
  Handbook of North American Indians. Vol. 15. Northeast. Smithsonian Institution, Washington, D.C. 1978.
Walthall, John A.
  Galena and Aboriginal Trade in Eastern North America. Illinois State Museum Scientific Papers, Vol. XVII. Springfield, Ill. 1981.
  Prehistoric Indians of the Southeast. Archeology of Alabama and the Middle South. University of Alabama, Tuscaloosa. 1991.
Williamson, Ray A.
  Living the Sky. The Cosmos of the American Indian. University of Oklahoma Press, Norman. 1984.
Yerkes, Richard W.
  Prehistoric Life on the Mississippi Floodplain. University of Chicago Press, Chicago. 1987.
Zawacki, April Allison, Glenn Hausfater, and Thomas J. Meyers.
  Early Vegetation of the Lower Illinois Valley. A Study of Floral Resources with Reference to Prehistoric Cultural-Ecological Adaptations. Illinois Valley Archaeological Program Research Papers, Vol. 1. Springfield, Ill. 1969.